ID0966383

the

golden tulip

Books by Rosalind Laker

THE SMUGGLER'S BRIDE

RIDE THE BLUE RIBAND

WARWYCK'S WOMAN

CLAUDINE'S DAUGHTER

WARWYCK'S CHOICE

BANNERS OF SILK

GILDED SPLENDOUR

JEWELLED PATH

WHAT THE HEART KEEPS

THIS SHINING LAND

TREE OF GOLD

THE SILVER TOUCH

TO DANCE WITH KINGS

CIRCLE OF PEARLS

THE GOLDEN TULIP

DOUBLEDAY

New York   London   Toronto

Sydney   Auckland

the

golden tulip

ROSALIND

LAKER

PUBLISHED BY DOUBLEDAY
a division of Bantam Doubleday Dell Publishing Group, Inc.
666 Fifth Avenue, New York, New York 10103

DOUBLEDAY and the portrayal of an anchor with a dolphin
are registered trademarks of Doubleday,
a division of Bantam Doubleday Dell Publishing Group, Inc.

Library of Congress Cataloging-in-Publication Data

Laker, Rosalind.
The golden tulip/Rosalind Laker.—1st ed.
p.   cm.
I. Title.
PR6065.E9G65   1991
823'.914—dc20   90-27591
CIP

ISBN 0-385-41560-5
Copyright © 1991 by Barbara Øvstedal

BOOK DESIGN BY CAROL A. MALCOLM

To the

memory

of Dorli

of Switzerland

AUTHOR'S NOTE

The paintings by the fictional Visser family and Hans Roemer are imaginary, but those by Jan Vermeer and the other great masters are as described. There is no record of Jan Vermeer ever having had an apprentice, but by letting my heroine enter his studio I have paid my personal tribute to the beauty and tranquillity of his work.

R.L.

CHAPTER I

For as long as ten-year-old Francesca Visser could remember she had been intensely aware of the colours of her world. The golden gleam of her mother's neatly dressed hair. The azure sparkle of Amsterdam's many canals under a summer sky and their frosty grey-green brilliance when frozen. Tall russet roofs made pale by mist and the ruby hues of tulips in the flower beds of the rear courtyard of her home. Above all else the treasure trove of her father's studio, where a few drops of linseed oil could make the powdery pigments, dark in their storage jars, burst gloriously into vermilion, lime yellow, deep blue and velvet purple for his palette and her own.

Yet today as she posed for him, wearing her best gown and seated on the studio rostrum, everything seemed sombre and shaded. A great crisis was looming up in the household and at the present time only she knew about it. She hugged the secret knowledge to herself, her heart heavy, and was afraid.

The house and the studio itself were as normal. There was the familiar slap of Hendrick Visser's dog's-hair brush against his canvas and the distant clatter of pots in the kitchen, where Griet, the maidservant, was preparing the noon meal under the direction of old Maria, who had been nurse to Francesca's mother and aunt before taking charge of the next generation. From beyond the diamond-paned windows came the slow clop of a horse's hooves as it pulled a loaded barge along the canal that divided the length of the street outside.

"You're letting your head droop, Francesca. Raise your chin."

"Yes, Papa."

As Francesca obeyed, shaking back her coppery hair, she thought it no wonder that her head had sunk with the weight of the forthcoming calamity on her mind, but she set the angle of her chin resolutely, determined not to lose her pose again. She knew from experience never to fidget or else her father would get angry and bellow at her. Hendrick did not mind talk from the rostrum, but he would not tolerate movement. It was the reason why neither of her sisters liked to pose for him. Aletta, who was a year younger than Francesca, became restless through nervousness, while Sybylla, who was younger than Aletta by thirteen months, was too energetic ever to be still, except when asleep. The fact was that Hendrick could never restrain himself from shouting, wherever he was, if anything upset him. His bushy, ginger-coloured brows would gather like clouds before a thunderstorm and his heavily jowled face would turn crimson, a sight dreaded more by Aletta than anyone else in the household. Francesca tried frequently to reassure her sister that the old proverb about someone's bark being worse than his bite applied to their father, but she never paid any heed.

It was not uncommon for Hendrick's temper to lead him into quarrels in the taverns and gambling dens of Amsterdam that he frequented too often for his wife's liking. Sometimes the trouble only started through an argument with certain of his fellow artists, hotheaded like him when they had been drinking too much, over something as easy to discuss as techniques in painting. Francesca had seen her mother roll up her eyes and let her hands droop in her lap upon hearing of this and similar causes of confrontation.

"Men!" Anna Visser would sigh with emphasis, putting a cold compress on her husband's black eye. Then he would grin, catch her hand to kiss the palm or fondle her rump through her skirts. She knew well enough that the next time he and his friends met, the discord would be forgotten until one or another subject controversial to artists came up again. Francesca, now that she was old enough to be more observant in such matters, could tell that her mother worried more about his gambling than his involvement in occasional brawls.

Sometimes her parents had wrathful spats between themselves. Then it was like an explosion of fireworks, for Anna was like most tolerant people in that she could give back as fiercely as she received when her temper was finally aroused beyond control. Yet these parental upsets did not trouble Francesca, for they were never of long duration, always ending upstairs in the marital bedchamber, where there was a great deal of bumping about before her parents emerged again, smiling and kissing, arms about each other.

Similarly Francesca never minded when the food on the table was plain and barely adequate, because whenever her father had money in his purse there would be plenty again. After a win at gambling he would come home with his arms full of largesse and, his breath smelling winey, toss gifts of toys and sweetmeats to her and her sisters. Then he would fill Anna's arms with flowers, taking one to tuck into her hair, before kneeling to place pink satin shoes on her feet. After that he would unwind the rolls of fine fabrics he had bought, whirling them out like banners to show there was to be a new gown for every female in the household before he piled the multicoloured velvets, silks and gilt-threaded brocades in Anna's lap. She would always smile and sometimes laugh, but often tears would trickle from her eyes no matter how he tried to kiss them away.

Yesterday there had been one of these exuberant performances. Janetje Veldhuis, who was Anna's younger sister and lived on her own in the house in which they had grown up, had been the recipient of a present simply because she had happened to be visiting at the time. Her pretty face had become as rosy as the rich brocade that Hendrick had draped over her shoulder.

"It's not my birthday," she had protested.

"Neither is it anyone else's," Hendrick had laughed.

Francesca had sensed instinctively that the pinkness in her aunt's cheeks had come from embarrassment. No doubt Aunt Janetje had thought that the money for her gift would have been better spent on settling a few of the Visser household's unpaid bills. Anna never complained, but Janetje knew how her sister had to scrimp and save and

3

keep at bay irate tradesmen at the door. But the incident of the brocade had occurred yesterday and today Aunt Janetje's blushes had stemmed from a different cause. Such misery welled up in Francesca at the thought of it that a noisy sob broke from her throat before she could stop it and the tears gushed at last.

"Whatever is the matter?" Hendrick, agile in spite of his portly girth, almost threw aside his brush and palette as he rushed to her. "Are you tired? I shouldn't have expected a second sitting from you this morning!"

She shook her head, wrapping her arms around his neck as he swept her up and held her to him. "It's not that," she sobbed. "I think Aunt Janetje is going to marry and then I'll never see her again."

He sat down on the edge of the rostrum and perched her on his knee. It was his belief that his sister-in-law saw Francesca as the daughter she had never had, which was why there was such a close bond between them. "Why should you get such a nonsensical idea into your head, child?" he asked, his eyebrows raised in surprise. "Your aunt is a fine-looking woman and would make any fortunate man a good wife, but she has never found anyone to suit her after an early disappointment and is fulfilling her life in other ways."

"She has found someone now. At the Korvers' house. I went there in my rest period, because Maria told me that Mama and Aunt Janetje had taken Aletta and Sybylla to play there."

Hendrick gave a nod. Heer Korver was a prosperous Jewish diamond merchant who lived at the far end of the street, and the friendship between the two families was of long standing. "So what happened?"

It all came pouring out. Young Jacob Korver, the eldest boy, had taken Francesca upstairs to the drawing room above the business premises to see a newly acquired kitten asleep in a basket there. She had found her mother in conversation with Heer Korver and his wife while Janetje sat apart by the window with a Florentine gentleman, Signor Giovanni de Leone, who had come to Amsterdam to buy diamonds. All were sipping wine, it being Heer Korver's hospitable custom to conclude a good transaction with some ceremony. What had disturbed Francesca was that for the first time ever she had not been greeted by her aunt with that special display of affection reserved for a favourite niece.

"Aunt Janetje hardly seemed to see me! It was the Florentine gentleman who held all her attention."

"I expect they were having an interesting conversation," Hendrick said comfortingly. "You know how your aunt enjoys a good discussion."

"It was more than that," Francesca wept.

"How can you tell?"

"They were looking at each other as you and Mama do sometimes. It doesn't matter what you're talking about, because your eyes and hers are saying something special."

He leaned her head on his shoulder and stroked her hair. Sometimes he wondered at his eldest child's intelligence and perception. "What do you think when your Mama and I exchange our thoughts?"

"I know it means that you love her and she loves you and you both love Aletta and Sybylla and me."

"That's right. Well, let us think what it would mean if Janetje and this Florentine gentleman should be finding love. It may mean a few weeks of friendship before he goes away again, perhaps never to return, or if they should marry he would most surely take her home to Florence, which is one of the great centres of Italian art. Michelangelo's city! Think of it!" He would have been at a loss many times for a nursery story to tell his children if he had not been able to draw on the lives of renowned painters and sculptors, adding some fairy tale touches of his own. The names of Michelangelo and Titian, Raphael and Botticelli were as familiar to Francesca and her sisters as that of St. Nicholaes, who brought gifts for children every year on the sixth of December.

But the tears were flowing again. "Aunt Janetje would be so far away."

"Part of her heart would always be in Holland and with us. Nobody forgets their homeland, child, or those they have left behind. When you are grown you could visit her and see all the wonders of Florence for yourself."

"Could I?"

He caught the more hopeful note in her voice and set her back from him to look into her tear-stained face. "Of course you could!" He pulled a clean paint rag from the pocket of his linen smock and dried her eyes with it. "Now, you little matchmaker, are you going to sit for me again, or have you had enough of being a model for one day?"

"I'll continue, Papa."

The sitting was resumed. Francesca occupied her thoughts by considering what marriage would mean to her aunt. Anna and Janetje had been born in Amsterdam at the family house. When Grandfather Veldhuis, by then a widower, died not long after the marriage between Hendrick and Anna, Janetje had stayed on there. She had never shown any sign of being lonely, although she was always eager to join in family occasions at the Visser home and to invite them all to her house. She had a wide circle of friends and in her charity work she held the role of regentess, as women governors were called, on the all-female board of an orphanage. It was an honourable appointment, for such positions were held only by those respected for their impeccable character and good works. Anna often visited the orphanage with her sister and afterwards never failed to say what a pity it was that Janetje was not married with babies of her own since she cared so much for little children. So marriage would bring her those babies. Francesca tried to fix her thoughts on that blessing for her aunt, but she was full of tears inside.

Hendrick, noticing that his daughter's face had not lost its woebegone expression, paused in his painting while he considered the best means of distracting her.

"Would you like to come for a walk with me this afternoon?" he asked. There could be no hurrying of the work in hand. Paint took a long time to dry, for it had to be built up in successive layers.

She nodded eagerly, too disciplined in her pose to turn her head. Walks with Hendrick were never dull. "Where are we going?"

"To call on Master Rembrandt. I've got that new book on Caravaggio that he wants to read."

She knew about the Italian artist Caravaggio. He had led the way in the chiaroscuro technique, the dramatic use of light and shade to sway the whole mood of a painting. Hendrick followed it, as did the artist they were to visit, but her father had said often that none could surpass

Master Rembrandt in creating pure spiritual feeling in his work. Similarly Hendrick and Master Rembrandt considered the category of so-called history paintings, which covered biblical, historical and mythological scenes, to be the highest form of art, a theory that was once prevalent before popular taste changed.

Francesca relaxed her pose as the tinkling of a little handbell in another part of the house announced that the noon meal was served and she sped with haste from the studio to the dining hall. She wanted to see her aunt again and discover if the glow in Janetje's eyes was still there. To her disappointment she found only her mother supervising her sisters as they took their places. No extra setting for her aunt was on the table.

"Where is Aunt Janetje?" The question flew from her. "I thought she would be eating with us today."

Anna's lips curled in a secretive little smile. "I thought the same, but that dashing Signor Giovanni de Leone invited her out with him and she is going to show him the Westerkerk and the Town Hall and a number of other fine sights that are to be seen in Amsterdam."

"She can't do all that in one afternoon!"

"I don't believe either of them expects to cover everything in a short time. I assume they will be spending time together for the week that he plans to be here. Now take your place. The food is on the table and your father is now waiting to say grace."

Stunned by this unexpected news of the romance developing so fast, Francesca stood behind her chair. Next to her was Maria, wrinkled, stiff-jointed through aches and pains and amply built, with impish-faced Sybylla at her left hand. Facing them on the opposite side of the table was Aletta, always quiet and reserved, her hair pale as moonshine, and also good-natured Griet, it being customary for a maidservant to eat with the family, except on formal occasions, if she was well liked and fitted in domestically. Anna, slender and full-bosomed, stood at the end of the table, looking towards Hendrick at the head. He bowed his thick mane of ginger hair and sent his deep voice booming over the table.

"Bless these victuals to our use, good Lord, and us to Thy service."

There was a clatter of chairs being pulled out across the floor's black and white tiles and everyone sat down to tuck into fried herrings, salad

7

and vegetables and crusty white bread. Francesca, although she ate well, was far from the table in her thoughts, following her aunt and the Florentine on their tour of the city. She did not think he would register any of Amsterdam's grand landmarks if he did not stop gazing at Janetje as he had done that morning.

When the meal was over Hendrick asked Aletta if she would like to accompany Francesca and him on their walk to Master Rembrandt's house. She shook her head and looked up at him with her huge, serious grey-green eyes that were much like his own

"No, Papa. I thank you, but I'm going back to play with Esther Korver again this afternoon. I promised her." She did not like going out with him when her mother was not there too. He had a way of drawing attention to himself all the time and thus, she felt, to her. Similarly, although she was like Francesca in loving to draw and paint, she dreaded his teaching sessions in the studio.

"Naturally you must go there," he said jovially. Then with complete disregard for his own lax ways, he added, "Promises must be kept."

There was a sudden shout from Sybylla as she rushed across the room, her corn-coloured curls abob, and clasped her father's legs. "Take me with you! I want to go too!"

Bending down, Hendrick loosened her hands and picked her up in his arms. "No, Sybylla. Not today." He did not like to deny her any-thing, always ready to indulge her, but he did not feel he could inflict her exuberant ways on Rembrandt at the present time. "If you are a good girl and make no fuss, I will bring you back some sweetmeats in my pocket."

Immediately she was all smiles again, and Maria, impatient with such bribery, drew her away. "Don't you bother your papa any more. You can help me fold linen this afternoon."

Sybylla scowled and stamped a foot in protest at the irksome chore, but the promise of the sweetmeats kept her from a tantrum.

Hendrick and Francesca left the house by the main door, stepping straight from the reception hall into the street, which was the style of all city houses, even those of the wealthy. She held the book under her arm, for it would have been beneath his dignity to carry it. He had no false pride towards his fellow human beings, whatever their station in life, but he had a huge personal conceit and among his idiosyncrasies was a delight in strutting along, swinging a cane that was fashionably shoulder-high with a red tassel dancing on it, and never burdening himself with anything. Even in dire straits, he would find a small coin somewhere in the recesses of his purse or pockets, often having to search for it, to give an urchin to carry for him a portfolio of drawings or a roll of canvas.

It was a gloriously warm and sunny afternoon. The iris-blue sky seemed to sparkle about the variegated gabled rooftops as if it had garnered the iridescence of the city's waterways. Linden trees, bright with vigorous green foliage, gave pleasing shade. With a tax imposed on width frontage, all the houses were tall and narrow, rising up through four, five and sometimes six floors to an attic, but each ran back a considerable length to a walled courtyard and occasionally a garden. A flagged passageway, incorporated into the side of many houses, gave access to these rear regions. Built usually of red brick that was soon mellowed by time and with sandstone ornamentation, each house had above its top window a hoist jutting out like a claw, for with awkward corners and narrow staircases within there was no other means of getting furniture to the upper floors except by rope.

A large cupboard was being hoisted to a fourth floor at one house as Hendrick and Francesca crossed a bridge. She paused briefly to watch it swinging suspended in the air before she darted forward to catch up with her father again. As she had expected, their progress was erratic. He could not pass any acquaintance without some conversation. If those persons were on the other side of the canal he would thunder his greetings across to them, making other people turn their heads to stare.

Before long they came to a street corner where an old seaman with a crutch and a peg leg stood propped against a wall as he played a flute. His cap was on the ground and Hendrick threw a stuiver into it.

"Play us your merriest tune!"

As the seaman obliged, Hendrick turned to Francesca and took her by the hand to lead her into a lively jig to the music of the flute, she following the quite intricate steps he had taught her himself last St. Nicholaes's Eve. Round and round on the cobbles they danced. A small crowd gathered. A few other people joined in and the seaman's cap became agleam with coins. There was applause as Hendrick led Francesca away. She smiled at him joyously. Nobody else had a father who could turn the most ordinary outing into an occasion of drama and entertainment.

They crossed a bridge over another canal and came into Breedstraat. Rembrandt's home was an imposing residence topped by a steep gable, the double windows of the attic having once given light to the pupils' studio, his being on the floor below. Hendrick, hammering on the door, supposed that this visit would be the last to this particular house, for Rembrandt was shortly to leave it, forced to by unhappy circumstances. Four years earlier, in desperate financial straits, Rembrandt had made an appeal for the liquidation of his property, thus saving himself in the nick of time from being declared a bankrupt. Legal procedures had enabled him to continue living in the house even after it was sold with all its contents by auction, but now time had run out and he was shortly to remove to a small and humbler dwelling.

Hendrick knew it must be admitted that much of Rembrandt's ill luck, apart from deep personal tragedies, was due to his extravagance and his failure to keep abreast with popular taste in painting. Hendrick was aware of being guilty himself on both counts, but a man could not change his nature. Although there was a warning in what had happened to a fellow artist, Hendrick was not unduly worried by it. He trusted to the generosity of Fate, which all through his life had rallied to him whenever a financial situation was particularly bleak. The natural optimism with which he was born had never yet deserted him.

The door had opened, but Francesca, who had paused on the lowest step of the entrance flight, had her gaze riveted at the Veldhuis family home farther down the street, where both her mother and her aunt were born. They could remember Rembrandt's late wife, Saskia, their ages twelve and ten respectively at the time of her death. But that thought was not in Francesca's mind now. She had seen, although her father had failed to notice, that Aunt Janetje and the Florentine gentleman had just alighted from a coach and were entering the house together.

"Who is this daydreaming on the steps?"

With a start Francesca looked up at the door, where Juffrouw Stoffels, who kept house for Rembrandt and lived with him as his wife, was smiling at her in welcome, capable peasant hands clasped together.

"It's only me," Francesca answered self-consciously. At any other time she would have responded more quickly to the little joke, but she had seen her aunt's romance set still further on the course of marriage. Janetje would never have asked any ordinary stranger into her home for tea and those delicious little cakes that she made.

"Come in, dear child. Why are you still standing out there when your papa is already indoors?" Round-faced with handsome dark eyes, warm-spirited, loving and maternal, Hendrickje Stoffels flung out her arms to the child. Francesca sprang up the steps into her embrace.

"How are you today, ma'am?" Francesca inquired, remembering her manners as the door was shut after her. Her mother had explained that Rembrandt and Hendrickje would have married long ago if it had not meant that by some condition in Saskia's will he would have forfeited a small allowance that at times had provided food for their table when otherwise there would have been none.

"I'm very well, Francesca, even though moving from here means that there's a lot to do."

Francesca had seen at once that the house was even more empty than the last time she had been here. The reception hall was completely bare, although the black and white marble tiles were as spotless as ever. She could see through the open door of the drawing room that everything was gone from there as well and she supposed it to be the same in the rest of the house. Yet she had been told that in his heyday Rembrandt had had over a hundred paintings on his walls, half of them by himself and many by his now well-known pupils.

Rembrandt's voice and her father's echoed hollowly from the studio upstairs, magnified as sounds always are when a house ceases to be a home. Hendrickje, taking Francesca by the hand, led her up there.

"Look who's come to see you, Rembrandt."

In the studio, devoid of everything now except a large easel and a table with the usual conglomeration of artists' materials, Rembrandt turned where he stood with her father. Clad in an old blue painting smock, a length of cloth wound into a flat turban about his head, his

1
1

white hair as curly in his fifties as it had been in his youth, he smiled at the piquant beauty of the child holding out a book to him.

"I thank you, Francesca," he said, taking it from her.

She in her turn thought that, in spite of the parting of his lips that lifted upwards the ends of his narrow moustache, his whole life-ridden face was full of sadness. Perhaps he was remembering all the happy times he had had in this house that would never come again.

"You may keep the book as long as you wish," she said swiftly, wanting to cheer him. "Papa won't mind."

"That's most generous," he replied appreciatively in his deep voice. "I may have to take my time over it, as I'm about to embark on a commissioned work."

"Shall you paint it here?"

"No." He cleared a space on the table and put the book down. "It's far too large for me to paint in this studio or at my new abode. I've always been permitted to set up my large canvases in the Zuider Church and I shall paint there once again."

Hendrickje put a hand on Francesca's shoulder. "Come down to the kitchen with me now and let the menfolk continue their talk."

Francesca accompanied her. "Is Cornelia here?" she asked hopefully. Hendrickje and Rembrandt's daughter was only a year younger than she and they always enjoyed meeting.

"No, she's gone with Titus to the other house in Rozengracht, where we're going to live. He's putting up some shelves and getting a few things ready. He and I are business partners now, you know."

Titus, who was now nineteen, was the fourth and only surviving son of Rembrandt's late wife, another boy and two girls not having lived more than a few weeks after their birth. Francesca liked him and thought of him almost as a brother, because one of his father's portraits of him as a boy hung in the parlour of her home and she saw it every day.

"Are you going to have a shop there?" she questioned with interest.

Hendrickje laughed. "Oh no! But together we are employing Rembrandt and paying him a wage. By that means he does not have to surrender his paintings to the Court of Insolvency. Now you shall try

1
2

some of the pancakes I've been making and I'm sure your father would like a glass of my apple wine."

Francesca was reminded of two other people taking refreshment together. On the way home again she saw the coach was still waiting outside the Veldhuis house.

For ten days nothing more was seen of Janetje. Then Francesca and Aletta arrived home from school in Maria's care at the usual hour of noon to discover an air of excitement prevailing in the house. Anna, full of smiles, met them with the news.

"Giovanni de Leone was here! As your father is Janetje's most senior male relative, albeit by marriage, the Florentine asked him formally for her hand. The wedding is already arranged for next week." She read the question in her eldest daughter's deep green eyes. "I know it has all happened very quickly, but he is due to return home in a matter of days."

Aletta spoke up. "Where is Aunt Janetje now?"

"Upstairs in the sewing room with a seamstress. Her betrothed has given her some beautiful Lyonese silk that he bought in Paris, not knowing then it would be for his bride's wedding raiment." Anna became aware that Francesca had neither moved nor spoken. She cupped her hand against the child's pale face. "I believe you knew of this match before any of us. Papa told me you spoke of it on the very day they met. It won't be any easier for Janetje to leave us than it will be for us to see her go. We must smooth the way for her."

Neither of them noticed that Maria, thinking that Anna and Francesca should be on their own together at this moment, had shepherded Aletta away with her. Francesca swallowed hard.

"Will she be happy for ever and ever with Signor de Leone?"

Anna drew her daughter to a cushioned bench by the wall. "Love isn't just being happy, Francesca. It's more than that. It is the willing commitment of one's whole heart to one person. That brings joy and ecstasy beyond measure and far ahead of your present understanding, but it can also bring pain and sorrow and the agony of being torn apart, not only by outside events but through the actions of the very two who care most for each other. Janetje will have special problems to face in going to a new country where another language is spoken, amid strangers and far from home." Fondly she smoothed back an unruly curl from her daughter's brow. "But true love can maintain its strength no matter what is hurled against it. I believe Janetje and Giovanni have found that kind of love for each other or else I would do everything in my power to prevent the marriage."

Francesca sensed, almost without being aware of it, that a great deal of what had been said had referred to her own parents' relationship as much as to what lay in store for Janetje. "May I go up and see her?"

Anna nodded. "She asked that you should go to her as soon as you came home."

As Francesca darted away upstairs, Anna went through the archway that led from the stair hall. When she entered the studio she was met by a strong odour of resin and animal glue with which, combined with ochre, Hendrick was preparing a canvas. He was whistling in high spirits, for after he had given his permission for Janetje to marry the Florentine a most generous offer had been forthcoming.

"My future wife's only reservation about leaving her homeland," Giovanni had said in his limited Dutch, "is her concern for her sister and nieces through your present financial straits. I want her to be happy and for her sake I am willing to give you a fresh start and settle all your debts from whatever source if you care to present me with the figures."

"I'm overwhelmed!" Hendrick had exclaimed.

"Do not thank me. I am doing it solely for Janetje's peace of mind and on the condition that you will never approach either her or myself for any financial help in the future."

"You have my word!" Hendrick had declared.

Anna, crossing the studio towards him, was grateful for Giovanni's generosity, but she had no hope of Hendrick being able to keep out of debt for long, even though he was to be given a clean slate. She linked her arms around his neck and rested her head on his shoulder. With the jar of gluey mixture and the brush still in his hands, he folded his arms about her, knowing that the forthcoming break with her sister was already causing her enormous anguish.

"I love you," he said softly, putting his lips to her temple.

1
4

She nodded. Had she not known that to be the truth she could never have borne the trials and tribulations that marriage to him had brought her. Slowly she turned her face up to his and immediately his hot, passionate mouth met its response in hers.

CHAPTER 2

Anna saved every one of Janetje's letters and wrote twice a year herself. With various wars raging around Holland's peaceful borders the passage of mail was precarious and it was best to entrust it to a merchant or traveller known to be going to Florence. Heer Korver had contacts there and he always sent word to Anna when he knew of someone prepared to collect and deliver a letter. The marriage between her sister and Giovanni was proving to be a good one. Janetje, although assailed at times by homesickness, was content in her new life, much absorbed by her sons, one having arrived nine months after the wedding and the second a year later.

Anna always had plenty of news to tell her sister, mostly domestic but including snippets about friends and neighbours that she knew would be of interest. Inevitably there were times when there were sad tidings to impart, and she shed tears that blotted the ink on the paper when she wrote that once again tragedy had struck Rembrandt in the death of Hendrickje Stoffels. He had aged noticeably afterwards, but work still flowed from him and recently he had been commissioned to paint the likenesses of a mutual acquaintance and his betrothed after their marriage. It was not to be a pair of bridal portraits, which was usual and had been expected. Instead he intended to paint them side by side. When Anna called on him one day, bringing him one of her cakes and a basket of plums from the tree in the courtyard, he explained his reason when answering her inquiry as to whether he would be attending the wedding.

"No, I'll not be there," he replied, biting into one of the juicy plums.

"I don't go anywhere socially these days. Work is my heartbeat. It's my eating and my sleeping, my going out and my coming in. I'm an old man now, you know."

She was facing him on the bench by the open parlour window, where they sat in the sun, and she exclaimed in protest, for to her he seemed ageless. "No, Rembrandt, no! Nobody would ever think of you as an old man!"

He smiled wryly. "That's kind of you, but nowadays I often feel at least a hundred years old!"

"You could come to the wedding with us. We'll all be going."

"No, Anna. It's thoughtful of you, just as it was to bring me cake and fruit today. But I don't want to see the bridal couple on the wedding day. They'll both be nervous and under strain. I want to create my first impression of them in their happiness when they have tasted the tender joys and sweet passion of love." He looked towards the door with his eyes narrowed as if visualizing their entrance into his house. "Why should they be separated on individual canvases when their lives together are in first bloom. There are too many partings of lovers in this life. I'll take no hand in that, even in paint."

She knew that Saskia and Hendrickje were in his thoughts. Two women quite different in character and from opposite backgrounds, but each had loved him and been loved, Saskia dying at thirty and Hendrickje only eight years older. She shivered as if a shadow had fallen across her path. He had noticed.

"Is there a draught? Are you cold?" He would have closed the window, but she stayed him.

"No! Please leave it. Somebody must have stepped on my grave." Then she regretted her use of the old saying in a house that death had visited again only a while ago. He saw her dismay and leaned forward to put his hand over hers and give it a friendly reassuring shake.

"Whoever it was will have to wait a long time for that chance!" His tone was deliberately cheerful, gaining a little smile from her, even if her eyes did not quite echo it. He tried a change of subject. "How are your daughters progressing with their art? Is their father pleased with them?"

Before replying she glanced out of the window to where Aletta and

Sybylla were playing with Cornelia. Francesca was not with them, for she had left school on her twelfth birthday in January, the age when girls were expected to receive increased instruction at home in the field of domestic arts in preparation for marriage. Today Francesca was being entrusted with the planning and cooking of the noonday meal for the family and the dinner in the evening, something she had done with success a good number of times before. Anna returned her gaze to Rembrandt, unable to keep a note of maternal pride from her voice.

"Hendrick continues to be astounded by Francesca's artistic ability at her age. Aletta is also far better than average." She gave a wry half-smile as she took a different tone. "As for Sybylla, she likes to play at being a painter sometimes, but that's the end of it, I fear. Unfortunately Hendrick doesn't like to be beaten at anything he undertakes and continues to teach her with the two older girls, hoping to coax some minor gift for art out of her. It would be far better if he didn't." She was thinking of the tempestuous scenes that resulted. Normally she could take such uproars in her stride, but since she had become pregnant again her nerves were constantly on edge. Maybe when her violent attacks of morning sickness passed she would regain the strength that was now drained from her at the start of every day.

"I assume that Hendrick has indentured the two older girls to himself?"

She was puzzled. "What do you mean?"

"Only that if he judges them to be as good as you say, it's high time he accepted them as his apprentices in preparation for when each will be ready to apply for a mastership of the Guild of Amsterdam. Nobody gets that honour without serving the obligatory six years under a master. Naturally neither may develop to that standard, but each should have her chance."

She remained doubtful. "I'm not sure that Hendrick would do as you suggest. He is happy enough to give the girls instruction when it suits him, but he hates to be tied down to anything not quite of his choosing. By making Francesca and Aletta his pupils officially he might feel himself to be under an obligation to teach them on a regular basis and that could be calamitous. As you know, it's the reason why the few apprentices he has had in the past never stayed with him. I wish he had

been more successful as a teacher. It must have given you great pleasure and satisfaction to see your pupils become splendid artists in their own right."

"That is true, Anna."

She recalled Hendrick's fit of wild jealousy when he had thrown out one hapless youth, who had been misguided enough to fall in love with her, and trouble had resulted over the refunding of the tuition fees, Hendrick being in financial difficulties at the time. Four or five other pupils had left of their own free will at various intervals, protesting to their parents that Hendrick had no interest in whether they progressed or not, a legitimate complaint that permitted the dissolution of their indentures. As a result, he had gained the reputation of being a poor teacher and the fees that supplemented the income of other artists never came his way.

"Nevertheless," Rembrandt continued, "I do advise you not to let the young years of your two older girls slip by without indenture papers."

She saw the wisdom of what he advised, but to confront Hendrick with an outright request for them would have the outcome she had mentioned.

Then there came an interruption as the faces of Aletta and Sybylla appeared at the window, both girls requesting that Cornelia return home with them for the noon meal and asking if afterwards they could continue the games they were playing.

"Yes, of course!" she replied willingly.

Her daughters exclaimed with delight and parted to let Cornelia through to the window. Her bright face, much like her mother's, beamed at Anna. "I thank you, Vrouw Visser." Then to her father, she added, "Am I allowed, Father?"

"Yes. You go and enjoy yourself."

"We'll see her home about six," Anna promised, rising to her feet. The streets were safe enough by daylight, but after dusk there were the same dangers in Amsterdam as in any other capital. The city militia patrolled the streets by night, but they could not be everywhere.

Rembrandt rose from the bench too. "There's no need. Titus will be in your area about that time and he can collect her."

On the way home, with the girls chattering together at her side,

Anna pondered over the advice Rembrandt had given her. That afternoon a downpour of rain, forcing the girls indoors, gave her an unexpected opportunity to do something about it. She sat the children down at the kitchen table, getting Francesca to join them, and introduced some word games on paper. When Hendrick, who had been out, came back home, Anna sent Sybylla to fetch him to add his name to each girl's fresh sheet of paper, which she had just handed out. Hendrick obliged, but did not stay while Anna collected all four sheets and improvised some guessing game about them.

Titus arrived at six o'clock. Anna met him, for the kitchen had been left to Francesca again and the other three girls had gone upstairs. "I trust I find you well, Vrouw Visser," he said cheerily.

"Yes, indeed," she replied.

"I've been delivering one of Father's etchings to a buyer," he explained, setting aside on a chair the leather folder that had held Rembrandt's work. Titus possessed no exceptional artistic talent himself but, unlike his father, was businesslike and practical. Those who were able to remember Rembrandt in his youth always said that his son looked as like him at the same age as another pea from the same pod, being of average height and broadly built with a roundish, smiling face and a shock of brown curls. "Is my sister ready to leave?"

Like all children when interrupted at play, Cornelia was not. Anna gained the girl another enjoyable half an hour by sitting to chat with Titus herself in the family parlour. She had a maternal fondness for him, having seen him grow up, and was pleased that recently he had begun courting a pretty girl, Magdelena van Lon, whose parents she knew well. As they talked he happened to glance up at the painting of himself as a boy on the wall.

"I'm still in a place of honour, I see," he joked.

"Only just!" she replied on a little laugh. "Francesca asked recently for your portrait to be hung on a bare peg in the studio, where she can have a friendly face to look at when she's on the rostrum with her gaze in that direction. She made the same request some long time ago, but Hendrick hung a landscape for her instead."

"I'm flattered that she should want to look at me! Does she pose often for Master Visser?"

"Not now. She is too busy with her own artwork."

He glanced at the painting again. "I remember that I was puzzling over some mathematical problems in my homework from school when Father first took up his brushes for that painting. As you know, he takes a great deal of time over all his works and in the end, when the problems were long since solved, I sat there daydreaming. But then I suppose that was what Father had been aiming for in the first place."

Anna looked up at the painting too. Much of the impasto had still been wet when it had come into Hendrick's hands. He had happened to meet Rembrandt in the street one day when the artist was desperate for cash, having been refused further credit by every supplier of art materials in Amsterdam. He had offered to sell Hendrick the painting of Titus for whatever he could pay. Hendrick had on him a purse that held the amount he had received from the Amsterdam art-dealer, Willem de Hartog, for the sale of two paintings of his own. Promptly he had pulled the purse from his pocket and placed it in Rembrandt's hands. Anna had come to appreciate the painting since then, but for a long time afterwards it had reminded her of how she had fainted away at discovering her husband had come home penniless when every stuiver in his purse had been urgently needed. It was Janetje who had kept the food on their table during the hard weeks that had followed until Hendrick sold half a dozen etchings and their fortunes took a turn for the better.

Titus remembered the hour and sprang up from his chair. "I really must take Cornelia home. She's almost as much at your house as she is at ours."

"Your sister is always welcome here."

When he and Cornelia had left, Sybylla came to ask for the papers from the word game. Anna gave her all except those bearing Hendrick's signature, which the girls had also signed. On her own again, Anna threw away Cornelia's paper before she went to an upper room. After turning the key in the lock, she began searching in a cupboard for a certain parchment document she knew to be stored there. Finding it, she took it across to a writing table where there was pen and ink, and sat down to copy the wording of Hendrick's indentures to the late Frans Hals of Haarlem onto the sheet of paper bearing his signature and

that of Francesca, incorporating them in the right places. She then did the same with Aletta's and Sybylla's. It was unlikely that Sybylla would develop into an artist at a later date, but it was not right to leave her out.

When all was done, the ink dry and the document returned to its drawer, Anna rolled up the three improvised indentures, tied them with a ribbon, took them into her bedchamber and placed them in her Oriental lacquered box, which held Janetje's correspondence and other items of importance to her. It was the only time in her life she had carried out a deception against Hendrick, but one day she would explain to him it had been for his good and that of their daughters. She smoothed the lace of her cuffs and brushed her hands down her skirt as if some evidence of what she had done might be clinging to her. Then, quite composed, she went downstairs.

It was almost time for the evening prayers and the family was gathering with Griet in the parlour. Anna knelt in her place beside Hendrick and glanced around at the little circle to make sure the children had folded their hands and were ready. Only Maria sat, for she could no longer get down on her knees. Then Anna bowed her head. Her religious faith was strong. She felt she was particularly blessed in having seen the face of Christ in Rembrandt's painting of Him. The Dutch Reformed Church rarely commissioned works of art, preferring its walls to be bare, and she thought it a sad loss to thousands of people that only a few of them would ever see the painting. Rembrandt, a devout man himself, had surely come as close as was humanly possible to portraying the Master's intense compassion and love. She knew that through the painting she had come nearer to Him.

Maria had been anxious about Anna's health, able to see that this pregnancy was taking its toll on her. Fortunately Francesca was a great help in relieving her mother of numerous chores, although Anna did not like any extra duties keeping the girl away from the time she could spend in the studio. Then, as the months went by, Maria was thankful to see colour returning to Anna's cheeks while her step grew more vigorous and her energy returned. It was clear she was set on a steady

course for the birth, which was due early in April. She was just into her seventh month when she came home from visiting a neighbour. Maria, who was teaching Sybylla a new embroidery stitch, told her that Aletta was playing at the Korvers' house. Leaving them, Anna went to look in at the studio. Both Hendrick and Francesca were at their individual easels, painting a landscape from sketches they had made, he having retained the colours in his memory while she, less experienced, had made some notes on her drawings to help her. Neither saw Anna and she went out silently again. She thought, as she had often done before, what a pity it was that painting out of doors on location was not possible. The sheer weight of a large, heavy easel and a good-sized canvas on its stretcher made carrying them prohibitive from the start, quite apart from transporting everything else that was needed. No wonder artists chose to go unhampered with nothing more than their sketch pads and then paint afterwards what they had seen.

At the Korvers' house Aletta was getting tired of waiting for someone to take her home. Heer Korver was with a buyer and his wife was supervising the arrangements for a family banquet to be held there that evening. Jacob, who would have taken her, was not home yet. He was serving an apprenticeship with another diamond merchant and, because the strictness of his indentures prevented his visiting his parents very often, there was always a celebration when he did come home. His grandparents and a host of other relatives were coming from far afield. Esther and the twins were up another flight to change clothing and there was nobody around to think of her. Even the old manservant, who usually escorted her home after sunset, had been dispatched on some special errand.

Impatiently she went to the window and looked out. Dusk had fallen but it was not yet completely dark. If she ran all the way she could be home in less than five minutes. Already in her cape, she did not bother to fasten it or pull up her hood, but set off at once down the stairs and let herself out the front door. No sooner was she outside than she found it was a little darker than she had realized. There was only one city wall lantern alight in the whole seemingly deserted street, but it was too late to go back indoors now. She could see well enough and that was all that mattered.

Swiftly she broke into a run, unaware of the dainty, mothlike appearance she presented, her primrose skirt billowing lightly and her mass of soft, silvery-fair hair dancing about her head like a tinselled cloud in the half-light. A roughly clad man, unshaven and half drunk, watched her with a stirring of his loins from the arch of a house's passageway on the opposite side of the canal. Draining the bottle he held, he set it down quietly instead of tossing it into the canal as he would have done otherwise. Tensely he waited to see if she would cross the bridge. If not, he'd take a quick sprint after her. There was nobody else about as far as he could tell and he'd take his chance. She *was* coming over to this side! He reached out a hand and tested the passage door to see if the house owner had bolted it yet for the night. He grinned as it swung open with a slight creak into blackness. He drew back into it, no longer able to see her, but able to judge her approach by her light footsteps getting nearer. Then, as she came level, he pounced.

To Aletta it was for one horrifying second as if a fairy-tale monster had sprung from the depths of the earth to seize her. Yet in the same instant she knew it to be a man. He had clapped a callused hand over her mouth, muzzling her screams, and grabbed a handful of her hair down to the roots as if he would wrench it from her scalp. Terror possessed her utterly as he half swung her into the passageway and slammed her against the wall to pinion her with his body there. Already breathless from the pace at which she had run, she felt she would suffocate from the stench of foul breath, stale sweat and filthy clothing that filled her nostrils like the odour of plague. His chin rasped her forehead and her eyes threatened to start with renewed horror from their sockets as she felt him slobbering over her head. She thought in fear-crazed disbelief that he was trying to eat her hair and she could feel some strange part of him through her skirts. Her struggling arms and kicking feet had no effect and he was muttering hoarsely. His words, although breathy, were audible and in the dialect of another province.

"Your tresses! So fine a colour is going to get you what you deserve!"

His saliva had begun running down her face. Worse—oh! much worse—she heard him pull the leather thongs of his breeches free and then his awful devil hand was bundling up her skirts. Her eyes rolled up

2
3

and her mind went blank with shock, her whole body rigid against violation.

Then, without warning, the passageway reverberated with the thunderous voice of the furious house-holder as he shouted to them from the rear courtyard. "What in hell's name is going on down there?"

Her attacker cursed, releasing her, and she fell to the stone flags as he bolted. The hostile interruption gave her no thought of help forthcoming from its direction. She was up and out of the passageway into the street like a homing pigeon released from a basket, guided by instinct more than sense or sight to cover the few yards to safety.

Griet, busy in the kitchen, turned in amazement as the back door went crashing open and Aletta, her face white to the lips, her eyes wild and dilated, dashed through, looking neither to right nor to left.

"Aletta! Wait! What's wrong?" Griet flew after her, but she had already disappeared up two flights of stairs to her room. Her bedchamber door gave an echoing slam. Turning about, Griet ran to the family parlour, where Anna and Maria sat sewing lace onto baby garments and Francesca was playing draughts with Sybylla. All looked up as Griet entered.

"What has happened?" Anna demanded on a rush of anxiety, putting her sewing aside.

"I don't know, ma'am. Aletta has come home in a dreadful state. She went tearing through the kitchen and up to her room!"

"Was anyone with her?" Anna was already out of her chair.

"No, ma'am. She had no cloak and her hair was all over the place."

Anna, moving swiftly for the door, gave her daughters their instructions. "You are both to stay here with Maria." Then to Griet she gave another order. "Fetch the master from the studio at once!"

"But he's not there, ma'am! He's out!"

Anna broke into a run as she made for the stair hall. She heard Maria shout after her that Aletta should be upbraided for breaking the golden rule of never being out alone after sunset. But this was no time for recriminations. All that was important was to discover what had happened and hope to put matters right.

In her overwhelming concern for her daughter, Anna had forgotten her condition completely. She took the narrow flight at a faster pace

than she had done since her pregnancy. It was as she swept around the top newel post to continue up the second flight that she inadvertently stepped on the hem of a petticoat that she had failed to bunch high enough to leave her feet free. It was a strong, hand-woven linen that did not give and she was hurled off balance, a victim of her own haste. Thudding with full force against the banister, she felt the handrail lash into her side like a bullwhip. Her first lightning thought was one of thankfulness that she had not struck her belly and she cupped a hand over her unborn child, but for a matter of seconds she could not move and remained gasping for breath. Downstairs Griet had come running into the hall to call up to her. "Are you all right, ma'am?"

Anna steadied herself and straightened her back, glad she was out of the maidservant's sight or else she would have had Maria's fussing to add to this present crisis with Aletta, whatever it might be. "Yes, Griet. Reassure Maria. I happened to stumble on my skirt hems."

It was a common enough occurrence and Griet did not come up the stairs to investigate further. Anna drew in a deep breath and thrust the pain from her mind. Time enough later to think about a few bruised ribs. She took the last stairs at a slower pace than she would have wished, and crossed the landing to Aletta's door. It was locked on the inside.

"Aletta! It's Mama! Open the door and let me in." There was no reply and she tried again. "Please do as I say. I know something has happened and I want to help you."

Still there was silence. Anna's fear rose sharply. Aletta was always particularly close to her. Never before had there been a time of trouble when Aletta had not run straight to her. It could only be some kind of shame that was keeping the child away. She shook the door handle urgently and banged the panel with the flat of her hand, calling through in as level a tone as she could manage, but getting no response. Then, happening to glance down, she saw that from under the door a trickle of water had appeared. She renewed her efforts, trying another tactic.

"Aletta! You must let me in! If this door has to be forced the whole household will be crowded around. Surely you would like to speak to me on your own."

She leaned weakly against the door, her brow against it. The daggers

2
5

of pain still driving into her side were nothing compared with the anguish over what she might have done to her unborn child and her despair over a little girl too shocked to seek her own mother's comfort. Her head jerked up as the key turned, but the door did not open.

She turned the handle and pushed the door open slowly, careful to restrain her wish to rush in and embrace her daughter. The room was in darkness and she turned back a step to take up the candle lamp from the landing table. It lit her way into the bedchamber. Then she halted to stand staring in shocked disbelief. Aletta sat naked in the middle of the room, her face hidden as she rested her forehead on her updrawn knees, her arms clasped about them. She looked like a shorn lamb. Scissors from her sewing basket showed how the damage had been wrought, for all around her on the floor were soft tufts and strands of her pure-coloured hair. To add to her pitiable condition she had poured water over her head from the ewer on the corner cupboard.

Almost in the same moment of registering the scene, Anna set down the candle lamp and shut the door, turning the key. Then she snatched up a couple of towels that lay folded by the china basin. Dropping awkwardly on one knee in front of the child, pain still stabbing at her side, she wrapped the towels about the shivering shoulders. Gently she raised her daughter's face and was met by a tormented stare. She had to choke back a cry at the sight of the livid bruises over mouth and jaw, the lips swollen and bleeding from pressure against teeth.

"Stand up, my baby," Anna said softly in the nursery tones of the past. "Mama can't lift you and you'll catch cold if I don't dry you quickly."

At first Aletta did not move. Anna coaxed again, holding out her arms, and then was nearly unbalanced for a second time as her daughter sprang forward into her waiting embrace, the tears coming like a torrent. At the first possible moment, Anna went to call downstairs for some things she needed. Then she finished drying the poor little shorn head where some of the hair had been wrenched out by the attacker, leaving raw patches.

Everything Anna had called for was quickly delivered, Griet having gained permission to enlist Francesca's help. Anna opened the bedchamber door only wide enough to receive each item and then closed it

again. There was a large jug of hot water, her medical box of salves and bindings, a heated brick wrapped in flannel and a mug of hot milk. The only time she held the door open for a fraction longer than necessary was to give Francesca some explanation of what had happened.

"It is as I feared. Aletta met somebody who handled her roughly on the way home, but she is going to be all right again."

"We're all so worried." Francesca's own drawn expression bore out the truth of her words. "Maria is in tears and begs you not to reprimand Aletta after all."

"I had no intention of doing that in any case. Aletta has been most cruelly handled and as yet she will not speak about what happened. But I can tell you that mercifully she has escaped the ultimate physical harm that can be done to a young, innocent girl. Let Maria know this. And tell Sybylla I shall sleep here tonight in her place. She can go in with you. Is there any sign of Papa yet?"

"None."

Anna closed the door and returned to attend to Aletta. Half an hour later Aletta was still remaining silent, lying in bed and staring up at the canopy. Anna sat by her, for all she wanted was her mother's reassuring presence. She started with fright when a tap came again on the bedchamber door and sat upright, speaking for the first time.

"Don't leave me, Mama!" she implored on a note of panic.

"I'm not going to," Anna assured her, giving her brow a kiss.

Francesca stood on the landing, her sister's blue cape in her hand. "Heer Blankert brought this cape he found in his passageway. He didn't know it was Aletta's until one of the other neighbours recognized it. He is very concerned, because he thought he saw a struggle taking place. I told him she is unharmed."

"Has he a description of her attacker?" Both she and Francesca were talking in lowered voices to keep their conversation from Aletta's ears.

"He rushed out into the street in time to see the villain running away and caught a glimpse of his face in the light from a window. He wants to speak to Papa about it."

"Then ask him to find your father for himself. He drinks enough with Hendrick to know his possible whereabouts." She shoved back the cape that Francesca held out to her. "No! That is to be burned. There's

more too." She slipped back into the room, where everything Aletta had been wearing was tied into a bundle, including hose and shoes, and brought it to Francesca. "Give this to Griet and tell her to burn every item. I want no reminders left of this dreadful evening."

When Aletta finally slept it was midnight. By her in the bed Anna lay awake, having finally been told of how the attack had come about. There had been more tears to dry, more comforting words to utter, and she hoped desperately that before long, with the resilience of the young, Aletta would be able to bury the experience in the depths of her mind. On the debit side was the reserve and modesty of the girl, which had been so flagrantly outraged, but on the credit side Anna knew there was in Aletta's character much of her own determination never to crumble under adversity, which, combined with more than a dash of stubbornness inherited from Hendrick, should stand Aletta in good stead.

Tentatively Anna ran a hand over her painful side. Surprisingly, considering she feared she might have cracked a rib, there had been almost no bruising when she had looked in the mirror while undressing. The baby in her womb was still as active as before, almost as if he wanted to let her know she need not worry about him when she had so much else to concern her. From the start she had been sure she was to bear a son this time.

She woke from a doze in the early hours of the morning to hear a commotion downstairs. Hendrick was home! With difficulty she sat up and reached for a robe. She checked that Aletta was lying undisturbed and then went downstairs as quickly as she could, holding on to the handrail and keeping her hems high. She was not angry with him for having been so long away from home when she needed him. There was no changing the way he was. But now she wanted to be held in his loving arms and given some tender words in her turn after all the anguish and physical pain endured, which still weighed her down. Together they could talk a little of how they might bring their beloved child out of her nightmare.

As soon as she came in sight of him in the stair hall she saw it was not going to be like that. Hendrick, flushed from earlier drinking, but sobered by the news he had received, stood with a crazed look in his eyes, his contorted expression blended of rage and frustration.

"How is she?" he shouted, taking no heed of waking anyone.

She put a finger to her lips and took the last few treads. "Asleep. We must be thankful she was spared the actual act of rape."

"The bastard laid hands on her! That's enough to earn him a rope! Blankert and I and a band of others have been searching for him in the streets and alleyways! We enlisted the aid of the Night Watch and combed the docks." His voice broke and he shook his head as if to clear it. "Dear God! I can't endure the thought of what would have happened to her if Blankert had not shouted in time." Then in remorse he drove a closed fist against his brow. "I should have been at home to meet her! That was the original arrangement, but I asked for it to be changed. There was to be a game of cards I didn't want to miss!"

She went to him. His big arms wrapped her to his broad body, but his head drooped onto her shoulder. Again she was the comforter.

In the morning Aletta rose at six o'clock with the rest of the household. It had not occurred to her that because of what had happened she should seek any privileges, even though the black horror of what she had been through had leapt into her mind upon waking. Twice in the night she had awoken in screams, but her mother had been there and the terror had been subdued again. There was no evidence in the bedchamber of how she had cleansed herself, except a damp patch on the floorboards, from which she averted her eyes. She wanted to build up a wall of blankness in her mind that would shut out everything that had happened. It should be possible, for she could not remember coming home, there being nothing between the shout in the passageway and the rush of cold water over her head.

Whether she could have faced the day without a solution to her appearance she did not know, but her mother had brought her a head-hugging little cap to wear. Caps of every kind were worn by many women and young girls. It was an old custom that had never lost its grip, although the French fashion of drawing the hair smoothly into a coil at the back of the head, leaving the neck free with a few curls dangling over each ear, had banished cap wearing for all those with an eye for mode. Anna had always dressed her hair in a pretty style and had never seen the need for her daughters to wear caps.

The one she produced for Aletta had come from the chest of accessories in Hendrick's storeroom where he kept a motley collection of robes, objects and artifacts for his paintings, much as strolling players had baskets of props. Aletta put the cap on. It was covered with bright beadwork, shaped to reveal a small semicircle of hair above the brow and then curving down over the ears to fit neatly at the back of the head. A damp comb had smoothed the little bit of her cropped hair that was to be seen and there was no longer anything unsightly about her appearance.

"There!" Anna exclaimed admiringly as Aletta stood regarding herself in the mirror. "It suits you well. Later today you may take any others you like from the chest. Several are in that style. Before long your hair will have grown again and in the meantime none will question your wearing a pretty cap."

Going down to breakfast in her mother's wake, Aletta thought that how long she had to wait for her hair to grow again was not important, for never more would she go with an uncovered head in public.

Sensibly everyone at the table, primed beforehand by Anna, made no comment, and before long the sight of Aletta always in a cap became natural to the household and to other people alike. For several nights Anna continued to sleep with her. Then one evening Aletta asked if Sybylla, who had shared her bed ever since growing out of the cot bed, could return to be with her. It was not that she did not prefer her mother's reassuring company, but any deviation from normal routine was reminder of the cause of it in the first place. Anna understood.

"Yes, of course Sybylla can come back to your room."

Sybylla was delighted. As the youngest she was the first to go to bed by half an hour. Since she never went to sleep early, she did not have so long to wait alone in the darkness for Aletta as she did for Francesca, whose bedtime was another hour after that. To add to Sybylla's joy in being back in the shared four-poster Aletta took her hand and held it, something never done before.

"Aletta?" Sybylla whispered.

3
0

"Yes?" The reply was half muffled by the goose-feather quilt that was as thick and soft as the mattress beneath them.

"We are going to sleep hand in hand. It's like skipping through a meadow or walking down a street or skating together."

"I suppose it is. Now stop talking. I'm tired." Aletta emphasized her desire for sleep by thumping her head on the pillow. She chose not to disclose that holding her sister's hand was for her own benefit. She had been wrenched out of childhood through no wish of her own and she felt vulnerable and insecure in the adult world into which she had been thrown before her time. Sybylla's fingers looped with hers made a link with her own innocence in the blissful days that would never come again.

Anna's realization that all was not well with her pregnancy came quite suddenly. She awoke earlier than the usual hour of rising to an unnatural stillness in her womb. It was still dark, but the curtains of the four-poster were apart and the embers in the fireplace gave some faint glow to the room. Hendrick was fast asleep, his arm around her. She lay for a while, trying not to be unduly alarmed and reminding herself that the baby was never constantly astir. Yet all her instincts told her that something untoward had happened. Her thought went against her will to the stumble she had had on the stairs. With concern for Aletta uppermost in her mind, had she reassured herself too quickly that no harm had been done? Was it possible that there had been deeper damage within that was now taking its toll? Merciful heaven! No!

Carefully she lifted Hendrick's arm from her and he grunted, but did not wake. Then she spread her hands gently over her round belly, praying that she was mistaken and willing the baby to give her some sign that his little heart was still beating with hers. For minutes that seemed like hours nothing happened. She had begun to tremble with apprehension. Then she almost cried out with joy as she felt a faint stirring. Tears of relief started from her eyes and she smiled at her own foolishness in giving way to unnecessary imaginings. Nothing was wrong after all. Strangely, that moment of feeling him move again after nigh-panic fear for his well-being had released within her heart the

fount of mother love that normally came with the first sighting of the infant. She felt as close to her son as if he were already in her arms. There was that sense of special togetherness that exists between a mother and her newborn child that is unique to the first hours and days.

Then pain pierced through her whole body like a sword. The force of her scream thrust her almost to a sitting position. Hendrick, waking with a great start, was in time to see her fall back again. She did not stop screaming and the whole house began to echo with banging doors and running feet. Ashen-faced, Francesca was first at the door as Hendrick flung it open. He had thrown on breeches and was thrusting his arms into a jacket.

"Stay with your mother! Don't let the younger ones in. Maria will most surely be here with you at any minute. I'm going for the doctor!"

He ran from the house, stopping only to bang the knocker on a neighbour's door. An upper window opened and a man's face appeared. Hendrick shouted up to him.

"My Anna! Her time has come too early! Ask your wife to go in to her at once!" Then Hendrick's running footsteps went echoing down the street.

For Anna there was only pain. Faces came and went at her bedside, accompanied by whispering and the crackle of starched aprons. For her previous confinements the midwife and helping neighbours had sufficed, for birthing was an entirely female affair, but this time the doctor was there as well. When he spoke to her his face seemed to hover in the most curious way and his cool hands on her arms made her realize how wildly she must be thrashing about. What he said to her she did not know, for she was incapable of listening or answering. Screams filled her head and her mouth as she and her son fought for their lives together.

When at last the pain eased she lapsed into a lulling quietude. There had been no newborn cry and she knew her adored infant had lost his battle. Yet the bond between them had not been broken.

"My beloved." It was Hendrick's voice, heavy with grief.

She opened her eyes. He was sitting at the bedside, holding her hand, and his poor, dear face was so doleful that she longed to take him into her arms, but she had no strength to raise them. There was no one else

in the room and she was in a fresh nightshift and lying in crisp, clean linen. Her gaze moved across to the corner where the crib had stood in readiness. It had been removed.

"Anna—"

"I know," she whispered. "Our son is waiting for me."

He had to bend his head close to catch her words. "No!" he cried out desperately. "Don't leave me, my darling. I can't go on living without you!" He gazed in agony at her face, deathly white from the terrible haemorrhaging, and pressed her hand to his lips. The tears ran from his eyes, which were already red-rimmed.

It had become almost beyond her to whisper now. "I'll never leave you in spirit, my love. Try to remember that."

"You've always been everything to me. My love, my world, my soul!"

"I have loved you in the same way and will do forever." She did not want to go from him, but all her fighting for life had been done in the past hours and she was now possessed by the most wonderful sense of peace. She wished she could explain it to him, for it confirmed that death was only a door. Her lids closed again, but she could not go yet and they fluttered open again. "Are the girls here?"

"Yes. I'll fetch them." He left the chair to open the door and beckon to his daughters, who stood huddled together, Maria and Griet with them. Francesca put an arm around Aletta, weeping on one side of her, and Sybylla on the other.

"Now smile for our mama!" she insisted. "It's what will please her most."

Somehow they managed it as each kissed her in turn. Anna whispered lovingly, "My darlings."

Maria and Griet came and stood at the end of the bed, able to see that the last moments were coming and there was no more time for personal farewells. The three girls together held Anna's hand that was nearest them while Hendrick half sat on the bed and drew her from the pillows into his arms, her head coming to rest against his shoulder. She made two or three little sounds in her throat and then she went from them on a sigh.

Francesca's life took an abrupt turn at her mother's death. She was just thirteen, newly come to womanhood, and her easygoing existence was no more. It was brought home to her the day after the funeral when she came down to breakfast, which was always eaten in the warm kitchen, to find there was no plate, knife, napkin or cup for her where she had always sat. Instead a place had been laid again at the end of the table at Anna's chair. She looked uncertainly at Hendrick, whose haggard face and bloodshot eyes were evidence of the alcohol he was consuming nightly to dull his grief. Listlessly he raised his hand and indicated she should take her mother's place.

The others watched her in silence as she went to it and stood there. She thought her heart must break anew, although she guessed the reason for this change. Hendrick could not endure looking at Anna's empty chair and it also established her position as female head of the household. It was to her that Maria and Griet must turn now for their instructions on any special matters arising and it also told her sisters that she was to be obeyed.

Hendrick said grace and all sat down. Since the day of Anna's going an uneasy silence had prevailed at mealtimes. Cheerful chatter was a thing of the past. Now and again there was a request for something to be passed along the table and Maria would make a comment about the weather, but that was all. Hendrick did not look at anyone, but sat in his cocoon of grief, eating automatically whatever he had on his plate. Normally he was a hearty eater who enjoyed his food, but now if something he wanted was not within reach he could not be bothered to ask for it.

This morning Francesca could sense that the new move of her taking Anna's chair had upset everyone, even Hendrick, although it had been done by his wish. The tension was building and she steeled herself for the moment when someone's tears would break forth. She hoped they would not be her own. Until now, in order to give some succour to her sisters and Maria, she had shed her own floods of racking tears in the privacy of her room and kept a brave face otherwise.

The sudden loud sob came from an unexpected quarter. It was Griet who covered her face with her apron and fled from the kitchen. Hendrick did not look up from his plate. Then Sybylla exploded into

hysterical tears, picking up her cup like a baby and smashing it down on her plate, spilling milk everywhere.

"I don't want Mama to be dead any longer!" It was the heart cry of the bereaved when after an initial state of numbing shock the empty gap begins to yawn. As Francesca sprang up to go to her, Sybylla added deliberately to her misdeed by picking up the basket of bread and throwing it across the room. But the attention she had expected from her father was not forthcoming. Instead of flying into a rage, he simply pushed back his chair and left the table to shut himself away in the family parlour, which he seemed to be making his place of retreat.

It was the first of many such scenes with Sybylla. She would throw tantrums and lie on the floor kicking her heels at the slightest provocation. Maria, finding her former means of discipline no longer worked on the child, called on Francesca to deal with her every time. Aletta, who had been closest to Anna, became deeply attached to Francesca and they would sit talking together as they never had before. First of all, it was about Anna and their memories of her, finding at last that they could laugh about funny things that had happened, which made her come more alive for them than remembrances of a more serious kind. Later they began to confide hopes and dreams.

They went together into the studio to look at the life-size portrait of Anna there. The studio had not been used for some time, because Hendrick had not been near it, and the half-finished painting of a mythical scene on the easel was as it had been on the day of Anna's death. The two sisters stood side by side to look up at Anna, whose twinkling eyes always looked right into the eyes of the viewer from any direction. Her laughing face framed by the banner of her hair, the flowing movement of her gown and the glimpse of one foot in its pink satin shoe showing beneath the hem, conveyed her whole warm presence to them.

"Let's set up our easels and start painting in this corner of the studio with Mama's portrait on the wall," Francesca suggested.

Aletta agreed eagerly. Nobody had encouraged them more in their art than Anna. This first step in beginning to paint again was like doing something for her.

Among Francesca's new domestic duties was the keeping of the

household accounts. She had been well taught in all domestic matters and running the house was not causing her any headaches. On the rare occasions when she sought Hendrick's advice, he would always give her the same reply.

"Do as your mother would have done."

That was well enough, but when it came to settling bills and there were only a few stuivers left in the housekeeping box she felt the time had come to get her father to work again. For six weeks he had spent his time shut away in the family parlour, where he drank by himself at all hours of the day, or else he went out to the taverns and idled his time away there. She spoke of the matter to Willem de Hartog, her father's art dealer, when she called on him one day, a leather folder of Hendrick's etchings under her arm.

To reach de Hartog's residence she had to cross Dam Square, which was the heart of this fan-shaped city of bridges that lived on and with water. Anna had always liked to buy vegetables and fish from the market stalls here, saying the produce was always fresh, and there was so much to see whatever the season of the year. There was a busy scene on any weekday, for here trading took place on several levels. City affairs were conducted at the Town Hall, which was a grand building ornamented with pilasters and cornices with great pedimental sculptures of sea gods. Cargoes from the ships dropping anchor by the Dam were dealt with at the weighhouse. The whole square and the streets leading to it thronged with people, wagons, coaches and handcarts. Pedlars bawled their wares, dogs barked and she kept out of the path of some drunken seamen who came reeling out of the tavern, singing raucously. Francesca paused to watch a team of tumblers in yellow-and-pink costumes performing to the music of a flute and a drum, which blended discordantly with the shrill notes of a trumpet being blown by a quack doctor's assistant to gain the attention of passersby.

It was far quieter when she thumped the silver knocker of Willem de Hartog's house. A maidservant admitted her, invited her to sit and then went to fetch the art dealer. The main ground-floor rooms of his house made up his gallery and in the reception hall where she sat there were many paintings set off by the walls of gilt leather.

Willem came to her at once. He was a tall, thin and dignified man

with brindled grey hair, his lean face trimmed with a moustache. He had attended her mother's funeral and had not seen her since, which was why he greeted her with a kiss on the hand and the cheek.

"What a pleasure to see you, Francesca! How is your father? Are you managing well?" He led her into another room where there were more works of art on the walls and they sat down at opposite sides of a narrow table on which she placed the leather folder of etchings. When he asked after Janetje she told him how deeply distressed her aunt had been to receive the news of Anna's death. "Her reply to my letter was so sad. She and my mother had always been close." Francesca talked easily with him, for he had been her father's friend and agent since before she was born. He had recently married a third wife, although his children by both previous marriages were grown up and wed themselves with no need of a mother. This was often the reason why a widower went speedily into a new marriage as soon as was decently possible. She did not think her father would take such a step.

"So you see," she said in conclusion after they had talked a while, "I feel I must get Father back to work in the studio, even if I have to use desperate measures. Not just because we've run out of money, but because he needs to work now more than ever. None of us will ever get over losing Mama." Her voice faltered, but she swallowed and carried on. "But she would have wanted us all to continue as if she were still in the house, which, in a way, she is with that wonderful portrait of her in the studio."

"I agree. Would you like me to talk to Hendrick?"

She shook her head. "That's most kind, but you know how easily he takes offence and I wouldn't want him to fall out with you after all these years."

Willem smiled. "I think I've broad enough shoulders to take whatever Hendrick should aim, knowing him as well as I do. However, I'll leave it to you to see what can be done, but if all else fails, do get in touch with me at once."

She thanked him and then opened the folder of etchings, explaining that she had gathered them from various drawers in the studio and hoped he would be able to sell them. He looked through them all. Most were of Amsterdam, but there were a few others of boats and barges on

the canals by windmills in the countryside. He guessed that Hendrick had been dissatisfied with each one for some reason or another, which was why he had never seen any of them before, but that had nothing to do with the matter now. Hendrick's daughter needed money for bread on the table and he would give her an advance on them to the full value of what he expected to get. This was a time when he would forfeit his commission, as he had done on two or three previous occasions when her father had been in desperate straits, not that Hendrick had ever known. His enormous pride was as touchy as his temper.

On the way home again Francesca shopped carefully. She practised all the economies she had been taught for difficult times. When she had deposited her purchases in the kitchen she went to Hendrick, who sat with a glass of grape brandy in his hand.

"Father," she said, steeling herself. "I took some of your etchings to Willem today."

He looked at her, bleary-eyed. "Did he take them? Good."

"There aren't any more. If you don't start painting again soon I'll have to take something else to sell. I could start with one of the smaller portraits of Mama that are hanging in this room. Later it may have to be the studio one."

He leapt out of his chair, hurling the glass and its contents into the fireplace, creating a roar of flame, and with his face a crimson mask of fury he swung up his hand to strike her. She faced him squarely, waiting for the blow to fall and did not flinch. His hand shook as he checked his action and then he let his arm drop to his side. He had never struck any one of his children and he realized painfully why she had goaded him as she had done. Reaching out, he drew her gently to him, cupping her head against his chest. His voice rumbled under her ear.

"I think I'll go along to the studio now and do some more work on that painting of Andromeda."

Francesca closed her eyes in thankfulness. Nothing was completely solved yet, but a beginning had been made.

Hendrick was never to work again as regularly as he had when Anna was alive. His commitment as an artist had not diminished, but at times

when a painting was almost finished he would break off and be away for several days at his own pleasures. It was as if he felt himself entitled to a reward for a spate of dedication to work in spite of his bereavement. This always infuriated Willem, waiting to sell the work, and exasperated Francesca, who continued to struggle to make ends meet, for nothing had changed in that respect.

Like her mother before her, she had become expert in juggling the creditors. When she received money for the housekeeping she would pay one tradesman in full and allow just enough to the rest to take the edge off their tempers. None of them had anything against her personally, any more than at Anna before her, for it was Hendrick they blamed for everything. Since they frequented the same taverns, their resentment would surge at the sight of him deep in his cups or flashing his money for any kind of wager when their account books had mounting figures of what he owed.

It was not only his new and erratic pattern of work that drastically reduced the tuition he gave his daughters. He had simply lost interest in teaching them. His resentment against giving instruction had come to the fore again now that Anna was no longer there to be pleased with their progress. It became obvious to the girls that their mother's generous praise for his efforts had been mainly instrumental in the close guidance he had given them in the past. Sybylla was overjoyed to be free of the studio. Her tantrums had subsided with the passing of time, but she waged a constant battle with Maria, who was determined to make her as competent at domestic chores as her sisters. Her exultation at leaving school on her twelfth birthday was dampened by the discovery of how many more hours a day she would have to spend mending and polishing and baking. On the day she had to scrub the stoop and pavement outside the house, normally Griet's task, she made a vow to herself, grumbling aloud to the soapsuds.

"I'm never going to do any of these chores when I'm married. Neither shall I be poor! Somehow I must find a rich husband quickly. Then I'll get away from Maria and have everything I want!"

During the next two years Sybylla kept a keen lookout every time she went to the Korvers' home. They were the only well-to-do people she knew and really rich men came to their house. When she was fifteen and her mirror showed her a pretty, dimpled face with sparkling mischievous eyes and a bosom of which she was proud, she thought she had found what she was looking for in Jacob Korver. He had come home from serving his apprenticeship and she had grown up in his absence. They looked at each other with new eyes. With his dark good looks and a future destined to be even more prosperous than that of his father, he filled her every requirement.

From him she received her first kiss. They were alone in the garden, hidden from the sight of the house. She melted towards him and was awakened to the first taste of the delights to be found in a man's arms, his lips warm and eager on hers.

"You're beautiful," he whispered, his face tender and adoring. He was totally infatuated with her.

"Kiss me again," she demanded shamelessly. It was even more thrilling the second time, for he placed his hand over her breast. They were breathless with delight and with each other.

"We shall be betrothed!" he declared recklessly.

But it was not to be. Heer Korver invited Hendrick for a glass of wine and they agreed amicably that a match between a Jewish boy and a girl brought up in the Dutch Reformed Church would not be suitable. They finished the bottle between them and parted in the same good neighbourliness as before. Jacob was sent off to learn about buying diamonds in foreign lands and Sybylla found herself back where she had started with a wedding ring as far away as ever.

CHAPTER 3

Francesca had many tempestuous scenes to settle with Sybylla over Jacob and there was no peace for anyone. Hendrick kept out of the way as much as possible, either leaving the house when trouble erupted or locking himself in the studio. Then, almost overnight, Sybylla accepted the situation. Nobody was more relieved than Francesca, for her painting had been severely disrupted, it being impossible to concentrate with such turmoil in the house. Looking in the mirror on the day she heard her younger sister laughing again, she wondered that she did not look thrice her age of seventeen years.

She was unaware of the extent to which her face had taken on an unusual and striking beauty, for she saw no symmetry in her features such as she admired in others and she was dismissive of compliments. Yet there was a haunting, fascinating quality to her expressive visage that Hendrick had long recognized in his paintings of her, and which was further enhanced by her lustrous green eyes, the upper lids weighed down by thick lashes. Her nose was narrow with delicately flaring nostrils and her neck was long, giving her a swanlike poise. Her cheekbones were wide, as was her mouth, but her lips were curved and her complexion was smooth as creamy silk.

She enjoyed men's company and, had she allowed it, could have been like any girl in becoming attracted to one or another handsome smile. It was not always easy to turn away, although by now the boys she had known since childhood had given up pursuing her, the older ones betrothed or wed elsewhere. The decision she had made long ago to be an artist had not changed and marriage was something she did not intend to contemplate for years to come, if ever.

The letter from Janetje was delivered one morning shortly before Francesca was to pose in another of many sittings for Hendrick, who was painting her as Flora, the goddess of spring. With about ten minutes to spare, she darted upstairs to her bedchamber, where she could read it on her own before sharing it with the rest of the family. Her hair, loosened in readiness for the sitting, hung in waves down her back and swirled out as she settled herself on the cushioned window seat, the sunshine through the panes making a red-gold aura of its coppery luxuriance. The fond link between her aunt and her had continued unbroken through their correspondence, Francesca writing to her much as she might have done to her own mother.

As usual, Janetje's letter was full of family affairs, from the progress her sons were making with their education to the banquet she and Giovanni gave to celebrate their seventh wedding anniversary. She expressed her intense eagerness for news from Holland, not having heard for several months, and Francesca hoped that by now the letter she had dispatched quite a while ago would have arrived. Any letter from her aunt that came at this time of year never failed to have a strong undertone of homesickness. It was clear that Janetje's thoughts always began to turn to the forthcoming Dutch Feast of St. Nicholaes, a family occasion which she had enjoyed both as a child and as an adult, and she never forgot to send a gift to each of her three nieces for the sixth day of December. This year of 1669 three pairs of scented leather gloves would be coming.

Francesca lowered the letter to her lap and began to fold it up again, her thoughts full of her aunt. It was pleasant to have read the letter by herself, here in her own room with its simple furnishings and the four-poster with the plain blue drapes. Nobody intruded on her when it was known she wanted to be alone. Her sisters still shared a room, although there were enough bedchambers for them to have had one each, but Aletta still had nightmares if she slept alone and Sybylla liked her company.

"Francesca!" Hendrick's voice boomed up the three flights like a distant roll of thunder.

"I'm coming!" she called back, not at all sure whether he would have heard her. She tucked the letter into her sash to take it to him, for she was already in robes from one of the atelier chests that she was to wear for the painting. Picking up a chaplet of silk flowers, she sprang up to cross to the mirror in a swish of heavy green satin, her sleeves of soft

and flowing silk gauze cut so full they almost draped to her hems, the wristbands encrusted with embroidery, as was her low-cut bodice. She put the chaplet on her head. In her lobes were large azure earbobs from the chest of trinkets and a necklace from the same source encircled her neck. After giving a final touch to her hair, she gathered up her skirts and hastened to descend the stairs.

Someone was hammering the knocker on the front door. Perhaps it was a tradesman expecting money, a pattern that never changed. If Hendrick had not called her she would have answered the door herself. Now she must leave it to Griet, who was equally well used to dealing with creditors. Her thoughts invariably went to her mother as she descended the second flight and turned by the newel post. She had no idea why, but she liked to believe she was being warned not to trip, for the last flight down to the stair hall was precipitous with barely enough room for two people to pass. By the time she reached the bottom tread the hammering had stopped. She sped from the stair hall, skipped two steps leading down from an archway into the corridor and hurried along it to reach the studio.

"I'm here!" she announced as she entered.

At the front door a tall, straight-backed young man in his mid-twenties had stepped from the stoop to regard the house with a frown. Was nobody at home? He had a shock of dark brown curly hair that grew fashionably to his shoulders and was kept temporarily in order by a black hat with a wide brim cocked at the side. His knee-length red coat was of good cloth, fitting well across his broad shoulders, and his bucket-topped boots were of fine leather. Under his arm he carried a lidded box. He had no wish to leave without fulfilling his mission and he looked upwards to see if a window was opening in response to his knocking, but nothing happened.

With no sign of life at the front of the Visser house, Pieter van Doorne decided he must try the back and went to the slatted wooden door at the side. Painted blue like the shutters and the main door of the house, it opened as he lifted the latch. His footsteps rang along the flags of the passageway within. The back door of the house was not the correct place to hand over the bulbs of a beautiful new tulip he had grown himself, they being worthy of a little ceremony, but there seemed no alternative. Normally he did not deliver his own wares, being far too busy and not through any sense of inflated pride, for he had built up his horticultural business the hard way and there was no humble task he had not carried out himself to establish it and ensure its success. It had happened today that he had found the staff on his market stall shorthanded due to illness and he had decided to do the delivery himself.

From the passageway he emerged into a sizeable and pleasant court-yard with trees, a trellis-shaded alcove for summer eating at a table, benches set by it, and borders of well-tended flowers. A broom propped against the table and the piles of swept-up leaves suggested that some-one had left the task to go indoors and would shortly return. The back door stood slightly ajar. Going across to it, he intended this time to give a shout, since knocking had failed to bring any response. The door swung back easily on its much used hinges to reveal a long shadowy corridor, doors and archways on each side, which ran the considerable length of the house to a room at the front. Within the frame of an open doorway, he could see a rostrum draped with a Persian rug, showing that it was Master Visser's studio. Illumined by its windows, it held the look of a stage set for a performance. All this he took in at a second and then in the next moment a slender girl with flowers in her copper-bright hair, her green satin skirts swirling, came into sight from another part of the room. The curious acoustics of the long corridor funnelled her clear voice to him as she addressed somebody else in the room whom he could not see.

"Aunt Janetje's letter arrived only ten minutes ago. I knew you'd enjoy reading it. How far have you got? Oh yes, you've come to the last part, where she describes a reception at the Pitti Palace. One day I'm going to visit her and see the splendours of Florence for myself!"

She flung back her head in ecstasy at the prospect, hugging her arms with her back arched. Pieter caught his breath at her unconsciously sensuous stance. He hoped she would look down the corridor and see him at the door. Instead she responded to some quip made by a man with a deep voice, whom Pieter guessed to be Master Visser himself. The girl's laugh was full-throated and merry. Twirling round, she stepped lightly up onto the rostrum, picking up a foliage-trimmed staff and a bunch of flowers lying there, and then stood in a graceful pose. "I'm ready, Father," she said, her gaze directed towards another part of the studio. Then, to his disappointment, the door of the studio swung closed, shutting off his sight of her as if her father had given it a push from where he stood by his easel.

Pieter grinned, shaking his head that he should have remained standing on this spot as if he had lost his power of speech at the tantalizing glimpse of that delicious girl. He did not think she would have been the one sweeping the courtyard and he would try his luck again.

"Hey!" he shouted, rapping the back door with his knuckles at the same time. "I've some bulbs here that I don't intend to leave on the doorstep!"

Down in the cellar, Griet, hunting for a sack in which to pack the leaves she had swept up in the courtyard, paused. Sighing with exasperation at the interruption, she shouted in reply as she mounted the stairs, "All right! I've heard you!"

Her irritability melted away as soon as she saw him. It was not often that anyone as personable came to the back door and his height and the breadth of his shoulders seemed to fill the whole doorway. Aware of being comely herself, she thrust out her breasts and smoothed her apron as she sauntered towards him, glad now that she was not trailing an old sack behind her.

"Good day to you, *mejuffrouw*," he said with a wide smile, holding a box out to her. "These are tulip bulbs for Master Visser. He ordered them at my market stall in the spring and asked for them to be delivered when it was time for planting. It was agreed there would be payment when they were delivered."

She took the box from him, knowing through long experience how to deal with those optimistic enough to expect ready cash for their goods, although she wished in this case she could have seen his account settled and gained a still wider smile from him. She liked the chiselled look of his facial bones that gave him such a striking countenance, the nose large, the jaw well set, and there was a tan to his complexion that came from the open air and the sunshine of the summer past.

"What is your name, *mijnheer?*" she asked, as much out of her own curiosity as the need to convey it to her master. Then, when he had

told her, she added, "The master is at work in the studio and can't be disturbed." It was a phrase that came glibly to her lips whether it happened to be true at the time or not. "I will tell him you were here."

This was the point when those who had had to wait overlong for payment in the past began to show aggressiveness and set a foot squarely in the door. This young man merely shrugged, his lively, clear brown eyes under the straight brows holding a twinkle she did not understand, for it was not directed flirtatiously at her, which she would have liked.

"Very well," he said casually. "I can't call back today, but the account is in with the bulbs and I will collect the money next time."

She felt a sense of shame that she could not warn him he would probably have to come several times before he saw as much as a stuiver. When creditors became ruthlessly demanding she could retaliate force-fully, seizing the first opportunity to slam the door in their faces, but she was certain that Pieter van Doorne was going to be a problem. He would remain polite but persistent, making it harder each time to turn him away without his just dues. Knowing the master, she was sure the most expensive bulbs to be had were in the box she had received. Although it was his personal debt, eventually it might prove to be a matter for Juffrouw Francesca to handle. Usually it was best to try to keep her out of it, because she would empty her own purse of whatever money she had, and it was always little enough.

"I thank you for calling. Good day to you, *mijnheer.*"

As Pieter left by the way he had come, he smiled to himself. The maidservant had no idea how pleased he had been when she had not fetched a purse to pay him. If luck was with him he would meet the artist's daughter the next time he called at the house.

As he retraced his steps along the street, he felt stimulated by the first breath of October, which had left September behind only the day before. The linden trees by the canal were golden and some late blooms still persevered in the flower beds that ran parallel with the water. He had been born in Haarlem and his tulip fields lay southwest of the old town, but recently he had bought a house in Amsterdam. He had always felt at home in the city's hustle and bustle, its salty atmosphere with ships in the harbour making a forest of masts as far as the eye

could see. Trade had caused the city to explode with wealth, and a political crisis in the Spanish Netherlands had brought an influx of Jewish diamond merchants, making Amsterdam the diamond centre of the world. The Hague was still the capital and the seat of government, but it was overshadowed by flourishing Amsterdam. It was here that the Dutch East and West India Companies had established rich trade routes to every corner of the globe. Holland, with its fleet of three hundred thousand ships, was the master mercantile nation, respected by all her rivals, even England, with whom there had been two recent short, sharp naval wars. Every merchant ship was heavily armed to meet with any skirmish involving old enemies or the privateers that plagued the seas. This defence ensured less risk also for those who invested in cargoes, something he had done himself to great advantage through the city's Exchange. He would later this very day plough some of his profits back into the same stream.

If there was any cloud on the horizon it was in the threat that France represented to Holland's peace and prosperity. It was obvious to many that Louis XIV had set his greedy eyes on the richest prize in Europe and it was impossible to dismiss the conviction that sooner or later he would pounce. It was odd how powerful men never learned from history. The Spanish had tried for eighty years, from the previous century into the early years of this one, to make Holland their own, using cruelty to captives that stunned the mind, but in the end it was mighty Spain that had weakened itself by widespread wars and its struggles against a little country where so much of the land had to be protected from the sea by dikes.

When Pieter arrived again at Dam Square, he checked that all was well at his stall. From there he set off to a coffeehouse where he had made an appointment to meet a merchant in order to discuss some business before they both went on to the Exchange. He was aware of smiling to himself again, thoughts of that vivacious girl dancing in his head.

In the studio on the rostrum Francesca now had a parchment map of Italy to look at. Janetje had sent it as a gift to Hendrick one St. Nicholaes's Day, telling him she wanted to be sure her nieces knew exactly where she was living. Francesca's gaze always lingered on Flor-

ence, Rome and Venice, the three cities she most wanted to see one day.

It was as well that the request she had once made to have the portrait of Titus hanging there had never been granted, for no matter what expression Hendrick might have wanted, her face could have shown only sadness when looking at it. In September last year Titus had died of a fever after only six months of marriage, just knowing that his wife, Magdelena, was pregnant with the baby they had both wanted. Again Rembrandt had found solace in work, but this bereavement had finally broken him and he had become a very old man, his hair completely white and his health failing. At least Cornelia was a devoted daughter and he, at the age of sixty-three, could never have managed in that humble little house on Rozengracht, forgotten and ignored, if she had not been there to take care of him.

"If we hadn't gone out to sketch those spring flowers in April and May when we did," Hendrick said from the easel, "those silk flowers you're holding and those on your head would have made a poor Flora of you."

"I'm sure they would, Father!" She had dropped her babyhood name of Papa for him on the day she had shouldered the responsibilities of the household.

"Now your garlands look freshly picked, even to a touch of dew."

"Is this the final sitting?" Her tone was hopeful. It was always hard not to be the one with brush and palette in hand.

"No. There'll be one more. I'll not finish by midday."

"I could sit again this afternoon." She spoke purposefully. "Then it would be finished."

"I have an appointment," he answered in a falsely self-important tone that did not deceive her, merely confirming that he was set on pleasure. It was one of those times when he had decided to reward himself with a break from work.

"You have another appointment with Willem tomorrow morning at eleven-thirty. Wouldn't you like to have the painting ready to show him? I'm sure he's expecting it to be finished."

"Willem can wait another day."

She breathed deeply. "Father! You try his patience to the limit. He's one of the best art dealers in Amsterdam and all too often you treat him like a pedlar!"

"He knows me well enough to realize I mean him no offence," Hendrick answered jovially. "He's my oldest friend."

"All the more reason why you should respect him and his efforts to sell your work." She chose not to remind him of Willem's constant and well-meant persuasion that he should paint subjects that would be easier to sell, because this matter, as well as Hendrick's whim in leaving work on the point of completion, were sore points between the two men. Nevertheless, it hung unspoken in the air and might as well have been said.

Hendrick changed one brush for another, taking a rich sienna onto its tip, and gave her a warning frown. "Don't nag me, Francesca. Your mother never did and I'll not take it from you. If you don't watch out you'll end up with a shrew's tongue." Then he grinned maliciously as angry colour flooded into her cheeks. "Your temper is spoiling your complexion. Fortunately I have finished your face," he concluded smugly.

She knew it amused him to goad her whenever he had the chance to get back at her for trying to keep him at work longer than he wished. But how could she not when persistently he ignored unpaid bills and continued to live as nonchalantly as ever. Apart from the monetary side of it, there was the waste of his great talent. His debauchery was taking its toll on his eyesight and his hands. After a night's carousal in a tavern his fingers shook too much to do a stroke of work, even if his aching head had permitted it.

To let him know her displeasure she made no attempt at conversation again. He retaliated by whistling tunelessly under his breath, knowing it to be an irritating sound and one she could not tolerate when she was working at her easel in the studio with him. Not for the first time she thought what an overgrown, undisciplined boy he was at heart. He ignored his fifty years as if they had taken no toll on his looks and physique. Yet maybe that contributed to the unassailable charm he could exert whenever it suited him. Very soon now he would tire of his whistling prank and make some promise to win her good humour. He never liked to be on bad terms with anyone for long.

"I'll tell you what we'll do to finish this painting in time," he announced cheerily ten minutes later.

"What's that?" It had taken five minutes less than she had anticipated for him to have a change of conscience.

"I'll come home at a reasonable hour tonight, and early tomorrow morning we'll start work again. Then, by the time Willem arrives, the painting will be done."

He looked so confident, his big smile enveloping her, that she wavered in his favour. "Are you sure?"

"Absolutely. It's only a matter of final touches."

"May I see the painting now?" she asked. He never liked his work to be viewed before the final stages.

"Yes," he said, standing back to study it. Then, emerging from the grip of concentration, he realized suddenly how much time must have elapsed since her last rest period. He did not like to have a clock in the studio, finding it distracted him. "You're overdue for relaxing in any case and I suppose it's getting near the time for the noon-meal bell."

She had put down her bunch of flowers and the staff to stretch her arms out before her, flexing her fingers. "I'm sure it is. I feel quite hungry."

Shaking out her skirts, she stepped down from the rostrum, her face alight with expectation. She had almost reached the easel when she swayed, all colour draining from her face. Hendrick grabbed her in alarm. Since losing Anna any sign of illness terrified him.

"You've modelled too long without a break! Let me help you to the couch and I'll fetch Maria!"

"No!" Almost desperately she thrust herself away from him, recovering herself. "It was nothing. Maria mustn't be called—you know how she fusses."

He saw the rose was returning to her cheeks. In his thankfulness he was irritable. "You should have reminded me you needed a rest," he said testily, shifting the blame from himself.

"Yes, I should have," she answered absently, confused by that inexplicable sense of dread that had assailed her as she approached the easel. She considered herself to be practical and levelheaded, not given to whims and fancies, but for a matter of moments it was as if the studio

had turned icy and there was a terrible threat to her that lay in the painting itself. Yet it was the work of a man who loved his children. How could it possibly portend any danger? Even the subject was close to her heart, for she was a lover of spring and its flowers, especially the tulip. Lifting her chin resolutely, she went to the front of the painting to come face to face with herself as Flora.

Instantly all her qualms fled. She uttered a little cry of relief and admiration. Before her was her father's best work for a long time and it had nothing to do with her being the sitter. When Hendrick painted like this he could have made a superb picture with a wooden post as the subject. Here was his masterly technique at its height in the fluid flow of the impasto. Anna's death had had a profound effect upon his work. His colours had become more sombre and he had dropped the theatrical and overemphasized gestures of his figures to take up a more restrained and sensitive approach that had benefited his work enormously, enabling him to convey a whole new range of emotion. Here Flora gloried almost shyly in the gifts she was bringing, the shadows of winter falling away behind her, and a more subtle use of his beloved red and gold and hot orange caught the sun's brilliance in her hair. His varied and expressive brushwork was at its peak, the sweet, fresh flowers tumbling from her arms seeming to emit their fragrance, the silks and satin of her robes almost to rustle.

"This is how you should always paint, Father!"

"Do I not?" he queried with an edge to his voice.

Too late she realized she had spoken out of turn. It was not for her to refer even indirectly to paintings that had fetched a poor price or remained unsold. She met his glinting eyes and answered frankly.

"I only meant that this painting will keep us fed and it is comparable with your portrait of Mama." She indicated its presence on the studio wall with a graceful little gesture. "You've always said it was your best work. Now you have achieved it again. It's almost like a new beginning, Father."

Her straightforward answer showed she had meant neither criticism nor reproach. He nodded, always knowing where he was with her. Even as a child she had had that open and honest approach to life, that strength of character that did not break in adversity, but renewed itself

5
1

on whatever had to be faced. He recalled how the pupils of her sea-green eyes had dilated at his bawling whenever her and her sisters' work had not pleased him. Her face had grown taut, but she had kept her stance solidly while the other two had run weeping from the studio.

"I'll demand a high price for it." Then he added what he knew would please her. "It should settle a number of tradesmen's bills."

She was looking at the painting again and spoke thoughtfully. "Maybe there would be some money over as well."

"What could be better than that?" He was glad she knew nothing of his current gaming debts or else it would have spoiled the moment for her. They were standing side by side and it would have been natural for him to rest a hand on her shoulder, but his fingers were aching painfully and he did not want to give their condition away through an involuntary spasm in his grip. It had hurt him when he had grabbed her, thinking she was about to fall, but in the confusion she had not noticed anything amiss. The trouble, whatever its cause, had made itself known during the previous winter with swelling in the knuckles, but with the summer it had gone again and he had never expected it to return. Then, after he had begun the Flora painting, the unwelcome aching had come back, coinciding with the crisper weather. It had slowed his work, but he was certain it would go again. On a surge of good spirits he chuckled mischievously. "I'd take any wager that we're going to make Willem's eyes pop."

She laughed with him, slipping her arm through his and looking up into his merry face. "What fun it will be! Let me be here with you when he views it."

"Indeed you shall."

At that moment there came the tinkling sound of the little bell being rung by Maria to summon everyone to eat. Francesca swung towards the door. "I'll change out of these garments before coming to table."

When she came down again to the dining hall everyone was waiting for her, nobody yet seated, for that could not be done before grace was said. Aletta's sharp glance under a sweep of lashes told her she had taken longer than had been expected. Today her sister was wearing a cap of starched linen, folded back from the brow and similar in style to

the one Griet habitually wore in her position of maidservant. It framed Aletta's oval, well-shaped face with the stubborn little jaw, large eyes that could be gentle with love for her family but which could become flashing steel if she was angry with them or anyone else, and her mouth was curved and rosy.

Ever since the morning after the attack she was never seen without a cap, except in the privacy of the bedchamber. She had a drawer and a shelf full of caps, many embroidered by herself, which were little works of art in themselves, and a wide selection of others in varying styles, including a number made entirely of Maria's homemade lace, each lined in a different colour. Every birthday and St. Nicholaes's Day brought her gifts of caps and she had one encrusted with pearls in Florentine work that had come from Janetje. All covered her whole head; even wisps of hair escaping at the nape of her neck were tucked up out of sight. She was becoming steadily more reserved, a very private person in all matters. Sybylla had once told her cruelly that she had the makings of an old maid and there were others who thought the same.

"I apologize for keeping everyone waiting," Francesca said, making for her place at the end of the long oaken table. She heard an impish tapping of a foot keeping pace with her swift steps and knew it could only be Sybylla. It stopped abruptly with an "ouch" of protest when Maria gave the offender a prod.

It was a poor repast that day, consisting of thin vegetable soup and the baker's blackest bread, certain sign of a low ebb in Hendrick's finances. In the general conversation, Sybylla managed to direct a private question at Francesca.

"Is the Flora painting almost finished?"

It was never advisable to question Hendrick about his work, because if it was not going well he would be moody about it. When Francesca nodded in reply, Sybylla sighed with relief and returned her attention to her soup. She was interested in the painting solely as a source of income for her father. Not once had she regretted the floundering of her own artistic talent, and the only painting that would have entranced her now was that of applying cosmetics to her face had it been allowed. At least she could do what she liked with her shining, corn-gold hair and she was forever dressing it in various styles, which sometimes drove Hendrick to exasperation point. He was never tactful when irritated.

"Is there some contest being held in Amsterdam as to which females can make themselves appear the most ridiculous?" he would demand, glaring at a ribboned topknot shaped like a steeple, or bunches of curls that danced high over her ears like cascades from a fountain. Then she would burst into tears and fly to her room, shrieking out that the women of Holland were always the last in Europe to follow French modes and she did not intend to be years behind the times.

What she said had been true in the past. It was not in the average Dutch woman's nature to squander on passing frivolities, however comfortably off her circumstances might be, but over the past decade this had changed and the latest fashions from France led the way.

Sybylla always took note of elegant women whenever she went about in the city, yearning more than ever to rustle in rich garments, to have costly jewels and ride in a coach. Had she not loathed posing on the rostrum, partly because she and her father always started quarrelling over her never keeping still, she would have gained some satisfaction in wearing the exotic garments from the studio chest, no matter that they were old and mended. But her feet never allowed her to sit quietly. It seemed to her that they were made for dancing and for setting out on new and adventurous paths. On the rare occasions when Hendrick had painted her portrait she had resented the results, for he never flattered his sitters and she did not consider he did justice to her fine looks. When she complained he took it as criticism of his work and that led to more trouble.

She was convinced that nobody in the house understood her. Least of all her father or else he would have gained rich patrons by painting the kind of pictures that were in demand and thereby earned enough to give her and her sisters handsome dowries to secure good marriages for them. What was more, he should be giving her special consideration after her disappointment over there being no betrothal. Her tears and anguish had been bitter enough at the time, but she was not pining deeply for Jacob. It had all happened and been over quickly, but it was galling to have lost such a prize. The Korvers were still her good friends and she was able to come and go at their house exactly as before, which

was fortunate, for she liked having a bolt-hole when she knew Maria was after her to carry out some tedious domestic task.

She glanced at Hendrick as she passed him the basket of bread that he had asked for. He talked at table these days and had no loss of appetite. In all respects he was himself again, except that there was more grey in his hair than before losing her mother, a day that was too agonizing to think about.

When the meal was over Sybylla was the first to leave the dining hall out of curiosity to view the Flora painting. She moved fastidiously in the studio, not wanting to snag her skirt on the framed paintings stacked against one wall or soil her garments with dusty chalk or dollops of wet paint. When she reached her father's easel and saw the likeness of her sister as the goddess of spring, a wave of appreciation of its beauty almost conquered her uppermost desire to estimate what it was worth. If all Hendrick's work had such appeal all his financial troubles would be over and they need never have a peasants' meal of vegetable soup and black bread again.

Sybylla wondered if perhaps she should grit her teeth and offer to sit for Hendrick herself. If he promised she should have a new cloak out of the price her likeness fetched, she would do it. Otherwise there was no point in submitting herself to his grumbling about her not sitting still and the general ordeal. She should have some personal gain.

The sound of the door opening made her turn hopefully, but it was Aletta come to view the painting. "Is Father still in the house?" Sybylla asked at once.

"I think he's just gone out."

Sybylla went to check for herself, only to find her sister was right. Too late she saw Maria, broad as a barge, waddling determinedly in her direction. "There you are, child. Why aren't you in your apron yet? It's your turn to brush down all the drapes in the bedchambers."

Sybylla sighed wearily. She thought sometimes that women through-out Holland fought with broom and scrubbing brush to keep their homes spotless as resolutely as the menfolk, with sword and cannon, had once withstood the might of Spain. At least that freedom had been won, but dust and dirt never surrendered.

Throughout the quiet afternoon hours Francesca and Aletta worked

in the studio on still-life paintings they had begun the previous week. In front of them, where they sat on stools at their easels, was a low table covered with a blue cloth on which were set in careful composition a number of items. Giving height to the arrangement was one of Anna's most treasured possessions, a nautilus as pearly as the faraway foreign shore from which it had been plucked to be set in silver on a finely fashioned stand. With it were a large hourglass, a bunch of black grapes lying beside a glass of wine and a fan with the light shimmering on its topaz-coloured feathers. A pewter plate had been placed to jut out over the edge of the table and on it lay a lemon with a knife's blade wedged in it while a long strip of peel, already cut off, curled as it dangled down. Three late rosebuds, which Francesca had fetched from the courtyard's little garden, lay across a tumbled damask napkin. It was an excellent exercise for the effect of light and shadow on various surfaces and textures.

Francesca always included flowers in her paintings whenever possible. It seemed to her that few pictures were complete without blooms, much as Holland would have looked bereft without the abundance of flowers that flourished everywhere from spring to autumn. They blossomed profusely in beds along the canals and streets, perfumed every garden, filled tubs and pots and, most dramatically of all, spread in glorious carpets of colour in the bulb-growing districts along the coast north and south of Haarlem.

She and Aletta did not talk as they painted. The atmosphere was completely harmonious between them. It was never quite the same when Hendrick was there, his personality tending to vibrate through the air. Sometimes he did not so much as glance at their work and at other times, particularly when he was in a restless mood, he would stump across to them at all too frequent intervals and find fault, not constructively as in the past, but with undue savagery. Aletta was long past her crying days, but she still blanched at times. Francesca thought the explanation was that he was troubled by his conscience at no longer having the inclination to teach them as much as he should.

What had become clear to both girls was that they had reached a crossroads with regard to their work. Each was fully aware of the potential in her skills, but totally frustrated by Hendrick's increasing

tardiness in giving them instruction. If they could have entered as apprentices in the studio of an independent master of repute it would have given them the opportunity to develop and advance beyond their present achievements.

The barrier to their joint aim was the fees involved and not that they were female, for in a studio it was only talent that counted. Francesca was a great admirer of the late Judith Leyster, who had studied with Frans Hals, as Hendrick had done, and Maria van Oosterwyck, a fine painter of flowers, who had been a pupil of Jan Davidsz de Heem.

In the studio the only sounds were those of Griet cleaning upstairs and the rattle of passing wheels or the clack of wooden clogs in the street outside. Then Aletta broke the silence between them.

"There is only one solution."

Francesca was able to follow her sister's train of thought. She smiled but did not pause in her painting. "What is that? A public notice to announce that two would-be masters of a Guild will sing and dance in the streets for donations to raise tuition fees?"

"I was dreaming of something better than that," Aletta confessed with a smile. "Wouldn't it be wonderful if we could both find rich patrons able to recognize our talent and willing to foot all expenses until we were masters. That's what happened to many Italian artists."

"But Holland isn't Italy. The attitude to art in that country is quite different. So many Italian painters and sculptors get commissions from the Church and from those holding political power. There is no munificence such as that here."

"How true that is!"

"Ideally we should complete our training under an independent master. Have we not discussed this many times? But I don't intend to be defeated by present circumstances and neither do you. Our path is one of hard work and more hard work. There are no shortcuts. The day Willem offers to sell our work we'll know that we're on the brink of true achievement and success."

"Like Father?" Aletta's voice was suddenly clipped in tone.

Francesca looked across at her. "He is as he is and not even Mama was able to change him. But you and I are both dedicated to our work to the exclusion of all else."

"So we must struggle on, must we?"

"Recognition will be all the sweeter when it comes."

"I suppose you're right." Aletta heaved a sigh as she continued painting. She was wondering what price this piece of work would fetch if she were able to sell it. A few stuivers? Or, better still, a couple of florins. Suppose she could find a way of selling her work unbeknown to anyone in the household. She could hoard whatever she received and, although it would take quite a long time, eventually she should have collected enough to attend the classes some artists took turns in holding where their own pupils gathered with those of other studios for joint instruction in painting from life. Amateur artists, willing to pay, were allowed in small numbers to sit at the back, but they received the tutor's guidance in their turn. If she attended regularly she would gain much from this source, but she had to get some money first. It was a problem she had to solve somehow.

Hendrick had not returned when they ate dinner that evening. Afterwards Aletta sat in the reception hall, playing on the virginal accompanied by Sybylla on the viol. The sweet music could be heard in the parlour, where Francesca sat by the fire reading. Maria was in a chair opposite her, making lace on a cushion resting on her ample lap, the click of the bobbins providing an accompanying rhythm. When eventually Aletta and Sybylla said good night and went to bed, Francesca put aside her book to go restlessly to the window. She cupped her hands to one of the diamond panes and looked out.

"Father promised he wouldn't be late home," she said on a sharp note that ranged from annoyance to anxiety. "When he's been drinking, as I'm sure he has tonight, I'm always afraid he will topple into a canal."

Maria glanced up from her lacework. "Your mother used to worry about that too," she commented phlegmatically, remembering how often she had seen Anna waiting by that same window, "but the only time it happened the cold water sobered him up and when he broke the surface the first thing he saw was an old leather purse full of gold coins lodged in a crevice. Anyone but your father would have drowned, but that's the sort of good luck that happens to men like him." She almost

said "rogues" instead of "men," but he was her employer and it would not have been the way to speak of him to his daughter, not even after all these years.

Surprised, Francesca turned back from the window. "I've never heard of that before. No wonder he can be so optimistic whenever trouble is staring him in the face. How old was I at that time?"

"About six months, if I remember rightly. That gold should have been a nest egg for him and your mother, but it all went on new gowns of saffron velvet and gold brocade for her and a painting for himself by a Venetian artist whose name I don't remember." She shook her head despairingly. "Money has always burnt a hole in his pocket."

"There is no Venetian painting in this house, Maria. What happened to it?"

"Need you ask?" Maria replied drily. "It had to be sold a year or two later when he couldn't raise funds anywhere else. It was nothing special. I like your pictures and Aletta's much more. The painting of tulips that you gave me last St. Nicholaes's Day makes me feel I have a vase of fresh blooms in my bedchamber all the year round."

Francesca was touched by the praise that was so sincerely meant and stooped down by the old woman's chair to give her an affectionate hug. "You're a dear, Maria. I want so much to be a really good painter and I've far to go yet."

"You'll get there, I know it." Maria kissed Francesca's cheek and then stayed her when she would have returned to the window. "Sit down now. There's no point in watching for the master. The only lamp in the street doesn't give you enough light to see any distance and your father is quite likely to set off home from wherever he is without thinking to borrow a lantern. It wouldn't be the first time that he was fined by the Night Watch for not carrying one after dark." She resumed her lace making, her fingers nimble with the bobbins. "I haven't made this pattern for quite a while."

"It's pretty." Francesca seated herself in the chair opposite Maria. "Is it for a collar?"

Maria gave her a direct look. "A bridal bodice, I hope."

"It's useless to have me in mind and don't pin your hopes on Aletta,

because she's as ambitious as I am!" Francesca's tone was firm. "Sybylla is the one most likely to wear it."

Maria sighed in exasperation. "I don't understand you. Suppose your heart should run away with you one day."

"I'll not let it." Francesca spoke confidently, leaning back against the cushions in her chair and resting her hands on the rounded ends of its arms. "The prospect of marriage is spectre enough for me to keep my head. The state of matrimony would stamp me into waiting on a husband and into motherhood as well as countless social duties that I can avoid now. Once a ring was on my finger I'd have no time to paint."

"Fiddlesticks! Of course there would be."

"Only if I married an artist."

"Why is that?"

"Because he would understand and cooperate."

"Then look for one."

"I'm not sufficiently interested."

Maria tried another angle. "But what of children? You're so fond of them and so maternal towards everyone in the household when the need arises."

Francesca turned her head and gazed into the fire. The glow of the flames flickered over her face, but her lashes shadowed her eyes and hid the expression in them. "I would like to have a child. Maybe when I have established myself as an artist there will be time before I'm too old to have a family of my own. But for the foreseeable future I've dedicated myself to an aim that will give me no peace until I have achieved it." She pushed back the cuff of her sleeve with a half-smile and regarded her wrist. "I think there must be a mixture of oil and pigment flowing in these veins."

"More's the pity," Maria muttered under her breath. When it was a choice between paintings and babies she would have chosen a third generation to watch over any day.

Francesca heard her, but made no comment. Maria could never comprehend the creative force in her that made it impossible to follow any other path. It was how it had been for her father and now it was the same for Aletta and for her. A beacon that was forever beckoning.

The sound of someone crossing the reception hall caused her to spring to her feet in relief. "Father is home!" But when she went to see for herself it was Griet coming from the kitchen. She had been spending the evening with a friend and was on her way up to her room. Francesca bade her good night and returned to the fireside. Not long afterwards Maria went to bed too.

Francesca settled down to wait a while longer, angry and disappointed that her father should have failed to keep his word yet again. Why was she always taken in by his promises? It was one of the many times when she had wanted to stamp her foot at his fecklessness, but she knew that if he should come staggering in now, displaying that shamefaced bravado that he adopted at such times, it would be hard not to let pity for him overwhelm her exasperation.

When the clock was well past midnight she left a lamp burning for him and took a candle to light the way upstairs. Ascending the flight, she pondered on the most tactful way to break the news to Willem in the morning that the Flora painting was not ready. Many times he had shown himself on the brink of refusing to handle Hendrick's work any longer and had issued a warning to that effect on his last visit. She feared that when he came on the morrow and found the long-promised painting unfinished, he would turn on his heel and go from the house forever. No other art dealer of repute would tolerate Hendrick's erratic ways. If her father should fall into the hands of rogue dealers he would never get a fair price for a painting again.

In the run of her thoughts she was gripped again by the sense of foreboding that had afflicted her earlier in the day, the same dread sweeping over her, and she gripped the handrail. In the glow of the candle fear was stark in her eyes.

CHAPTER 4

On the stroke of half past eleven the next morning, Griet opened the door to Willem de Hartog. He greeted her courteously and stepped indoors onto the long Persian rug that was always laid down to honour expected visitors. He handed her his cloak and gloves but not his large hat, since headgear was worn by men as much indoors as out. He doffed it to Francesca as she came across the stair hall and through the archway into the brightness of the reception hall. A silver-framed Venetian mirror reflected her approach. He was struck anew by the unusual beauty of the girl with her blazing hair, gold earbobs in her lobes, and her simple gown of russet wool.

"Good day, *mijnheer*. Welcome to our home again," she said.

He observed her serious smile and was alerted to things not being quite as they should be. It could only mean what he feared. "I thank you, Francesca. You're looking well. I trust it is the same with Hendrick and your sisters."

"They are in good health. Please sit down. Griet has gone to fetch refreshment for you."

He remained standing and a frown gathered his brows together ominously. "Is the painting not finished?"

"If you will just sit for a few moments, I will tell you about it." She sat down herself by the large stone canopied fireplace that was inset with blue Delft tiles patterned with dancing figures and where peat burned with a cheerful flicker of flame. Her hope that he would take the chair opposite her came to nothing, for he did not move from where he stood.

"Do you mean that Hendrick is not even here to receive me?" His voice held a rising note of rumbling anger.

"I'm hoping for his return at any moment."

"What time did he go out?"

She drew in a deep breath. "Yesterday afternoon."

"Bah!" He threw up his hands in exasperation, his complexion tinged red with annoyance. In his own mind he took a guess as to how those hours of absence had been spent by this errant artist. There would be gaming with cards, but something more as well. He was not setting himself up as a moralist, but he thought marriage a great deal tidier for such matters. But Hendrick would never marry again and the reason was obvious. No second wife must ever enter Anna's home and domain. It would continue to be hers in Hendrick's eyes until the end of his days.

"Aletta and Sybylla have been out an hour looking for him." Francesca was disturbed by the way Willem was pacing up and down on the Persian rug, his fingers twitching as if he wished they were around Hendrick's neck. He did not appear to have heard her.

"I gave the idler a last warning when he agreed to paint you as Flora! I said that if he disappointed me once more I'd wash my hands of him. Let him fall into the clutches of the thieves and charlatans of the art world if that is what he wants!" He halted in front of Francesca so abruptly that he rucked the rug under his heel. "I'll have my cloak and gloves back again. It's no fault of yours, but your father is impossible!"

She sprang to her feet again. "Please don't go! The painting needs no more than a morning's work. It's the best thing he has done since Mama died. He's calling it *The Goddess of Spring*. I'll show it to you."

That calmed him down, but still he hesitated. "I thought it was the rule in this house that only Hendrick showed his work for the first time."

"In the present circumstances I'm breaking it!"

Slowly he smiled at her. "Are you indeed? Well, it's time Hendrick discovered he can't ride roughshod over us all." Out of the corner of his eye he had seen the maidservant bringing a tray with homemade wine and cakes. "I'll drink to that after I've seen the painting."

Francesca led the way to the studio, Willem following her. He considered Hendrick to be a very good artist, equal to several whose names were better known, but his work always fell short of reaching the peak. In his painting of Anna that was hanging in the studio and into which he had put his whole heart, he had come close to genius, but he had

kept the essence of his wife to himself, too possessive to share what he had hidden in the tantalizing likeness of her. It had caused the painting to slip past greatness into a lesser mould. Rembrandt always withheld something of each person whose portrait he painted, intriguing the viewer and arousing the urge to discover more of that elusive, indefinable quality that lurked behind the faces captured, but he also gave generously and therein lay the difference. Not that Hendrick's work came anywhere near Rembrandt's extraordinary masterpieces. Neither did anyone else's, to Willem's mind, but in dealing with temperamental artists on one side and wealthy clients on the other, it was not politic for him to voice his own opinions.

They had come to the studio and Willem leaned forward in front of Francesca to open the door for her. She went in with swift steps to the painting on Hendrick's easel. "Here it is!"

To reach it he had to pass the two still-life paintings that she and Aletta had left propped on their easels the previous day. Willem stopped to stand back and regard each in turn. He recognized the girls' individual work instantly, having observed their progress since they were young children. Each still showed errors and weaknesses, which could be corrected under the right tuition, but the remarkable standard of their work set them far ahead of other rising young artists of their respective ages. Aletta, being the younger, was as yet less mature in her use of colour and in composition, but Francesca's still life had a jewel-like quality with tiny reflections of the objects and even of the window in the silver base of the nautilus.

He lifted the painting from the easel and took it to the window, where he scrutinized it closely. "Your work is coming on extremely well."

She blushed at his praise, knowing he did not give it lightly. "Not fast enough for my choice."

"How many hours' tuition a week does your father give you?" When she did not answer immediately he looked up sharply at her. "None?"

"He guides and advises us sometimes when we're in special need of assistance," she replied staunchly.

"None," he repeated caustically, undeceived, and returned his atten-

tion to her painting. "I like to keep an eye on your progress. Have you anything else you've done recently?"

"Yes, I have, and so has Aletta. But wouldn't you prefer to look at my father's painting first?"

"No. I'm concentrating on yours now." He shot a smiling, half-teasing glance at her. "Never distract an art dealer who's showing interest in your work. You'd better learn that lesson now."

She laughed and went to a stack of paintings propped against the wall. Due to the necessary economy of linen canvas, all were small and she and her sister frequently painted over earlier work. She took four of Aletta's pictures to him first, never supposing it was hers alone that he wished to see this time. He looked at each one, was struck again by the quality of the work and gave some helpful criticism to be passed on to her sister. Then she showed him three of her own.

He studied each in turn, taking his time. The first was of Griet in the courtyard, hanging up newly laundered sheets. The little picture throbbed with life and movement, making it possible to believe one heard the flapping of the damp, billowing linen. Then came a landscape with windmills, depicted on a warm day when a vaporous mist, sparkled through with sunshine, lay gently over water and fields. The third painting was of Maria at her lace making, her gnarled hands given a strange beauty at their delicate work. Dealing in the art world had made him cynical and blasé over the years, but he was pleased to discover he could still experience a sense of excitement at the promise of a new and dazzling talent, such as he saw in this girl's work.

"I see that in each of these you have a flower," he commented without showing expression. "There are wind-tossed tulips in the courtyard, a single wild iris showing in the landscape's canal bank and Maria's lace has a pattern of lilies."

"You're very observant," she said with a smile. "I admit I like to include flowers at any opportunity. When the day comes for me to sign my work for all the world to see, I shall include one in my signature."

"Ah! As was done by the illustrators of manuscripts in past centuries. Keep to your notion. I like it." He knew the presence of a flower would not sell a picture in itself, but it would catch the eye and be remembered when seen again. It might even make a direct appeal to a prospec-

tive buyer and in his business that could weigh the balance in a sale. He had no doubt at all that if Francesca's talent was nurtured and brought to fruition she had it in her to rise to immeasurable heights in her work. "Do you wish to concentrate on being a flower painter?"

"No. I will say that my eye ranges much farther than that."

"It's as well." He had not taken his concentrated gaze from her still life that he held. Now he looked up with a quizzical smile. "Had you kept to a rose in your paintings I would have suspected you had love on your mind."

Her eyes danced. Pure love between a man and a woman was symbolized in a picture by a rose held or pleasingly arranged, whereas a fallen one on the ground depicted either the pain of love or unchaste love, according to the subject of the painting. The rosebuds in her still life could be interpreted as the dawning of romantic love, but that had not been intended, although there was much that was symbolic in the picture. The nautilus represented wealth, exotic shells of all kinds being costly, while the fan was a symbol of extravagance. The hourglass warned of the passing of time and the foolishness of piling up riches on earth, while the pewter plate, poised precariously, told how easily life could be cut off. The grapes and the wine symbolized Holy Communion and Christ with the hope of resurrection. An artist's choice of this *vanitas*, as it was called, was wide, with many more components that everyone recognized. Often a painting was not what it appeared to be at first impression, but either illustrated a proverb or was in the popular theme that Francesca and Aletta had used to make the observer contemplate his or her moral frailty, the swift passing of the years and the worthlessness of the sheer pursuit of pleasure.

"You can be sure," Francesca said, carefully returning her paintings to where they had been stacked against the wall, "that love is the last thing on my mind at the present time."

The little joke had been enjoyed by them both. Willem replaced her still life on the easel, noting again how much careful thought had gone into the selection of each item in the *vanitas*. "Now I'll take a look at your father's version of you as Flora."

He strolled over to it. She drew near and watched him anxiously as he stood looking without expression at the painting for what seemed an

interminably long time. At last she was unable to bear his silence any longer.

"What do you think?"

"I'll speak frankly," he replied meditatively, still studying the portrait. "I had not thought to see a painting as superb as this from Hendrick's brush today. It's one of his best! I'm full of praise. A morning's work on it, did you say?"

"That's what he told me."

"Then try to keep him to that." Some artists would go on adding touches forever if they could, never wholly satisfied. His immense pleasure in the painting was tinged by disappointment that, as with the painting of Anna, it did not reach the heights of greatness that it might have. Yet he continued to hope that would come about. Some artists painted better than ever in old age, but it had to be remembered Hendrick was unpredictable in all things. At least this picture would attract eager buyers. The sheer beauty of the girl's expressive face would set it in high demand and her armful of flowers, held as if she was about to shield herself from the viewer's gaze, added both sensual mystery and charm. "This painting will fetch a good price."

Francesca clasped her hands together eagerly. "Four hundred florins?" she queried hopefully, daring to add a hundred more than the figure Hendrick would have in mind.

Willem did not look taken aback as she had feared. "If I should have the right buyer I would expect to double that figure and more."

Neither of them had heard Hendrick in his soft house shoes come through the studio door, which had been left ajar. His voice thundered out, reverberating against the walls. "What if I should decide not to sell?"

They turned to face him. Francesca straightened her shoulders and refused to back away before his furious expression. "Direct your anger at me, Father. I invited our guest in here."

"I need nothing from him!" With a theatrical gesture Hendrick pulled his purse from his pocket, jerked the thong free and threw it to the floor. A shower of guilders sprang from it and rolled in all directions. In the silence that followed, Willem put out his foot and prodded a spinning coin to a standstill.

"So you've had a change of fortune on two fronts, Hendrick," he remarked calmly. "You've painted a splendid Flora and in addition the cards and the dice have favoured you. My felicitations on both. You must be a very happy man."

Hendrick, mollified by the praise, stuck his thumbs into his belt and swaggered forward, highly pleased with himself, but still aggrieved that his showing of the painting had been forestalled. He was sober, but his colour had a purplish tinge and his eyes were bloodshot and tired from lack of sleep. "The stakes last night were the highest I've known and I didn't stop winning. I cleared my gambling debts and all the way home I've been ladling money out to greedy tradesmen in settlement of bills. Now I owe not a stuiver to any man. What's more," he added boastfully, "there's enough over to keep my family and myself in meat twice a day for months to come." He was taking immense satisfaction in having the upper hand over Willem. "So you see, I'm in a position to keep the painting."

"Indeed you are," Willem agreed mildly and then stemmed any further discussion by bowing his head to Francesca. "My business being at an end here for the day, I should like to avail myself of that glass of wine you offered me."

"Yes, of course." She looked inquiringly at Hendrick. "You'll join us, Father, won't you?"

"What? Yes." Hendrick felt uneasily that he had been manipulated in some way and sought to assert himself. "I'm not a fellow unable to forgive an error of judgement. You were both at fault, but I'll overlook it this time."

"That's most generous of you." Willem's voice held a dry note that Hendrick missed but which was not lost on Francesca. She went ahead of the two men to pour the wine.

After Willem's departure she returned to the studio and picked up all the money, putting it into one of her father's spare leather purses. When she handed it to him he thanked her cheerfully as if nothing amiss had occurred, all his ill temper completely forgotten.

He finished the painting that same afternoon. Perhaps he realized he would be at a permanent disadvantage with Willem if he failed to do as was wished of him this time. He knew his old friend could not wait to

get his hands on the painting. They could judge each other well enough in that respect, just as Willem would have known he had every intention of selling, no matter what he had said in anger. When finally he put his brushes away at the hour of four o'clock, Francesca sprang from the rostrum to hug him exuberantly.

"You've done well, Father! This evening we are to have a special dinner to celebrate the completion of *The Goddess of Spring.*"

He grinned. "What is it to be?"

"Your favourite dish! No other!"

"What a treat!" He could not spoil her pleasure by telling her that only the evening before he had dined on that same deliciously spicy concoction of capon and sausages cooked with several good meats and vegetables in wine, all served garnished with boiled chestnuts. He had sat down to it at her table. With her big soft body and welcoming arms, she was the only one able to assuage in any way the loneliness that gnawed at him in his darker moments. It was in the house of a woman named Margretha that his luck had turned at the cards, although it had worried her when he had settled to those high stakes.

"Sybylla has also been busy making a special pudding with eggs and cream," Francesca told him happily as she helped him off with his linen smock. Then, instead of hanging it on its wooden peg, she was overcome by what she had to say to him and unknowingly clutched the smock to her. The intense appeal in her face prepared him for what she was about to request.

"Don't take such dangerous risks with the cards again," she implored. "Because if they had gone against you yesterday it could have meant ruin. I know how you miss Mama and need a social life with people other than family. But you have the taverns where artists gather, the skittle alleys, the homes of friends who invite you to table, the art auctions you like to attend and a host of other diversions from watching the sailing races in summer to the ice sports in winter." She threw aside the smock and caught up his hand to press it to her cheek in an almost childlike plea. "I'm not asking you to give up cards altogether, but please play only with those who can afford to lose no more than you."

She looked exactly like her mother across the eyes at that moment, almost as if Anna had chosen to endorse their daughter's urging that he should turn over a new leaf. He was deeply moved. Whenever he listened to his sluggish conscience he did avoid tables with fierce stakes, but there were times when the siren call that gamblers hear in an inner ear promised a winning streak and was impossible to resist, no matter that it sometimes proved false. "I'll be more careful in future," he promised, swayed by the moment. It had brought a note to his voice that rang true.

Francesca drew back with her face bright with hope. "I believe you!"

Again he saw Anna in the girl's eyes and he shifted uncomfortably. Such expectations were a burden on him, but he should do something about them. Exactly what, he did not know, for he was aware of his own weaknesses, his good intentions having fallen by the wayside so often, but he should take some action now while the mood was still with him. He knew Anna wished it.

On sudden impulse he pulled the purse of silver from his belt again and thrust it into Francesca's hands. "Take this into your charge. Keep it in a safe place and spend it on household needs. I want no part of it."

It was a moment or two before she found her voice. "I shall use it wisely," she vowed emotionally, thinking thankfully that there would be no more bills mounting up and she could go shopping for weeks to come without facing the ire of honest tradesmen who had not been paid.

"I know you will." He was smiling at her.

An answering smile curled the corners of her mouth and her eyes twinkled. "But don't expect meat twice a day."

He guffawed. It was, and had been, a joke in every respect, for few people in Holland ate meat more than once a week, because, apart from this time of year when animals were slaughtered before the winter, there was little fresh meat to be had. Fish, morning-caught from the sea, was cheap and in abundance, as were vegetables, preferable in any case to salted meat, and there was no country anywhere that had a better choice of good cheeses.

"Just let me have a plate of fried herrings once a week and I'll make no complaint," he teased.

"You shall have them," she promised merrily. "I'll go and put this

money away now. After I've changed and put on an apron I'll come back and clean your brushes."

As soon as she had gone from the studio he looked at his hands and eased his painful fingers. The knuckles had ached so much during the afternoon that once he had dropped his brush. Fortunately Francesca had not suspected the reason or else she would not have caught his hand in hers as she did. He had almost winced.

Suddenly he felt overwhelmingly tired, the previous night's lack of sleep catching up with him. He poured water from a pewter jug into a bowl of the same metal and washed his hands carefully, not sure whether the cold water eased or aggravated the aching. After drying them on a linen towel, he bent to pick up his smock and place it on his peg. Then he went from the studio.

Sybylla must have been waiting for him, because when he crossed the reception hall to the parlour she came darting after him.

"Father! I must speak to you."

"Does it have to be now?" he asked tolerantly, not sending her away as he would have done anyone else who had approached him at this particular time. He had planned to have a peaceful, uninterrupted doze before dinner and sank down into a leather chair by the fire to stretch out his long legs and close his eyes. "I have been working all the afternoon."

She did not take the hint and leave. Instead she shut the door after her and came to kneel by his chair. "I know, but it's most important."

He felt the familiar tug at his heart strings. This was the baby of the family, the apple of his eye, coming to him with some pretty notion in her head and he must listen to her. At least he did not think it would be about some madcap betrothal. He shifted his large body into a less relaxed position and gave her his full attention. "What is it, little one?"

She was encouraged by his pet endearment for her. From Aletta she had heard, almost with disbelief, that he had come home with plenty of money in his purse, but without the gifts normal to such occasions, rare though they were these days. She came straight to the point, seeing no need to offer to sit for him after all.

"Father, I do need a new cloak for this coming winter. I'd like one with a fur-lined hood, which I've never had before."

He was able to picture exactly what she was requesting, for if he had not expected Willem to be at the house that morning he would have bought one for her and loaded himself with gifts for the others too. But it had suited his mood to face Willem in a spirit of independence, which was why, for the first time ever, he had allowed the full clearance of debts to take priority. He had made up his mind to be as lavish with the remaining bounty on the morrow as he had been in the past, but those few extraordinary seconds when Anna had seemed to look at him out of his eldest daughter's eyes had changed that arrangement. He had never listened in the past when Anna had begged him to be more practical and less extravagant, and it was satisfying to know he was pleasing her over that matter at last.

"You have at least two warm cloaks, Sybylla," he said with a firmness directed as much at himself as at her. Not even his dearest child could compete with the wishes of the beloved wife he had lost.

"Neither of them have fur and I feel the cold so badly," she wheedled, her gaze aimed to be beguiling, her expectations high. "I also need silk for a new gown to be made up in time for St. Nicholaes's Day. I've seen the loveliest material in gillyflower pink—"

"The cloak and the silk must wait for another time."

"Why?" She pouted prettily, not yet taking him seriously. "You can afford a few luxuries for every one of us again now."

He smiled, shaking his head. "Far from it. As a matter of fact I haven't as much as a stuiver in my pockets. All the money I brought home with me is under lock and key for housekeeping expenses under your elder sister's jurisdiction."

Sybylla was aghast, but all was not lost yet. "There's still the painting. You are going to sell it, aren't you, Father?"

"Yes, but that won't be tomorrow. I know Willem. He'll hang back for a week or two, thinking to make me fret for a sale. It'll be his way of getting even with me for not making him a promise this morning that it shall be his to offer whenever he likes."

"Suppose he doesn't come back?" She was anxious, thinking of the funds for her new garments lying dormant in that painting on the studio easel.

"He'll be back, never fear." Hendrick closed his eyes again, sleep dragging at him. Sybylla leapt up from her knees and darted away as quickly as she had come. The cloak and the silk were practically hers! It was exasperating having to wait, but if her father and Willem were engaged in a battle of wills, she would have to be patient somehow.

Next morning Francesca made sure Hendrick had enough money when he left the house to buy a new supply of pigments. She wanted no more accounts run up to high figures that became so difficult to meet; in future cash was to be paid for all purchases, whether for the household or for the atelier. Hendrick did not demur at her ruling. He had quarrelled too often with every artist's supplier over denial of credit at various times not to enjoy the rare experience of slapping down coins on their counters as if casting pearls before swine.

When she heard him re-enter the house only a few minutes after leaving it, she supposed he had forgotten something and expected him to go into the studio to collect whatever it was before going out once more. Then, when the front door did not open and close again, she went to see if anything was the matter. She found him sitting in one of the chairs in the reception hall, staring unseeingly before him.

"Are you not well?" she inquired anxiously.

Slowly he raised his head to look at her, his mouth jerking with anguish. "I heard some sad news in the street. Rembrandt died yesterday."

Involuntarily she cried out in distress. "Oh! Can it be true?"

He answered her in a voice heavy with grief. "He is to be buried in the Westerkerk. It is not just our country that has been bereaved. The world has lost the greatest painter who has ever lived."

She took up his hand and cradled it against her cheek, sharing his sorrow. One of her earliest memories was of being taken by him to see Rembrandt's painting of the Militia Company of Captain Frans Banning Cocq that was hung in the wing of that same militia's headquarters. The scene had been captured at a busy moment when all were getting ready in good time for the Night Watch. She had stood awed, staring up at the vast painting where diffused sunlight and shadow played across a scene throbbing with activity, and Hendrick, who never took

account of her extreme youth, spoke to her as he might have done to an adult. He explained that this group painting was entirely at variance to the conventional static settings normally used in this type of commissioned work in which every face was turned in the direction of the viewer. The explanation had meant little to her then. She was only aware of the teeming life on that canvas where all the militia were going about their affairs, the foreground dominated by the captain in black and a fellow officer in yellow. She seemed to hear the clatter of arms, the rattle of drums, the barking of the dog and all the tumult of the men's voices. Best of all at that time, she had liked the presence of the small girl in the painting, whose gown was similar to her own that day. She supposed the child to be with her father just as she was with hers, except that Hendrick was an artist and not a wearer of armour and military sashes. One thing about the little girl had puzzled her.

"Why has she a chicken with golden claws hanging from her belt, Papa? Has she brought it for their supper?"

"Maybe she has and maybe she hasn't. The significance of it lies in the fact that the escutcheon of this company bears golden claws and so Master Rembrandt has introduced the emblem. See how he has applied highlights of thick white impasto to the yellow, all against a darker ground, to achieve the shimmering effect of the feathers as well as the rich fabric of the little girl's skirt. Can you spot somebody you know in the painting?"

"Who?"

"Master Rembrandt."

She knew it was a long-established tradition, going back to the great Italian painters, that an artist frequently included a likeness of himself in a populated painting. Slowly she let her gaze pass along the faces of those more in the background than the rest, each person there having paid according to the amount of space on the canvas individually occupied.

"There's Master Rembrandt!" She laughed and clasped her hands with delight. "He is just behind the man in armour! One day I'm going to do that! Paint myself showing part of my face as he has done."

In retrospect, looking back now to that moment, Francesca was

certain it was when the spark had been kindled in her to follow the path of a painter to the exclusion of all else.

"I should like to offer Cornelia a home with us, Father."

Hendrick nodded willingly. "That should be done without delay."

"I'll go to Rozengracht at once!" She took a step towards the stair hall.

He stirred in his chair. "I'll not come with you. I've no wish to go out again today." Wearily he rose to his feet. "I'd like to spend the rest of the day quietly in my studio."

She understood. There was no better place in which to mourn a fellow artist than in one's own studio. When she arrived at Rozengracht it was to learn that Cornelia had already been taken into the care of kind relatives and a good home for her was assured.

Four days later Hendrick attended the funeral at Westerkerk and saw Rembrandt laid to rest beside Titus and Hendrickje Stoffels. Throughout the following weeks Hendrick was as cast down as if it had been his own knell that he had heard. The painting of Titus drew him as though it were a new acquisition and had not graced his home for a long time. The depth and meaning of the work, combined with its beauty and harmony, moved him till his throat ached, so great was the admiration that swelled his heart. He also began pausing to look at the Hals painting that he owned: a toper with the drunken flush to his cheeks, merriment in his eyes and a tankard in hand. Hendrick marvelled anew at the glittering brushwork, the pulse of life created by those gashlike strokes of colour. It was inevitable that his own technique should have been influenced by such a tutor, whose temperament had been so much like his own and to whom laughter, alcohol and good company had also been all-important. Three years ago Hals, an old man in his eighties, had died and now Rembrandt, only sixty-three, had followed him. Both had ended their days in abject poverty, virtually forgotten by society. Was that to be his own fate too?

One morning as he stood in front of the painting of the toper, Francesca came and stood beside him. She was wearing her gardening apron, and gloves were tucked in the pocket. She comprehended the mood that was depressing him and slipped her arm through his.

"You know," he said in a voice torn by regret, "I should have gone to

see old Hals before he died. I kept meaning to make the trip to Haarlem, but somehow I never did. I suppose, having heard he was still painting, I thought he would go on forever, but of course none of us do."

"Why not make the trip to Haarlem one day and pay your respects at his last resting place?" Francesca suggested. "If you went by passenger boat on the canals you could either stay the night or be home again by midnight."

He gave a nod but did not commit himself. "I'll think about it."

She continued on her way out to the courtyard. It was a fine morning on which to plant the tulip bulbs that had come from a field somewhere near Haarlem. Griet had told her about the delivery, the order for which Hendrick had forgotten to mention, and said that the tulip grower would call for payment another day. It was only the previous week that she had replanted the bulbs she had taken up in June, but she enjoyed gardening and was always content at it, even when engaged in the more monotonous chores of digging and weeding. Aletta shared her interest and would have helped her with the bulbs if she had not gone out to sketch a view of the Amstel by one of the old bridges.

Kneeling down on a folded rug, Francesca dug holes in the sandy soil at regular intervals and set in the new bulbs, which were of excellent quality, being hard with skins that were a good rusty colour. When they came into bloom she might gather some to take indoors and begin a floral arrangement for her canvas, painting other flowers as they blossomed in turn, until a huge bouquet from the different seasons was completed, a not unusual procedure.

The tulip would always be her favourite flower, its long-stemmed grace and elegance surpassing to her eyes even the beautiful centiflora rose that presented such an abundance of tinted petals as to resemble a confusion of petticoats. Maybe the romantic in her had been irrevocably drawn to the tulip when long ago she had heard how supposedly it had first come into being. According to the Persian legend, it was when Fernad had pined in anguish for his love, the exquisite Shirin, that the wild tulip had sprung up from where his tears had dyed the sand, its

petals blood red. She could never look at tulips without remembering their association with tender love and deepest passion.

It seemed strange to her that although they had been cultivated in the exotic gardens of Persia and Turkey, it was not until just over a hundred years before her birth that the tulip had reached Europe. An ambassador to Turkey from the Court of the Holy Roman Emperor had been so impressed by the tulip that when he returned home to Vienna he took with him some seeds and bulbs, which he presented to Ferdinand I. These grew and flourished until soon other countries were transplanting this new flower shaped like an eastern turban. There were many tales as to how it eventually came to Holland, but the most likely was that a cargo of bulbs arrived by ship in Amsterdam. Whatever its means of travel, the tulip took to Dutch soil as if Holland were its natural habitat and it had always belonged there.

Red, yellow and also white tulips, as well as some striped ones, had grown in the Visser garden for as long as Francesca could remember. She had no real preference in colour, finding something to admire in every one, but she looked forward to the bloom that would be produced by the recently delivered bulbs. It was to be a shaded crimson with feathered petals, and was more expensive than any she would have chosen. At least it did not come into the category of the rare hues that commanded top prices and had made many a horticulturist extremely prosperous. Yet never again would bulbs fetch the exorbitant prices they had done some years ago when what had become known as "tulipomania" had swept the country. People from all walks of life became speculators in bulbs expected to bring forth new patterns or exceptional colours and which might soon become worth their weight in gold. Houses with all their contents were exchanged for a single bulb; livestock from farms, tools of trade and premises and family heirlooms all went in the general madness as fortunes were made overnight. Often a bulb changed hands figuratively several times, the buyers and the sellers never seeing the actual product, exactly as financial deals were carried out at the Exchange in Amsterdam, and at those in London, Paris and elsewhere.

This horticultural madness came about through the cultivated tulip's unique way of producing its own variations through a natural breaking

down of the bulb into new forms, the colours of the offsets staying virtually steadfast. Those who had never gambled in their lives before threw caution aside and the wild speculation was maintained throughout every month of the three years that the fever lasted, giving opportunities to tricksters and swindlers in a whirlwind of fraud. When the market crashed many were left without a roof over their heads. Hendrick had been in the first years of his apprenticeship, but he had gambled a small inheritance and, with the good luck that rallied to him at certain times, he had emerged from the chaos with a thousand florins more than the sum with which he had started.

Francesca rose from her knees, brushed dirt from her apron and picked up the rug. Her task was done. In the early spring she would come out each day to watch the first shoots emerge. She went back indoors with a lighthearted step.

When Aletta returned home she had made several detailed sketches. Francesca looked at them with interest. "You have worked hard, Aletta."

She did not notice the gleam of excitement in her sister's eyes. "I'm going to have no time for anything else except work now," Aletta said as she took the sketches from Francesca and carried them away upstairs.

To Francesca's surprise Hendrick had taken more note of her suggestion about making a trip to Haarlem than she had supposed. As his spirits recovered once more, he made the announcement at breakfast one morning that there was to be a family outing to the old city of his apprenticeship.

"We'll go tomorrow to pay our respects at my old master's tomb and then take a look around. It will be Saturday, so there'll be lots to see. I'll borrow a horse and sporting cart to get us there. Its owner owes me a favour." It was not the most comfortable form of transport, being much like a wooden tub on wheels, and passengers were rocked about, but it was much quicker than the canal boat and it was free.

Sybylla clapped her hands excitedly. "An outing! What a treat!"

Aletta looked uncertain. "It's getting colder every day. Suppose it should snow and hinder our return."

Francesca thought it was unusual for Aletta to make such a com-

ment. It was almost as if she were seeking any sort of excuse to prevent the trip. "I don't think we need worry about that," she said firmly.

"Indeed not!" Hendrick endorsed. In any case, once he had decided on a course of action that suited him personally he could rarely be persuaded otherwise. He raised a quizzical eyebrow at Francesca. "We can afford it, can't we?"

"Oh! Yes!" she replied with a laugh, excited herself at the prospect. It was the custom at the week's end for families to pour out of the towns and cities for picnics in summer, or to country taverns and the entertainments provided there when the weather was colder. As a family in the past there had been many such expeditions, but since Anna had died there had been none. Hendrick had not been able to endure any avoidable occasion that emphasized her absence. Francesca was sure that this outing would be good for him and for all of them. Neither she nor her sisters had ever been to Haarlem, although it was only thirteen miles away. "We'll take a picnic!"

"Be sure you include a bottle of wine with the food," Hendrick insisted jovially.

Francesca had another thought. There was only one outstanding debt in her household ledger and that was for the bulbs. "Do you happen to know whereabouts near Haarlem I could find the premises of the tulip grower van Doorne, who supplied the new bulbs?"

Hendrick shook his head, puzzled as to why she should have asked. "I ordered them at the market here in Amsterdam. Do you need more?"

"No, there are plenty, but I would like to pay him."

Hendrick's gesture tossed such an unimportant matter aside. "He'll be back for his money soon enough."

That was what she hoped to avoid. By making direct payment at van Doorne's premises it would be a way of erasing all those distressing times when she and all the household, except Hendrick, who usually managed to disappear, had been pestered for money. At least van Doorne's location should not be hard to discover once she was in Haarlem.

Maria sighed. "My old bones won't allow me to go on this outing."

Francesca sympathized and then Aletta spoke up defensively. "I won't be going tomorrow either."

They all looked at her in surprise. "Why not?" Hendrick asked.

"I want to finish my painting of the bridge over the Amstel."

"There'll be other days."

"No." She had her obstinate look. "If I'm to be a serious artist I can't drop everything for a day of frivolity."

Sybylla looked at her pityingly. Aletta was becoming as old in her ways as Maria. She herself was not interested in visiting Hals's tomb, but she was in seeing the shops and whatever Haarlem had to offer, particularly in its young men. Maria kept far too close an eye on her at home and it would be wonderful to be free of her for once.

"You're becoming more of a stick-in-the-mud every day, Aletta," she gibed.

"Better that than to think of nothing else except ogling anything in breeches that walks along the street!" Aletta countered fiercely.

Sybylla's face flushed a guilty scarlet. "Listen to that viperish tongue! Can I help it if men look at me and not at you?"

It was not entirely true, for it was only Aletta's natural hauteur that discouraged advances. At the moment there was a flush of angry pink in her cheeks. "I'm not interested in riffraff, Sybylla!"

Hendrick had become exasperated. He had no tolerance of quarrels that he himself had not instigated. "Be silent both of you! Aletta shall stay at home if that is what she wishes. I'll not discourage anyone from work." His faintly pious note might have led a stranger to suppose he was never away from his easel himself. "At least Aletta will be here if Willem can't hold back any longer from collecting the painting."

It was decided that an early start should be made. Even so, Aletta was up before anyone else in the morning and already in the studio at work when breakfast was served.

"Aren't you coming to eat?" Sybylla asked, looking in at the door. She had Hendrick's virtue in never sulking and, again like him, she quite enjoyed a clash of temperaments, feeling invigorated by it. This morning she would willingly have embraced her sister in reconciliation if it had been necessary, but Aletta had already forgotten their tiff.

"I've eaten." Aletta did not glance away from her canvas, but continued to paint steadily. "I told you yesterday that I wanted to get this painting finished."

Sybylla noticed a half-eaten slice of bread and cheese on a plate that

must have forced a space for itself on the cluttered side table. Whatever drink had been left in a cup was now cold and soaked up into a carelessly cast-aside paint rag that had landed across it. "I'll fetch you a fresh drink anyway. There's hot chocolate this morning." She went across to pick up the cup and then stood to study the painting of the bridge and neighbouring buildings. "What's so vital about this one? Why the rush? Have you a buyer for it?" Her words had been intended as a jest, but Aletta looked so startled that Sybylla paused, grinning triumphantly at her. "So that's it!"

Aletta rushed to the door and closed it to avoid anyone overhearing before she came back to where her sister stood. "I think I have. That day I was sketching at the bridge I included a row of property with a bakery in the foreground. The baker's wife came by, looked over my shoulder as people do, and offered to buy my sketch. I told her it was for a painting and she became quite excited and said if it was good she would buy it as a surprise gift for her husband's fiftieth birthday. He would be so proud to have such a painting to hang in his shop."

"What!" Sybylla was as outraged as their father would have been. "As a family we've been in low straits more times than I care to remember, but never has a painting or drawing or etching signed with the name of Visser been displayed over a shop counter!"

"Maybe if it had, life would have been easier for Mama without all the scrimping and saving she had to do and which Francesca has had to carry on doing ever since!" Aletta's eyes flashed like streak lightning. "I've no false pride. I want money for a reason of my own and if my painting becomes covered with flour and sultanas until it looks like a bun I shall not care in the least."

Sybylla gave a gurgle of laughter. "I think you would!"

An unwilling smile came to Aletta's lips and she inclined her head in agreement. "You're right," she said more calmly, "but it makes no difference to my wanting the sale to go through. I asked a good price and had to hide my surprise when the woman agreed without hesitation to pay it." Abruptly she gripped Sybylla's arm. "Don't tell Father or Francesca about this, will you?"

For once Sybylla did not taunt or tease as she liked to do whenever an opportunity presented itself. From personal experience she under-

stood the importance of money to those who had never had any, since she could number herself among them. "I won't say anything," she promised, "but isn't it a rule of the Guild that anything painted by pupils in a studio belongs to the master in charge?"

"Yes, it is, but I don't consider myself to be Father's pupil any longer!" Aletta spoke fiercely. "It's many weeks since he last made a remark about my work and it was neither helpful nor constructive. So I'm taking the risk. He need never know."

"But why are you doing this? Do you want to buy something fine to wear?"

Aletta smiled again. "Nothing like that! What I want costs far more than a garment. When I've saved enough I'll tell you what it's for."

"It's quite a while since we shared a secret. Last time was when I told you Jacob wanted to marry me."

"And I told you not to raise your hopes."

Sybylla made a rueful little grimace. "You were right, of course. But I'll not tell you the same, because I'm sure the baker's wife is going to be pleased with what you've done. I'll fetch your hot chocolate now."

"No, wait!" Aletta removed her painting smock. "I'll come with you. If Father should look in here before leaving for Haarlem he would see that I've almost finished and insist on my going too."

"Yes, he would."

Companionably, the two girls went from the studio together. Half an hour later Aletta stood with Maria to wave her father and sisters on their way in the sporting cart. Griet rose from her knees where she was scrubbing the stoop and waved in a shower of soapsuds white as snow.

The recent cold, dry weather had made the rutted road hard and the wheels of the sporting cart sped along. Francesca and Sybylla shrieked and held on to each other with laughter as they were almost bounced off the seat at times. The October sun was pale in a sky atumble with clouds, for the wind was strong and the great sails of the windmills were all turning. It did not matter that the countryside was totally flat as far as the eye could see, for it was a lush green and there was always a gleam of water as if large opals had been sprinkled everywhere. With much of the land below sea level it was a constant battle to save it from flooding and the huge dikes, built of earth and rock, were sometimes

overcome by exceptionally rough tides, which resulted in the loss of life and livestock. Here and there little bridges gave access across canals and waterways, the wooden passageways being constructed so each could be raised to allow laden barges and small boats to pass underneath.

There was plenty to see on the road itself. People trudged along on foot, and they passed farm carts filled with produce. Now and again Hendrick would draw aside to let the lumbering coaches of the wealthy burghers go by, the paintwork agleam. He had to give way again whenever they met a stage wagon racing along at full speed, for the coachmen took a pride in keeping down the time taken from one destination to another, no matter that the passengers were tossed about like dice in a box. These vehicles raised a small sail as soon as they were out of town, if the wind was in the right direction, which allowed the horses to maintain a full gallop as if the load they were pulling was weightless. It was not uncommon for accidents to happen on the rough roads. The highlight of the journey for Sybylla was when she and Francesca received waves from two young officers of the Guard on horseback, handsome in their huge black hats and velvet and lace, white teeth flashing between thin moustaches and arrow-sharp beards. She looked after them wistfully as they disappeared ahead into the distance.

At Haarlem, Hendrick drove through the fourteenth-century gate with its helm roofs and octagonal towers, smiling to be entering the territory of his youth again. He looked about him whenever the traffic allowed, memories of petticoat chasing and carousals coming back to him. Frans Hals had been strict enough in the studio, but he still had such weaknesses himself in those days and turned a blind eye to the lusty activities of his apprentices as long as they were sober and on time in the morning and worked hard under his tuition.

Haarlem followed the layout of most Dutch towns in having a large central square with the church facing the town hall across it. Mediaeval buildings flanked the two remaining sides and brightly painted signs were suspended over the doors of those that had been put to commercial use. A busy market was at its height and Sybylla looked at it eagerly as Hendrick drove past and into the old vegetable market alongside the Church of St. Bavo, where small shops were set against its walls. Vertical shutters had been lowered to form counters on which were piled fabrics

and lace and other fancy wares that caught her eye. Hendrick tied up the horse and helped his daughters alight from the sporting cart. Sybylla would have darted across to the little shops if Francesca had not restrained her, for Hendrick was waiting for them to follow him into the church. He removed his hat as he entered.

Within it was a place of light with its double rows of immensely high windows of clear glass and almost every slab of the great floor was a memorial stone to those interred beneath.

Hendrick located the last resting place of Frans Hals in the choir by the high gilded screen. As he stood with his daughters, looking down at the plain black stone inscribed with his late master's name, he bowed his head in respect, memories flooding back. He remembered that merry, drink-raddled face, the hearty laugh that had rocked the whole of the man's broad frame and the generous praise freely given when a pupil's work was well done.

The wealthiest and the grandest of Haarlem's citizens had commissioned their portraits from Hals, whose work had blazed with life and wit and sometimes irony. Not for him the quiet landscape or the history painting. He had liked to paint people from all walks of life: the topers he got drunk with, the tavern maids who fought his hand up their skirts, the jokers who told a jolly tale and anyone else who reminded him that life was for living to the full. And always those stately and often self-satisfied faces of the rich, some of whom never suspected he had painted them with his tongue in his cheek!

Hendrick wiped a tear from his eye and took out a kerchief to blow his nose vigorously. In the end this genius of a man had had to beg for a charity stipend from the city to keep him and his wife from starvation in their old age. Finally, the bill for his funeral had, through necessity, been on the city's accounts—he who had given Haarlem more in his lifetime than any other man who had ever been born there. Francesca, who had brought a small bunch of foliage and a few late flowers from home, laid the bouquet on the tomb.

As soon as they emerged from the church, Sybylla made a beeline for the stalls selling fripperies. Hendrick followed his daughters around quite amiably, although with the bored expression common to men while their womenfolk shop. Several purchases were made, including a

blue shawl for Maria and a string of coloured beads for Griet, gifts to be kept for St. Nicholaes's Day. They ate their picnic on a bench by a canal and afterwards Hendrick showed his daughters Hals's old house, where he had served his apprenticeship, narrowly missing being run down by horses and a wagon when he stepped into the street to point out which windows had been those of the studio.

Nearby was the house where he had had accommodation and with his face full of anticipation he knocked on its door, Francesca and Sybylla standing at his side. A maidservant answered the door and showed them into a drawing room. A few minutes later a grey-haired woman in a dark red silk gown came to meet them. She was the eldest daughter of the couple with whom he had lodged and was of his own age.

"Joan!" Hendrick exclaimed on a roar of delight.

In spite of the passing of time she recognized him at once. "Mercy! It's Hendrick Visser!" She made them welcome and refreshment was served. Her good-looking son was at home and he and Sybylla were taken with each other from the start. The only sad note was when Hendrick learned that Joan's parents had died. They had taken him into their home when, after meeting him with Hals one day, they heard he needed somewhere to lodge.

Then it was time to leave if they were to make a short detour on the way home to visit van Doorne's place of business before dark. Joan gave them directions. Sybylla and the young man were in close conversation until the last minute, and he walked with them to where Hendrick had left the horse and sporting cart. Francesca noticed that Sybylla had a satisfied smile on her lips when she took her seat in the sporting cart. It was easy to guess she had had plenty of flirtatious compliments.

A lane led in a southwesterly direction to the van Doorne bulb fields, bare now in November with nothing to hint at the glory that would come in the spring. They came to what must have been a farm building at some time, its walls of stone and its dark brown thatch as neatly clipped as a head of hair. A sign proclaimed it was the van Doorne office. Hendrick and Sybylla stayed in the sporting cart while Francesca alighted to knock on the door and enter. A middle-aged man with a quill pen stuck behind one ear came from a desk to bow.

"Good day, *mejuffrouw*."

"Am I addressing Heer van Dorne?"

"No, I'm his clerk. He is here if you should wish to see him, either at Haarlem Huis—that's his home just beyond the trees, although it can't be seen from this office or the lane—or else somewhere near at hand."

"No, I don't wish to speak to him. I've only come to pay a bill."

"Certainly. Such an intention is always good news." His jovial air showed that it was not the first time he had made that particular jest.

Francesca paid the monies owing and left immediately, Hendrick having already turned the equipage in readiness for departure. She took a backwards look at the old thatched building. Its centuries-old form and its setting would make a fine landscape. She registered the scene in her memory, something at which she had become an expert.

Then the trees slid across her view of it and as she turned back in her seat they were passing an orangery. In the same instant a tall young man emerged from a doorway and he and Francesca looked right into each other's eyes. For an extraordinary moment the excitement she sensed in him seemed to course through her. She saw astonishment and recognition in his gaze, which she was at a loss to understand, and she was sure there must be bewilderment in hers, for to the best of her knowledge she had never seen him before. If she had she would have remembered. A grin spread across his face, his teeth as white as the keys of a virginal. To her further amazement, he dashed forward, leapt over a low fence and took a couple of running paces to catch the horse's bridle and cause Hendrick to draw up.

"Your pardon!" he exclaimed to Hendrick. "I'm Pieter van Doorne. I didn't want to see you leave without a word. You are Master Visser of Amsterdam?"

"I am."

"I trust the bulbs delivered to you were satisfactory."

Hendrick regarded him with amusement. "I can scarcely tell until they flower."

Pieter laughed. "I didn't mean that question to be as foolish as it sounded. It was whether the condition of the bulbs themselves was up to your expectations."

"It's pointless to ask me. I'm no gardener." Hendrick glanced over his

shoulder into the sporting cart. "Francesca, you are the one to give judgement."

She smiled reassuringly at Pieter, who had come to stand looking up at her. "I have no fault to find. I'm looking forward to the blooms."

Sybylla spoke up, not wanting to be left out of this conversation. "So am I. We came here specially to pay your bill after being in Haarlem for the day."

Pieter turned again to Hendrick. "Before you start on your journey home allow me to offer you some refreshment at my house before you leave."

Hendrick shook his head. "I thank you, but I want to go most of the way before darkness sets in. The evenings close in early at this time of year. Good day to you."

With a flick of Hendrick's whip in the air, the horse moved forward. Pieter held Francesca's eyes with his demanding stare. "Another time, then," he said as if to her father, but the message in his gaze was for her.

The horse went trotting on its way. Before the lane curved to the road, Francesca felt herself compelled to look back and saw that Pieter was watching them out of sight. He raised his arm and waved to her. She responded and then he was lost from view.

CHAPTER 5

Three weeks had gone by since the trip to Haarlem when Hendrick received Willem in his studio. It pleased him that the art dealer should find him at work. On the rostrum was a scrawny beggar in rags, whom he had sighted pleading for alms near the steps of the Exchange. He was painting him in the act of reaching a clawlike hand for a large jewel that was to be depicted in a watery gutter. Like the azure earbobs that Francesca had worn in the Flora painting, the jewel was only a worthless fairing from one of the trinket boxes in the storeroom.

Willem stood back to view the painting. Like Hals, Hendrick rarely made a preliminary drawing, but sketched in paint straight onto the canvas, his loosely applied brushstrokes giving spontaneity to his work. This painting looked as if it might be a worthy successor to his Flora, although the subject would not be to everyone's taste.

"A silver florin would be more plausible than a jewel of that size," Willem remarked. "Half of Amsterdam would have sighted that gaudy geegaw from a mile away."

"Why do you assume that the setting for my painting is in this city?" Hendrick growled belligerently. "There are beggars in every land. Maybe it's in a slum alley in London."

"Has a thief dropped the jewel, then? The wearers of such gems as that piece of glass is supposed to represent don't usually wander about in dubious areas."

Hendrick paused in his painting and glared. "Don't jest with me! You know well enough that the jewel in this particular context symbolizes the world's wealth that is out of reach of the poor everywhere. And that includes artists whose agents never sell their work at a good price!"

Willem breathed deeply and let the matter rest. There was no one more bullheaded than Hendrick when his temper turned. Allegoric paintings and symbolic touches were more popular than ever, but symbols had to be a natural part of the picture, further enhancing its subject or theme. The jewel in Hendrick's painting jarred the eye, as did so many touches that he had persisted in adding to his pictures over the years, always surprised when one or another of his works fetched abysmally low prices. "I've come for *The Goddess of Spring.*"

Hendrick resumed his painting. "Have you a buyer?"

"Better than that. I have several potential buyers, but I want to speak about that to you in private."

Hendrick put aside his palette and brushes, telling the beggar to take a rest. Then he and Willem left the studio. In the parlour the art dealer explained he had let the word spread that he had an exceptional work, which he was reluctant to sell, partly because he saw it as an investment, but more for the beauty of the model herself who had posed as Flora. Already he had had keen inquiries, but he had acted mysteriously

and evasively, not saying whether he would let it be viewed by the public or not.

"I need hardly say that the curiosity of certain people is almost more than they can bear. I've had offers for it unseen and when I let this be known more demands for the first right to buy came in."

"So what is to happen next?" This stratagem appealed to Hendrick.

"I shall have it veiled in a room in my house and that will intrigue still more. When I have the right buyer and the right moment, I shall reveal the painting of Francesca and settle the deal."

Hendrick laughed exuberantly. "Well done, old friend!"

Willem remained sober-faced. "I'm doing this as much for Francesca as for you."

Hendrick frowned. "What has my daughter to do with this?"

"I want to see the sum that you get for this painting put to the best possible use. Let it pay for her tuition in the studio of an artist who would teach her well and release the fount of talent that's ready to burst forth."

Hendrick's gaze shifted and he half turned away. "Do you think I haven't wanted that? My own patience has run out and, although I have tried to carry on instructing my daughters, it's as if a wall has come between them and me in that respect. Teaching was never my forte and now I seem to have lost whatever ability I had in that direction."

"Then do as I say!" Willem urged. "You'll have it in your hands to give Francesca the apprenticeship she deserves."

"But whatever I receive from the sale of the portrait would never run to her tuition and keep for the necessary six years."

"She doesn't need six! Two years at the most would combine with the instruction she has already received from you."

Hendrick faced him again. "I'm not sure that you realize the difficulties involved. I don't know a single artist of my acquaintance who would take a woman pupil. It's not through prejudice against the weaker sex, but the sheer mechanics of finding space elsewhere for them to draw and paint plaster figures of classical origin when there's a nude model on the rostrum. My daughters have been brought up to accept nudity in the studio and had their first lessons in life drawing almost from the start, although my male models have always kept their

genitals covered at my instruction whenever the girls were present. No, it will not be easy to find a master willing to take Francesca as his apprentice."

Willem's confident expression had not changed. "I know of someone," he stated firmly. "He's of the school of Delft."

Hendrick considered, rubbing his chin thoughtfully. Each of the seven states of Holland had local schools of painting attached to their main towns, and he would have preferred the Guild of Amsterdam for his daughter. Admittedly Delft was a good choice in that Rembrandt's pupil Carel Fabritius had gained fame there before his untimely death, and it could boast of the presence of Jan Steen and other painters.

"What is the name of the artist you have in mind?"

"Johannes Vermeer."

Hendrick looked at Willem blankly. "I've never heard of him."

"Don't be surprised by that. Few people have, outside of Delft. On the whole he paints very little and his favourite model is his wife, to whom he is devoted. They have several children."

"How does he support them, then?"

"For a short while he ran his late father's tavern, but he has now rented it out. These days he deals in paintings, which is how I first met him."

"A tavernkeeper!" Hendrick's tone was so outraged that a stranger might have supposed him to be one who had never crossed a threshold where alcohol was sold.

"An artist of the highest merit," Willem corrected. No need to add that he had met no one yet outside Delft who shared this view. It was simply his own personal conviction that Vermeer was a great painter. "He would be the ideal choice as a tutor for Francesca," he continued. "He is easy-tempered, a conscientious man of thirty-eight years who has no other pupils and will devote time to her. You need not fear that he'll make any immoral advances, because, as I've already said, he has eyes only for his wife."

"Hmm. Nobody can be sure of that." Hendrick reflected that no man could love a woman more than he had loved Anna, but that did not mean he had not strayed from time to time.

"Then be sure of Francesca instead. She has a head not easily turned."

"Agreed." Hendrick spoke proudly and then his voice took on a sarcastic edge. "What qualifications does this Vermeer have besides being able to fill tankards with beer?"

"Don't grind on about that short period in his life. He is a master of the Guild of St. Luke, having served his six years' apprenticeship in Delft, the city of his birth."

"So I should expect."

Willem ignored the gibe. "There are two other important reasons why you should consider Vermeer as a tutor for Francesca," he pressed on. "Both she and Aletta have developed their own individual style, which pays tribute to the teaching you gave them in their early years, and there's something about Francesca's work that reminds me each time of Vermeer's. I'm certain the two would work in harmony."

"How do you know he would take Francesca as a pupil?"

Willem smiled with compressed lips. "I've already paved the way. She would be his only pupil. Think what an advantage that should give her."

"Yes, that is so."

"There are only two things more. I shall want some of her recent drawings and at least one of her paintings to show the Guild committee. I shall also need the document of her indenture."

"There isn't one."

Willem stared at him for a few moments. "I don't believe this. Are you telling me you never indentured your daughters?"

Hendrick answered carelessly. "I suppose I never thought about it. They came into the studio at such an early age."

Willem almost ground his teeth. "You realize that this will mean Francesca has to start from scratch. It will have to be the full six years."

"I can't afford that."

Willem slammed his hands on the chair arms. "Then think! Rack your brains! Have you anything at all to show she has been painting for most of her life? A letter? A written entry anywhere? What about Anna's papers? Would she have kept anything? Whatever comes to light may not prove enough, but I'll have to present some documentation."

Hendrick thought deeply, leaning his head forward. "I can't think of anything, unless my sister-in-law, Janetje, ever commented in her letters

on something Anna might have told her about our daughters' progress. Anna kept all the correspondence, just as Francesca has ever since."

"Then look through those letters! Now! Today! Let me have whatever you find. All this means that on no account must Francesca have an inkling of what we are trying to arrange. Neither of us wants her hopes to rise only to be dashed again. In any case it will be the New Year at the earliest before *The Goddess of Spring* is sold, and some time after that before I can visit Delft again and set my appeal on her behalf before the Guild members. I'll take my leave of you and let you start your search."

When Willem had left, Hendrick went upstairs to the bedchamber, where Anna still haunted him, and opened the lacquered box that held the only papers that had been hers. He had had to glance through them after her death to find the deed of trust that her late father had drawn up at the time of their marriage, securing the house and its effects to her for her lifetime, which in turn had saved it from being sold over their heads when at different times his creditors had become nasty about their unpaid dues. Anna had bequeathed everything to him, which was probably not what her father had expected, thinking it would pass to his grandchildren. Upon learning of the contents of her will Hendrick had immediately resolved never to take again the gambling risks on a grand scale as he had done before when he had been safe in the knowledge that whatever happened they would always have a roof over their heads. His father-in-law had not been a rich man, but Maurice Veldhuis had made a small investment for each of his daughters, enabling both Anna and Janetje to draw the interest in their lifetime, the capital to go to their offspring after them. On a sigh, Hendrick thought of how often what should have been Anna's spending money had gone to settle mounting bills incurred through his selfishness.

Grief had been blinding him when previously he had had to look in this box, but now he was able to see exactly what Anna had treasured and kept locked away. Here were letters tied with ribbon that he had written to her during their courtship. Beside these was early correspondence from Maurice Veldhuis and his wife when Anna and Janetje had been sent to an aunt's house in the country when plague was sweeping through Amsterdam. Taking up a great deal of space were the children's

first baby drawings with their later poems and birthday greetings. Then came a thicker package of Janetje's letters, Francesca having added each new one as it came, and he thought it would be a long dull task to go through every one. As he lifted them out he saw that among a few minor items still left in the box was a thin roll of paper tied with ribbon. He took it out, removed the ribbon and unrolled it to find it consisted of three sheets, each indenturing one of his daughters to him, the script in Anna's neat hand and bearing his own signature and those of the three girls. Anna had signed her own name on each indenture as a witness with the date clearly inscribed.

He had no idea how this had been done, having no recollection of the subject having been brought up, except on rare occasions and then only in passing. To the best of his knowledge Anna had never thought of the girls becoming his apprentices officially any more than he had. Yet with exceptional foresight she had done this for her daughters.

He put her signature to his lips and kissed it. Then he rested a hand across his eyes and sat for some time, letting memories of Anna flood over him. When he did move again it was to return Aletta's and Sybylla's indentures to the box with everything else, taking only Francesca's downstairs with him.

When he had sealed it into a letter of explanation he gave it to Griet for immediate delivery to Willem's home. No sooner had it gone than he was struck by an uneasy thought. How could he send one daughter for tuition and not the other? Maybe he should paint a portrait of Aletta as Ariadne, daughter of King Minos of Crete, but then he dismissed the idea. Aletta was such a modest, retiring girl and would never agree to removing her cap to reveal her beautiful hair, which had such an exceptional colour, so pale and yet full of lights. She was unselfconscious about it if they met by night or morning on the landing when it was hanging loose down her back, but it was clear she had never forgotten that horrific experience in the passageway and still felt safer wearing a cap in public.

"We'll let her be," Anna had said to him. "In time she will come to realize that it was extreme ill fortune that caused her to suffer and she need not go through life fearing it will happen again."

Since there had been no recision of the vow Aletta had apparently

made to herself about keeping her hair covered, a history painting with her as a model was out of the question. In any case she was rarely in the studio these days, always off somewhere on her own when she should have been at hand, as Francesca was, for those moments when he chose to give tuition. Aletta's chance of an apprenticeship would have to wait. There was no hurry since she was a year younger. At some time in the future, if funds were in hand again, her work could be assessed and the situation reconsidered.

With his mind easily settled, Hendrick re-entered the studio, where he was assailed by the stench of the beggar's rags. He saw that the fellow had taken an orange from Francesca's recent still-life arrangement and had dripped juice, the peel scattered. Hendrick went to the window and opened it wider to fill his lungs with fresh air.

"There's a draught," the beggar grumbled.

"You should be used to that," Hendrick replied heartlessly, although he did draw the window in slightly. "Resume your pose."

He took up his palette and brush again as well as his maulstick, the ball-topped stick on which a painter rested his hand. There were spells when the pain in his knuckles made it difficult for him to paint without it.

Aletta went out every day except Sundays to sketch in the city. Although she often showed her drawings to Francesca she preferred to paint upstairs in a side room with a communicating door that led off the bedchamber that she and Sybylla shared. Previously it had been a little parlour where either of them could read or entertain friends on their own. Aletta took whatever materials she needed from the studio and Sybylla with Griet had helped her carry up a spare easel. There was nothing unusual about this move to work alone, because it was known that Aletta liked solitude and her concentration was always disturbed in the studio when Hendrick was there too. Working on her own there with Francesca was a different matter.

"Why do you never show anyone except Sybylla your finished paintings?" Francesca asked one day. "Your eye for perspective is so good. I'd like to see them."

"They're not up to your standard and Father would tear them to pieces with his criticism. When I paint one that satisfies me I will show you."

"Is that a promise?"

"It is indeed."

Francesca was reassured. She knew how it was to feel full of doubt about a project in hand and sometimes one needed to work out difficulties on one's own.

At Martinmas in November, Hendrick took his three daughters to see Amsterdam's great sailing event of the year on the river Ij. Aletta had made her usual excuses about work, but Hendrick had swept them aside.

"This is a day for families to be together and enjoy themselves," he insisted. "Everything else must take second place to the racing at this time of year."

She had no choice but to obey and then gladly joined in the spirit of the occasion, realizing how long it was since she had allowed herself any relaxation. Enormous crowds massed along the banks, but by arriving early the Visser family secured good places at the front near one of the winning posts, the distance varying according to the type of race. The day was cold, but the girls were wrapped in warm cloaks and their hoods protected them. The wide brim of Hendrick's hat flapped in the wind, but he had jammed it on well before leaving home. It was a splendid sight to see the hundreds of little sailboats and rowboats gathering for the various competitions. Everyone was in a merry mood and pedlars did good business in selling sweetmeats and fairings and sticks with streamers to wave. Sporting rivalry was intense among the competitors and this gave spice to the atmosphere. All were excited and there was plenty of wagering among the spectators.

A pistol shot started the first race. Cheers roared out as a host of brown, yellow and cream sails billowed in the lively wind and the light craft went skimming along the water, the bows veiled in spray.

Pieter van Doorne was among the competitors, but he did not see the Visser family until a couple of hours later when he and a friend entered a rowing race and took their craft first past the finishing post. As they leaned over their oars, gasping breath into their blown lungs, he

happened to glance up through a tangle of his hair and saw the family cheering and applauding him. Francesca's vivacious face, framed by her hood, was full of laughter, her cheeks nipped pink by the cold air, and he felt the same attraction that he had experienced when he had first seen her in her home, and again that day when she had paid his bill. She was making it clear that she and those with her were rejoicing over his win, her clapping hands raised to signal her congratulations. He was too far away to hear what she was saying, and in any case it would have been impossible in the din, but he could tell she was calling, "Well done!"

Francesca had told Aletta who he was and then forgot him, for another race had already started and she strained forward with everyone else to see who was in the lead. Yet the sight of him must have stayed with her, for the next morning she awoke remembering it was high time she put the usual mats of straw over the beds of tulip bulbs to protect them against the heavy frosts that had begun to sparkle the ground each morning. As she carried out her task she thought of him again. His eyes had seemed to pierce right into her.

Two days before the Feast of St. Nicholaes the first snow came and all blemishes in the city were masked. In the Visser household there was much jollity as final baking was done and the last gifts purchased or, if they were home-sewn, placed into bags of linen. Aletta and Sybylla had their final rehearsal together for the concert they would give on the evening of the saint's day. Playing the virginal by candlelight after sunset, when it was impossible to paint, had become Aletta's only relaxation. As children, she and her sisters had believed it was St. Nicholaes who filled their clogs with sweetmeats and novelties. Now that they were grown they themselves prepared a pair of large wooden clogs, which were painted with the saint's emblem and into which they put crystallized fruit and other dainties for all the household to enjoy.

The awaited day dawned with a new layer of powdery snow. After gifts had been exchanged, the Visser family, with Maria and Griet, all went to see the street puppet shows, the stalls selling dolls and effigy candles and the jugglers and tumblers and the strolling players that entertained the crowds, all to the cheerful noise of lutes and drums and

flutes and singing voices. Then Francesca and Griet returned home ahead of the rest to have the special dinner ready for the family.

Afterwards there were the last-minute preparations for the party to be given that evening. When the time came to dress, Francesca chose a currant-red velvet gown, the rich colour setting off her hair, which she wore in the style that fashion dictated. It was drawn smoothly back from her brow into a coil at the back of her head, leaving the neck prettily bare with falling curls over her ears. This evening she wound a string of small, bright beads into the coil, which gave a glittering effect.

At seven o'clock Hendrick stood ready to welcome guests in to Maria's homemade wine and a barrel of beer. They began to arrive in a flood, but fortunately there were plenty of sweet cakes and other delicacies. Best of all was a long roll of almond paste shaped into an "S" for St. Nicholaes, baked within a crust of light pastry and served cut into short lengths.

The reception hall and the drawing room opening out of it presented a merry scene. All were in their best velvets or silks and sat chatting together or stood in small groups, the buzz of cheerful noise punctuated by the clink of glasses and tankards. Every sconce was alight and the central bronze chandelier, suspended from the crossbeamed white plastered ceiling, blazed with thirty candles.

When everybody who was expected had been in the house for an hour or more, there came another knock on the front door. Griet, giggly with wine, went to answer it. To her astonishment it was someone she had never thought to see again. Forgetting her training, she shouted back over her shoulder to make herself heard above the general conversation. "It's the tulip grower from Haarlem! Heer van Doorne!"

Hendrick, always hospitable, boomed out a welcome to the young man on the stoop in the snow. "Come in, *mijnheer!* Griet, hold the door wider. Nobody stands on the threshold on the Feast of St. Nicholaes!"

All looked towards the door. Francesca smiled in wonderment at this unexpected surprise. Then Pieter made an unwittingly dramatic entrance in a flurry of snowflakes, stepping onto the strip of Persian carpet that had been laid down by the doorway for the evening. He seemed to loom into the room, for his big black hat, powdered with snow, added to his fine height. More snowflakes clung to his plum-coloured cloak,

which reached to the ankles of his white knee hose, his shoes silver-buckled. As Griet swiftly closed the door behind him to keep out the cold, he doffed his hat to bow first to Hendrick and then to the company, his keen eyes locating Francesca where she sat.

"My greetings, Heer Visser," he said to Hendrick, "and to all here."

Hendrick, who had heaved himself out of his chair at the arrival of each guest, had done the same now and gone across to him. "On behalf of all present I give you ours in return and bid you welcome to my house."

Then Pieter took from under his cloak, which Griet was waiting to take from him, a Delft pot filled with dark earth from which was sprouting a tall and strong-looking shiny green shoot. "As you are a new customer," he said to Hendrick, "I'm taking the opportunity on this Feast of St. Nicholaes to bring a hyacinth to this house. It should bloom for Christmas."

There were exclamations on all sides, those in the drawing room crowding in to see the plant, many startled by this aberration of nature. Nobody thought of witchcraft or knew fear. It was just that the hyacinth belonged to spring and had no place thus out of order. In any case, what could be expected of this shoot, healthy though it appeared, at a time when bulbs should be dormant?

But Hendrick always appreciated a good surprise. He held the potted plant high for everyone to see.

"Look at this miracle, my friends! The seasons are being reversed!"

Aletta nodded appreciatively and Sybylla darted to him, clapping her hands at such a gift. Francesca, who remained sitting on the bench, could feel that Pieter was as aware of her presence as she was of his. Incredulously for her, it was as if a fuse had been lit and was sizzling silently and invisibly between them.

He stood with a smile in his eyes and on his lips as he surveyed the room. His long green jacket fitted him well across his broad shoulders, while his hair, the curls too unruly to submit much to any comb, glinted with spangles of melted snow.

"Now you must meet everyone, my friend," Hendrick declared, turning back to him. Still parading the plant, he led Pieter up and down the long room, making the presentations. Then they reached Francesca and

suddenly she and Pieter were face to face as he took her hand and bowed over it.

"I'm honoured to meet you again, Juffrouw Visser," he said formally, although there was nothing stilted in his smile or in the look of pleasure that he gave her.

"May your time in this house be blessed," she replied in the same formal tones, "and I thank you most sincerely for the gift you have brought us." The colour had risen to her cheeks, for she was momentarily unnerved by the forceful contact that seemed to exist between them, but she thought he would not notice anything amiss. There were so many people already pink-cheeked from the wine and the heat generated by so large a company. Hendrick was already drawing him away and out of the corner of her eye she watched him complete his tour of the room. A married couple who were present knew him already and, having met everybody else, he entered into conversation with them. Why then, Francesca asked herself, did she still feel that he was sending out invisible rays from his mind and his body towards her?

There came a tap on her shoulder to draw her attention and Sybylla bent her head to whisper in her ear. "What fun this should happen! I believe Pieter van Doorne has come to see you again more than anything else."

"What nonsense!" Francesca replied forcibly.

"Not at all. I saw the way he looked at you in the sporting cart and again on the river." With a laugh Sybylla went off with a swing of her hips to present her platter of almond delicacies to the newcomer and the two guests with him. All three of them took a piece and Pieter looked amused at whatever she said to him, making some riposte in return that obviously delighted her. It was clear there were to be no barriers in their getting to know each other. Francesca turned on her seat and joined in talk about lace making with the two women at her left-hand side. It was dull enough to be an antidote to Sybylla's ridiculous suppositions.

As a result she failed to see Pieter return to her until he spoke, causing her to look up quickly. He was holding the plant. "Your father just gave me this back again to hand on to you. As with the bulbs, he

says you're the one with green fingers and you should take care of such a rarity."

"I'll do my best," she said, taking the Delft pot from him. As she had expected, he sat down at her right side, where there was a vacant place.

"It's always enjoyable to talk to a fellow gardener," he said, although by the way he was smiling he appeared to have anything but gardening on his mind.

"I wouldn't class myself in your category. Our garden consists of a few flower beds."

"I know. I saw them when I delivered the bulbs at the beginning of October. But lack of space doesn't mean that the flower beds there can't produce in minor quantities anything as fine as I grow."

"I'd like to think that. Gardening is a hobby of mine," she admitted, "and I like producing flowers to paint."

"You're an artist too?"

"So is my sister Aletta. There are three painters under this roof, but only one master."

He gave her an encouraging nod. "Perhaps one day there'll be three masters."

"That's what Aletta and I hope for most of all."

"With all sincerity I wish you both well."

"I thank you." She thought he meant what he said. "I shall paint the hyacinth when it blossoms."

He looked pleased. "What an honour for it!"

Aletta's voice broke in as she came with a silver-lidded flagon of wine in one hand and a glass for him in the other. "There is beer if you prefer it."

"I thank you, but I'll take the wine."

He had risen to his feet to hold the glass as she poured. "It's quite potent," she warned him seriously.

"I'll remember that, Juffrouw Aletta."

She looked directly at him as he spoke her name and she returned his smile. Sybylla had conjured up her own reason for his visit, which she had already divulged to Aletta. Whether there was any truth in it or not did not matter to Aletta since she was not the one singled out for his interest. It was always Francesca or Sybylla who magnetized men's

eyes, and that suited her. Yet she liked this man for his friendly air. He had been particularly courteous when Hendrick had presented him, but it had been natural to her that she should add her thanks for the gift he had brought to her home.

"I'll be back when your glass needs refilling," she promised.

"That's most obliging of you."

Aletta held her flagon up questioningly at Francesca, who indicated she had a full glass on the shelf behind her. As Aletta left again Francesca would have twisted round to lift the glass, but Pieter reached for it and handed it to her as he sat down again. He raised his own glass to her, the wine ruby red, the glass sparkling.

"To you, *mejuffrouw.*"

On her visit to his Haarlem home he had seen with satisfaction that at close quarters her eyes were green and lustrous. The currant-red dress she was wearing this evening echoed dramatically the glints in her coppery hair. In her lobes were gold earbobs that shone against her milk-white skin. She put both her fine-looking sisters in the shade, although the youngest was so ripe for plucking that at a touch she would be off the branch.

"Your good health," Francesca said in reply to his toast.

"It was most hospitable of your father to invite me to stay this evening." He glanced over his shoulder and smiled at a loud burst of laughter that followed a joking remark made on the other side of the room.

"Did you celebrate earlier today with your own family?" she asked.

He frowned sombrely. "I regret to say I have no close family now. I had two younger brothers, but they died with my parents within four days of one another."

"What a terrible tragedy!" Her voice was full of deep compassion.

His jaw flexed. "The plague took them all. That was seven years ago. I was at university at the time."

"Did you continue your studies?"

He shook his head. "That was impossible. I had been bequeathed the family home and the farm, which I ran for a few weeks while I formulated my plans and settled my future. Botany had been my source of study at the university and horticulture my interest from boyhood. My

father had always allowed me to have an orangery. Gradually I changed the layout of the land and converted farm buildings into greenhouses as well as erecting new ones. I also built the new orangery, which you saw the day you came there."

"It must have been hard work to get everything in order."

He shrugged with a smile. "The results have been worth all the effort. The soil is good and each spring my land turns to ribbons of tulips and hyacinths. I grow other flowers too, but in lesser quantities."

She had seen such carpets of flowers, the colours almost taking one's breath away. "I always think it's a sad sight when the barges transport huge mounds of those glorious tulip heads to dump them."

"They have to be cut off the stems the first year if the bulbs are to be a commercial proposition. Did you ever thread some of those blooms together when you were a child?"

"Yes, we did," she replied with enthusiasm. "A friend of my late mother used to bring us a huge basket of them. My sisters and I would sit in the courtyard and choose from all the different colours to make garlands to wear on our heads and hang around our necks. I still like to see those tulip chains draped over doorways and festooning wagons and sailboats." She gave a little laugh. "I remember always wishing I could lie on a bed of those blooms!"

Her words innocently conjured up such a seductive image for him that he needed to change the subject. "You're still nursing that hyacinth on your lap. Let me put it aside for you."

"I don't want it out of my charge now that I've been entrusted with it," she declared lightly, but with seriousness behind her words. "You must have made this Feast of St. Nicholaes an outstanding one for all your new customers by giving them such bounty."

His hesitation before he answered her could only have lasted for a matter of seconds, but during that lapse their eyes held and the realization dawned on her forcefully that no other customer had received anything. His reply, skirting her remark, confirmed indirectly what Sybylla had whispered to her.

"Most of my customers have been established with me for quite a while."

She returned her attention to the plant in order to hide her racing

thoughts, her lashes lowered. "How often should the earth in this pot be moistened?" she asked quickly, "and where would be the best place in the house for it to stand?"

It was entirely new to her to have a plant in the house and that was the general rule. Flower beds, public and private, might blossom and flourish everywhere in season, delighting the eye on all sides, but blooms were rarely brought indoors. The fastidious Dutch housewife had no place for a film of dusty pollen or dropped petals on her spotless surfaces. It was why paintings of flowers were so popular, giving the beauty without any of the mess, quite apart from the exorbitant cost of choice blooms.

When she had received from him all the advice she needed, Francesca seized on the chance the hyacinth had given her to break up their conversation. "I'll go now and put this plant in a good position."

He stood up as she left the bench. "May I come with you?"

Before she could answer him, Hendrick and two other men had stepped in to draw him into conversation about garden landscaping. She heard him say it was something he specialized in before she carried the potted plant away from the chatter and laughter into the quietness of a side room. There a candle lamp gave a soft light and a fire glowed in the grate.

Carefully Francesca placed the Delft pot on a side table under the window where it would get plenty of light while being out of any draught. She could hardly wait for it to bloom. What a subject for painting at this time of year! Then she became thoughtful as she remained standing by the table with her fingertips resting against the sides of the Delft pot with its blue-and-white pattern. Sybylla had been right. Francesca knew as surely as if Pieter had told her himself that this plant had been a ploy to gain an entrée into her home and further their acquaintance. To herself she commended him for his initiative, although, despite her attraction to him, it was misguided. Had her display of enthusiasm for his winning the race on the river led him to believe she would welcome this move of his?

She turned her head to where a Venetian mirror hung on a side wall and saw her own reflection within the gilded frame like a painting in a candlelit setting. The face of the girl she saw there was not exactly

troubled, but there was disquiet in the countenance. According to Maria, she was long overdue for courtship and kissing, but she had made her decision. Work and more work made an antidote to natural physical desires.

Just recently, for no reason that she could think of, Hendrick had taken a fresh interest in her work, although she knew it was an effort for him, and he had given her some tuition that had been most helpful. It was not on a regular basis and only when he was in a good mood, but she was grateful for it and felt she had made some advancement. She did not want disruption in her organized existence from Pieter van Doorne with his determined chin and penetrating eyes. This same evening she must squash any designs he might have on her time, for she had none to spare. She would be polite, but more distant. By this means she had discouraged a would-be suitor last year and the same young man was among the company in the reception room this evening, his newly betrothed with him. She turned with a swish of red velvet and lace-edged petticoats to go back to the merrymaking, but Pieter stood in the doorway.

"Sybylla told me where to find you."

Francesca realized that it was just the sort of thing her mischievous sister would do. She indicated the plant where it stood on the table. "I've found a good place for the hyacinth, as you can see."

He went across to it and she guessed it was not so much to check on where it stood as to delay her leaving the room. As she had half expected, he turned from it to rest his weight against the edge of the table, more than ready to prolong the time with her.

"I have a confession to make," he said quite seriously.

So he was about to confirm what she already knew. "Oh? What could that be?"

"I used this hyacinth as an excuse to meet you again. There was no chance to talk last time and even less on the two previous occasions."

"One, don't you mean?"

He shook his head, smiling. "No. I saw you the first time when I stood delivering the bulbs. I could see right through to the open door of the studio. You were in costume with a wreath of flowers on your hair. It was just a glimpse and then your father pushed the door closed."

She gave a little laugh, her eyebrows raised. "You are full of surprises, Heer van Doorne!"

"Call me Pieter, please. May I address you as Francesca?"

She shrugged lightly. "If you wish."

"Tell me more about your work, Francesca." He glanced about the room. "I'm certain none of these paintings is yours. I know that one over there is a Seghers."

"That's right." She recalled her mother's distress over Hendrick's extravagance when he had come home with it from an auction. In the past his acquisitive nature had made it impossible for him to turn away from anything he wanted and the house was full of paintings, contemporary and otherwise, that he had been unable to resist. The Seghers had caused one of those sharp quarrels between her parents, which had ended in the usual way upstairs. Now, in adulthood, she understood fully how much her mother had loved Hendrick, Anna's forgiving, generous heart unable to hold out against his wiles. "The only work of mine hanging in this house is in Maria's bedchamber. I would not dream of letting any of my paintings take a place beside the works on these walls even if my father allowed it."

"But the day will come."

She regarded him with amusement. "How can you possibly know that?"

He thrust himself away from the table and came across to her. "I don't, but I'm sure about it. Will you show me your painting of the hyacinth when it is done?"

It was a request she could not refuse. "Yes, of course," she said willingly.

He took a step closer. "I should like to see you often, Francesca."

This was her chance to stem their acquaintanceship before it advanced any further. "I have little time to myself. When I'm not painting I'm dealing with domestic matters."

"But there is always the spare hour. Everybody needs some relaxation. We could go to the theatre—there's enough to choose from in Amsterdam—and to concerts. We could talk and walk and really get to know each other."

She had never been more tempted. His height, his smile and the

1
0
5

sheer attractive physical presence of him threatened to blot out every-thing else for her. "I think not," she managed to say and was saved from any argument by the notes of the virginal striking up melodiously from the reception hall. "My sisters' concert has begun. Let us go quickly!"

She led the way and, looking through the archway into the reception hall from the stair hall, she saw that everyone was well settled and listening attentively. Not wanting to disturb anyone with a late arrival, she indicated the stairs.

"Let's sit here," she whispered to Pieter.

She had expected him to sit on the tread above hers, but he chose to squeeze in beside her, his hip and thigh against hers. Two of the audience had already glanced in their direction and she decided to stay where she was to save any further distraction. She set her mind to concentrate on Aletta's solo piece and away from this virile young man.

Aletta's piece came to an end and there was enthusiastic applause. Then she and Sybylla began to play together. Sybylla's viol produced a soft resonance and was really an instrument more suited to Aletta's temperament than to hers, for even when the music was fast it sounded placid. Perhaps that was why it appealed to Sybylla, who was unable to moderate her own emotions, but at heart she was a true musician. She had her eyes closed as she played, lost in the music, the bow in her hand held from underneath with her fingers touching the stick, each note beginning and ending in gentleness.

Francesca's artist's eye was struck by the picture her sisters made and her fingers itched for paper and pencil. Tonight, no matter how late the guests left, she would make a sketch while this view of her sisters was sharp in her memory. Then in the days ahead she would set them on canvas. Aletta would be seated at the virginal, which was painted green and decorated with Dutch scenes on the raised lid. The back lacing of her figured silk gown was as straight as her spine, her oval face reflected in the mirror sloping from its nail in the wall above the instrument. Sybylla, who though not having received either of the new garments she had hoped for, would appear as now, wearing Maria's gift of a deep lace collar, which had been added to her rose silk gown shortly before the guests' arrival. It lay on her shoulders, delicate as frost.

Then, shattering Francesca's concentration, Pieter took hold of her

hand. He must have felt her whole body jerk in reaction, for when she would have pulled her hand away his cool, strong clasp tightened and her hand was trapped, palm against palm, fingers entwined. She sensed that he glanced sideways at her, but she kept her gaze rigidly on her sisters, nothing to show the effect the meeting of his hand with hers was having on her. She had no idea that handholding could be so sensual or so curiously intimate, aided as it was by the shadows in which he and she sat and the little distance that shut them off from the rest of the gathering. Even the music helped, as if it were being played specially for them. Her pulse was racing and when he moved his hand slightly, making a caress of his clasp, she was aware more strongly than ever of some intangible bond by which he was seeking to draw her wholly to him.

He released her hand only to let her applaud and then regained it, even though she tried to keep it from his reach. When he took it from her lap she gave up the contest.

As soon as the concert was over she sprang to her feet. "I must check now to see that everyone gets more refreshment."

He grinned as she flew from him to busy herself among the guests. Sybylla had vacated the chair on which she had been playing and he took it to speak to Aletta, who sat sideways to the virginal, thanking people for their compliments. When they had moved off, he added his own.

"You play so well. I admire such musical talent."

"I thank you," she said shyly. "Are you travelling all the way back to Haarlem tonight?"

"No. I've a house here in Amsterdam," he answered, "which I bought two years ago. I shall be staying there."

"It's as well you have two homes in this case. I peeped out of a window before Sybylla and I sat down to play and I was going to warn you that it is snowing hard. I'm still marvelling over the hyacinth you brought us."

"It was an experiment in culture and some interpollination that I'll not make public again. Several people here were at pains to point out to me that a house is no place for plants of an experimental nature or otherwise."

"Nevertheless, the hyacinth will be appreciated by my family. I shall make it the subject of a painting before it fades."

"Francesca intends to do the same."

"I thought she would, because she loves flowers so much."

"She has promised that I shall see her painting when it is finished. May I see yours too?"

"Yes, indeed you may. Please tell me more about your plants and bulbs and flowers. Do you have stalls other than the one here in Amsterdam where my father ordered the bulbs?"

"Yes, I have another stall at Haarlem and at a couple of towns within easy reach. I take every outlet I can for my produce." He smiled slowly, his eyes narrowing. "I'm as ambitious as you and Francesca. I leave no stone unturned to get my name known."

Sybylla had returned to pull up another chair and sit on his other side. "You're aiming to be a rich man, are you?" she asked with a giggle, having just caught the tail end of what he had said.

He gave her a dancing glance. "I intend to be successful and if riches come with that state of affairs I'll be well satisfied."

She tossed her head provocatively. "That's too long for me to wait. Plants and flowers can't be hurried out of the ground."

"So you wouldn't want to invest in my venture, Sybylla?" he joked.

"No!" she squealed back delightedly. "Or to be your wife either! Whoever you marry will have to help you weed and sow and snip off the tulip heads. I want an idle life where I'm waited on hand and foot."

He laughed, entertained by her. Normally Aletta would have checked her sister severely for her behaviour, but something Pieter had said seemed to offer a solution to a certain problem that somehow she had to solve. It had come like a ray of light, but she could not talk about it here.

"How often do you have your stall in Amsterdam?" she inquired.

"Not at all now until the spring." He saw disappointment pass across her face and wondered what lay behind her question, but she gave no clue and let her sister dominate the conversation.

Guests had begun to rise to their feet to leave and Pieter did the same. Outdoor garments were fetched and donned. Aletta seized the chance to speak to Pieter more privately.

"Is there somewhere in Amsterdam where I might find you one day soon? I can't make it any more definite than that. I should like to seek your opinion on a certain business venture."

He looked at her searchingly. Since she obviously intended to come on her own he could not invite her to his home, but must keep the rendezvous to some public place. "I go to the Exchange at noon on the last Wednesday of every month."

She nodded gratefully. "I'll remember that."

Francesca stood at Hendrick's side to bid each guest good night. Farewells were quickly said and there was no lingering on the stoop outside, because each time the door was opened the snow swirled in. Pieter stood ready to depart.

"May this evening have seen the first of many such hours that we shall spend in conversation together, Francesca."

She shook her head slightly. "Although it will always be a pleasure to see you at my home, I have to say again that my time is completely taken up."

"Nevertheless, I remain hopeful. Good night to you." He moved on to thank Hendrick for his hospitality and gave a last long look in Francesca's direction before he clapped on his hat and went out into the swirling snow.

When the door was finally closed on the last departing guest, Francesca's thoughts turned to the clearing up, but Griet's married sister had been hired to be in the kitchen that evening and once the glasses had been gathered up from tables and ledges there was little left to be done. Maria was persuaded to go straight to bed and Hendrick followed shortly afterwards, reeling slightly and having difficulty in placing his feet on the stairs. By the time Griet's brother-in-law arrived to escort his wife home there was hardly any sign that a party had been held. Francesca locked up while her sisters and Griet went yawning to bed.

Alone in the warm kitchen, having brought a sketchbook and pencils from the studio, Francesca settled down to draw by the rosy glow of the firebox. She did not feel in the least tired, too stimulated by all the happenings of the evening. An image of Pieter persisted in coming between her and her drawing, as if he had gained a mental and physical grasp on her. Eventually she stopped what she was attempting to do

and deliberately sketched him instead. Her pencil seemed released, almost as if it were following familiar lines by its own volition, and the result was a startling likeness. She covered the drawing over quickly, knowing she would never be able to complete what she had intended to do with it in front of her, still more vivid now than he had been in her mind's eye. Then she found that having exorcised his haunting, she was able to finish her sketch of her sisters to her satisfaction.

Then suddenly she was tired. She blew out the kitchen candle lamp and took an extra candlestick that had been left for her to light her way to bed. At the foot of the stairs she hesitated, feeling herself drawn to look once more at the plant that had been forced into growth especially for her. She retraced her steps into the side room. This time she took notice of the pattern on its Delft pot. She saw that it depicted sailboats and rowboats on a river.

CHAPTER 6

As the days went by Francesca tended the plant and called everyone in the house to see each stage of advancement as the budding flower thrust strongly through the waxy leaves. Maria had distrusted it from the start.

"It's a heathenish growth," she muttered, but her curiosity was such that she still viewed it daily. Griet also never missed, her work taking her into the room each day in any case. On her own she would regard the plant wistfully, wishing it had come as a personal gift for her instead of to the family. She had her share of beaux, but the only one she cared anything for was at sea and there was no knowing when he would be home again.

There were few special Christmas preparations in the house apart from an extra-thorough cleaning from cellar to attic with every curtain and all bed drapery freshly laundered. With all the jollity and giving of gifts having taken place at the Feast of St. Nicholaes, the Holy Day of

Christmas was a quiet family occasion with church attendance and Bible reading at home.

The hyacinth flowered fully on Christmas Day. It was short and small-sprayed, but of a deeper blue than anyone had expected and with a sweet scent. Maria was won over in spite of herself.

"I must admit it is lovely to behold," she said, inhaling the perfume and deciding it had absolved itself from its unnaturalness by giving forth its beauty for the Holy Day. It was her suggestion that it be placed in the reception hall, where it could be admired by all in a place of honour.

Francesca had begun her painting of her sisters the morning after she had made her sketch, but that was put aside for the priority painting of the hyacinth once Christmas Day was over. It had to be painted while it was still in its prime. She placed it on a stand in the studio while Aletta arranged some drapery of green and grey behind it. The snow-bright light through the window heightened the bloom's sapphire brilliance. In silence both girls began to paint.

By now the weather was bitterly cold. Since before Christmas ice had closed the river. Small boats rested at odd angles along the banks, cushioned in the snow with their masts and rigging lacing the skyline. Sleigh bells jingled everywhere and people of all ages skimmed along on long wooden skates, twice the length of their feet, the metal runners curling up in the front like ships' prows. Speedy traffic on runners had turned many of the canals into fast highways, and quieter areas were chosen by those wishing to play ice golf and other such sports.

Sybylla skated at every opportunity. It was exhilarating to speed away from Maria's watchful eye, although even then she had to stay with approved friends. Sometimes Francesca would join them and they would form a snake, one behind the other, and have a merry time. Aletta never came with them. Often she was absent for hours at a time, carrying a linen bag full of her sketching materials, but when her mittened hands were so cold that she could barely grasp a pencil, all outdoor sketches were rapidly and roughly executed and she would return home to paint in the warmth of her studio-parlour. Since Hendrick never went to his daughters' private rooms and had made it a rule

never to be bothered with any domestic details, he knew nothing of this pattern of work Aletta had set for herself.

It was as Francesca skated on her own one day, coming home from the fish market, that she happened to see Aletta coming out of the shop of an artist's supplier with a roll of canvas under her arm. When Aletta arrived home some time later she found Francesca waiting to challenge her.

"Why are you buying your own canvas? I pay these days for everything that is needed for work and you have always been able to take whatever you wanted for your studio-parlour upstairs."

"I want to be independent," Aletta replied defiantly. "If it's my own canvas I can use as much as I like and make my paintings the size I prefer."

"I wish you'd show me your current work. You lock yourself away in that studio-parlour and nobody else ever enters it, not even Griet since you have taken to cleaning it yourself. I respect your wish for a sanctuary, but why are you so secretive? You painted the hyacinth still life at my side in the studio, and whenever you carry out any other work there you are open enough about it. I simply don't understand."

Aletta put her arms affectionately about Francesca and then stepped away again. "Please be patient with me. I'm set on a path of my own that is right for me at the present time. When I can share it with you I will."

"I'm thankful to hear that. I should never want any kind of rift to come about through your cutting yourself away from the rest of us."

"It never will," Aletta promised fervently. "You have my word."

"I'm so thankful to hear that."

As Aletta continued on her way upstairs she was relieved that she had come through her sister's questioning as well as she had. She had not wanted to spend any of her precious savings on canvas, but as she already had orders for commissioned pictures it would have been only a matter of time before someone noticed how quickly the studio rolls of canvas were diminishing. She could count herself lucky that Francesca's suspicions had not been aroused, and the truthful cover of hard work had been her saving.

Her market had extended beyond any bounds she would have be-

lieved possible in so short a time. Housewives had spoken of her to one another and the word had passed around. She had painted many houses and little shops and now, wearied by drawing outside in this cold weather, she was concentrating mostly on interiors. She found that the people who commissioned her work were delighted to have paintings of their rooms. More often than not a family or a couple would group themselves in their kitchen or parlour to be included in the painting. These pictures were the most profitable, for she would charge per head above the basic price of the painting, which was the custom with any group portrait.

Since she dealt only with strangers in parts of the city where she had no acquaintances, she used her mother's maiden name of Veldhuis as an extra precaution against being identified or linked in any way with her father.

Her patrons, all of them hardworking people of a lower order, but with money in their purses from their toil, thought her to be little more than a pedlar of her artistic talents. She felt humiliated, for that was her true position, and also she knew the paintings she sold lacked the pure quality they would have had if she did not have to rush through her commissions. When asked to sign a painting she used a monogram of "AV" in a curling form, which impressed her patrons, who were never critical. She hated the deception of not being known by her own name, but consoled herself with the resolve that the day would come when, as a master of a Guild, she could put her full signature to her work.

Willem de Hartog called in mid-February, two days after Sybylla's birthday, to collect the painting *The Beggar and the Jewel*. In the studio he happened to see Francesca's painting of her sisters playing the virginal and the viol. It was propped against the wall where it had been placed when finished. After studying it, he left the studio to go in search of her and, finding her in the kitchen, he questioned her about her work.

"I made my original sketch after watching my sisters play by candle-light, on St. Nicholaes's Day," she told him. "I decided afterwards to paint them in daylight. They gave me a sitting for that."

"What title have you given it?"

She smiled. "I haven't really thought. It was just an exercise."

"Why not *The Sisters' Concert?*"

She nodded. "I like that."

He praised the painting, which pleased her, while privately he thought again how strange it was that at times her work should run so closely to that of Vermeer's, which she had never seen and knew nothing about. Here was the same flooding of clear light and female forms in a quiet domestic setting, not with the same polished skill, but nevertheless with enchanting and brilliant results.

Hendrick, measuring a length of canvas, looked around when Willem came back into the studio, flourishing Francesca's work.

"I could sell this painting many times over!" Willem announced enthusiastically, totally unprepared for Hendrick's explosion of wrathful sarcasm.

"You would sell a daub!"

Willem regarded him sternly. "Be fair to your daughter's work. Naturally, as yet all her paintings belong to you, but I see no harm in letting her work be seen at this stage by those with an eye to the future, especially those who keep a lookout for the work of any young and promising artist."

"Has the renowned Willem de Hartog stooped to scraping up a florin or two where he can for substandard art?"

Willem was outraged. "Francesca's work is exceptional and you know it! Why else did you agree that she should have an apprenticeship after you had admitted failing her in tuition?"

"Damnation to you!" Hendrick grabbed the painting from him. "Yes! She needs instruction! That's why I've never allowed her yet to put a brush to anything of mine in the filling in of backgrounds and drapery!"

"Bah! Both she and Aletta could have carried out those straightforward tasks for you long ago, but everything you do has to be entirely your own. You were the same when you had full-time apprentices here. Never must anyone else put a brush to your work even in the humblest capacity. Rembrandt could allow it of his pupils, as did others of high repute, but not you! Your conceit would not allow it! Or was it that the day might come when their brushwork might be better than yours? Don't condemn your daughter's work to me!"

Hendrick's colour deepened horribly and he spluttered in his rage. "No painting bearing the name of Visser leaves this studio that doesn't reach my standards! To the devil with yours!" He then hurled the painting away into a corner.

Willem went to snatch it up again and study it for damage. Fortunately there was none. He was fuming, but struggled to calm himself. "I'll take this painting to show to the Guild of St. Luke in Delft. Has Francesca missed those sketches of hers that I have already?"

"No, but she'll miss that." Hendrick was still scowling.

"You can tell her I've taken it to get another opinion on the way her work is developing, which does happen to be the case." Then, without another word, Willem took the picture of the beggar, which had been made ready, and carried both to his waiting sleigh. He was furious, but he was also amazed to think he had known Hendrick all these years without realizing the full extent of the jealous depths of his nature. Hendrick had been jealous over Anna, but that was understandable, for he had been stupid with love for her, but this new outburst was in another vein altogether. Willem shook his head in despair. Why were artists so troublesome?

Francesca knew nothing of the clash between her father and Willem, having been out of the house at the time. It pleased her to know that the art dealer had taken her painting to be viewed by somebody he knew. Hendrick warned her that it could be a long time before she had the outcome passed on to her, but she was puzzled that Willem should not have given her a direct criticism himself. Yet it sounded promising. Was it possible that a sale might be in the offing? She hoped most sincerely that might be the case, for she had the butcher to face that afternoon with no more than a few stuivers in her purse and until *The Goddess of Spring* and *The Beggar and the Jewel* were sold there would be no more money coming in. "Father, the housekeeping box is empty. How much can you spare me?"

It turned out that he had had a moderate win at faro the night before and she left the house later with enough in her purse to pay off the amount owed to the butcher and to get a piece of salted beef. She

was about to leave the shop with a basket on her arm when there was some commotion at the far end of the street and the butcher came to the door to look out with her. They could see people running and shouting, some waving sticks, before disappearing around a corner into another street.

"It's another demonstration against the French," the butcher said phlegmatically. "Ever since Louis XIV marched into the Spanish Netherlands and took possession we've had trouble. Ordinary people are letting the burghers and the merchants know that we don't intend to let the French be masters here."

"That can never happen!" she protested. "Remember how Spain tried in vain to master us for eight decades!"

He wagged his head. "Things were different then. We didn't want the Spanish Inquisition established on our good Protestant soil, or our own independence taken from us when we had fought so hard already against the sea for our low-lying land. No man or woman, be he or she Protestant, Catholic or Jew, need go in fear throughout the whole of Holland. Should Louis come it could be another matter."

"I've heard that opinion voiced in my own home."

"And rightly so. Nevertheless, take a route back to your house that keeps you away from the demonstration. There are always hotheads in any mob and innocent bystanders can be caught up in such events."

She heeded his advice and took a side street that she did not normally use. What had been said stayed with her. She and her father and sisters and many friends were all with those who wanted to keep the country free of foreign domination. Previously few would have faulted the governing of the states of Holland by the Pensionary, Johan de Witt, who had shouldered the burden when Willem II had died a month before his heir was born. But it had gradually become apparent that de Witt was not standing out against the overtures of Louis XIV of France as firmly as was wished by all the people except the important burghers and the powerful merchants, who feared for their fortunes in the event of war. Hopes that the twenty-year-old prince, Willem III, might speak out on the people's behalf had come to nothing, and yet it was said that he distrusted Louis, whom he saw as Holland's most fearsome enemy.

Francesca's route took her through a narrow alleyway. She was half-way along it when she heard running feet and the din of raised voices, which meant the mob must have changed direction and was some-where nearby. She hesitated, not sure whether to go on or to turn back, for by some trick of the alleyway's acoustics the noise seemed to be coming from both ends of the passageway. Then she saw that this was in fact the case. Ahead of her the yelling crowd was in full pursuit of a terror-stricken young man in a torn coat, his hair awry, who was racing towards her, while over her shoulder she saw a band of the local Civil Guard in grey with wide-brimmed hats and broad sashes coming at a run from behind her. In spite of the din she could hear the shouts from the mob, which told her the cause of the fugitive's fright.

"Catch the French spy! Throw him in the canal! Get him!"

As the young man passed her she looked back again and saw he was making for the protection of the guards. She herself was trapped in the middle of what was going to be a violent and bloody clash! Feeling as terrified as the fugitive, she darted for the entrance of a warehouse. The doors were locked and she pressed herself against them, clutching her basket close. She saw the guards part to let the young man through their ranks and then they closed together in a phalanx. The captain fired a pistol into the air, shouting for the crowd to halt. A few in front did pause briefly, but they were thrust onwards by those at the back and the surge forward continued, the mob intent on its prey. So great was the pressure in the narrow alleyway that when the yelling horde came past Francesca her basket was knocked from her arm and she herself was caught up like flotsam on the sea, forced to run with them or be trampled underfoot. She heard pistol shots ring out, but it appeared the firing was still into the air, for nobody fell. Then she was in a maelstrom of fighting men, civilians and the guards in a tumult of shouts and curses, her own screams among them. Suddenly a man, felled by a bludgeon, staggered against her. She screamed again as she felt herself going down with him. Then a strong hand grabbed her wrist, almost wrenching her arm from its socket, and she was clutched hard against a Civil Guard's thick leather jacket. She was half lifted, half swung off her feet as he thrust her through his own ranks out into safety beyond the alleyway. A moment later she saw it was Pieter who had saved her.

"Are you all right?" he demanded almost angrily.

She nodded, unable to speak. A combatant's elbow had thudded into her breast as he had hauled her through the melee and she felt sick with pain. Pieter smoothed her dishevelled hair back from her face and saw there was blood on her forehead. "Listen to me. My house is in the street running parallel with this one. It has crimson shutters and an oak door with a bronze knocker. Go there! My housekeeper will look after you."

Then he was gone, running back into the scrum, and she saw she was being stared at by people who had gathered quickly to watch what was going on from a safe distance. A motherly-looking woman came forward and put an arm around her. "I'll help you there."

At the house the woman banged the knocker and saw her safely into the care of the housekeeper, who did not make the least fuss. It might have been every day that a girl with a torn sleeve, bleeding forehead and loosened tresses appeared on the stoop.

"I'm Vrouw de Hout," she said as she removed Francesca's cloak and sat her on a chair by the fire in a comfortable parlour that was very light and bright with red curtains at the window and a black-and-white-tiled floor. "I'll get some water to bathe your wound and then we'll see if you need to have it bound."

The blood was stemmed with some clean linen, for it was simply a deep scratch from somebody's sleeve button. The pain in her breast subsided, although she supposed it would be bruised, and she was given a brush and comb with which to re-dress her hair. A cup of hot chocolate completed the treatment. Throughout this procedure Vrouw de Hout, who was a middle-aged cheerful-looking woman, chatted, saying that she was a widow and this position of housekeeper suited her very well, because both her married daughters lived in Amsterdam and she was able to see her grandchildren quite often. When Francesca asked about Pieter being in the Civil Guard, she was told that he was in the reserve and fulfilled so many hours of duty a year.

"He joined for three years when he bought this house. It's a community service and also he enjoys the social side. The rule is that the officers of any militia corps may not hold more than one banquet a month at their headquarters, but the eating and drinking goes on for

two or three days. Not that he is able to attend more than about once in two months, because he is often in Haarlem or—to be more accurate —at his house and bulb fields, which lie a short distance from that town."

"I know. I visited there last autumn."

"I've not been there myself. Now how do you feel?"

"Much better and rested." Her private regret was that she had lost that precious piece of salted beef, which would have fed the family at dinner for two nights and would have made a good broth for two or three meals more.

"I think you should wait here for Heer van Doorne to return," Vrouw de Hout said quite firmly. "I'll look out and see if there is any sign of him."

Francesca was in no hurry to leave. She hoped that Pieter had suffered no injury and she would like to see him to be sure, as well as to thank him for his timely rescue. Vrouw de Hout returned to the parlour. "We can carry on talking for a while yet," she said, drawing a chair closer to the fire. "My own parlour is on an upper floor, which is virtually a little apartment all to myself. I'd like to show it to you sometime in the future when you are feeling stronger."

"I'm not feeling in the least weak, I do assure you. It was a shock to be in such a frightening situation, but I've recovered from that now."

"You did indeed have a lucky escape."

"I hope nobody was seriously injured."

Vrouw de Hout looked across to the window as a shadow passed across it. "We shall soon know. I believe that is Heer van Doorne now."

She hurried to the front door and Francesca heard Pieter's voice. Rising from her chair, she stood facing the door. As he entered the room he smiled to see her on her feet. He had lost his hat, but seemed unharmed.

"I'm glad to see you recovered, Francesca!"

"And I to see you safe. Whatever was the cause of the attack on that young man?"

"He was a Frenchman drinking in a tavern and boasting of the size of his king's armies. Several Dutchmen there took offence and one accused him of being a spy for Louis. A ridiculous suggestion, of course, as no

genuine spy would openly proclaim his allegiance, but in the people's present mood it was like a match to tinder, and after a scuffle the Frenchman took flight. The cry of 'French spy' was taken up and more joined in the chase. He's recovering now in a safe house and I've a feeling he will be leaving Amsterdam at nightfall."

She had sat down again and he took the seat that his housekeeper had vacated, she not having returned to the room after seeing him into the house.

"I can't thank you enough for having come to my rescue."

"I must say I could scarcely believe my eyes when I saw you in the midst of that battling throng."

"Were many people badly hurt?"

"There were a few cracked heads and broken limbs, but nobody was killed."

"How many hours of duty do you do?"

"The rota is flexible for someone such as myself who has business commitments in another city. These corps of militia were formed for a serious purpose in the days when our forebears were fighting the Spanish, but now we are local keepers of the peace with few calls on our arms. Pray God it remains so."

"Do you take the French threat seriously?"

"I'm afraid I do. In my opinion Louis is too set on expanding his borders to listen to placating words from de Witt. Nevertheless, no Frenchman shall be mobbed in the streets of our cities and this case today is the first we have had to deal with."

"I hope it is the last."

"So do I." He gave her a broad smile. "Especially if there's any danger of your getting involved again. I might not be at hand another time."

She smiled in turn. "I should be getting home now."

He was on his feet again. "I'll take you. Allow me a minute to fetch another hat."

When they arrived at her home she took him at once to her father, knowing that he would wish to thank him too. Hendrick was horrified to hear of the danger to which his daughter had been exposed and full of gratitude to Pieter for saving her. He would have sent for wine, but Pieter insisted he had to report back to the militia headquarters imme-

diately. Hendrick saw him to the door, still repeating his grateful thanks, while Pieter bowed his farewell, giving Francesca an intense look as he left.

After telling Maria there was no salt beef for dinner that evening and seeing Griet, who was also in the kitchen, go without a word to take some vegetables from the cellar for soup instead, Francesca went up to her bedchamber to change her torn garments. She was shaken to realize that it was not her escape from being trampled by the mob that was foremost in her mind, but the look in Pieter's eyes as he turned to go down the street.

As Willem had anticipated, it proved difficult to find a buyer for the painting of *The Beggar and the Jewel*. It was one of Hendrick's best works, equal to *The Goddess of Spring*, making it one of those tantalizing brushes against genius that had punctuated Hendrick's career. But the picture was completely lacking in public appeal. The beggar's suffering was too acute, the starkness of his misery creating unease even in the least sensitive of those who viewed it. Willem was himself aware of the painting's power to disturb. It was a picture too uncomfortable for anyone to live with, and although several serious collectors considered it, they still turned away without making an offer. Others covered their inner reactions by objecting to the size of the jewel, as he had known they would in any case, but for once Willem knew that Hendrick had been right and he himself had been wrong. The very blatantness of the gem accentuated the torment of the starving man unable to grasp it. Eventually he sold the painting for a paltry sixty florins, knowing it to be hugely undervalued, but on a personal level he was thankful to get it out of his house.

Still *The Goddess of Spring* remained veiled in his gallery. He had removed all the paintings previously displayed there into another room, where they could be viewed equally well. By letting Hendrick's painting be on its own the mystique was increased and its importance emphasized. Yet he knew he must not let his ploy run on too long, and he judged the exact time to have come when he could let those who had made the six best offers for it come to the gallery in turn. With luck he would only have to show it to one. He sent an invitation to the first on the list, a gentleman who lived in the grandest residential area in

1
2
1

Amsterdam on Heerengracht, the Gentlemen's Canal, which was also known as the Golden Bend as a mark of the wealth of those who lived there.

In the shadows of Willem's gallery a well-dressed man in a wide-brimmed hat and sweeping blue cloak, holding a fashionably tall cane, stood waiting impatiently for the first sight of the painting that was hidden by the curtain drawn across it, as valuable works often were when there was need to protect them in a sunny room. Here in the gallery the shutters were closed today, candles giving some illumination, for the art dealer intended to reveal the painting in the full light of day with increasing drama.

"Pray sit down, *mijnheer,*" Willem invited, knowing full well how to prolong suspense.

Ludolf van Deventer took the large chair set squarely in front of the curtained work of art, watched the art dealer go without haste to the first shutter and fumed inwardly at the deliberate dawdling. For weeks he had been intrigued by the talk of this work that might, or might not, be sold. He had wanted to make it his from the first hearsay. Greed was in his whole nature, possessions all-important to him, such as often happens with those who have started life with nothing. His offers to purchase the painting unseen had been turned down each time, increasing his determination to have it. With all knowledgeable Amsterdam speculating about this new Flora, it would give him increased prestige to become its owner, an important factor being that it was by an artist of the same city and he needed to play up his interest in all things Dutch. This was not the time for him, a Dutchman born and bred, to reveal in any way his secret allegiance to France. No matter that everything French was increasingly fashionable, a trend he had followed earlier than most, he had too much at stake not to be seen as a staunch patriot. Anonymously he was even trying to trace a collection of old Dutch paintings which he had sold very foolishly ten years before.

At the same time he continued to associate with those wealthy burghers and merchants favouring friendship with Louis XIV. Naturally they were fearful of war, wanting to maintain their prosperity at all

costs. Yet they were fools! Did they imagine that a Catholic king as strong and autocratic as Louis would not weigh them down with taxes or let their Protestant ways remain unchanged and undominated? Ordinary Dutch people, jealous of their freedom and willing to fight for it, spoke openly of the French menace, but they had no one in authority to voice their viewpoint and their threat to Louis was minimal.

He alone was on the right path. By working undercover for France now he would lose nothing and gain everything when Louis was master of the Netherlands. There would be a glittering ministerial post and rewards beyond measure. Power was everything! He had hopes of eventually becoming Louis's choice as the Stadholder, able to govern from the palace at The Hague. But all that was in the future. The immediate matter was the purchase of this painting about to be revealed to him.

"Come, come, Heer de Hartog!" he snapped impatiently. "I've waited long enough."

Willem had unfastened the second set of shutters and the gilt-leather walls of the gallery had begun to gleam and glow with touches of light, the perfect setting for a picture of importance.

"You are the first to see this painting since it came into my hands," Willem said smoothly, moving on to the next window.

"Most obliging of you," Ludolf replied drily. After the figure he had already offered for the work it was not surprising he should get priority.

The last window completed the flooding of the gallery with light. Willem went across to the little silk curtain covering the painting and with a final flourish he drew it back. "I present Flora, the goddess of spring."

Long habit enabled Ludolf to keep his face composed, but his hand tightened convulsively on his cane. Inwardly he was stunned, not only by the splendour of the painting but by the extraordinary beauty of Flora herself. It was by no means the classic symmetry of features normal to the feminine ideal, but there was a fascinating blend of the sensual with the ethereal that fired his senses.

"Who is she?" he demanded throatily.

"That I shall reveal only to the purchaser," Willem replied blandly.

"Damnation to you! You know I will have the painting!" Ludolf sprang up and went to study the face of Flora more closely.

1
2
3

"I've had a higher offer than the last one you made."

Ludolf turned a hard and glittering gaze on him. "Name your price."

Willem smiled to himself. This was the best deal he had made for many years.

When Willem went to see Hendrick the next day, the angry words they had exchanged when they had last seen each other were uppermost in his mind. But the artist was his usual self and greeted him without the least animosity, although there was a sharp complaint about the meagre sum the painting of the beggar had fetched.

"I've made a sale that will more than make up for that," Willem replied. They were in the family parlour, where he had found Hendrick sprawled out in a chair by the fire. It was an all too familiar sign that he had slackened off work with a spate of cards and dice.

"The Goddess of Spring?" Hendrick's eyes sharpened with interest.

"Yes. You will be pleased to hear that after all my hard work I landed a buyer who may prove to be a very big fish indeed."

Hendrick jerked forward in his chair. "How much?"

Willem was determined to hold him to his daughter's training. "Enough to give Francesca two years' tuition in Delft, with bed and board as well as a box of new clothes. There is also a sum over that, in itself twice as much as any figure I've managed to raise on any one of your paintings before."

Flinging back his head, Hendrick uttered a huge bellow of triumphant laughter, slapping his hands on his broad knees. Dame Fortune was smiling on him again. He had done well at cards recently and now this bounty was to be poured into his coffers. You've done splendidly, Willem! We may have had our differences in the past, but I doff my hat to you. When you use your wits you know how to sell the works of a great master!"

Willem's lips twitched wryly at Hendrick's excessive display of self-satisfaction, but he also nursed intense regret that this fine artist could not be classed in that exclusive category. "I've still more good news to tell."

"You have?"

"Yes, the buyer is a rich ship broker. His name is Ludolf van Deventer. He has commissioned you to paint his portrait."

Some of Hendrick's exuberance waned. He lowered his head and shifted uneasily in his chair, reminding his companion of a bull at bay. "I'm not sure. You know I've never liked to paint portraits to order."

Willem knew that only too well. Many commissions in the past had come to nothing through Hendrick offending the sitters by bellowing at them for fidgeting or else becoming too bored with their faces to finish the work. "If you make a special effort this time I think you can be sure of this man's patronage for a long while to come. He also bought that little painting of yours of the head of a Trojan warrior that I had on display. Your work interests him."

"Hmm." Hendrick lodged an elbow on the arm of his chair and rubbed his chin. "What sort of fellow is he?"

"A man who has had to make his own way in life and is now at an age when he wants to enjoy his hard-earned money. Why not invite him to dinner? His wife would not accompany him, as she suffers from ill health and never goes out. If you spend an evening with him you'll be able to judge for yourself whether or not you feel able to accept the commission."

"I suppose it would be a good idea." Hendrick still looked uncertain. "He's rich, you say?"

"Very rich."

Hendrick heaved a sigh. "Well, I've thought several times that I should give Aletta her chance of tuition—that is, if her work merits it. At the moment she's acting like a recluse with her painting, but she's at a foolish age."

"Aletta has never seemed anything but sensible to me. I've always liked her work. When your finances permit she should be placed in a studio too."

"Then I'll invite van Deventer here."

"One thing more. I'll be leaving soon on a tour of studios throughout the provinces, during which I'll be staying in Delft to settle Francesca's apprenticeship with Vermeer and the Committee of the Guild. I must impress upon you to continue to keep matters to yourself. I have to allow for any unforeseen snags."

"Very wise." Hendrick tapped a finger against his nose. "Not a word until you are back from Delft with good news."

When Willem left the house he was confident that everything had been arranged for the best.

CHAPTER 7

Aletta sat in an anteroom at the Exchange, waiting to see Pieter. She was breathless, having run part of the way to get to the building before its closing hour. She had left home in good time, but she had not gone far when she had seen a neighbour, who was pregnant, slip and fall in a street left treacherously muddy by the thaw. She had rushed to help her up and then, seeing that Vrouw Zegers was much shaken, she had walked her slowly back home. Since their houses were side by side, Aletta had found herself starting out again with half the time to reach the Exchange, but she had reached it with a quarter of an hour to spare.

She looked down at her skirt hems. As she had feared, there was mud on them where they had trailed on the wet road. The thaw that had produced these conditions was welcome nevertheless. It had set in early, allowing crocuses to burst forth in cushions of purple before February was over and once more boat traffic was able to move along those waterways that were impossible to keep open with savage winter weather. Yet the winters were not as harsh nowadays as they had been during the past hundred years when the canals had been frozen through to the end of March at times. It was far from warm yet, but the sun was gaining strength every day as if determined to be ready for the first day of spring.

Aletta was the only one in the anteroom, but a thunderous rumble of male voices came from some inner part of the Exchange. A messenger servant had been sent in to fetch Pieter to her. Her glance went to a high inside window and she wondered what might be seen of this male sanctum from there. Her curiosity overcame her. Telling herself sternly that she was behaving as Sybylla would have done, she climbed up onto the bench below the window.

Before she had even raised herself on tiptoe to look through it, the door of the anteroom burst open and a vigorous, well-dressed and good-looking black-haired young man in a red-plumed hat came striding in. She flushed deeply at being discovered in such an ignominious position, wanting to curl up with embarrassment, but he was smiling approval, greenish eyes twinkling.

"What an excellent notion!" he exclaimed enthusiastically, leaping up onto the bench beside her. "I saw you through the glass panels of the door and decided to follow your example." Being tall, he was able to look through the window with ease. "This is a position of advantage, isn't it? There's somebody I want to make sure is here today without bothering to go into that melee to search for him. Yes! He has come. There's my banker, old van Jansz, doing all the donkey work on my behalf!"

He did not seem to notice she had not added anything to his stream of talk and any further chance was stemmed, much to her relief, as a swarm of half a dozen young men and women, a riot of colour in their silks and velvets and plumes, came through the door he had left open into the anteroom. At the sight of him standing on the bench they exclaimed loudly, each shouting a protest.

"What are you doing up there? Is there no end to your pranks, Constantijn? You said you were going to dive into the mob, not dally about here! You're wasting time! We want to be on our way!"

He grinned at them from where he stood and made a mock-placating bow. "Calm yourselves! My business is done. I'm ready to go."

He sprang from the bench, slid his arm about the waist of the loveliest girl in the group and led the way out. They were gone like a flock of parrots, slamming the door after them.

All the time Aletta had stood as though frozen. Now she relaxed slightly and, risking discovery again, decided she could not resist looking through the window after hearing Constantijn's descriptions of the gathering within as a mob and a melee. She wondered what his surname might be.

On tiptoe, and holding the sill with her fingertips, she could just see into the heart of the Exchange. It was a huge rectangular courtyard, open to the sky, where a noisy throng of men milled about, some shouting or arguing or simply standing, heads lowered, in deep and private consultation with a fellow investor. More than a few were giving way to the most extraordinary histrionics. Hats and wigs were being torn off either to be waved triumphantly or thrown to the ground and stamped on, according to whether good or bad news had been received. She was used to explosions of temperament from Hendrick and Sybylla in her own home, which usually upset the entire household, but it was thoroughly entertaining to watch such displays from a detached viewpoint. Foreigners who thought her fellow countrymen to be dull and placid fellows should be allowed to peep through this window as she was doing. They would soon revise their opinions!

There was Pieter threading his way through the crowd. She sprang down from the bench, caught her heel in a petticoat hem and fell full length on the floor. She just managed to scramble to her feet before the door opened and Pieter came into the anteroom with a broad smile.

"You're here at last," he greeted her. "I had begun to think you had decided I wouldn't be of any help to you after all." His glance took in the severe furnishings of the anteroom. "It's not very comfortable here. I suggest we go elsewhere to talk."

She hesitated. "Did I take you away from anything important?"

"Not at all. My business is finished here for today." Side by side they went out of the Exchange and down the steps to the street, he asking on the way about the health of her father and sisters.

"They are well. I didn't tell anyone that I was meeting you today or else I know they would have sent their compliments."

They soon reached a tavern where the enterprising landlord had turned one of his rooms into a coffeehouse for people of both sexes, unlike the segregated clubs for coffee drinking, which were a fashionable quirk. He held the door for her. "Here we are."

The superb fragrance of freshly roasted coffee beans met them as they entered the warm atmosphere. The drinking of coffee was no longer the privilege of the wealthy and coffee was starting to rival the more expensive China tea. Here, as in every coffeehouse where mixed

company was served, all who waited at the tables were female. The place was very busy, but a waiting maid showed Pieter and Aletta to a booth with high-backed settle seats. From it they had a good view of the large copper coffeepots from which coffee, flavoured with cloves, cinnamon or ginger according to taste, was poured from little taps. Aletta had never been in a coffeehouse before, because it was cheaper to drink beverages at home.

She lowered the hood of her cloak. Her customary cap that hugged her head and kept her hair under strict control was of cream linen today with a modest edging of lace. Pieter thought it more suited to an older woman. She was too young to detract from her fine features with such severe headgear. Had the cap been of velvet, or silk with beads or embroidery designed to flatter, it would have been a different matter.

"I should like the cinnamon-flavoured coffee," Aletta replied when he asked her what her choice would be.

"Sweetened with sugar or honey?"

She chose honey and he ordered his own to be unflavoured and unsweetened. He also asked the waiting maid to bring a selection of the gingerbread and cakes that were made on the premises. While they waited for it all to be brought to them she ventured a question.

"What made you decide to buy a house in Amsterdam?"

"Through certain business interests I like to be in close touch with the Exchange, and it may surprise you to know that winter can be a busy time for me. It's when I see people who want their gardens newly designed and made ready for the spring, and since I get a great deal of my work from Amsterdam it seemed sensible to have a pied-à-terre here."

She smiled at him. "In your own way you are an artist too, but in earth and trees and flowers instead of pigments and oils. Do you like that side of horticulture?"

"Immensely. People sometimes take time to make up their minds, wanting more variations planned on paper than they need, but that is all part of it."

As they chatted he tried not to reveal that he was taking note of her sibling resemblance to Francesca. It came and went in a flicker of expression almost too swift to register and in the way her lips curled

slightly before a smile broke forth. But there was nothing in Aletta's grey-green eyes of the allure he had glimpsed in Francesca's. The girl sitting opposite him was contained within herself, small and composed with some inner defence to keep her from the emotional upheavals that usually afflicted young women. Aletta's prim air seemed unassailable. How was it possible for the same parents to have produced both her and Sybilla? They were as different as chalk and cheese. Perhaps Francesca was a little like both her sisters, with the calm of one and the passion of the other. Whatever the true facts, he knew her now to be the woman for him.

The coffee came with the cakes and gingerbread still warm from the oven. "Now," he said, when he and Aletta had taken their first sip from their cups and sampled a bite of cake, "tell me why you came to see me today."

She began by telling him of her aim to be a master of a Guild. How and when that would be achieved she did not know, but somehow she would fulfil her dream. Meanwhile there were classes she wanted to attend. As she talked he thought it inexcusable that Hendrick Visser should not be helping his daughters by making them officially his apprentices and seeing them through the whole of their training. It revealed the total selfishness of the man behind the joviality.

"I've been taking commissions unknown to my father," Aletta continued, "and introducing myself by using my mother's maiden name of Veldhuis to conceal my identity. I doubt if any of my patrons would have heard of Hendrick Visser, because they are not in the range ever to buy from his dealer, but I had to be sure that no chance meeting gave me away. Father talks to all and sundry wherever he is." She went on to tell of the paintings of houses, workshops, interiors and even the fish stall she had done.

He looked amazed. "Have you any spare time at all?"

"Almost none, because I use every spare minute to build up a stock of pictures to sell whenever it should prove possible. It's with such money I'll be able to attend those drawing and painting classes I've already mentioned."

"Where is this work to be sold? In picture shops?"

"No. I did approach several, but it was the same in every one. They're flooded with stock and nobody would look at mine."

"Where else, then? Many taverns display pictures for sale."

"That would be far too risky. My father has drinking companions in every tavern in Amsterdam. Some of them have been to our home and should I be seen in such places they would recognize me."

"I see your difficulty. What does Francesca advise?"

"She doesn't know and mustn't suspect, because she would say I'll never be a painter if I don't devote my time to serious work."

"Is she right, Aletta?" They had dropped into the use of Christian names almost without realizing it.

"What I am doing is serious enough for me, but the kind of work she means awaits me in plenty at those classes. In the meantime I'm learning and improving even by the rough means of speed that I've chosen. I can tell whenever I paint in the studio now that I have acquired more skill. Even my father had a good word to say about my painting of the hyacinth. But Francesca is going from strength to strength. Recently her work has become quite beautiful. She seems to have leapt a gap that was keeping her back."

"What would the reason be?"

"Father takes the credit for having resumed his teaching of her, but I think it's a natural progression. Like a fledgling taking wing."

"Does he think highly of her work?"

"He does, but he is very sensitive about his own. Francesca must never become his rival, at least not in his studio."

"Could that happen, do you think?"

"I believe she is destined to be a splendid artist. She did a painting of Sybylla and me that was so good that Father's agent, Willem de Hartog, is getting it viewed for an independent assessment of her work." She took another sip of coffee, savouring the treat she was having.

"If," he queried, "your father has resumed his teaching of Francesca, why aren't you benefiting from it too?"

"I'm not often in his studio, because I have my own upstairs. He gets irritated enough having to instruct Francesca and to deal with two of us again would be too much for his temper. After my mother died he reverted in his grief to doing only what he wanted to do, and it has

stayed that way. I understand. It has nothing to do with his love for Francesca or for me."

"You are very tolerant." He regarded her in a friendly and encouraging manner. "Perhaps you should explain now the full purpose of this meeting. We haven't come to that yet and my guess is that you have mapped out a role for me to play in this plan of yours for class attendance." His grin was merry. "Am I to sell your paintings for you?"

It was said in jest, for he believed she had been leading up to asking for a loan to let her attend classes, and he had made up his mind that she should have it. To his dismay she seized on his remark avidly, her usual calm expression changing to one of thrilled and overwhelming relief.

"Oh yes! I never expected you to offer. I dreaded asking you. Just a few at a time along with the bulbs and flowers at any one of your stalls in Amsterdam or elsewhere." The words were tumbling from her joyously. She scarcely drew breath. "You'll take a commission from every sale as if you were a real art dealer. It won't be much, but it will mount up as my share will with time." Then her voice trailed away and her eyes became stark as he threw up his hands and shook his head regretfully.

"I'm deeply sorry, Aletta. I fear I misled you with an ill-timed joke. I had no idea that was what you wanted of me."

"What were you expecting?" she asked flatly.

"The request for a loan. I would have met you on that."

She shook her head. "That's out of the question. When I start my lessons I'll have no time to paint anything for sale and there would be no way of paying you back. I must have the money in hand first."

He sighed and leaned both arms on the table. "I have no time to sell pictures and neither have my assistants. You know how busy stalls are on market day. Why not rent one for yourself for a day? You'd probably sell out. I've seen picture stalls doing a good trade."

"I can't do that." The anguish of her disappointment was catching at her throat. "I'd be in the public eye. My father seldom goes to the flower market, but people who know me do and in no time I'd be in the deepest trouble. Worst of all, it would be the end of any classes for me."

132

He nodded sympathetically. "I see your difficulty. Do you know anyone else who would be willing to sell for you in return for commission?"

"I daresay our maidservant's sister would do it. I know she would be glad of a little extra money. But as I said, a stall is out of the question."

"Suppose you were allotted a small space at the end of one here in Amsterdam. Would that be enough?"

Her whole face became suffused with hope again. "Do you know someone who would be agreeable to that?" When his smile provided a clue she clasped her hands and brought them up against her chest. "You, Pieter! How can I ever thank you?"

"Wait a moment," he insisted in a serious tone. "If you do decide to employ your maidservant's sister, it must be understood there can be no encroaching by your pictures beyond the space allowed."

"There won't be!"

"Good, but I haven't finished yet. You'll have to agree to a special condition."

His expression was so implacable that she lowered her hands to her lap again. "What is that?"

"You will tell Francesca about the arrangement. I'll do nothing behind her back."

She looked long at him, seeking the reason in his eyes. "I'm not proud of keeping anything from her, but I fear she will never approve. She would not give me away to my father, but she'd want me to go back into the studio, although she knows I've always found it difficult to work at his side." Then she bit deeply into her lower lip, which was suddenly tremulous. "Even if I could persuade her to agree to my plan I realize now I can't accept your offer. How foolish I was to trouble you in the first place."

He leaned towards her. "You're thinking that you couldn't pay rent for a section of my stall as well as letting someone else receive commission, because you'd make no profit at all. But, if you are willing, I'll take your painting of the hyacinth in lieu of any rent."

She raised her face again with an expression of disbelief. "You haven't even seen the painting yet."

"I'll take a chance."

For the first time tears glinted in her eyes. The rise and fall of her hopes had not made her weep, but his generosity at this point had moved her. "I think you're the kindest man I've ever met."

He smiled and picked up the platter of cakes. "Take another of these and don't exaggerate. I'll order more coffee too."

She took one to allow herself time to regain her composure. "I'll speak to Francesca at the first suitable moment."

"You may not find her as obdurate about this matter as you fear."

Her lips compressed ruefully. "You don't know what she's like when she is against something. Nothing will sway her."

"Would it help if I discussed it with her?"

"No." Aletta was firm. "I have to do this on my own."

"Then let's meet here again next Friday. By then you will have had time to speak to Francesca."

"Come back home with me today and see the flower paintings. If all works out well, I wouldn't want you to think you've made a bad bargain."

"I've no fear of that, but I can't come today."

"Next week, then?"

"That would suit me well." He hoped, but would not ask, that he would see Francesca also.

Aletta had no chance to say anything to her sister that day. Upon her return home she was met by Griet with the news that the pregnant neighbour, whom she herself had helped up from the ice that morning, had gone into labour. Maria had hobbled in next door to be with the woman while Francesca had rushed for the midwife and then for the husband from his place of business. Afterwards there were the young children of the family to be fed and cared for.

It was late when Francesca and Maria finally came home. Aletta in her nightshift looked over the banister.

"What happened?"

Francesca raised a tired face. "It's a girl. She's very tiny and we pray that she will live."

"Oh yes! Who's with Vrouw Zegers now?"

"Her mother and her married sister have arrived from their village."

Maria patted Francesca's shoulder. "You go to bed now, child. It's been a long time since this morning."

For five days there was suspense over the infant's chances of survival. During that time Francesca was in and out of the house next door, helping however she could. Then, miraculously, the baby began feeding properly and all was well.

No sooner was this crisis over than a woman cousin of Hendrick's arrived to stay two nights in order to attend a wedding. Hendrick did not like her, nor did she have any patience with him, and the atmosphere was tense. All this time Aletta was watching for a chance to speak quietly to Francesca on her own, but the moment was never right.

It was during this cousin's visit that Sybylla came perilously near to disclosing Aletta's secret ahead of time. The cousin, who dressed in the best of fabrics with taste and style, had some valuable jewellery and wore it discreetly in turn. After watching her leave for the wedding in a hired sleigh, Sybylla had spoken scornfully.

"Why did she wear only those topaz earbobs and a single brooch. If I'd been her I'd have worn all my jewellery today for everyone to see. What's the use of having lovely things if you don't show them off and make everybody jealous! That's what I shall do when I'm rich."

Aletta, her nerves taut, turned on her. "Can't you think of anything except wealth and how to flaunt it?"

Sybylla was indignant. "How can you say that? Nobody is more greedy for money than you!" Then the sudden drained look on Aletta's face made her bite back whatever else she would have said.

"Don't talk foolishly, Sybylla," Francesca said from the table where she was writing in the housekeeping ledger. She had not glanced up or else she would have noticed the tension between her sisters. "Aletta is the last one at whom you should throw that accusation."

Later, when they were upstairs in their bedchamber, Sybylla apologized to Aletta, who answered patiently.

"I was at fault too. I appreciate your keeping to yourself what I have here." She pushed open the communicating door into the studio-parlour. Her easel stood by the window, and stacked around the three walls were the extra pictures she had painted and was storing as stock.

Most were on wood, which many artists preferred for being tougher than canvas, particularly if their work was to have rough handling between markets or auctions before sale. She had had a windfall of wood when she had painted a view of a carpenter's home and he had a store of pieces of plain panelling that he had removed from an ancient house. It was too thin for re-use for its original purpose and he had sold it all to her for a guilder, cutting it into suitable sizes as part of the bargain. There was still more in his cellar for her when she was ready to collect it, since, having no storage space, she could only take a little at a time. He had wanted to deliver the wood to her, but she was quick to decline the kindly offer. She dared let nobody discover her address.

"It can only be a question of time before you're found out," Sybylla warned bluntly. "Suppose Francesca should come into this bedchamber one day when you had forgotten to shut that door. She would see at a glance that you're not painting to standard up here as you do in the studio. Then think of the questions she'd let fly at you!"

"I've thought of that all along. I decided last week to tell her, but she's been so busy I've had no chance. Now she's compiling a menu for the evening when Heer van Deventer comes to dine. I know she's not going to approve of what I'm doing."

"That's true. I shouldn't say anything to her until after Cousin Leisbeth leaves this afternoon."

Aletta felt desperate. That left only one day with van Deventer coming to dine in the evening before she met Pieter the following morning. Who would have thought it could be so difficult to have a simple heart-to-heart talk with one's own sister?

After breakfast on the morning of the dinner party Francesca went to the big oak cupboard in the stair hall. There were three such cupboards in the house, for a large stock of linen was every Dutch woman's pride and Anna had been no exception. In this particular cupboard, which was the grandest, the best linen was kept, while another in a side room contained that of medium standard, and it was the much used supplies in an upstairs one that gave Sybylla her practice in patching and mending. Francesca took from a middle shelf the best damask cloth and napkins. Aletta came to her side and spoke urgently.

"May I talk to you sometime today?"

Francesca looked gently at her. "Is anything the matter?"

"No. I just wanted to ask you something."

"I'll be quite busy today. Why not wait until tonight at bedtime?"

It was a time when they had talked so often after Anna's death, curled up together against the pillows.

"Yes," Aletta said, pleased. "That's best."

At seven o'clock that evening Francesca went into the dining hall to see that all was perfect with the dinner table. Hendrick appeared in the doorway. A letter he had received that morning seemed to have put him in an exceptionally good humour, although he had not revealed the contents to anyone.

"How do I look?" He had always asked Anna that question before any social occasion, for she had been quick to spot an overlooked blob of paint on his hair and made sure his collar was smooth on his shoulders. From habit after her death he had let Francesca check his appearance when necessary.

"You look magnificent," Francesca declared. She had steamed and brushed his purple velvet garments, which with the full-cut breeches were flattering to his portly figure, and he was wearing the crimson hose Aletta had knitted for him for the Feast of St. Nicholaes.

"You look very fine yourself," he commented, not recognizing an apricot silk gown that she had refurbished yet again with some new ribbons. "I may paint you in that raiment one day." Then he was reminded anew of the purpose of the evening ahead and his expression changed as he became intensely irritable. "Damnation! This is all going to be a waste of my time! I don't want to paint this wretched ship broker!"

"Wait until you've met him," Francesca advised calmly. "You may find before the evening is out that you like Heer van Deventer well enough."

"*Liking* has nothing to do with it! I'd paint my worst enemy if he agreed to sit anytime I felt like painting him. I won't be tied down to set hours."

"No, Father." She slipped an arm through his, amusement quivering the corners of her mouth, and she turned her face into his shoulder to

hide it. He sensed her mood and took her by the chin to tilt her face up to him. The mirth in her eyes coaxed reluctant laughter from him.

"I am an old bear, aren't I? Why aren't you afraid of me?"

"I'm not easily scared." She laughed with him. "But maybe you'll be able to browbeat your new patron into dancing to your tune."

He sighed. "I doubt it."

She moved over to the table to straighten a fork. "Why didn't you invite Willem to supper this evening? After all, he was responsible for this forthcoming meeting and you might have found it easier to have his company too."

"I would have if he hadn't been away at the present time."

A hammering came from the front-door knocker. She made an alert little movement of her head. "There's our guest now."

Hendrick sighed again more heavily and raised his eyes theatrically to the ceiling. "May the Lord grant me patience." Then he left the dining hall and paused with an exasperated air as Griet went scurrying to admit the guest. At the same time Aletta and Sybylla came down the stairs.

Francesca made a quick dash to the kitchen to check that all was ready. When she turned into the stair hall it was to see the front door standing wide, her sisters waiting at Hendrick's side. A liveried servant, cloaked and wearing a flap hat, had knocked for his master's admittance, and had now returned to the grand coach. Ludolf van Deventer stepped from the coach onto the muddy cobbles. He was a large, vigorous-looking man, deep-chested and slightly above average height, clothed in fox red and grey with a flow of white ostrich plumes in his hat. Griet bobbed as he entered and was quick to shut the door. Francesca judged him to be about her father's age.

He greeted Hendrick genially. "I've been looking forward to meeting you, Master Visser. I've become an admirer of your work. This is indeed a pleasure."

"And an honour for me! You are most welcome, *mijnheer*. Allow me to present my daughters." He saw with slight surprise that Francesca had not come yet and proceeded to introduce her sisters.

Francesca shivered, blaming the chill air being let into the house and yet horribly aware of dread dragging at her. In the same instant she

realized she had experienced the same sensation in those few moments before she had viewed the painting of herself as Flora. Then she straightened her shoulders fiercely to quell the dark illusion. But she still stood seemingly rooted to the floor of the stair hall.

Griet passed Francesca, carrying the visitor's cloak to deposit it on her way back to the kitchen. She was burning with indignation. Not only had he flung it off carelessly, half smothering her with it, but he had not even wiped his feet! She wished she had the strength of a neighbouring maidservant who had lifted an Englishman off his feet to remove his muddy shoes when he had begun leaving footprints all over her clean floor. No doubt Heer van Deventer had travelled widely and adopted the slack ways he had found elsewhere.

Aletta and Sybylla were following Griet from the reception hall. They were to help her fill the two dishes for the first course. Maria was competent at presiding in the kitchen, but could no longer do anything active. Francesca ignored her sisters' questioning glances as they went by, but she caught Sybylla's whisper.

"Francesca is going to make a grand entrance. I wish I had thought of that!"

How far Sybylla was from the truth! Something of that whisper must have reached Ludolf's ears, for he turned his head quickly and looked towards the stair hall. Involuntarily Francesca rested a hand against the old oak of the archway as he sighted her. His smile spread slowly, revealing teeth that were broad and square, well suited to the shape of his face. He was not without good looks, but there was a coarseness to his features. His brows were of a sandy hue, as were the thin moustache and the small pointed beard, matched by the thickly curled periwig that reached to his shoulders and down his back. The lids of his sharp, alert eyes were deep and his nose was wide, as were his nostrils and his mouth, his chin thrusting and pugnacious. He was not a man to cross.

"Ah! The goddess of spring herself!" he exclaimed. "Master Visser, pray present me to this lovely Flora."

Francesca drew in a deep breath before gliding forward to be presented and to dip her best curtsey. Ludolf handed her up and would have retained his hold on her fingers if she had not slipped them free as

she made a conventional reply to this greeting. "I endorse my father's welcome to a stranger in our house."

"But a stranger no longer, I trust." He kept his gaze on her while addressing Hendrick. "You have a fine bevy of daughters, Master Visser. It will be my pleasure to call your eldest by her Christian name without formality, not from any ill manners, I assure you, but because Francesca graces the banqueting hall of my house with her likeness as Flora and it is as if she had always belonged there. I have only one fault to find with that painting. It does not do her justice. She is far more beautiful."

Two points of colour had appeared in Francesca's cheeks, not at the oily compliment, but that he should be speaking about her as if she were an item of goods on display with no tongue in her head. This had always been a house where women spoke their minds, and her annoyance was high. She saw that Hendrick was also irritated by the veiled criticism of his work. It was time to intervene. She gestured graciously.

"Pray come through to dine. All is ready."

The atmosphere at the table was easier than Francesca had expected. Ludolf was a fluent talker with a wide knowledge of the world from his travels abroad. Deliberately she crushed down the dislike she had experienced at first sight of him, wanting to be fair-minded towards a guest in her home. He was courteous in the extreme, encouraging her and her sisters to express opinions, for he was also a good listener, and this suited Hendrick's garrulous nature. It was easy to see he had won her father over completely. Hendrick had forgotten his earlier qualms and was relaxed and merry. She guessed it had much to do with Ludolf's firm request to view one day soon any paintings her father might have that Willem had overlooked. She knew that nothing would delight Hendrick more than that he should place with this patron pictures that the art dealer had declined to handle.

The extremely good dinner ended with bowls of crystallized fruits and ginger. Ludolf patted the stickiness from his lips with his napkin. "I think we should now discuss your painting of my portrait, Master Visser."

It was the moment for the girls to withdraw. "We shall leave you two gentlemen to your business talk," Francesca said.

1
4
0

"We shall not be long," Ludolf replied, rising from his chair as she and her sisters left the table.

Away from the room Sybylla poked Francesca playfully in the arm. "He sounded as though he thought you might miss him," she teased.

"The reverse is the case," Francesca replied somewhat sharply.

"Did you notice his rings?" Sybylla rolled her eyes. "They dazzled me!"

Aletta, seating herself in the drawing room, looked speculatively at her elder sister. "You don't like him, do you?"

Francesca took a chair opposite her. "My feelings about him are rather mixed, for a reason that is wholly foolish in origin. All that matters is that Father should find him agreeable. They are the two who will be seeing each other."

"I agree." Aletta reflected that Francesca probably felt much the same about the man as she did. Feminine intuition had told her there was something about him that did not ring true. It had been like having dinner with a playactor who was sustaining a chosen role even after leaving the stage.

In the dining hall the moment had come for Hendrick to refuse the commission. He had seen almost from the start that Ludolf was a man of intelligence who would be sensible enough towards the finer feelings of others, his conversation throughout the meal having confirmed this. Had it not been so, Hendrick knew he would have had second thoughts about the decision he had made, for having gained this patron's good-will it would have been folly to throw it away without making a supreme effort to please him. They were both mellowed by wine and good food, which was also conducive to maintaining the relationship already formed.

"I fully appreciate your offer of a commission to paint your portrait, Heer van Deventer. Unfortunately the way is not clear for me to accept it."

Ludolf looked down at the napkin he still held and laid it with more care than was necessary on the table beside his plate. "Not clear?" he said on a quiet note of surprise. Then he shifted round in his chair to regard Hendrick steadily. "My good fellow, please explain."

1
4
1

"It may be difficult for a layman to understand, but I happen to be among those artists who can't be governed by the clock."

"I envy you," Ludolf replied with a sigh. "Most of my days are mapped out hour by hour."

Hendrick warmed to his own words, for everything was going so well. "I can only feel hamstrung by arranged appointments." His memory dwelt briefly on times in earlier years when he had thrown his brushes into the air and yelled at some pompous burgher or his plain wife that he could not paint to another's timetable. The price paid for Francesca's painting as Flora had lulled him into considering this new commission, but he was thankful to be rid of it. "I must paint at midnight if the mood takes me, but at an hour that might suit you for a sitting I might have no wish to hold a brush. Total freedom is important to me and brings forth my best work, any of which in the future can be offered to you for your consideration first."

Ludolf nodded in the most friendly manner. "I like a man who speaks his mind, and is not freedom the natural right of every Dutchman? Show me all your future work. I have time at last to start a collection of paintings. Until recently the pressure of business left me with no leeway for leisurely pursuits, but I have begun to delegate much of the work that was mine to others with no ill results." He reached out and clapped a hand on Hendrick's shoulder. "At least I know genius when I see it and it was in your painting of Francesca. Such men as you can't be tied down."

The praise fed Hendrick's conceit and the modest little lift of his hand was made invalid by his satisfied smile. "You do me much honour, *mijnheer.* Now that is settled I think it is time we joined my daughters in the drawing room."

Tea was served. Conversation was light and all three girls noticed their father's exceptional good humour. When the tea was drunk Hendrick gave his guest the choice of chess or cards and the latter was chosen. It was the girls' chance to withdraw, for unless it was a mixed card party it was customary for the women of the household to leave the men on their own for gaming. Good nights were said and Francesca led the way upstairs, her sisters following one behind the other.

No sooner were they halfway up than Ludolf showed himself to be

seized by an idea of importance and tapped his forehead with a finger. "I've had such a good notion, Master Visser! Would you be kind enough to call Francesca back for a few moments?"

"Yes, indeed." Hendrick left the half-open drawer from which he had been taking the cards and went to the foot of the stairs. "Wait, Francesca! I'd like you to come down again for a minute."

She raised her eyebrows at her sisters, signalling her wonder at this unexpected summons, and they drew back against the banister to let her pass. As Francesca reached the foot of the stairs, Sybylla caught hold of Aletta's arm. "Let's listen!" she whispered.

Aletta answered fiercely. "No! Any kind of eavesdropping is loathsome and surely you've heard enough of that man's voice for one evening. I know I have." She moved to go up the next flight and when Sybylla did not follow she returned to beckon her crossly. Still ignored, she shook an angry finger and then continued up to the third floor.

Downstairs Francesca was invited to sit down by Ludolf as if it were his home instead of hers. Then from where he himself was seated he addressed Hendrick.

"With regard to my portrait, which you have declined to paint, I have thought of a means by which my disappointment can be overcome."

"What is that?" Hendrick had drawn his chair to the table, where he had set down the pack of cards, impatient for play to begin.

"Simplicity itself. Francesca shall paint my likeness instead."

She was aghast. "That's impossible!"

Ludolf smiled directly at her and shook his head. "I disagree. There could not be a better solution."

"But my work can't be compared in any way with my father's!"

"I realize that, so don't worry on that score. De Hartog told me that he had the highest faith in your future as an artist and he commended the way you work daily from morning to evening in the studio. Therefore, since you keep regular hours, there should be no difficulty in our arranging sittings to suit each other."

Hendrick jerked in his chair as if he had been struck across the face. He could scarcely begin to comprehend how easily he had been brushed aside. His eyes blinked on the tempest of outrage that swept through

1
4
3

him. Like a drowning man clutching a spar, he seized on the only excuse against her accepting the commission that would conceal his own mauled pride.

"It can't be done! Francesca is to be apprenticed very shortly to an artist named Vermeer in Delft!"

They both looked at him, Ludolf with a flash of anger and Francesca in complete stupefaction. She rose slowly to her feet and went across to sit opposite Hendrick at the table. "I don't understand, Father!"

He waved his hands agitatedly as he struggled with the turmoil of temper and indignation within him. "I only received the news this morning. Willem wished it to be a surprise for you when he returns from his journey. However, in view of what our guest has put to you, I've had to speak about the matter sooner than I'd intended."

"Is Aletta to go with me?" Francesca asked swiftly.

"No. Her chance will come later."

She had a thousand questions tumbling in her mind to ask him, but she was constrained by the presence of a stranger. "This is marvellous news," she exclaimed breathlessly. The promise of Aletta following after her was all she needed to complete her joy at what had been opened up for her. "Should I have heard of Master Vermeer?"

"No chance of that. He has other means by which to live and doesn't confine himself to painting, but Willem thinks most highly of his work. So," he added to Ludolf, "you have my most profound apologies that your commission can't be undertaken by my daughter."

"Is that so?" Ludolf's manner had chilled. "That is a very great pity. It is a blow to all my expectations."

The significance of his words was lost on Francesca, who could have thrown her arms about her father's neck for his spurning, with such a wonderful disclosure, Ludolf's high-handed assumption that she would jump at the chance he had offered her. Apart from anything else, she would never have trodden deliberately on her father's exclusive territory. There were none more wary of his pride than his own household.

Unsuspected by her, the momentum of Ludolf's threat had hit Hendrick hard. Had he and his daughter obliged the man's whim all would have been well, but a second refusal in one evening would not be tolerated. Sweat began to gather on Hendrick's forehead. He fought for

calm and would have drummed his fingers on the table as his thoughts raced to find a means by which to solve this crisis, but pain in his knuckles shot through his fingers and he covered them quickly with his other hand. He did not realize that Francesca had noticed the involuntary tremor of his fingers or that he had made her aware of how often recently she had seen him take that action of cushioning his knuckles. Hendrick cleared his throat. "I regret to hear that. No offence was intended."

"I did not suppose that it was." In spite of Ludolf's conciliatory acknowledgement the same iciness persisted in his voice. He glanced at the clock as if he might be changing his mind about staying for cards after all. It was a clear indication that if he went he would be taking his patronage with him.

Panic rose in Hendrick. Suddenly he saw Ludolf as a bastion between himself and a poverty-stricken old age. The spectre of Frans Hals existing in his last years on charity and poor Rembrandt's pitiful end haunted him in his depressed moments, as did those of other artists he had known who had been reduced to ignominious circumstances. The old fears surged through him once more. He liked living with a certain dash and it was clear that the luxuries of life would be plentiful under Ludolf's patronage. The cost was his pride, but for once in his life he must sacrifice it. He could not let everything that had been dangled before him that evening slip through his fingers, the painful condition of which was likely to get worse as the years advanced. A tolerant patron, as Ludolf had shown earlier that he could be, would never hasten work when the end result would be all that was desired.

"I don't see this situation as an impasse," he said in an attempt to sound at ease. "Francesca's departure for Delft needn't be hurried." Deliberately he ignored the look of alarm that had flown into his daughter's face. "No date has been considered yet as to when she will be leaving Amsterdam. There would be time for her to paint you first."

Francesca cried out in protest. "Such a portrait could not be rushed."

"The time will simply be extended until it is finished." Hendrick beamed at his guest. "That's settled then. I can promise you'll not be disappointed in the result, *mijnheer*. I shall personally add any necessary touches. Naturally it won't be the masterpiece you would have had if I

1
4
5

were able to undertake the commission, but Francesca has a gift for capturing likeness that is commendable." Then he reached over to her, acting a show of enthusiasm, and clasped her wrist harder than he had intended. The burning needles of pain driving into his fingers almost made him grimace. "Thank our new patron, Francesca."

She had felt him wince and, under her lashes, she saw at close quarters that there was a slightly swollen look about his knuckles, nothing that was noticeable in the normal way, but following that involuntary tremor it was a sign that meant a great deal. Torn by regret, she felt her will to refuse the commission dissolve away in pity and filial love. How long had he been concealing this rebellion of the joints that was every artist's fear, linked as it was to cold studios and draughts and sketching when chill winds blew in from the sea. No wonder he did not want this commission to go by, whatever the toll on his conceit. The least she could do for him was to achieve her best work to date. She swallowed hard, smiled at him and then turned her head to meet Ludolf's waiting gaze.

"I thank you, Heer van Deventer," she said, feeling like an obedient child instead of a grown woman with an independent mind.

He was smiling benignly, his eyes very bright. "I suppose we need to discuss details."

She knew he was referring to the pose he should adopt, the colour of his garments and so forth. The financial side would not be mentioned between them, for whatever was received would go to Hendrick. "We can fix a time one day that is convenient for you."

"Why not when I come to view your father's paintings by daylight? That can be tomorrow. I'm eager to see them."

Since arriving at the house Ludolf had formed his own opinion of Hendrick and summed him up as a bombastic, self-satisfied fellow who would be easy to manipulate. He had in his possession at home a full report from an investigation into the artist's background that gave gambling as his weakness. It was Ludolf's policy never to do business with anyone, not even the simple commission of a painting, without knowing all about the person he was dealing with. He had good reasons. There were shadows in his past that he never wanted to stir up again by chance. The knowledge he gained also gave him a tremendous advan-

tage and he compared it to having seen the hand of an opponent in a game of cards before play began.

Francesca was the unknown for him in this house. He was magnetized by her. Her allure was almost beyond physical endurance. It was difficult to keep his eyes from her, the racing of his blood so fast that it was a wonder it did not thunder in his veins like a river in spate. He felt like a man who had been denied the sight of a woman for decades. He wanted to eat and drink her, drown her mouth in his and turn her every way until there was no part of her not known to him. Countless women had aroused him fiercely throughout the years, but never before had he been so fascinated and enthralled, weak as a youth in love for the first time. Had he not been able to disguise his feelings he would have given himself away when he sighted her standing in the stair hall, candlelight falling on her pale, oval face and flaring red-gold sparks in her hair. Although he was already more than familiar with her likeness as Flora, her sensual and unusual beauty in the flesh had all but driven the breath from his lungs. In those few seconds the alarming realization had dawned that he had become totally obsessed by her.

He had had to keep an expressionless face again in the dining hall when Hendrick had declined the commission for himself. Instantly it had become apparent how it would be possible to be alone with Francesca, not once or twice, but for as many hours as it would take in sittings for her to paint his portrait. His ruse had worked and from it all he desired would come. It was many years since he had set out to seduce a chaste virgin. It could be argued that at fifty his sexual mores had grown too sophisticated for such a young man's game, but there was an exception to every rule and she would be a delight to teach and would be quick to learn.

"I'll bid you good night once more," she was saying to him.

"Good night to you, Francesca. We shall meet again tomorrow morning."

He would have liked to walk with her to the stairs, to have seized her in the shadows and taken her violently against the wall, thrusting himself into her warm, moist depths while kneading her breasts, his hungry mouth swallowing hers. As she went through the archway his hooded gaze devoured her until she had disappeared from sight. He

took a lace-trimmed handkerchief from his pocket and, unseen by Hendrick, wiped his sweaty palms.

Upstairs on the third landing Francesca found Sybylla waiting for her and she was given no chance to speak. "I listened! Isn't it marvellous news about the apprenticeship!"

"Yes, it is." Francesca laughed happily as she was pulled by the hand into her sisters' bedchamber. Aletta, already in her nightshift and robe, rushed to embrace her.

"You deserve this wonderful chance more than anybody! All my felicitations!"

"It will be your turn soon!"

Aletta stood back and held her by the arms. "It's a heavy chore for you having to paint that man first," she said sympathetically, "but it shouldn't take you too long and then you'll be away. Think of that all the time he's sitting on the rostrum."

"I will!" Francesca hooked her arm through Aletta's and they sat together on the edge of the four-poster bed. "I could see Father felt obligated to fulfil his new patron's wish."

Sybylla, having removed her gown, bounced onto the bed in her petticoats and knelt beside her sisters. "Where's the money coming from for the tuition? Has father had a huge win at gaming?"

"I think he's had some small wins over quite a long period, because he has kept my household coffer regularly supplied. It's my belief that my apprenticeship is being financed by the sum Father received for *The Goddess of Spring.*"

"Would that be enough?"

"There is also a little money of Mama's that was placed in trust for each of us when the need arose. I expect my share will be added."

Sybylla's face lit up. "I never realized I had a dowry. How is Aletta's apprenticeship to come about?"

"That's obvious. When an artist has a rich patron his work is far more sought after. Father can count on a bigger income from now on."

"I still hope Master Vermeer is paid in advance," Sybylla stated bluntly, "because you know what Father is! We'll probably have creditors at the front and back doors again within a month of your going away, Francesca."

Aletta gave Sybylla a push that sent her backwards across the bed. "Stop that talk! We don't want Francesca to go off to Delft full of worry."

Francesca's expression changed to one of anxiety and concern. "Do you suppose I haven't thought of that? I'll organize everything and try to cover any emergency before I leave, first for you, Aletta, and then for when Maria takes over. I'll make sure that Father agrees that this is how it shall be or else I'll not take the apprenticeship. Having a new start last autumn with creditors paid and money in the household coffers has enabled me to keep abreast with all expenses. Although Father is still gaming, he does seem to have made an effort as he promised and kept to modest stakes. Now at least when he loses it is not a disaster."

Sybylla was back on her knees again. "Neither of you has spoken about letting me be in charge when you're both absent," she pouted. "Why should it be Maria?"

Aletta answered her crisply. "Because you and Father would throw all his money away between you in no time at all. You both need keeping in check."

"That's unfair!"

"No, it's not. It's the truth and you know it. You're always trying to wheedle the fripperies you want from him."

Sybylla's face blazed. "I never received that new cloak, did I? That's how much he listens to me!"

Francesca could see a sharp quarrel was soaring up between her sisters. "Be quiet, Sybylla! You'll be heard all over the house and we'll have Maria coming from her bed to see what's the matter." Having silenced Sybylla, she spoke again to Aletta. "We'll talk about all this again tomorrow, but you wanted to ask me something, didn't you? Come along to my room with me now."

Aletta shook her head. "It was nothing important." Out of the corner of her eye she could see the frantic signals that Sybylla was making behind Francesca's back, indicating that she should go. "It was a question that has more or less answered itself."

Francesca looked doubtful. "Are you sure?"

"Quite sure. Go to bed now and sleep well."

As soon as Francesca had gone from the room Sybylla sprang from the bed. "I thought you were going to tell her of your plans."

"What happened this evening took away any chance of her agreeing with them."

"How can you be sure?"

Aletta slipped off her robe and climbed into bed. "She would say that my need to sell my pictures was eliminated by my forthcoming apprenticeship."

"I suppose she would be right."

"Yes, she would be," Aletta sighed. "Now finish getting undressed and come to bed. I can't sleep until the candle is blown out."

Sybylla came to the bed to stare hard at her on the pillows. "You don't think your apprenticeship is certain, do you?"

Aletta hesitated. "Mine isn't settled with a studio like Francesca's. Until it is I feel I must carry on with what I'm doing."

"You're being pessimistic."

"I see it as being realistic."

"You always have wanted everything cut and dried. That's why there's nothing romantic in you. You never expect to find anything waiting round the corner for you, not even love."

Aletta rolled up her eyes. "Spare me your philosophizing at this hour."

Sybylla was pondering another point and paid no attention. "I suppose it's just possible that Father said you'd be getting an apprenticeship later on to make sure Francesca accepted hers. She would never have agreed otherwise to preferential treatment with you the loser."

"Don't malign Father on that point. He always means what he says at the time. It's not that I don't think he wants me to have my chance, it's simply that he may not be able to arrange it for me when the time comes." Aletta sat up abruptly. "You must keep what I've said to yourself! Francesca must not suspect my uncertainty. You are quite right in thinking that if she should start questioning Father it could end up with her refusing to go to Delft."

"I won't breathe a word. I haven't given the secret of your commissions away and I'll keep all that's been said here to myself too."

Aletta lay awake long after Sybylla's regular breathing showed that

she slept. She had known that as soon as Willem had been mentioned in connection with the arranging of her sister's apprenticeship it would be secured. He was the most reliable man and would make no false promises about what could be done, but for herself it was a different matter. Her apprenticeship depended on her father's work pleasing Ludolf van Deventer indefinitely and there was no guarantee of that. Only yesterday Hendrick had started a painting of a tax collector. Who would want such a picture? Tax was a sore point with everybody and with the rich most of all. He had alienated so many would-be patrons in the past with his temperamental outbursts and his inflated pride. No matter how good his intentions, or how deep his love for those involved, circumstances of his own making all too frequently defeated him.

She was not looking forward to the morrow. Facing Pieter without having spoken to Francesca was going to be difficult. All she could hope was that he would understand how the events of the evening had created a barrier that she had not anticipated and would be satisfied with her promise that as soon as Francesca's apprenticeship was confirmed she should be told everything.

Aletta had another thought. Sybylla was wrong about there being no romance in her. She was fully aware of Pieter as just the man whom she might have loved, for she admired everything about him from his looks to his kindness and his integrity, but she must close the door on those feelings and turn the key. Only a fool would fall in love with a man whose heart was almost certainly centred on her sister.

CHAPTER 8

Pieter received the news from Aletta of Francesca's apprenticeship in Delft with surprise and mixed reactions. "I understand this is a wonderful chance for her," he said thoughtfully, "even if I deeply regret it means she will be leaving Amsterdam. Nevertheless, I still cannot agree to anything being done behind her back. She has to know."

In desperation Aletta pleaded. "It may only be for a short time that I have to keep her in ignorance, and maybe not. I can't make any promises about that. For all I know, my apprenticeship may never materialize and then without those classes I should have lost every chance I ever had to reach the standard for which I am aiming." She put her hand on his arm where they sat again in the coffeehouse, her face desperately anxious. "Please, Pieter! Give me a time limit of twelve months if you must, but in mercy's sake don't take from me the one opportunity I have to get where I want to be."

He could be hard and obdurate when there was need, but in this case her argument was such that the just side of his nature questioned his conscience about refusing her. He knew what it meant to be able to fulfil an ambition and had he been denied the career he had chosen he would never have gained satisfaction in life. Although his silence while he considered her plea was of little more than a minute's duration, it seemed like an hour to her. Finally he gave a slow nod of his head.

"You shall have that section of my stall. I'll not set a time limit, because it's immaterial whether it's a week or a year when we are both keeping from Francesca what she has a moral right to know." He frowned ruefully, although he had spoken without reproach, simply stating a fact. "This business sets me at a disadvantage with her. The conspiracy between you and me will be at the back of my mind every time I see her."

She was glad he was not looking at her at that precise moment or he might have seen the searing regret twisting her face that he should care so much about keeping her sister in the dark. "I know that."

"I admire her," he said as if she might not have grasped fully how he felt.

She managed a cheerful smile. "That's to be expected. She's a fine person. You granted the favour to me originally because I happened to be her sister, didn't you?"

"Yes. I'll not deny it."

"Do you intend to court her?"

"I do."

"Others have wanted to," she warned, "but Father has shown them all the door at her wish."

He laughed under his breath. "I'm not easily discouraged."

"You'd be wiser to look elsewhere. There must be plenty of pretty girls in Haarlem and wherever else you go."

"Plenty," he agreed, the creases appearing at the corners of his smiling eyes causing her to guess he had explored that discovery to the full.

"Are you saying there's only one Francesca?"

"That's it." Again he laughed quietly. "I'll take my chance with her just as you are going to take yours at my stall."

"I wish you well," she said genuinely, suppressing whatever might have arisen within her at the moment.

"As I do you, Aletta."

She reached for her gloves, it being time to leave. "Shall you be able to come home with me to see my hyacinth painting today?"

"I've been looking forward to it."

On the way she told him of the commission Francesca had received from Ludolf van Deventer the previous evening and how it had all come about. "I don't envy her having that man as a sitter," she said thoughtfully, "but maybe all will go well for her."

"Is there any reason why it shouldn't?" He had his own reservations about Ludolf van Deventer. Nobody in Amsterdam appeared to know where he had come from and there was talk at the Exchange that not all his business dealings were quite aboveboard.

Aletta meditated for a few moments. "He has an interesting face, but it's like a mask, never showing much feeling. With people like that it

can often be very difficult for an artist to bring character to the face. It's almost as if there's a shield behind which they are protecting their private selves from the world." She shrugged, slightly embarrassed. "I'm not trying to sound profound. It's just that a painter learns to observe people in this way."

"I'm impressed. I know van Deventer by sight. You say he bought a painting of Francesca as Flora?" It galled him to think of such a man possessing a likeness of her. "Do you know anything about his roots or his background?"

"No. He talked a lot at dinner, but now that I think about it he rarely mentioned himself in any situation. All we know at home is that he's rich and a ship broker and has travelled extensively."

"That's all anyone seems to know. I've wondered about his origins, where he made his money and so forth. From what I've heard he has only lived in Amsterdam for about ten years, although he gives the impression he has owned the business he has now for much longer elsewhere."

"Probably he moved to Amsterdam when he married. He is starting a collection of paintings for his house now."

"Doesn't that strike you as odd? Why should a wealthy man only be collecting now?"

"He told Father that he had never had time before. Business has occupied him completely."

"I suppose that's logical," Pieter admitted.

"He may still be at my home when we get there. Father planned to show him every single painting in the studio this morning."

When they arrived at her home a red-and-gold coach was drawn up outside. "I can see he is still here," Aletta remarked. Once indoors she asked Griet the whereabouts of the visitor in the house.

"He's still in the studio with the master and Juffrouw Francesca," Griet replied. "They've been there for ages. When I went past the door just now I saw that pictures were ranged all around the studio for Heer van Deventer's inspection."

"That probably means they will be there a while longer." Aletta turned to Pieter. "Sit down by the fire. I'll go upstairs and fetch my painting."

She hastened away. Left alone, Pieter did not sit down, preferring to remain standing. He wondered if he would see Francesca before he had to leave again.

In the studio there had been a few tense minutes for Hendrick and Francesca when Ludolf had first entered with them and had seen the painting of Anna on the wall. He had strode across to it immediately, gesturing towards it with his fashionably long cane.

"I'll take that! It's magnificent! There's one of the same model in your reception hall. I'll have that too."

"Your pardon," Hendrick had replied stiffly. "Neither is for sale."

Ludolf turned sharply to him with a frown of displeasure. "You brought me in here to show me your work, didn't you?"

"Yes, but that is my late wife."

"Are you telling me that you keep what is surely a splendid likeness of her in this untidy place?" Ludolf's tone had a sarcastic edge and his contemptuous sweep of the arm encompassed the whole studio. It was clear that he doubted the truth of what Hendrick had said, almost as if suspecting the painting of Anna was being withheld for another patron.

Francesca explained. "My mother was so often in this room with my father that all of us in the family like her to be here still."

His frown disappeared. "My apologies are due."

After that all went well. Francesca helped Hendrick to show a number of his history paintings that had remained unsold. Ludolf chose a scene following the conquest of Troy with a Greek commander looming over a deep-breasted Trojan woman on her knees before him. She was pleading for the lives of her household, including her children, who huddled in the background, and was offering food and wine in appeasement. The dish in her hands held oysters, one of the many erotic symbols that were instantly recognizable.

His second choice was a naked Venus, wet from the sea, which again had its own connotations. The third was an imaginary landscape, harsh with rocks and cliffs, which he said reminded him of a foreign land he had once visited.

Hendrick was inwardly jubilant at these sales, from which Willem could not expect a percentage. When the business was done Francesca entered into a discussion with Ludolf about her forthcoming painting of

1
5
5

him. It had to be decided how his pose should be, portrait sitters always having definite ideas about how they wished to be shown. She suggested it would be appropriate to include the model of a ship in his portrait and Hendrick promptly fetched one from a shelf of various objects. It was a delicately made replica of a merchantman with sails of parchment curved as if in full sail and the rigging and all else accurately reproduced to scale. When Ludolf gave his approval, Hendrick lifted a small table of the right height onto the rostrum beside the chair. After Francesca had swung some drapery over it, she placed the vessel in position. Then she sat down herself in the chair beside it and demonstrated a pose, her elbow on the chair arm, her fingers supporting her chin.

"I'm not sure about the hand," Ludolf said uncertainly, tilting his head as he viewed her. "Perhaps I should hold the ship."

Obligingly she held it. When he shook his head again she replaced the model on the table and changed her pose. "Does this please you?"

Everything about her pleased him. He was keeping her on the move for the sheer enjoyment of watching her. There was the soft movement of her breasts beneath her bodice as she turned, the cling of her skirts to her hip or her knee, and the milky whiteness of her skin against the rich colour of her hair hinted tantalizingly at the further beauty that her clothes concealed.

"I do believe the first pose was best after all," he said, again indecisive.

But Francesca had seen what he was about and rose quickly from the chair. "I agree," she said, giving him no further chance of making an exhibition of her. "Have you decided what you will wear? I need to know, because of the background drapery that I shall arrange."

There was no hesitation about that. He would be in black and gold. At this point she was free to leave him with her father and she was thankful to escape. She had loathed the way Ludolf had looked at her, stripping off her clothes with his eyes. At least during the sittings she would be in her painting smock, the most concealing of garments, and with the pose she had settled for him his gaze would be directed away from her.

Entering the stair hall, she was caught off guard by the unexpected sight of Pieter standing in that eternal male stance with his back to the

fire, hands linked behind him and feet apart, a proud tilt to his head on the strong neck and broad shoulders.

"I've been hoping to see you," he exclaimed.

"Pieter!" She went across to him, her footsteps light in her happiness that he should be back in her own home again. "I didn't know you were here."

"I've just arrived at your sister's invitation."

"Did you meet Sybylla somewhere?"

"No. It was Aletta who asked me. I'm to see her hyacinth painting."

"It's very good. Is she fetching you some refreshment?"

"I have no need of any. She and I had some at the new coffeehouse not far from the Exchange."

She wondered why Aletta had been in that part of the city and supposed it was for another of those street scenes her sister claimed to find especially interesting. "I've heard of it, but I haven't been there."

"Let me take you one day soon. We should celebrate this news of your forthcoming apprenticeship."

"I don't know when that could be arranged," she said truthfully. "I've received my first commission and that must take priority in order that it may be completed before I leave for Delft."

"Aletta told me about it, but Heer van Deventer won't be coming every day. Why not—" He broke off as Aletta returned, carrying her painting turned towards herself. He guessed that she was anxious again in case he should think he was getting a bad bargain when he saw her work. He smiled at her encouragingly. "I've already heard from Francesca that your picture is good."

Aletta shot a grateful glance at her sister and then, somewhat nervously, she reversed the painting for his viewing. Immediately the hyacinth bloomed for him. It had been portrayed in meticulous detail and on the silk swathed about the pot an ant crawled as if attracted to the flower's scent and perhaps set on ravishment, a typical symbol of the frailty and vulnerability of all living things. He knew enough about art to see Aletta's talent shining through. Any doubts he had had about being drawn into her ambitious schemes were swept away. The girl should have her chance.

"I like your painting. It is all I thought it would be." His straightforward statement told Aletta what she wanted to know.

Francesca observed the look they exchanged. It was almost as if there was some shared secret between them. Then there was no more time to think about it, because her father and Ludolf were coming from the studio. She saw that Hendrick was exuberantly good-humoured and knew immediately that his new patron had bought an extra painting after all, there having been some hesitation by Ludolf over a particular one earlier. Sighting Pieter, Hendrick bellowed a hearty greeting and promptly presented him to Ludolf.

"This is the tulip grower and designer gardener, Pieter van Doorne. You will remember I spoke of him to you yesterday at supper."

"I recall every word." Ludolf was interested. He had mentioned that the layout of his garden was not to his satisfaction and the artist had told him of this young fellow with the extraordinary horticultural talent. Perhaps someone of such keenness could produce a design more unusual than those he had rejected from other gardeners, who had simply drawn variations of what he already had. Indicating Aletta's painting, Hendrick explained that the girls had painted the famed hyacinth that had bloomed at Christmas.

"You should see Francesca's painting of the hyacinth too," Hendrick said to both Pieter and Ludolf. He patted his daughter on the shoulder. "Go and fetch it, my dear."

"Not now, Father." Francesca spoke firmly, determined not to spoil Aletta's moment. Pieter, by the very timbre of his voice, had shown such appreciation of her sister's work that it had gladdened her to see Aletta so encouraged. His simple comment had meant far more than any number of gushing compliments. "I'll show it another day."

Hendrick was, as always, irrepressible when his mind was made up. "This is no time for modesty. Aletta! You fetch it!"

Aletta went willingly to the studio, where it had been put with other work by Francesca in a cupboard. Their father had not wanted any diverting of Ludolf's interest by a chance sighting of anything done by anyone else until his own works were sold. He had never questioned why his second daughter had removed all her past work from the studio

some time ago. Aletta's guess was that he simply appreciated more room for his own canvases.

She had to sort through a number of paintings before she came to the hyacinth. Never once had she felt the least jealousy towards her sister's work, even though, as she had said to Pieter the previous week, it had recently surged ahead. Who was to say the hyacinth had not been a turning point? Perhaps the very surprise of it coming at such a time to a lover of flowers had proved to be a spark to tinder. Pieter had a right to see the results and he was too sensible a man not to expect Francesca's version to be superior to hers.

In the reception hall Ludolf took advantage of the few minutes of waiting for Aletta's return to speak to Pieter about the growing of the hyacinth. "I'm most intrigued. How did you go about it?"

"I've been experimenting for some time. I made several errors of judgement before I succeeded in getting roots by keeping the bulbs cold and moist under several inches of peat. Then, a year ago, I was fortunate enough to get a bloom about a week after the apex shoots had shown themselves. The whole experiment was simply to increase my knowledge in another field, but I'm well pleased that the hyacinth proved to be an inspiration to two artists." Pieter glanced across at Francesca.

"Naturally you would be." Ludolf continued by asking, "Please name some persons of repute for whom you have designed gardens."

Pieter raised a chilly eyebrow. "I don't give the names of those who have employed my skills. If they choose to recommend me, that is their affair and of great benefit to me."

Ludolf approved this. Here was a young man who knew how to keep whatever he saw or heard to himself. It was well never to let a gossiping tongue near one's abode. Servants learned early in the van Deventer home not to discuss their master or anything that happened under his roof. Unpleasant things happened to those who did, always seemingly by accident, but the message went home and new servants were warned by their seniors to obey this special rule.

"Come back with me now, van Doorne. I should like you to take a look at my garden with a view to redesigning it."

Pieter knew what would be wanted. Symmetrical parterres, some

classical statuary, a fountain or two and, if space permitted, whatever would pass as an avenue of trees. With everything French having become so fashionable, all those who could afford it wanted their gardens to resemble the park of the palace of Versailles. His own rules were for colour, fragrance and harmony, making house and garden complement each other in whatever he designed. Whether he took the commission being dangled like a carrot was another matter.

"I can't make any other calls today, Heer van Deventer," he said, "because when I leave here I'll be on my way back to Haarlem and my home nearby where I have my orangery and my bulb fields."

"Then let us make another appointment for two weeks from today at this hour." It did not occur to Ludolf that he might get a second refusal and without waiting for a reply gave his address in Heeren-gracht, a street of exceptionally fine property facing a canal, and added that his house had a double flight of steps to the entrance and his name was above a ship moulded in the pediment.

Even if he had not mentioned that he lived in the area known as the Golden Bend, the description of his house would have been a testament to his riches. Well-to-do people had a flight of steps to the entrance of their homes, but the rich had twin flights. Pieter, who had done extensive garden work for the owners of such properties, would normally have welcomed this chance to gain another client, but his doubts about Ludolf van Deventer's integrity put this possible commission in a different light. Early on in business he had been swindled by such a man over some landscaping, but it was a valuable lesson and he was a great deal wiser these days. He was almost on the point of saying he was too busy to handle extra work now that spring had come, which was virtually the truth, when he considered Francesca's involvement with this ship broker. If he accepted work from van Deventer he could keep an eye on her interests at the same time.

"I shall call on you, *mijnheer,*" he said, giving Ludolf the customary bow. If it was less deep than usual nobody noticed, for Aletta had returned with Francesca's painting. Ludolf exclaimed over it.

"What a splendid picture for a young artist on the road to achievement!" He knew enough about Hendrick now to be certain that praise for the work of others, particularly his daughters, should be moderated

in his hearing. Ludolf wanted nothing to interfere with his getting a hold over the man, which was why he had let him win heavily during their game of cards the previous evening. It was far from the first time he had caught a fool in a net and Hendrick should be easier to trap than most. "So much talent in one house. From the mighty oak two saplings have sprung." He bowed to Hendrick and then to the girls. "If I had wanted proof of how good my portrait is to be," he added to Francesca, "it is here in this fine example of your art."

The difference in the quality of the two hyacinth pictures had been apparent to Pieter at once. In Francesca's the flower positively glowed in its glory. Moreover, there was no symbolic ant or anything else to warn that nothing is perfect. The whole painting was a tribute to the flower itself.

"My felicitations," he said directly to her.

Her face had become strained at Ludolf's extravagant praise, but cleared at his words. This did not go unmarked by Ludolf, who was annoyed with himself for not having judged more accurately how she would receive flattery. Most women could not get enough of it. He covered his blunder by a few words about making his departure.

Farewells had been said when Sybylla arrived on the step just as Ludolf went from the house. She bobbed a curtsey, giving him a twinkling glance that came from sheer exultation that he had returned as had been arranged, a visit that heralded anew the prosperity he was to bring to the house. Francesca seized the moment of diversion to speak to Pieter on his own.

"Please stay and share our noon meal with us. You have a long journey back to Haarlem ahead of you."

"I accept gladly."

At table he was given the seat next to Sybylla. "Did you see Heer van Deventer's handsome coach outside?" she asked him as the food was being served.

"I did. If Aletta had not told me to whom it belonged I'd have thought it was the Prince of Orange visiting your father."

She liked that. "Who knows! Perhaps that will happen any day now that Father has such a wealthy patron."

1
6
1

Hendrick in his exuberant mood slapped the table in appreciation. "Well said, Sybylla!"

"The coachman let me sit in that handsome equipage," she announced to the table at large.

Maria glowered. "You had no business to take such a liberty!"

Sybylla ignored the reprimand. "It's upholstered in the softest velvet with gilded tassels." She tilted her face provocatively at Pieter. "When are you going to have a coach like that?"

He answered half seriously and half in jest. "When I can produce a tulip of a new colour that everyone will want."

Francesca from her seat at the end of the table looked along at him. "Is that your ambition?"

"I think it is every tulip grower's wish."

Hendrick gestured with his fork. "Don't revive tulipomania. That's all I ask!" He laughed heartily at his own joke. "It was all over before you were born, young man, but you must know plenty about it."

"I do. My father was one of the successful investors, but he had friends who lost everything."

"I was also fortunate in that I came out of it unscathed. It was an enjoyable gamble while it lasted." Hendrick began to reminisce, relating tales that his family had heard countless times.

Pieter listened in spite of what was happening under the table. Unbeknown to anybody else Sybylla had kicked off a shoe and with her stockinged toes was trying to twist his hose awry. His garters at the calves were firm, but as the meal progressed she succeeded in dragging one loose and he had to reach down and jerk it tight again. When he glanced sideways at her she was eating docilely with an air of total innocence, but there was such mischief and sexuality dancing in her eyes under her downcast lashes that he was sure it was only a matter of time before someone at the table became suspicious. He believed that if anyone in her family should challenge her she would denounce him as being at fault. It was not a comfortable meal.

When it was over he had a short while on his own with Francesca in the reception hall. "You heard when van Deventer and I arranged for a meeting in a fortnight's time, which means he won't be here that day. Say you'll meet me early that afternoon?"

She agreed and arranged where they should meet. If it was fine they would take a walk after leaving the coffeehouse, but if wet they would sit longer over the coffee.

"That sounds a splendid arrangement." Her eyes were smiling.

"I'll be looking forward to it."

When he had gone she tapped a finger thoughtfully against her cheek. Had she been foolish to agree to that meeting? Then she reminded herself that soon she would be going to Delft and then this short, sweet spell of knowing him would be at an end.

As always when Amalia van Deventer heard her husband return home she hoped he would not come to her apartment, where she lay on her couch, propped up by cushions. With so many hours to lie there thinking over the past, she had wondered more times than could be counted how she had ever supposed herself to be in love with him. Now, knowing he had been to the studio of an artist named Visser to buy paintings, she was certain he would come to report to her, for on the surface there was nothing to fault his behaviour as a husband in the eyes of others.

Her suite of rooms was most luxuriously furnished in the French style with gilded panels and rich furnishings, as was the rest of the house, the outcome of visiting France ten years ago on a wedding tour. Through her connections she and Ludolf had been invited to stay at several grand châteaux, and upon their return to Holland nothing would satisfy him except that the house he was building should reflect something of the splendours they had seen. He had his own wealth, but it was her money that he had used. In spite of her protests, everything that she had treasured, either as heirlooms or out of reverence for the craftsmanship of a past century, was allowed no place in the new house. She had wept to see beautifully carved oaken cupboards and chests and tables, once used by her mother and grandmother before her, carted away in wagons. Her first husband, who had left his fortune to her, had been a collector of early Dutch art, but there had been no room in Ludolf's house for his pieces. All had been sold hurriedly with no thought to their true value, which for her was beyond price. Some French paintings had replaced them, all mediocre to her eyes.

Since he had been more than enamoured with anything French, it puzzled her that now, when many were beginning to look towards France for inspiration in interior decor as well as fashion, he was becoming ostentatiously Dutch-minded, and a year ago he had let it be known that he was starting a special collection of contemporary Dutch art. He was such a devious man, with no real concept of the truth unless it suited his purpose, that she could not help being suspicious that he had some ulterior motive. He had always talked about business trips he had made to France, but coinciding with the start of this new collection he had stopped talking about visiting there. Probably only she would notice all these odd little pieces of a puzzle, but then she had so much time to dwell on any slight thing that stirred her curiosity. On second thoughts she was almost sure that her personal maidservant, who had been with her since shortly before her marriage to Ludolf, took note of everything as keenly as she did, not that the matter was ever mentioned between them. Neeltje was the perfect maidservant in that she never gossiped and kept herself apart from the rest of the domestic staff, as befitted the sole attendant on the lady of the house.

Amalia thought again what a pleasure it was to have Dutch paintings around her once more. Shortly before last Christmas, Ludolf had begun talking about a mysterious painting that de Hartog might, or might not, sell, and knowing Ludolf as she did, she was not surprised when eventually he outbid everyone else to acquire it. To her it had been another little piece in the not-yet-put-together puzzle of his newfound patriotism, for all Amsterdam had been talking about the unknown picture and his name was on everyone's lips as soon as it had become his.

When she saw *The Goddess of Spring* she thought it a beautiful painting and a splendid acquisition, and was not surprised when it replaced his favourite French painting in the banqueting hall. There was no doubt that Hendrick Visser was a painter of talent, but not even his *Flora* could supplant her particular fondness for a work by Pieter de Hooch, which hung in her dayroom exactly where she could gaze at it. It was a tranquil interior which reminded her so much of her childhood

home that when Ludolf had brought it in she had asked for it to be hung in her apartment and he had agreed. The disadvantage was that he brought guests to see it, which meant she had to play the hostess, elaborately gowned and coiffured, either from her couch, if she was particularly weak that day, or from her chair, for the wasting illness afflicting her had drained away her energy, making it difficult for her to walk or stand for any length of time. She did fulfil her duties as hostess whenever possible; otherwise she remained in her apartment, which suited her and the husband who hated her.

He was coming! She knew his footsteps all too well. With an effort she raised herself and reached for the hand glass lying on the low table placed conveniently by her side. On it she had books, a decanter of fruit juice, an enamelled casket that kept her bottles of physic out of sight and another, covered with embroidery, in which she kept her cosmetics. It was this casket that she would need.

Her hand glass showed her a face that had once been striking if not handsome, her brows thick and dark, as were her lashes, her eyes hazel with corn-coloured lights and her chin prominent. Her illness had drawn purple shadows under her eyes and given a yellowish tinge to her skin, which had once been like alabaster, and drawn it tight over her facial bones until there was a skeletal look to her. Yet she must always be correctly painted and powdered for her own self-respect and not from any wish to please Ludolf. When she was too weak to apply her cosmetics, Neeltje, who was also her nurse, would apply them for her.

A touch of carmine on the lips! A dab of powder! Both were applied and the casket closed as he came into the room. He gave her his customary greeting. "How are you today, Amalia?"

"Much better, I think." It was the lie he expected.

"Good." He rubbed his big hands with the thick fingers in an exuberant manner, not because he was cheered by her answer, but through some happening that she knew he would soon disclose.

"Did you see anything you liked at the Visser studio?" She wished he would stop rubbing his hands. She always tried to avoid looking at them. They had done such dreadful, unspeakable things to her during the night hours when she had shared a marriage bed with him. If there

could be any blessing in her illness it was that it had released her from Ludolf's perpetual lust.

"I've bought four paintings. The artist is a most agreeable fellow. I've invited him to an evening of cards. One day soon my clerk shall send out invitations to a banquet. Visser, who is a widower, and his three daughters will be the guests of honour."

She dreaded these banquets. However poorly she happened to feel, she had to attend, even for a little while, and to date she had always managed. What puzzled her was this sudden benevolence towards the artist. Ludolf never did anything unless it was for his own ends. "How many do you intend to invite?"

"Twenty-five to thirty. You may add whatever names you please to the list that my clerk will bring you."

It was the usual procedure. Friendships made during her first marriage had fallen away and only a few faithful childhood friends still kept in close touch. Although they preferred to visit her on her own, they would come for her sake to the balls and banquets that he gave.

"You must have a new gown, Amalia." He was striding about in his exhilarated mood, going to the window and back again. None could deny he had a good bearing.

"I have so many gowns." She supposed some might argue that he was being generous, for he would be paying for it, and not many husbands were eager to subscribe to yet another expensive garment for a wife when her closet was already full of them. It was of no account that he had squandered her fortune on the house, his jewels and clothes, his carriages and sleighs and his stable of thoroughbred horses.

He dismissed her faint protest. "It doesn't suit my rising position in society for you to be seen in the same gown twice over on a grand occasion. I'll select the fabric to save you the exertion and the seamstress shall come tomorrow."

She knew better than to argue further. "Whatever you say." At least he had an eye for colour and would choose a shade flattering to her present sallow complexion and greying hair. As for his social ambitions, she thought, as she had done often before, that he should have been born a Frenchman of quality, for Holland lacked those close-knit aristocratic circles that existed in France and he would have revelled in the

pomp and ostentation that played no part in Dutch life. It made it all the stranger that he was now so secretive about any business that compelled him to travel to Paris. He never spoke of any invitations received there.

"When is your gaming session to be?"

"Next week. There'll be only four of us playing. Visser and I played a few hands after supper last night. I could tell that he likes a serious game and I shall see that he gets it."

That meant the stakes would be high. "Are you sure he can afford it? Artists are usually of moderate circumstances."

"This fellow can. He has a well-built house and appears to keep a good table, although I suppose the best was put on for me, including the wine, which was excellent. Visser is also in a position to apprentice his eldest daughter to a Delft studio and the second is to follow shortly. What's more, he has a hawk of an agent in de Hartog, who knows how to press up prices for his work."

He was satisfied he had presented a convincing picture. Had he not known of Hendrick's tendency to fall easily into debt, apparently controlled to a degree at the present time by Francesca and, according to his paid informant, frequently having to exist on a few wins at the tavern tables, he would have thought the Visser household to be on a solid financial foundation. It was his guess that Francesca had to look at every stuiver and make it stretch far. All that would change for her in the future. She would want for nothing. At first the apprenticeship at Delft had seemed like a setback, but by the time she had finished his portrait even that obstacle to his pursuit of her should be eliminated.

Amalia's mind had been put at rest by Ludolf's assurance. It had been the mention of the artist's daughters that had concerned her. Bankruptcy, with its attendant misery for the family, was all too often the fate of a painter and she did not want Hendrick Visser hastened towards it while under this roof.

As soon as Ludolf had left the apartment, Neeltje brought her tea on a tray, for she always needed something to revive her after being in her husband's presence. Sometimes she wished she could find oblivion in alcohol, but she had never liked it in any form and when guests were present a juice resembling wine was always poured into her glass.

"How prompt you are, Neeltje," Amalia said gratefully as the cup of fragrant China tea, sieved of its leaves, was handed to her.

"I try always to be prepared, ma'am."

The exchange was a familiar little ritual that had evolved over the years.

Neeltje was in her forties, plain-featured with fading fair hair, always neat and spotless in her starched cap and apron, with large peasant hands that could be gentle when nursing and strong in supporting the frailness of an invalid when slow steps had to be taken from one room to another. She was a wonderful companion in every way and often Amalia would talk to her of days gone by and of her first husband, Stephanus, although Neeltje had never known him. Friends did occasionally mention him when on their own with her, but she had been widowed five years before marrying Ludolf and that had been over a decade ago.

It had been an arranged marriage with Stephanus, a widower and thrice her age, she only fifteen on her wedding day, but he had been good and kind. She had grown to love him, but it had not been love of the heady, romantic kind. That had passed her by entirely. Maybe that was why she had lost her head and allowed herself to be swept out of lonely widowhood by Ludolf, who had flattered her and wooed her and seduced her into marriage. Trusted friends had warned her, saying that nothing was known about this stranger who had been a sleeping partner in an admittedly reputable ship-brokering business and had only just made an appearance. She had replied that it was the death of his partner that had brought him home to Amsterdam from his travels securing business overseas. Why was it, then, they had countered, that nobody of their acquaintance in such circles knew of him? She had pointed out lightheartedly that the world was wide and Ludolf had confided to her that he made the best deals through quiet negotiations.

It had been a triumph for her when she met, and was able to present, two merchants who spoke highly of Ludolf, each of whom had met him in the New World. One had received vital supplies of gunpowder from him when none was available, and the other the replacement for a vessel wrecked beyond salvage. Later, when she was disillusioned and far wiser, she wondered if those two men had been bribed by Ludolf to

make those statements, for neither of them had ever crossed her path again.

"There's to be another banquet soon, Neeltje," she said on a sigh.

"Then you must rest well beforehand, ma'am," Neeltje replied solicitously.

Amalia smiled wryly to herself. She did little else to survive from day to day. The collapses she had endured had been frightening, but each time she had rallied, astounding her doctor. He explained it as her strength of will. What he did not suspect was that her elixir of life was a hatred of her husband that was equal to his own for her. Not even Neeltje guessed how it sustained her and was her strength. She knew she was living on extended time, but her vengeance would be if she could deny Ludolf the freedom from her that he wanted by outliving him!

The next day in the parlour, Willem stared incredulously with a rise of anger at Hendrick. "You have done what?"

Hendrick was unperturbed. "Letting Francesca take the van Deventer commission was the only way I could get out of accepting it myself. I'm giving her the chance to earn some money for herself before she goes away, because I shall share with her whatever price you set on it. That's generous of me, don't you think?"

Furiously Willem shook the apprenticeship papers that he held. "These are signed and sealed stating she will start at Vermeer's studio next month. She must be there!"

"Impossible," Hendrick replied casually.

"Damnation to your folly. I gave up a lot of time to arrange all this! Do you imagine it was easy getting the Guild of St. Luke to grant Francesca three years to become a master instead of six? What's more, the committee is prepared to consider only two if she should reach their expectations."

"But you had that document of indenture."

"That showed she had been trained in your studio from the age of twelve, but no work was displayed to the Guild of Amsterdam at what should have been the end of the apprenticeship span on her eighteenth

birthday. The document was also queried because it was not written on parchment, but it was decided it would hold up legally, which is why the Committee eventually decided leniently in her favour. The strength of her sketches and the painting of her sisters did much to sway them in her favour."

"What reason did you give for the switch of studios?"

"Circumstances!" Willem was glaring.

Hendrick did not probe. He suspected that neglect of tuition had tipped the scales. "That's it, then."

"What are you saying?" Willem looked as if he might explode. "I haven't told you before, but Vermeer wasn't enamoured with the idea of having a pupil. I had to do a deal of talking about Francesca before he would consider taking her. Now that he has agreed, giving her a golden chance at moderate terms such as you'd never get anywhere else, you have to sabotage everything! Don't you realize he could either sue you for her nonappearance or—worse still for her—take this opportunity, and be within his rights, to declare her indentures with him to be null and void! Where is she now?"

"Upstairs being fitted for new garments."

"Send for her."

Hendrick, as ever when knowing himself to be in the wrong, became belligerent. "I'm not having her upset by you in your present temper."

"Then I'll seek her out myself."

Willem strode from the room and took the stairs two at a time. These upper regions were unknown to him, but he would shout for her. The landing branched curiously, as happened in so many Dutch houses, his own included, and another narrow staircase wound upwards while a long corridor with closed doors lay to his right. Only the one at the end stood half open and from it came a buzz of female chatter.

"Francesca!"

There was a moment of surprised silence and then Francesca herself appeared in the doorway attired in a gown of tawny velvet that was partly held together by white tacking stitches. Astonishment and amusement blended in her face at the sight of him. "Have you lost your way, *mijnheer?*" she asked with laughter in her voice.

"I have to speak to you. It's most important."

Her smile fled at the sternness of his request. She spoke to the seamstress in the sewing room and then left to go to her own room. "We can talk in here."

In her bedchamber, on the cushioned bench, he explained the situation. "I can't say what action—if any—Vermeer might make. He is an amiable man and might be persuaded to overlook a delay, although that's impossible to guarantee."

She sat very straight, absently lifting her left sleeve occasionally, for it was slipping away from its tacking at the shoulder. "Whether he would or would not is beside the point. An agreement has been made in good faith on both sides and not to abide to it is breaking one's word. Similarly a bond has been agreed in my accepting van Deventer's commission."

"Could you finish the portrait in five weeks?"

"I could if I had the studio to myself, but Father is working on his painting of the tax collector. When he's in the mood for work he has to paint. It's like breathing to him. I daresay I could share Aletta's studio-parlour, but I'm not sure that she would want me there and there's scarcely room for two of us in any case." She tilted her chin. "But there are other rooms in the house and I will fulfil my obligations somehow."

"You have to consider the possibility that van Deventer's engagements might keep him from coming for sittings as often as you would wish. But I've a suggestion. I could ask him if you could use one of the rooms in his house as a studio. Then he would be able to sit for you whenever he has five minutes."

Her face cleared. "That would be the solution to everything!"

"I'll go straight from here to his house. When everything is explained to him I feel sure he will agree."

She smiled gratefully. "You are such a good friend."

He returned her smile. "I've known your father too many years not to want to help whenever I can and I was fond of your good mother."

"I can't find enough words to thank you."

In the sewing room again, as Francesca stood having the new garment readjusted here and there by the seamstress, she thought of the meeting she had arranged with Pieter. If she was to go daily to the van Deventer house it might not be possible to meet him as planned, but at

least she knew he would be at the same house on Friday morning and she could tell him then if it proved impossible.

Early that evening one of Ludolf's servants delivered a letter to Hendrick. In it Ludolf wrote that a room had been converted already into a studio for Francesca and it had been fully equipped with an easel and canvas, oils and brushes and everything else she might need. This meant she could keep the appointment already arranged on the morrow for his first sitting. He would be sending his coach for her. All this information was somewhat overwhelming, for she had planned for a man with a handcart to take what she would need.

"It's too much," she said uneasily to Hendrick. "I only expected space with a good light, a chair for van Deventer and a side table for the model of the ship."

"It goes to show what a considerate man he is," he replied. "After all, he sent his coach for me last night for that evening at cards at his house. Naturally he would do the same for you."

It had been a most gratifying evening for Hendrick. Three of his paintings were hung prominently in the card room and the fourth in the supper room of that splendid house. After a slight setback, he had won handsomely from Ludolf and his two friends. Never had he drunk better wine or seen gentlemen lose with such good grace. They had congratulated him at the night's end and expressed their pleasure when he had invited them to his house to play again, giving them the chance to win their money back. But he had been laughing to himself. He knew from long experience that when his luck was in full spate it would carry him through many such games yet. A few more such wins and he would be able to send Aletta to Delft too.

When Sybylla heard that Francesca was to ride in the van Deventer coach she insisted on going with her. "Do let me! I'll be very quiet and not disturb you when you're painting."

"When have you ever been quiet!" Francesca teased.

Sybylla became frantic. "Don't begrudge me this chance to see inside that house!"

Francesca relented. "You can come, but any foolishness and you will have to leave." She shook a warning finger.

"I'll be so good! I promise."

The coach came for them at eight o'clock the next morning. Francesca carried her painting smock and the roll of draperies for the portrait's background, while Sybylla held the model of the ship. Throughout the ride Sybylla was on the lookout all the time for anyone she knew. Then she would wave and dip her head graciously as if aping Prince Willem of Orange when he rode out from the palace at The Hague. Once she kicked her feet with delight after a girl she disliked intensely had gaped in envious amazement as she rode by.

The mansion with the twin flight of steps faced the canal. Ludolf had mentioned that he had had it built on the site of an ancient property that had been torn down. It had a wider frontage than the older houses, although, as with them, there was little more than an inch between its walls and those of its neighbours on either side. Elaborate pilasters adorned the frontage, the sills and casements carved with twirling foliage. In the pediment up by the gables was the ship in full sail by which Pieter had been directed.

Sybylla would not go up the same flight of steps as Francesca, but like a child at play took the other to arrive at the opened door at the same time. Ludolf himself met them in the reception hall, already resplendent in black velvet with gilt braid decorating his fashionable longish coat, loops of ribbons at the shoulders and bunches again on the garters of his hose meeting the full-gathered calf-length breeches. If anything his shoulder-length periwig was even more carefully curled than before. Francesca suspected he had donned a new one in readiness for his portrait. If he was surprised to see Sybylla as well, he did not show it.

"Good day to you both and welcome to my home. What a splendid arrangement it is that you should have a temporary studio here, Francesca. I was told by Heer de Hartog that we have just five weeks before you leave for Delft. You may be sure," he insisted, "that I shall cooperate in any way I can."

"I think you have already shown that by your kindness." She had to give him credit for being so obliging.

Sybylla was wide-eyed at the size and splendour of the reception hall. A hundred people or more could have danced there with space to spare. There was so much gilt agleam, the walls silk-panelled, and huge crystal

chandeliers were suspended from a ceiling depicting whales and vessels and stormy waves in the ornate plasterwork. Set into the blue marble floor was a circular design of dolphins with a ship in the middle, the twin of the one in the pediment outside. It added to her awe that two liveried menservants should attend them, their cloaks taken in one direction and her sister's painting smock and the model of the ship borne away upstairs to the location of the studio. She had supposed the coach servants doubled up for work indoors, for a tax was levied by the state on employers of menservants, but that was not the case. The ship broker must have florins to throw away! She turned her enthralled gaze on him. Somehow she must do her part to ensure favour for her father and, at the present time, her sister with this Heer van Moneybags!

"You needn't fear Francesca will rush your portrait in any way just because she's going to Delft at the end of April," she volunteered.

"Such a thought never entered my head," he answered, intent on showing his goodwill. "Before we go upstairs to the studio I should like you both to meet my wife."

"That is what I hoped," Francesca replied. Knowing that Amalia van Deventer was an invalid, she had brought with her a box of sugared sweetmeats that were her culinary speciality.

As they turned into a corridor lined with tapestries Ludolf explained that his wife's suite was on the ground floor to enable her to walk about a little sometimes without the exertion of the stairs. Yet when they entered Amalia's dayroom and saw her lying against her cushions it seemed impossible to either Francesca or Sybilla that this woman could have the strength to rise from them. She looked so delicate, almost as if the embroidered silken quilt covering her legs might be too great a weight for her. Painted, coiffured and fully dressed in spite of an hour early for an invalid, she extended a hand, thin as a bird's claw, to welcome the two girls to her side.

"How kind of you to come and see me. I know you, Francesca, as Flora here in this house. And this must be Sybilla. Oh, what have you brought me? How prettily the box is decorated. Shall I peep inside now? These look delicious!"

Francesca could see that this woman, who had every material benefit she could wish for, was genuinely touched and delighted by the unex-

pected gift. Ludolf waited until some conversation had been exchanged and then drew the sisters away, both of them promising to see her again before they went home.

Francesca was amazed by the size of the room that had been allotted to her as a studio. A four-poster hung with embroidered curtains had been pushed back against a wall to give maximum space and was partly concealed by an Oriental screen. Four large windows gave her north light and the view was of the long garden that Pieter was to redesign. A large carved chair and a side table had been placed in the right position to benefit from the north windows, and an easel with a prepared canvas on it stood together with a stool. She went at once to a side table where much more than she would need was laid out.

"Who mixed the oils and pigments?" she asked Ludolf.

"The supplier. Has he done well?"

"Indeed he has." A manservant was waiting to see if she wanted anything changed and she asked for another screen to be set behind the carved chair on which she could arrange her drapery. When this was done she nodded approval to Ludolf. "Now let us begin!"

He helped her on with her smock while Sybylla put the model ship on the table at the angle Francesca wanted. Then he took his hat from the chair and put it on. It was in the latest French mode for men, with a stiff and narrow brim and an ostrich plume that stood upright, the fronds dipping over a high crown. Then he sat down, his pose comfortable, with a relaxed air. Sybylla settled herself on a chair to watch at an angle from which she could see his likeness taking shape on the canvas. She had brought nothing to occupy the time, knowing in advance that she would be too excited by her surroundings to concentrate on anything else.

Francesca was rarely troubled by anything when she painted. Normally her cares fell away from her and it was only occasionally, such as when she found thoughts of Pieter persisting, that she was not able to give her whole attention to her work. Today she was fully concentrated. Nothing existed except her and her sitter. She was getting to know his features, noting how his nostrils curved, the way his brows met sparsely in a V above the bridge of his nose, and how his thick lower lip had a faint indentation as if once it had suffered a cut from a fist. There was also a scar by his left eye. As for his periwig, that would be an exercise in itself, all those gleaming highlights and curling shadows.

Ludolf talked, which sitters usually did. Only professional models kept silent. The conversation was mostly between Ludolf and Sybylla, who was as garrulous as Hendrick, but Francesca did answer when necessary, one part of her mind alerted for it. She gave Ludolf a rest after twenty minutes, which was as much as most sitters, other than professionals, could take at a time. She continued working, seated on her stool, while he went across to the window to discuss his hopes for a new garden with her sister.

The sitting had been resumed for only five minutes when Sybylla was unable to contain her enthusiasm any longer. "This is a beautiful place!" She sprang from her chair to almost dance about the room as she looked at paintings and porcelains, silver trinkets on a French toilet table, and was unabashed when she opened a cupboard to find a silver chamber pot inside.

When she came into Ludolf's line of vision again he watched her rapt face as she ran her hand over a carving and stroked a brocade hanging.

"Why don't you look at the rest of the house," he invited expansively.

"May I?" Sybylla pressed her palms together with delight.

"If you should get lost there's a bellpull in every room. One of the servants will come and find you." As the door shut behind her he rose immediately from the chair. "I'll take a rest now." In the next moment he was viewing the beginnings of his portrait. It was still no more than a rough sketch in paint, but there were decisive strokes and already there was a masterly commitment to his likeness. "Should you leave my portrait at this stage all would know it was I!"

She put down her brushes and rectangular palette to rise from the stool. "My father's whim is that nobody should see his work until it is almost finished. I'm not as strict as that, but I'd prefer you didn't look at this canvas again until I invite you." She did not want him seeking any excuse to peer over her shoulder and this rest he was taking was far too soon.

"It shall be as you wish."

176

"I thank you."

"I want only to please you." His voice lowered slightly, shot through with meaning, and he moved closer to her. "Do you understand me, Francesca?"

She thought her bile must rise. Did he suppose even for a moment that she might be flattered by the advances of an older man of wealth? Deliberately she misinterpreted his words. "Then when you return to your chair try to keep your gaze in the direction we arranged. It will be most helpful to me if you don't turn your head during this first stage."

He gestured with a hand that came near to touching her, his eyes smiling. "Then try not to be a magnet to me."

She regarded him impatiently. "Please understand that here in the studio I'm a craftswoman wanting only to depict you as the man of property and position that you are. Don't reveal to me a side of yourself that you would not wish others to see, because, whether I wanted it or not, it would show in the finished portrait."

He was taken aback. "Are you that sure of your talent?"

"It's not a question of skill. To me it is a flaw, because in portraiture I find I paint as much with the inner eye as an outer one. How much better it would be not to reveal the blatant facts and leave whoever views the result wanting to know more of the nature and the thoughts of the person within the frame. So much given and so much held back. That's how people are to one another in life. Nobody can ever know somebody else's whole soul."

"You think deeply, don't you?"

"I'm not naïve about my fellow men and women."

He reflected that he had never been more neatly rebuffed. And twice over! She had put him in his place with a skilful warning over his advances and again in telling him clearly that she was not one to have her head turned. "So if a man was secretly in love you could portray it?"

She saw the line he was following again. "It would probably surface just as hatred or greed or anything else that would show when the face of a sitter is studied long enough. If anyone should ask if there was one thing taught me by my father that I valued above all else, I would say it was the development of that inner eye, but I have yet to master it and bring it under my control."

"Is that what you expect to happen at Vermeer's studio?"

She relaxed and a look that was both meditative and joyous came into her face in her yearning to be there. "I hope for everything at Delft!"

It was a further rebuff, whether she knew it or not. He could see that it was not going to be easy to win her, but that only incited further his resolve to make her his own. With an amiable remark and a show of good grace that was far from his true feelings, he returned to the chair and she took up her work again.

CHAPTER 9

At Ludolf's house there was no repeat of the incident of the first day. It was between Francesca and him as if it had not happened; his conversation with her was easy and friendly and devoid of any innuendo whether during the sittings or when she and Sybylla ate the noon meal with him. She reminded herself there were many men who could not resist an opportunity for seduction, and she judged him to be no better and no worse than most. It was to his credit that he had taken notice of her clear indication that she wanted none of it.

As the days went by the routine settled down. When Sybylla continued to accompany Francesca to the house every day, the novelty showing no sign of palling, it seemed time to mention the matter to Ludolf.

"I hope you have no objection to Sybylla being here so often," she put to him.

He was quick to reassure her. "Indeed not. I'm extremely pleased that she should be here, because I can see that already my wife delights in her cheerful company. And who would not?"

Francesca was equally glad that a friendship had been struck between his wife and her sister that took no account of the difference in their ages. Amalia had an interest in fashion that matched Sybylla's own and they had long discussions about it and other topics, including the interests of the Visser family.

"It's splendid that Francesca should have obtained an apprenticeship in Delft," Amalia remarked one day. "She must be a truly gifted painter."

"Oh, she is," Sybylla assured her. "I wish you could see the painting she did of my sister and me playing in concert, Aletta at the virginal and I on my viol."

Amalia's face lit up. "The viol? Are you telling me you play the viol? It was my mother's favourite instrument and as a child I spent many happy hours listening to her playing." She hesitated. "I suppose—would it be asking too much—I mean could you possibly play for me occasionally?"

"Of course!" Sybylla was genuinely enthusiastic. "That would be marvellous, because I love playing. I'll bring my viol with me in the coach tomorrow morning."

"Your sister's lively company," Amalia said to Francesca a few days later, "does me more good than any physic the doctor brings. She is like a ray of sunshine whenever she comes into my apartment and we share a love of music. I can't tell you how much pleasure she gives me when playing her viol."

If Amalia needed to rest Sybylla would visit Ludolf's library or wander about the house or garden, only his study and apartment closed to her. Once she happened to see Neeltje coming out of the study and locking the door after her. Sybylla, who was sitting curled up, her feet under her on a window seat, would have thought nothing of it if the woman had not glanced about swiftly before darting away, putting the key in her pocket. She did not notice Sybylla, who wondered if she should mention the incident to Amalia, for it was obvious that Neeltje should not have been there, but after consideration she thought better of it. For all she knew Neeltje had been there at Amalia's instruction, finding out some matter of interest that Ludolf had no wish to disclose. Perhaps Amalia suspected him of having a mistress, which was more than likely. She had seen the sly way he looked at Francesca, and even with herself he was too fond of seizing any opportunity to slip an arm about her waist and glancing at her bosom as if he could see right through her bodice. She often felt his eyes following her naturally swinging hips when she left his presence.

One of the times of day that Sybylla enjoyed best in the van Deventer house, apart from being with Amalia, was the noon meal, for there was always delicious fare served from silver dishes. Mostly she and Francesca were alone to eat, Amalia always taking her meals in her apartment and Ludolf frequently not at home. Adding to her enjoyment of being in this fine residence every weekday was the knowledge that Maria could not get at her for all those boring domestic chores.

Francesca's work went well until the morning when she was to meet Pieter. Then her glance strayed constantly to the clock. She had the studio to herself, Ludolf being elsewhere and Sybylla keeping Amalia company, which meant she had nothing to distract her except her own unwarranted rise of anticipation as the hour for his arrival at the house drew near. Slightly ahead of time she discarded her painting smock, checked her appearance in a mirror and then hastened downstairs to be in the reception hall when he came. She arrived exactly as he banged the knocker. A manservant went forward to open the door.

There was Pieter on the doorstep, outlined against the sunny morning. He had not seen her yet, speaking to the manservant as he was admitted and giving his name.

"Heer van Deventer is expecting me." Then he did see her, dazzling her with his look of surprise and pleasure. She believed with regret that had she wished it, there could have been something very deep between them. As the manservant went to announce his arrival, she explained the reason for her presence.

"I'm sorry, Pieter, but I can't leave my work to meet you later today. I'm here on the understanding that I complete the portrait within five weeks and that means using every minute."

Before Pieter could reply, Ludolf's voice rang out from the far end of the reception hall. "I wouldn't think of being the cause of any disappointment to you, Francesca. Heer van Doorne is more than welcome to take the noon meal with us. Then at least in the time available you will have the chance to keep part of your appointment."

It was not what either of them wanted, but Pieter accepted the obviously well-intentioned invitation. Then Francesca returned to her

work in the studio and he went out with Ludolf by another way into the garden. Upstairs she put on her smock again and went to the window. The two men stood in deep discussion at the top of a flight of steps leading from a stone-paved terrace, Ludolf's gestures indicating that the position of the flower beds and lawns were not to his satisfaction. Now and again Pieter nodded, making notes in a workbook he had taken from his pocket and occasionally pointing in various directions himself. When the head gardener joined them Ludolf went back indoors. After a short conversation the gardener left and Pieter was on his own.

Until then the wide brim of his hat had half hidden his face from her sight, but now he looked up sharply and unerringly at her window. It was as if some extraordinary communication between them told him from the first second that she was watching him, for he had not known where her studio was located or seen her go upstairs. He waved and she waved back before slipping away from the window, for he had work to do and she had hers.

She stole a moment a while later to look out at him again. He was on one knee by a distant rose bed, examining the soil. Ludolf happened to enter the studio while she was at the window. He made no comment about her not being at her easel, simply taking his place in the carved chair. It had become a pattern of his sittings that he came to the studio whenever he had time to spare.

"There's half an hour left before the noon meal," he said, settling himself comfortably. "I thought you could put my presence to good use."

"Even ten minutes is a help," she replied, switching brushes and colours, having previously been filling in some background detail. He only changed into his black and gilt-braided clothes when he was able to sit for longer periods, but his hat was kept in the studio and he put it on each time.

When the noon hour struck they left the studio and went downstairs together. Sybylla came from Amalia's apartment and was the first to find Pieter waiting in the reception hall while passing the time looking at the paintings on the green silk walls.

"Good day, Pieter! So you're here, are you?"

"I've been invited to stay for the noon meal."

"What fun!" She giggled mischievously. "Are we to sit together at table?"

But that was not to be the case. Ludolf sat at the head with Francesca at his right hand and Pieter next to her. Sybylla was shown to a chair opposite Pieter, who gave her an impudent wink. He was telling her without words that the table was too wide and they were too far apart for her to misbehave this time. Her mouth twitched with barely controlled laughter. She was not able to calm it until she had had a sip of wine. Always a chatterbox, she was irrepressible today, more at ease through Pieter being present than she was when Ludolf was on his own with Francesca and her at the table.

Francesca noticed that Ludolf never minded her sister's garrulity in the least. He laughed at her joking remarks and even argued with her most amiably over some small matter. Sybylla was always at her most entertaining self when she held male attention.

Pieter had no chance to have a few words alone with Francesca, for when they rose from the table Sybylla took him to see Amalia, who wanted to discuss the landscaping of the garden.

"I would like you to include a sheltered corner for me," Amalia said to him. She was feeling better that day and was seated in a chair by the window, which was a rare treat. "I have not been outside since last summer, because unless there is a day without a breeze there has been no place for me to sit."

"I've already thought of that, ma'am." He proceeded to point out through the window where he thought a little bower should be. She became quite animated as he spoke of a gently sloping terrace to eliminate stone steps, the protection of a wall and bushes, the shade of trees. Sybylla, listening intently, thought how closely he had considered the needs of an invalid, even planning that the bower should be close to the house for easy access and yet giving as much privacy as was required. Then Amalia echoed her thoughts.

"It sounds perfect," she said, pressing her thin hands together. "How soon will it be ready?"

Pieter inclined his head slightly. "That depends on whether my plans

meet with your husband's approval. If they do, you may be sure that your bower will be finished first."

She had become subdued at the reference to Ludolf and nodded with dignity. "I would appreciate that." Then she changed the subject, asking if he lived in Amsterdam, and he stayed talking to her for quite a while.

When he left her apartment Sybylla went with him to guide him through the corridors and he interrupted her chatter to ask where Francesca's studio was located.

"Upstairs," Sybylla replied, "but I can't take you there now. Heer van Deventer is sitting for her again and he wouldn't want you taking up the precious time he allows her. He's a busy man."

He frowned. "Doesn't your father object to Francesca being alone for hours with van Deventer in that studio?"

She trilled with laughter. "Why should he? Vrouw van Deventer is always in the house. I'm here too, much of the time. Servants go in and out with coffee and refreshments and to mend the fire. In any case, when Francesca is at Delft she will be leading an independent life subject only to the rules of apprenticeship. Father knows she has a sensible head on her shoulders and can take care of herself or else he'd never let her go."

"How long is it now before she goes away?"

Sybylla reckoned up. "Ten days and that's not counting the day she leaves. Just before her departure Ludolf is holding a grand banquet. Father and I and my sisters have all been invited." Her glance teased him. "Don't you wish you could be there too?"

He countered that easily in the same vein. "Only if I could have Francesca at my right hand and Aletta at my left."

She threw back her head and trilled again. "You'll never forget that meal at our house, will you! You're such a joy to torment, Pieter. You can count yourself lucky that I don't want to marry you!"

They continued to banter merrily until he was out on the steps of the house. As he went away down the street he turned in the direction of the Visser home. Sybylla was too talkative for him to have told her why he was going there and in any case it was a matter between Hendrick Visser and himself at this stage.

Griet smiled widely when she saw it was he at the door. Then she

1
8
3

shook her head when he asked to speak to her master. "He's painting and he has a model on the rostrum, so he won't see anyone who's not expected. That's true," she added, as if he might remember the excuse she had given him when he had first come to the house with the bulbs and expected immediate payment. "Would you like to wait? All the three young ladies are out, but I'd make you tea." She was hopeful he would accept.

"I thank you, Griet, but I'll come another time. Will there be a model here tomorrow?"

She thought carefully, adding up how long her master had been painting his tax collector picture. "It's difficult to say. The model wasn't here for several days and this could be the final sitting."

"I'll take my chance tomorrow, then." If he had not fixed another appointment that day he would have waited, no matter for how many hours he had had to drink tea, for he had a sense of urgency about speaking to Francesca's father as soon as possible. There was so little time before she left home. He wanted above all else to be able to visit her in Delft.

Ludolf was equally aware of the swift passing of the days. He had been congratulating himself on winning Francesca's confidence and her trust after that first unwise move on his part. She was relaxed in his company now and had responded to his friendliness. He saw he had pleased her with his tolerance of her imp of a sister and she appreciated the frequent sittings he gave her. To lull any doubts she might still have about him, he always talked encouragingly of how she would enjoy being in Delft, her eyes shining as she listened to him while she painted. It was all part of his campaign to make the disappointment more acute when she discovered her apprenticeship there was not to be. That was going to be so easily managed and he dismissed as unimportant Pieter van Doorne's interest in her. There must be several young men with an eye for her. Hendrick had spoken of having shown the door to would-be suitors at her request, and later conversations with Sybylla on her own had further endorsed his understanding that Francesca was dedicated to

a future in art above all else. He believed the way clear for himself by the means he had planned.

It was to be certain of this that he had offered hospitality to Pieter, wanting to view the situation at close hand. On the surface there had been nothing at all to suggest anything really serious between them, but there had been the incident of finding her gazing from the window. Yet that might have been only female curiosity to see what was going on.

At least the trap for Hendrick was well and truly set now and when it snapped shut Francesca would be equally securely imprisoned by it. With his prior knowledge of Hendrick's gambling weakness, he had let him win that first time at the Visser house. Then at his own home it had been arranged again, two of his cardsharp henchmen acting the gentlemen and Hendrick leaving with large winnings. Tonight was to be the denouement.

In the early hours of the following morning Hendrick sat ashen-faced in the firelight of the drawing room. He was bowed over, forearms across his knees and his hands hanging. The whole house was sleeping and he was alone in his torment. He had not been in such desperate straits since he had had Anna to turn to, when, without a word of reproach, she would calmly count up what could be sold this time. Another piece of her treasured jewellery would always top the list until that was all gone. They had quarrelled about many things, including his gambling and womanizing, but at times of crisis she had turned her thoughts only to how she might save him from disaster. At least, through her father's foresight, the roof over their heads had never been endangered. Unfortunately, because of a legal technicality that had been overlooked, that protection had not been continued for her children. It was why he had made a supreme effort since his bereavement not to be as reckless at gaming tables as he had been previously, comparatively minor debts always settled sooner or later.

Until tonight! He groaned aloud. The evening had started off superbly. Ludolf and the two other players, Claudius and Otto, with whom Hendrick had played previously, arrived in good spirits in anticipation of the return card session. Both the newcomers to the house had

admired his painting of Anna in the reception room, as people with an
eye for art so often did. Following what they had already seen of his
paintings in Ludolf's home, it was obvious they would soon be wanting
some of his work too. Francesca had set a buffet supper on a side table
with several decanters of wine and then left them to begin their game
in the drawing room.

At first the size of the stakes suggested had almost made his eyes
bulge, but luck was running in his fingers and he knew he could not
lose. It was not time yet for that winning streak to start playing tricks
and he could feel his own power.

"Why not raise the stakes still higher, gentlemen?" he had suggested.
He had seen that only Ludolf had not been taken aback, giving an
approving nod, and the other two recovered themselves and agreed.

How well the play had gone! The cards adored him. They purred as
he fanned them out and if he had seen them switch suits to please his
play he would not have been surprised. His winnings mounted from the
first hand. By the time a break was taken for food, the glasses having
been replenished by each to his own requirements during the game, he
had two mountains of shining florins beside him and knew there would
be more before the night's end.

It was after supper that everything began to go wrong. He would
lose and then win again with the resurgence of power, only to be
dashed unexpectedly in the next hand by rogue cards that ruined everything. His winnings began to diminish, but he was in a trap of his own
hospitality, giving him no chance of withdrawing from the game on
some pretext of having to leave, and more so by his own conviction
that luck had not deserted him. He always sensed when that was
happening, even though he might choose not to take notice, but that
was not the case tonight. There was no trickery afoot with the three
other players, for even when he dealt he lost in the same way.

Eventually all his winnings had gone and he went on, getting deeper
and deeper into the mire, Ludolf keeping him company, but then his
patron had had the poorest cards all the evening. Sweat ran down into
Hendrick's eyes and his shirt was sticking to him. The perpetual pain in
his knuckles began echoing in his chest, a sensation he had not experienced before, and he loosened the strings of his collar. Then, when he

had a winning hand in his clasp again, almost making him weep with joy that his luck had returned in a way that would sweep him on to the whole night's jackpot, they fell from his nerveless fingers as his chest seemed to contract and he began gasping frantically for breath, lurching back in his chair.

The others sprang up with exclamations. Ludolf wrenched Hendrick's shirt wide open at the neck, aided by Otto, while Claudius rushed to throw the window wide. Mercifully the pain began to subside as quickly as it had come, and as Hendrick began to sit up and mop his brow, his companions relaxed, showing relief that he had recovered.

"Too much wine," Ludolf jested kindly. "Combined with the heat of the room, it overcame you."

Hendrick could not answer, concentrating on getting some regularity back into his breathing. To his dismay he saw the cards he had dropped lay on the floor amid those that had been scattered by his fellow players when they had leapt to his assistance. There was no chance of retrieving that golden hand of hands and playing on.

"I think we should call this night to a close," Ludolf continued, taking Hendrick's agreement for granted and glancing at the other two, who acquiesced graciously. "We'll play again at the first opportunity. Let the final score be tallied and then Hendrick and I can write our promissory notes."

Otto immediately obliged and then Claudius checked his results before handing them on to Ludolf, who seated himself at the table again. While he wrote his promissory note, Hendrick was shown the amount he owed. He could scarcely comprehend that the figure he saw there applied to him. Ludolf handed his notes to the two fortunate winners, and Hendrick, with a violently shaking hand, set the quill scratching as he saw himself signing away the value of all he owned and more.

He had only the haziest recollection of seeing his guests out of his house. Afterwards he had slumped down into the fireside chair and had not moved. The money to send Francesca to Delft had gone, but that was only a fraction of his losses. With his poor credit no bank or individual would advance him a loan of such a size as he had brought down upon his own head tonight. There was no way that he would be

able to pay without selling the house. Anna's home! This was where he still glimpsed the flicker of her golden hair through a pattern of rose glass in the windows and dreamt of her passionately at night in their bed. Her loving presence was everywhere in the house and in losing it he would lose her forever.

A great yell of mingled heartbreak, frustration and hopelessness rose in his throat and drove him up with it from the chair to his feet, his face contorted into a grimace of utter despair, his fists bunched high. As his voice roared forth he slammed his fists against the fireplace with such force that the searing pain from his knuckles, worse than anything he had experienced earlier, hurled him off balance and he fell sprawling to the floor. There he rolled over on his side, his cheek against the cold marble tiles, his bleeding hands spread out. He did not weep from physical agony but from the anguish of his spirit.

"Anna!" He sobbed her name. The acoustics of the house were governed by twisting stairs, odd-shaped corridors and thick doors. No sound reached the upper bedchambers and those who would have come to him slept on.

When Griet washed the floor of the drawing room, which was her first task after lighting the fires every morning, she found the bloodstains. Immediately she assumed that somebody had broken a goblet during the previous night's card game and cut a hand at the same time. She looked about warily for any glittering shards but was unable to find any. It was not like the master to clear up anything after himself or his guests, but he had been careful about the glass this time.

Shortly afterwards at breakfast she saw that both his hands were bound up in clean linen and the tips of his fingers, which were all that could be seen, were swollen and pulpish. Francesca had to cut his cheese and spread his butter. He was totally subdued and quiet, quite unlike himself, and his explanation to his concerned daughters was that he had injured his hands by falling in an awkward way.

"Drunk again," Maria muttered under her breath. She was getting deaf and did not realize how audible her pithy remarks were becoming.

But she had only said what everybody thought, although Griet alone

knew of the evidence in the forgotten window left open and the cards kicked about all over the floor. She had been quick to tidy all that out of sight, only thankful that no thief had taken advantage of an easy entry, and she had not wanted Maria or any of the girls to see the evidence of drunken revelry. Why she should cover up for the master she did not know, but she was pleased to do it.

When breakfast was over Francesca, about to get ready for Ludolf's house, put a hand on her father's arm. "Why not come with me today? You can't paint with your hands as they are and Ludolf would make you welcome. He's most hospitable. As I told you, he invited Pieter to stay for the noon meal yesterday."

"No!" He spoke more sharply than he had intended, but his patron was the last person he wished to see. He was trying to subdue his memory of that fateful card game that had reduced him to such humiliating and degrading circumstances. It was enough that he was faced with a horrendous debt that had swallowed him up. There was no time to waste in bemoaning why it had happened. He had decided during his sleepless night to spend the day ahead in trying to raise loans throughout the city. There were many people he had never approached for money before. Some faint stirrings of his old optimism made him hope that here and there he might receive a generous hearing. Whether his paintings would be accepted as collateral he did not know. Tradesmen sometimes took paintings in lieu of payment for outstanding bills, but he was uncertain about the sort of businessmen he would be seeing on today's awful tour of supplication. Never before had he been forced to beg, which was what it amounted to, and the crushing down of his pride was torment.

"I'll find plenty to do." He was unable to raise the faintest note of cheer in his voice. "There's an auction of foreign works of art being held today. I'll look in at that."

Griet popped her head into the room. "The coach is here."

"I'm coming," Francesca replied. Then as Griet went again she embraced her father and kissed his cheek. "Don't be cast down. Your hands will soon heal. But if you take my advice you will show them to the doctor today. He may also be able to suggest some treatment for that

swelling of your knuckles, for that is more than just the result of the cuts you've suffered."

He met her eyes. "So you've noticed?"

She smiled at him fondly. "Of course I have, but it's my secret and yours. Nobody else has any suspicion. So will you do as I ask?"

He thought to himself that she had no idea there was no money now for anything such as treatment from doctors or—far worse—an apprenticeship. If he was not successful today she would have to be told, but how he could bring himself to break the news he did not know. She was so happy and excited about going to Delft, her boxes half packed and her new clothes almost ready. He *must* raise some money somewhere! "I may call at the doctor's house on my way to the auction."

"Yes. Do that, please."

As she left him she hoped he would keep his word. Men were such difficult patients; they thought they were dying if they had a bad cold, but if it was something really serious they would be resolute and foolishly courageous, wanting to avoid medical attention at all costs. She found her younger sister already seated in the coach.

"I'm going to miss all this luxury when you've finished the portrait, Francesca," Sybylla said petulantly as the wheels of the coach rolled forward.

"I thought you said you're going to continue visiting Amalia."

"I shall. We get on so well. Somehow I can always entertain people."

Francesca smiled. "That's your great gift."

"Is it? I never thought of it in that light. But visiting there and being shown straight to Amalia's suite won't be the same for me as it is now. I like to pretend it's my house and I really live there."

"I'm not sure that's a wise fantasy to have. You might lose sight of true values."

Sybylla turned to her on the velvet upholstered seat. "I'm not belittling our home! I know there's more love there than that mansion has ever known, but money makes life so much easier." She paused fractionally as if uncertain whether to continue and then decided she would. "I've had another dream too. But you mustn't laugh if I tell you about it."

"I won't."

"Well, I hoped when I went with you that first day and ever since that I'd meet there a young, rich and handsome man, whom I could never find in our circles, and who would fall in love with me and offer marriage."

"I haven't seen anyone there to fit that description!"

"Neither have I," Sybylla sighed heavily, thoroughly disgruntled. "People come and go all the time. Clerks and businessmen and friends of Vrouw van Deventer, but not a single one who would suit me."

Francesca put her hand over her sister's. "Don't give up hope," she said, half seriously, "there's still the evening of the banquet to come."

"So there is!" Sybylla brightened.

"I should be able to put the last touches to the portrait that morning," Francesca added. "Then Ludolf will be able to hang it for the occasion, which is what he wants."

She was willing enough to please him, because she could not fault his behaviour towards her since she had made her attitude clear. Out of a sense of fairness she had to admit that no one could have been more considerate. He had spent some part of each day sitting for her, often coming twice and even three times, occasionally prepared to sit for half an hour without a break, which was good for anyone not a professional model. As a result she had made steady progress with her work and saw no reason why that should not continue. He had not seen her painting of him as yet, and had declined only yesterday when she had invited him across to her easel.

"No, I can wait until it is finished now. I'm a patient man."

She thought this was probably true. As she painted with her inner eye attuned to her subject, she saw no indication of an impulsive nature, more that of a man who would judge his timing, which was probably why he had been so successful in business. Greed was there, conveyed unwittingly by the eyes, but his hooded lids and brushlike lashes disguised it sufficiently for it not to appear obvious in her portrait, although if he had been looking directly at her, instead of his gaze being lodged elsewhere, it would have been registered. Nothing could hide the fleshy fullness of the lips, indicative of a lustful nature, nor would her painting, for this was not a likeness depicted for his conceit.

One of the first lessons Hendrick had taught her was to set down the truth of what she saw.

"Shall you be glad when the portrait is finished?" Sybylla asked.

"What a question!" Francesca gave a happy laugh. "I'm totally interested because it is my first commission, but I'll know when I apply the last brushstroke that it's the eve of one day less before I leave to begin my apprenticeship."

Sybylla made a little grimace, unable to think of anything more dreary than setting off for three years of concentrated work.

When they arrived at the mansion Francesca found Ludolf, resplendent in his black-and-gold garments, waiting for her. "I have a morning free of engagements," he said, "and so I'm at your command."

"How fortunate! I particularly wanted to detail your hands today and your rings."

He talked even more than usual from the rostrum. At midmorning hot chocolate was brought. She moved with him to take one of the chairs, each with a silk velvet cushion in beautiful colours, which were placed on either side of the fireplace that was giving such a steady warmth to the room. No peat was burned in this house. The flames were constantly replenished with expensive logs, no doubt from cargoes of timber imported from Norway, a country with which Holland did much trade. A boy servant was detailed exclusively to take care of the fires and the one in the studio was timed to be at its best when refreshment was taken.

After all the conversation of the past hours Ludolf was silent as he held his porcelain cup and looked into the flames. There was no sound except the spitting and crackling of the birch logs. Then he looked across at her.

"I hope that during the time we have spent together here you have come to know me well."

"A bond does form between artist and sitter," she conceded. "That is inevitable."

"Have you not forgiven me for my indiscretion?"

"Of course I have," she said generously.

He looked again into the flames. "You have seen for yourself that I am a lonely man. Amalia has been wife to me only in name for over

four years. My compassion for her has kept me faithful and devoted. I do all in my power to ensure she has everything possible to relieve the burden of her ill health, but I have to confess that my own life is empty. Can you wonder that I forget myself completely when I am alone with you?" His eyes were on her again, full of appeal.

Her sound common sense told her to be wary and not to be fooled. She had glimpsed too much in his eyes and studied his face too closely not to have summed him up as a man of lusty appetites who would not settle easily to celibacy. But then maybe he had spoken the truth; men who loved could be faithful in the most difficult circumstances. There were many beautiful things in Amalia's suite that were gifts from Ludolf, not only on birthdays and special occasions but also when he happened to see something he had thought would please her. Even the Pieter de Hooch painting was to have been hung in a prominent display elsewhere in the house, but Amalia herself had said that specially to please her Ludolf had placed it in her dayroom. At his orders spring flowers were delivered to her daily, her suite always full of pale hues of the delicate blooms, and there were tulips of every colour. More than once Sybylla had told her of seeing him arrive home with an extra posy. The occasional gift might be in keeping with a married man's troubled conscience, but so many gifts were an expression of fond concern. In any case, Francesca did not think he would be bothered by qualms about any indiscretion.

"I told you," Francesca said gently, determined to be fair-minded, "I don't consider that incident to have formed a barrier in any way."

"I'm in love with you. But," he added quickly, seeing her dismay, "I ask for nothing from you in return."

She breathed quickly, having been fearful he would spring from his chair in an attempt to embrace her, but he had made no move except to put his cup aside and spread his hands wide as a man might do to show himself unarmed.

"Let us not talk of this matter ever again," she declared, still fully alert.

"Nevertheless, as your father's patron and through my feelings for you, I want to shoulder a certain amount of responsibility for his well-being and that of his family."

"That is not necessary!" She was adamant. "Buying my father's paintings puts you under no obligation whatever."

"But I want him to know that if at any time he is in trouble or difficulty he will turn first to me. Will you tell him that?" When she did not reply, her face turned resolutely away from him, he continued, "I think you should. Who is to say what he might not drift into with you away at Delft and no one to keep hands on the household reins?"

That startled her. "I have everything organized."

"I don't doubt that, but I have come to know your father well enough to see that he has his weaknesses."

Her filial loyalty surged. "Do not dare criticize him to me!" she gave back angrily.

"That was not my intention. I'm speaking of him as a friend. To the best of your knowledge does he always keep his word?"

Her jaw set rigidly. "I don't want this discussion to continue. I have my father's assurance that all will go well in my absence and I trust to that."

"If it should not be, you can be sure I will stand by him. That should give you greater peace of mind at Delft."

"I know you mean well—"

"I do and I implore you to remember that, Francesca. No matter what happens, and if any calamity should befall you, I would lend all my strength and power to make things right for you again."

The vehemence of his declaration alarmed her. It was almost fanatical. She decided to calm things down immediately. "I will remember what you have said. To satisfy you, I'll pass your message to my father. Now I think I should get back to work."

Her reassuring words had the desired effect. He kissed her hand as a mark of his gratitude before the sitting was resumed. Later, on his own, he estimated how long it would take Hendrick to come to him for a loan. He knew from well beforehand there was no one else in the city who would be prepared to lend Hendrick—or any other artist for that matter—the sum required. He had been certain from the start that Hendrick would ask him, but time was short and he didn't want any dithering about.

There was no doubt that the little talk he had had with Francesca

had gone even better than he had hoped. He was certain he had won her over now. All Amsterdam knew of his kindness to Amalia, his solicitous attention to her comfort, and of the doctors he had brought from far afield to see if anything new could be done for her. When she died—as she would when her gradually declining strength finally ran out, according to every medical opinion—he wanted it to be seen and known that his hands were clean. Her death had to be natural and in its own time.

It was why he had wanted Amalia to have her personal maidservant always in attendance by day and within earshot by night from a truckle bed at the foot of her four-poster. When he had spent most of Amalia's fortune and she was no longer of any use to him in bed, it would have been easy enough to hire someone to rid him of her, but never again should there be suspicion about him as there had been once in the past. In any case it was of no consequence to him how long Amalia lived. He went his own way and there was nothing she could do to interfere. Being a lady in the true sense of the word, she never spoke of their estrangement even to her closest friends. Only Neeltje, waiting on her day and night, would know of the emptiness of their relationship, but even she could not deny his solicitude.

He hoped to make Francesca a willing mistress. He wanted her to come to him eagerly with outstretched arms and let him do whatever he wished to her. It was not easy being near her day after day while she was at her easel and only the Chinese screen divided off the four-poster bed. If she had responded with encouragement that first day he would have swept her up onto the bed and possessed her then and many times each day afterwards.

Once again Hendrick sat with his head in his hands. Beside him on the parlour table was a bottle of grape brandy and a glass, which he had filled and re-emptied several times. He had had a terrible day and had been ill received everywhere. Interviews that had started off pleasantly had soon changed in atmosphere when his purpose became known. Sometimes he was blatantly shown the door and at others a thin veneer of politeness had not softened another disappointment. The promise of

a few hundred florins from an old friend and fellow artist least able to afford it was all he had to show for his day.

"Master," Griet repeated when he took no notice of her addressing him the first time, "you have a visitor."

He looked up blindly. "What?"

"Heer van Doorne is here to see you. He came yesterday afternoon, but you were in the studio." She thought he did not seem to be grasping what she had said. "You had a model there. That man who's posing as the tax collector, and so I didn't disturb you."

Hendrick passed a bandaged hand across his forehead. Yesterday? Was it so short a time ago that he was painting there without a care? It seemed like a lifetime. He didn't want to see anyone. "Isn't Francesca at home?"

"Not yet, master. But even if all three of your daughters were here it's still you he's asking for."

Hendrick groaned under his breath. "Show him in, then."

When Pieter entered the parlour he experienced a sense of shock when he saw the greyish pallor of Hendrick's face. "Are you not well, mijnheer?"

"Well enough." Hendrick waved Pieter to a seat. "If you have come for conversation I'm afraid I'm not good company today."

"I'll make only one request and then I'll go."

"What is it?"

"Would you allow me to court Francesca and visit her sometimes at Delft?"

Hendrick stared at him with bloodshot eyes. Delft? Francesca? But that was finished. He was going to tell her later and would have to drink himself almost into a stupor before he found the courage to do it. "Didn't you know it's her wish that I never give my permission to any suitor wanting to call on her?"

Pieter was undaunted. "That was for others. Not for me."

"Why should she think differently about you?"

"No reason that I can give you, but I'm sure she does."

Hendrick had had enough of this persistent young man. He wanted to be on his own to plan in his tired mind how best to break his daughter's heart, for that was what it would amount to. Unhappy

memories of the times he had brought Anna to tears were persecuting him at this moment. He had never thought he would ever have to inflict any misery on their firstborn and he was being torn apart. He gestured impatiently, remorse pulling grotesquely at his mouth.

"If Francesca is willing I raise no objection. Marriage would be good for her, because her apprenticeship is no more."

"I don't understand. I thought everything was settled."

Hendrick shook his head, rocking as if mortally wounded. "There's no money anymore. I've been a fool, Pieter. I lost myself in a card game that ruined me."

"Surely it can't be as bad as that. The bank—"

"I've been there. In fact I've been everywhere I can think of today. This house will have to go. I'll have to rent a small place somewhere." Hendrick's voice cracked completely. He put a shaking hand over his eyes and gestured that Pieter should leave, too choked to say any more.

Pieter only drew a chair up close to Hendrick. "I'll loan you the money for Francesca's apprenticeship. Interest-free. You can pay me back whenever you like. If that never proves possible, so be it. She must have her chance."

Slowly Hendrick raised his head again. He looked dazed, as if unable to comprehend what had been said. "Did you say—?"

"Yes. Tell me the sum required."

With effort Hendrick cleared his thoughts. Something momentous was happening and he must deal with it without confusion. "An initial payment was made by Willem de Hartog when the indentures were secured. That came from my sale of Francesca's portrait, but it doesn't end there. The rest of the fee for her tuition and working materials has to be met biannually and there's her keep in lodgings."

"As I said before, tell me what you need for her."

Hendrick, still undecided, looked at him askance. "There's no evidence that she'd have you at the end of it."

A deep flush of anger swept over Pieter's face. "It's not by putting her under an obligation that I intend to win her. Far from it! You'll tell her nothing of this arrangement between us!" There echoed in his mind all that he had fixed with Aletta, equally to be conducted without Francesca's knowledge. He felt he was wading in again towards sabotag-

ing all that he wanted to be with her, but once more this was an exceptional circumstance.

"In that case I'll accept your kind loan." Hendrick saw a first ray of hope. Maybe all would be well in the end after all. Not only were there more sources to tap, but right here in his own home, without even looking for it, the funds to solve his first immediate problem had come to him. The awful dilemma of having to shatter Francesca's dreams had been dispersed. It meant he need not tell her of his present dreadful difficulties and she could go off to Delft in blissful ignorance. If the facts did have to come to light, he would try to keep them from her as long as possible. But could he dare to believe that his luck had taken an upward swing again?

"What time is Francesca expected home?" Pieter wanted to know.

Hendrick blinked at the clock. "About six o'clock. She finishes painting around five, but always visits Vrouw van Deventer for a little while before she leaves."

"Then I'll go before she comes. Now let us get down to facts and figures." Pieter took his workbook and a pencil from his pocket. "I'll arrange for the money to be lodged at the bank and for it to be drawn by a second party—I suggest my lawyer—whenever payments become due."

Hendrick stuck out his chin belligerently. "Don't you trust me? Do you think I would endanger my daughter's future again?"

There was an obvious answer to that, but Pieter did not make it. "Suppose you are not able, in your unfortunate circumstances, to keep your creditors at bay. I should not want them claiming what is due to Francesca."

"That's sensible, I suppose," Hendrick was forced to agree.

During the next quarter of an hour he and Pieter settled the figures. Then Pieter accepted a drink and left soon afterwards. When he had gone Hendrick realized he had not asked him all the questions that a man should put to a prospective son-in-law, but at least he knew the young man had a good business and had funds enough to meet a totally unexpected outlay.

Francesca and Sybylla arrived home in the coach together shortly after Aletta. They all three thought their father seemed a little brighter

than he had that morning. When Francesca was on her own with him later in the evening while changing the linen bindings on his hands, she asked him about the visit he had promised to make.

"What did the doctor say?"

For a moment his mind seemed a vacuum. A good supper had dulled the effect of the grape brandy, but her reference to the doctor puzzled him until he remembered that aeons ago that morning she had asked him to seek medical advice. "He said it's nothing serious if I take care," he lied glibly. Then his inventive powers carried him along. "Such as wearing mittens in the winter when I paint."

"You do that anyway when the weather is exceptionally cold. What treatment did he suggest?"

He was nonplussed as to how to answer her. Then he recalled that when a child he had seen his mother caring for his grandmother's knobbly old fingers. "Soak my knuckles in warm oil to loosen the sinews."

She nodded, still bandaging. "I've heard of that and it's easy enough to do. We'll start the treatment when these cuts are healed."

He thought irritably of the inconvenience it was going to cause him, wasting time with his fingers dabbling in bowls. "Once a week was often enough, the doctor said."

She frowned, puzzled. "That can't be enough. You must have misheard him."

"I'm not deaf," he retorted sharply, proud of his keen hearing. "He said I could hold my hands in hot water for a little while each time I wash them." Then, seeing she was about to question him further, he curtailed whatever she was about to say with something he knew would silence her. "Pieter van Doorne called on me today to ask my permission to court you."

Her fingers paused for a second in the tying of the knot in the binding, but that was the only sign that this information had had any impact on her. "What did you say?" she asked evenly.

"I gave him the usual answer, but he wouldn't accept it."

"So?"

"He seemed convinced you wouldn't be averse to his courtship.

There was no question of his wishing to rush you into marriage. It's important to him that you should finish your apprenticeship."

"Three years is a long time and I may have all sorts of plans at the end of it. You know that I want to go to Italy at some point in my life. The Renaissance was the very fount of great art and I must see some of those masterly works for myself and be free to paint there."

"Pieter is not tying you down to anything. All he asks is that he may see you sometimes during your apprenticeship."

She did not speak again until she had finished rolling up the surplus linen and putting it neatly with her scissors into the little basket on her lap. Then she gave a slow nod. "I'd like to see him there, but not in courtship. If that is understood there is no problem."

"Shall I tell him or will you?"

"I will. I also have something to pass on to you." She paused. "I had an odd sort of conversation with Ludolf today. Through becoming your patron he feels patriarchal towards us as a family."

"I've never heard of that happening before."

"Neither have I, but his goodwill is towards you, Father."

"Very kind of him. He's a most considerate man." A vagueness had clouded Hendrick's eyes even as his thoughts shied away violently, almost with a sense of horror, from looking for a loan in that quarter. It would be a final, rock-bottom humiliation that he could not face. He had presented himself as a man of comparative means, a successful artist well used to the kind of price for his work that the portrait of Francesca had fetched. Ludolf, on the basis of what he had paid the first time, had bought those surplus pictures from the studio at figures that were higher than those a more renowned artist might have looked for. Hendrick knew that if he approached his patron humbly, confessing to the abject folly that had carried him away, he would not only destroy his position in Ludolf's eyes but would similarly degrade the value of his work on both the artistic and monetary sides. His patron might never buy from him again.

The following evening, on his way home with slow dejected footsteps, Hendrick stopped on a bridge over the Amstel River and looked down into the glinting water. Suicide was strongly in his mind and he leaned his arms on the parapet in blackest misery. Nobody except for

Pieter had offered him as much as a stuiver throughout the whole day. He wished he could send to Janetje for a loan, but that brief acquaintanceship with her husband had told him that Giovanni was not a man to relent on a promise extracted and she would be allowed no voice in the matter. Similarly he could not approach Heer Korver, knowing his neighbour's strict views on gambling. Hendrick clenched his hands on the parapet in deepest despair. How good it would be to feel the river close over his head and take his troubles from him. He remembered the time when he had fallen drunk into a canal in the dead of night and survived with a purse of gold as a bonus. That couldn't happen again even though his need for himself and his daughters was greater now than— His daughters! A horrifying realization flashed through his mind. Dear God, if he killed himself the debts would devolve upon them! That was intolerable! With a shudder he moved away from the parapet.

"Salted herrings! The best in Amsterdam!" A pedlar with a barrel of the small silvery fillets was plying his trade just beyond the bridge. Hendrick opened his purse strings and bought six fillets. Holding each up by the tail end, he tilted back his head and dropped the cheap street delicacy into his mouth. Spiced and salty, they inflamed his thirst and his step was lighter as he turned into the nearest tavern to start quenching it until he was as oblivious to his misfortunes as if he had drowned himself in the Amstel.

Francesca had expected Pieter to come again to her home to hear what decision she had made, but he did not appear. Neither did he come to Ludolf's house, although he was not yet expected there. When he did present his plans they would not only show the new layout of the garden; there would also be drawings of important areas, and all flowers and bushes and any additional trees would be listed.

Ludolf was also awaiting a visitor. Every day he expected to see Hendrick standing before him with hat in hand. He had heard from his informant that the artist was in a permanent state of semi-intoxication while making the rounds of everybody from whom he had the remotest chance of raising a loan. One day he had gone to Rotterdam, where he had some connections, but that had obviously been without result, because the next day he was again on the same mission in Amsterdam.

Ludolf judged that it had reached a point where Hendrick's only option was either to approach one of the many notorious moneylenders, whose rates of interest topped any others in the city, or to come to the one man he least wanted to ask. There was no certainty of knowing which way the scales would dip, but it was hard to believe the artist, pompous and conceited though he was, would not realize eventually that in the choice of two evils he should turn first to his patron, whatever the consequences.

Hendrick's hands might have healed more quickly if he had not knocked them afresh when reeling against doorways and once slithering down a flight of steps on a wharf. This spate of drinking distressed all three of his daughters and they decided among themselves it was due to his frustration in not being able to paint all the time the cuts remained open. One morning when Francesca repeated her invitation that he should spend the day at Ludolf's house he agreed to go with her, but on a harsh and tragic note with something like the glint of tears in his red-rimmed eyes. Sybylla promptly burst into tears, moved by his distress that she could not comprehend, and buried her face against his chest.

"Don't cry, little one," he said, raising his hand automatically to stroke her hair consolingly. "I'm only still a little drunk from last night."

Francesca also spoke to her. "Why not fetch Father's favourite brushes and his palette. He may feel able to put a few correcting touches to my painting of Ludolf at this morning's sitting."

Sybylla seized on this chance to do something that would lift her father's curious melancholia. As soon as she came back with what she had been sent to fetch, she went ahead on her own in the coach while Hendrick and Francesca walked to the van Deventer home.

"I need fresh air," he had explained.

She enjoyed the walk too, her arm threaded through his. If it had not been for Sybylla's enjoyment of the ride she would have walked every morning. It was only in the evenings, when she was tired from working all day, that she was glad of the coach waiting for them, even more so when it happened to be pouring with rain.

When Ludolf entered the studio and saw Hendrick discussing Francesca's painting with her, he knew that the artist had finally succumbed

to the only real outlet open to him from his financial difficulties. The intense strain of the past days showed in that haggard face and the artist's whole frame seemed to have shrunk. Alcohol and despair had certainly taken their toll.

"I'm extremely glad to see you, Hendrick!" They had been on Christian-name terms since the first evening of cards. "You will stay to eat with us, of course. What do you think of your daughter's work, then? I've yet to see it."

"She has done well," Hendrick replied. "Why not look at it now? It's in the final stage when I would permit the sitter to view."

"Oh no!" Ludolf laughed with every show of good nature, raising a hand against the invitation as he sat down in the chair. "I'm waiting until Francesca tells me it is completely finished."

Hendrick did add a few touches to the painting, just able to hold his brush with the aid of the support of the maulstick. It stimulated the yearning in him to get back to work on his tax-collector painting, but like a weight on his brain was the moment when he must throw himself on his patron's mercy. He decided to approach him after they had eaten.

The moment came when they rose from the table. As Francesca returned to the studio and Sybylla went from the room with her, Hendrick cleared his throat. "I wonder if I might have a word in private with you."

"Not now, I fear, my good fellow." Ludolf glanced at the clock and then drew his pocket watch out of its embroidered cover to check the time. "I have to be at my warehouse in twenty minutes."

"It is a matter of utmost urgency."

Ludolf showed surprise. "Do you intend to prepare me for not liking Francesca's portrait of me?"

"No. Nothing like that."

Ludolf looked pointedly at the clock again. "I really must be going. I'm busy tomorrow, but the day after the banquet at midmorning—"

"That's almost three days!" He dared not risk meeting either Otto or Claudius at the banquet with the promissory notes still unpaid. Neither could he risk offending Ludolf by staying away. "I can't wait that long!"

For the first time Ludolf appeared to take note of Hendrick's desper-

ate expression. "Hmm. I can see you are troubled. Ride with me in the coach and we can talk on the way."

In the coach Hendrick thought that if the situation had been contrived to be as awkward as possible for him it could not have surpassed these circumstances. How did one begin to ask a man short of time for a huge loan with all the distractions of a busy street passing by? To add to everything else, Ludolf had a sheaf of important-looking papers in his hand, at which he kept glancing and which were obviously uppermost in his mind.

"Ludolf," he began, and then hesitated.

From the opposite seat, Ludolf looked across at him. "Well? Speak up, my friend. What is it?"

The amiable courtesy could not veil a slight impatience. Somehow Hendrick found his voice. "First of all I should like to thank you for not having mentioned my ill fortune while we dined today, or during your sittings with Francesca." He had thought that a good way to start, but now he was not sure of anything anymore.

"I know the prim attitude most women hold towards gambling losses," Ludolf replied with a shrug. "It's best to keep them in ignorance of occasional bouts of ill luck." He chatted on flowingly about how he tried to keep from his sick wife whatever he thought might distress her. Frantically Hendrick awaited his chance to speak again. Had he not known his patron for the kindly man he was, it would have been possible to believe the delay in letting him speak was deliberate. Perhaps it was! Anyone as rich as Ludolf would have become adept over the years in thwarting appeals for money. Then, even as Hendrick felt it was impossible to go on with what he had intended to say, Ludolf gestured encouragingly.

"I'm talking too much. Pray pardon me. As I daresay you've noticed," he added with a touch of humour, "the only time I'm silent is when I'm concentrating on play at the tables. We really must have another evening of cards again soon—not just on the evening of the banquet, when the players in the card room will be an assorted bunch, but us four keen players on our own again. That should give you the opportunity to recoup your losses."

"That chance can't be mine." Hendrick clasped his shaking hands

together. Into his artist's mind there sprang a picture of how he must look and the title of such a painting came with it. *The Abject Borrower.* "I'm in a most terrible predicament. I've not yet settled my debts to our fellow players and I can't foresee any time in the near future when I'll be able to!"

Ludolf looked extremely grave and he put the sheaf of papers on the seat beside him as he leaned forward. "This is a dreadful admission to hear. I had no idea that this was what you wanted to speak to me about. I thought— Well, no matter now. How did this situation arise?"

Although Hendrick gave the best explanation possible, saying that he was carried away by the excitement of the game, it sounded weak and feeble even to his own ears. No matter what he said, nothing could take away the fact that his playing for stakes beyond his capacity was tantamount to theft. Moreover, settling gaming debts quickly was a matter of honour, and failure to do so meant ostracism and disgrace in any gaming circle. He struggled on and when he had finally managed to utter his request for a loan he lapsed into a stunned state of misery, seeing how deeply he had shocked his patron, who was perhaps his patron no longer.

Ludolf sat back in his seat, shaking his head slowly as if words failed him at this lamentable disclosure. When eventually he did speak it was in a slow and weighty voice.

"It is entirely against my principles to lend money for gaming debts. No man such as you with a family should jeopardize his responsibilities in such a foolhardy—I will say criminal—way. And to such a vast sum! A fortune, *mijnheer,*" he emphasized, as if Hendrick might not be fully aware of it.

A rebellious streak in Hendrick made him want to retort that it would not be a fortune to Ludolf, wallowing in wealth, although it was to him. "I know," he croaked, closing his eyes to shut out the black abyss waiting to drag him down. Refusal was in Ludolf's every intonation. "I'm a lost man if you don't help me."

There was a seemingly endless silence before Ludolf spoke again and then more leniently. "You've been a fool, but you've placed your problem before me and as your patron I must think how best to solve it for you." He stroked his pointed beard as he looked unseeingly out the

window as if deep in thought, fully aware that the distraught artist was waiting on tenterhooks. "My first move must be to purchase your promissory notes. That would lift from you the immediate need to sell your home and give you breathing space."

Hendrick almost wept with gratitude. "What can I say? This—"

"Wait!" Ludolf frowned at him sternly. "There is no guarantee that either Claudius or Otto will sell. They may feel an example should be made of you and take you to a debtors' court. If I should be successful in taking over your debts," he added after a pause of meditation, "I would set conditions and expect some collateral."

"Anything I have is yours."

"Anything?"

"Yes, on my oath! I ask only to keep my paintings of Anna."

Ludolf nodded. "I'll give you my word that I'll leave no stone unturned to do my best for you and your family. I'm thinking particularly of Francesca, who must be uppermost in your mind in the midst of all your troubles. When do you intend to tell her that her apprenticeship is not to be?"

Hendrick was glad to have something good to tell. "That has been spared me. Her stay in Delft is already financed. Whatever happens to me won't touch her."

With a sense of shock Ludolf saw his intended grip on Francesca loosened. "In what manner did that come about?" he barked harshly.

Hendrick thought miserably that surely his personal dignity had suffered enough. There was no need to let Ludolf know the true source, and in any case Pieter had wanted it kept between themselves. "Anna left all three of our daughters some money that was her own," he said, which in itself was a truthful statement. "That's how I'm able to keep Francesca from knowing anything about my present straits and I'm going to try to keep it that way for as long as possible. Once she is installed at Vermeer's studio she will be compelled by the law governing apprenticeship to fulfil her indenture time, however much she may wish to be at home with me during what may be difficult days."

At any other time Hendrick might have noticed Ludolf's reaction to what had been said in the sharp flare of nostril and ugly twist of the mouth, but neither his sight nor his reason was wholly under his com-

mand in his present taut and anxious state. With an almost puppetlike jerk of the arm, Ludolf snatched up his sheaf of papers and spoke in a clipped manner. "We have reached my warehouse. You had better alight here at the gate." He tapped fiercely with his cane for the coach to stop.

"How soon shall I know if you've been successful?" Hendrick asked, making no immediate move to alight, although he could see his patron was impatient for him to be gone.

"I'll send a messenger to your house when I'm ready to see you."

"And the debt itself, if all should go well? How am I ever to repay you?"

"This whole affair must be taken one step at a time." Ludolf's face was hard and expressionless. "We can discuss what is to be done next— whatever the outcome—after I've made my attempt to salvage you from this sordid catastrophe. Now good day to you."

Hendrick stepped out of the coach. As the door shut and Ludolf was carried forward into the cobbled yard of his warehouse he hurled the papers from him. As they fluttered about he slammed a fist into the palm of his hand and swore viciously. He had planned everything down to the last detail, but he had not allowed for an unexpected fund to weaken his total hold over the situation.

During the frequent sittings Ludolf had plenty of time to reconsider his strategy towards Francesca in view of the unexpected hitch. Since there was nothing he could do to prevent her going to Delft he would make sure that she was lodged where she could be available to him when the time came. In fact this turn of events could prove to his advantage in the end, for it was inevitable that she would be homesick at first and he would be the comforting friend visiting her until such time as she succumbed to him as his mistress. It was fortunate that he had connections at Delft, which he did visit on business of his own from time to time, and therefore none would question him calling to see the daughter of an artist whose patron he happened to be, Amalia least of all. Knowing his wife as he did, he could be sure that she would want news of Francesca, and she would be innocently pleased that he should apparently go out of his way to see the girl.

His eyes slid under their lids in Francesca's direction. As always he marvelled at his own patience in stalking her, but he needed more from her than he had ever wanted from any other woman. Once she was his mistress he doubted if his obsession would ever be slaked. He almost resented her for the savage pull on his senses, the madness she had inflicted in his blood, and it caused him just as much satisfaction to contemplate how he would punish her for it as it would be to pleasure her.

He returned his gaze to where he was supposed to be looking. She had not said anything about his erring from it and he supposed she was busy painting his wig or the fine linen cravat at his throat or some other part of his raiment. One of the marks he could count up to his own favour in this heady pursuit of her was that she had addressed him early on by his Christian name, which had been at his request.

"You may rest now if you wish, Ludolf."

He smiled across at her, thinking that maybe it would not be long before she was whispering the reverse of that invitation in the night hours.

CHAPTER I0

On the eve of the banquet Francesca stood back from her portrait of Ludolf and studied it critically. She could see her own faults, which she must strive to correct during her apprenticeship, but the overall likeness that she had captured should please him. During the hours they had spent together she had come to know him well enough to realize he would not mind that she had shown his ruthlessness, for in conversation he had made it clear that he enjoyed power and business intrigue. In her painting she had also revealed his sharp intelligence while the sly twinkle in his fierce eyes betrayed an

appreciation of bawdy humour. The whole portrait had been a challenge in more ways than one and she was thankful it was finished. She wished she could call Ludolf in to see it now, which would save her coming back in the morning, but as he was absent from the house this afternoon he had told her he would view it first on the morrow.

When she had cleaned her brushes and removed her smock, she tidied her appearance and then left the studio. Normally she spent an enjoyable half an hour with Amalia before going home, drinking tea with her, but today Neeltje waited at the foot of the stairs.

"My mistress begs you to excuse her, but she is unable to see you today."

"Is she very unwell?"

"No," Neeltje replied. "She is saving all her strength for her appearance at table tomorrow evening."

"That's sensible. Give her my good wishes."

As Francesca left the house she thought it was fortunate that Sybylla had not visited today, but had been occupied at home preparing what she would wear at the banquet. It had given Amalia all day to conserve her strength. Rain was pelting down and she ran down the wet steps to the waiting coach and was quick to get into it. Its door had not yet been closed when there was a slight scuffle outside. Leaning forward, she saw that the coach servant holding the door was trying to push Pieter away.

"It's all right," she exclaimed quickly. "I know this gentleman. But I'm getting out to walk with him."

The coach servant looked worried. "Pray pardon me, *mejuffrouw*. Anyone of your acquaintance has the right to ride with you."

"I know." She was stepping out, Pieter having put out his hand to her. "You were only doing your duty, but this has nothing to do with that." It was obvious to her why Pieter had come and she did not want to talk to him in Ludolf's coach, almost as if somehow it would taint their conversation. This instinct reminded her of her first impression of Ludolf. All her efforts over the past weeks to overcome her initial dislike of him were swept away and she realized how her dread of him had never lifted. She drew closer to Pieter than she had intended and he threw his cloak over hers for added protection. Rain was running off

the wide brim of his hat, but she was close enough to him to escape the drips.

"I was lucky to catch you at this moment," he said. "I understood from your father that you usually leave a little later." Beside them the coach rolled away.

"I do. There was a slight change of programme today."

"I was far down the street when I saw you come out of the house and I sprinted all the way. I had to talk to you on our own. I called at your home half an hour ago and Master Visser told me that you would be giving me your decision about my seeing you in Delft. I'll take you to a hostelry out of the rain."

"No, we can't talk with other people around. Let's walk."

"I'll not see you soaked. Come home with me."

She agreed. They hurried along, heads down against the increasing downpour, and finally they broke into a run along the last stretch of the street that brought them to his house. Vrouw de Hout came hurrying to take their wet cloaks, pleased to see Francesca again, and having a pair of buckled shoes ready for Pieter to change into. She darted away to return a minute later bringing Francesca a pair of house slippers from a cupboard of such footwear kept for guests in almost every home.

Pieter took Francesca through to the same parlour she had sat in after his rescue of her from the mob. The curtains were drawn against the early twilight and there was a good fire burning. This time she did not sit down, for Pieter, after closing the door behind them, held her lightly to him within the circle of his arms. Her face, upturned to his, bore an expression of intense seriousness.

"How shall I begin?" she said as much to herself as to him.

"Be totally frank with me."

"That's how I would want to be now and at all times." She wished that his eyes were not looking so deeply into hers and that she was less conscious of his physical presence so near her. "I value your friendship most highly, and I will even say most dearly, but there is no room in my life for commitment in courtship or in any other way, except that which I hold for my work. I have an aim to fulfil which has been with me since I was a child and there is no turning away from it."

"I understand that and also I know of your hopes of living in Italy for a while."

"I don't remember mentioning that to you."

"You haven't. But the day I delivered the bulbs and saw you for the first time there in your father's studio, you were speaking to him of your dreams of going to Florence one day. I've not forgotten the enthusiasm with which you spoke of it."

She spread her hands outwards a little and then put palms and fingers together. "For all I know, when that chance comes I may decide to live there permanently."

"I can't believe from what I know of you that you would ever be able to cut yourself free from your Dutch roots. But I'm not asking for promises now or tomorrow or at any specified date in the future. I'd never cage a bird. Do you think I'd do less for the woman I love?"

She caught her breath at his tender words and stepped away from him. "Don't speak of love!"

He eyed her keenly. "Why should that alarm you?"

"Because it's only friendship that I want to discuss or even to consider. Nothing more."

"I'm not against that, but why should I not try to make you see that I'd never allow myself to be a barrier to your art?"

"You haven't begun to comprehend the situation!" She was vehement. "Don't you see? It is my work itself that would divide us, not you! My need to paint would take hours from any life we might share! The studio would take priority over the kitchen. Grinding pigments would come before playing hostess to company. How could I create on canvas when the only creating that you or any other man in Christendom expects from a wife is the conception of children!"

He showed no surprise at her outspokenness, because it was what he had asked of her, but he raised an eyebrow, his lips curling wryly. "What an argument! You must have given a great deal of thought to the matter."

"I have over the past three or four years—long before we met. I decided that in fairness to any man I would never be a wife. It would only cause trouble and unhappiness. If you can accept my decision—

2
1
1

and you must be sure about it—then we can meet sometimes in Delft and it will gladden me to see you."

He shrugged resignedly. "Then I'll abide by your terms. Friendship it shall be. Let the future look after itself. Neither of us knows what it will bring, but we should place a seal on our agreement."

He took her about the waist with one arm and placed a quick, light kiss upon her lips. She was relieved that all had gone so well and was about to speak when his other arm went about her and he almost lifted her from her feet as he crushed her to him, his lips sweeping hers apart. She felt a swift, unbidden flame of yearning sear up from the pit of her stomach and she clung to him as his warm mouth possessed hers in a deep and passionate kiss such as she had never experienced before. It was an awakening for her, a releasing of emotional and physical desires that she had long kept subdued. Swept away by the moment, she surrendered to the fierce glory of his mouth on hers.

When their kiss ended she opened her eyes dazedly and was instantly aware of where she was and that he was still holding her. She spoke huskily. "I didn't know it was to be such a special kind of friendship."

His smile was serious. "Have no fear. It will not make lovers of us."

She nodded, knowing she should be reassured. "I must go home now or else everyone will start worrying about me."

As on the previous occasion when she had been in his house, he escorted her home. The rain had stopped and the sky had cleared. At her door he drew back, emphasizing the distance she had put between them. As she bade him farewell and entered the house, she was conscious of a sense of loss, almost as if she had left something of herself with him. Then she dismissed the notion determinedly. Nobody questioned why she had not come home in the van Deventer coach, for Pieter had not been seen.

Later in the evening when she was on her own with Hendrick she told him of the agreement that had been made. He nodded and patted her hand, his thoughts seemingly elsewhere. His unrelieved melancholia was having a dampening effect on the whole household and was worrying Aletta and Sybylla as well as Francesca. It had been hoped that his spirits would lift when he began painting again, but this was not proving to be the case. Francesca was reminded all too vividly of his state of

mind after her mother's death. She tried to talk to him about his dreadful gloom.

"Take heart again, Father," she urged. "Damaging your hands as well as the painful swelling in your fingers was a frightening experience for you, but they have healed and are becoming more mobile every day. I believe that the special concoction of herbs that Maria made for you to drink each morning is having more effect than the treatment with warm oil."

He gave a heavy nod. "I know."

"Just try to remember that we have no worries at the moment. Everyone is well, which is more important than anything and we are not in debt. You have an enthusiastic patron in Ludolf and you told me yourself that the two gentlemen with whom you played cards expressed an interest in your work. It seems as if it is the start of a new stage in life for you."

She was not to know that every word she spoke pierced him through. He managed what he supposed was a ghastly smile, but she did not seem to notice anything amiss. "Don't let any mood of mine blight your excitement over going to Delft," he insisted, still smiling. "I rejoice that you are to have your great chance. I'm a little low at the present time, but all will soon be well again."

"Indeed it will!" She thought she detected a spark of his old optimism in his voice and took it to be a good sign. He had made an effort to smile again, forced though it was.

He was relieved when, after a little more conversation, she left him to himself. There was so much he had to think about. He had heard nothing from Ludolf. Almost hourly he had expected word to be sent, but nothing had happened. All day he had worked on his tax-collector painting, but each brushstroke had been almost automatic, for he kept an ear primed for a knock on the door, having instructed Griet to bring him any message immediately.

He stole a glance at the clock. At this hour tomorrow he would be in the midst of the festivities at Ludolf's house and he did not doubt that Otto and Claudius would both find a chance to challenge him about his debts to them. His whole future was hanging in the balance.

He gazed into the parlour fire. Why had Ludolf not been in touch with him?

Ludolf enthused over his portrait to Francesca and applauded it exuberantly as if it had been unveiled for him in a public place. "Your work should be displayed in the best public gallery in Amsterdam!"

"Oh no!" she protested, shaking her head.

"But you have captured me exactly. My bad points are there as well as my good ones and I wouldn't have it otherwise." Stepping forward, he lifted the portrait in its newly carved and gilded frame from the easel. "Now you shall see where I intend to hang it."

Together they went downstairs to the reception hall, where a pair of library steps had been placed by the marble-canopied fireplace. A French landscape, which had hung above it previously, had already been removed and propped against the wall. Ludolf went up the steps and hung his portrait in its place.

"Is it straight?" he asked her.

"Not quite. Adjust the top right-hand corner. Yes! That's it!"

He climbed down again and stood at her side, looking up at the portrait with her. "What do you think?"

There was no doubt but that it made a striking impact on the eye. The austere composition, Ludolf posed in a broad-based triangle, gave drama to the portrait. That face of marred good looks was all the more arresting through having been painted without any concessions, further dramatized by the plumed black hat and the flow of periwig, the white lace collar, the sheen of velvet, the glitter of braid and jewelled rings, all against crimson drapery. The whole picture was set off against the dark green silk-panelled walls of the reception hall with the white marble canopy below and the snow-bright plasterwork of the ceiling above.

She had had Hendrick's permission to sign the painting if she made her signature inconspicuous. In the lower right-hand corner it was just visible. Only if one peered closely was it possible to see that the "r" of Visser swept downwards to curve at the end and enclose a tiny cream-coloured tulip.

"You've done me much honour by hanging my work in such an

important place. Everyone who comes into the house will see it," she commented.

"That's what I want. I'm particularly pleased that it will be viewed by so many people this evening."

She went across to the French landscape. "Where shall you hang this one now?"

"Help me decide." He snatched it up. "Let's go from room to room until we find the right place."

Although the house was newish it followed in many ways the style of older houses, having a number of small rooms leading off corridors, frequently at different levels on the same floor and linked by steps. Either he or she found fault with every place in which they tried the painting, he holding it up against the wall until it became quite a joke between them. Buoyed up by her own private happiness that her task was done, that the start of her apprenticeship was now only hours away and, equally important to her, that she and Pieter were still to meet and retain their friendship, she laughed easily and readily, able this morning to forget that she had no real liking for this man whose face she had come to know so well. She declared herself reminded of childhood games of hide-and-seek as they went up and down steps and seemingly around in circles. Finally they settled on hanging the landscape in the library, trying a new place they had missed when in there before.

"Yes! That's just right," she declared, studying the position of the picture, and she stepped back to view it from further away. She had not known that Ludolf was standing close behind her and her heel came down on his foot. For him it was more than he could bear after weeks of restraint. The fragrance of her hair and skin was in his nostrils and something seemed to explode in his head. Before she could turn, laughing, to apologize he seized her by the arms as if to support her being off balance, and jerked her back against him. Her spine became rigid, her mirth swept away by an overwhelming fear of this man whose face she could no longer see, all too aware of his quickened breathing.

"I hope I didn't hurt your toe," she voiced with apparent calmness in an attempt to level the situation. "You may release me now."

But his hands did not loosen their grip. "Francesca," he breathed against her hair, "I'll never release you."

To her alarm it sounded like a vow. She felt as if the library had become a trap, for she was shut in here with him away from the rest of the house. The prospect of being kissed by him was abhorrent to her, but a far greater dread was mounting, the fear that he would use his powerful strength to put his hands on her flesh, combining with still more terror, unnamed and unfocused, that was chilling her whole body.

"You're creasing my sleeves," she protested mundanely in a further attempt to defuse his mood, certain that if she struggled to free herself he would whip her around and into his embrace. If she kept her wits that could be avoided. "And you're bruising my arms with your hold. Let this game be finished."

To her relief he obeyed her, but even as she would have stepped swiftly away he had cupped his hands over her breasts and buried a passionate kiss into her neck.

"No!" she cried out frantically, plucking desperately at his hands. Neither she nor he had heard the library door open or knew that Neeltje was present until that moment when she spoke. "The mistress wishes to see you, master."

Francesca felt a tremor pass through him as though even in the instant of being discovered in his indiscretion he could scarcely bear to loosen his limpetlike clasp. Then freed by him, she whirled away and saw him turn abruptly towards Neeltje like a towering giant with a temper-ridden visage that would have quailed any but the strongest-willed, his whole frame shaking.

"This is not your mistress's apartment," he roared threateningly. "How dare you come creeping in here!"

Francesca stepped forward quickly, not at all sure that he was not about to strike the woman to the floor. "Would you fetch my cloak, please, Neeltje? I'm leaving now."

"Yes, *mejuffrouw*. Would you care to accompany me?" It was as if nothing untoward had been witnessed or interrupted by the woman.

Ludolf spoke harshly. "Francesca! Wait!"

She paused in the doorway to look back at him coldly. "Didn't you hear what Neeltje said? Amalia is waiting to see you. I would never come between husband and wife on any occasion!"

Neeltje trotted slightly ahead, her soft-soled house shoes making no

sound on the marble floor. Francesca thought it odd that the woman had made such a timely appearance in the library, almost as if it had been planned to the second. No word was exchanged between them until Neeltje had put the cloak about Francesca's shoulders.

"You will be back for the banquet this evening, won't you, *mejuffrouw?*"

"I don't know." Francesca was tying the strings of her cloak. That intense fear of Ludolf had not subsided and she could not wait to get out of this house as quickly as possible. She could still feel his squeezing hands on her.

"You must, *mejuffrouw*. That is, if you care anything for my mistress."

Francesca stared at the woman. "What do you mean?"

"If you don't come to the banquet this evening, you who have painted the portrait that is to be displayed to some of the master's most important friends, what is Vrouw van Deventer to think? Do you suppose she doesn't know how attracted her husband is to other women? She imagines she keeps everything to herself and normally I wouldn't have spoken to you in this way, but I don't want her to have the least suspicion about what happened between you and the master today."

"I'm thankful that you came."

"It was not by chance that I arrived when I did. I know his nature. There have been young maidservants in this house who have had to leave, the reason always kept from my mistress. I owe you an apology for not coming sooner, but I had to remind Vrouw van Deventer of something she wished to speak to her husband about, which gave me a plausible excuse for interrupting."

"I'll always be grateful for your consideration."

"I did it for my mistress as much as for you."

"I realize that, but it doesn't change anything. In view of what you have told me, I'll come to the banquet this evening, but I implore you to see that my place at table is nowhere near the head of it."

"I'll do my best, *mejuffrouw.*"

With her cloak about her shoulders, Francesca crossed the reception hall, making for the entrance door, which had been opened for her so many times during the past weeks. Now when she had almost reached

it, the manservant ready to swing it wide, Ludolf's voice rang out to her.

"Francesca! Pray do not be late this evening. You are my guest of honour."

She did not turn, but lifted her chin, choking back all she could not say. "I'll be on time," she promised crisply. Then she swept out of the house.

He smiled to himself. So once again she was to be more forgiving than he had expected her to be. All the consideration and kindness he had shown to her previously during her time in his house, all at great cost to his own emotions, had paid off. As an artist's daughter she had shown herself to be more worldly than most young women of her age, obviously able to grasp that there were times when a man's self-control broke when tempted by the proximity of a beautiful woman. Desire for her still ran hot in his veins.

He turned for the stairs and on his way spoke quietly to the manservant on duty, giving a summons that was to be obeyed by the person concerned. While the man went on the errand, Ludolf continued up the flight and along to the studio. Francesca's easel still stood in its place, ready to be returned to the supplier as arranged. She had packed up all the materials the previous evening and they were neatly stacked, the brushes cleaned. He sensed her everywhere around him, able to see her face, her slim form and the sweep of her skirts whichever way he turned. His obsession for her throbbed in his brain and gripped his loins. He paced the floor until a certain maidservant, buxom and prettier than the rest, came into the room.

Out of habit she locked the door behind her, even though it had not happened in this room before. She pulled up her skirts and looked at him inquiringly, hoping he was not in an ill mood, because bruises were not always easy to hide. He knocked aside the screen and gestured towards the bed. Then he followed her to it. Talk did not come into their arrangement. He had obscene signs for everything.

Amalia started to dress early that evening. Neeltje had to do everything for her, from slipping her diamond earbobs into her lobes to kneeling to

2
1
8

place her feet right into her satin shoes, for she lacked the strength to do anything for herself. How she was going to get through receiving the guests she did not know, although Ludolf allowed her to sit in a chair instead of standing at his side in the reception hall. When she had to move he would support her with a strong arm to her place at the opposite end of the table to his. Throughout the feast he would appear to keep a fond eye on her, occasionally lifting his glass in a silent toast to her alone, and all the time she would go through with the masquerade, her breeding and upbringing, and even her natural good manners, preventing her from upsetting others with any indication that all was not as it appeared.

"How do you feel now, ma'am?" Neeltje asked anxiously.

"Am I ready?" Amalia had kept her eyes closed while seated before her mirror, as if by concentrating on feeling better she might achieve it.

"Yes, ma'am. Shall I help you to stand now?"

"Wait a moment. How long have I?"

"A while yet before you have to leave your apartment. I meant only to see you through to the couch in your dayroom."

"That will also lessen the distance I'll have to walk to my door when the time comes," she said, making a little joke.

Neeltje helped her to stand and she saw herself in a full-length mirror. Her seamstress had recently had a wicker frame made on which to fit her garments, so that she was spared the ordeal of standing. Now she was seeing herself in the new gown for the first time. Ludolf had surpassed himself in his selection. The gown was of a rich orangey-pink taffeta, which gave its own warmth to her skin, and it parted from waist to hem, cut in such a way as to reveal an ivory underskirt, ornamented with wide bands of gilded braid running down the middle and along the hem. It rustled enchantingly. If only it had been a gift of love from him instead of a smug tribute to his own generosity towards a sickly wife for others to see. How often she had heard the whispered adjectives "devoted" and "adoring" applied by others to his attitude towards her.

"A step at a time, ma'am," Neeltje urged gently.

Her pace was slow and she saw the couch beyond the open double doors of her bedchamber as distant as if it were a thousand miles away. How was she ever to reach it? She knew she was going through one of

her low periods when the least exertion was really too much for her, but Ludolf had insisted on her presence and her sense of duty compelled her to obey him.

They reached the couch at last. She sank back against the cushions while Neeltje arranged her sleeves and skirts to avoid unnecessary creasing. "I thank you, Neeltje. What should I do without you?"

"Shall I leave you now until it's time, ma'am?"

"Yes, but allow an extra quarter of an hour to see me through to the reception hall. Your master likes me to be in my chair there well before the guests are due and I don't want to hurry."

While Neeltje went to tidy the bedchamber, replacing lids on cosmetic jars and putting away discarded garments, Amalia lay gazing at the Pieter de Hooch painting that could always transport her back to her childhood home. Daily it had become a greater source of comfort to her as she imagined she was going along its passageway, holding her mother's hand, to the sunlit street that could be glimpsed at the end of it.

But that was all in the past and she must bring herself back to the present and the ordeal of the banquet ahead of her. If only she could lie here until the morning she would have more strength again. There was a curious pattern to the rise and fall of her condition. She could have been carried about the house in an indoor sedan chair had she wished. Ludolf had had one made when her strange illness had first come upon her, but the doctor had advised that she should walk whenever possible, fearful that she might lose the use of her legs. Perhaps this evening she should take a dose of the potion prescribed for such emergencies. She did not like to take it and her doctor did not encourage it, for it made her strangely light-headed, but it did release some inner strength in her, enabling her to believe she could walk any distance and even run, although that was a mere illusion.

She reached for her casket of medicines, but in taking care not to disarrange her sleeves she misjudged the lifting of it as she had on one or two previous occasions. A sharp cry broke from her as it crashed to the floor, scattering its contents. As Neeltje hurried in from the bedchamber, Amalia saw that the flask of the potion she needed had cracked and the liquid was spreading into a dark patch on the floor.

Upstairs Ludolf left the ministrations of his valet, well pleased with his appearance. His new clothes, ordered specially for this occasion, fitted him perfectly. The long coat of corn-coloured heavy silk was slightly curved in at the waist, flaring fuller at the knee-length hem, and was fastened with twenty gold buttons. There were more gold buttons on the deep, turned-back cuffs, and a cascade of Flemish lace at his throat was newer than the wide collars that many men still wore. His breeches were of velvet in the same shade as his coat and there were large chased gold buckles on his shoes. He was proud of having kept his figure, and if his stomach was less hard-muscled than in his rougher days, at least he had no paunch. His wigmaker had informed him that the new periwig, now caping his shoulders, was made entirely of a virgin's hair, which amused him, and he had made a lewd joke that startled the fellow, who was not attracted to the opposite sex.

Downstairs he made a tour of inspection. There was a general last-minute bustle of servants, but everything appeared to be ready. The banquet table, now set for forty people, had ten silver candelabra shining down its length to supplement the glow from the crystal chandeliers suspended from the painted ceiling. He stopped in front of the painting of Francesca as Flora, and for a moment he almost hated her for driving him demented in his obsession for her. Wherever he was and whatever he was doing, she was never out of his mind. Well, tonight should settle everything. He intended to hold Hendrick to ransom and the price to be paid was Francesca.

He strolled back to the reception hall expecting to see Amalia in the brocaded chair that had been placed ready for her, but she was not there. This was surprising, for normally she liked a considerable rest after the exertion of moving from her apartment and before the first coach would draw up outside. He had sent his own coach to fetch the Vissers, but when he had established Francesca in a house of her choice —where she could paint to her heart's content when he was not there —she should have a coach of her own. While she was in Delft any serious rival who might seek her favours could be easily disposed of on a dark night. Neither was there any chance of a runaway marriage, because no son or daughter under the age of thirty could marry without a parent's consent and Hendrick would be hamstrung over that.

Ludolf's thoughts switched again to Amalia. Where was she? He looked impatiently down the corridor along which she should come, but she was not to be seen. It would be at least twenty minutes before the first guest could be expected and as yet only the menservants on duty were at their posts in the entrance hall that led to the reception hall. Usually if she needed to be carried from her apartment to the reception hall in the sedan chair, Neeltje would come to let him know, but that annoying creature, who had made such an unwelcome appearance in the library, must still be with her mistress. Normally he never went to Amalia's apartment on these occasions, knowing that sometimes the simple effort of dressing was enough to make her rest again for a while. Never once had she failed in her duties as hostess, except during those periods when she had been totally bedridden in the doctor's care.

He paced up and down. It was important that Francesca, arriving for this occasion of splendour, should see him, a well-built, still virile man, totally uncomplemented by this thin, fragile wife at his side, who would appear almost waiflike in spite of her grand clothes. Francesca could not help but excuse him further for his behaviour that morning and would pity him being tied to a poor wretch who could give him neither sexual comfort nor children. It was one thing to see Amalia as an invalid and another to see her failing to match a husband and host of his standing.

Realizing that his increasing annoyance had brought about a need for him to relieve himself, he went from the reception hall into a corridor that ran parallel to that leading in the direction of Amalia's apartment. On the way he met four maidservants hastening to take up their posts for collecting the guests' outdoor garments.

"Hurry up!" he snapped brusquely before entering the privy room. When he came out again a quick glance into the reception hall showed him the maidservants giggling quietly together, their backs turned to him and Amalia's chair still empty. Fuming, he decided he would fetch her, or at least discover the reason for her delay. He took a shortcut through the library, which brought him out by her apartment. When he flung open her door he was amazed to find her still lying prone on the couch and making no attempt to rise. Since she was alone he let his wrath fly.

"In the devil's name, why aren't you in the reception hall instead of lying here?"

Fear had leaped into her strained, white face at his furious tone. "I lack the strength to move, Ludolf. My legs won't support me at the moment."

He came and loomed over her where she lay. "Where's Neeltje?" he demanded. "Why hasn't she sent for your sedan chair?"

"She was worried about me and has gone to Dr. Mattheusz's house."

He saw she did look extremely unwell, as happened during her lapses. It maddened him that it should have occurred on this evening of evenings. "What about that special potion? It always sees you through half the evening and I excuse you the rest."

"I was clumsy and spilt it. That's why I've sent Neeltje for more."

"How long has Neeltje been gone?"

"Only about ten minutes."

She had no inkling that her simply given information should come like a revelation to him. With a terrible rise of exhilaration he saw that, without warning or the least forethought on his part, fate had presented him with a unique and totally unlooked-for opportunity to rid himself of the main barrier that all along had stood between Francesca and him. Every one of the devious ways he had thought of to get around it could be cast aside. The servants were busy. None had seen him come here. Neither could Neeltje return under another quarter of an hour.

"Never mind, Amalia," he said thickly and on a dangerously gentle note. "You did right to send for the potion. I'm very pleased that you did."

Those were the last words she was ever to hear. Even as terror swept through her at the sudden glint of murder in his eyes, he snatched the satin cushion from under her head and a second later was holding it pressed down over her face. Her arms flailed helplessly, her cries muffled.

She struggled longer than he had expected. Then abruptly she became limp, one slim hand dangling. Slowly he lifted the cushion away. She might have been sleeping. Apart from a slight dishevelment of her hair and a smear of carmine left by her lips on the cushion there was no sign of violence. He raised her head and slipped the cushion back into

place. Then he turned her face sideways into it, making sure the smear was exactly level with her lips. He tidied a strand or two of her hair, smoothed her skirt where it had become twisted in her struggle and then stepped back from the couch. He felt excited and released, intoxicated with liberty, but he had yet to return to the reception hall without being observed.

Swiftly he went to the door and opened it a crack to look out. The corridor was deserted. He slipped out of the apartment at once and closed the door silently after him. Within seconds he was in the library, where he drew breath and wiped the ball of his hand across his brow. He had murdered before and killed more men than he could recall with his sword during the years he had absented himself from Holland, but surely no death could have been less premeditated than that of his own wife. He had done the one thing he had vowed never to do, but then he had never supposed such perfect circumstances would deliver her into his hands.

Leaving the library, he hastened back to the privy room. Once inside he listened until he heard another clack of heels. Then he emerged, adjusting his coat. There had been witnesses to his going in there and this witness to his coming out again was the maidservant who had her own way of obliging him. She had a raw cut on her lip where he had probably bitten her and one eye was swollen and closed, purple as a plum, while her kitchen attire showed she was to be kept out of the guests' sight. She stopped to let him go by, but her gaze was reproachful. He slid a pearl ring from his little finger and slipped it down her cleavage. Then he patted her cheek meaningfully before strolling on into the reception hall. Almost in the same instant the first guests were being admitted and he was there to welcome them.

Half of those expected had arrived when Hendrick appeared with his daughters. The artist's face was so hangdog with anxiety that Ludolf could have laughed. He went forward swiftly to clap a hand on Hendrick's shoulder and speak in a low voice into his ear.

"Take heart, my friend. All is not lost. The promissory notes are mine."

Hendrick's relief was like the sun coming out. From a dragging walk he seemed to bounce on his toes. Ludolf's hooded lids hid the incredu-

lous look in his eyes at the change in the man. Hendrick was still as deep in the mire as before, but the fact that he believed himself in debt to a more tolerant person had created the most extraordinary upsurge of good humour. But Ludolf had no time to think more about the father when there were the daughters to greet, and Francesca in particular. From the moment of her entry her desirable beauty had hit him as it always did. She was attired in a currant-red velvet gown she had not worn in his presence before. The effect of it with her brilliant hair, dressed this evening with seed pearls wound into the coil, was dazzling. Out of caution he greeted her sisters before turning to her.

"My dear Francesca, you do me more honour by coming this evening than you could ever know."

She read the apology in his words, but was not softened by it. The incident in itself had been nothing. Ardent young men had embraced her and sought her kisses many times in the past and in reality there should have been no difference in this incident. But there had been and it lay with Ludolf himself, impossible to define and pinpoint, except in the certain knowledge that he was a man too sophisticated and ruthless to be easily diverted from whatever he wanted.

"Where is Amalia? I can't see her anywhere and I'm most anxious for Aletta to meet her."

Ludolf looked around and raised his eyebrows as if in surprise that his wife was not present. "Is Amalia not here yet? No, I can see her chair has been put back against the wall. When she has not appeared by a certain time it means she has decided not to be present after all."

Francesca became anxious. "Then she is not as well as she had hoped to be?"

"I fear not."

Aletta, who with Sybylla was still at Francesca's side, shook her head regretfully. "I've heard so much about your wife," she said to Ludolf, "and I was so sure that I was about to meet her at last."

He leaned towards the sisters in order that other guests should not hear. "I daresay she would like to see the three of you on your own for a few minutes later on. Her nonappearance usually means she is not up to talking to many people throughout a whole evening."

Francesca was uncertain. "We wouldn't want to tire her still further."

"Amalia has told me that your company and Sybylla's never fail to lift her spirits." His gaze switched to Aletta. "And I can be sure that you would be as welcome as your sisters." Briskly he stepped back with an extravagant gesture. "There are many here wanting to meet you this evening. Now let me present a few of these people to you."

He saw them into one group and then left them with another, returning to greet more arrivals. Just as the last of his guests had been welcomed, Ludolf saw that a number of them had gathered in front of the imposing fireplace and were admiring and discussing his portrait. "Ah, my friends," he said, crossing the hall to join them, "I see you have discovered this remarkable addition to my collection of paintings. Now let me introduce the very gifted young artist who has recently completed this striking work—Francesca Visser, daughter of Master Visser, who I'm sure is known to you all and whose abilities she has undoubtedly inherited."

He would have taken Francesca's hand to lead her forward, but she moved swiftly to avoid his touch. There was a general clapping of hands, exclamations and congratulations, which she acknowledged with a graceful curtsey.

Ludolf would have liked to take Francesca into the banqueting hall, but wisdom had prevailed ahead of this evening's unexpected development. It would only cause offence if he did not take in the wife of the city's most prominent burgomaster. When all were seated at table he saw that Francesca was much farther down than he would have wished, but perhaps it was as well in the present circumstances.

It was from then onwards that he began to keep check of the passing of time, having estimated that by now Neeltje should have returned. He kept expecting a manservant to approach him unobtrusively or, if the doctor had decided to check on his patient's condition, for that little man to appear from the corridor. Perhaps even Neeltje might rush in hysterically, with tears streaming. He was quite pleased that he would be in everybody's gaze when the message was eventually brought for him to go to Amalia's room. His expression would be either that of gravity at the summons or of absolute shock, according to the manner in which it was delivered, and he was fully prepared. He had done many

things in his life and a spell of acting as a lad with a band of strolling players had stood him in good stead throughout the years.

At first he was in high spirits. Amalia's empty place at the far end of the table might have been a silent accusation to any other man, but Ludolf had only to raise his eyes to see *The Goddess of Spring* hanging on the wall behind the vacant chair and the thought of who was to replace her made his blood sing. After the first course he did have Amalia's chair removed together with the place setting, which emphasized to the company that until then he had hoped his wife would make a last-minute appearance.

Francesca was seated on the opposite side of the table to her sisters and none of them were near enough to converse, but all three were marvelling at the change in their father. He was now in the most buoyant of moods, eating more heartily than he had done since he had first cut his hands, flirting outrageously with the women on his left and right, both of whom were responding to him, and his roar of laughter at any joke frequently punctuated the general buzz of conversation.

Ludolf noticed the glances the sisters gave towards their father and then at each other with smiles and puzzled raising of eyebrows. He could have explained everything. His paid henchman Claudius was present that evening and had been most cordial to Hendrick, which came easily to him, for he had served a prison sentence as a confidence trickster, after which Ludolf had decided the rogue would be useful to him, coming from Antwerp as he did and being unknown in Amsterdam. Otto had not been included in the guest list, for even after the number of years that had elapsed, Amalia might have recognized him as one of the so-called merchants introduced to her during their courtship.

Francesca was happy to see her father enjoying himself. Perhaps this social occasion had turned the scales for him in such a way that from now on he would be his own self again. She could see that her sisters were also having a very good time. Aletta was in animated conversation with the gentleman on her left. This evening her hair was concealed by a gold-beaded cap and in profile only a small, shining V of her tresses showed drawn back from her brow, coral earbobs setting off her elegant neck. As for Sybylla, seated further along, she was being her usual exuberant self, although there were no handsome young men present

such as she had hoped to meet. An older man in a dark periwig, aged about forty-five, was seated next to her and had that familiar besotted look that Sybilla could induce in any male face whenever she tried.

Francesca glanced towards Ludolf and saw him take a swift, surreptitious look at his watch. He put it away immediately and resumed eating and conversing. She would have thought no more about it, except that not long afterwards she noticed him turn slightly in his chair to look at the clock by the wall. It hardly seemed likely that he was in a hurry for the banquet to end, for he was expansive in his role as host and full of ready humour. She supposed that even though he had had Amalia's chair removed he was half expecting she might appear. Not wanting to catch his eye by chance, she returned her attention to her neighbours at table, both of whom were lively conversationalists.

As one course followed another, Ludolf became increasingly tense. Why had nobody come to him? Had Amalia not been quite dead when he left her? But that was impossible, for he had checked her pulse twice and there had been nothing. It was almost two hours now since he had left her. Was Neeltje grieving privately and waiting until the evening was over before she broke the news to him? His anxiety was becoming acute.

In another part of the city Neeltje was recovering consciousness on a cushioned bench in a room she had never seen before. Her whole head was aching and there was an excruciating pain in her side. She would have put a hand to her brow, but her wrist was seized gently.

"Lie still. You were attacked in the street."

She recognized Dr. Mattheusz's voice and cried out on a sob, "I was trying to find you. My mistress—"

"Yes, you told me when I found you outside my door that she had need of that special potion in order to attend her husband's banquet." It was his own opinion that Amalia van Deventer should be spared all large social gatherings and he was well pleased that without his potion she would be resting quietly as she should be. In any case the feasting would be over by now. "You needed immediate medical treatment that had to have priority over all else. Apart from the gash on your head, you have two broken ribs, which I have bound up."

A wave of horror swept through her and she clutched the doctor's hand. "Was I—?"

"No, Neeltje, you were not raped. Your attacker wanted your horse and nothing else."

Neeltje closed her eyes again. That hateful horse. She was a nervous rider and it had known that, tossing its head and trying to get the better of her. It had taken any excuse from a drunken shout to somebody running across the street to make her haul on its reins, fearing the animal would bolt. Had one of the grooms selected a mount for her it would have been a gentle and placid animal, but they had all been in their best livery to attend the guests' coach horses and she had had to leave the choice to a stableboy to saddle up for her. She recalled now that it was a lad whose ears she had once boxed for impertinence and guessed this had been his means of revenge. His ears would be stinging again the next time she was in the stables!

"I must get home. My mistress will be anxious about me."

"Not yet, I think. She will assume I have been called out and you are waiting here for my return. I'll take you home myself when you have rested a little longer. Then I can see how Vrouw van Deventer is at the same time."

Neeltje closed her eyes thankfully again. She could understand more fully now how her mistress must dread rising from her couch when she felt least like doing so. But a certain disquiet remained. Why was that? Then it came back to her. In the meagre street lighting she had taken a wrong turning, which had delayed her arrival at the doctor's house. All the details were coming back now. Just near her destination a man had leapt from the shadows, grabbed the bridle and with one huge hand had hauled her from the saddle, letting her crash down on the cobbles. Dazed and bleeding, she had heard her attacker ride away and, terrified of being run over by a coach in the darkness, she had crawled from the street to the house steps. Somehow she had stretched up to reach the knocker, collapsing from pain as the door opened. She could not remember now who had been standing there or what she had said before she fainted. But she must have been away from home for a very long time!

"I must get back now!" she exclaimed, attempting to sit up. "I took

longer in the dark to get here than I had expected and my mistress was very poorly indeed when I left."

He took more notice then and soon afterwards she was being assisted down the steps, the doctor on one side and a manservant on the other. She felt giddy and it was difficult to breathe, which she blamed on the tight binding about her ribs, but soon her mistress would be reassured about her and she would be in her own bed.

When the van Deventer house was reached, Dr. Mattheusz could hear that dancing was in full swing in the reception hall. The music drifted on the night air and he considered it wiser to instruct his coachman to drive around to a rear entrance. He was one of many of his fellow countrymen who disapproved of dancing, believing that it raised passions that led to immorality, but he did not wish to disrupt the gathering by appearing with this injured woman in her bloodstained clothing. He had no personal malice against those enjoying themselves. He had come to this house to care for the patient at his side and to attend to the one who awaited him.

"I must go to my mistress," Neeltje insisted when helped from the coach, but she was almost fainting with pain and the doctor forbade her.

"Go straight to bed. I'll explain everything and another maidservant can wait on Vrouw van Deventer tonight."

Neeltje was reluctant, but she had to obey.

Ludolf was dancing a slow courante with Sybylla, their hands linked shoulder high and the steps slow and graceful. Out of a jealous whim towards Francesca he had invited no youngish bachelors on this occasion, and the only men present without partners were widowers, two in their forties and the rest older than himself. All three Visser girls danced well, Aletta having informed him during an earlier dance that Sybylla kept both her and Francesca abreast of all the new dances. He had not yet danced with Francesca, wary now of the slightest risk of gossip, but he had partnered five other women in addition to her sisters.

"Whatever did you say to Father to make him so merry?" Sybylla questioned with a giggle. "Look at him over there." She indicated where Hendrick was all smiles in the dance.

"Why not ask him?" Ludolf suggested, knowing that whatever Hendrick replied the true reason would not be given.

She looked at him quizzically. "Aletta did and he said you were going to buy his painting of the tax collector."

"Well?"

"I think that's most unlikely." She glanced upwards and around at the sumptuous room. "Why should you wish to hang a painting of a representative of those for whom you surely have no liking?"

He laughed heartily, deciding that he would endorse Hendrick's lie by buying it. "Perhaps that is the very reason. I can put the painting facing the midden or the most costly item in the house that I possess. The joke will be mine."

She giggled. "You are the most outrageous man!"

"Don't deny that you like me all the better for it!"

Her eyes twinkled at him, but she did not take the bait. "Do you think Amalia is able to sleep with this music playing and all the noisy chatter?"

He could guess what was coming. Aletta had hinted at it, but he had brushed aside her reminder of his half-promise. "She doesn't sleep well at the best of times. Why do you ask?"

"You did say when my sisters and I arrived this evening that we might see Amalia later. It seems so hard that she should have tried to gather enough strength for this evening and then, when she failed, not to have a single visitor."

Sybylla was honest enough to admit to herself that had there been any dashing young men present she might have forgotten Amalia completely. But she was genuinely fond of her new friend and was glad that she had remembered her lying in her apartment away from these exciting festivities with only Neeltje for company.

Ludolf thought quickly. Suppose he did take the three girls to Amalia's apartment? He was convinced that his wife's death would not be attributed to foul play, but why not strengthen his apparent innocence still further by going willingly, and seemingly unsuspectingly, to find his wife had expired at last from her illness. He could count on hysterics from Sybylla, to which he would add his own restrained display of bravely borne grief. Most important of all, he would be able to satisfy his curiosity as to why he had not been called away to the apartment.

"Then gather your two sisters when this dance is ended and we'll find out if Amalia will see you. If so, I'll have to return to the dancing, but you may judge how soon you should leave her again."

As the music stopped Sybylla left his side to summon both Francesca and Aletta. Before Ludolf could make any move himself Hendrick blocked his way.

"I was hoping we might have a little chat on our own for a few minutes," Hendrick said significantly.

Ludolf struggled with his annoyance that the artist should approach him at this particular time. "I realize you are eager to know the details, but they can't be hurried through."

"I'm at your command. Shall I call on you?"

"Yes. We don't want to be overheard or disturbed. Come tomorrow at three o'clock. It's not a very convenient time for me, but I will cancel another appointment."

Cheerfully Hendrick accepted this arrangement. Then his daughters went with his patron to the invalid wife's apartment and he strolled away to watch some games of cards at tables in one of the drawing rooms. He longed to be playing too, but a man with empty pockets and debts deeper than the Amstel could only be a wistful spectator.

Ludolf opened the door of Amalia's room, the sisters behind him. With a rush of dreadful apprehension he saw that the couch was empty, the carmine-stained cushion having fallen to the floor.

"As I expected," he stated after a fractional pause, "my wife has retired. I'll go first on my own into her bedchamber."

The girls waited as he strode for the double doors, which opened before he could reach them. Both Francesca and Sybylla recognized the short man in black clothes and a white periwig who stood there, having been presented to Dr. Mattheusz when he had called on Amalia one day.

"Heer van Deventer," the doctor said in solemn tones, "I arrived here only a few minutes ago and was on my way to find you. I regret that I have the gravest news for you."

"What's happened?" Ludolf's question was almost inaudible.

The doctor looked towards the girls and then back at Ludolf. "Do you wish me to say in the presence of others what I have to tell?"

Ludolf gave a nod, relief at what he was obviously about to hear giving him a soaring sense of power that once again he had manipulated events to his benefit. "I believe you have already prepared us. Two of these young women have drawn close to my dear Amalia quite recently."

"Then with great sorrow I have to say that your wife died alone here this evening after sending her maidservant to fetch a potion from me. Unfortunately the woman was violently attacked and injured just as she reached my house and collapsed as I opened the door. It was not until she had recovered her senses that I understood your wife was in an extremely low state, and so I decided I should visit her while bringing the injured woman back at the same time."

Ludolf groaned in a heartbroken fashion, bowing his head, and the sisters drew closer together, Francesca and Sybylla pale with shock and with tears in their eyes. Only Aletta spoke. "The poor lady!"

The doctor stepped forward and, being too short to guide Ludolf by the shoulder, placed a hand on his back. "Come now and see her. She is at peace."

Ludolf dropped his hands to his sides and, like a man bereft of all he had cherished, went slowly into the bedchamber. The doctor did not accompany him but stayed in the dayroom, closing the doors to let him be alone with his late wife. Then, seeing that two of the sisters were thoroughly distressed, the third with an arm around each in comfort, Dr. Mattheusz went across to them.

"It may ease your grief to know that Vrouw van Deventer did not suffer," he said kindly.

Sybylla, who had not behaved as Ludolf had expected, looked at the little doctor with swimming eyes. "How terrible that she was on her own! To think that we were all in the banqueting hall and then dancing while she—" She broke off, covering her face with her hands.

Aletta spoke to her soothingly and thought, as she had many times before, that Sybylla, for all her superficiality, had a tender heart. "As Vrouw van Deventer was in bed, it's almost certain she went in her sleep."

"That is sound thinking," the doctor confirmed. It was not for these young women to know that he had found Amalia half fallen from the couch. The satin cushion under her head had slipped, taking her with it. Having known her as a woman always fastidious about her appearance, he had guessed how she would have hated to be found in an ungainly position and, out of charity, he had picked her up and carried her through to lay her on her own bed. His personal regret was that the delay in Neeltje's errand of mercy had prevented him getting to Amalia in time to summon her husband to her bedside for her last moments.

The bedchamber doors opened again and Ludolf emerged. The doctor noted that he looked extremely sad, but not totally devastated, and he supposed that Amalia had been in such a weak state for so long that this devoted husband had been partly prepared for her demise at any time.

"Would you be so kind as to make an announcement to my guests, Dr. Mattheusz?" Ludolf requested brokenly.

"Of course, *mijnheer.* I'll do it at once." The music had been jarring on the doctor's ears, for this was now a house of mourning. He hurried from the room. Francesca guided her sisters to follow while all three of them murmured condolences. Ludolf thanked them with a bow. Away in the reception hall the music trailed away and silence fell. As they went to receive their cloaks Francesca knew afresh the horror of the struggle in the library. To think that it should have happened almost within Amalia's last hours. If Ludolf felt any remorse it had not shown in his eyes when he had looked at her. Her loathing of him made her flesh creep. When she and her sisters reached the reception hall the same stricken look was on every face. Hendrick came to them at once and spoke sympathetically. Francesca, her heart heavy with grief at Amalia's lonely passing, was glad of his comforting arm about her shoulders and saw how Sybylla cuddled up to him on his other side as if she were a child again.

While all the guests had made their departure, Ludolf remained alone in the apartment. The one question that was still causing him anxiety was who had entered the room and moved Amalia's body from the couch to her bedchamber. It was greatly to his relief when Dr. Mattheusz returned and explained what he had done.

"I knew you would be puzzled when, in time, your wife's maid told you she had left her mistress on the couch in a very weak state, virtually unable to have moved to her bedchamber alone."

Ludolf was all gratitude. "A most kindly thought, Doctor. I thank you with all my heart. Apart from what my dear wife would have felt, had she known, it would have been a terrible thing if those three young women had entered the room and seen my wife lying dead. The shock would have been most distressing."

Once alone again Ludolf, with his hands on his hips, surveyed Amalia's dayroom. When a suitable time had elapsed he would have the whole decor changed here and the rooms refurnished to become integrated with the main house again instead of being a separate apartment. The Pieter de Hooch painting caught his eye. It had been wasted hanging here. He would have it rehung in a drawing room where it would be better displayed. Naturally he would have to play the role of a grieving widower for a long time to come. Yet he knew to the very day what length that period should be and, as it was already into the early hours of a new day, it would date from tomorrow.

Hendrick felt somewhat uncertain about keeping an appointment in a house so suddenly tipped into mourning, but no message was sent to cancel it and so he set off for the van Deventer house in good time. The manservant who admitted him had bunches of black ribbon on the shoulders of his livery and two maidservants, hurrying across the reception hall, wore black lace aprons. This place of hushed voices was in sharp contrast to his own home, where friends and neighbours were calling in all the time to wish Francesca well with her apprenticeship and hand her little gifts.

Ludolf was waiting to receive him in a room where they had first played cards with Claudius and Otto. Hendrick thought it a poor choice of venue, considering the reason why he was here, but perhaps it had been deliberately selected. The new widower was in unrelieved mourning attire, even to plain black buckles on his shoes.

"It is most courteous of you to see me on such a sorrowful day," Hendrick said after uttering conventional condolences in the sepulchral

tones reserved for such times. He had taken the seat that had been offered him, although Ludolf chose to remain standing, resting a hand against the rose marble canopy of the Delft-tiled fireplace, as if showing from the start he intended to dominate this interview.

"There are matters to be talked out that can't be delayed," he began without preamble. "I want to marry Francesca."

Shock and disgust shook through Hendrick. "You dare to stand there in the raiments of bereavement with your late wife barely cold—"

"This is no time for sentiment," Ludolf broke in, his expression hard. "I have set my period of mourning for the minimum six months. After that I shall court her."

"You take a great deal for granted!" Hendrick snorted, outraged.

Ludolf continued as if there had been no interruption. "During those first months I'll not see her at all, except when she is at home on a visit, and then you will invite me there at all times to enable me to start my courtship without giving rise to public gossip."

"That won't be often," Hendrick retorted with grim satisfaction. "Apprentices are only allowed to visit their families at Christmastide or in an emergency."

Ludolf snapped his fingers contemptuously as if those conditions could easily be overcome. "I'll not interrupt her apprenticeship, knowing how important it is to her, and my one aim is her happiness, but at the end of it she shall become my wife."

"I'll not give my consent!"

Ludolf regarded him with mild surprise, much as if a tiny gnat had dared to sting him. "What is your objection? Is she promised to someone else?"

"No."

"Has she spoken of wishing to be anybody else's wife?"

"No. Quite the reverse."

"Well, then?"

Hendrick rubbed his hands uneasily over the arm ends of his chair. "She doesn't want to stay in Holland once she has been granted membership of the Guild of St. Luke. She aims to go to Italy."

"I'll take her."

Hendrick shook his head stubbornly, finding this whole interview far

more difficult than the one conducted with Pieter, which had been without selfish demands. Neither had he come prepared for this sudden development. The sooner it was nipped in the bud, the better, because he had come to talk over his debts and he wanted to get on with that quickly. "Francesca is set against marriage. She wants to be an artist first and foremost with no hindrances, emotional or otherwise, to hold her back."

Ludolf left the fireplace and strolled across to the nearest window and stood looking out into the street. "Would you prefer that I make her my mistress?"

Hendrick sprang from his seat with a huge, vibrating roar, shaking his fist. "You dare to say that to me! Her own father!"

Ludolf moved to lean back leisurely against the windowsill and folded his arms. "To whom else should I make my intentions known? They are honourable, are they not? I was simply pointing out that I intend to have her either way."

"Damnation to you! I'm going!" Hendrick started for the door, but he did not reach it, for Ludolf had drawn the promissory notes from his sleeve.

"Aren't you forgetting something?" Ludolf inquired drily, flicking them to and fro in the air.

Hendrick's heightened colour took on a greyish hue. "That's a different matter altogether," he spluttered. "My debts are between the two of us. Nobody else comes into them."

"That's not entirely correct. I'll remind you that you said on oath that I could have any collateral that I required and I've chosen Francesca."

Hendrick became desperate. "You surely didn't imagine I had included my own daughter?"

"Why should I suppose otherwise? Women are men's chattels. You have every legal right to dictate whom your daughters should marry."

"But I have never held that attitude towards them. I'm a freedom-loving man myself and when Anna was first pregnant she and I decided that our sons and daughters should be brought up on an equal footing. We had no boys, except the stillborn infant who cost her life, but our

girls have grown up with independent spirits and been encouraged to have opinions of their own!"

"But Francesca will obey your will."

"She would never be forced into anything! You know nothing of her if you haven't discovered that!"

"Why not try persuasion? If she should have to be told what the alternative to marrying me would mean for you and her sisters, as well as that old nurse of whom she is so fond, I can't see her refusing me."

"What alternative is that?" Hendrick queried cautiously, slack-mouthed with fear.

Ludolf slowly paced the room as he answered. "I would drag you through the public debtors' court into bankruptcy and claim everything you own from the roof over your family's heads to your paintings of Anna. You'd languish in prison, because that's where I would put you, and your womenfolk would be confined to an almshouse for the poor."

Hendrick dropped back into his chair and began to weep abjectly. "Merciful God! What have I done!"

Ludolf came to stand nearby and allowed time for the wretched man's misery to sink deep into his body, mind and soul. The only sounds in the quiet room were of Hendrick's distress and the subdued noises from the street outside. Then Ludolf spoke again.

"Take heart, my friend. I'll be a good husband to Francesca when the time comes. There's not another father in Amsterdam who would not jump at the chance of giving a daughter as a bride to me. She'll want for nothing and if my generosity to her should spill over to you and her sisters I'll raise no objection. What's more, I'll make a marriage gift to her of the promissory notes and she can tear them up in front of you."

Hendrick, his face sagging like a hound's, his eyes red-rimmed, gave a choked appeal. "As I said once before, I don't want her or her sisters to know of my losses. That must never be!"

"Then I'll give the notes to you. Think of it! From this day forward your debt to me is in abeyance and you may continue your life as if nothing had ever been amiss. On the day that I wed Francesca you can rejoice as you burn these scraps of paper. Your future will be assured and secure as you wish it to be. By that I mean that never again would I step in to save you from your own stupidity."

"I've learned my lesson." Hendrick bowed his head brokenly.

Ludolf eyed him cynically. Gamblers always made such vows, but at least it was certain that never again would the artist be such a fool as to go to stakes that were beyond him. A few paltry guilders would be all he would allow himself from now on. "Then it is agreed?"

"It is." Hendrick's head sank still lower and his voice was slow and heavy. "At the end of Francesca's apprenticeship, and if she has not already agreed to marry you, I will inform her that she must become your wife."

"By then my courtship will have taken full effect and I'm confident that it will never be necessary for you to make such a stipulation. Now we shall sign the marriage contracts. A lawyer was here early this morning and I had them drawn up while he was dealing with Amalia's will and other papers as well."

Dull-eyed and full of loathing, Hendrick looked up to see his patron take two documents from a drawer, for they would each keep one of them after signing. What sort of a man was this who could callously engage a lawyer to handle his late wife's estate, whatever was left of it, and prepare contracts for a new marriage at the same time? Hendrick was aware of not being particularly perceptive in everyday life when his "inner eye" was not in use as when he was painting, but he knew that here, in this room in private interview, he had seen a side of Ludolf's character that was not normally revealed. The lawyer, whose discretion could be relied upon, would have seen it that morning, but the rest of the world had no inkling of a heartlessness beyond measure.

Listlessly Hendrick took the contract Ludolf handed to him and read it through. While this was happening Ludolf flicked open the lid of a silver inkwell in readiness and tested one of the quill tips against a finger.

Hendrick looked up with a questioning frown. "Who's this widow mentioned here?" He peered closely at the name again. "Vrouw Geetruyd Wolff?"

"I investigated the family Francesca was to stay with and considered the atmosphere there to be too lax. Therefore I've cancelled her going to that house and arranged for Vrouw Wolff to meet her off the stage wagon tomorrow and take charge of her. One thing further." Ludolf

placed another sheet of paper before Hendrick. "This is a letter to Vrouw Wolff setting out the rules that Francesca is to obey. I wish you to copy it, so that the woman knows it comes with your parental authority. I shall see that she receives it by a special messenger, who is waiting to depart."

As Hendrick's eyes followed Ludolf's writing, he gave a mirthless and exasperated laugh. "What's this condition of Francesca being chaperoned unless she is with her sisters, or me, or with you and also being forbidden to be alone in male company at any time? My daughter is going to Delft to work. Not to jeopardize her chances by dilly-dallying with young men!"

"She must be protected at all times."

"So," Hendrick said bitterly, "you couldn't have done all this today. You've been working on this agreement for some time. If your wife hadn't died last night it would have been a bill of sale awaiting your receipt that I'd be holding now instead of a more honourable marriage contract."

"That's correct. I actually had one ready, but there is a clause in it that if I became a widower in the interim of three years, then Francesca would marry me as we have arranged."

Hendrick could contain himself no longer. "You ruthless bastard!" he yelled with all the power of his lungs, shaking the contract that he held. "May you rot in hell!"

Ludolf sneered at him contemptuously. "I thought you'd come to that kind of verbal abuse sooner or later, but let there be no more of it if you want me to continue as your patron. Finish reading what has been written, copy and sign it, and then we will complete the contracts."

There was nothing more Hendrick could say. His eldest daughter had been trapped even before marriage became possible. It had always been his hope that when she had achieved her ambition of becoming a master of a Guild, she would find happiness in marriage with a man of her choice, supposing that otherwise she might be tempted to take a lover when she was a mature woman. But this coercing of her while still a girl was the other side of the coin entirely. In this case he must be thankful she was to become a wife and nothing less, and even then he

had his doubts that Ludolf would allow her to complete her apprenticeship but might attempt to buy off Vermeer.

He copied the letter and then went with it to the table where the marriage contracts had been laid. Both he and Ludolf signed the documents and duly exchanged them. Hendrick left the house immediately afterwards. As he walked homewards through the busy streets, he was too wrapped up in mulling over what had happened to be aware of the passing traffic, the shouts of the pedlars or the clash of cymbals for a dancing bear. He hoped that Francesca's apprenticeship would be blissful and carefree. In spite of all Ludolf's promises of what she should have as his wife, it was unlikely that love and happiness would ever be hers.

When he reached home he could tell by the chatter in the parlour that still more company were gathered there and the stack of gifts on the table in the reception room had increased during the time he had been out. He went straight to Anna's portrait in the studio and stood before it, wanting her forgiveness and understanding of what he had done. As he studied her laughing face, set off by the swirl of her gleaming hair, he realized that Ludolf's threat of annexing her portrait had affected him more deeply than having to accept the fate that had been allotted to Francesca. He had thought his heart must stop.

CHAPTER I I

At dawn the whole Visser household was astir in readiness to have breakfast with Francesca before her early departure. Alone in her bedchamber she finished lacing up the back of her bodice and smoothed her collar into place while she tried to think if there was anything in the organizing of domestic affairs in her absence that she might have overlooked. Maria had been given charge of the household funds and Aletta the little box that always contained some cash for personal needs. All had promised her that everything would be run

as if she were still in charge. She wanted the flower beds to continue to thrive, for her tulips were in full and glorious bloom, the new ones adding their rich red and feathery petals to the beauty of the courtyard. To herself she had long since given them the new name of "Pieter's tulips." Aletta was to care for the flower beds with the help of Sybylla, who had already given an assurance she would mind her manners, would not misbehave and would respect whatever instructions Aletta gave her for her own good.

It was Hendrick who worried Francesca most. There had been a brief respite when he had seemed his normal self again at the banquet, but the tragedy of that night must have revived his melancholia again. His hands were almost back to normal, causing him little discomfort, but he had agreed to continue with the treatment. Although he complained that Maria's concoction was foul enough to poison him, the fact that he never failed to take a dose each morning showed he had faith in it. At least he was working hard, giving himself no rest at the present time, which was a helpful sign in itself.

Glancing around the room, Francesca checked that nothing was forgotten that she wished to take with her. The travelling chest with her clothes and other possessions had been taken downstairs the night before and only a small casket, which she would carry herself, still stood open on the cushioned bench. In it she had placed last-minute things, such as her comb and hairbrush. She added her hand glass to the casket and, as she did so, noticed in its reflection that her face was drawn. A natural sadness at leaving home for the first time was also touched by the sorrow of Amalia's demise. Even yesterday, amid all the excitement of friends and neighbours coming and going, she and Sybylla had exchanged a look that showed they had not forgotten her.

Firmly she closed the casket and picked it up by the handle. Then she gathered up her cloak, which she had put ready earlier, and left the room where she had slept since she was twelve months old, the birth of Aletta having removed her from the cot in her parents' bedchamber into a little bed that had once stood in the place of the four-poster of her growing years.

At breakfast there was a strained atmosphere. Everyone was making conversation as if they were strangers, needing to cover what her leav-

ing meant to them. Never before had she been away from her sisters, or Hendrick, or even Maria for more than a day or slept a night under any other roof.

"You must write and tell us all about your work," Aletta said with feigned brightness, "and then I'll know what to expect when my turn comes."

"I will," Francesca promised. She glanced with concern at her father. Yesterday evening when she had been alone with him after all the well-wishers had departed he had become very emotional, actually having tears in his eyes when he spoke of her going away. He had said she was always to know that whatever happened her happiness mattered more than anything to him. It had been an odd sort of conversation, almost as if he were keeping back the whole reason for it. Just as she was getting to her feet he had added suddenly, "Oh! One other small matter. I decided to change your accommodation in Delft and so I've arranged for you to stay with a widow, Vrouw Wolff, who will welcome your company. She will be meeting the stage wagon."

Francesca was taken aback and puzzled, but the sight of Hendrick's increasing distress, his head dropping into his hands, had convinced her this was not the moment for questions or arguments. She had put a gentle hand on his head and assured him that she knew he only wanted the best for her.

Sybylla was voicing a request to her. "Willem said that Master Vermeer always paints his wife in handsome clothes. Be sure to describe her gowns to me in detail."

"Yes, of course."

Maria spoke in gruff disapproval. "You always get people to gossip, Sybylla."

"I like to know whatever is interesting," Sybylla retorted pertly, "so I ask the right sort of questions. There was nothing tattletale about what Willem said. He had heard it from Catharina Vermeer herself after he had admired a painting of her drinking from a glass in a rose-and-red velvet gown."

"I expect the setting was an interior," Hendrick commented, helping himself to more of the good white bread that Griet had earlier taken hot from the baker's tray at the door. "My only reservations on what

I've heard of Vermeer's work is that he is not much interested in landscapes. So, Francesca," he added with emphasis, "make sure that aspect of your training is not ignored."

"I'm sure it won't be," Francesca replied. Then she shot a fond smile at Aletta. "If it is, I shall have to go out by myself at times as you do to sketch your outdoor scenes." She missed seeing how deeply her sister flushed at her remark, for there had come a knock on the front door. She gave Griet no time to move but sprang up from the table herself. "I'll go."

She flew through the house to fling the door wide. As she had hoped, Pieter stood there. "I'm so glad you've come," she said openly.

"What are old friends for if not to see one another off on journeys?" he queried with a half-teasing grin as he stepped into the house, handing her a bunch of violets tied with a flowing ribbon. "I knew you would be busy yesterday and so I thought I'd come this morning instead."

"I'm so pleased that you did. These violets are beautiful." The delicate scent of them hung in the air between them and she cupped the dewy posy in both hands to raise it to her nostrils. "Such a fragrance."

"Are you quite ready for leaving?"

"Yes, I am. Come through to the dining hall."

They found that only Hendrick was still at the table. Everybody else had moved from it. When they heard that Pieter had ridden from Haarlem, starting before dawn, Hendrick waved him to a seat and Griet set food before him. Francesca, who wanted a final word with Aletta and Sybylla, went from the room to find them. They were to accompany her, and now it seemed Pieter, to the stage wagon. Maria also went hobbling off, taking Griet with her, for the porter had arrived to collect Francesca's travelling chest and there were other final matters to supervise.

Hendrick was well pleased to have the opportunity to speak to Pieter far sooner than he had expected about seeing Francesca in Delft, for yesterday's development had changed a number of things. It was necessary now to try to crush at all costs the relationship between his daughter and this young man. If Pieter had not been paying for her tuition he would have forbidden him to see her ever again, but that was

scarcely possible in the circumstances with all the financial arrangements completed. It was a great nuisance that Pieter had become involved, because there was no doubt now that if Ludolf had been asked at the time he would have forked out the money to be her sole benefactor. Not that it wasn't a good thing to be free of an even greater debt to him.

"I have to speak to you about visiting Francesca in Delft," Hendrick began authoritatively after clearing his throat. "I must insist on her work being uninterrupted and I would prefer you to stay right away from her."

Pieter was dangerously quiet in his reply. He had finished eating and rested an arm on the table as he looked penetratingly at Hendrick. "It was arranged with your consent and Francesca's agreement that she and I should meet occasionally. How can you go back on that now?"

"I've had time to think things over," Hendrick blustered.

Pieter was studying him. "Has something happened?" he asked perceptively. "Have your financial matters deteriorated still further? You and your family never need to be homeless. I have a property in Haarlem."

"No!" Hendrick assured him hastily. "Everything is in hand again. I still have my huge debts, but I've been given a long time in which to settle them."

"Is it all being properly handled? I'm not a professional financier, but I have a good grasp of money matters in all forms and would willingly guide you. You're not being charged interest at an exorbitant rate, I trust? I'd change that, for a start."

Hendrick shook his head vehemently. "All you can do for me is to keep away from Francesca. I have good reason, Pieter, and I implore you to heed my request. You want her to be a great artist as much as I do. Put her first. Think of her future before you consider your own wishes. I warned you not to raise your hopes."

Pieter felt he had been tricked. His skin had stretched over his strong facial bones and the set of his mouth was angry. "I shall think over what you have said. I make no promises and that is all I can say now."

There was a tap of heels approaching and Francesca returned cloaked and gloved for her journey. "I'm ready now," she announced. Then as

Hendrick pushed back his chair and rose to his feet, she flew into his arms, hugging him tightly. "Take care, Father! If ever anything should happen that means you should have need of me at home I'd come at once."

"Of course you would, dear child, but I don't foresee any catastrophes." He kissed her brow, heavy-hearted with shame at the conditions to which he had consigned her and of which she was unaware.

As she stood back from him her face was full of filial love. "I can never thank you enough for this marvellous chance you've given me. You alone are enabling me to take this great step towards the fulfilment of my dearest ambition."

Pieter left father and daughter together and went into the reception hall, where both Aletta and Sybylla were in their cloaks and waiting by the open door. He felt no resentment that Francesca should suppose her father to be entirely responsible for giving her the apprenticeship. It was enough for him that he had been able to step in and secure it for her when it had almost been lost. If staying away from her should benefit her work he would have to do so, but later on, after she had settled down at Vermeer's studio, he would be better able to judge whether he was an interloper and a hindrance to her progress.

Francesca reappeared on her own. "Father and I have said our farewells." She went to kiss and embrace Maria, who wept all over her and released her reluctantly. Even Griet was full of tears. Francesca had been a buffer between her and Maria's wrath in the early years of her employment, and had been specially kind to her more times than could be remembered.

"May good fortune attend you, Juffrouw Francesca."

"I thank you, Griet." Francesca felt choked. Then, as if physically tearing herself away from home, she went at such speed out of the house that Pieter, carrying her hand casket and already on the doorstep, just managed to catch her hand in his as she darted by. He squeezed it in understanding and she gave him a grateful little smile, slowing her pace to let her sisters catch up with them.

It was a windy morning and their cloaks billowed out like colourful tulip petals when they reached the square where the stage wagon was waiting. Francesca's travelling chest was already aboard the long open

wagon, the roof of waxed cloth stretched over hoops of iron. She had a few last words with Pieter, telling him of the change in her accommodation in Delft.

"Why was it rearranged?" Pieter asked her.

She gave a little shrug, still puzzled herself. "It appears it was no longer convenient for the first family to have me, but on thinking it over I am sure Father really has another reason for making the change. He had become nervous of my being away from home in a new town among strangers. He thinks I will be better cared for by a widow glad of my company. Her name is Vrouw Geetruyd Wolff."

"I'm sure you will. Shall you have time to write to me?"

She answered in a gentle jest. "My evenings will be my own unless I get lessons in the tonal light of lamps and candles after dark."

He surveyed her teasingly. "Is that so? Somehow I don't think that will happen very often."

"We want letters!" Sybylla declared firmly.

Aletta gave a laugh. "It won't be a one-way correspondence, I promise you, Francesca."

Pieter became more serious. "What of your studies, Francesca? All jesting aside, I'll take no time away from you in letter writing to me that should be spent on your art."

She gave back her reply with equal seriousness. "If ever I should find some conflict arising between our friendship and my work I would tell you."

"That's a promise?"

"It is."

An increasing bustle of activity around the stage wagon showed that it was about to leave. For a few seconds more they looked deeply at each other before he kissed her with such intensity that Aletta and Sybylla stared in astonishment. Then she embraced her sisters in turn, cheeks kissed and last-minute advice and instructions given and returned. Pieter helped her up into the wagon by the steps placed alongside it. She took a seat where enough space had been left by the waxed roof covering for passengers to see out. With a shout from the coachman and the crack of the whip the high wheels rolled forward over the cobbles, bearing her away. Aletta and Sybylla both ran a few steps along

to keep level with her, although Pieter remained where he was. All three waved to her. "Farewell! Take care! God speed you!"

She waved back until the stage wagon rumbled over a bridge and a row of warehouses blocked off her view of them. Her first action then was to find a safe place for her violets and there was a crevice by her seat in which she was able to wedge the stalks in their ribbon binding. It was as well that she took such a precaution, because, as she had expected, it was a bone-shaking journey. The high wheels thundered along as the little leather sails were raised on the roof to catch the wind and aid the speed of the four galloping horses. Passengers cried out in alarm and were tossed against one another whenever the stage wagon tipped dangerously in a deep rut. All the time the madman with the whip drove on his horses and yelled in triumph when he passed another stage wagon going in the opposite direction, a sign that he was keeping up to time and maybe even surpassing it on this particular journey.

Occasionally there was a much needed halt at a hostelry when horses were changed and some passengers disembarked while others came aboard. For those making the full journey from Amsterdam to Delft there would be just time to snatch some refreshment at the hostelry or use the privy, but rarely both. The coachman would blow his horn as a signal he was about to depart again and he did not wait for latecomers. It became a common sight to see men almost choking themselves to down the last drop from a tankard or come running to scramble back onto the stage wagon still tying the strings of their breeches.

Francesca had a packet of food wrapped in a white napkin to sustain her on the journey, together with some of the fruit that friends had brought as farewell gifts, most of which she had left behind for the family. She had a change of fellow passengers beside her three times throughout the journey and each time they chatted, which helped to pass the hours.

The late-afternoon sun was shining when the stage wagon eventually rumbled into Delft and Francesca looked out eagerly. The prosperity of this charming old town was founded on its cloth, its breweries and its shipping, being connected by canals with ports on the river Maas. Over the past hundred years there had been such a growth in its potteries

2
4
8

producing Delft tiles and every kind of domestic utensil, ornamental and practical, that there were now thirty establishments in the town.

She thought that Delft with its innumerable bridges appeared to be more webbed by canals than Amsterdam, and whichever side of a street she looked at there were grey- or rust-red-roofed mediaeval, Gothic and Renaissance buildings unchanged by the passing of centuries. Leaded panes winked in the sun and ancient doorways lurked in the shadows while shutters shone blue or green or brown and sometimes crimson. Trees, misty with blossom or sharp with new green, combined with flowering plants and brilliant tulips to bring added beauty to the old town. Surely there was no better time to come to Delft than on a sunny May day!

There was a bustle of activity outside the hostelry in the street where she alighted, her posy of violets in one hand and her casket in the other. She had ensured that her travelling chest had been unloaded and set down beside her before she saw in the milling throng of people the middle-aged woman whom she guessed to be Vrouw Wolff. The widow spotted her in almost the same instant and came forward. Although soberly dressed in a short cape over a white-collared black gown and a plain hat without plume or ribbons, she had a certain style that belied her prim attire. In her early forties with a fine figure, she was not an uncomely-looking woman, her face triangular, her brow wide, her chin sharp. She was smiling in welcome, but her grey eyes were as hard and bright as glass in her assessing scrutiny of the new arrival.

"I believe I'm addressing Juffrouw Visser," she said, her black silky brows raised inquiringly.

"My greetings, Vrouw Wolff. Please call me Francesca."

"Since I am to guard you as if you were my own child that would be appropriate. Is this all your baggage?" She looked somewhat disparagingly at the old and much battered travelling chest on the ground and the single hand casket that Francesca held in one hand, her beribboned posy in the other.

"Yes. I'll hail a porter."

"No need. I already have one standing by." Vrouw Wolff half turned to signal with a raised hand to a youth waiting with a handcart. When the baggage was loaded she made him go ahead of them, suspecting

that he might try to tamper with the contents if he was behind their backs. It would not have occurred to Francesca to doubt his honesty, but later she was to discover that Geetruyd Wolff rarely trusted anyone.

It was only a short distance to the narrow crooked street called Kromstraat, where Geetruyd lived. Her house was five storeys high and at some time in the past it had been tarred to protect the bricks from corrosion by the damp climate, which made the sandstone ornamentation stand out attractively. Across the casement windows at street level the ochre-coloured half-shutters were closed to give privacy while allowing light to penetrate through the upper halves. The entrance door, with its iron knocker, when opened by Geetruyd, was thick enough to have done justice to a church porch. Inside the effect was of gloominess, partly through the light being reduced by the shutters and also a choice of dark wall panelling, but there were some pieces of particularly fine furniture and a display of beautiful Delftware.

A maidservant named Weintje guided the porter, who had hoisted the travelling chest onto his back, up a precipitous staircase that rose from an inner stair hall as in Francesca's own home, although here it was L-shaped, which hid the flight from the view of anyone in the reception hall. Geetruyd led the way for Francesca, who followed her up the staircase, which was handsomely carved, in the wake of the maidservant and the porter.

"These old houses," Geetruyd said over her shoulder, "have many rooms, and some years ago, in order to improve my modest circumstances, I started giving accommodation to travellers when the hostelries were full. Since then I have built up a clientele of merchants, who travel regularly and always come here, because they can be sure of a quiet night in respectable surroundings with a good bed and an ample breakfast in the morning." She had reached an upper floor and was nimbly ascending the next flight.

"Are there many guests staying at any one time?"

"No. Usually only two or three or four at the most. I accommodate only those gentlemen who are known to me, although I do oblige the landlord of the Mechelin tavern by providing a room sometimes, because I know he would never send me anyone unsuitable, which is important. You will hardly know when there are guests in the house,

because I have four large bedchambers downstairs with wall beds dating from the days when people often lived and slept in the same room, as they still do in parts of the countryside till this day. Breakfast is always served in the rooms, so none come into my dining hall, which leads off the kitchen on the ground floor."

"I noticed through two open doors that we passed on the first floor that you have upstairs parlours."

"Yes, there are three and also an office where I keep my books and deal with paperwork linked with my charity work. I am a regentess on the committee of several almshouses for the elderly and other charitable institutions."

It was a declaration of the high respect with which she was regarded in the town. Having reached the second floor, she went trotting off along a corridor to where the porter was emerging from a doorway after setting down the travelling chest. Francesca went to him, loosening the ring of her stocking purse with the intention of paying him, but Geetruyd held up a restraining hand and paid him herself.

"I have received a fund out of which to pay sundry expenses," she explained. Then to Weintje, who was hastening out of the room to let her mistress and the new arrival enter, she said, "Bring a vase for Juffrouw Visser's violets."

Francesca was pondering over this fund and could only suppose that Willem had suggested to her father that a little extra cash should be provided, because she could not believe that Hendrick would have thought of it by himself. He certainly hadn't mentioned it when he had given her a bag of money for her purse, saying that it included her share of what was due to her from Ludolf's portrait. She had noticed that the bag was heavy and had expected to find a number of stuivers in it, but on opening it only seconds ago she had been amazed to see that it contained quite a number of florins.

Her panelled room with its brocade-curtained four-poster did not have much light, for it had only one window and that looked down into the street. Yet it was furnished with all she would need, including a silver-framed mirror and the luxury of a Persian rug on the floor by the bed.

Geetruyd was eyeing her speculatively. "I was told you are a responsi-

ble young woman dedicated to art and, if I was not misled, I think you and I should get on well together." She moved across to the door and paused there to look back over her shoulder. "I'm leaving you to unpack. Weintje will bring you a cup of tea to refresh you after your journey. When you are ready you will find me in an east-facing parlour that is directly below this bedchamber. We shall have a talk before supper and I'll outline my duties towards you. I have undertaken to become your chaperone throughout your time in Delft, and it will be to our mutual advantage if we erase any possible difficulties from the start."

Half an hour later Francesca went in search of the east-facing parlour. She looked closely at every picture on the way. Mostly they were etchings of Delft, including one of Willem I's magnificent tomb in the New Church, the high tower of which she had seen on her way from the final stage post. Clearly depicted at the feet of the effigy of the Prince of Orange was his faithful dog, who had pined for him, refusing to eat, and who had died soon after his master. If ever she should be directed to paint a picture of that man it would be with his dog frisking along at his side.

The talk with Vrouw Wolff did not consist of an exchange of views, for Francesca had to listen to a number of stipulations laid down by her father in a letter to which the widow referred. Among everything else she was amazed to hear that she was not to associate socially with any male. Vermeer's home and studio were only a short walk away, but in the mornings and at the end of the day she would be escorted by Geetruyd's cousin and companion, Clara Huys.

"You'll be meeting Clara at dinner," the widow said in conclusion after adding that she herself would accompany Francesca to any social gatherings she deemed suitable. "Is all that understood?"

"Indeed it is!" Francesca was thoroughly displeased by what had been dictated to her, although upon reflection she saw now that her father had really not been quite sane over these past weeks, for he would never have set down these rigid rules in a normal frame of mind. Regretfully, it was also typical of him that he should have avoided telling her all this directly, but had left the unpleasant task to somebody else. "Since this is how my father has mapped out everything for me at the present time, I

must abide by his wishes. However, I'm sure that after I've been here for a while and he has become used to my being away from home, he will relax these absurd rules."

"Don't count on that."

"Whether it happens or not, there is one person whom I will see on my own. I made that clear to my father and I had his agreement. The name is Pieter van Doorne."

Vrouw Wolff had Hendrick's letter on her lap and now she unfolded it to glance at it again. "Yes, it is as I have told you. No exceptions are to be made."

"That's not possible!"

"See for yourself!"

Francesca took the letter handed to her and saw in her father's own hand exactly all that Geetruyd had said to her. "This letter is an expression of anxiety about me. He has not been himself recently. He will soon rescind these instructions."

The widow took the letter from her again. "Until that time—if it should ever come—I shall carry out all that has been requested of me to the best of my ability."

"You can't stop me from seeing Pieter!"

"You're mistaken." Geetruyd regarded her calmly. "It is obvious to me that the young man is an unsuitable suitor from whom your father wishes to protect you. Among the institutes and almshouses of which I am regentess is a home specially for wayward young women. I am the consultant on how they should be treated when special means are needed. If you should disobey me I would have you incarcerated as a disobedient daughter to let you cool your heels and come to your senses."

Francesca sprang furiously to her feet. "You're mad! Punishment has been virtually unknown in my home. Father would never condone such an extreme and wicked penalty!"

Now the widow became equally fierce, bounding to her feet and shaking a finger in Francesca's face. "Don't dare ever to insult me again! I'm your father's representative and as such will do everything in my power to keep you on the path he wishes you to tread. Recall what you read in his letter. Did he not write that I was to have complete author-

ity over you since he knew whatever decisions I made would be for your own good."

"You've misconstructed the whole situation. My relationship with Pieter is set on a course of friendship and nothing more!"

"I've heard that before! You're not the first young woman I've had to protect against her own foolishness. That is why you were sent to me."

Francesca made for the door. "I'm not spending a night under this roof! I'll seek refuge with the Vermeers and tomorrow I'll make other arrangements for my accommodation."

"You'll do no such thing!" Geetruyd moved with surprising swiftness to slam shut the door that Francesca had been opening. "I will have the guards from that home of correction after you in no time at all. It's located nearby. You'd miss the first day of your apprenticeship and perhaps a whole week, or a month, according to how long it might take you to become repentant. Should you ever try to see Pieter van Doorne after all the warnings I've given you I'll have you shut away for a minimum of eight weeks. How will your training fare then?"

Francesca had become ashen, unable to think immediately of any way out of this totally unreasonable state of affairs. "I'll write to Pieter tonight telling him about this tyrannical rule you have imposed on me and I'll send it in the morning."

"You may write that one letter to him, putting an end to meetings and any further correspondence, and I shall read what you have written before it is sealed."

"This is intolerable. If you think I'll submit to censorship—"

Geetruyd cut in. "It only applies to this one letter. I've no wish to act as a gorgon towards you. Everything can be perfectly harmonious during your time with me if you simply take notice of the rules I expect you to obey."

Angrily Francesca opened the door and hastened away up to her room. There she paced the floor, thumping her fist in fury against a bedpost and anything else that came into range as she struggled to come to terms with the conditions by which she was being forced to live. She felt trapped! Caged like an animal. All the joy with which she had approached this time of coming to Delft had evaporated. With everything falling to pieces around her would she find other setbacks

waiting for her at Vermeer's studio? What if he should prove to be as temperamental as her father? Suppose he had only taken her on as a pupil for the money and not because he believed her work had promise. He had had no experience as a tutor and might find it impossible to convey his knowledge through no fault of his own. Not once had she contemplated any of these aspects of her apprenticeship. Instead she had seen it as a blissful fulfilment of her dreams, never imagining that anything could go seriously wrong.

Again she thumped her fist, this time on the top rail of a chair, and she followed it up with another against the window frame. She scarcely dared to allow herself to think of Pieter, whose visits were now banned. Downstairs in the east parlour she had been confident at first that Hendrick would not want these restrictions on her exercised for any real length of time, but if he should have become slightly crazed by his melancholia would he ever consider her case logically?

She came to a standstill and drew a deep breath. Losing her temper was no solution to solving what she had to face. Always she had tried to be practical when meeting difficulties and it was particularly important now. She would write to Pieter as Geetruyd had directed, but follow it up with a second letter explaining the situation. Later when Hendrick began to emerge from his dark state of mind, which she was sure he would with time, she could enlist her sisters' help and Willem's to get her released from her bonds. Even then it was likely Hendrick would have to be pressed continually to get results. Kind at heart, he would genuinely intend to do as he was asked, but if absorbed in a current painting he would have no thought for anything else. In a cheerful frame of mind he would toss off matters that he took to be exaggerated —as when he was told tradesmen would wait no longer for their bills to be settled—and it was highly likely he would regard the restrictions imposed on his daughter in Delft in the same light. There was also the hurdle of his not liking to write letters. It was to be hoped that Aletta would compose the necessary letter to Geetruyd and that he would sign it. She had been surprised upon seeing how fully he had written to the widow. A few hastily scrawled lines were all she had ever seen from his hand before.

A tap came on the door. She whipped it open and saw a very small,

nervous-looking woman, no longer young, who was full of little fluttery movements, twitching at her collar and then at her rings. Once she must have had reasonably good looks, but the passing years had darkened the pigmentation about her sunken eyes and flecked her complexion as well as the back of her hands. Her wispy hair, showing beneath her starched cap, showed traces of pale gold amid the grey.

"I'm Clara Huys." Her shyness was such that it gave her a cowed look as if she expected constant hostility on all sides. "I hope you're going to be happy during your time with us."

"I thank you, but I'm afraid certain things will have to change before that is possible." Francesca stood aside for her to enter, but she declined.

"I've come to call you to dinner."

"I'm not sure that I'll be welcome at table."

"But you will! When my cousin Geetruyd has had her say she doesn't keep on about it."

Francesca knew that Clara was supposed to be watching over her, but there seemed to be no malice in the woman and even an apparent wish to be friendly. "Then I'll come," she said. "It's an old tradition that troubles should be put aside when sitting down at table and I'll abide by that."

"That's sensible behaviour. Try always to do what is right in this house and then all is peaceful."

At dinner, which was good and plentiful, Geetruyd chatted as naturally as if the scene between Francesca and her had not taken place. It was obvious she had no wish for sustained unpleasantness and what had happened was an incident on its own. Francesca maintained her courtesy and talked in return. Only Clara did not open her mouth, except to say "Please" and "I thank you" like an obedient child when a dish was offered to her. It was too early yet to be sure, but it seemed to Francesca that Clara had surrendered her whole personality and, being a gentle person, had been moulded by her more dominant employer into the role of a shadow in this house.

After dinner Francesca wrote to Pieter, telling him of the new rules about their relationship that she was forced to obey. She had propped her drawing of him, done on the night when he had brought the hyacinth to her home, against the vase of violets, the fragrance of which

made her feel close to him, although the words she was writing were to keep him away. She hoped he would read between the lines and realize the letter had been written for another pair of eyes.

Mercifully Geetruyd did not devour the contents of the letter, but only glanced through it in a crisp, businesslike way. "That's well done." Then she sealed it. "I shall see it's dispatched tomorrow. You can look forward to the first day of your apprenticeship without any other task being put on you. Now good night and sleep well."

As soon as Francesca had gone to her own room Geetruyd sat back in her chair and gave a little sigh. It was never easy during the first weeks of looking after someone's wayward daughter in need of discipline.

Yet, if she judged rightly, Francesca was more intelligent than most of the girls that had been in her charge, some of whom she had had incarcerated for their own good. Moreover, Francesca had a dedicated purpose for being in Delft and would be sensible enough to avoid any folly that might interrupt her apprenticeship. It should not take long before there was submission to the rules of the house and then all would run smoothly for the rest of her stay.

There was nothing unusual in Ludolf's messenger coming to give such short notice about the girl. It was usually a crisis that triggered off the banishing of a daughter to more capable hands. Since Ludolf was the patron of the artist concerned, it was natural that he should have been called upon to help arrange stricter accommodation after some sudden alarm on the father's part over Pieter van Doorne, whom Francesca had been most anxious to see. And unchaperoned, indeed!

What had been startling was the news that Ludolf sent, together with his urgent request for her to take the girl in, that Amalia had finally died. Her immediate thought had been that he was free at last! When his aim for political power and position were fulfilled, he and she would be able to take up again where they had left off and on a very different basis.

It was a long time since they had first met and too long since she had last seen him, although they were in touch through what might be called business matters. It was due to his generous payments that she was able to enjoy some of the luxuries of life, although at the same time

she was proud that everything she owned came from her own hard work. Nothing had come to her easily.

Her brute of a father had married her off when she was fourteen, neither knowing nor caring how she would fare with her old husband in Rotterdam. Dirck Wolff had been parsimonious to the extreme, begrudging money for everything. She was his third wife and soon became no more than a housekeeper, poorly clothed and poorly fed, and he kept a stick at hand with which to beat her if she spent a stuiver more than he had allowed at market.

She was twenty-five and had been married to Dirck for eleven wretched years when she had met Ludolf, suntanned from seafaring and well dressed, being ashore again after months at sea. The attraction between them had been instant.

It had been so easy to meet. Her old husband liked to keep at the fireside or shut himself away counting his money. There was a hostelry with a rear entrance in an alley where she could enter with little chance of being seen. It was where Ludolf had taken her for the first time. Never before had she seen a man in red silk undergarments and she had been amazed to learn that such male finery could be had in several magnificent colours. It further astonished her when he removed everything he had on before making love to her and expected her to do the same, which she had done quite shamelessly. All that had happened had been a revelation to her, including her response to him, and before she left his arms she was in love with him.

Often he was away for a year or two at a stretch, although there were also times when his ship needed repair or some other cause had arisen when he could reappear after three or four months, which meant that every day she awoke in the knowledge that she might see him again before nightfall. It had sustained her through the bleakness of her marriage and it was he who had eventually rid her of her old husband. She had admitted him into the house after dark while Dirck snored by the fire. Ludolf, entering the room silently, had slit his throat. She felt faint with horror once the deed was done but had kept her head, her own alibi well prepared. As soon as Ludolf was well away from the house and she could be sure he had reached the safety of his ship, which

was sailing at dawn, she began screaming and rousing the neighbour-hood.

In the will she had been left only the house and half its contents; the rest, with all Dirck's money, went to his adult children, whom she had never seen. Having previously arranged with Ludolf where he could find her again, she left Rotterdam and moved to Delft, where she rented the house in Kromstraat. There she had set out to establish herself as a respectable member of the community.

It was a far more natural state to her and suited her temperament, for respectability brought its own strength and protection. There was nothing hypocritical in her service to the community, for she had always had a sense of duty drilled into her, first through filial obedience to her father and then, still young enough to be malleable, by her husband's demands that put her at his beck and call.

It had been no surprise when Ludolf had married Amalia, because she understood his motive. At the time she had been agonizingly jeal-ous, but throughout the years he had made intermittent visits to see her and their passion was undiminished. Then, when they had set up their line of work together, it had been advisable for him to stay away and not to correspond, although she did send him reports by those whom they could both trust.

"I bid you good night, Geetruyd." Clara had put her head into the room.

Geetruyd stirred in her chair. "Are you still about? You need your rest. Don't forget you have to escort Francesca in the morning."

"I'm looking forward to it."

As Clara went up to the next floor, Geetruyd went downstairs to check that all was securely locked for the night. One of her first actions upon coming to Delft had been to take Clara as a companion, not caring to live alone, for at that time she had dreamed too often of that horrific occasion in Rotterdam. She had plucked Clara from an orphan-age where she had grown to adulthood from birth and ostentatiously given her a home. Her charity had not gone unmarked by the board of regentesses and had stood her in good stead later. Clara, a meek crea-ture, already cowed by a particularly strict regime, had been easy to

manage from the start and was gratefully loyal for having been removed from institutional life.

Going upstairs to bed, Geetruyd paused by Francesca's door. There was no sound of tears. Some girls cried themselves to sleep for nights after first leaving home. Stifling a yawn, she went into her room.

Francesca had not heard footsteps pause outside her door. She had expected to lie awake, but after climbing into bed and sinking down between the lavender-scented linen into the soft feather mattress, she had realized for the first time how exhausted she was, not only from the journey but from the stress of all that had happened since her arrival. It was as if she had only just closed her eyes when Weintje came clumping into the room with a container of hot water to put on the tile-topped table.

"It's six o'clock, *mejuffrouw*. Breakfast is at half past," she said on her way out.

Francesca leapt from the bed, stripping off her night shift as she went. Today was the day! All her doubts and trepidations had vanished with a good night's sleep. She bathed herself with the hot water, put on fresh undergarments and then dressed her hair before putting on one of her new and practical gowns in violet and deep blue.

When ready she went downstairs to the dining hall. As at dinner the previous evening, Geetruyd was perfectly amiable throughout breakfast. Again Clara said nothing, but she was waiting by the entrance door when Francesca came with her tapestry bag holding a clean smock, palette and brushes. Remarking on the fine weather, they fell into step, Francesca looking about her with interest. They turned into the opposite direction to that by which Francesca had entered Kromstraat with Geetruyd the previous afternoon and came into a street that led them across a bridge over the canal at Oude Langendijk and then on into the large market square. At the east side was the great New Church, looming in its mellow hues with the tower piercing the sky, while facing it to the west was the magnificent Town Hall with its giltwork aglitter in the sun, its blood-red shutters flung wide at all its many windows. Gabled houses, many of some grandeur and others with shops at ground level, lined the north and south sides. As in Dam Square in Francesca's

own home city there was a busy scene with stalls set up and people thronging around them.

"There's Master Vermeer's house!" Clara pointed to a corner house on the north side of the square close to the church. "The narrow alleyway running alongside, leading out of the square, opens into the little street of Voldersgracht, where he was born. He can look out of his back windows into it."

"It's a large house," Francesca remarked as they approached it across the square. "At least double the frontage of its neighbour."

"That's because half of it is the tavern, known as the Mechelin, and the residential half on the corner side is usually referred to as Mechelin Huis. Master Vermeer's late father, Reynier, was a silk worker and dealt in art as a sideline. The family went through hard times, but eventually Reynier prospered and he bought the Mechelin and turned it into a thriving tavern. Probably whoever built the house originally had lived in the town of Mechelin, or why else should that place name be in the pediment?"

It was clear that the little woman enjoyed passing on all this information. Her face was animated with bright spots of colour in her cheeks as if she were blushing at this position of importance her role as guide was giving her.

"Do you remember Reynier Vermeer?" Francesca wanted to know.

"Indeed I do!" Clara's hands flapped at the memory. "Such a boisterous man! He would use his fists to deal with troublemakers in his taproom and then toss them out into the square. His son had to help him at times."

The house and the tavern each had its own entrance. By the lack of symmetry it was apparent that the latter had been inserted when the property was first turned to a commercial purpose. The door was painted green like the shutters and stood open, a buzz of voices from within showing that business was already in progress. The residential half had a very fine old door of dark oak, its bronze knocker gleaming. The white stoop was damp from its morning scrub, as was the individual pavement of grey tiles that fronted the property, those of the tavern no less clean.

"I was told before I came that Master Vermeer rents out the tavern," Francesca said after Clara had knocked and they stood waiting.

"That is correct. He gave up everything to do with it after his father died, which was shortly before his marriage."

The maidservant who admitted them was an amiable-looking young woman, her hair hidden under a white kerchief knotted at the back, while her blue apron showed that she had been engaged in the usual morning routine of washing every floor throughout the house.

"The master is not in at the moment, Juffrouw Huys," she said to Clara while her bright eyes took in Francesca from head to foot with a surreptitious side glance. "He has gone to send a picture by canalboat to Leiden, but my mistress wishes me to take Juffrouw Visser straight to her."

"Very well, Elizabeth." Clara turned to Francesca. "I'll leave you now, but I'll be back at six when your day here ends."

The door was shut after her. Elizabeth bobbed as she said, "This way, if you please, *mejuffrouw.*"

The house seemed so light and bright after the one in which Francesca had awakened that morning that she almost blinked. It was well furnished in the sparse Dutch style that set off each piece to advantage with pastel walls hung with maps and paintings, chequered marble floors and bronze chandeliers suspended from white plastered ceilings with black crossbeams. There were the usual steps between different levels on the ground floor and a maze of corridors through which Elizabeth led her before stopping to tap on a door. A woman's voice replied from within.

"Enter!"

Elizabeth opened the door for Francesca, who went into the room alone. Catharina Vermeer sat serenely suckling her baby, at whom she was gazing. With her blue bodice unlaced to reveal the whiteness of her chemise and the pale curve of her naked breast, she could have been posing for a painting of the Madonna and Child. An aura of light from the window shone about her neatly dressed head, giving a sheen to her light brown hair and touching the down on the infant's head. Slowly she looked up and for a moment the illusion held, for her expression was one of sweet contentment. Then, like an awakening sleeper, she

emerged from the euphoria of single-minded motherhood and became alert again to her other duties as mistress of the house, her face animated and smiling.

"You're here! I hadn't heard you arrive. I'm Catharina. There's no need for any formality between us. Come and sit down. Have you breakfasted? You can't paint on an empty stomach and I can send to the kitchen— Oh, you have eaten. I've heard Vrouw Wolff keeps a good table. Jan won't be long. Oh yes, I call him Jan, although he is Johannes to most of those who have known him longer than I. That's eighteen years and we've been married for seventeen of them. Our elder son is named Johannes too."

Francesca had warmed to her immediately, for she exuded an open friendliness that was entirely without guile. She had a round face with a creamy complexion, very sparkling brown eyes under arched brows, a pretty nose with a slight tilt and when her smile was wide it curved her mouth like a crescent moon lying horizontally. In all it was a well-formed, expressive face which any artist would want to paint, and Francesca thought it not surprising Willem had said that Catharina was her husband's favourite model.

"What is your baby's name?" Francesca peeped down at the infant guzzling its milk.

"This is Ignatius—a long name for such a mite, but I'm almost running out of names that I like for our children. I've been put off so many by people I know. I would have invented lovely names if it had been possible, but then children have to live with them all through school and you know how children hate to be different from one another."

Francesca was highly amused, for it had all been said with tongue in cheek and yet with a basis of truth. This was a charming woman who, in spite of constant pregnancies and all the many tasks a large family created, had lost neither her sense of fun nor her youthful looks.

"It might have been possible to name them after tulips," Francesca joked. "Semper Augustus would have sounded very grand, or there's Laprock, which would suit a prince in a fairy tale as well as a handsome male child."

Full of laughter, Catharina plucked the baby from her breast and held

him high to look into his sleepy little face. "You might have been called Catolejn's Red and Yellow! How would you have liked that, my sweeting?" The baby burped just as if he had made a disparaging reply and she gave a shriek of mirth which blended with Francesca's laughter, and hugged him to her before removing him to her shoulder and patting his back. With dancing eyes she looked across at her husband's new pupil. "You must be a gardener or a great lover of flowers to know those names."

"Both. I could say the same about you."

Catharina shook her head. "No, but I've heard so much about flowers from my mother, who lives in Oude Langendijk, the street near where you are staying. She has a garden with parterres and trees that is quite perfect and yet she lets my children play there. We have no garden here. Look out of the window and you will see."

Francesca went to the window and leaned out. Below her a narrow canal shimmered alongside the rear wall of the house and those of its neighbours as far as she could see up and down the length of the street of Voldersgracht. Small bridges gave access to it from the alleyways leading through from the square. She saw at a glance that the almshouse of red brick opposite had been depicted in a painting that she had noticed on her way to this room and which only could have been painted from this very window.

"I saw this view on the corridor wall," she said, having retained an instant impression of the painting's beauty and peacefulness. One of the inhabitants of the almshouse was sitting in an open doorway with some sewing, exactly as another woman had been portrayed in the picture.

"That's one of my favourite works by Jan," Catharina said happily. "He called it *A Little Street in Delft*. When I particularly like one of his paintings he lets me keep it. That's why when people come to his art gallery, thinking to buy one of his works, they find nothing there and do not know what we have in the house."

Francesca returned to where she had been sitting. "My father painted several portraits of my mother that he'll never part with. To return to the subject of your mother's garden, how often do your children go there?"

"As often as they can. I'm afraid they run riot when they get there,

but my mother never minds. She grows the most superb tulips and one year two of the children tripped and fell among some of the best. You should have seen that array of broken stalks!" Catharina rolled her eyes in dismay.

"Perhaps your mother would let me make some sketches of her flowers and then I could create a floral painting later on."

"I'm sure she would. Mind you, I don't think you'll get much flower painting with Jan, although I'm sure he'll let you please yourself sometimes as to what subjects you choose. You won't find him a hard taskmaster, although he can be terribly strict at times. He has to be with the children and so do I, or else he'd get no peace in which to work. I think that's why the children get so exuberant when they're in my mother's garden. There they can make as much noise as they like."

"Does Master Vermeer paint many portraits of them?"

"No! They're far too fidgety and restless. He has drawings of them, but if you didn't know we had offspring you'd think when viewing his paintings that there was not a child in the house. Except," she added as an afterthought, "he has painted me during two or three of my pregnancies."

"How many children have you?"

"Eight now." Then Catharina's face clouded and her eyes went to the baby in her arms. "We have lost two children, the second only last summer."

"I'm so sorry."

"I can't talk about it."

"I would not expect you to," Francesca declared sympathetically. Out of consideration for the woman's feelings she took up another subject. "Is there one of your husband's paintings in this room?"

Catharina looked up again and shook her head. "There are a few in other rooms in the house and a half-finished one in the studio. Maybe you would like to go along there and see where you will be working while I change the baby's linen before putting him down to sleep?"

"Yes. How do I find it?"

Francesca would have found her way easily from the clear directions Catharina gave her, but before she reached the studio she met three little girls waiting for a glimpse of her.

"Good day, children," she greeted them. "I'm Francesca Visser and, as I expect you know, I've come to complete my training as an artist with your father. Would you like to tell me your names?"

The tallest girl, with a prim air and hair the colour of honey, bobbed respectfully. "I'm named Catharina after my mother, but Papa started calling me Rina and that is how it stayed. I'm nine."

"Are you the eldest girl?"

"Oh no, that's Maria, who is fifteen."

Francesca spoke to the second girl, who was bright-eyed and freckled. "And you?"

"I'm Lysbeth. On my next birthday I'll be eight."

The youngest, a merry-looking child with impish eyes, jumped up and down now that it was her turn to speak. "I'm Beatrix and I'll soon be five!"

Rina gave her a shove. "Be still now. You'll wake the baby with all that noise." To Francesca she added, "Our new brother is three months old."

"I saw him. He is a fine baby." Francesca knelt down and put an arm around Beatrix, drawing her close.

Both the other girls knelt down too, Rina to move into the crook of Francesca's free arm while Lysbeth, conscious of her appearance at all times, spread her skirts carefully around her. They started to ask Francesca many questions about her home and family, wanting to know if she had any more sisters and if she had brothers too. In the animated conversation none of them noticed the sound of footsteps along the corridor until Francesca saw out of the corner of her eye that someone in a pair of bucket-topped boots had come to a halt beside her.

She looked up from where she knelt. Master Jan Vermeer, hands resting on his hips with elbows jutting, a black hat thrust to the back of his head, was grinning down at her. His face registered with her before he spoke. It was long and oval, framed by a shoulder-length mass of frizzy brown hair, eyebrows arched over twinkling eyes. The thin nose, turned down at the end with a slight crookedness to it as if at some time it had been broken, had nostrils flaring back. The mouth was wide and sensual, revealing small, uneven teeth, and his chin was firmly

rounded. He leaned over her, thoroughly entertained by finding her in the midst of three of his offspring.

"Are you a new nursemaid or my apprentice?"

"Both at the moment!"

He reached a friendly hand down to her and raised her to her feet. "Welcome to Delft, Francesca!"

CHAPTER 1 2

As Jan led the way through several rooms to the studio he asked Francesca about the training she had received from her father and nodded approval when he heard that basically it had followed the pattern of Hendrick's own apprenticeship.

"Here we are!" He flung open the studio door for her to enter.

It proved to be a somewhat grand room for an atelier and was a full twenty feet or more in length. Situated at the front of the house, it looked out on the market square, but as the ground floor was above street level there was no question of anyone being able to look in, even though one of the windows with its coat of arms set in coloured glass was open. An ornately fashioned chandelier flashed back the brightness of the morning and the walls were cream-coloured, one half draped in a rich wool tapestry in shades of russet, dark orange, yellow, green and a sharp blue. A darker blue cloth over a brown one covered one table and on another was all his artist paraphernalia. In the middle of the black-and-white tiled floor stood two easels with stools in front of them. She guessed that one was for her, but she went to the other, on which was propped a painting that was all but finished.

She saw at once that Jan Vermeer was an artist who used pure light like paint on the tip of his brush. It was as if she was seeing her own aims made visible, for here was the masterly technique that she had always worked for without ever having seen anything that came near it. What had always been in her head and in her heart was before her in this painting of Catharina, the whole scene bathed in clearest daylight that caused textures and surfaces to refract, absorb and reflect its intensity, all there for a purpose, nothing by chance. Francesca's gratitude sped out to Willem, who had seen something in her work that was akin, in a small undeveloped way, to that of this master. She was too choked to speak and took in every detail of the subject matter in silence.

The painting showed Catharina in a yellow silk jacket trimmed with ermine and a skirt of slightly deeper hue, sitting with a lute in her left hand as if interrupted while playing. Her right hand was upraised and holding a letter that had just been handed to her by Elizabeth, who was clad in the same white kerchief and blue apron in which she had opened the door that morning.

Both Elizabeth and Catharina were viewed through a doorway and not only was the painting astonishingly beautiful but there was also much symbolism in it. The maidservant's encouraging smile and the woman's half-startled, half-wary look showed that she was uncertain whether the letter would contain good news or bad. That it was from a lover was made clear by her lute, linking music with the pleasures of love, and there were several sheets of music on a chair in the foreground. Lying on the tiled floor was a pair of shoes, symbol of sexual passion. Yet Francesca knew, as any other viewer would have known, that all would be well with the romance, for a seascape hanging on the wall behind the woman was of a ship on a calm sea. Had it depicted a storm with rough waves then the outcome would have been different. A broom, shown propped by the shoes, further endorsed that the woman would be a good housewife. In all it told a story full of love and desire that was destined for a happy ending.

"There can be only one title to this painting," Francesca said quietly, "and that is *The Love Letter.*"

"Correct," he answered.

She glanced keenly about the studio. "You didn't paint it in here, did you?"

"Not in the beginning. I chose the dining hall. I wanted part of that colonnaded fireplace for the composition and the richness of the gilded leather on the walls. I wasn't popular with Catharina," he added with a

rumbling laugh, "for choosing to stand my easel in that doorway at intermittent intervals, blocking the way. We all had to eat in the kitchen until the painting had reached its present stage, when I could move back here."

"I like the theme of the letter."

"It's one I've used many times before and I daresay I'll use it again." He did not offer an explanation and she did not question him. Her gaze was held again by the painting. Suddenly she spoke low and intently as she turned a desperately serious face to him.

"Teach me to paint with those condensations of crystal light! That quicksilver play over silks and satins! Nothing in this work of yours is indifferent to the brilliance of day and yet, whether figure or object, all is in total harmony. Show me what I must do!"

He did not answer her immediately but rested a hand on the corner of the painting's stretcher frame, his eyes narrowing at her. "I would say from your painting of your two sisters that you're more than halfway there."

She became pale at his praise. "I thank you, but there is still a long way to go."

"Agreed, but I wouldn't have taken you on as a pupil if you had not been thus far advanced. As you may or may not know, I simply don't have the time to start from first rules. The instruction and advice you receive from me will be concentrated and that is what you need."

"You'll find me attentive to all you say."

"Good. De Hartog told me that your training with your father had all but faded out. Yet you should always be grateful to Hendrick Visser, because it is he who has given you the rocklike foundation on which to build your work."

"I realize that. I've heard him say often enough that so much can be taught and so much is basic talent, but the interpretation of a visual experience onto canvas comes from the very soul of an artist."

"Indeed it does."

"Long before I understood its meaning, my father used to quote Leonardo da Vinci's advice—observation, experimentation and analysis."

"A golden rule for any artist." His gaze became more speculative. "I

269

see you as one of those diamonds that find their way to the gem dealers of Amsterdam. Your ability as an artist has been rough-cut by an experienced hand. My role is that of polisher. What happens during that latter process will be entirely up to you."

"I want only to strive forward."

"Then I foresee a future of achievement for you, perhaps beyond the realms of your present imaginings, but time will tell." He relaxed on a more jovial note. "At least by coming into my studio with so much training behind you, all the chores usually allotted to an apprentice in the first year are far behind you."

She gave a little laugh. "I was well taught in that respect. Everything from making brushes to binding drawing pads!"

"My daughters Maria and Aleydis are my willing assistants when I require their help in that respect. My elder son Johannes used to be mainly in the studio, but gradually he realized a painter's path was not the one he wished to follow. Now he is apprenticed in Haarlem to a silk merchant, learning to design silks, as did my father at that age. By rights I should have done the same, because that was what I was taught when I was growing up in my childhood home on Voldersgracht. My father still had his silk business when he became more prosperous and began to deal in works of art. When he bought the Mechelin he continued to buy and sell paintings as well as spirits, wine and beer."

"You have only kept to art dealing in addition to painting yourself?"

"That's right."

"So who is to follow in your footsteps?"

He shook his head. "If you mean as a painter, none of my children as far as I can tell. Unless Ignatius should surprise me one day." He grinned as he mentioned his youngest son.

"May I see your gallery when you have time one day to show me?"

"What better time than now?" He threw out his hands. "You can't work this first morning when you are getting to know us all. You'll meet the rest of the family at the noon meal, except, that is, Johannes. As he is an apprentice, he is not often at home."

The gallery had once been an extra-wide corridor with a wooden floor along which barrels had been rolled to a door into the Mechelin's taproom. That door was now locked, but Jan had retained the corridor

when leasing the tavern, for it had its own entrance from the side alley with good light from two large windows. Down the length of it was a long oaken table stacked with etchings and drawings for customers to browse through and the walls were covered with paintings of every size. A cool place in summer and able to be kept moderately warm in winter, it was perfect for paintings, especially for those on wood, for panels would crack or split apart in extremes of temperature.

She wandered around looking at the work. "I'm sure you sometimes get paintings to sell that you'd prefer to keep."

"Quite often. I've a little masterpiece here by someone who taught me much about painting when I was young, but as I have three of his works already, I have to let this one go." He beckoned her across to a painting on the wall that she had not yet reached. "It's by the late Carel Fabritius, a former pupil of Rembrandt. I'll be offering it to de Hartog next time he's here, but I'll not like to see it go. Superb, isn't it?"

She nodded and yet the subject matter saddened her. It was a goldfinch perched on a wall box and held by a chain about its leg that was only long enough to let it flutter a few inches into the air. Many people kept captive birds, but there had never been one in her home, because that would have gone against Hendrick's principles of freedom. It was odd that he should have deprived her of that same freedom now. She was chained as securely by his and Geetruyd's restrictions as that beautiful painted goldfinch on its box.

Something of her thoughts must have shown in her face, for Jan's gaze became hard on her. Leisurely he perched his weight on the edge of the table, speaking straightforwardly.

"What's all this about your having to be escorted everywhere? Vrouw Wolff came to see me yesterday, full of demands that you should never be allowed out of this house to sketch anywhere on your own and other such tomfoolery. I heard her out and I'd like to hear your side of things. I abhor tyranny and all that Geetruyd Wolff said smacked strongly of it."

Francesca explained fully. Since she was to spend many months under his tutorage she was glad to have the situation clear from the start. Jan listened to all she had to say, frowning deeply when he heard of Geetruyd's ugly threat about the institution.

"Are you sure there is no other reason why these stipulations should be laid down?" he queried when he had heard everything. "Has your father any cause for personal dislike of Pieter van Doorne?"

"None at all. I would have known. My father can never hide his feelings. Yesterday, when I was leaving home, he welcomed Pieter to the table to eat with him. Yet all the time that letter had been written to Geetruyd Wolff. I simply don't understand and, as I said to you, I can only blame it on some quirk of his melancholia. Even a while ago when Pieter asked his permission to court me, my father did not just send him away, which was an arrangement he and I had about suitors. Instead he gave me the chance to think again about Pieter. That can be summed up as my father encouraging me towards a courtship as never before, except that I stipulated friendship with Pieter instead."

"So what are you going to do?"

"For the moment my hands are tied. Until my father relents, which I hope won't take too long, I am a prisoner of Geetruyd Wolff's unnecessarily harsh discipline."

He smiled grimly. "I do advise you most strongly to beware of her power. She is a tartar, the scourge of many a committee, and will not be crossed. I could have saved you all this if I had insisted in the first place that you had bed and board under my roof, as is usual for apprentices, but I thought that, as you were older, it would be better for you to be accommodated with some liberty away from the studio. Also—to be frank—I wanted to spare my wife from having another adult female in the house. It did not work when my late mother lived under the same roof for the first year of our marriage, and although the circumstances would have been entirely different, I vowed then that it should never happen again."

"I quite understand."

"I do sympathize with your predicament, and should you find yourself in special difficulties at any time, please remember Catharina and I are here to help."

"I appreciate that."

Francesca felt cheered after talking to him. Just before the noon meal she met his three other daughters, Maria and Aleydis, who had been spending the morning with friends, and Truyd back from school. The

girls were full of talk and not in the least shy, all pretty and slender and vibrant.

"If you want any pigments mixed," Maria offered willingly, "Aleydis and I know exactly what to do and even Truyd is learning."

Aleydis nodded, brown curls dancing, a myriad dimples in her laughing face. "We are experts, especially if you favour yellows and blues and greys and whites as Father does."

Catharina had appeared from the direction of the dining hall and Francesca, remembering those colours had dominated the painting in the studio, looked at her inquiringly. "Doesn't your husband like to use the whole palette?"

"He did in his earlier work and he has painted me twice in red gowns, but I admit he does prefer a softer range now and always his beloved yellow."

As soon as they reached the dining hall Francesca recognized it instantly from the setting of the studio painting. There was the colonnaded fireplace, the handsome wall covering of gilded leather and the seascape hanging above the chair where Catharina had sat. During the noon meal Catharina told her that originally it had been arranged, in agreement with Willem de Hartog, that Francesca should stay next door with some good neighbours during her apprenticeship.

"It would have been so convenient for you, Francesca," she continued, "being so near. It was such a surprise and disappointment to us yesterday when Vrouw Wolff arrived to inform us she had been given sole responsibility for you."

Jan supported her words from the head of the table. "At least we must be thankful you are not farther away."

Catharina nodded encouragingly at Francesca. "We hope that you'll spend time with us after working hours whenever it is convenient."

Francesca smiled appreciatively. "I should like that very much. It's good to know that I have friends in this house."

That afternoon Francesca started work, deciding she would paint the market square within the frame of the window. Jan provided a small wooden platform for her to stand on to improve her view and stayed to discuss what she was doing. It was time for her to go back to Geetruyd's house almost before she realized it.

Jan showed her out through the drawing room, which had been hidden from her view by closed double doors when she had arrived at the house that morning. Now, coming into it by another door, she saw it could have been called a music room. At one end of the long room was a clavichord, a particularly large and graceful instrument with a shaped lid that was raised when the keys were being played. Beside it was a viola da gamba and on the wall hung a lute. At the opposite end of the room were two virginals set apart and a guitar lay on one of them. She looked at Jan with delight.

"I can see this is a house of music as well as art!"

"It is. Do you play?"

"The virginal."

"Then you must join in our family concerts."

"I should enjoy that so much." She had paused to look at another painting of Catharina. Again there was the theme of a letter, but the atmosphere was entirely different. It showed her in the last months of pregnancy, dignified and beautiful, wearing a blue silk jacket that swelled out over her extended figure and was tied with ribbons. She was standing in front of the studio table with the light streaming over her while the tranquillity and tenderness that prevailed were almost palpable.

"You see," Jan said at Francesca's side, "even when my good wife is pregnant she poses for me."

"She told me about that."

"The title is simply *A Woman in Blue Reading a Letter.*"

Francesca was studying it keenly. "I know exactly what is portrayed here. This is a woman who has just received a letter from her husband, who is far away. Perhaps he is at sea and has sent it from a foreign port. Or else he's on business in a distant Dutch town. Either way he is concerned about her bearing their first child. She's very alone and aware of it. Even that chair in the foreground on the right creates a barrier between her and us. Yet she is full of love because it is a married love letter that he has sent her."

There was a pause before he spoke. "What can I say? That is what I aimed for and you have voiced it all. When I told Catharina what I wanted to bring out in this painting she took all the love letters I had

written to her during our courtship and reread a different one every day."

She felt her heart contract on some emptiness within herself. Her voice came quietly. "It sounds as if you and Catharina exchanged many letters."

"We did. They were of extreme importance to us when it seemed as if we were never to be allowed to marry. Both our families were strongly against the match. I was twenty-one, only recently finished with my apprenticeship, a brand-new member of the Guild with no money and little prospect of ever having any. Since Catharina was Catholic and came from a well-to-do background while I was the Calvinist son of a tavernkeeper who didn't want me to take on the responsibility of marriage so soon, I suppose it was not a surprising impasse."

"How did you win through?"

"My parents finally gave in when they realized how resolved I was to have Catharina, and her mother relented when my former master made an appeal on my behalf."

"No wonder you showed such understanding of my simpler problem over a friendship."

"There is nothing new under the sun, is there?"

She returned his smile. "I suppose not."

Outside the double doors, which would be opened for social occasions, Francesca found Clara patiently waiting for her, seated on one of the sapphire-blue, lion-headed chairs. She was eager for talk and questioned Francesca all the way home.

That evening after dinner, Francesca sat down in her own room to write another letter to Pieter. This time she explained the situation in full. She wrote a different letter to Hendrick and her sisters. After telling them about the Vermeer family and her first day she added a description of Fabritius's painting of the chained bird. She knew it would hold a message for her father, aware that she was using the symbolism of it in her letter much as it might have been used in a work of art. Hendrick would associate her with the captive bird and himself as the one who had fashioned the chain. It would touch his sensibilities far more than any written plea would have done.

Catharina had also been writing letters to invite family and friends to

come to Beatrix's fifth birthday party in July. When the last invitation had been written she arose from the table at which she had been sitting in the upstairs room where Jan dealt with all business matters. Picking up the branched candlestick that had illumined her task, she left the room, crossed the landing and went into every bedchamber where her children lay sleeping. All was well.

This was the time of day that was important to her, when she could feel free to spend a little time on her own with Jan. The candlelight showed the way for her as she set off downstairs, knowing where her husband was to be found, for the resonant notes of the viola de gamba came from the drawing room, sounding much like the hum of a particularly melodious bee.

When she hastened across the hall her new silk petticoat, a gift from her generous mother, rustled about her ankles. Catharina thought it was a measure of Jan's tolerance that he never showed resentment over his mother-in-law's generosity or the children receiving gifts, which were often ill timed. They frequently came when he was going through a lean period with a lack of sales in his art dealing and debts began mounting up again. Yet he knew that nothing his wife received from any other source could compare with the gift of large pearl earbobs that he gave her as a marriage-morning gift after their first night together.

Their marriage was satisfying in every way. Jan with his kind heart was both her lover and her friend, which made the essential qualities in a good husband. Kindness in a man covered everything from shared pleasure in bed to concern for everything else important in family and everyday life. If anything, she loved him more now than in those first halcyon days of their passionate union. She was also proud of him for being held in such high regard in Delft. It was to him that the local authorities turned for advice on works of art, and he who had to approve paintings offered for public auction in the town.

Catharina passed a richly carved cupboard on her way to find Jan at his music. It was one of the items that had come with her as part of her dowry, together with some lavish furnishings, including the costly Turkish rug that draped a table in the drawing room.

But the house was not without its own grandeur, for Jan's father had been in comfortable circumstances when he died and the house had

been furnished accordingly. His widow had not been able to take everything she would have liked when moving from the Mechelin after a year of living under the same roof with her son's wife—a year filled with domestic conflict. Digma Vermeer had left behind those items of furniture she knew Jan preferred, for he had been the apple of her eye, even if she had never approved his choice of a wife.

Catharina entered the drawing room. Jan was seated at the far end on one of the lion-headed chairs that his mother had bequeathed him. He had the large viola da gamba propped at a comfortable angle and supported by his spread knees on each side of it, the fingers of his left hand high on the strings, his right hand drawing the bow. She thought how, at that moment, he personified the close link between painting and music. He looked up and smiled as she came towards him, but did not interrupt his playing. She put down the branched candlestick and seated herself to listen quietly until the last note hummed into silence.

"I like that piece," she said approvingly. "Are you going to play it on the evening of the party?"

"I thought I would." He rose from the chair and carried the instrument across the room to prop it in its place near the clavichord. "Is everything quiet upstairs?"

"Yes, peace at last! How did you get on with your pupil today?" She patted the velvet cushion of the couch for him to join her there by the fire, for it had turned unseasonably cold that evening and Elizabeth had lit it for him at his music.

"I think Francesca will excel, given time and the chance to strengthen certain aspects of her work. My only anxiety is that she is already baulking at the conditions laid down for her by Vrouw Wolff." He gave his wife a full account of all Francesca had told him. "So I hope there is not going to be so much harassment as to interfere with her concentration."

"You'll have to put your foot down with Vrouw Wolff if it does." Catharina made a little grimace. "Five minutes with that self-righteous woman was more than enough for me." He had put an arm about her and she rested comfortably against him.

"In addition to everything else, it appears that Francesca has been forbidden to see or write to a young fellow of whom her father previ-

ously approved even to the extent of encouraging her to agreeing to courtship."

"Who is the young man?" she asked.

"His name is Pieter van Doorne, a horticulturist of Haarlem. Did Vrouw Wolff mention him to you?"

"No. It was all the stupid nonsense that she spouted to you. She seemed to take it for granted that you would always accompany the girl and I didn't disillusion her."

"With this threat of incarceration in a house of correction hanging over her, Francesca had to write and let Vrouw Wolff read and approve a letter telling van Doorne not to visit Delft."

"That's despicable!" Catharina was outraged.

"I agree." He leaned forward without taking his arm from her to boot a piece of burning peat, which was threatening to topple, deeper into the heart of the fire. When he sat back again his hand rested familiarly and caressingly on her breast. "I can't understand what all the fuss is about. Francesca told Vrouw Wolff, as she told me, that she and van Doorne should be able to meet as often as they wished since there is only friendship between them. The girl is really upset about it."

Catharina half raised herself to look with mock surprise into his face. "You believe it's only friendship, do you?"

"Francesca was quite definite about it."

"It sounds to me as if she were trying to convince herself more than you." She tapped his chest with a forefinger. "Women don't go up in the air about friendship. There must be more to it than that."

"You've missed the point. There is a principle at stake and I agree with her. If she's responsible enough to be apprenticed like a man, then she should be equally capable of looking after the social side of her life without interference."

"Agreed, but I'm sticking to my romantic theory." Catharina raised herself higher and kissed him on the lips. His arms closed around her and he held her to him, lengthening and deepening their kiss.

"Let's lock the doors," he said softly.

She leaned her head back to regard him playfully. "We have a perfectly good bed upstairs."

"Do as I say, sweeting."

There was a velvet look in his eyes that in itself was a promise of all sorts of sweet treats for her. She slipped from his arms to cross to the double doors and then to another through which she had come into the room, turning the key in each. He was a man who needed the width of a bed for his lovemaking and there was no question of the narrow couch being used, although he had taken the cushions from it to toss them down in front of the fire. These were followed in a swirl by the Turkish rug, whose rich hues made an exotic spread for her. He pulled off his jacket and she released her ribbons. Within seconds of her petticoat being discarded he encircled her warm nakedness in his arms and drew her down to the rug with him. They surrendered to their mutual passion in the combined glow of the candles and the fire.

In the morning Francesca placed the letter to her father and sisters in a silver bowl in the hall. Geetruyd had told her it was for incoming and outgoing post. She knew it would reach her father swiftly, for Holland had an excellent postal service with sorting offices in all the main towns, which she had heard was without parallel in Europe, but it was expensive. Although her sisters had spoken of corresponding with her, she could be sure they would have to wait and send letters to her only when someone they knew personally could deliver them, Vrouw Wolff had mentioned what the postal rates were the previous evening and she put the necessary money on top of Hendrick's letter.

As soon as Clara had left her at the Vermeers' house, Francesca went to Catharina to ask if Elizabeth could take her letter to Pieter to the postal office. "I had to tell him the truth of this bizarre situation," she explained after ensuring that Jan had told Catharina everything as he had promised he would.

"Of course Elizabeth shall post your letter for you," Catharina said willingly. "Give it to her now and then it will be sent without delay. Afterwards go along to the studio and forget your troubles. Things have a way of working out and I'm sure that eventually it will be like that for you."

Francesca passed a peaceful day in the studio. Jan was also there for the morning and she was not surprised to learn that he spent nine or

ten months over each of his paintings, for his brushwork was meticulous, deep thought behind every stroke. He had some business that took
him away from the house in the afternoon, but she had enough of the
market square on her canvas for his helpful words to have had effect.
She found herself using small angular touches such as he had shown her,
and took note of his warning that if she should create the foliage of the
trees by placing blue on yellow, which he favoured in his work, she
should remember that with time the blue would predominate and allow
for that.

As on the previous evening, Clara was waiting for her and the little
woman's question was the same. "What have you accomplished today,
Francesca?"

It was clear that a pattern had been set, but Francesca answered her
tolerantly, aware of feeling much more relaxed than she did after a
similar day's work in her father's studio. The reason dawned on her. At
home there were so many interruptions. Maria or Griet frequently
sought her advice on some domestic issue, or she would have to stop
work herself to go to the market, receive a visitor or make some
obligatory call on a neighbour. Here she was completely free to concentrate on her work with nothing else to think about. It could have been
like that to a degree when she was painting in Ludolf's house, except
that there were distracting influences of another kind. Foremost had
been the strain that his presence put on her, almost as if it had been a
tiger instead of a man she was painting, never quite sure when danger
might spring on her. There were also those bewildering emotions over
Pieter that had troubled her before everything had been settled as
friendship between them. She would never want to go to Ludolf's house
again now that Amalia was gone. Pieter was due to start the landscaping of the garden there this week, but, as he had told her on the way to
the stage wagon that last morning, the beautiful little bower he had
planned for that sweet-natured invalid was no longer to be included. At
least it was possible to be certain that Sybylla's bright company and her
playing of the viol had brought Amalia much pleasure and comfort in
her last days.

Clara led the way into the Wolff house. Francesca, following after

her, saw Geetruyd standing in the hall to await them—with one hand behind her back as if she was hiding something from view.

"Good evening to you, Francesca," the widow greeted her. "We have something to discuss."

Out of the corner of her eye Francesca saw Clara scuttle away. It could only mean some new trouble ahead. "What could that be?" she queried coolly.

"This!" Dramatically Geetruyd brought forward her hand from behind her back and waved to and fro a letter with Francesca's own handwriting on it. It was the one to Pieter that had been dispatched by Elizabeth only that morning.

"Where did you get that?" Francesca demanded furiously.

"It was sent to me from the postal office by the official in charge. I told you I was not without influence in this town. It is not the first time he has been alerted by me to intercept forbidden correspondence, and I had warned him that you were likely to bribe Vermeer's servant or one of his children to send a letter secretly on your behalf."

"How dare you interfere with my private correspondence!" Francesca was trembling in her fury and she held out her hand for the letter.

"It has not been read." Geetruyd held up the letter and turned it about almost with the air of a conjurer to show that the seal had not been broken. Then deliberately she tore it into several pieces. "I shall see that this evidence of your disobedience is burnt. Mark this as a last warning, because you know what will happen if you attempt to disobey me again."

Francesca went with dignity to the stairs, her head high, but torn by wrath and frustration within. How was she ever to endure such close surveillance? It was imprisonment! She felt she could not breathe. If only there were a flower garden to the house where at least she could escape its four walls. Then she thought of Catharina's mother, Vrouw Thin, who had a garden and lived nearby. Perhaps after she had met Vrouw Thin she might be allowed to sit there sometimes to draw the blossoms and the trees. This small ray of hope, linked as it was to the chance of some liberty, helped her to bear up under Geetruyd's new act of tyranny.

When an opportunity arose during the next day Francesca told Cath-

arina what had happened to the letter. Catharina advised her to write it again here in the Mechelin and Jan would post it when he visited some other town, but Francesca declined the kindly intended offer.

"I don't want to cause any bone of contention between you and Geetruyd. As you know, she is a dangerous woman. I must be patient and await a chance of my own to send a letter to Pieter. I feel it will not be long before Willem de Hartog comes to Delft again and he would take letters for me." She then broached the subject as to whether Vrouw Thin might allow her to visit now and again, explaining the reason why.

Catharina immediately gave her approval to the idea. "Nothing would please my mother more than to have a fellow flower enthusiast appreciating her garden. It is not right that you should have to spend summer evenings cooped up with Vrouw Wolff. Leave everything to me."

When Clara called for Francesca at the usual time, she flew into a panic at hearing that her charge had finished work early and had gone home with Vrouw Thin to the house on Oude Langendijk. She set off for the address, almost running, but before she reached it she met Catharina, who took her by the arm and turned her around to retrace her steps, walking with her.

"I've introduced Francesca and my mother to each other," Catharina explained. "When they have finished inspecting and discussing every bloom in the garden, Francesca is going to dine there."

"So late! When am I to fetch her?"

"There's no need. She will come home in my mother's sedan chair borne by two of the most reliable bearers in Delft. Neither you nor Vrouw Wolff have any cause to worry."

At Vrouw Thin's house Francesca spent another hour with her new acquaintance in the lovely formal garden with its neat parterres and straight paths, its sundial and shady mature trees. She and Catharina's mother were now choosing which blooms should be the ones to start her off on a flower painting, which she had decided she would paint stage by stage as other flowers came into bloom, just as she had thought of doing at home in Amsterdam before she knew she was to go to Delft. It would be in addition to the painting she had begun of the

market square and any others that might follow. They had agreed that morning picking was essential and that Francesca would come for the first of the flowers on her way to work one morning when the canvas was prepared and she was ready to begin this new venture.

"It's a pity the tulips are over," Vrouw Thin said regretfully. She was diminutive and full-bosomed, friendly in face and manner, handsomely gowned in dark green satin. Her eyes were round and blue with thin little eyebrows of a shape that made her appear permanently surprised by all she saw, which would not be the case, for she was a worldly woman. "I would have let you pick the choicest of them all."

"But remember, this flower painting will be a year on canvas," Francesca said smilingly. "I'll add the tulips when spring comes again."

"Splendid! Of course you will!"

When Francesca arrived back at Vrouw Wolff's house in the sedan chair Geetruyd was surprisingly amiable about the unexpected outing. The reason was soon revealed, if unwittingly.

"Vrouw Thin is most generous to the fund for maintaining the almshouses of which I am a regentess," Geetruyd said smugly. "I and my committee invite her to meet the inmates once a year. You have my permission to visit her whenever she is gracious enough to ask you to her home."

Francesca breathed an inward sigh of relief that there was to be no opposition. She had been given an open invitation by Vrouw Thin to go to the garden whenever she wished.

As the weeks went by, the Delft jug, which had been given a permanent place on a table in Jan's studio, was to hold a succession of choice flowers morning-picked from the Thin garden. As peonies gave way to clematis and then to roses and gillyflowers, Francesca's first impression that Jan was the best master possible for her had been more than confirmed. He was the type of teacher who could fling doors wide to a new vision and understanding, able to make more penetrating that precious inner eye. In a few words, or with the demonstration of a brushstroke, he could give the exact knowledge she needed.

Unlike her father, who could never have followed such methodical

ways, Jan planned every detail of a painting in advance. For as long as anyone knew, artists had used gadgetry to help them in their craft, not all as free-painting as Frans Hals and Hendrick, and the camera obscura had been employed for over a hundred years. Jan introduced Francesca into the use of it, as Hendrick never had. The principle of the device was that a lens, inserted in a box, would reflect in reverse into a darkened area whatever the artist had set up to paint in the light. A canvas or a piece of paper was pinned to the wall to hold the image while the artist drew around the shapes reflected. When the drawing was put the right way again, the artist had his subject matter ready for painting.

Jan had enlarged on the idea. With the aid of screens and a lid he could erect a large box against a wall into which he could step into complete darkness. A fine lens, locally made in Delft, where the fashioning of high-quality lenses was fast becoming an industry, gave a perfect reflection in full colour of the subject matter he intended to paint, a great improvement on the smaller boxes, and she admired his ingenuity. It was not that Jan or any other artist could not have drawn the subject matter of a painting in free hand, but the camera obscura saved time while shadows, forms and architectural detail were captured with perfect accuracy. Francesca found Jan's version most helpful at times, although—like her master—she did not use it for every work.

Jan was away from home more than Francesca had anticipated, but since art dealing was his principal means of livelihood it took priority over his painting. She asked him once why he did not paint more himself and make dealing in other people's work a sideline.

"As you've seen for yourself," he replied, "I am a slow painter. Even if I were not, my work has no appeal outside Delft. I've no idea why that should be, but I'm not complaining, because everything I paint finds an immediate buyer within the town itself. My neighbour Heer van Buyten, a master baker, has purchased some of my works. The book printer Jacob Abrahansz Dissius is also a keen collector of my paintings and has twenty. There are others locally who will buy whenever one becomes available. The prices I receive are far higher than I could expect to obtain in places where I'm not known, although I do have a good patron in Antwerp. I never sell my own paintings to de Hartog

because he could only raise a few guilders for anything of mine in Amsterdam."

She knew that on the very day Jan had declared *The Love Letter* finished it had been snapped up by Heer Dissius. She wondered if the fact that Jan painted so little and had such ready purchasers was a double handicap to his work reaching a wider field and surely the general acknowledgement that it deserved. It would be interesting to talk this over with Willem when he should come, but that had not happened as yet.

At the present time Jan was making preliminary drawings of Catharina in various poses for another painting with a letter theme. When she saw him crumple up and throw away those that did not please him, she asked if she might have the next that would otherwise be cast out. He agreed, saying she could have her pick of them. She chose three of these exquisite drawings and at her request he signed them for her, his signature consisting of "Meer" with a vertical dash above, one of several variations of it that she had seen on his other work.

These three drawings were the first works of art to be displayed on the walls of her bedchamber. They were a distance away from her own drawing of Pieter, which was propped on her table and tucked away in a drawer when she was absent. She could never be sure that Geetruyd would not destroy it if she should see it and guess whose likeness it was.

Daily she yearned for a letter from home. She knew there was no chance of hearing from Pieter after the brusque message she had been forced to write to him. If she had known then that the second letter was not going to reach him she would have written more fully the first time. Yet this was easy to feel with hindsight and she reminded herself that she had been almost too distressed to think properly that first terrible evening.

Her daily routine had settled to light and shade, the bright hours being those she spent at the Mechelin Huis and the clouded ones those passed under Geetruyd's roof. Often when her day's work in the studio was at an end she would stay on to dine with the Vermeers, a concession that Catharina had won on her behalf from Geetruyd. Then she would help put the younger children to bed, enjoy a card game with the older girls and sometimes play the virginal when dinner was over. It had not surprised her that music should be appreciated in this house as much as art, for there were few homes where families did not encourage singing and playing of musical instruments. Jan always escorted her home, Catharina often coming as well when the evening was fine and she felt in need of a walk. It was usual at these times for a long detour to be made in order that Francesca could have interesting and historic features of the town pointed out to her. She had been for walks with Geetruyd and Clara and went to church with them every Sunday, but their company lay heavily upon her and it was not the same as being with the Vermeers.

Francesca was overjoyed one evening to see that there was a letter for her in the silver bowl. It was from Aletta and had been delivered by hand. A wave of homesickness swept over her and as soon as she was on her own she brushed a hand across her eyes before the swim of tears subsided to allow her to read. As she had hoped, it was full of family news. Hendrick's knuckles were much improved and the mobility of his fingers had fully returned. Maria boasted that the cure was her doing, but not in his hearing in case he became contrary and refused to drink her decoction of herbs another time should the need arise. He insisted that extra work had done the trick. Two commissions had come in for history paintings and Ludolf had bought through Willem the painting of the tax collector, although at a moderate price. The best of the good news was that Hendrick was not gambling. He met his drinking companions in the taverns most evenings, but frequently came home sober. As a result there were no tradesmen hammering on the door for money, and life was comparatively peaceful.

I have seen Pieter several times, Aletta continued. *Whatever has made you change your mind about seeing him in Delft? I have no idea what you wrote to him, but whatever it was he is far from pleased over it. Your letter to us was most welcome, although I have to remind you on Sybylla's behalf not to forget to describe Vrouw Vermeer's clothes next time. Our neighbour Heer Zegers will be delivering this letter when passing through Delft, but will have no time to delay. I hope next time we may find a bearer who will be able to collect a reply from you. We all miss you, especially Father, who was morose and irritable for days after we heard from you, which is a sure sign that your well-being is much on his mind.*

Francesca sat meditatively when she had finished the letter. So her description of the caged goldfinch had made its mark on Hendrick and her message had gone home. How long would it be before he had a change of heart towards her circumstances? She dropped her head in her hands as she anguished over Pieter's disappointment in her. Somehow she *must* get in contact with him. Perhaps the solution was to tell everything to Aletta and let her inform him. But she could not be sure that Aletta would hold back from taking up arms on her behalf against Hendrick, and the last thing she wanted was to create strife in her home during her absence. Yet this seemed to be the only path open to her. Although the hour was late she wrote to Aletta at once, impressing on her not to rile their father in any way and to call on Sybylla as a last resort.

She was about to get into bed when she heard a knocking on the entrance door of the house. Her window was open and she looked out in time to see a traveller admitted. There had been several comings and goings during the weeks since her arrival, but only once had she come face to face with one of the overnight guests. The man was from Utrecht and they had had a short conversation in the hall when leaving the house at the same time, she to go to the Mechelin Huis escorted by Clara, and he to catch a stage wagon to continue his journey. Although Geetruyd liked to emphasize her modest means, her way of living did not match her words, and it seemed to Francesca that the widow liked to pretend genteel poverty while actually having a good income, or else her visitors paid her exceptionally well for their accommodation. The former seemed the most likely. It would explain Geetruyd's fine gowns, good wines and rich food. Only when she attended one of her charity meetings did she dress in plain grey or black and even then the fabric was of the very best.

Francesca would have gone to sleep without another thought for the traveller if the muffled sounds of a quarrel had not reached her from one of the ground-floor rooms. Since she was two floors above there should have been no chance of any noise reaching her, but this was an old house and she supposed some hollowness in a wall, or perhaps a deep crack in the plaster somewhere, was funnelling the disturbance through to her. More than once the banging of a door in that downstairs room had made her sit up in bed or look towards her door in the momentary illusion that it was close at hand. She could not distinguish the words of the quarrel and neither did she want to, but there were the unmistakable shrill tones of Geetruyd and the angry rumble of a man's reply. Perhaps he had left last time without paying his bill and was about to be shown the door. Then as Geetruyd's voice rose to a piercing note a scrap of what she said came through. ". . . she'll re-member your face, you fool!" After that there was six or seven minutes of sustained quarrelling in lower tones before Geetruyd left the traveller and came up to bed, the sharp tap of her heels seeming to convey that her anger was unabated.

Normally Francesca would not have looked out of the window when she heard a guest departing early in the morning, but this time she did. As he crossed the street and hurried away she saw to her surprise that it was the man from Utrecht to whom she had spoken on his previous visit. He was either catching an earlier stage wagon than before or else he could not get out of the house quickly enough. Not that he would have avoided meeting Geetruyd again, for she was always dressed and downstairs to receive her travellers' payment before they departed.

Francesca pondered over what she had heard. Why had Geetruyd been so furious about someone remembering his face? Surely the widow could not have been referring to her? Why should it matter in any case? If Geetruyd, for some obscure reason of her own, wanted her guests to have the ultimate privacy at all times, she should not have had an apprentice to stay in her house, for the odd chance of meeting was always there. One thing was clear. If this was a typical incident, she was on far more familiar terms with her travellers than she had admitted. Francesca frowned. Since Geetruyd had not been present when she had had her conversation with the man from Utrecht, Clara must have reported it. Unfortunately it put Clara in a new light as Geetruyd's spy, something that Francesca had not considered before, and she supposed that everything she told the little woman about her work and her home was reported back to build up some kind of casebook about her. What a mercy it was that she could forget everything connected with this house at the Vermeers'!

Before leaving for the studio Francesca went across to the fireplace,

which was the source of the voices and sounds that had reached her. Careful examination revealed that at some time the fireplace had shifted slightly, leaving a gap between itself and the panelling, which was not unusual in a house of great age. Putting her hand to it, she could feel a draught, showing there was a definite funnel somewhere from the room two floors below. She had some spare paint rags and she stuffed them into the aperture, not wanting to overhear any more conversations not meant for her ears.

Aletta was on her way to see Pieter. She was anxious not to delay in telling him of the restrictions being placed on Francesca's freedom and correspondence, which she had read about with shock and dismay in the letter received only an hour before. She knew where to find him, for only yesterday he had told her that the flagstones for Ludolf's paths were being delivered and laid this morning and he would be there to oversee the work. She did not think she could just go through to the garden without making her presence known, and duly presented herself at the entrance door to the house.

"Is Heer van Deventer at home?" she inquired when it was opened.

The manservant recognized her as having been at the banquet with her father and sisters. "No, *mejuffrouw,* Heer van Deventer is away from home for several weeks."

"Oh, I am sorry to have missed him. I also want to speak with Heer van Doorne, who I understand is to be here supervising the work in the garden this morning."

The manservant smiled obligingly. "Heer van Doorne has been here for some time. If you will follow me I will take you through to the garden."

He showed her through to the drawing room, where doors opened out onto the terrace. There Aletta paused to gaze appreciatively down the stretch of the beautiful garden. She had no idea of how it had looked before Pieter had refashioned it, for it had been dark on the evening of the banquet when last she was here, but it was now a vista of parterres and lawns with a little avenue of newly planted half-grown trees that carried the eye forward to a glade with a fountain and the

promise of more secluded areas of peace and charm beyond. She thought sadly how it would have enchanted Ludolf's late wife. She could not see Pieter, but his gardeners were everywhere. As she was about to go down the steps in search of him a woman's voice spoke to her.

"Juffrouw Visser."

Aletta turned to see a fair-haired woman in a white cap and black gown that proclaimed her to be a servant of the van Deventer household. "Yes?"

"I heard what you said at the door." The woman bobbed to her. "We have not met, but I'm Neeltje. I was the late Vrouw van Deventer's personal maid until her tragic death. Would you mind if we went down to a sheltered seat that is hidden from the house? My master has gone away, but I should not be seen idling and I have a warning to give you for your sister, Juffrouw Francesca."

Aletta, her curiosity aroused, went with her down the stone steps and along to the seat. There they sat down, turned slightly towards each other. "What is it you wished to say to me?" Aletta prompted.

But Neeltje was not to be hurried, and she began to tell Aletta about herself. "I was orphaned when I was twelve and had to get work wherever I could. My only asset was my ability to sew and eventually I obtained regular employment with a seamstress making garments for well-to-do women. It so happened that I was given the task of making a wedding gown of blue satin for my late mistress's second marriage, this time to Ludolf van Deventer. When I heard that her personal maid had no wish to move with her to Amsterdam after she was married I went specially to ask her to let me become the replacement in her service. That same evening I was able to move out of the hovel where I had lived into the home that had been hers and her first husband's. I finished the wedding gown there."

"I'm sure it was the beginning of a much happier time for you."

Neeltje's eyes became hard and glittering. "It would have been if I had not seen her married to that monster!"

Aletta drew back startled. "What are you saying?"

"Van Deventer is a liar and a hypocrite! As soon as I can find other

work better than that of linen maid, which I have become, I shall leave. I tell you that Juffrouw Francesca is in danger from him!"

"You must be mistaken," Aletta exclaimed. "She is working in Delft and will be there for a long time yet."

"Van Deventer's hand can reach out anywhere!" Neeltje made a grabbing gesture in the air. "Did your sister tell you that she would have been subjected to indignities by him if I had not entered the room in the nick of time?"

Aletta felt chilled. She guessed why Francesca had said nothing, wanting to spare her a revival of memory that still brought on the occasional nightmare. "When did it happen?"

"On the day of the banquet. Only hours before his wife—died." Neeltje had almost said "was murdered," because she was sure it had not been a natural death. Weeping with grief, she had laid Amalia out, in spite of the pain of her cracked ribs at the time, for she had been determined that nobody else should perform this last service to the woman who had always been good to her. It was then that she had seen a faint bruise at the jawline and almost under the ear. In addition, three fingernails were broken. A terrible suspicion had seared through her. At the first opportunity she had secretly examined the couch and found clawed threads in the silkwork. There was also the smear of carmine on the cushion consistent only with Amalia turning her face fully into it. In her own room she had held a cushion over the lower half of her face before a mirror and seen where knuckles of a hand holding it down with force might well have caused such a bruise as she had seen on her mistress. Her conclusion had made her shake so much that it was as if an ague had come upon her. She knew the identity of the murderer as surely as if he had confessed. When the doctor came to see her again, in order to make sure her breathing was not affected by the state of her ribs, all she had intended to say to him about the conclusions she had drawn was silenced by his first words.

"You were the last to see Vrouw van Deventer alive, Neeltje. How exactly was she at that time?"

Immediately she had seen that if foul play did come to light, she would be the first to be accused. No one would suspect Ludolf with his constant show of devotion that she knew to be totally false. So she had

held her tongue while burning with rage and hatred against him. He had twice brought devastation into her life, even though he probably did not remember the first time, but that was something she had long kept to herself and was not to be divulged to this gentle-faced girl. "I would not wish van Deventer as a husband for my worst enemy and it is my belief that he means to have your sister as his next wife."

"She would never marry him! Neither would my father permit it! Your fears are groundless!"

"That's as may be. I tell you that van Deventer is a man easily obsessed by violent ambitions and at the present time he wants your sister above all else. He is besotted by the likeness of her as Flora. It draws his eyes as if he were magnetized by it and thus it was when she was in the house. He guarded himself when others were present and even when she looked directly at him—until that last time when they were alone. I had long observed him with her from the shadows and my own watch points in the house, and I saw such lust in his face that I trembled for her safety and I still do."

Aletta could see that the woman meant every word said. "Why should you take such a risk yourself to tell me all this? How do you know that I will not speak of it and bring about your banishment from this house sooner than you anticipate?"

Neeltje was unmoved by this testing. "Because I have heard your sisters speak of your love of family and your integrity. Both of them, especially your younger sister, brought such happiness to my late mistress in the last weeks of her life that I'll always feel indebted to them. It is for that reason that I am asking you to let Juffrouw Francesca know that her whole future might be hanging in the balance."

Aletta felt sick with dread. This well-meant and yet awful advice coming on top of her learning of the restrictions on Francesca's freedom, even though her sister had emphasized all that the Vermeers had done for her, made it easy to believe some disaster lay ahead. "I must tell you there is one person in whom I feel it is essential to confide all that you have told me."

Instantly Neeltje was wary. "Who is that?"

"Heer van Doorne, who has redesigned this whole garden. I know he is in love with Francesca and should some threat be levelled against her

he is the one best able to deal with it. He will respect my confidence and I trust him completely."

Neeltje gave a nod. If the Visser family trusted him that was good enough for her. "Inform van Doorne by all means. I have done all I can for your sister by telling you what I believe. It is up to you, and those you can rally to help you, to see that what I fear never comes about." She rose from the seat to go back into the house.

Left alone in a daze of foreboding, Aletta went to ask one of the gardeners where Pieter was to be found. She almost ran in search of him.

Indoors Neeltje returned to the linen room, one window of which looked down into the garden. She kept her chair by it, partly because it gave her a good light over her left shoulder, but most of all because she liked to glance out at the work in progress. She sat down and picked up the damask tablecloth which she was in the process of mending. The garden would look very fine when it was finished, but it would never have what had once bloomed in a small tulip bed outside the humble cottage that had been her childhood home.

She let her hands rest with needle and thimble as her thoughts drifted back to those days. Times had been hard and money always short, but her parents had been good and kind, her childhood a happy one. They had had a cow and Neeltje had helped her mother make the cheese and butter that they took to market together with the vegetables that her father grew. Long before tulipomania had swept through the land he had been given half a dozen tulip bulbs, probably believed to be of inferior quality, in lieu of payment for produce, and he had begun to grow tulips for sale.

One morning, not long after her mother had died and tulipomania was in full spate, he had rushed into the cottage where she was baking bread. He was shaking with excitement.

"Come and see!"

He had grabbed her by her floury hand and rushed her outside to look at a tulip on the point of bursting into bloom. It was that rarest and most sought-after colour which all growers were seeking to achieve —a black tulip!

Both of them knelt on the earth gazing at it. She felt bound to warn

him against disappointment in case it should prove to be no more than a dark purple. "My dear child," he had said, "it will be black, you'll see."

He was right. When it came to its midnight-hued bloom there had been an almost velvety look to it. The local pastor, who could be trusted to keep the secret, came to bear witness to the colour and write a testimonial while impressing on them both not to let a slip of the tongue betray them before the time of selling. But her father was so jubilant that he could not resist a word in confidence to one neighbour and then another.

Then on the evening before he was to take the bulb into town, two well-dressed strangers called at the cottage, a large man and a youth of about seventeen whom he introduced as his son. They had come to make an offer for the bulb before it reached the open market and mentioned a sum of so many hundred guilders that her father had stood openmouthed, for it was far more than he had ever expected. Although she was twelve at the time she was still shy in the presence of strangers and she kept back out of the way, watching everything. While her father and the large man talked, she studied the face of the youth, trying to think where she had seen him before.

Proudly her father brought out the precious bulb and the testimonial to place them on the wooden table. When the man asked if he might hold the bulb, her father willingly agreed and the youth took up the testimonial to read it. Then in the next second the man deliberately dropped the bulb to the floor and crushed it to pulp with his heel while the youth hurled the testimonial into the fire.

"What have you done?" her father shouted heartbrokenly. "That was the only black tulip in all Holland!"

To which the man had given an extraordinary reply. "On the contrary! Only yesterday I bought another, which is now the only one. If you had sold yours on the open market it would have halved the price of mine! Now you have no proof that yours ever existed!"

Her father had never been a violent man, but he was so incensed that he grappled with the man to stop him leaving, shouting to her to run to the neighbours for help. But the youth had drawn a heavy bludgeon from under his cloak and struck him such a mighty blow across the head that he fell with a cracked skull and blood spurting. Then both

men fled to their horses and galloped away. It was a neighbour who heard her screaming and came running to find her temporarily out of her wits with shock.

After a while she did remember where she had seen the youth before. It had been in the marketplace when a band of strolling players were taking their bow at the end of a performance and he had been among them. Inquiries were made, but he had left the company on the day of the murder. When eventually the bulb of the black tulip had surfaced in the open market it had changed hands too many times, frequently in taverns, where many such deals took place, for the two criminals to be traced.

Yet Neeltje had never forgotten the youth's face. When she saw him again many years later she had recognized him instantly, although in no way did he connect her, a mature woman in her thirties, with a child he had barely noticed in the shadows of a candlelit cottage. Taking up her mending again, she thought how satisfying it was to be thwarting Ludolf van Deventer's chances with Francesca Visser, but it was not enough. True vengeance was needed. Not for one murder only, but for two.

CHAPTER 1 3

Hendrick pondered over Aletta having received a letter from Francesca. The fact that she had not shared it with him or, to the best of his knowledge, with anyone else in the household was confirmation of what it contained. During the day he had seen the flash of accusation in her expressive eyes before she had lowered her pale lids and scurried away upstairs. Her speed had suggested that she was afraid of what she might say to him if she stayed any longer in his company.

That evening at dinner Aletta did speak of the letter from her sister, giving the information that Francesca was well and working hard. "She writes that Master Vermeer has an almost ethereal control of his brush, able to create vividly as well as sensitively and accurately. With a single touch of paint he can reveal the gleam of a pearl such as Francesca has never seen done before."

"That's nice," Sybylla commented mundanely, her thoughts busy with her own affairs. She had two suitors at the present time and had no intention of marrying either, since both were craftsmen of moderate standing with no chance of ever making a large fortune, good-looking though they might be. If Francesca had written only of painting she was not really interested in seeing the letter, although it was odd that Aletta had not offered to let her read it.

"Well?" Hendrick prompted, wanting to hear more of Vermeer's technique.

Aletta's glance fell on him as coldly as a dousing of canal water. She spoke meaningfully, knowing he alone at the table would grasp what lay behind her words. "Francesca didn't include anything else about her work or that of her master in the letter."

He stared her out with the bravado he could summon at times. "Then the rest of what is written can be of no interest whatever to me!"

When Aletta dropped her gaze he knew that she understood she should not try to intercede on her sister's behalf for any change of the arrangements in Delft.

Maria, always concerned for the well-being of the three girls, did not notice the tension between Hendrick and his second daughter any more than Sybylla had. "When you write again, child, tell Francesca always to wear a straw hat in the sun."

"I will," Aletta replied in a strained voice.

Griet, who was observant, was curious to know what the trouble was. She wondered if the master ever realized that Aletta, in spite of her docile appearance, could be as stubborn as he when the need arose.

Willem made a visit to Delft to collect the Fabritius goldfinch painting that Jan Vermeer had kept for him. Their business was settled, Willem taking several other paintings by lesser artists as well, before he went along to the studio to see Francesca.

"How good to see a friendly face from home!" she exclaimed. "I trust I find you well. What news of my father and my sisters?"

All the time he was answering her he had one eye on her work. She had chosen as her subject one of the younger Vermeer children, the little girl called Beatrix, who was shown sitting on the floor in the full light from the window and playing with a doll. Not only was it enchanting, but Vermeer's influence showed in the impression of a single captured moment. Some portrayal of movement could have been expected with an active child at play, but by the tilt of the young head and the hand hovering over an arrangement of the doll's gown Francesca satisfied the beholder that all would have been still in that brief moment of contemplation. As with the master, so it was with the pupil. Francesca was learning fast and putting her own interpretation on canvas.

"It is good that you came to Delft, Francesca," he said in a congratulatory tone.

"I'm thankful for every day in this studio," she said enthusiastically, "but I should like to move from where I am staying into other accommodation." Quickly she explained everything, including all she had been forced to write to Pieter. "You know Father so well that I'm sure your backing would make all the difference when Aletta feels the time is right to appeal to him."

"I'm an old-fashioned man," he said staidly. "I believe young women should be chaperoned every step of the way. It is how my own daughters were guarded and I happen to think it's right for you here in a strange city. To be frank, I always thought you and your sisters had far too much liberty at home. Frequently you all went here, there and everywhere without escort, just as Aletta and Sybylla still do. For a long time Maria has been far too old to keep a properly caring eye on three pretty girls. I can't be sorry you are under the guardianship of a regentess. To me, that shows you could not be more safely protected. For once in his life, your father has made a wise move in my opinion."

"What of Vrouw Wolff's terrible threat of shutting me up if I should disobey her?"

"If you are obedient you have nothing to fear. I see that warning of

hers as a deterrent to waywardness, such as a birch in a teacher's firm hand can quell uproar in the classroom without action being taken."

She was bitterly disappointed that she had not gained his support. "Would you at least take a letter to Pieter for me and have it delivered when you are back in Amsterdam? I have one that I wrote a while ago and I have kept it here in the studio until such time as I could ask someone to do this for me."

"My dear girl," he said gently and not without sympathy, "I can't go against Hendrick's wishes. If he changes his mind at any time I will take any number of letters to this young man for you, but until then I have to refuse."

The disappointment in Francesca's face and the sad droop of her hands distressed Willem. He moved over to the window, troubled by the hurt he was causing and remembering how burdensome Francesca's life had been during the past five years since her mother's death. Not only had she shouldered increasing domestic responsibilities, but she had coped with a totally unreliable father whose drinking and gambling left her to struggle with debts on every side. As for Pieter van Doorne, it was possible that Hendrick's present unaccountable state of depression and melancholia might have caused an unreasonable aversion towards a young man whose advances he had previously encouraged. A very different life from that once enjoyed by his own daughters!

Willem turned back to Francesca. "Don't be so upset, dear child. I'm not sure I'm doing the right thing but I will take your letter to Pieter. As it may be some time before I return to Amsterdam I will post it in the next town I visit. But this letter only—no more until Hendrick gives consent!"

Francesca's gratitude and thanks were overwhelming. True, she was still tied to Geetruyd Wolff, but she told herself this might prove only a minor setback and she was herself again by the time Clara came to walk back to Kromstraat with her.

The morning of Beatrix Vermeer's fifth birthday Francesca worked on her own in the studio. Upon her arrival earlier she had handed her a gift of a little wooden doll in a green gown, which had delighted the child.

It was almost noon when Truyd and Rina came bursting into the studio with the birthday girl, who was prancing about in her excitement.

"No more work for today, Juffrouw Francesca!" Truyd and Rina chorused happily. "As soon as the noon meal is over everyone is to get ready for the party!"

Francesca had brought a best gown with her that morning to change into, as she always did when invited to one of the Vermeers' social functions. Twice Heer and Vrouw Dissius, who had such an enviable collection of Jan's paintings, had included her in invitations to musical evenings with her master and Catharina. On other occasions she was made welcome next door to the Mechelin tavern, where the master baker Heer van Buyten lived with his wife and family. Among the Vermeer paintings on their walls was a charming one of Catharina in a yellow gown playing the clavichord accompanied by a gentleman with a guitar and a woman singing. It was exactly how she had seen the Vermeers grouped with friends on their musical evenings.

Francesca changed in an upstairs bedroom. A mirror enabled her to check her appearance in her gown of grape-green silk with its falling frill of lace around the scooped neckline. In her lobes she slipped the gold earbobs that had been her mother's and her thoughts turned to the times when she had prepared for parties at home. With a pang of yearning she recalled the evening when Pieter had brought the hyacinth to the house. Her longing to see him again had become a persistent ache that she could only overcome by concentrating on her work.

When she came downstairs guests were beginning to arrive. There were plenty of young children. All the adults, in the old custom of bringing *kindermaal*, carried cakes and other delicacies to add to the feast. These good things were placed on the long damask-covered table in the dining hall. Catharina's face was joyous as she greeted everyone with a kiss and embrace, having a special word for every child. She looked beautiful and elegant in a gown of heavy cream satin with a little ermine-trimmed yellow silk jacket that she had worn for *The Love Letter* and in which Jan had painted her several times previously. Her mother, Vrouw Thin, was present, also handsomely gowned, and watching fondly her grandchildren at play.

At the height of the fun Jan was called away to see someone who

had come to the house. When he returned soon afterwards it was to speak quietly in Francesca's ear.

"Elizabeth had shown a visitor into my gallery, thinking he was a buyer, but that was not the case. He is waiting in the more comfortable anteroom and would like to speak to you."

Her eyes widened, but Jan turned away without giving her any clue as to who it might be. Yet she knew—and did not dare to know! She went swiftly from the room and by the time she was near the gallery she was running. She flung open the parlour door and saw Pieter within. Joy and panic rose simultaneously in her.

"Pieter!" she breathed.

He rushed to meet her and she flew without further thought into his arms. His kiss took away her words, her breath, her very will. The realization of how much she had missed him made her lose herself in his kiss, almost as if in a frenzy, and she clasped him tightly around his neck as he held her crushed to him. It was as if they would never be able to part again, but eventually sanity returned and she thrust herself out of his embrace. She was trembling and rested a hand on the lion head of a chair as if for support. Her voice came huskily, scarcely above a whisper.

"It is well meant that you are here, but you shouldn't have come."

"After what Aletta told me of all you had written to her and then a letter from you, posted in Leiden, reached me yesterday afternoon, do you suppose I could have stayed away?"

"At least you know now why I wrote to you the first time as I did." She could not think what was the matter with her, for even her lips were tremulous.

"That first letter, coming so soon after your giving me your word you would say if our friendship threatened to interfere with your work, made me believe you had reached the decision on the journey to Delft."

"I guessed that."

"It also added up with what your father said to me on the morning of your departure about my not seeing you at all."

Her head shot up. "He said that to you?"

He frowned, puzzled. "Didn't you know?"

She shook her head wearily. "I don't understand what has come over him. Did he give you an explanation?"

"Only that he wanted you to concentrate on your work with no distractions."

She gave an empty laugh. "He said that and yet I'm forced to live chaperoned almost night and day and under constant threat of incarceration in a house of correction if I disobey the rules! I try to put all that from my mind when I start work in the mornings, but sometimes when Geetruyd Wolff has made some niggling complaint at breakfast I find it hard to slam a mental door on her."

He took her hands into his. "I've something very serious to discuss with you about Ludolf van Deventer."

She half turned her face away in disgust. "I don't want to talk about him! I'm thankful to say I've neither spoken his name nor heard it mentioned until now since leaving home. Aletta did write that he had bought another of Father's paintings, but that was an unwelcome reminder of someone I want to forget."

"That may never be possible if your father has promised that you will marry him!"

She stared at him incredulously. "Whyever should you suppose such an outrageous possibility? It could never happen. Father knows my views on marriage."

"He also knew of your love of liberty and independence, but has he respected that?"

Becoming very still, she looked searchingly into his face. "What have you heard?"

He led her across to a cushioned bench, where they sat down together, he continuing to hold her hands. He proceeded to tell her all that Aletta had told him of Neeltje's warning. Since he had given his word to Hendrick never to let her know of her father's dire straits, linked as it was with his own secret payment of her apprenticeship fees, he could not reveal his conviction that it was Ludolf to whom Hendrick owed a huge debt. During various conversations he had had with Aletta, she had all unwittingly revealed that the friendship between her father and his patron, which had started with card playing and visits, had cooled most noticeably. It had not been hard to deduce after

Neeltje's comments that it was this debt that could give Ludolf such a hold over Hendrick that anything could be demanded by the man. He saw Francesca's cheeks colour when he spoke of Neeltje's timely arrival in the library.

"That was a hateful experience," she exclaimed grimly. "I was foolish to have let him catch me unawares, because I had long since judged him to be the man he proved to be. I told nobody about it, because it was pointless to cause a breach between my father and his patron when I was going away in any case, never—I hoped—to see Ludolf again. But my father would never value any man's patronage above the well-being and happiness of his daughters. I feel you are placing too much importance on Neeltje's words."

"I choose to believe otherwise. I wanted to put you on your guard. Should such an arrangement be made for you I'll get you away to Italy by the first ship. I'd take you to your aunt in Florence out of harm's way."

"You would do all that for me?" she said wonderingly.

"I'd do anything for you!" he declared vehemently.

"But Ludolf could follow me to Italy."

"It would be a wasted journey for him, because by the time he arrived I would have married you with your aunt's permission. Dutch laws do not apply in Italy."

She gave him a long, steady look. "We agreed on friendship."

His smile was serious, as were his eyes. "Lovers are fortunate when they are friends as well. I'd leave you to study in Italy until such time as you wished to come home to me."

She could tell that uppermost in his mind was the certainty that once they had shared a marriage bed she would never be able to stay away from him, however much she might try. Her heart was opening to him like a rose unfolding its petals to the sunshine, all the love she had suppressed released at last to blossom fully. She spoke in a whisper. "Then what would happen?"

"We would live together in marital harmony, you with your work and I with mine. Maybe we could entice Neeltje into our home to take charge of household duties and relieve you of all domestic chores. If not, we'd find somebody else."

She uttered a soft laugh at the manner in which he was knocking all obstacles aside. He grinned, releasing her hands to put his arms about her and catch her close to his chest. She put her hand fondly against the side of his face.

"Have you forgotten what else I listed in my case against marriage?"

"No," he said, serious again, "but if we have a family while we're young and guard against it spreading out indefinitely, you'll have years and years in which to paint when the children have flown the nest and we're on our own again."

"And in the meantime?"

"Surely you'd let a nursemaid take charge for some hours of every day."

He looked at her in such despairing appeal that she smiled, stroking the frown away from his forehead. "You're finding ways to overcome all my arguments. You were not so adamant the first time we discussed this matter."

"I did not know then if you would ever love me. When two people love each other any difficulties can be overcome."

"I believe that too, and I do love you, Pieter."

His mouth took hers with such passion that she was lost to everything except the pressure of his lips, the strength of his embrace and her own sweeping desire. His whole physical presence seemed to be in her breathing and in her blood. When he caressed her breast she strained against him, wishing she could tear away the fabric that made a barrier between her flesh and his touch. She sank against him when their kiss ended, her head on his shoulder, her heart beating so hard that she was sure he must hear it. He passed a stroking hand over her hair and she felt that she arched like a cat straining for more fondling. He put his fingertips under her chin and raised her face to his.

"I'll come to see you as often as possible," he promised. "All the time Vrouw Wolff doesn't know who I am, I can come and go in Delft quite easily."

"But you must never be seen with me!"

"Don't be afraid. I'll act wisely. If Master Vermeer allows me to meet you here that will solve everything."

She sat up and away from him, although she kept a hand resting on

his wrist. "If he or Catharina should suggest it, that would be wonderful, but I can't ask them. It wouldn't be right for me to see you during studio hours, and later, when normally I should be back at the house in Kromstraat, would be dangerous. If Vrouw Wolff became suspicious she might well find some means of discovering the truth by questioning the children or the maidservant, and she would cause trouble for the Vermeers all over Delft. I know, Pieter, as do Jan and Catharina, that she is a dangerous woman."

"I understand that. Do you ever go sketching alone?"

"I'm going out into the countryside tomorrow, but Catharina and the children will be with me as on previous occasions and we're taking a picnic." She leaned towards him. "Perhaps another time I could arrange to be on my own."

He took her face between his hands and kissed her lips softly. "Somehow I'll have to find a means by which to let you know when I'll be in Delft again."

"You can't write to me here at the Mechelin Huis. Any letter bearing my name would go straight to Geetruyd Wolff, whatever the address."

"Maybe I can find a messenger to send one to you during your studio hours."

"That would be the only way."

Francesca felt it was time she returned to the party, having been half an hour or longer away from it, and after all she was a guest. In the gallery she reminded Pieter of their original agreement as he held her in his arms once more.

"After all we've said to each other an amendment is needed," she said.

"What would that be?"

"It has become a loving friendship."

His smile broadened. "I've no objection to that." Then he kissed her hard before leaving by the gallery door into the side street.

It was to be quite a time before he was able to find someone he felt able to trust to deliver letters to Francesca at the Mechelin Huis and to bring him hers in return. Then an old friend from childhood, Gerard Meverden, happened to call in at the farmhouse while he was in his office.

"Business is expanding all the time," Gerard said to Pieter after preliminary conversation. He dealt in potash, which was used in the bleaching of linen, and had recently bought a large house in Haarlem, having previously lived next to his warehouse. "I've opened up some outlets in Delft now."

"Shall you be travelling there often?"

"About once every six weeks, I expect. Why?"

"You're just the one I can ask to do me a favour."

"Ask away! What is it?" As soon as Gerard heard what was requested of him, a grin spread across his amiable face with its broad nose and heavy chin. "So I'm to play Cupid, am I? That's a new role for me. Give me your letters, old friend. I'll deliver them with pleasure."

When he returned from his first visit to Delft, he reported on how well he had been received by Catharina Vermeer, who had happened to open the door to him.

"Did you see Francesca?" Pieter demanded impatiently.

"Indeed I did. She had a letter in readiness in case of an opportunity arising, and I give her a little time to add a few lines to bring it up to date before I left again." He took it from his pocket and handed it over, his laughter-crinkled eyes bright. "She's a beauty. You're a lucky man. If any other purpose had taken me to the house, I'd be after her myself!"

Normally Griet would never have disturbed Hendrick when he was at work in his studio, but she felt that this caller at the door should be made known to him.

"Pardon my interrupting you, master, but there's somebody asking for Juffrouw Anna Veldhuis."

Hendrick jerked his head toward her. To hear his wife's maiden name again had been like an arrow shot through him. "Did you ask this person in?"

"No, master, because it's not the late mistress whom she wants to see, but an artist of the same name."

Puzzled, Hendrick went to the door himself. He was wondering if a long-ago acquaintance of Anna's had come with some muddled mem-

ory of her. He found a woman of middle age, wearing the modest black clothes of an artisan's wife, her linen cap as crisp as her collar.

"It's a young woman I wish to see," she explained. "Juffrouw Veldhuis painted a fine family portrait at the home of my son and wife during the winter. Now that their new baby is four months old and somewhat delicate they would like him put in the group now instead of waiting until later."

It was not unusual for successive children to be added to a family portrait over the years, often making it appear that the parents had a dozen or more offspring around the same age, frequently in the same clothes when good garments had been handed down. Hendrick sympathized for the need for haste in this case, but he could think of no artist other than himself in this particular vicinity. It must be an amateur for whom the woman was searching.

"What made you think the young woman lived here?" he questioned, still curious about the coincidence of the name.

"I'd been told she was seen going into a house in this street. When I asked a passerby where I might find an artist he pointed to your door."

"I fear you're on a wild-goose chase here, ma'am."

She bobbed politely. "I'm truly sorry to have troubled you."

Hendrick closed the door and returned to his work. Veldhuis was not a particularly uncommon name, but it was a strange coincidence that it should have been spoken again on the threshold of his home.

He could not be sure why the incident of the woman calling at the house should have stayed with him, but every now and again in the days that followed he thought of it. He supposed it was the aftermath of a flicker of hope he had experienced in thinking he was to see someone who had known Anna in days gone by. Those who had never been harshly bereaved had no realization of what a comfort it was to engage in talk of the one who had gone. Too often people refrained from talk from misplaced good intent, not knowing that whenever he heard Anna's name spoken she lived for a few seconds again.

He was in the process of a self-portrait. A mirror had been placed at the right height by his easel and he glanced in it as he painted. He was in a rich-looking costume from one of the atelier chests with a velvet hat on which a long feather was fastened with a jewelled clasp in the

style of a hundred years earlier. To be thus grandly dressed was to emphasize his standing as a successful artist, which Rembrandt had done in his heyday. To Hendrick it was an act of defiance against his hated patron as if it might show that he was not dependent on any one man's munificence. Aletta should have been in the studio to paint him in these robes while the opportunity was hers instead of sketching scenes of the city to paint afterwards in that room upstairs.

His brush suddenly hovered between palette and canvas as a twinge of suspicion dawned. A young woman painter! Aletta could fit that description. Then there were the names—Anna Veldhuis and Aletta Visser—linked by the same initials. There was also a witness to a young artist coming into a house that might, or might not, have been his. He wanted to dismiss out of hand a growing conviction that there was some connection between his daughter and the family portrait that had been mentioned, but it persisted. Finally, his concentration shattered, he went from the studio to mount the stairs at an increasing pace until he reached the bedchamber that his two younger daughters shared. The door into the studio-parlour was locked, but with a hefty shove from his broad shoulders it swung inward with a crash.

For a few moments he stood glaring around at the paintings propped against the walls. He picked up the first one, which was painted on oak that was not from his supplies. His eyes threatened to start from his head when he saw it was signed "A.V." How dare Aletta sign her work without his authority! All doubts began to fall away and the hot colour surged up his neck to flood his face, rage making his hands shake. He threw the painting down to snatch up the next within range. Then he went from one to another, certain now that his daughter and the young painter who had been inquired about were one and the same. These roughly executed works, showing a talent debased by speed, careless perspective and too hasty use of colour, were all in the east and south of the city, where craftsmen and ordinary traders lived, none in the west, where the wealthy burghers and merchants had their grand residences. A half-finished painting on the easel of a family grouped in a simply furnished room was the final, conclusive evidence in his eyes. All the anxiety and misery he had endured, his whole mental torment of the past months since that disastrous card game, finally took its toll. Something seemed to snap. All self-control vanished.

With a thundering roar of rage he dashed to the window and threw it wide. Then he gathered up the paintings, breaking some across his knees, and hurled them down into the courtyard. Maria, sitting outside in the sun shelling peas, gave a cry of alarm as the paintings descended to smash and splinter on the cobbles. She was out of harm's way, but fright made her start in her chair, causing the bowl to slip from her lap and all the green peas went bouncing and dancing away.

"What's happening?" she cried out in a quavering voice. "Has Aletta gone mad?"

Griet had come running to see what was happening and she put a reassuring hand on Maria's shoulder. "It can only be the master! Juffrouw Aletta went out a while ago."

The last painting had descended. Griet moved forward cautiously to look up at the third-floor window, but Hendrick was already on his way downstairs. He appeared in the back doorway. Out of the setting of the studio he was an incongruous figure in his fanciful robes and feathered hat.

"Where's Aletta?" he demanded loudly.

Griet, stooping over the mess of painted wood to see if any picture had survived, straightened quickly. "Out for the day at her sketching, master!"

Maria, outraged by what had happened, had hauled herself out of her chair. "You can't expect Aletta to paint as well as you!" she hissed, totally misinterpreting his destruction of the paintings. "When did you last give her any tuition? Have you no conscience about what you have done to her work?"

He glared at her, his eyes narrowed and glinting dangerously. "I've put it where it belongs, old woman! Ready as fuel for the fire." Then he pointed an authoritative finger at Griet. "You will burn every scrap of the rubbish strewn about this courtyard! There must be only ashes when I return home. Where can I find Aletta?"

"I've no idea. She doesn't tell me where she's going."

He turned his demanding gaze on Maria, but her face set stubbornly. "If I knew I wouldn't tell you when you're in this mood!"

3
0
8

"Then I'll find her for myself!" He swung back into the house, pulling the velvet hat from his head and shedding the brilliant robes, leaving them in a trail behind him. Clad in only his shirt and breeches, he hastened back to the studio, took his hat from a peg and snatched up his jacket to plunge his arms into it as he went from the house, taking swift strides.

He made first for those streets and corners that he had recognized in Aletta's work. It was not hard to deduce that she had been painting to sell, not only to individuals who had commissioned work from her, but in the case of views of Dam Square, the Town Hall, the various churches and the harbour, to offer for sale generally. He looked in every picture shop as he went by, but saw nothing of hers and neither did he expect to, for a girl offering her work would have to be an exceptional artist if she was to be given serious consideration. That only left the market or a fair for output.

He came into Dam Square from a street that opened into it from the opposite side to where the market stalls were clustered. He shouldered his way through the crowds and when he reached the stalls he wound his way in and out, ignoring those selling fruit and vegetables, pottery, stacked cheeses, clogs and old clothes. At each picture stall he scanned through the work there with such thoroughness that he was taken as a potential customer and forced himself to voice the question that was abhorrent to him.

"Have you anything painted by—Anna Veldhuis? She signs her work with her initials."

The answer was always in the negative, which was a tremendous relief each time. It was doubtful whether he would have seen that there were paintings at the end of a flower stall if he had not caught sight of a face he recognized. It was that of Griet's married sister, Helena, who had come often to his home to give a helping hand domestically whenever it was needed. It crossed his mind she might have seen Aletta that morning and there was no harm in asking. As he drew nearer he saw she was assisting at the stall from which he had bought tulip bulbs, long before its owner had become known to him. With all flowers being expensive, it was one of only two stalls selling them, but there was a fine show and well-dressed folk were making purchases.

To his astonishment Helena was at the far end of the extended stall on which was arrayed a number of paintings. Even from where he was he recognized the work. So Pieter van Doorne and Helena and Aletta were all in a conspiracy together! He thought he would explode with fury. Purposefully he charged to the end of the stall. When Helena saw him standing in front of the paintings she turned a guilty scarlet.

"Master Visser," she stammered. "It's a fine day, is it not?"

His bellow made heads turn several stalls away and with a sweep of his powerful hand he sent his daughter's pictures crashing to the cobbles. People stared in amazement to see him snatch up those that remained to hurl them after the rest. Then he leaned across the stall to seize Helena by the shoulders and shake her in his temper.

"Who put you up to this? Was it Aletta? Or van Doorne? I want the truth!"

The two stall women selling the flowers had come dashing to Helena's aid. "Let her go!" one of them shouted angrily. "What do you think you're doing?"

"See the mess you've made!" shrieked the other, throwing up her hands at the strewn pictures.

He ignored them. "Answer my question, Helena!"

She was badly frightened, for his congested face was only inches from her own and his fierce grip on her shoulders was bruising her. "Ask your daughter! Not me! I'm only working here. There's nothing wrong in that!"

"There is when you're selling work with an unauthorized signature!"

"You're hurting me!" In her struggling to be free of his grasp she caused the stall to shake. The section on which the pictures had been lying knocked against the main one and the vibration caused a tub of roses to topple. Both stall women cried out in dismay.

"Help! There's a madman here!" they shouted as they tried to save other tubs from disaster.

Spectators, drawn to the scene, moved back as three burly men left their own stalls to grab Hendrick by the arms. "Leave that woman alone, you!"

Hendrick was jerked back, his hold on Helena broken. In his blind rage he swung about to give one man a full punch in the face while a

second man received a thrust in the chest that sent him staggering back against some bystanders, adding to the confusion. Before the third man could seize him, Hendrick took hold of the picture section of the stall to send it hurtling onto its side and out of his path. Helena began to scream hysterically as he came lunging through at her, but those whom he had struck aside had recovered their balance and with the third man they leapt forward to grab him. He whirled out again with his fists and in the resulting melee the main stall tilted and fell, causing the cobbles to become slippery underfoot from water and crushed flowers as he fought to free himself of those attempting to restrain him. A shout had gone up for the Civil Guard to be fetched.

Aletta, who had completed a full day's work, arrived home at five o'clock to be met by grave faces, filling her with a rush of apprehension. Willem was there and he broke the news to her.

"Prepare yourself, Aletta. Your father has been arrested and charged with causing a breach of the peace."

"Oh no! What happened?"

Before Willem could reply, Sybylla, who was red-eyed from tears, cried out accusingly. "You may well ask! It was all through your wretched paintings! He smashed them up here and at the market stall!"

Aletta did not hear Sybylla burst into further sobs, for shock had caused her to faint. She would have fallen on the marble-tiled floor if Willem had not caught her in time.

Hendrick languished for six weeks in a prison cellar in one of the city's oldest gatehouses. He, who loved freedom of the spirit, body and mind, thought he would soon lose his reason and die. Weight fell away from him. He shared his dismal confines, the only light coming through a small barred window, with twenty other men awaiting trial for various offences. He had nothing for his comfort except a thin layer of straw. Food had to be purchased from the guards. It was of poor quality and, as he had no appetite, he would hand it on, after a couple of mouthfuls, to poorer prisoners, who gobbled it up. When his purse was empty,

food continued to come to him, which meant that his family, or perhaps Willem, was paying for it. He hoped it was not Ludolf, for that would have turned what little he did eat to ashes in his mouth. He thought constantly of the chained goldfinch in the Fabritius painting that Francesca had described, but he no longer saw her as the captive, for it was he who was learning the true meaning of the word. She was still able to paint each day while he sat on the straw-strewn floor, chained at the ankle, his hands dangling from his updrawn knees. He no longer had pity for anyone except himself.

It was no consolation that Pieter had not pressed charges for the damage done at the stall, for it was enough that the three stall holders had accused him of assault and battery, which could combine with the new harshness of the law against rioters to earn him a ghastly punishment. He might be exposed in a pillory in front of the Town Hall for all Amsterdam to see with his head sticking out of a wooden bell and his misdemeanour emblazoned on a placard. Or he might be paraded through the streets with a smashed painting around his neck or in a ludicrous flowered hat as a symbol of his wrongdoing. There was no telling what humiliation and degradation he would have to face. He might even receive a long prison sentence as well. If that happened madness would be his fate. He was so full of dread he was in an almost permanent state of nausea.

It was a hot September day and the sky over Amsterdam was a clear Delft blue when Hendrick was taken from the cellar and conveyed to court for his trial. He sat in the cart with his face hidden in his arms, wanting no one to recognize him. The previous morning Willem had gained permission to see him and to bring a lawyer and, equally welcome, a razor and a change of clothes, or else a beard and unkempt hair would have disguised him.

Mercifully the trial was over quickly. The lawyer presented a strong defence of provocation caused to a master upon seeing unauthorized signed work by a pupil from his own studio. Willem also spoke on Hendrick's behalf. Lastly Aletta took the witness stand and admitted that she had done work for sale without her father's knowledge. The judge publicly condemned her as a wayward daughter, which caused her intense shame. The punishment imposed on Hendrick was restricted to

a heavy fine, which Willem paid on his behalf. Hendrick was careful not to show his jubilation at how lightly he had got away. Once again good fortune had nudged a path through tribulation for him. But as he left the courtroom a free man again, the sobering realization came to him that his debts, now increased by a further six hundred florins, held him in thrall as securely as the prison bars he had left behind him. He would not be truly liberated until Francesca was married to Ludolf.

As he went down the steps into the street, Willem and Sybylla with him, he saw Aletta standing there, but he ignored her. Without a glance in her direction he took a seat in Willem's coach, which was waiting. His pride had suffered another almost insupportable blow and he could not forgive her. Had she used her own name and not gone about her clandestine painting under the name of her mother, he might have found it in his heart to forgive her, but to his mind she had insulted Anna's memory. When he saw Sybylla hesitate as if she would go to Aletta he beckoned her fiercely.

"Get in the coach!"

She obeyed reluctantly. Her eyes, full of sympathy, were on her sister. Willem, wanting to bring Hendrick and Aletta together again, spoke to him persuasively.

"Surely you would like both your daughters to ride home with you on this day?"

"No!" Hendrick sat forward with a grimace that was almost a snarl. "Aletta shall never paint again under my roof! Or be welcome there! That is to be the punishment of a daughter who has offended against her father!"

Willem sighed and took the seat beside him. As the coach moved forward Willem saw that Aletta stood with her head bowed in distress. It was to be hoped that before long Hendrick's basic good nature would surface and there would be a reconciliation between them. Willem, having heard both sides of the story, thought that Aletta had erred, although he understood and sympathized with her reasons.

As was to be expected, Hendrick was hungry for news as to what had been happening in Amsterdam and elsewhere, for little information about anything had reached the damp confines of the gatehouse tower.

Then, as the talk in the coach turned to the trial, Willem spoke of Ludolf.

"Had he not been away from Amsterdam on his business travels, I would have asked him to speak as well on your behalf. I wrote to tell him of your predicament, asking his clerk to see that the letter reached him. With the interest he has in your work and your well-being, I'm sure that upon his return he would have moved heaven and earth to get your release if the worse had come to the worst."

Hendrick gave a snort. "I'm sure you're right. Naturally he wouldn't want me to be incarcerated. It would undercut his plans."

"What do you mean?"

Hendrick realized he had let slip too much and covered it quickly. "Only that he wants to fill his walls with my paintings without too much delay. Has word of my tribulation been kept from Francesca?"

"It has. You asked me that yesterday."

"Did I? To have freedom again has set my head in a whirl."

Sybylla leaned towards him from the opposite seat. "All will be well when you're home again, Father. Please try to forgive Aletta for being the cause of so much trouble."

Again his face contorted fearsomely, causing her to draw back in her seat, and he made a threatening gesture. "Don't mention your sister's name to me! Forgiveness was drained out of me in prison. I don't know yet if it will ever return."

When Hendrick's home was reached Willem remained in the coach, letting him go in on his own with Sybylla. Maria and Griet must have been watching out, desperately anxious to know the result of the trial, for the entrance door opened wide before they reached it.

Maria wept with relief and happiness to see Hendrick home again and he suffered her kiss, prickly with whiskers, on his cheek. Then he went straight to his studio. The familiar aroma of chalk, oil, paint and ink had a reviving effect, almost as if his blood had been dormant and was now coursing through his veins again. His self-portrait was exactly as he had left it and he eyed it critically, able to see already where more work was needed. Then he looked in the mirror that was still in its position at the side of the easel and was shocked by the change in his appearance. His face had become thin, his jowls hanging in dewlaps and

his eyes were sunken. As for his hair, that had become quite white, almost no trace left of its coppery colour. He had been aware of his loss of bodily weight, but he had not realized that incarceration had also stamped old age into his features.

He shuddered and took the half-finished portrait from the easel to place it in the storeroom out of sight. There was no point in finishing it now. Later he would paint over it and do another likeness of himself once his self-esteem had returned and the memory of prison had faded. In the storeroom Aletta's easel was propped against the wall, her palette and brushes on a shelf above. Whether this had been done through orders he had sent through Willem or whether it had been prompted by Aletta's conscience after his arrest he did not know. He tilted the palette and touched a scrap of paint left on the surface. It was hard and dry.

With the memory of her careless work vivid in his mind, he no longer had any faith in Aletta's future as an artist, all thoughts of an apprenticeship for her dismissed from his mind. She should concentrate now on marriage. He would give her free choice, even though he was denying it to Francesca. There was nothing that could make him change his mind about seeing Francesca wed to Ludolf. Not even for his beloved firstborn could he ever face prison again.

Hendrick was not aware that he was making Aletta a scapegoat for all his troubles. Having made his way home without speaking to her, it remained that way. She might have been invisible for all the notice he took of her. She in her turn had become exceedingly quiet, having lost the more open attitude that had resulted from her going out to sketch and meeting people of many walks of life. That had been a time when she felt she was her own person, making her own decisions and deciding the pattern of her life for herself, no longer overshadowed by Francesca's beauty and Sybilla's exuberance. Now all that had gone. She withdrew into herself, going silently about full-time domestic duties in the house that relieved both Maria and Griet of a number of chores.

Yet she was changed. Her temper, which she had only ever shown before under extreme provocation, now flared more easily, exploding

like a firework before she retreated again into her shell of quietness. No one was spared either in the household or out of it.

"You poor child," Maria said well-meaningly to her one day. "With your father scarcely speaking to you there's no life for you in this house at the moment."

Aletta, stripping a bed at the time for laundry, hurled her bundled-up sheet halfway across the room, her cheeks flaring and her eyes flashing. "I'm not a child. I'm a woman with a mind and a will of her own. If Father had any compassion in him he would never have deprived me of the lifeblood of painting that is as vital to me as it is to him!"

It added to her personal torment that she who was to have spoken to Hendrick on Francesca's behalf had failed her sister. He might have listened to her eventually if all the trouble had not occurred. That same evening in her misery she confided Francesca's plight to Sybylla, who was not particularly sympathetic.

"I'm not surprised Father wanted her chaperoned when she's away from home. It would have been the same for any one of us. Remember, she's probably homesick and that would make everything appear much worse to her than it is."

"But will you appeal to him on her behalf?"

Sybylla sighed. "Very well. I'll go to him now."

She went to the family parlour, where Hendrick was sitting, but returned almost immediately.

"What happened?" Aletta asked anxiously.

"I asked him if I could speak about Francesca's accommodation in Delft and he said, 'No.'"

"Didn't he say anything else?"

"Yes. He told me not to speak about you to him either." Then Sybylla made a sensible suggestion. "Why don't you go and stay for a week or two with Francesca in Delft? You must have enough money from the paintings you sold. Maria, Griet and I can manage well enough here."

Aletta's face cleared. "Oh yes! I'll go tomorrow."

If her father wanted to see her again after she bade him farewell in the morning he would have to send for her.

316

CHAPTER I 4

When Aletta went to the studio and told Hendrick she intended to go to Delft he did not glance in her direction, but continued to lace a canvas onto a stretcher. Then, when she turned to leave, he slammed the stretcher down on the table and swung around to roar at her.

"Go! Stay away forever, for all your absence matters to me!"

She halted and stood her ground. "Am I never to be forgiven?" she replied as fiercely.

"Never in my lifetime! Get out of my studio."

She was ashen-faced, but not cowed, her lace-capped head held high. "You need never see me again. I'll make a living for myself away from Amsterdam."

"It will not be at painting," he retaliated cruelly.

The taunt struck at her so deeply that she flew from the room.

. Next morning at breakfast he was the only one who did not speak to her and he shut himself away in his studio while farewells were being said. When he heard her leave the house with Sybylla he went on preparing the canvas he had been stretching the day before, and did not look towards the window in case she should stand on tiptoe outside to take a last glance at him through the glass.

Aletta sat silent in the stage wagon and did not chat to her fellow passengers. It was as if she had been drained of all emotion. She felt numb, cut off from the rest of the world. The many weeks of conscience-stricken misery and the harshness of her father's attitude since his return home had finally taken their toll. She had brought two lots of hand baggage with her, and when she had found employment in Delft, Sybylla would send on a chest with the rest of her belongings. Sybylla, who so often did not think before she spoke, had unwittingly exacerbated Hendrick's taunt of the previous day by suggesting that Aletta could give drawing and painting lessons to bring in an income.

"That's the last thing I'll ever do!" Aletta had hissed. "I'll use a scrubbing brush and a bucket, but never a dog's-hair brush or a palette again."

It was not only a thoroughly uncomfortable journey in the stage wagon, but noisy as well, for the weather was rough and wild. Rain drummed on the waxed cloth overhead while the force of the wind caused it to whip and billow as if at any moment it would be ripped away from the iron hoops. Every now and again the wheels would slither in the soft surface mud, the ground below still hard from a long, dry spell. Halts at hostelries meant heads down against the driving rain and some passengers chose not to alight, wanting to avoid sitting in damp clothes for the rest of the way.

It was towards the end of the journey when Aletta heard comments being made by those familiar with the area about the speed of a coach approaching from behind along the road. It was obvious to them that the coachman was intent on overtaking the stage wagon before reaching the bridge that lay ahead, for whoever crossed it first would have command of the route for the rest of the narrow road into Delft. Naturally the coachman did not want to follow the stage wagon's slower pace, it having been impossible to put up its little sails with a high head wind blowing towards them.

From where she sat Aletta was unable to see that the coach was gaining ground speedily, but she was kept informed by the talk around her and she recognized the actual moment when the devil, who lurked in every driver of a stage wagon, came to the fore. There was a crack of the whip and a surge of speed that made her cling to the seat. Some of the women passengers began to murmur in alarm, their husbands and the most staid among the menfolk shaking their heads at this folly on a slippery road, a few calling to the driver for caution. They in their turn were shouted down by three boisterous younger men, who cheered as the stage wagon lengthened the distance between it and the coach that was following. But it was only a temporary gain, for the coach horses had a far lighter load and, under a cracking whip, they began to advance

steadily, the wheels sending up fountains of muddy water from the road. Soon the coach was drawing level.

It was at the approach to the bridge that the accident happened. There was an enormous, bone-shaking crash as both equipages slithered and struck against each other. All the passengers in the stage wagon were thrown from their seats and women screamed as the whole vehicle skidded violently, dragging at the frantic horses. The ordeal was not to end there and renewed screaming resounded as the stage wagon began to slide backwards from the road and down a bank until it came to a thudding standstill at a precipitous angle with its back wheels lodged in a strip of grass above a canal.

It seemed to Aletta that every woman was weeping or crying out except herself. She was shaken, but she had suffered no harm, except for some buffeting that would result in bruises and a gash on her ankle where somebody had scraped a clog when attempting to get up from where he had fallen. Suddenly afraid she might have disarrayed her cap, she clutched her hands to it, but found it still firmly in place. People were alighting and she took her turn moving over to where helping hands half lifted her down. Two elderly women were deeply shocked and distressed, but they had family with them in attendance. Aletta held up her hems as she stepped across the soggy grass to climb up the bank to the road. Then she saw with horror what had happened to the coach. In the collision it must have swung out to smash down on its side against a wall, causing part of it to cave in. Men from the stage wagon were pulling on the wedged door lying uppermost in an attempt to get through to the one passenger within. The coachman had been flung from the box and had struck the framework of the bridge. Some-one had already covered his dead face with a kerchief. Others were calming the terrified horses, the snorting and whinnying of the unhar-nessed animals mingling with shouting from men and the sobbing of women.

The door finally gave, one helper having been handed an axe to demolish it, and another man lowered himself into the coach. His distressed voice sounded clearly.

"Merciful God! This man's legs are trapped. Give me that axe to free him and I'll need help here!"

Two men went into the coach immediately to give assistance, there being no room for more. The whole equipage shook as they struggled to extricate the victim. People had come on the scene from a nearby farmhouse. A youth among them was sent back by the farmer to bring a horse and cart to transport the injured man to Delft and the nearest doctor. Eventually he was lifted out, wrapped in shawls and a blanket, and supported by many willing hands he was carried towards the waiting cart. His head lolled, for he had been senseless from the moment of impact, his black hair blood-soaked.

Aletta, standing near the cart, recognized him immediately as he was borne past her, although momentarily she could not remember where she had seen before that wide brow and haughty, prominent nose, the strongly shaped jaw and the well-cut lips, which were colourless now in his present pitiable state. Then it came to her. He was the young man who had leapt so effortlessly onto the bench beside her in the Exchange anteroom the first time she had gone to meet Pieter. His name came back to her. Constantijn. She was overwhelmed by compassion for him and hoped his injuries would not prove to be too fearsome. Macabrely the dead coachman was placed alongside him in the cart.

People had been collecting their baggage from where it had been thrown in the collision and Aletta found hers. The farmer's wife, with the assistance of her sons, took charge of all the horses. Shouts had gone up for the driver of the stage wagon, vengeance in the voices, but he was nowhere to be seen. It was believed he had taken to his heels until the young man on the cart, already driving across the bridge, pointed to the water. Then he had to wait while the drowned body was pulled out of the canal and laid beside the coachman.

By now it was getting dark. Aletta was taken into Delft, together with the other women passengers and the baggage, by the farmer in his hay wagon, the men walking at the side, the ride ending by the Old Church. When Aletta asked to be directed to Vrouw Wolff's house in Kromstraat, a married couple who had travelled with her took her to the door.

Francesca, coming downstairs for dinner, gave an exclamation of joy at seeing her sister with Geetruyd in the reception hall. "Am I dreaming? Aletta, are you really here?"

They flew to meet each other and hugged and kissed and hugged again. "I've come to stay here for a while," Aletta explained. "Vrouw Wolff has agreed that I should share your room to save expense and we have settled the terms of my board."

"That's wonderful!"

Upstairs, washing her face and hands after her journey, Aletta told Francesca about the accident and the coincidence of recognizing the victim from a brief encounter in Amsterdam. A tremor in her voice betrayed delayed shock over the incident. "It's why I was so late getting here."

"Were you hurt at all?" Francesca inquired anxiously.

"Nothing of any importance." Aletta paused in drying her hands. "But I'm haunted by what happened to that young man. And to think there should be two fatal casualties is so terrible." She shuddered, shaking her head.

Francesca put a comforting arm about her shoulders. "Let us be thankful there were not many more, which could easily have happened."

At dinner Aletta had little appetite. Geetruyd, hearing about the accident, wondered who the victim might be, for she knew many well-to-do families in the town through her charity work. "I daresay I shall soon hear more about it at my meetings and elsewhere as news of the accident spreads."

"I'll send word to Father straight away," Francesca said, "and then he'll know quickly that no harm has befallen Aletta."

Later, when the two sisters were on their own, sitting side by side against their propped pillows in bed, Aletta told Francesca about their father's imprisonment, not sparing her own part in it and accepting all the blame. Francesca was shocked to hear how much had been kept from her over such a lengthy period.

"You should have let me know. I would have come home!"

"That's what we didn't want. You couldn't have done any good. He wasn't allowed any visitors until the day before the trial and then only Willem and a lawyer. We didn't want your work to suffer."

"But yours did. I had no notion as to why you were forever out sketching in the city, or your ultimate purpose. Now I know why you

wouldn't show me any of your finished paintings. By the very subject matter I would have guessed that all wasn't as it should be."

"I hope none of my work was as bad as Father declared it to be," Aletta said painfully, "but then I'll never be sure. I was so upset and guilt-ridden when he was arrested that I think if I had taken up a brush to paint again it would have scorched my hand. All I did was to anguish over his being shut away through my actions while I clung to the hope he would forgive me whenever the nightmare was over."

"You say he was released in mid-September and now we are into November and yet he still has not softened towards you? What has come over him? He never was one to harbour a grudge for long. Perhaps this break of yours away from home will give him time to reconsider."

"I wish I could believe it," Aletta said tonelessly.

"He has been harsh towards both of us. How is he with Sybylla?"

"She can still make him laugh and she has always played up to being the baby of the family. Yet he wouldn't even listen to her when she tried to speak to him on your behalf."

"I only thought of Sybylla as a last resort. You're the one with the tact. When Sybylla wants something she so often blunders over it." Francesca mused, resting an arm behind her head. "I realize now that Father must have been awaiting trial when Pieter was here in late August."

"He told me he was going to see you when he called at the house one day to ask if we'd heard the date of the trial. He also said that you're able to correspond with each other through a friend of his who lives in Haarlem and makes business trips to Delft."

"That's right. Gerard Meverden is his name and he brings Pieter's letters to Mechelin Huis and I always have one ready myself for him whenever he comes." She tapped her sister's arm. "You haven't explained why Pieter gave me no word of what had happened to Father."

"I asked him not to tell you. That's why Sybylla and I didn't send letters with him. We were afraid you might read between the lines and sense something was not right at home."

Francesca gave Aletta a sideways glance. "Isn't it time now that you also told me what role Pieter played in letting your paintings be sold on his stall?"

"You mustn't blame him in any way!" Aletta sat up from the pillows. "He wanted me to tell you from the start, but I begged him not to insist on that condition. I knew you would have argued against what I wanted to do and I was determined not to have any interference with my plan." Abruptly she covered her face with her hands. "But he was right and I was wrong! If you had known and stopped me in time I wouldn't be facing a life in ruins!"

"Aletta," Francesca said softly, taking her sister's wrists and gently pulling her hands away from her tragic face, "you're still only seventeen. Nothing is over yet. You've had a setback, but that's just a passing thing. Maybe you have developed bad habits in your recent work through painting too swiftly, but that can be undone."

Aletta shook her head. "I haven't told you yet the worst that has befallen me. Before Father was even home again he sent a message by Willem that whatever the result of the next day's trial, I was never to paint under his roof again. His one thought has been to be rid of me. I fear it's because every time he looks at me he is reminded that I was the cause of his being chained up like a dog in that gatehouse."

"My poor, dear sister!"

"That's why I'm never going home again, and I told Sybylla and Maria that before I left." Aletta's jaw jutted resolutely. "I asked Vrouw Wolff if I could stay here until I get employment that will provide me with a bed as well."

"But your painting!"

Aletta looked stonily ahead of her. "That was a dream that has been shattered. At the moment it doesn't seem to matter much. I can't feel anything anymore. I haven't for weeks, except to become angry with everybody at the least provocation. When the moment of the accident occurred I knew no fear. I didn't care if I lived or died."

"Yet afterwards you sorrowed for the injured and the dead."

"That must have been some last flickering part of me not yet snuffed out."

"Come to the studio with me tomorrow. I'll be on my own, because Jan is away again. Just sit and absorb the atmosphere. After all you have been through you need to rest and go through a period of healing. Just

to look at Jan's beautiful and tranquil paintings will be a step towards restoring your spirits."

Aletta's voice was hard. "I'll never set foot in a studio again!"

Francesca would never have believed it possible for Aletta to be so changed. All gentleness seemed to have been crushed out of her and she was like tempered steel. "At least come to the Mechelin Huis with me and meet Catharina. She is just the one to ask about finding employment for you. I'm sure Geetruyd would find you work scrubbing the floors of her almshouses and institutions, or cooking in the kitchens, but—"

"I don't suffer from Father's excessive pride," Aletta broke in sharply. "I'll do any chore."

"I know you would and so would I if the need arose, but you have such talents that could be put to good use. You sew and embroider, dress hair like a professional, even though you never do more than brush your own and twist it up under your various caps, and you can play the virginal with your soul in the music as Sybylla does with her viol. You would be able to teach all those skills and perhaps eventually have a little school of your own."

For the first time since their meeting Aletta smiled, slight though the smile was. "You've always had the right words of cheer and comfort for me."

"I hope I've said to you what Mama would have chosen to say."

"I'm sure you have."

"Now I think we should blow the candle out and sleep."

It was as if they were children again. Francesca drew the bed curtains after extinguishing the candle flame and they tucked down under the goose-feather quilt. Aletta's last thoughts before she slept were of the injured young man. She uttered a silent prayer that he would live.

In the morning, when it was time for Francesca to go to the studio, Clara was waiting as usual to play escort, although she knew Aletta was to accompany her sister. Francesca was so used to it that she never thought of there being any change in the situation, but Aletta did.

"There's no need for you to come today, Juffrouw Huys," she said with such iron firmness that Clara stepped back automatically, having

caught a resemblance to Geetruyd's tone when no argument was to be brooked.

"But I always do," she protested, recovering herself.

"In my father's instructions to Vrouw Wolff," Aletta countered, having been given all the details by her sister, "he insisted, as I'm sure you were told, that Francesca had no need of extra chaperonage when in the company of a member of her family and that included being with her sister."

"I think it was in the plural—sisters."

"A sister in the singular," Aletta bluffed, not entirely sure on that point. "I'll also walk home with Francesca when she has finished work."

"Won't you be back for the noon meal?"

"Not today. After I've delivered my sister I want to explore Delft." Aletta took Francesca by the arm and set off at a brisk pace before there was any chance of Geetruyd coming to intervene.

"Not this direction, but the other," Francesca said with a laugh, drawing Aletta to a halt and turning her around to leave the crooked, narrow street at the east end.

"I came by way of the west end of Kromstraat yesterday evening."

"So did I when I first arrived, but this is the quickest route."

As they walked along, Francesca pointed out Vrouw Thin's home, which could be seen in the row of gabled houses from the bridge over the canal at Oude Langendijk. In the square Aletta wanted to know how more recently the New Church there was built in comparison with the Old Church, by which she had alighted from the hay wagon.

"Well, the old one dates from the thirteenth century and the new one from the fourteenth. The Vermeers like to worship at the former, which means I rarely see them on Sundays, because I go to the latter with Geetruyd and Clara."

"Are you never free of those two women?"

"Never for as long as I would wish."

When they reached the Mechelin Huis, Francesca was disappointed when her sister declined to go in with her.

"Not today," Aletta said. "It might not be convenient. In any case, as I said to Clara, I want to get some idea of my whereabouts today and to see the sights of interest."

"If you're sure," Francesca said uncertainly. "I finish here at five o'clock on these darker winter evenings and even for the last half hour I carry out sundry chores in the studio as soon as the light gets bad."

When Francesca had gone into the house, Aletta felt an enormous sense of relief at being quite alone and unknown to anyone, a stranger in a strange town. There was nobody to hail her, none to greet or chat with and, best of all, no further need to keep a bland countenance with a heart being torn apart when well-meaning acquaintances asked after her father, wanting to know if he had recovered from his ordeal. She had seen in every pair of eyes that awareness of the judge's condemnation of her as a daughter. They were not to know of the self-punishment to which she had sentenced herself. Giving up painting, with or without Hendrick's permission, was the only way she knew of atoning for all she had done.

It was a damp, dull day with the cobbles everywhere still wet from the day before, but as yet there was no rain. She spent a long time in the New Church, where she viewed the spectacular tomb of Willem the Silent and the memorials to other members of the House of Orange. From there she went to the old palace, once a convent, where Willem the Silent had lived. She had not expected to see in the wall of the staircase the gaping holes where the bullets of his assassin had lodged. Having been in close contact with death the previous day, she felt the same chill of horror come upon her and she hastened from the building to cross the bridge of a narrow canal into the Old Church. There she sat in a secluded corner until that renewal of icy shock had subsided again. She thought of many things as she sat there, including what Francesca had told her of Jan Vermeer's work. Perhaps, since he worshipped here, he had been inspired to capture in his paintings the same pure light that flooded the whole church through the great high windows of clear glass. The effect on pale walls and pillars devoid of ornamentation and the great carved pulpit with extraordinarily beautiful workmanship was breathtaking.

When she left the church she bought a bun at a bakery and ate it on the premises. It was enough to keep her present small appetite satisfied and, well wrapped up in her hooded cloak, she walked along narrow streets and followed canals as she came to know her way about. But at

four o'clock the rain, which had held off all day, finally descended and she ran through the heavy drops to Mechelin Huis. Catharina, who had heard about her unexpected arrival from Francesca, welcomed her in to hot tea and a warm fireside.

Aletta, fearing what she might hear from the hard-faced Geetruyd about the victim of the accident upon her return to Kromstraat, asked Catharina if she had heard any news about the young man.

"I have," Catharina replied. "What happened is the talk of Delft today because the young man in question is the only son of one of the town's wealthiest wool merchants. Only three months ago there was great rejoicing in the de Veere family when Constantijn—that's the young man's name—became betrothed to Isabella van Alewijns, the eldest daughter of a prosperous Gouda merchant in the cheese trade."

"How is he? Do you know?"

"Alive. That's all that can be said. I was told that his father has sent to Amsterdam for the best doctor in the city." Catharina paused. "The news is grave. Both legs had to be amputated and Constantijn is fighting for his life. It is all so sad, because he excelled at sailing and every other kind of sporting activity."

Aletta sat motionless, staring into the fire. "It should never have happened," she said bitterly.

"That can be said about any accident," Catharina said quietly. "For a moment of speed and folly, lives can be shattered."

"Where does Heer de Veere live?"

"Do you mean the father or the son?"

Aletta raised her eyebrows. "Have they separate establishments?"

"I told you they were a rich family. Directly opposite this house, on the other side of the square, is the de Veere office and above it is the apartment that the young man occupies. His parents used to live there before they built a house out in the country, but Constantijn was taken to his own place last night, because it was considered too dangerous to continue transporting him any further to his parents' home."

They were sitting in the firelight and Aletta rose to go over to the window and look out across the square at the house opposite. Every window there was bright with candle glow from the office to the attic. So he was nearby. She had a sudden superstitious notion that if he died,

3
2
7

so would she. Not perhaps in the physical sense, but to lose her true grasp on life and become cantankerous and lonely as Sybylla had long prophesied. She was aware from her recent behaviour to being well on the way to that state.

"Your sister has told me of the difficulties you have been having at home and that you hope to find employment in Delft," Catharina said from where she sat.

"Yes, I do." Aletta returned to her chair. "Today I made a mental note of several possibilities. The baker's wife seemed to be shorthanded and I came across a little shop selling embroidered items including caps, which I can say I'm quite expert at making. I should like to start work soon while I still have enough money to take a small room somewhere."

"Won't you stay on with Vrouw Wolff?"

"I couldn't afford to, much as I would like to continue living in the same house as my sister."

"I've a suggestion. I know from all Francesca has told me that you are a clever young woman. I wondered if, as a temporary measure and until you get something more suited to your abilities, you would consider giving me a helping hand with the children. It would give you a breathing space and you wouldn't have to rush into anything just because you need to get work quickly. I couldn't afford to pay you very much and you'd have to share a room with Ignatius, who is nine months, but you would have some hours of liberty every week and nobody goes hungry in this house!"

Aletta was keenly appreciative of the offer, but uncertain. "I understood from Francesca that your husband never wished to have another woman staying in the house."

"That's true, but he is away at the present time and all matters are under my jurisdiction."

"I've had no experience in looking after children."

"But you like them, don't you?"

"Of course I do, but I want to be perfectly honest about everything. I should like to work here, but I seem to have little patience these days if anyone crosses me."

"All the better. My offspring need a firm hand." Catharina lowered her voice confidentially. "I'm almost certain that I must be pregnant

again. I'm not sure yet, but I'm queasy at the oddest hours. Elizabeth is a good maidservant, but she has enough to do and for once, just for my husband's sake when he returns, I'd be glad not to have my mother fussing over me."

"When would you like me to start?"

"Tomorrow?"

"I'll move in tomorrow morning when I come with Francesca."

Later that evening Aletta wrote to Sybylla and asked her to send on the chest of belongings that had been left packed in readiness. Francesca kept to herself her doubts about how Sybylla and Maria would manage, but Aletta brought up the subject.

"Maria won't let go of the purse strings, no matter how hard Sybylla might try to get hold of them, and Griet will feel herself in charge, paying only lip service to the other two. I think we sometimes forget how long she has been with us, how much she has learned and what a competent housekeeper she has become. In spite of what Father said to me, I wouldn't have left those at home in the lurch if I'd felt they couldn't manage without me."

When Aletta moved into Mechelin Huis she found that her room, which was on the third floor and at the front of the house, gave her an uninterrupted view of the de Veere house opposite. Even as she looked out, a mud-splashed coach with tired horses drew up outside its entrance, which she guessed had brought one of the doctors from Amsterdam, and this was confirmed when a man in the customary black garb of a doctor hastened into the house. She tried to guess which was Constantijn's bedchamber. Living quarters were most likely to be on the floor above the offices, which meant he would be lying behind the windows that were on a level with hers, the grandest rooms being usually at the front of the house.

All the Vermeer children took to Aletta, although they soon found that she had a will of iron and would have discipline. They respected her for it, for they were then clear as to what the situation was and it was satisfying to have a framework of rules to kick against when they felt rebellious. By their natures they bore out to her, even as she had learned from her own childhood, that parents who showed love for each other bred affectionate children. They were a warmhearted bunch,

329

incredibly naughty at times, but there was also a great deal of laughter in the Vermeer house, which Aletta enjoyed on the surface while inwardly she remained frozen and bereft. She liked Jan Vermeer as much as his wife, for he was most kindly towards her and in return she tried to keep out of his way as much as possible, although she supposed he had no objection to her being in the house since he knew it was a temporary measure.

Catharina was not pregnant after all, but had been afflicted by some curious illness that made her giddy with pain in her head, forcing her to lie down. There were some days when she could not rise from her bed, but then she took a turn for the better and was full of hope that she would be well enough to bake and prepare for St. Nicholaes's Day.

"I've already started the baking," Aletta said to her one morning, "and I've the girls to help me, teaching them at the same time. Even Beatrix has been removing the skins from almonds after they have been given a dip in hot water."

In the end Aletta did everything for the celebrations, including buying the gifts for the children, since Catharina was not yet well enough to do any purchasing herself. Aletta and Francesca also made or bought their own presents for all the family, and they sent a small package home by canalboat, which contained gifts from both of them to everyone there.

"You had better not put my name as a half-donor on those fancy coat buttons for Father, or else he'll never use them," Aletta had said.

"I'm doing it anyway," Francesca said, "and when I go home at Christmas I'll sew them on his best coat myself if it's not already been done."

As yet Aletta had been kept so busy in the Vermeer household that she had not found time to look for other employment and in any case Catharina still had need of her. Not once had she been in the studio, but she had lingered many times in front of the paintings in the house, appreciating those by other artists as well as Vermeer's. Totally detached, she viewed these works of art as if she herself had never painted, unable to feel the sense of loss which she was sure was crushing her inside.

Almost daily there was some word spoken of the patient across the

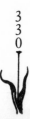

square. His mother was constantly at his bedside. Since he had lost so much blood she refused to allow anyone to bleed him further and two of several doctors had left in a huff. All sorts of potions were being prescribed to help him regain his strength, many with a vile taste, according to hearsay.

"Do you remember the ingredients of the specially nourishing broth that Mama used to give us when we were ill?" Aletta asked Francesca after hearing of these vain attempts to restore the invalid.

"Yes, I made it often enough after I was put in charge of the house-hold. It needs bone marrow and eggs with everything else, including just enough of the right spices to encourage the most jaded appetite. I believe I can guess what you have in mind."

"I thought you would. If we made the broth and presented it at the de Veere house on St. Nicholaes's Eve, nobody could take offence or think our action presumptuous."

"I agree. That's a splendid notion. I'll buy all we'll need."

"And I'll ask Catharina if we may make it in her kitchen. I'm sure you don't want to ask any favours of Geetruyd!"

Catharina was only too willing and insisted that they used her spices, which saved expense. When the day came Francesca had to work in the studio, but she had written out the ingredients to present with the broth in case Vrouw de Veere should wish to make it again for her stricken son.

That evening Jan accompanied Aletta across the square with the jug of broth, having offered to present her, for he knew Constantijn's parents, who had bought paintings from his gallery several times. Francesca had already gone back to Kromstraat with Clara.

"You take it as your gift," she had said to her sister. "After all, you were the one who suggested it in the first place."

The entrance into the de Veere house was next to the one into the office. Jan and Aletta were invited in and on the first floor the two parents, a couple of about her father's age, dignified and gracious, received them in a splendidly appointed room.

"How kind of you," Heer de Veere declared heartily when Aletta had explained the purpose of her visit. Previously she had only seen him from a distance as he went in and out of the building and now, at close

quarters, she could see the strain in his face over the tragedy that had befallen his son.

"Your thoughtfulness is more appreciated than you could ever realize," his wife said to her. "Friends and neighbours have been wonderful with their support and to think that you, whom I know to have been in the stage wagon at the time of the accident, should come with your offering for our son's well-being touches me deeply. I have seen you and your sister come and go at the Mechelin Huis during the many hours when I've sat by the window while my son has slept." She dropped her gaze to the recipe for the broth that Aletta had given her with the jug, which had been sent to the kitchen. "I do believe this recipe is very similar to one that my grandmother used to make and which I have been unable to find. I know it to be good."

"How is your son now?"

The woman exchanged a look with her husband as if it were getting harder all the time to answer such queries. "He is still desperately ill and sleeps most of the time." Her voice caught on a tremulous note. "My greatest fear is that when he is stronger he will lose his mind."

Heer de Veere interrupted quickly. "My dear, I've advised you not to consider that terrible possibility."

"But how can I not?" she exclaimed emotionally, both to him and to their visitors. "Constantijn has put up such a fight to live, but once he discovers his legs have been amputated he will suffer the most dreadful mental torment. He was such a sportsman, you see."

Jan nodded compassionately. "There was none to match him on ice or in a *kaatsen* team bashing that hard leather ball."

The woman dabbed her handkerchief to each eye. "But that can never be again."

Both Jan and Aletta saw it was time to take their leave. Vrouw de Veere thanked them again for coming. "I'll go up and give my son some of your broth. It should be heated and ready by now."

Heer de Veere saw the two visitors to the door. He echoed his wife's thanks, but did not suggest that either should come again, which they had not expected in any case. After they had gone he went with slow steps back upstairs. He had been glad of the little diversion of a visit for his wife, for they were both stunned by more bad news to bear, news

which had been received only an hour before but which they would have to keep to themselves for a while yet.

Before going to bed that night Aletta stood for a few moments at her window, as she always did, to look across at the one level with her own. Vrouw de Veere had shown such interest in the broth that she was sure it would be made up again and regularly if Constantijn should be like other sick people in appreciating its flavoursome goodness.

"You must live, Constantijn de Veere," she whispered aloud. Then she closed the curtains again and went to look at Ignatius sleeping in his crib. He was a good baby and rarely woke at night. She leaned over to tuck his quilt closer about him, and a little necklace of coral, hanging over the end of the crib, rattled gently. It was an heirloom, such as was owned by most families and always handed down to the newest baby, for coral was known to have healing qualities and could ward off illness. During the day Ignatius wore it under his bodice, but when he was old enough not to snatch at it as babies did he would wear it outside his gown until his fifth birthday, when he was breeched, or Catharina had another baby, whichever was the sooner.

If at her home the Visser coral necklace had not been handed down to Sybylla, who had it in a drawer until she should have children, it would still have been in Aletta's possession and she knew she would have taken it across the square and asked for it to be put under Constantijn's pillow, as was sometimes done when an adult was sick. But since she did not have it she must trust to the wisdom of his doctor and the recipe for the broth. Neither detracted in any way from the strength of her prayers for him every Sunday in the Old Church, which she attended with the Vermeers, nor from those she said before she went to sleep at night.

Pieter was on his way to Delft. After St. Nicholaes's Night the year before when he had taken the hyacinth to Francesca's home, he had no intention of not seeing her this year as well. He had chosen to go on horseback, for after much rain a recent cold snap had hardened the roads and the puddles had become glittering ice.

He had seen Francesca only once since he had called at the Vermeers'

3
3
3

house during the birthday party. It was during the time when Hendrick was still in prison and Aletta had implored him not to let her sister know of their father's predicament. The arrangements for the meeting had been made through Gerard. Francesca had been waiting for him by the helm-roofed towers of the east gate that August morning. As he had ridden into sight, she had come running across the bridge to meet him, a slender figure in a green gown and a straw hat. She carried sketching materials, which provided the official reason for her being out all day, although she had taken Catharina into her confidence.

He had set her up on his horse and they had ridden out into the countryside where they could be alone. It had been an idyllic day with a picnic he had brought with him, which had included a bottle of wine. He had watched her make sketches of the sparkling canal and the cornfields beyond, distant harvesters to be seen and a red windmill seeming to preside over the whole tranquil scene. He had feasted his eyes on her lovely face composed in concentration on her drawing, the sunshine trapped in her glorious hair and the vulnerable beauty of the nape of her neck just above the white cambric collar.

There had been more tender moments when they had lain side by side, exchanging lovers' whispers in the high grass that was full of wildflowers and aflutter with butterflies, wings as jewel-bright and trans-parent in the sun as stained glass. He had kissed her mouth, her face, her throat and the nipples of her pale breasts, aching to possess her. Once he had buried his face in her lap with such yearning, his arms clasped about her hips, that he had felt her quiver and gasp with desire. But she had raised herself to take his head between her hands and drawn him up to kiss his lips lovingly, her wide-open eyes telling him that the time was not yet, no matter that she might long for it as much as he.

When the hour had come for them to go their separate ways again she had given him a drawing of herself that Jan had done in a matter of minutes at her request. It was of her head and shoulders, an exquisite likeness and quite small. She had preserved it from creasing by placing it in a leather folder of the same size. He tucked it into his jacket next to his heart.

"Please convey my thanks to Master Vermeer," he had said, his arms about her. "When is he going to paint you?"

"Catharina would like him to do so, because when he does have some rare time in which to paint it is not always convenient for her to leave everything to sit for him."

"Well, then?"

"He would never take working hours away from me."

"Then paint a self-portrait."

Her smile teased him, but not her eyes. "Not yet," she had said with the same warmth of promise with which she had restrained his passion earlier. Shortly afterwards they had begun their regular if intermittent correspondence, his obliging friend, Gerard, always letting him know when a trip to Delft was in the offing. It was an exchange of love letters. Never before had he set down his innermost feelings as he did to her and they had both found that the old adage about absence making the heart grow fonder was true, except that the deepening and enriching of the love they already felt for each other went far beyond mere fondness.

Now, on this winter evening, he rode into Delft at dusk. Sounds of merrymaking and children's laughter came from most of the houses as he rode past along the narrow streets. He planned to stay at the Mechelin tavern. It would be the first time he had stayed overnight in Delft, having left the town before nightfall on both previous occasions, putting up at hostelries on the road home. Now he had become more confident that all the time he remained unknown and unrecognized in Delft he would incur no danger to Francesca.

The tavern was crowded and he had to wait before the landlord's wife at the desk could give him her attention. "I'm sorry, *mijnheer*," she said in answer to his request for a room, "but this is St. Nicholaes's Night and every room is taken by those coming home for family celebrations. You will find it is the same with every hostelry in the town."

"Can you recommend a private house where I might find accommodation?"

"Again I have to say no on this night. But wait a moment." She leaned back from the desk until she could see her husband and shouted to him, "Has Vrouw Wolff any vacancies left?" When he shook his head

she shrugged her shoulders apologetically at Pieter. "That is how it is with every house which normally obliges us with an overflow."

"At least may I leave my horse in your stables?"

"Certainly. They are a short distance away, but you'll find an ostler outside who will take your horse there."

After removing the saddlebag, Pieter left his horse in the ostler's charge and took the few steps that led him to the front of the well-lit Mechelin Huis. His intention of surprising Francesca was certainly going awry. She had told him that Catharina had promised that when he could call again they should have some time on their own together. Now he had to complicate matters by asking Catharina if he might spend the night under her roof, if only in a chair. He felt it was an imposition to ask, but he himself would never have wanted anyone of his acquaintance to spend a freezing night in a doorway and he was certain she would be of the same mind.

He asked for Catharina as soon as he was in the entrance hall and Elizabeth, rosy with happiness over the gifts she had received, having been treated as generously as if she were one of the children, bobbed to him. "I'll tell the mistress that you are here."

He and Catharina had not seen each other before, for it was only her husband whom he had met on his first visit to her house, but she welcomed him as if they were well acquainted.

"I've heard so much about you, Pieter. What a happy surprise Francesca is going to have! You can join our party without any worry, because we are only close family this evening. My mother is here, but she knows the situation and will not give away your presence in Delft. Where are you staying?"

He then explained his predicament. Normally she would have invited him to stay without hesitation, but she had gained special permission from Geetruyd for Francesca to stay the night and she was uncertain about having two people passionately in love with each other under her roof at the same time. She knew if she and Jan had been spending the night in the same house during their courtship days nothing would have kept them apart. Then the solution came to her.

"I've thought of something." She left him for a matter of minutes and then returned, her crescent smile wide. "I've spoken to my mother

without Francesca hearing and she is willing that you should stay at her house, where she has plenty of room."

"I'm most grateful."

"Now I'll tell Elizabeth to show you where you can wash and tidy up after your journey. Meanwhile I'll organize everything so that all the party can join in your surprise arrival, just as it was last year in Amsterdam. Francesca told me about the hyacinth!" Although they were on their own she whispered to him as to how he should make an entrance and he agreed willingly.

After washing, he changed into a clean shirt from his saddlebag and put on a fresh cravat of plain linen. Having already removed his riding boots, he put his feet into buckled shoes. He flicked a speck of dust from his sleeve and was ready to play his part in Catharina's reorganization of his sudden appearance at the St. Nicholaes's Night celebrations. Elizabeth was to give her mistress a prearranged signal.

At the party Aletta and Francesca were sitting on the floor playing a game with the children in which a ring was passed secretly from hand to hand while the child in the middle, who happened to be Beatrix, tried to locate it. She was quite wild with excitement. Looking around the circle on the floor, Beatrix pounced on Francesca's hand like a boisterous puppy. "You have it!"

She was right and it was the moment Catharina had been waiting for. "That means Francesca must pay a forfeit!" she announced merrily, clapping her hands to make herself heard above the mirth. "She shall be the first to be blindfolded in a game of chase-and-capture."

Francesca submitted willingly to having her eyes bound with a clean kerchief by Jan. Then all the children joined in spinning her around until she lost all sense of direction. They were nimble and dodged her. She was certain she almost had someone within her grasp when lace flicked across the tips of her fingers as she had her arms stretched out before her. Too late she realized the trick that had been played on her as she felt the cooler air of the adjoining room on her face and the communicating door slammed behind her, muffling the sounds of the party. Laughing, she fumbled at the knot at the back of her head.

"Let me do it for you," Pieter's voice said, releasing it.

The blindfold fell away and her delighted eyes absorbed the sight of

him for no more than a matter of seconds before she was in his arms. It was the hammering of the children on the other side of the door, demanding her return, that eventually brought an end to their kissing.

"This time I'm able to join the party," he said as he led her to the door.

Catharina watched them enter together. She saw how they looked at each other with the eyes of lovers for a brief moment before they turned simultaneously to smile at those in the room, and she thought them more blessed than they probably realized. Only those who had experienced the constant threat of being parted forever, whether by parental opposition or any other kind of catastrophe, fully appreciated love and life together when eventually it was achieved. Jan was already welcoming the new arrival. What a perfect evening it was turning out to be!

Aletta had gone forward eagerly to greet Pieter, who kissed her hand and her cheek. Catharina, still watching, saw something in Aletta's face that might have been love too, but it was only there for a fleeting moment and was gone almost as soon as it had appeared.

When the party was over Pieter and Francesca had a little while alone to exchange their gifts and make their own loving farewell. He gave her a necklet of pearls, which was of the fashionable length to be worn high about the throat, a single drop pearl hanging from it, and he fastened it on for her.

"It's beautiful," she breathed, looking at her reflection in a mirror. "I'll treasure it always."

She had a gift for him. It was a small painting of the view taken from the sketch she had made on the August day they had shared together. Within its frame he saw again the canal asparkle with sun-diamonds, the cornfield and the windmill beyond.

"It's splendid, and you've signed it!" He peered closer at her signature. "There's a tulip within the signature. How apt!"

"Jan gave me permission to sign it. As my master everything I paint belongs to him and he has sold most of my work, but he allowed me to keep this one for a token sum, so it's not a costly gift that you have received."

"You're mistaken." He looked fondly at her. "It's the first painting of yours that I've ever owned and that makes it beyond price to me."

From the entrance hall Catharina called tactfully through the door that was standing ajar. "My mother is ready to leave, Pieter."

At Vrouw Thin's house he was given a good bed in a warm room. In the morning, although he rose at an early hour, the servants were about and he was served a hearty breakfast.

"Snow is on the way," a manservant warned while pouring out steaming coffee for him. "I was born on a farm and I know all the signs of bad weather. It's my belief that a blizzard is not far distant."

A few flakes were falling when Pieter went to collect his horse at the stables, but there was no wind and it was less cold than on the previous day. He covered the many miles back to Haarlem without any delay, relieved that the forecast had so far not proved to be right.

Haarlem Huis was always at the centre of activity, even in winter. The most constant chore was that of cosseting the orange trees, a careful check on the lamps thrice daily ensuring a steady temperature, whatever the degrees of frost might be outside the orangery. Pieter was planning to build another such orangery very shortly, for this expensive tree was much in demand.

Whenever business elsewhere caused him to be absent from his bulb fields more than he would have wished, at least he could be sure that all would be efficiently run while he was away, for he had an excellent manager, who lived on the site in the old farmhouse. It had been the van Doorne family home until Haarlem Huis had been built on the profits of the short, sharp spell of tulipomania, from which Pieter's late father had emerged successfully.

Pieter, well satisfied with his own investments in cargoes, was able to follow the latest shipping reports even from Haarlem Huis, for Holland had more newspapers in circulation than the rest of Europe put together. He was reading one of several that he took regularly when Gerard called in at Haarlem Huis to see if there was a letter ready for him to take to Delft.

"Not this time," Pieter said after they had settled at the fireside, each with a glass of wine. They had been friends since their school days and were totally relaxed in each other's company. "Neither Francesca nor I

expected you to be going there again before Christmas and what we would have written is to be said instead when we see each other very soon now in Amsterdam. I'm banned from calling at her home, but we shall meet at my house."

"How did your trip to Delft go?"

"Extremely well."

"Good fortune must be smiling on you."

"I'll drink to that," Pieter replied firmly and raised his glass while Gerard did the same.

But the toast was to no effect. Neither Pieter nor Francesca was able to get to Amsterdam for Christmas. A great blizzard swept across Europe, blocking roads and causing many of those trapped by it to freeze to death.

Hendrick, looking out the window at the driving flakes, which made it impossible to see across to the houses on the other side of the canal, was selfishly thankful for the storm. He had dreaded meeting Francesca face to face. She had the uncanny ability to see through him at times, being much like Anna in that respect. Not only would she have challenged him about the restrictions of Vrouw Wolff's chaperonage, but she would have gone up in the air about his treatment of Aletta.

He was not without shame at his harshness towards his second daughter, especially when he had heard how narrowly she had escaped injury in the accident, but he did not want her home again. For a while after she had left, Sybylla had been sulky, saying he had driven her sister away, but she had soon recovered from that phase and was full of life again, happy in her favourite game of playing off one would-be suitor against another. He knew she was a little minx, but she had been spoilt since birth through being the youngest and it was too late to change that now. It would be a dull house when she finally settled on a husband and moved into her own home, which was why he was in no hurry for her to marry. When she did it would leave him with only Maria's gloomy face at mealtimes, for the old woman missed sorely both Francesca and Aletta and her main pastime was the same unceasing bickering with Sybylla.

At the present time he was painting Maria. He was like Rembrandt in finding old faces interesting subjects. She came daily into the studio

to sit for him, ensconced in a comfortable chair, and he had thought to capture the sad look that had settled in her eyes since the departure of Aletta, but that had not been possible. Instead she had fixed him with a fiercely resentful gaze that pleased him better, for those who viewed the portrait would interpret the look as that of a still young spirit trapped in an ancient body instead of a pent-up grudge against him for causing further emptiness in the house.

Hendrick did not know if Ludolf would like or want the finished work, but freedom in the studio was all that was left to him, for his patron could not dictate subject matter even when holding jurisdiction over everything else in his life. Mercifully Ludolf had been absent from Amsterdam for quite a time, away on business in Antwerp, where he had shipping interests. Before he had left, Hendrick had had an igno-minious summons to Heerengracht.

"I'll probably be away through the rest of my period of mourning," Ludolf had said, seated grandly in a gilded chair while Hendrick stood like a schoolboy in disgrace with no invitation to sit. "Naturally I shall make a point of returning in time for Christmas, when Francesca will be home. As I said to you previously, I intend to start my courtship then."

Recalling that haughty statement, Hendrick watched the snowflakes being hurled with increasing force against the windowpanes and he smiled grimly. No doubt Ludolf had expected to sail home to Amsterdam from Antwerp, but no ships were putting out of harbour into the present rough seas and the roads were impassable. It was a true saying that it was an ill wind that blew no one any good.

In the new year there was no return of what had been termed every-where as the Great Blizzard, but heavy falls of snow continued to make travelling hazardous. Traffic was much easier on the frozen canals once they were cleared of snow, and the air rang with the tinkling of bells on sleighs and sledges. In the de Veere house Constantijn was making steady progress. It was said that when he had recovered enough to realize his legs were gone he thought the amputation had been done only recently, for in the hazy coming and going of his senses he had still been able to feel his legs and even his toes. He had not wept or cried

out when he had faced the awful truth that he would never walk again, but a terrible anger had possessed him and showed no sign of abating.

Aletta understood that anger. It was in her too. He had lost his legs and she her painting.

Constantijn, propped up by pillows and wedged in by them in the four-poster bed with its rich brocade curtains, did not open his eyes when he heard his mother enter the room. Another meal of slops, he thought. It would be easy to believe that everyone from the kitchen staff to his mother was trying to finish him off with steamed fish or coddled eggs or gruel. It would make an interesting inscription on the stone under which he would lie in the New Church with his forebears. *Constantijn de Veere, who died of a surfeit of curds and whey.*

Then a tantalizing aroma reached him. It was vaguely familiar and he was reminded of moments of rich living, intimate dinners with a beautiful woman, carousing with riotous friends in celebration when a match had been won and even family feasts on special occasions.

"What have you brought for my noon meal today?" he asked, his eyes still closed. "It smells like real food."

"It's broth made from a recipe left with me on St. Nicholaes's Eve. A whole jug of it was brought for you, but I only gave it to you once."

His eyelids lifted and he regarded her with weary astonishment. "You had it in the house and didn't give me any more of it?"

"The doctor happened to call at the time and thought it too rich."

"Ah, I might have known. Why has it been made again for me now?"

"Your diet is to be strengthened. You're to be allowed red meat and red wine from now on."

"May heaven be praised," he said drily.

She set down the silver platter with the bowl of broth on it. "It was a young woman who originally made the broth for you. She is temporary nursemaid to the Vermeer children and sister to Master Vermeer's female apprentice."

She had told him all this when she had put a spoonful of the broth to his mouth on St. Nicholaes's Eve, thankful to see him take every drop, but he had forgotten so much from that time when it had been uncertain whether he would live or die.

"I've seen her."

"When?" She wondered if he had retained some image conjured up by her words at the time.

"At least I think it must be her. A young woman pulls the curtains back every night from the window level with mine across the square. Only for a minute or two. Then she closes them again."

"As you should have yours closed," she said brusquely, not quite sure what to make of his observation.

He guessed what was going through his mother's mind. "She's in full attire."

"So I should hope!"

He thought to himself it would have relieved the tedium of being confined to his bed if the young woman had not been clothed! Nevertheless, he appreciated her thoughtfulness over the soup. There had been countless gifts and notes from well-wishers, many of the senders well known to him and others from his parents' acquaintances. The only letter that had held his pain-racked interest had been from Isabella, to whom he was betrothed. Mostly he had fallen asleep during his mother's reading of the good wishes and it was still easier to doze than to be awake. Perhaps he was sleeping his life away as very old people did and it tempted as a soothing way out of the crippled future to which fate had condemned him.

"Here's the broth, dearest boy. Are you sure you can manage?"

He looked into her sweet, kindly face as she fussed over spreading a napkin for him and handing him a spoon. Whether she realized it or not she was in her element at having him as helpless as a baby again, all her maternal instincts having come to the fore once more. He both loved and pitied her. All that had happened was as great a trial for her as it was for him, but he did not know how much longer he could endure the nursery atmosphere that she had induced into his bedchamber.

"I can manage well, Mother."

It was still an effort to feed himself, there being so little strength in his arms. At first he had dropped the spoon several times and food had been spilled, increasing his sense of humiliation. Fortunately the doctor had brought in a nurse, a stolid, middle-aged woman with a rear as wide as a barge, to deal with all the private menial duties concerned with

nursing. From the start she had also kept out everyone else, his mother included, during the dressing of his stumps. He would always be thankful that she gave him a wad of linen to bite on and stifle his groans, which sometimes escaped him when the dressings still stuck while being changed. He did not know what screams he must have uttered during the cauterizing after the amputation, for he had no recollection of that night.

His mother chatted while he enjoyed the broth. She did not mention what he most wanted to know and he interrupted her. "Is there no word yet of when Isabella will be coming to see me?"

"The roads are still bad for travelling. She will come as soon as it is possible. More snow fell during the night."

He cursed the snow. As yet he had received no visitors, although local friends had called many times. They would have been too cheerful and hearty, embarrassed at not knowing quite what to say, and he could not have endured his fellow sportsmen's poorly disguised sympathy that he, who had outrun, outraced and outskated them all, should have been reduced to such terrible straits. After Isabella had been to see him and they had talked over this new situation that had arisen, he might feel differently about receiving visitors. But for the present time he was curiously in limbo.

CHAPTER 1 5

Ludolf had returned to Amsterdam from Paris by way of Antwerp. He was careful to cover his tracks these days. It was all very well for the burghers and merchants to show favour towards France, but when Louis XIV moved to annex Holland there might be a swing of feeling among them to match the hostility of the people towards the possibility of French rule. On this visit he had been received at Versailles itself, his flourishing bow to the Sun King as flamboyant as any Frenchman's.

His first action upon re-entering his home after his absence was to sort through the stack of letters awaiting him. When he found a note from Willem de Hartog he tore it open, doubtful of what he might read. To his relief it told him of Hendrick's release. He had not received word of the artist's arrest until he was about to leave Antwerp on his homeward journey, only to be trapped there by the Great Blizzard, which had delayed his return by another three weeks. Had Hendrick been heavily sentenced, his own hold over him would have been considerably diminished. A smile touched the corners of Ludolf's thick lips. As it happened, everything had worked out in his favour. Now that Hendrick had had a taste of prison, he certainly would not want to set foot in one again.

There was a letter from Geetruyd, written before Christmas, and in addition to more important matters, it reported that Aletta, the sister of the young woman in her charge, had come to stay in Delft and presently had employment caring for the children of the Vermeers. He tapped a fingernail thoughtfully against the letter in his hand. Nursemaids usually had very little free time, which made it unlikely that Aletta's presence would ease Francesca's chaperonage in any noticeable way. When he had made that family clause in the letter which Hendrick was forced to copy, he had never supposed that either of Francesca's sisters would ever get to Delft, except possibly on a special visit with their father.

Ludolf crossed to the window and looked out onto his white garden. It was impossible to tell whether the flagstones had been replaced during his absence before the snow came. It was months since van Doorne had declared himself dissatisfied with the quality when they had been unloaded from a wagon and had had them sent back. The base of sand and rubble had been laid, but Ludolf was impatient for the whole project to be finished.

"It is important to the whole harmonious layout of the garden that the flagstones should be of exactly the right colour, which in turn would compliment the house," van Doorne had said, showing him a piece of stone to illustrate its faults.

Personally Ludolf had not been able to see much wrong with it, but he had learnt over the years to defer to experts while retaining the

3
4
5

information they gave, for it was one of the ways by which he had hauled himself up from his rough beginnings to the position he held today with higher things to come. Similarly his polish and fine manners had come from careful observation. He prided himself on never having lost sight of his aim to gain wealth and the authority that came with it. He had been inwardly amused when Sybylla, during the time when she had been visiting Amalia, had confided to him that she wanted a rich young husband. The hint had been there for him to arrange a few introductions, but he never did anything for anybody that was not ultimately for his own benefit, even though he had seen in her the same avid lust for wealth that had been his already when he was her age.

While he had been at Versailles recently a *comtesse*, naked and scented in her soft bed, had stroked his chest and remarked on the number of scars on his body. He had given her the reply he always made at such moments.

"Those were gained in the service of my country."

This useful lie always melted a woman's eyes. Geetruyd was the only one of her sex to know that his wounds had been received from the weapons of seamen fighting to prevent their richly cargoed ships and themselves from being captured. Privateers were notoriously merciless with regard to prisoners. The only ones he had ever allowed to live had been those he had been able to sell to Arab slave traders along the North African coast. In contrast to his violent means of livelihood at that time, he had invested as soon as he was able in a legitimate ship-brokering business in Antwerp and later Amsterdam, always through an agent, and each had created its own rich profits, for his prices were competitive and nobody liked a bargain better than a Dutchman. There were other projects too, in which he had invested with equal success.

It was originally for these businesses that he had adopted the well-sounding name of van Deventer. Abandoned as a baby and brought up in an orphanage, where the authorities had baptized him Ludolf, he had no knowledge of any rightful surname, and during his years at sea he had used a variety of common names, changing from one to another when circumstances made it advisable.

At forty he had retired from the sea, a rich man from several sources, whereas others of his trade had drunk, gambled and wenched their

money away, but then they had been content to spend the rest of their lives at sea. For him it had only been a means to an end. What was more, he was secure in the knowledge that there were no survivors from his more brutal exploits to rise up and accuse him of his crimes, while those who had been his companions were unlikely ever to cross his path. Money was power and he had it at last, not knowing then that it was not to be enough and a new lure was to be one of political mastery.

Not long afterwards he had married Amalia. He had enjoyed using her money, but he had not married her just for her wealth, or for the fact that in those days he had found her desirable. Overriding all else had been her good breeding and her lineage that had had links with the House of Orange in generations gone by. Marriage to her had elevated him to the secure status that he had needed, gaining him an entrée into the best families in Amsterdam and, on their marriage journey, in France as well. That was when the scales had fallen from his eyes and he had seen how it was possible to live in ultimate luxury. He had become obsessed by all things French, which had led eventually to his being enrolled as a spy for France. The military information he had supplied this time had been rewarded with a complimentary word from Louis himself.

Leaving the study, Ludolf went through to the banqueting room. There he shut the door behind him and went to gaze, as if he had been starved, on the likeness of Francesca. His period of mourning was well and truly over. Not the slightest suspicion had fallen on him. He was free to go in pursuit of this lovely girl as soon as matters could be arranged.

In another part of the house Neeltje was going up a back staircase with some folded linen in her arms. So Ludolf was home again! From a window she had watched him come into the house, hatred in her eyes. The murderer! Tonight she would take her secret keys and go through his mail and whatever papers he had brought home with him. She had often come across love letters from women, but her mistress had been too private and dignified a person to sue for divorce with all its attendant scandal. In any case, as Ludolf was never physically cruel to her, a few letters would not have been enough to secure her freedom. His affairs never lasted long and the only regular correspondence from a woman was from one who wrote in an entirely different tone. She was Geetruyd Wolff, who lived in Delft and wrote obliquely on what could only be business matters about ships and deliveries and people referred to by their initials. Yet Neeltje's feminine intuition told her this woman had some feeling for Ludolf. In those letters there had been only one reference to Francesca, saying that the young woman was now in her charge and that she intended to carry out the father's wishes most strictly. Neeltje had not passed this on to Aletta, seeing no need, and in any case she had not wanted to be asked how she had come across this information. She hoped to find something of interest when tonight she would go through the mail that Ludolf should have opened by now. She had resisted the temptation to deal with it before his return. A hot knife slipped under a wax seal was effective, but she had not dared in case by ill chance her hand should slip in her nervousness and smudge the softened wax. Ludolf had sharp eyes. It was safer and easier to read the letters after him. It gnawed at her that when she had gained precious evidence of murder against him, which would have put him to a savage execution, she had been powerless to use it.

She paused on the stairs and drew breath. It was not ascending the flight that normally caused her any discomfort, for she was a strong woman with good lungs, but there were times when she still suffered a twinge in her ribs during any exertion and then it was best to rest for a minute or two. Through a window she could see the garden. Her warning to Aletta about a possible threat to Francesca from Ludolf had been conveyed to Pieter van Doorne, with immediate results. The young man had stopped the unloading of the flagstones on some pretext, leaving the way open for him to come to the house whenever it suited him. During the laying of the base materials on the paths she had given him an opportunity to speak to her, which he had taken.

"If ever you have more information that would help me protect Francesca," he had said, "please leave a message at my Amsterdam address."

He had given it to her and she had tucked it away in her pocket with a nod, going back indoors again. To thwart Ludolf over the issue of

the young woman he wanted would be a triumph. There were more ways than one of killing a cat.

Geetruyd was on her way home from a meeting of the orphanage board of the regentesses. She had to skirt a noisy demonstration in the square. Supporters of the Orange party, in favour of the Prince, the States party, who backed de Witt, and a third party, who shouted loudly and did not seem to know what it wanted, were coming close to a free-for-all, there being many angry faces and shaking fists.

Snow was slushy underfoot in the late February thaw, but her high-built shoes were of the best-quality leather, soft and supple while keeping her feet dry. She could have afforded her own sedan chair with bearers employed as menservants if she had not had to keep up her image as a widow in modest circumstances. She knew Ludolf well enough to know that he paid her generously only because she did not make careless blunders in her secret work on his behalf. There had been one slip when Francesca had been able to spend time talking to the agent from Utrecht long enough for her to have registered his face and voice. Not a serious matter in itself, but it had been necessary to raise the point with him in order to quell a rising interest in him towards the girl, the last thing that could be allowed to happen.

She arrived home and, after kicking the wet snow from her shoes, she entered. Weintje came to take her cloak and hand her a pair of buckled house shoes.

"You have a visitor, madam. Heer van Deventer is in the drawing room."

Her throat seemed to close with anticipation. It was so long since she had last seen him! "I thank you, Weintje," she managed to say. "He and I will have much to talk about. See that neither you nor Juffrouw Clara disturbs us. I suggest you both stay in the kitchen region in case I have need to ring for anything."

"Yes, *mevrouw.*"

When Weintje had gone from the entrance hall, Geetruyd whipped off the staid linen cap she wore to her meetings and thrust it into a

drawer. Then she smoothed her hair into place and went into the drawing room.

Some while later she smiled at Ludolf as he stirred from his doze in the bed beside her. They were in her bedchamber, where they had come soon after their first embrace of reunion.

"You were mad to come to Delft, you know," she said. "We had agreed on almost no contact and only essential correspondence."

He grinned lazily. "I used to visit you."

"But that was before your involvement in French affairs." She traced a forefinger over his shoulder. "It's like old times again. Nothing has changed, has it?" She wanted to hear confirmation from him. Now that they had both established themselves away from all that lay in their past and with Amalia dead, the future had opened up for them again. Naturally she did not love him blindly now as she had when he had first come into her life. Certainly some of his ways, which she had once endured in a devoted and submissive haze, wanting only to please him, would be intolerable to her now. Perhaps in truth she no longer loved him at all, but he was what she had wanted then, and what she still wanted and had always been determined to have when the time was right. It was not right yet, but when France had gained control of Holland and Ludolf was raised to a high ministerial post she would do him credit as his wife. All subterfuge and dreariness would be a thing of the past. She would be able to extend her not inconsiderable intelligence and educated taste in literature by holding salons in the French style.

He was giving her waist an absentminded squeeze, his thoughts moving rapidly away from her as he considered the important matter that had brought him to Delft, her question only just lodging with him. "We've known each other too long now for anything to change."

He threw back the quilt and left the bed to start dressing. She watched him luxuriously. He still wore red silk underwear. After the passage of time she might have expected him to look faintly ludicrous in it, but he was still a formidable man with nothing about him to raise the slightest ridicule. His hair, which he wore cropped for convenience under his periwig, had receded slightly and had some wings of grey in it, but baldness was still far from him.

"You still haven't told me why you've come to Delft," she said, hoping it was simply to see her, although she did not expect that to be the reason. There was not a grain of sentiment in him. His reply confirmed it.

"It's time you and I talked about branching out on a new tack of getting to know what the defences are at Muiden and other places where the sluices control the sea water. There was deliberate flooding to keep the enemy at bay during the Spanish war and it's a method of defence likely to be used again. However, I have a legitimate reason for being here in your house, if not in your bed! Being the patron of the artist whose daughter is staying with you, it would be expected that I should inquire after her welfare from you in order to report back to her father."

She sat up, holding the quilt to her. "I believe in caution and still more caution. Of course we need to talk this time and you can't be here too often for me, but we were wise before and must continue to be. Although the minimum period of mourning for Amalia is over for you, there can be no question of us marrying until your spying for France and my involvement in it has achieved its purpose."

He was arranging his collar in front of a mirror, his back to her, and he was thankful she could not see his shift of expression. Marry her! Did she still expect that after all this time? It was she, more than he, who had always spoken of it. If she had inherited her old husband's wealth, as they had both expected and which had been the major factor in their getting rid of the old man, he would have made her his wife instead of Amalia. It had been his full intention, for he had seen how they might mould their future together, but when he had returned from the sea to discover she had been left almost nothing, he had looked elsewhere for a bride. Geetruyd was still pleasurable to bed, and was extremely useful to him as the kingpin of a house where information could be received and dispatched under perfect cover, but that was all. She would come to terms with his marrying someone else as she had done before. He had never found her difficult to manage and he did not expect any complications now. He turned and smiled at her approvingly.

"Tell me about Francesca," he said, sitting down to pull on his knee

hose. "As I said before, her father will want to know how she is behaving and whether she sees much of her sister."

"I've had no trouble with her after the first day or two. I find her agreeable and quite like her company, but whether she is conducting any correspondence against her father's wishes is impossible for me to say. There is a limit to how much control I can exercise. At least I know no such letters addressed to her have arrived in Delft and frankly I don't believe she is receiving them by any other means. She acknowledges my rules for a peaceful existence, totally unlike so many girls I've had here, but then she has her painting to absorb her. I've heard from Master Vermeer himself how hard she works. Whenever she goes out with Aletta I always insist that Clara go with them. In all, I've had nothing serious with which to upbraid Francesca. She always asks my permission before visiting with the Vermeers or seeing Vrouw Thin."

Ludolf was dressed, even to his periwig, and he jerked his cuffs into place. "Surely you've had to keep a few young men at bay?" he queried casually.

"No doubt if Francesca had encouraged them there would have been plenty, but that hasn't happened. The first letter I made her write as soon as she came here was to that young man, van Doorne, putting an end to any possible visits from him. She wrote it was only friendship between them and now I'm sure that was so."

"Good." Then he added, almost as an afterthought, "Her father will be pleased."

"Where are you going now?"

"To pay a call on Master Vermeer. It is on Hendrick Visser's behalf. When it is over I'll walk Francesca back here. There'll be no need to send Clara today. Then this evening I think we should all go out for some entertainment—a *musico* or a concert, maybe a play. What is on in the town?"

"There's usually a *musico* at the Mechelin, but I couldn't be seen there."

"But such evenings of music and dancing are always in a room separate from the taprooms."

"Nevertheless, it would do my reputation no good with my fellow

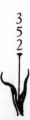

regents and regentesses to be seen anywhere near a tavern. They are narrow-minded beyond belief!"

He accepted her argument, for although wine and ale were to be had in every household, it was the drunkenness that took place in taverns that was condemned and kept many away, not the alcohol itself.

"Where else could we go?" he asked.

"There's a concert at the Town Hall."

"Excellent. That's what we'll do, then. Francesca might like Aletta to come too."

"I'm sure she would."

When Ludolf opened the entrance door into the gallery at Mechelin Huis he was surprised by the length of the room and how well lit it was by the windows on each side of the door that reached to a high ceiling. He presumed that the man setting a painting into a frame was the one he had come to see.

"Master Vermeer?"

Jan put down his work and came forward, interested to see a prospective customer who was new to him. "That is I."

"Allow me to present myself, Ludolf van Deventer."

The name meant nothing to Jan, for Francesca had never mentioned Ludolf to him or his wife. "In what may I interest you, *mijnheer?* Do you wish to look at what is on the walls here or have you a special kind of picture in mind?"

"It's not a work of art that I require," Ludolf said, although he glanced with mild interest at what was on the wall nearest him. "I have other business with you."

Jan's immediate and decidedly gloomy thought was that this well-dressed stranger was a lawyer sent by one of those to whom he owed money. "What might that be?"

"You have a pupil. Francesca Visser."

"Indeed I have."

"I'll come straight to the point. I'm here to buy her out of her apprenticeship. She is to be placed in another studio in Amsterdam."

Jan perched his weight against the end of the long table and folded his arms. "I've heard nothing of this from Francesca," he said coolly, thoroughly offended.

"She doesn't know yet. It is to be a surprise for her."

"Is that so? And on whose authority do you act?"

"Her father's. I saw him only yesterday before I left the city." Ludolf was glancing at more paintings as he strolled leisurely down the gallery. Then he paused to take a folded paper from his pocket and toss it across the table for Jan to pick up. "Read his wishes for yourself."

A few steps farther along Ludolf halted before a painting. It was a riotous tavern scene and the laughing, red-faced man raising his tankard was not unlike Hendrick. Yet the artist had had anything but a merry face when summoned to Heerengracht the previous day.

"Francesca won't like your interference," Hendrick had said, glowering, "and the same amount of money already paid will have to be returned to the source from which it came."

"That is no problem. Just put your signature to this document, giving me the necessary authority to take the matter in hand. My clerk has drawn it up for you."

"What if I refuse to sign?"

Ludolf had not bothered to answer and after a second or two Hendrick had picked up the pen. Once again the artist had taken warning.

Jan spoke. "Whom does Heer Visser have in mind as a new master for Francesca?"

Ludolf turned and took up the paper that had been replaced on the table. "Pieter de Hooch."

"Ah. I knew him well when he lived in Delft. His work was remarkable then for his harmonious, rich colours and the tranquillity of his domestic scenes."

"I was told that your style influenced him."

"That's as may be. Is he willing to take her?"

"Only with your agreement."

"That was to be expected. Neither he, as an old friend and fellow artist, nor any other painter of repute would filch an apprentice from another studio, whether that pupil was almost fully trained, as Francesca is, or simply a beginner. Have you found out if she is willing to make such a change?"

Ludolf scoffed smilingly. "One doesn't consult a woman. She will accept whatever is arranged for her."

"You think so? What made her father decide on de Hooch?"

"For the reason I just gave you. Your style and his are not all that far apart, which will make the transfer easier for Francesca than if she were to be placed with anyone else."

"I don't understand Master Visser's motive. Surely he is aware that de Hooch's work has changed in his new surroundings? It has become mechanical and mannered in his bowing to popular taste for grander scenes with men and women in French silks and satins."

"He is still the best choice."

"No!" In a blaze of fury Jan slammed a fist into his palm. "Even if I were prepared to let Francesca go, which I'm not, I'd refuse to see her fluid style and her individual control of light broken down and lost!"

Ludolf frowned and tapped a finger on the table. "I don't want that sort of aggressiveness. Perhaps I haven't made it clear that you are to be well compensated for the lost year or two you would otherwise have given her."

"She is not up for sale!"

"You're twisting my offer. It was not made in that vein. I have her interests at heart too. But it will not be long before she is a wife and mother. Painting can never be more than a hobby for her. So what can a change of style matter?"

Jan, supposing that this man had caught some gist of Francesca and Pieter's eventual marriage plans, decided it would be wiser for their sakes to make a show of ignorance on that point. "Her personal life doesn't come into this discussion. It matters to me"—here Jan rammed a thumb to his chest—"that she may reach the ranks of our best contemporary artists and I'll not see her chance thrown away."

Ludolf's face was thunderous. "Enough of this argument. I'll pay you double what you would have received for three years! Plus another two thousand guilders to cover any sales you might make of her work! Don't tell me you don't need the money, because I never do any business without finding out everything it is possible to know about the one with whom I'm dealing. You owe your baker so much it was only through borrowing from your mother-in-law that you narrowly missed having to give him a painting in lieu of your debt, which is still not fully settled. I'll not trouble to list all the other debts you have out-

3
5
5

standing in this town. The Great Blizzard kept away potential customers from other towns, adding to your financial difficulties." Ludolf
paused for breath and straightened up, for he had leaned forward men-
acingly when speaking, an old trick when intent on intimidating, which
he had learned long ago. His voice evened out. "Now we have bargained
long enough. I'm a generous man. How much do you want?"

"You've already had my answer." Jan spoke with icy ferocity, not
raising his voice. His control exacerbated Ludolf's anger.

"Don't be a fool!"

"Leave my premises!"

"Not before I've seen Francesca! She'll not go against her father's
wishes." Ludolf believed now that Francesca herself might prove to be
his trump card.

"Oh? So she's to be brought into this after all, is she? Do you suppose
you can browbeat her into changing course?"

"Surely you wouldn't keep her against her will?"

"In her case it would be for her own good, but should she prove
adamant about taking up this new chance, I might feel obliged to
reconsider."

"Now you are being sensible." Ludolf could feel mastery of the situation coming back into his hands. "Send for her."

"No, I've a better idea. I want her to make up her own mind
independently, without any persuasion from me or coercion from you."

"You have a blunt way of stating my part in it," Ludolf remarked
caustically, "since I represent her father."

Jan shrugged. "You can scarcely expect me to pick my words! Now,
next to the studio is a room that goes up through two floors, much as
this gallery does, and there is an aperture with a wooden balustrade
from which it is possible to look down into it from a parlour at mid-
level. I'll take you up there and you can watch and listen while I tell
Francesca her father's wishes. You must make no interruption until she
has made her decision. Is that agreed?"

"If you do not attempt to influence her in any way."

"You have my word."

Jan took Ludolf to the room with the balustrade, a common enough
feature of Dutch homes with a variance of floor levels. He did not like

what he was having to do, but on second thought it had seemed the fairest way. For all he knew, it might cause Francesca much distress not to follow her father's bidding. Should she ask to be released from her apprenticeship in order to return to Amsterdam, Jan knew he would agree to it, but he would not accept the compensation. It had not been offered as a normal settlement, but as an insulting bribe.

Francesca was surprised when Jan opened the studio door and asked her to step into the next room for a few moments. She left her work at the easel and went to him. It struck her how serious he looked.

"I have just received a disturbing request from your father, Francesca."

When he told her what was proposed she let her hands rise and fall in disbelief. "This is outrageous! My father has always been inconsistent, but this is going to extremes. I can only guess he has sold a painting for an exceptionally large sum and the money is burning a hole in his pocket. Why else should he think of taking me away from here and putting me to Pieter de Hooch's studio? I'll not go! Nothing shall make me!"

"You must think this over very carefully," Jan advised.

"I have. Surely you wouldn't force me to abide by such a thoughtless whim?"

"No, I won't, Francesca. Nobody shall remove you from my studio. You'll be a member of the Guild before that happens." Then, as she closed her eyes in her immense relief, he added, "Would you like to send word of your own decision to your father, explaining why you want to stay, by the messenger who brought his letter here?"

"Who came?"

Jan indicated the aperture high in the wall and saw shock register in her face. Ludolf was resting both hands on the rounded top of the balustrade, his expression dark. He was not angry with her, only exasperated that she had made everything much more difficult for him than it had needed to be. She had taken a few steps forward as she looked up at him, her head tilted back.

"What on earth are you doing up there?" she demanded fiercely.

"It will be a lengthy explanation," he stated crisply. "I've voiced my

reasons for being here once in this house already. I'd prefer to talk to you on your own elsewhere."

Jan had looked from Francesca to Ludolf and back again. "How well do you know this man?"

"He's my father's patron," she gave back impatiently. "Come down from up there, Ludolf. If you wish, you may walk back to Kromstraat with Clara and me. My working day is about at its end." Then, as he disappeared from view, she turned to Jan. "Why did he have to be there? You wouldn't have agreed to it without just cause."

Briefly he told her all that had taken place.

When she emerged from the house there was no sign of Clara, but her sister was waiting with Ludolf. Aletta explained why she was there. "Vrouw Wolff has invited Heer van Deventer and me to her house for dinner this evening and afterwards we are to attend a concert."

"Are we?" Francesca spoke sharply. She had had enough of everybody exerting pressure on her from all sides. This latest whim of her father's to switch her apprenticeship had exhausted her patience. "Well, Ludolf, let me hear your promised explanation for supporting Hendrick's mad scheme to get me back to Amsterdam. I have heard from Master Vermeer that you pressed him most strongly and wrathfully for my release." She set a swift pace for Kromstraat and he and Aletta fell quickly into step with her.

He answered her as sharply as she had spoken to him. "I had promised your father that I'd do everything in my power to see that his wishes were fulfilled. Why should I not? I told you long ago I held a patriarchal attitude towards Hendrick that included his family."

"Maybe you also wanted me back in Amsterdam yourself!" she challenged hotly.

"I'll not deny it. Don't be so uppish with me, Francesca, because I'm in no mood for that. In the gallery I lost my temper with Vermeer. It was the last thing I intended to have happen, but he riled me, as I did him. It's understandable that Hendrick should miss you and wish you apprenticed nearer home."

She came to an abrupt halt. "I'm nobody's chattel! When will you and my father realize that? I'll not be moved about like a chess piece!"

He raised his hands placatingly. "Calm down! This is getting out of

control. You want to stay in Delft and Master Vermeer has every lawful right to keep you. There's the end of it. I've other places to visit after Delft and by the time I return to Amsterdam your father may well have forgotten all about his idea to switch you back there."

Aletta thought that Ludolf had shown a keen insight into Hendrick's character. "That's most likely," she agreed.

Francesca made a weary gesture. "I'm sure you're right."

Aletta put her arm about her sister's shoulders and the three of them walked on together to Geetruyd's house.

Over dinner, which was served on silver dishes kept for special occasions, conversation flowed normally. Aletta asked Ludolf if he had seen Sybylla before leaving Amsterdam.

"No. I've not been to your home since my return from Antwerp. Your father came to see me about calling in at Delft and seeing Master Vermeer on his behalf." He had already told Geetruyd about this during the first course of oysters.

Aletta did not want that subject brought up again, for her sister had become silent and very straight-backed as she had been before. Quickly she looked towards Geetruyd, who sat at the head of the table in a flattering gown of deep lilac-blue silk. "Had you and Heer van Deventer ever met before today?"

Geetruyd took a sip from her glass. "Yes. Through a mutual acquaintance some years ago. Isn't that so, Ludolf?"

"Indeed it is," he replied blandly before turning to Aletta. "How do you like living in Delft?"

"I've settled down very well. The Vermeers have been extremely kind to me, but it's high time I found somewhere else to work. I only went there on a temporary basis."

Francesca smiled meaningfully across at her sister. "I'm so glad you could be spared from nursery chores to be with us this evening."

"Catharina was very willing that I should come. The two older girls are so efficient at helping put the younger ones to bed that I'm hardly needed, although I can manage Beatrix much better than anyone else when she's in a mischievous mood." Aletta gave a fond little laugh on her thought of the child. "But I must find some other employment soon."

If Francesca had not been in the house already, Geetruyd would have offered Aletta board and a room and employed her to help Weintje with the domestic chores, but even if Master Vermeer was not going to heed Hendrick Visser's latest whim, she herself was going to obey his orders to the letter. To have a sister in the house might give Francesca cover for more freedom and that was not to be allowed.

Geetruyd noticed that Ludolf was talking to Francesca again. She did not wonder, for the young woman had a bloom on her these days that enhanced her remarkable looks and Ludolf had always been a womanizer. Not that he was making much impression, for Francesca gave him no special response and talked more to her and Aletta and Clara than to him. Yet there was something in the air between the two of them, a tension that was almost palpable. Geetruyd thought how easily men gave themselves away when they were strongly attracted to a woman. The frequent glances, the easy laughter and the deliberately casual air were so transparent to any other female watching them, particularly wives, and she herself had been more than a wife to Ludolf through all they had done together, which was why thinking of herself as his mistress grated on her. It would not be hard to believe that Ludolf had become bewitched by Francesca's unusual beauty. By the time the evening was over Geetruyd was convinced she was right.

The concert had been most enjoyable. Francesca and Aletta sat side by side with Clara and Geetruyd in the seats between them and Ludolf. He stayed at the Mechelin for almost a week, seeing Geetruyd on her own by day, which gave him plenty of chance to list those agents whom she was to direct to certain areas, and also to slake through her the desire that just seeing Francesca roused in him. Each evening, after dinner at the house, he took Geetruyd and Francesca to other concerts and twice to plays. Aletta did not attend again, reluctant to ask Catharina for further time off at the busiest hours of the day. Francesca would have liked the same reason to have stayed at home, but her excuses were overridden each time, for Geetruyd was determined not to give Ludolf any loophole in which to leave on his own from wherever they were and return to the house, where Francesca would have been alone.

"You're a fool," Geetruyd said to him one day. "Francesca isn't going to allow herself to be seduced by a man of your age."

"My dear woman," he had countered with laughter and mock astonishment, "how could you suspect me of such a purpose?"

He knew in his own mind that Geetruyd would be less amiable and less amorous if she suspected that he intended more than the seduction of Francesca. It occurred to him that he was leading two women, twenty-four years between their ages, gradually along a certain path. Geetruyd to an acceptance of his not taking her as a second wife and Francesca to a point where she would come to accept him as her husband. He felt he had made some progress on both counts.

Everything seemed peaceful again to Francesca when she no longer had to see Ludolf every evening. Even without Neeltje's warning she would have come to the conclusion that it had been more he than her father who had tried to engineer her return to Amsterdam. She had never expected to be pleased with Geetruyd's chaperonage, but she had been grateful during his visit. The woman had never left them on their own.

Aletta did not move far when eventually she left the Vermeers' employ, her new position being next door in the home of the van Buytens. Her task was to give first lessons to the two youngest children before they went to school in the spring. What would happen then she did not know, but in the meantime she had a comfortable little attic room. Although she was now two floors higher than the bedchamber where across the square Constantijn de Veere slept, she still looked towards his lighted window every night before she went to bed. It was said on all sides that he was well out of danger and would live, but as yet he had not left his room.

She thought she knew why. Just as she could not face going into a studio, unable as yet to adjust to a life without painting, so it was for him. His was a far greater void to enter than hers, for he was without the limbs with which he had once skimmed the ice like a bird.

CHAPTER 16

From his pillows Constantijn looked towards the bedchamber door as it opened and put aside the book he was reading. His father entered, a written note folded in his hand.

"Isabella is here," Heer de Veere said. "She and her parents arrived about half an hour ago. Your mother and I have been engaged in serious talking with them."

"So Isabella has come at last," Constantijn commented wryly. She had written to him at quite regular intervals, encouraging him affectionately to be well again and sending him news of mutual friends. There had been very many excuses for her not coming to see him, which ranged from the dangers of travelling in severe weather to the imminent demise of her great-grandmother.

"She wants you to read what she has written first." Heer de Veere held out the letter. When no move was made to take it from him he laid it on the quilt in front of Constantijn, who, with a single sweep of his hand, knocked it to the floor.

"Surely you should read it, my son."

Constantijn looked at his father's grave face framed within the grey periwig. "Why? I know what it says. She no longer wishes to be my wife."

Sadly Heer de Veere sat down on a bedside chair and rested a hand on each velvet-covered knee. "Isabella can be held to the marriage contract. The law is with you there."

"I'll marry no woman against her will."

"A sum double the original dowry has been mentioned voluntarily as compensation."

"I don't want a stuiver of it. I set Isabella free. She is no longer bound in any way to me."

"How long have you known that she had changed her mind?"

"When she did not come to see me as soon as was possible after the accident. I kept hoping that the loss of my legs would not change the relationship between us, but at the back of my mind I knew I was deceiving myself. The Great Blizzard gave Isabella an excellent excuse to avoid visiting me for a while longer and now when she has run out of reasons to stay away she has had to come. You must have guessed the truth of it, Father, even if Mother couldn't accept that anyone might reject her son, whatever the circumstances."

Heer de Veere sighed and passed the tips of his beringed fingers across his forehead. "We knew on St. Nicholaes's Eve. Isabella's father wrote that under no circumstances could he allow his daughter to marry you now. You were too ill to be told then and afterwards we continued to hope that he would revoke his decision."

Constantijn smiled cynically. "The poor old fellow was covering up for Isabella. It would have been her decision and that of her mother, but not his. He is a mild man, too kind for his own good with such a wife, and I'm sure he would have come to see me out of concern and goodwill if she and Isabella had not forbidden it. Yet he must have dug in his heels over Isabella giving me my ring back herself or else I doubt if she would have come at all."

"I'm of the same opinion myself."

Constantijn pushed aside the bedclothes. "I want you to help me into the chair, Father. I'll not appear bedridden when Isabella is here. Find a shirt and all else I need. I'll have the coat and breeches of crimson velvet."

While his father took the clothes from drawers, Constantijn pulled his nightshirt over his head and then thrust it under the pillows out of sight. Normally his nurse fetched whatever he wanted before he sat in the chair, but now his father was at hand. He had become expert at dressing in bed and hauling on his own breeches. When he was ready he was given a lift across his father's back and then lowered into the nearby solid chair with its broad arms and leather upholstery in which his mother had sat for so many hours. He removed the wide belt that normally strapped him to it, for several times he had forgotten his handicap after reading or dozing and had fallen when he had automatically thought to stand.

"Put the belt away somewhere," he said to his father. He could not endure the thought of Isabella seeing him strapped in. A rug was tucked around him and that would be the only visible sign to his visitor that he was not exactly as he had been at their last meeting.

"Tell Isabella to come up on her own, Father."

"I will."

Heer de Veere wondered as he went downstairs to the next floor if Constantijn hoped to win Isabella back to him if they could talk alone. She would be his first visitor, although he had been well enough for some time to have received visitors many times over. It was as if he had been waiting for her before he could start mending his life again.

Constantijn became consumed with impatience as he waited. He had been confined to this bedchamber for a long time, first through physical weakness and then through his stubborn refusal to be carried downstairs, which he thought of as being carted about like an infant.

He had borne the time of convalescence stoically, but now, waiting while Isabella put one foot in front of the other on her reluctant way up the flight, it seemed to him that she was taking all eternity.

His father had left the door ajar and for a split second before Isabella saw him he glimpsed dread in her eyes as she looked towards the bed, expecting to see him there. Had she supposed he might have been without covers over his severed limbs? Then she saw him and relief flooded her fine face with its clear pallor and sloe eyes, her lips pink and moist as oysters ready for serving.

"How well you look, Constantijn! Thinner, but that suits you."

He held out his hands to her, but she pretended not to see them, seating herself in a chair his father had put ready beforehand and plucking nervously at the deep lace collar of her azure gown. She was holding something small within her left hand and he guessed what it was.

"You're not wearing the betrothal ring I gave you." He was angered already that she had chosen not to come in with it on her finger, but was cupping it in her hand like a cheap fairing. If she was set on returning it to him she should have drawn it with dignity from her finger in a moment between them as private as when he had given it to her, no matter that the whole mood had been reversed.

"As I said in my letter—"

"I didn't read it. I want to hear from your own lips why you no longer want to marry me." He watched her mercilessly, determined not to spare her.

She flushed uncomfortably. "I discovered my feelings were not as strong as I had believed. People make mistakes about love sometimes."

"Then it has nothing to do with my losing my legs?"

There was a start of guilt in her eyes before she shook her head too quickly. "Of course not!"

"Have you met someone else?"

"No."

"Then there are no obstacles in our path after all. We've been apart too long, Isabella. That is all there is to it." His voice softened deliberately to the tender note that in the past had never failed to have an effect on her. If only she was nearer he could touch her, for he knew her intimately and how to arouse her to fiery desire under his caresses. "Remember the last time we made love when we escaped to the stairs during your parents' dreary party!"

"For mercy's sake keep your voice down!" She half rose from her chair in panic as she looked towards the door that she had left open. "Mother may be on her way up here! I've only been allowed a few minutes to be on my own with you!"

"Or that time in the rose garden?" he urged, not mocking now, for on a sudden renewal of hope he saw that he was getting through to her after all.

There was anguish in her eyes. "Those days are gone. I did love you, Constantijn. I suppose I still do."

"Then give me my ring that you're holding and let me put it back on your finger."

She opened her hand and looked down at the ring lying in her palm, a large emerald set in pearls and winking with all the colours of the sea. "No," she said, her voice thick with regret.

"Why not? Nothing has really changed."

"But it has." She raised her sloe eyes swimming with tears, but all unconsciously her lips twisted with aversion. "I could never marry half a man."

For a brain-splitting second he thought how easy it would be to slip from the ultimate pitch of rage into murder. Beyond speech, he held out his hand for the ring. She left the chair to give it to him and was within his reach at last. He seized her by the wrist, which sent the ring flying, and brought her falling with such force against him that the chair rocked as if it might have tipped them both backwards. Before she could get away he drove his fingers into her hair to hold her head as he kissed her violently. Lost in their passionate struggle, neither heard her mother enter the room with a shriek of outrage.

The woman flew forward and struck him about the head. It was when she wrenched her daughter free that he was jerked forward and toppled, unable to save himself. He fell face downwards to the floor, landing with a heavy thud, his arms sprawled awkwardly. Isabella gave a piercing scream and would instinctively have knelt to him, only to hesitate when she realized the covering rug now lay tangled beneath him. As she saw him without his legs, which previously had given him such a fine height that she had had to stand on tiptoe for his kisses, she began to scream again hysterically. Her mother, who had a fierce hold on her arm, drove her forward out of the room. He heard the piercing sounds continue with increasing force as she was bundled down the stairs. Then for the first time since the accident, and for as long as he could remember, he wept where he lay.

That night when Aletta looked out of her window across the square before closing the curtains, her heart seemed to stop. There was no light in Constantijn's window. The whole house was in darkness. In the morning her fears were confirmed. He had left Delft and, as yet, no-body knew where he had gone.

Sybylla continued to suppose that her only chance of finding a rich husband was at the Korvers' house, but she did not visit as often as in the past, because the girls were all wed and away from home. Yet she never forgot that her Aunt Janetje had met her husband there, which sustained hopes in that direction. She no longer expected any invitation to be forthcoming from Ludolf when his period of mourning should come to an end and she blamed her father for that. Hendrick was

scarcely civil when Ludolf had taken the trouble to call and say he had seen Francesca in Delft. There was always a show of bad temper if Hendrick had to see his patron on business.

"Why do you have to scowl whenever there's anything to do with Ludolf?" she had asked him once. "He buys your paintings and yet you make it so obvious that you don't like him."

"I would wish my work to hang in any house but his," Hendrick had growled in reply.

"But why? You should be exceptionally considerate towards him since he is in mourning."

"Huh!" Hendrick had given a hollow, derisive laugh before stamping off into the studio and slamming the door behind him.

Aunt Janetje had sent each of her nieces a gold bracelet for the last St. Nicholaes's Day, the designs varying. They had come late, not reaching Amsterdam until well into the new year, and the two for Francesca and Aletta had not been sent on, but were being kept until Francesca made a visit home, which should have been at Christmas and was now overdue. Sybylla was particularly proud of her bracelet, it being the prettiest she had ever owned, and she had taken to wearing it daily. She loved the feel of it on her wrist and its expensive little tinkle when she rested her arm on anything. Maria did not approve.

"Such fripperies are for best wear, Sybylla. If you don't keep it for special occasions you'll lose it one day, mark my words!"

Sybylla took no notice. She liked always to be stylish and had developed an instinctive knowledge of what suited her. She recalled that when a child she had been amazed when a visiting cousin had not worn all her jewels; now she knew that a single piece of adornment could set off to perfection a lovely neck, or arm or hand. Whenever she played her viol she knew that the glint of gold about her wrist further enhanced her graceful movements, almost as if the links of the bracelet were dancing to the music.

Eventually Maria's warning came true. Sybylla lost the bracelet somewhere between Willem's house and her own. She had been on an errand for her father and remembered glancing proudly at it as she drew on her gloves while Willem bade her good day. There had been no marketing to do on her way home, which had been a relief, because she was like her father in hating to carry anything in the street and it did not please her to have a basket on her arm with cabbages or cauliflower or the tail of a fish sticking up out of it. Fortunately Griet was taking over the running of the house more and more, which even Maria welcomed in her increasing infirmity. Sybylla was congratulating herself on Griet having gone to the butcher's that day, relieving her of the chore, when she sensed an emptiness about her wrist. She turned back the cuff of her glove and gave a sharp cry. Her precious bracelet was gone.

She panicked, tearing off her glove and pulling up her sleeve. Frantically she shook the side of her cloak and skirt to see if it had fallen and caught on the cloth, but there was no welcome sound of it falling to the cobbles. In despair she began to retrace her steps, searching as she went. Such a light object could have been unknowingly kicked aside by passing feet and she zigzagged as she returned along the way she had taken. It was difficult when she had to cross a road where there was traffic, for wagoners shouted at her for being in their path and some coaches came at speed. Once she was caught in the middle of a flock of sheep being driven home from market. She was almost back to Willem's house when somebody spoke to her.

"Juffrouw Visser! What have you lost? May I be of assistance?"

She looked up and saw a man in his mid-forties whose face she remembered, although she could not think where they had met. Then it came to her. "Heer Cents! We sat next to each other at Heer van Deventer's banquet last May! Oh, I'm in such trouble. I've lost a gold bracelet and I can't find it anywhere."

"Have you just missed it?"

"No, but I've searched a long way back without result. All that's left is just round the corner to a house there."

"I'll help in looking for your bracelet. I'm going in that direction in any case. I'm to meet my nephew at an art gallery."

"Willem de Hartog's gallery?"

"Yes. Of course you know him! I remember now that your father is an artist and it was your sister who had painted that fine portrait of van Deventer."

"That's right. I last saw my bracelet when I was leaving Willem's house."

"Perhaps we'll be lucky in finding it near there, then."

He searched as carefully as she did, but they reached the double flight of steps leading to Willem's entrance without result. They decided there was just a chance she might have dropped the bracelet inside the hallway and when the door opened she preceded him into the house. The maidservant who admitted them knew nothing of anything being found, but Heer Cents said they would ask her master. He was pleased to renew his acquaintance with Sybylla, having enjoyed the sight of her pretty face and lively company at van Deventer's table at what otherwise would have been a long evening for him, for he neither gambled nor danced. Then the evening had become a tragic one for everybody through Amalia van Deventer's death. Had he himself not been a confirmed bachelor he might well have made a point of seeing Sybylla again.

The door to the gallery stood open and the first thing Sybylla saw as she went in was her bracelet lying on a side table. "It's been found!" she exclaimed, running to snatch it up and cup it in her hand.

Willem was nodding at her. "So it is yours? I thought it must be. If you hadn't come back I would have had it sent to your house."

"Did you find it?"

"No, I did," somebody else said.

She turned and saw the man she had been searching for as diligently as she had been looking for her bracelet. Tall and fair-haired with lean-faced, handsome looks, his whole appearance conveyed an impression of wealth from his white-plumed hat, its wide brim curled like a huge saucer, to his diamond-buckled shoes and the large ruby on his finger.

"Allow me to present my nephew to you, Juffrouw Visser," Heer Cents was saying. "He is my sister's son, Adriaen van Jansz."

Those of the Visser household who knew Sybylla well would have seen that already she was aglow with the extra charm she could summon up at will. The name of van Jansz was a highly respected one in Amsterdam, the family being bankers and powerful merchants, which made her doubly dazzled by having a young man of such rich background here in the same room with her. She curtseyed to him and as he raised her up by the hand, making the usual conventional pleasantry of being honoured to meet her, she gave him the full benefit of her round blue eyes ashine with suppressed tears of gratitude.

"How wonderful that you should have found my treasured bracelet! It has the deepest sentimental attachment for me, having been sent all the way from Florence by my aunt, for whom I've had the greatest affection since my childhood days."

"I recognized it as Florentine work."

"Where did you happen upon it?"

"On the bottom step of the flight outside. I think you'll find the clasp is loose." He bent his head close to hers as they examined the bracelet.

"Yes, it is," she agreed, thinking he must have been barbered just before leaving home, for his skin smelt fresh and clean with the faintest hint of verbena. It was hard to restrain her eyes from sliding in his direction instead of focusing them on the bracelet, but she had learned a great deal about enticing men since Jacob had been infatuated with her, and to appear too eager was always a mistake. "I shall go straight from here to a jeweller and have it repaired."

"Allow me to drive you there. My coach is waiting."

She exclaimed prettily, "That is most kind."

"Will you pardon me while I have a final word with Heer de Hartog about some works of art I was about to decide upon at the moment when you arrived."

"Yes, of course."

Heer Cents chatted with her while they waited for his nephew and Willem to finish their business. She saw Adriaen had purchased a Raphael and six Michelangelo drawings. Obviously his taste ran to Italian work. Willem was promising delivery of them and it was clear that Adriaen was a valued customer. It seemed to her that her feet barely touched the ground as she went with the uncle and nephew out of the house. The coach was far more elaborately ornamented and gilded than Ludolf's and there were four matched greys in the traces. Had she been in a less agitated state when she arrived at Willem's house she would have taken more notice of the splendid equipage. As if in a dream, she sat down on the seat upholstered in sapphire velvet and saw to her amazement that the roof above her had painted panels depicting

mythological scenes. Heer Cents was seated opposite her and Adriaen sat down at her side.

"We're going straight to the best jeweller in the city," he told her reassuringly.

She came close to panic. There were only a few stuivers in her purse and there was no way she could pay for an expensive repair. She had counted on Heer Korver doing it free. "I'd prefer to go to a jeweller known to me," she insisted swiftly. "He is a diamond merchant I know well since he lives in the same street as I do."

"What is his name?"

"Heer Korver."

"I've heard of him. He has a good reputation. It will suit me to go there too. I'll be interested to see what he might have to show me." He glanced across at Heer Cents. "What of you, Uncle? Do you mind a delay in our viewing that property?"

"Not at all. My time is my own."

As Adriaen gave the changed address to the coachman through a small aperture, Sybylla almost wriggled with delight. Not only would she bring Heer Korver a new and very rich customer, but her time with Adriaen would be extended and she could show an admiring interest in the diamond pieces displayed that would be remembered by this young man at a suitable time in the future. She could see that he was much taken with her. She knew the signs only too well. Never had she been more glad that since coming to womanhood she had kept her sensual impulses in check. She would donate her virginity to the marriage and he his riches. It would be the best of bargains.

All these thoughts were darting about in her head as she directed her dancing glances at both men, trilling at their little jokes and making all the pretty movements of her head and hands that she knew to be captivating. Never in her life had she been more determined to get what she wanted. If claws had suddenly grown from the tips of her fingers she did not think she would have been surprised.

Everything went swimmingly. While Heer Korver's assistant mended her bracelet clasp, Adriaen was shown sets of diamonds suitable for mounting into coat buttons. She surprised him by talking knowledgeably about the various cuts and tints of diamonds, but then he was not

to know that she had long since thought she should learn as much as possible about them in readiness for when she would wear such fine stones herself.

"How did you learn so much about diamonds?" he questioned with interest.

Smilingly she invited Heer Korver to answer for her, which he did. "Sybylla has been in and out of my house since she could walk and has heard as much about the diamond trade as my own children. Then, in later years," he added with twinkling glances at her, "I have allowed her into my workshop on occasions."

She turned with a mischievous little laugh to Adriaen. "I wasn't a very well-disciplined child, which was why it was barred to me previously."

"So you have changed," he challenged flirtatiously.

"On the surface anyway," she gave back.

"I'm intrigued."

Heer Korver, seeing there would be no sale at all if Sybylla continued to work her wiles over van Jansz, making him forget everything else but her, produced two more sets of diamonds. "These are from India," he said, drawing the young man's attention back to the glittering array, "and are mogul-cut."

The final selection took a considerable time, neither Adriaen nor Sybylla wanting to hurry this time together. Several times Heer Cents, sitting patiently on a chair, took out his watch to look at it. Eventually Sybylla, having heard from Adriaen that the diamonds would become buttons for an evening coat of moonshine silk, advised a set of symmetrically rose-cut diamonds with a peach tint, saying they would give a warmer sparkle.

The usual decanter of wine was brought in to round off the transaction, which gained Sybylla further time to cement this new relationship with Adriaen. She had drawn away tactfully when prices were discussed and had no idea what the diamonds had cost, although there was a clue towards their value in Heer Korver having produced his fifteenth-century Venetian goblets for the wine, for these only came out for special customers and high transactions. Perhaps it was also the first time he had had a member of the van Jansz family in his house.

Outside, her bracelet safe on her wrist, she declined an offer of a further ride in the coach, saying she would walk the short distance across the bridge to her home. Adriaen accompanied her on foot, which she had expected, and their stroll was leisurely while Heer Cents rode in the coach that lumbered slowly behind them. At her door Adriaen spoke of taking his sister to some musical gathering arranged for the following afternoon in aid of charity. He had extra tickets. Would Sybylla care to attend with her father as his guests? She hesitated deliberately until she was sure that disappointment was gathering in him as he feared a refusal. Then she accepted on her father's behalf and her own. On this happy note they parted.

No sooner was Sybylla inside the house than she flung herself into a wild jig, clapping her hands and laughing exuberantly, her petticoats aswirl. She danced into the studio and then remembered that Hendrick was out that day. Promptly she rushed along to the kitchen, where Maria was dozing in her favourite place by the hearth, her slippered feet on a foot warmer. The old woman was jerked awake when Sybylla let the kitchen door slam behind her.

"I've found him!" Sybylla's voice was exultant and she flung her arms around the old nurse to kiss her on both cheeks.

"Who, child?" Maria exclaimed in bewilderment, slightly dazed by her rough awakening.

"The man I'm going to marry!" Sybylla drew back to make a deep curtsey, "You see before you the future Vrouw van Jansz!"

"Oh, my!" Maria pressed a hand against her ample bosom as if to quieten her heart. "Don't play such tricks on me!"

"It's no trick. I've met him and it's true." Sybylla flung herself down to rest her head in the wide lap and look up into Maria's wrinkled face. "He's already falling in love with me."

"My dear child," Maria said sadly, stroking the girl's golden curls, "if he is of *the* van Jansz family such a marriage could never come about. Money marries money. You have no dowry."

"There's some money Mama left for Francesca and Aletta and me."

"It's very little. Nowhere near the amount your father would be expected to offer. My guess is that it would have to be many thousands of guilders with land and property as well."

"If Adriaen loves me, a dowry won't be important."

"Not to him, perhaps, but it would be to his parents. Put this dream aside. It can never be fulfilled."

Slowly Sybylla raised her head. "It has to be. I'll never have a chance like this again to secure all that I want from life. I know how to make him want me so much in his turn that his head will spin and he'll overrule all opposition."

"Hush! That's wanton talk. I'll not listen." Maria held up her hands as if to keep it at bay.

"No, it's not, Maria. I promise you that Adriaen van Jansz shall never regret the day I become his wife."

Maria, although she foresaw only trouble ahead, relented and cupped the girl's fervent face between her soft palms. "You were always foolish and headstrong," she declared with loving exasperation, a quiver to her lips.

Sybylla beamed. "All will be well. You'll see."

Hendrick received the news of the connection Sybylla had made with far more enthusiasm than she had expected. Unlike Maria, who saw only gloom and doom, he looked at it in a keen and hopeful light. A rich son-in-law would solve all his troubles. At the right moment, after Sybylla was well and truly wed to Adriaen van Jansz, it would be a simple matter to confide his misfortune at cards that had led to the dreadful trap in which Ludolf held him and Francesca. The sum needed to settle those debts would be nothing to a van Jansz and the hired wits of the best and most expensive lawyer in the city could make that marriage contract, which had been signed under threat, null and void. He himself would have his freedom again and Francesca need never know how nearly he had ruined her life for her.

"I'll attend this afternoon charity affair with you," he said jovially to Sybylla, his face brighter than it had been for many weeks.

She linked her arm through his and hugged it. "I'm so glad! I was so afraid you'd be busy or wouldn't want to come."

He grinned at her. "If you really fancy this Adriaen van Jansz, I'll not stand in your way. You've taken long enough to make up your mind."

Maria snapped at them both. "On the strength of two or three hours, mark you!" All her misgivings had returned and she felt she had blun-

dered when she had shown in a weak moment her devotion for the girl, who was still childish in so many ways. It was when she should have mustered all past authority into her voice and put her foot down, squashing Sybylla's notion once and for all. She thrust to the back of her mind the possibility that it would have made no difference. Hendrick had come across to her.

"Don't be sour, Maria," he chided genially. "I knew as soon as I clapped eyes on Anna that she was the one for me. Love at first sight happens more often than you think. I believe that something very special happened between those two young people this afternoon and we'll soon be hearing wedding bells."

Maria snorted derisively and clattered plates. Never had she seen the likeness in character between Hendrick and his youngest daughter stronger than at this moment. With that same buoyant optimism, which took no account of possible disappointments, they already had a marriage band on Sybylla's finger.

"There's many a slip betwixt the cup and the lip," she warned them ferociously.

To her intense annoyance they both laughed.

At the van Deventer house Pieter was checking the laying of the flag-stones. He had a good foreman and there was no need for him to be there personally, but he wanted to see Neeltje. He had received a full account from Francesca of Ludolf's visit and the attempt to disrupt her apprenticeship. Now that she knew Ludolf and Geetruyd were well acquainted she was convinced that the last-minute switch of her accommodation had been due to his conniving and her father had simply fallen in with his patron's wishes.

Pieter, knowing much more about the whole situation, had not the least doubt that it was as she believed, for he was certain that Ludolf was using Hendrick's gambling debts to virtually blackmail the artist into doing his will with regard to Francesca.

Ludolf was wandering about the garden, watching the work in progress, which meant that Neeltje would not appear. Pieter was impatient for the man to be gone, but he did not seem to have any other

commitments that morning. Pieter did not dare send a note to Neeltje, fearing that Ludolf inspected all correspondence that came to the house before it was passed on.

Pieter glanced upwards at the house several times, but there was no sign of the woman. For all he knew she might have been dismissed already. Disappointed, he left his foreman to complete the work and went from the house. At the first corner of the street he found Neeltje waiting for him.

"I've been hoping to see you!" he exclaimed.

"That's what I thought. I saw you look up at the house several times."

"Can you tell me anything about your master's relationship with a woman in Delft named Geetruyd Wolff?"

"Only that she writes to him on business matters occasionally. She has mentioned Juffrouw Francesca only twice—once when she first went to Delft and secondly when Juffrouw Aletta went there too." Neeltje saw Pieter's gaze sharpen and realized she had given herself away. She jerked her shoulders back defiantly. "Yes, I read his correspondence. I have my reasons."

"Maybe if you confided those reasons to me we might work together on them."

She regarded him steadily for a few moments as she considered what he had said. Then she spoke abruptly. "Shall I come to your house this evening?"

"I'll be there," he said, and gave her directions.

She hurried back along the street to the house without saying farewell. There was no point in wasting time when she would be seeing him later. For the first time since Ludolf had cast a shadow across her life she felt a glimmer of hope. If all went well this evening she would have a strong ally in Pieter van Doorne.

She arrived at his house after dark. His housekeeper served them tea and cakes by the fireside and then withdrew. Neeltje was grateful for Pieter's relaxed attitude and easy manner. No pressure was being put on her to confide anything if she should have second thoughts. It helped her tremendously and she supposed he knew that. She drained the last

drop of her tea from the little bowl of Chinese porcelain before returning it to its saucer and putting it to one side.

"I was still a child in those mad years of the tulipomania," she began.

He listened quietly and attentively as she recounted the horrific experience of the destruction of the black tulip bulb and her father's brutal murder. It astounded him to learn whom she believed the murderer to be. She gazed into the fire all the time she was talking. Although she did not weep he saw the firelight reflected like tiny sparks in the tears that gathered in her eyes, but which she blinked back. He was full of compassion for her and when at last she fell silent he shook his head sympathetically.

"I've never heard a worse story of treachery and foul murder," he said. "You say you remember Ludolf as being the younger of the two men when you saw him again. Are you absolutely sure that it was he?"

She turned her head slowly and looked directly at him. "I'm absolutely certain. As I said, when I saw him in my home his face was already familiar and this caused me to study his features. That's why, ever since I entered my late mistress's employ, I began to check on him, hoping to find something incriminating against him. I've been shameless in reading his correspondence from the time I first managed to get a duplicate key made to his study, the first of several I collected through patient waiting and watching until I could gain access to all his private letters and papers wherever they were kept. It's my belief that what he was paid as an accessory in the destruction of the black tulip enabled him to buy a half-share in a ship. Eventually he must have done well enough to own his own vessel before becoming a ship broker. At the time when inquiries were made it was believed he had gone straight to sea. Never did I suppose that the day would come when I would be wanting to make him atone for a second murder as well."

"A second?" Pieter queried alertly.

She folded her hands in her lap. "If this were to be my dying breath I would swear that Ludolf van Deventer caused the death of his wife. He smothered her with a cushion! He had to be rid of her in order to marry Juffrouw Francesca!"

"What are you saying?" he demanded.

She told him everything. He was convinced that the truth was in all

she said, and he questioned her closely about the correspondence she had followed through the years.

"What sort of business is it that causes Geetruyd Wolff to keep in touch with him?"

"I don't know. She used not to write at all, except for one letter that came from Delft some years ago and which he burnt immediately. I found the ashes of it in the fireplace and kept a tiny scrap of paper that had escaped the flames. I matched it up with other writing, but never found its like until she began writing these business letters three or four years ago. It was undoubtedly her handwriting and I believe it was a love letter that he had put to the flames. He must have told her that he thought it was too risky to write in such a manner again."

"That is only supposition," he pointed out practically.

"It's what I believe. But to get back to what she writes now. It's sometimes about a delivery of which she's had a good report that it will please him to hear about and so forth. She only refers to people by their initials."

"Perhaps he has a half share in her house, just as he may once have had in a ship, and she is referring to the number of guests she takes in. When I tried for accommodation the last time I was in Delft, the wife of the tavernkeeper asked her husband if Vrouw Wolff had any vacant rooms."

"Maybe that's it," she agreed. "I thought the occasional references to a ship might mean that he handles investments for her."

Mentally he stored away all that she had told him. They talked for a little while longer before he saw her home. She told him not to go farther than the corner of the street nearest the van Deventer house, but he watched until her lantern, bobbing along at the side of the canal, disappeared down into the servants' entrance under the double flight of steps to the main door. Satisfied that she was safely indoors, he returned to his own home.

Some duties in the reserve militia kept Pieter in Amsterdam for another week. The present standard-bearer was getting married, which meant that a replacement would soon be needed and Pieter heard that his

name had been put forward. It was an honour given only to a bachelor, for the standard-bearer was expected to wear the richest clothes and finest sashes with gold or silver fringes, all of which mounted up to a considerable financial outlay, and it had been agreed long since that a married man with other responsibilities should not be expected to take on this expense. In conversation during one of the meals Pieter had enjoyed in the Visser house, before being barred from there, Hendrick had talked of Frans Hals's only time in Amsterdam when he had been commissioned to paint the officers and subalterns of the Civil Guard.

"Hals was so homesick being away from Haarlem," Hendrick had said, "and he disliked Amsterdam so much that he only painted the left half of the painting and then went home again, leaving somebody else to finish it off. But you can be sure that the standard-bearer with his lace and silver, his white boots and golden spurs and his orange sash with enough fabric in it to make a woman's skirt was in Hals's completed section. The standard-bearer always draws the eye and Hals wouldn't have wanted his replacement to belittle that splendour."

Pieter, after being officially approached, agreed he should give his reply to the whole corps and he chose a moment about an hour after the start of a three-day banquet that had begun that evening. At these gatherings, restricted solely to officers and subalterns, music and singing provided breaks in the eating and drinking, the speeches and the toasts.

"You do me much honour, gentlemen," Pieter said, standing at his place and looking up and down the table at the seated company, "but I have to decline the esteemed appointment as standard-bearer that has been offered me."

"Are you taking a bride too?" someone shouted out jovially.

Smiling, Pieter shook his head. "Not yet. My reason is that I shall be in Amsterdam less and less during the months ahead and I wouldn't wish to be absent on any important occasion when a standard-bearer should be present."

There was a rumble of disappointment, but his reason was accepted. Pieter sat down again to enjoy two or three hours of good talk and feasting before he made his departure. When he did leave he had reached the hall when one of his fellow officers who had seen him go from the table came after him.

"Van Doorne! Wait a minute. Are you going already?"

"I'm returning to Haarlem tomorrow. I need to get some sleep."

"I won't delay you long, but you know the artist Hendrick Visser, I believe."

Pieter compressed his lips slightly. "I have an acquaintanceship of sorts with him."

"Good. A vote was taken at the last meeting, which you were unable to attend, that it was high time another group painting was commissioned. It's several years since the last one and there are many new faces among us now, including that of the captain. It was suggested that you should see the artist and talk terms and so forth."

Pieter nodded, welcoming a legitimate reason to break the ban of calling at the Visser house that had been placed on him. "I'll be pleased to do so. Out of interest, why was Master Visser selected?"

"One or two people had seen his work in the van Deventer house and also elsewhere."

"I'll call on him before I leave Amsterdam tomorrow and send you a written report from Haarlem afterwards."

Next morning at the Visser house Griet expressed her pleasure at seeing Pieter again. "It's been such a long time, *mijnheer!* Come in."

"How are you, Griet?" he inquired.

"Very happy indeed. My sweetheart is home from the sea and we've become betrothed." She was so full of excitement that he guessed the betrothal was very recent.

"That's excellent news. My felicitations!"

"But I'll not be leaving here, because after we're wed he will be returning to sea before very long."

He regarded her with understanding. "It will not be easy for the two of you to part again, but I'm sure this household is very glad not to be losing you."

"I don't know how they would ever manage without me." Then she clapped a hand over her mouth. Heady with joy over this new turn of events in her life, she was not her usual discreet self that morning. "Take no notice of me, *mijnheer.* I'm forgetting myself. I'll tell the master you're here."

"You'd better state my business too." Pieter was not at all sure that

Hendrick would see him otherwise. "Tell him I'm here to commission a group portrait on behalf of the Civil Guard."

It was not long before Pieter was shown into the studio. Hendrick was alone but at work. On his canvas people were at table and a richly robed man had risen to his feet with an expression of such fear and alarm on his face that Pieter guessed the subject to be Belshazzar's Feast. The paint had been built up thickly on the jewelled brocade cloak and Hendrick was carving it away with a knife to promote the rich texture.

"What's all this about a group painting?" Hendrick questioned gruffly without greeting, his eyes on his work. When what was needed had been explained to him he gave a snort. "I don't paint portraits on demand. I choose faces to my own liking."

"I remember Francesca telling me that." Pieter paused deliberately. "Before a ban was placed on our meeting."

"Why did you come here, then?" Hendrick shot at him with a scowl.

"I came with regard to the commission. I thought it might suit you to paint the individuals in your own time and when the mood took you. I would arrange that you had a generous time limit."

Hendrick pondered, recalling that Rembrandt had taken four years to paint that militia company preparing for the Night Watch, for although he had let his pupils do much of the groundwork and the garments, he had taken other commissions in between painting the faces and the important details.

"The officers would come when it suited me?" Hendrick checked.

"I would make that stipulation on your behalf."

"Hmm." Hendrick thought the matter over. The canvas would be too large to set up in his studio, but he was not far from the Zuider Church, where Rembrandt had been allowed to paint, and since he and his family worshipped there, he was almost sure the same privilege would be extended to him. This meant that he could hire an artist to do everything except the faces and anything else he particularly wanted to do himself. The fellow would not be under his feet, something he had never been able to abide in his own studio.

It was still not a commission that appealed to him, but he was wearied of painting solely for Ludolf, who took unerringly whatever he produced. The history painting he was finishing now had been commis-

sioned originally by somebody else, but Ludolf had taken a fancy to it. It had meant making an excuse for a delay while another was painted for the merchant, who had wanted that particular subject, and Hendrick was not surprised when the commission had been taken from him and given to somebody else. If Ludolf had paid as he did originally it would have sweetened the pill a little, but he had revealed a tightfisted streak that had not been apparent before. A group painting of the Civil Guard would be the last thing Ludolf would want on his wall.

"I accept the commission," Hendrick stated firmly. Then, because enough time had elapsed for him to overlook Pieter's role in Aletta's misdeeds over her paintings, he stopped working and addressed him more civilly. "I thank you for coming. It could not have been easy for you. Had I been in your shoes I would never have come to this house again."

"I had a dual purpose in coming."

Hastily Hendrick held up a hand. "Don't ask me to let you renew your courtship of Francesca, because nothing you could say would move me on that."

"I didn't expect it since Ludolf van Deventer has forbidden it."

Hendrick looked taken aback. "Why should you suppose he has anything to do with my decision?" he blurted.

"Until you clear yourself of debt to him he will continue to dictate to you about Francesca."

"So you've worked that out." Hendrick let his shoulders rise and fall resignedly as he spoke in a dry and wearied voice. "I thought you might."

"The man is evil!"

"Do you suppose I don't know that?" Hendrick sat down on a stool, a hangdog expression on his face. "I would never have stood between you and Francesca. Far from it. You proved yourself to me by shouldering the expense of her tuition without wishing her to know anything about it. To me that showed you loved her unselfishly. Different from that devil!" he exclaimed on a rush of pent-up bitterness. "He makes a show to me of considering her in all matters, but already he has tried in vain to switch her apprenticeship. Can you guess why?" He did not wait for a reply. "He thought that after ending one apprenticeship with all

its rules and regulations about no marriage for pupils and so forth, he would marry her before she took up another! Except that it wasn't to be an alternative apprenticeship he had planned for her. It would have been private tuition as a married woman!"

"Francesca would never marry him!"

Hendrick's chin had sunk low on his chest. "Not by her own free will."

Pieter was seized by a terrible suspicion. "What do you mean by that?" When the artist did not answer, he went forward and shook him vigorously by the shoulder. "Have you contracted her to him? Is that it?"

Hendrick put a hand over his eyes. "I had no choice," he admitted miserably. "If I had not agreed he would have put me in prison for debt under a sentence of many years." He confided in Pieter the sum that was owed.

Pieter breathed deeply. "When do you intend to be honest with Francesca about what you have done?"

Hendrick jerked up his head. "Not yet! To my dying day I'll be grateful to Vermeer for refusing to release her. At least she still has some carefree months ahead of her. It is my fervent hope that she will need the three years instead of only two before she gains the membership of the Guild. Perhaps by then the situation will have changed."

"In what way?"

Hendrick's voice lifted on the thought of what his youngest daughter might inadvertently do for him. "Sybylla is being escorted here, there and everywhere by a van Jansz, his married sister acting as chaperone. Everything is in the bud as yet, but the signs are promising. With time I hope to prevail upon a rich son-in-law's generosity."

Pieter thought Hendrick was foolish to raise his hopes in that direction. The van Jansz family was not known for being charitable to others. "Which van Jansz is Sybylla seeing?"

"Adriaen van Jansz. Do you know him?"

"Not personally. I designed a garden for an acquaintance of his once on the Golden Bend." Pieter was not prepared to say more on the subject. The client had been a married woman with whom Adriaen van Jansz had been involved since he was seventeen. She was twice his age

and the husband was old and complaisant, the result being that the affair had caused a scandal in certain circles for a considerable time. It had provided his fellow officers with a succession of bawdy jokes, but he had never paid much attention to the name of van Jansz and there was too much else to discuss without dwelling on Sybylla's chances now. "What if Ludolf should tell Francesca of the marriage contract?"

Hendrick answered confidently. "He won't. Not now that he has to wait longer than he had anticipated for her. I know from what he has said he thinks to win her as a willing bride. It's hard to suppose that such a man is capable of love, but it can't be denied that he is infatuated by her."

Pieter paced slowly over to the window, deep in thought. At the present time he had too many commitments to raise the sum required to settle Hendrick's debts together with the interest, which would have been mounting up. Had it not been for a large colonial investment he had completed recently, he might have scraped it together, but it would not end there, for inevitably a long and expensive battle would follow in the courts to break the marriage contract, with no guarantee of success, especially when Ludolf could show that he had saved Hendrick from bankruptcy and prevented him and his family from being turned out into the street. It seemed to Pieter that his original plan to get Francesca away to Italy still remained the only way by which to save her.

"I shall be making a visit to Delft as soon as it proves possible," Pieter said, returning to the middle of the room. "There's no need to look alarmed. Ludolf won't be hearing that he has a rival. With the busy tulip season ahead I can't make definite plans yet. All my various stalls will need to be supplied."

"With amateur paintings too?" Hendrick questioned sarcastically, a sore wound reopened.

"Not this time. If necessary I shall speak to Aletta, but as Francesca has most surely told you, her sister has not sketched or painted anything since she left her. But if she had work to sell I would gladly give her the opportunity again."

Hendrick frowned angrily, rising to his feet. Then his temper subsided almost as quickly as it had come. He had not forgiven Aletta,

whom he now saw as a heartless daughter who had deserted her father, and anyway Ludolf was too much a constant thorn in his flesh for him to have much anger left over for anyone else. "That subject is a closed book in this house. I wish you well with your new stall, but for mercy's sake keep away from Francesca. Just through caring for her you present the greatest threat to her present safety. Don't endanger her, Pieter."

"It would cost my life first."

They parted on restored good terms. Two hours later Pieter was back at Haarlem Huis. With spring fully arrived again it would be only a short time before his bulb fields burst forth into colour.

CHAPTER 17

"Have you heard what Constantijn de Veere has done now?" Geetruyd asked Francesca, her tone showing she had gained another snippet of gossip at a meeting of regentesses.

"I hope it is something that will benefit him." Francesca knew, as everybody in Delft did now, that Constantijn had had himself carried out of the house on the square into a hired coach and gone off into the night, letting nobody accompany him.

"It turns out that he went to his country house just outside of town on the night of his departure. While still in the coach he called for the housekeeper and dismissed her and all the domestic staff except for an old maidservant who was there in the time of his grandparents, from whom he inherited the place. Most of the rooms have been shut up and he's living there on his own while the elderly woman cooks and cleans. He sees nobody. The gates are kept locked and a guard with dogs keeps everyone away, even Constantijn's own parents. After all the selfless hours his mother spent at his bedside! Obviously he lost his mind as well as his legs in that accident."

Francesca saw the situation in another light and spoke with deep feeling. "I only hope he hasn't taken to his bed to die."

"Perhaps he has." Geetruyd's voice did not hold a note of pity.

"My sister will be very sorry to hear all this about him. Aletta has taken such an interest in his progress."

"I have been slightly involved myself. The old maidservant wants someone to fetch and carry and do the scrubbing of floors and so forth. At this morning's meeting at the orphanage my fellow regentesses and I considered her request for an orphan and turned it down. That house with a madman is no place for any of the young ones in our care."

Francesca made no comment, for she was thoughtful, an idea having come to her.

In the morning she sought Aletta out before going to the studio, ignoring Clara, who tried to keep within earshot. As she had expected, her sister had heard the same news about Constantijn shutting himself away. Aletta had something more to add.

"It is said that it was only after all the domestic servants had left that he allowed the coachman to lower him onto the steps of the house before driving away. The old maidservant could never have lifted him, which means he must have levered himself up the flight to get indoors. The next day he sent for the man who used to coach him in his ice racing and other sports, and who now keeps guard." Aletta's face was tragic. "When Constantijn de Veere showed such courage on that first night, why couldn't he sustain it instead of making a hermit of himself?"

"You have a chance to ask him."

"What do you mean?"

Francesca explained and Aletta's eyes widened when she heard of the work she might get there. "I'll go today. I can't risk anyone else applying for the post there before me."

"What of the children's lessons?"

"I'll speak to their mother. Only yesterday she asked if I had secured any other employment yet, because they will be starting school next week."

Later that morning Aletta was on her way. She had packed up all her belongings in readiness for transport, determined that somehow she would secure this new post. She left the town by the East Gate and knew she had a walk of two miles ahead of her. When eventually she

left the road it was to follow a gravelled drive flanked by elm trees which brought her half a mile further on to the locked gates of an old house of mellow brick with many windows. A flight of wide steps led up to the entrance. Even as she reached for the iron bellpull of the gates a great barking went up and two snarling dogs came rushing across the gravelled courtyard to throw themselves against the ironwork. She stepped back quickly. A gruff voice called them to heel and a big burly man in good clothes roughly worn, his cravat askew, his coat incorrectly buttoned, inquired her business.

"I'm the new maidservant," she claimed boldly.

"I've heard nothing about that. You must have come to the wrong house." He turned away and went striding off.

She clutched at the railings and called after him. "The de Veere housekeeper sent to the orphanage for someone to help with the work! Ask her! She'll confirm it!"

He halted and turned about to come back to the gates, taking out his keys. "Why didn't you say so in the first place? I knew an orphan was expected, but I thought one of the regentesses would arrive in a coach with a child. Where's your baggage?"

"That will follow."

He saw that she edged away from the dogs as she came through the gates. "These won't hurt you. They're hunting dogs and I've trained them to keep guard. Pat their heads. Show you're friendly. You'll only find them dangerous if you start running away from them and then they'll see you as prey."

She was unused to dogs, except for the little one in the baker's house. It wore a collar of bells, which was to avoid accidents underfoot with the elderly father, who lived with the family and was blind. Summoning up her courage she patted each of the guard dogs and when they responded with an enthusiastic wagging of tails she was reassured. "What are their names?"

"Joachim and Johannes. I'm Josephus. How's that for a trio?" He laughed heartily, relocking the gates. "And you?"

"Aletta Visser."

"Come with me, Aletta, and on the way I'll give you a few tips to remember about the outdoor rules. The master never comes down to

the front of the house, but that doesn't mean you can swan about here when you feel like it. Secondly, he doesn't go out into the garden at the rear of the house either, but as his windows look out on it he won't want to see you taking a shortcut to the orchard or the kitchen garden. You'll keep to the paths allotted to the servants of the household, which are hidden from sight of the main windows by tall hedges. At the present time there's only Sara, you and me and the gardeners, who don't live on the premises and are gone by three o'clock in winter and by five at this time of year."

"Does Heer de Veere ever go outside?"

"No, he doesn't and you call him the master when you speak about him. He stays in his own apartment all the time. Old Sara will tell you why."

"I already know."

"Then don't ask foolish questions. He doesn't go out for two reasons. The first is that he can't walk and the second is that he won't be carried. Common sense should have told you that." He had brought her to steps that led down to a door at basement level. "You go in there. If old Sara is not about you shout for her."

Aletta found herself in the most neglected kitchen she had ever seen. There was a mountain of unwashed plates and dishes and cutlery stacked beside a bowl of cold and greasy water on the washing-up table by the pump. The copper pans, which should have reflected light like mirrors, had not seen a polishing rag for many a day. An iron pot of boiling water was steaming away pointlessly on the firebox, causing condensation to run down the walls of Delft tiles, which had a charming pattern in yellow, russet, green and blue of fruit and herbs and vegetables. The floor tiles had not seen water for some time and the white ones were almost indistinguishable from the black. Then the door opened and a harassed-looking woman who looked to be in her mid-sixties rushed across to the boiling pan to remove it to the cooler ledge at the side of the firebox. She was neat and clean in herself, but a long strand of grey hair had escaped from her folded cap. She was about to tuck it back when she sighted Aletta. Promptly she threw up her hands in dismay.

"Oh, my! You're an older orphan than I expected!"

Aletta realized that the battle to secure a position here was not yet won. "I'm not an orphan, Sara. My father is living. Surely my being eighteen is all to the good. I'm better able to do hard work than any child could manage." She removed her cloak as a gesture of determination to stay.

"But the master won't like it!" Sara was agitated.

"Why not?"

"Because you're a young woman, of course. Until he became betrothed there used to be plenty of females coming and going in the grand rooms of this house, but he wouldn't want any woman to see him now."

"You see him."

"That's different. He remembers me from his childhood. I used to smuggle his favourite foods to him whenever he'd been sent to his room without supper for one of his mischievous antics. His grandparents were stricter with him than his own parents, but I'm softhearted where children are concerned and didn't like to think of him being hungry." Sara straightened her shoulders determinedly. "You'll have to go. Now. Before he knows you've been let through the gates."

Aletta stood her ground. "The orphanage isn't going to send you anyone. I know that for a fact. And," she added, glancing about disparagingly. "it seems to me that I'm greatly needed here. This is a Jan Steen kitchen if ever I saw one!"

She was using a phrase that had crept into the Dutch language through the popularity of paintings by Jan Steen, who drew a moral from disorderly domestic scenes. Sara, knowing the criticism to be just, sank down on the nearest chair, her face crumpling. "I know it is, but I can't manage everything. There used to be a fully trained staff here until he sent them away. I could manage well enough cooking and cleaning for him, Josephus and me, if he didn't ring that bell of his a hundred times a day. I'm up and down stairs all the time. Occasionally in one of his rages he will break everything in the room. Sometimes he rips up his sheets in his fury and then I have to replace all the bed linen." She shook her head despairingly. "So you see, you have to go. He gave me permission to have a child to help me, but he'd never tolerate you in the house. I daren't disobey him. I tell you, I'm fast reaching my limit." She clapped weary fingers over her eyes.

Aletta looked about for a caddy of tea, spotted it and put a spoonful of the precious leaves into a teapot. After ladling some of the steaming water into it, she left the tea to draw while she found two cups. She was about to hand a cup to Sara when in the outer kitchen a bell jangled. The woman jerked nervously in her chair.

"There he is again. I'll have to go."

Aletta put a restraining hand on her shoulder, continuing to hold the cup in front of her. "Let him wait another minute. You drink this and I'll answer his bell."

"But I told you—"

"He'll either tell me to get out or he'll let me stay. Give me the chance!"

The tea tempted Sara and her back ached. At least if the girl answered this summons, whatever the outcome it would save her one trip up those stairs. "Very well, but be warned. He has never thrown anything at me, but there's no telling what he'll do when he sees you."

"I'm not afraid. Tell me how to find his room."

Aletta went from the kitchen and reached the hall. It was quite a grand house but not pretentious. Plenty of good carving, some paintings of what were no doubt ancestors, including one of a military man in a handsome frame carved with banners, drums and bugles, and fine displays of Chinese porcelain. Upstairs she found Constantijn's door without difficulty. She knocked and entered an anteroom furnished with a writing table, a painted cupboard and a chest from the Zuider Zee area and a gilded clavichord. Another door led into the bedchamber. Once more she tapped before going in.

She was immediately assailed by a winey aroma that reminded her unpleasantly of her father's drunken bouts. For the moment Constantijn was hidden from her by the high end of the couch on which he lay fully dressed with a table to hand on which stood an elegant glass with a tall, twisted stem and a silver-topped wine flagon. A fire burned in the grate and although the flames were bright enough now there was a smoky atmosphere as if previously a gust of wind in the chimney had sent smoke billowing into the room. A four-poster, neatly made and hung

with yellow silk curtains, was set between two windows, both of which were closed. Constantijn did not turn his head, merely indicating the flagon with a forefinger.

"Fill it up again, Sara," he said in slurred tones. She looked down at him as she picked up the flagon, but his eyes were shut and he was too drunk to sense there was a stranger in the room. When she returned to the kitchen Sara sprang up anxiously from her chair. "What did he say?"

"He only asked for the flagon to be refilled." Aletta held it up. "He didn't notice that I wasn't you. How often does he drink like this?"

"Whenever he's weary of reading or tired of beating Josephus at chess or cards. Then boredom sets in and he drinks himself into oblivion. After he arrived that first night he drank himself into a stupor that lasted for days."

"So he's not drunk all the time?"

"Not yet, but his bouts are becoming more frequent. You had better fetch that wine. He doesn't like to be kept waiting. You'll find the door to the cellar in the outer kitchen. Take any bottle from the wine racks there. It's only when he's sober that he states a preference. Otherwise he doesn't care."

"When did he begin this present drinking session?"

"When he woke this morning. He had had either a poor night's sleep or one of those nightmares when he thinks he's running or skating again. Twice he's hurled himself out of his bed in his sleep and I've found him on the floor." Then Sara gave a startled exclamation, for Aletta had rinsed out the flagon from a bucket of water and was now ladling fresh water into it. "What are you doing?"

"In future he will get wine only with his meals and a gentlemanly glass or two of brandy after dinner. If he is thirsty at other times he can drink water instead."

Sara let herself flop back into her chair, not knowing whether to laugh or weep. "You're mad," she shrieked on a rising note close to hysteria. "He won't tolerate that!"

Aletta shrugged. "What can he do about it? You and I control everything that goes up to his room."

Sara gasped at such audacious thinking. At a loss for words, she watched Aletta leave the kitchen again with the flagon of water. Then

she set her elbows on her knees and let her head drop into her work-worn hands, waiting in dread of the outcome.

Constantijn heard returning footsteps and the faint clink of the lip of the flagon against the glass, followed by the sound of pouring. Still with his eyes closed, he held out his hand for the glass to be put into it. Then he took a gulp of the contents. Astonishment made him swallow the water and as he sat forward, propping himself on one hand, he saw a young woman crossing to the nearest window and opening it onto the balcony.

"You need some fresh air in here," she said, her back to him as she thrust a curtain back to let the spring-scented air enter unhindered.

For no more than a second he had the impression that he knew her, but it passed in the same instant as he yelled at her. "Who the devil are you? You've no right to be here!"

She turned regarding him calmly, and answered as she strolled past to the door. "My name is Aletta Visser and I have every right to be here. I'm the new maidservant. It's of no importance to me whether you have legs or not. My artist father, for all his faults, is an enlightened man in many ways. My sisters and I were brought up to accept the sight of the naked human body in all its forms. When I was ten years old I was set to draw an almost nude man born without legs, which neither frightened nor disgusted me. My only terror in childhood was of my father's temper. So don't suppose that, having lost a couple of limbs, you're in any way unique. What's more, the model I told you about normally had to beg for his living on the streets of Amsterdam. He couldn't lie on velvet swilling wine."

She was gone from the room. White-lipped with fury, Constantijn realized he was still holding the glass of water and he hurled it at the closed door, where it burst into a silvery shower of sparkling shards. Then he reached for the bellpull and tugged it hard.

Outside the apartment Aletta was leaning against the wall of the landing, and she had shuddered at the impact of the glass against the inner door. Her palms were pressed flat against the panelling for support. Had she gone too far in speaking to him in such a manner? It had not been her intention to mention the beggar who had propelled himself about the streets on a wheeled board, but comparison between his

pitiable circumstances and those of Constantijn had sprung the words from her before she could stop them. Shakily she moved away from the wall. Halfway down the stairs she met Sara ascending pathetically at a slow and weary pace, a flagon of wine in one hand. The woman spoke accusingly.

"I told you he wouldn't accept water instead of wine! He must be swinging on the bellpull if the clangour in the kitchen is anything to judge by."

Aletta felt her strength surge back. She had to do whatever she could for Constantijn while she was here. Sara was indulging him now as she had done when he was a child and probably it had been as wrong for him then as it was now. Deliberately she blocked the woman's way.

"Don't take the wine to him! Can't you see how he will end his days if he isn't stopped now? My father would have gone down the same path after my mother died if my sister hadn't found a means to force him to take up life as a painter again."

"But your father had legs! That's the difference. There's no future for that poor lad up in his room. He lost the young woman he wanted to marry and all that mattered most to him. He has a right to anything that gives him solace."

"I won't let you help him to become a senseless drunkard!" Aletta grappled with Sara and wrenched the flagon from her. "Now go in and tell him that I've taken the wine! You'll also inform him that I'm staying!" She swept away down the stairs.

Sara stood dithering, not knowing whether to go after her or continue on her own way empty-handed. Then the authoritative tone that Aletta had used weighed the balance. Since first entering domestic service at the age of twelve, Sara had always had someone in authority over her to direct her at all times. In spite of having to face her master's wrath, she felt no resentment that Aletta was obviously set on usurping her command and, in fact, had already done so. Sara knew well enough that she herself had no ability to organize. It gave her a welcome feeling of security to know that the burden of this house would no longer rest entirely on her shoulders. That was, if the master allowed Aletta to stay.

Praying in her heart that he would, she stepped over the mess of glass and water in his room and went to stand before him. To her surprise he

did not ask why she had not brought wine and, although his speech was not entirely articulate, his encounter with Aletta seemed to have sobered him up. He was glowering at her.

"What's your explanation for introducing a young woman into my house instead of a child?"

"She's all I could get," Sara pleaded, "and she is more than willing to stay." It was beyond her meek nature to quote Aletta's dictatorial statement.

"Did you know she refilled the silver flagon with water?"

Sara nodded nervously. "She says you will be allowed wine with meals and grape brandy after dinner."

His jaw throbbed. "The devil she did!" Then his eyes narrowed fiercely. "In future she is to be at my beck and call. Whenever I ring she is to come, no matter how many times a day. Is that understood?"

Sara felt enervated by relief that Aletta was to be allowed to stay. She could hardly answer him, but finally managed to say, "Yes, indeed." Then she looked troubled. "Surely not the double rings too?"

"No. Josephus will still help me bathe, and since he made me that conveniently low closestool in the closet, he will continue to attend to it."

Sara moved towards the scattered glass and the water. "I'll clear this up before I go downstairs again."

"Let Aletta do it."

"I haven't shown her yet where I keep my upstairs supply of cloths for such accidents."

"It wasn't an accident, Sara," he taunted, "and you know it. I threw the glass deliberately."

"If you say so, master."

When the task was done he told her to take the flagon of water away. "Tell Aletta to fill it up with grape brandy and bring it to me. I doubt if she ever saw anyone drunk at the orphanage and I intend to expand her education."

Aletta, who had her sleeves rolled up and her arms covered with suds, was washing up the dirty dishes and shook her head when his order was repeated to her. "He shall have a glass or two after dinner, as I said, and not before."

After the dishes were done she kept them stacked in a clean place until she had washed all the cupboards and shelves. Then she started work on the Delft-tiled walls, the furniture and the doors, finishing off by scrubbing the chequered floor until it shone. All the time the jangling bell of Constantijn's room did not cease its clangour until she stood on a chair and wedged its clapper with a linen cloth. Sara prepared the noon meal. She was a good cook and happiest to deal only with food. She could see it would be easy to get along well with Aletta. When the whole kitchen was spotless and the noon meal was ready, Aletta replaced her borrowed apron for a clean one supplied by Sara. Then she picked up the silver tray on which Sara had arranged Constantijn's noon meal of asparagus soup with a delicious aroma, crusty bread, cheese, salad, fruit and a small flagon of wine.

Constantijn greeted her caustically. "So you've deigned to come at last!" Then he scowled as he saw her balance the edge of the tray on a side table while she put the flagon on it before bringing his noon meal to him.

"I've been making a start on putting the house to rights," she said, making sure the tray, which she had set down on a low table, was within his reach for everything. "How Sara has managed here at her age I just don't know. It's far too great a burden for one elderly woman on her own. This afternoon I shall fetch my immediate belongings and hope to find a porter willing to bring my travelling box here as soon as possible."

"Wait a moment! I expect the domestic staff to answer my bell promptly and you appear to be deaf when it comes to hearing it and in obeying orders. Unless you are prepared to change your attitude over that matter I shall instruct Josephus to lock the gates after you and not to admit you again."

She had unfolded a starched linen napkin and she spread it deftly in front of him. "That would be your loss," she commented crisply.

He eyed her curiously and watched as she went to pour the wine into a glass only a little distance from him, but too far to allow him to grab the flagon. Since she was not afraid of him, and was not repelled by his being an amputee, it might have been possible to read a sexual promise in her words, but he could tell that had not been her intent.

She had a cool, touch-me-not attitude like an invisible shield and in that head-hugging white cap looked what she was, as virtuous as a nun. When she handed him the glass of wine he raised it to her with a taunting air.

"To your shrewish tongue."

"The master of the house doesn't raise his glass to a maidservant unless present at her wedding."

"You're too uppish ever to have been a servant. What are you doing here?"

"If you mean why am I in Delft, there is a simple answer. My father in Amsterdam wished to be rid of me. Secondly, I'm here in your house for the work and a roof over my head. I've already been a nursemaid to the Vermeer family and a teacher to their neighbour's two children."

"I thought you were from the orphanage."

"So did Sara. But the regentesses wouldn't send anyone to the house of a recluse."

"Ah!" he exclaimed bitterly. "So you can be tactful when you choose. Why didn't you say it was because without my legs I'm a sight to frighten children?"

Her composed expression did not change. "Enjoy your soup before it gets cold and stop feeling sorry for yourself."

"You're going too far!" he yelled at her dangerously. Then he saw she had picked up the flagon to take it with her from the room. "Give me that wine!"

She answered without turning her head. "You'll not drink yourself to death while I'm in this house. I'll be back to pour you a second glass."

Outside the door she held her breath, afraid that this time he might throw the bowl of soup. It was worse. A thunderous crash told her that he had hurled the whole tray and everything on it in the direction of the door. The echoes reached every corner of the house.

Josephus had come indoors for the noon meal in the kitchen and both he and Sara stared at Aletta when she set the flagon down on the table. She was very pale. They did not have to ask what had happened.

"I promised him another glass," Aletta said firmly, "so I'll have to go back with it soon. I fear he'll bar me from the house this time. I'd better prepare a second tray."

"You sit down and have some soup," Sara insisted, getting up herself. "I'll see to the tray and take it up to him this time. He'll be in a dreadful mood."

"No." Aletta was adamant. "I'll go. I won't let him intimidate me!"

Constantijn's hostile silence greeted her. Aletta was aware of his cold, hard gaze on her as she set the tray beside him once again. She poured him a glass of wine and, when he made no attempt to take it from her, she put it down on the tray. Not a word was spoken as she went about the clearing up of the debris. Her final task was to wipe up the spilt soup and wine. It was when she was leaving the room that he spoke in icy tones.

"Send Josephus up here. I have certain instructions for him with regard to the gates."

Her step almost faltered, but her inherited pride would not allow him to see what a blow he had dealt her. Her chin jerked higher until she was outside his apartment. Then she stood, hands clasped, struggling not to break down. She had failed. He had banished her. His life and hers were both doomed. At least she was thankful she had never mentioned the times she had seen him before this day.

Sara burst into tears when Aletta told Josephus that his master wished to see him about the gates. "I know what that means! He's given you the boot!"

Josephus sighed as he left the table and paused to speak kindly to Aletta. "Sara told me what you tried to do and it was high time somebody took the master in hand, but Rome wasn't built in a day, you know. You should have taken your task in easy stages."

Sara, still full of sobs, drew Aletta to the bench at the table and sat her down. "Try to eat something before you leave," she urged brokenly, ladling soup into a bowl. "I thought my troubles were over, but things can only get worse from now on. I could never stand up to the master as you have done."

Aletta took a spoon into her hand, but whether she drank the soup or not she did not know, too full of grief that she should have blundered so foolishly. She heard Josephus's footsteps returning but did not look up until he spoke. Then she saw he was smiling broadly.

"I'm to give you a key to the gates, Aletta. What's more, the master

said I'm to drive you into town to collect your travelling box and to bring you home here again."

Joy suffused her face. Sara hugged her and Josephus shook her by the hand. It was as if a battle had been won, even though the war remained.

Josephus took her into town in a sporting cart and they were just drawing up outside the van Buytens' house when she saw Willem de Hartog coming from the Vermeer gallery. She waved to him and he smiled in recognition, coming to help her down from the cart. As she had expected, he knew all about the rift with her father, having been told by Hendrick himself, but he had not known until coming to Delft and speaking to Francesca in the studio that she had turned her back on art.

"I don't like to think of you letting all these months go by without drawing or painting," he said. "But it will come back to you once you start again."

"That was another life and I've put it behind me."

"Nothing can destroy talent when it's only lying dormant. The day will come when you'll not be able to hold back from painting once more. Whatever your father said about your work it was voiced in anger in the heat of the moment and not heartfelt."

"Has he said that to you?" she asked distantly.

"No," Willem admitted, "but you could prove yourself again."

"I think not. He condemned my meagre talent all too vehemently." She was full of pain at these reminders of a time in her life she wanted to forget.

"It grieves me to know of this gulf between father and daughter."

"Why? Is he ailing?"

"No, he is well and so is Sybylla. As for Maria, she looked just the same as usual when I saw her at your home only a few days ago. How shall I report back to them about you?"

"My father won't want to hear my name mentioned, but tell Sybylla and Maria that I'm in good health and have secured new employment." She explained what she was doing and he noticed a rise of enthusiasm in her tone.

"Francesca told me she intends to take a long-delayed visit home soon. Will you be accompanying her?"

"No." She was adamant. "It will be a long time—if ever—before I see Amsterdam again."

"Then I'll hope to see you whenever I'm in Delft. In the meantime I wish you good fortune. Just remember one thing—once an artist, always an artist. I've dealt with enough painters to know that."

The old adage he had quoted lingered with her after they had said farewell, he to visit another gallery in Delft and she to go with Josephus into the master baker's house. But, she thought, there were exceptions to every rule.

When Aletta returned to her new place of employment she found that Sara had made ready a bedchamber and an adjacent parlour for her that had previously been occupied by the housekeeper. They were the two most comfortable rooms in the domestic quarters of the house, and her status had been established. On a table was a large bunch of keys on a ring.

"These are yours now," Sara said, gladly resigning all authority to her. "Josephus and I will call you 'ma'am' in future, as befits your position."

Thoughtfully Aletta picked up the keys. "I'm going to make changes."

"Whatever you say."

"There will be no more meals served to the master on trays. He's not an invalid. His lolling on that day couch will have to stop. From now on he can eat buckled into an armless chair with the table in his room drawn close to his chest. There will be a clean damask cloth and napkin every time as well as the best silver and porcelain. Josephus can carry a tray with the heavy silver dishes of hot food under covers to that long side table in the anteroom and I will serve the master from there."

"Yes, ma'am." Sara was smiling. This issuing of orders was like old times.

"Before I unpack I want to make a tour of the whole house and the cellars."

"Only the wine cellar is open. The rest, taking up about two-thirds of the space under the house, have been locked up for many years."

As Aletta began her tour with Sara she thought how her family would have recognized her commanding tone. It would have prompted Sybilla to taunt again that she was destined to be a sharp-tongued

spinster for the rest of her life. Going from room to room, Aletta found the dust sheets and shuttered windows depressing. "How long have these rooms been like this?"

"Since after the house was opened up for the last party held here about three years ago. Previously the master always preferred living in Delft or in Amsterdam. That's why only a skeleton staff was kept on here."

"It will take us time, Sara, but gradually we'll work our way through all the rooms and make each clean and polished and habitable as we go. The master is never going to be tempted out of his own pleasant apartment if the rest of the house remains in shrouds."

"He ordered that they should be kept closed."

Aletta made no reply, only setting her chin more determinedly, and Sara saw at a glance there was to be a tussle of wills between the new housekeeper and the master.

When viewing the wine cellar Aletta spared Sara any more stairs and went down alone. It was a large and square space with racks in a number of alcoves, two locked doors leading into the closed sections under the house. She tried the largest keys on the ring, but none opened the locks. As with most cellars, including that of her own home, sound was cut off from the rest of the house and she did not hear Sara call to her until the woman shouted from the top of the stairs.

"The oldest French brandies are in the far alcove. The master likes them when he asks for brandy."

"I thank you for telling me. Where are the keys to these cellar doors?"

"I don't know. They've never been opened in my time. You don't want to clean in there too, do you?"

Sara sounded so incredulous that Aletta laughed. "No! But the flagged floor here must be washed regularly, even though the bottles must remain undisturbed in their dust and cobwebs."

"Some of those wines were put down years and years ago."

Aletta noted carefully where all the rarer wines were stored. Lastly she took a bottle of the old French brandy back to the kitchen with her. A glass of it would make a fitting end to the dinner Constantijn should have in style that evening.

The next Sunday afternoon, when Francesca expressed a wish to see Aletta, Geetruyd was more than ready to escort her.

"It will be a most pleasant walk, Francesca. Naturally you want to tell your sister that you are going home for a week." Geetruyd particularly wanted to see inside the de Veere country house and this seemed a splendid opportunity, although she suspected they would not be shown into the main part of the house. She had also heard of the manservant and the two ferocious dogs that kept guard. What she had not anticipated was that after Aletta had been fetched by the watchman to the gates they were not even admitted inside the grounds. Aletta came outside the gates to talk to them.

"I regret I can't invite you in, but nobody except Sara, Josephus and myself is allowed in any part of the house. Even the gardeners are not permitted to enter the kitchen."

"Is it true that most of the rooms are shut up?" Geetruyd inquired inquisitively, her gaze roaming over the front of the house.

"Yes, they are, but I'm keeping them fresh and clean." Aletta took her sister's hand. "It was good of you to walk all the way out here to see me."

Before Francesca could reply, Geetruyd spoke again. "Where are the rooms that Constantijn de Veere uses?"

Aletta's expression hardened. "I don't think he would care to be discussed at his own gates."

Geetruyd's eyes glittered with annoyance. "It certainly shows a lack of courtesy that he doesn't allow his maidservant's own sister and her chaperone to be received with some refreshment." Then she added on a vicious note, "Is he a slave driver? I've never seen you look more tired. It's a pity you didn't consult me before you accepted employment here."

"I haven't been sleeping well," Aletta replied truthfully. There was conflict with Constantijn every day, and at night she could not dismiss it from her mind.

"Dear me!" Geetruyd shrugged indifferently, and began to wander along the railings, peering through as if she might glean something of

interest for herself. Both sisters were glad to have her out of earshot. Francesca put an arm around Aletta's shoulders.

"Are you sure you want to stay here?"

"I do!" Aletta affirmed vehemently. "Don't worry about me. It's good to see you."

"I came to tell you that at last I'm taking a trip home. It's not just because I've received the date of Griet's marriage, but there's something else. Sybylla has written to tell us that she has finally met the man of her choice and is to become betrothed." Francesca took the letter from her purse. "Read what she says for yourself."

Aletta read it, sighed and returned it to her sister. "All she can say is how rich he is and how handsome and what a fine coach he has and the rest of such nonsense. As if any of that mattered! She never once says that she loves him."

"I noticed that too."

"So you're going home to see our future brother-in-law for yourself."

"I want to be sure that she's not making a mistake."

"Knowing Sybylla when her mind is made up, you wouldn't be able to do anything even if she were set on marrying Ludolf van Deventer."

"Heaven forbid!"

Francesca looked so aghast that Aletta laughed. "At least this Adriaen van Jansz must be better than he."

Francesca smiled agreement. "Sybylla wants both you and me to be at her betrothal party."

"I read that. Our sister is still a child. She is just as Father used to be before he developed that unforgiving streak. Sybylla always thinks that trouble can be easily forgotten if one pretends it never happened in the first place, no matter that a serious aftermath still remains. She doesn't give the slightest indication that Father has softened towards me in any way and it wouldn't have made the slightest difference if she had. It's my guess that this young man of hers has a united family and she wants to present us as being the same, no matter how Father and I feel towards each other."

"We were close once."

"That ended with Mama's death. Nothing was ever the same again. You'll have to go home on your own. When shall you leave?"

"Next week."

They had a few more minutes together before Geetruyd returned to them, impatient to be on the way home again. Aletta went back inside the gates, waved and then walked slowly back to the house. It was no wonder that she looked tired. She had become Constantijn's antidote to boredom and had to bear, through his goadings and taunts, all his pent-up frustrations. He never smiled unless cynically, never laughed unless savagely, and was at his worst during periods of deepest melancholia. Curiously he never protested again about her limiting his drinking and would sometimes not take or finish a second glass of wine, but he took his revenge by getting wildly drunk periodically from a source that she could not trace. The key to the cellar was in her possession, and since both Sara and Josephus had declared on oath that he did not get his supplies from them, she could only conclude that he had a stock hidden away behind a secret panel in his apartment, for he never went out of it. He gained immense enjoyment from seeing her search for it as she tapped the panelling and tried in vain to shift sections of skirting or carving.

"Why not take up the floorboards?" he would gibe. "Or look on top of the bed canopy?"

On one occasion, having found him insensible with empty Holland gin and grape brandy bottles beside the couch, she had fetched a short ladder and climbed up to look into the well of the carved canopy, to find nothing there. She knew he was considerably active, for although she had never seen him move from one place to another, he did much for himself and had a rope tied to his bed by which he was able to haul himself into it. What he would not do was to go outside, although he would have a chair on the balcony on fine days.

When she entered the kitchen his bell was jangling, as it did count-less times a day. She wondered what he would want now as she went up the stairs. He took malicious pleasure in calling her upstairs to tell her to fetch him a book from the library downstairs or some such errand and then, when she had brought whatever he had requested, he would send her back again to get a second book, or a duplicated item. She had replaced Josephus as his partner at chess and cards, because she was able to beat him sometimes, and it was all part of the constant battle between them. Her victory would come on the day when she saw him take up the threads of a reasonable life again, going about, entertaining and receiving friends. Perhaps then her own shattered life might take on some meaning again. Opening the door, she went in to him.

Geetruyd and Clara, as well as the Vermeer children, came to see Francesca leave on the stage wagon for Amsterdam. She waved until she could see them no more. Then she settled for the journey. She was going home! To see family and friends! To Pieter and to liberty! She felt intoxicated with excitement.

Jan had allowed her to take home her latest painting to show her father, which was a kindly concession on his part, for he could have sold it the day after it was finished. All her work found ready buyers and her flower painting, which she had completed with the first of Vrouw Thin's tulips, had fetched quite a good price. She was glad about that, for she knew that Jan, with so many children to support, was more often in debt than out of it. He had finally finished and sold his exquisite painting of Catharina seated with pen and paper at a table, a brooch sparkling on her greenish-yellow bodice, her favourite pearl earbobs in her lobes and a pretty lace-trimmed cap covering her hair. *Lady Writing a Letter with Her Maid* had been the clear choice for the title, for Elizabeth stood behind her with arms folded, obviously waiting to deliver the letter when it was finished. Currently he was halfway through a painting of a local woman standing at the virginal in the drawing room, her hands on the keys.

"I'm going to change the picture on the drawing-room wall for this work," Jan had said to Francesca beforehand. She knew how careful he was always to have the right background, for every detail added up to the whole message of the finished painting.

She had helped him lift down a large painting by Theodor van Baburen, entitled *The Procuress*, which would not have been at all suitable. Together they had replaced it with another from the opposite wall, which had appeared in two or three of his earlier paintings. It showed Cupid holding up a card, signifying that love should be confined to one person. Since the local woman was known to be happily and faithfully

married, it was an appropriate picture to be shown hanging on the wall behind her in Jan's painting.

He had already planned a companion painting—not that they would be sold as a pair. Since one portrayed pure love, he thought it would be interesting to paint profane love in the same subtle fashion.

"My model playing the virginal in the companion painting will be as grandly gowned," he had said to Francesca as well as to Catharina, who was in the studio at the time. "I see her in dark blue silk, the skirt of deep yellow."

Catharina gave Francesca a little wink. They both knew she had such a gown in her closet and that Jan would want to borrow it for his model. Since the model would probably be his daughter Maria, who now sat for him at times, it would present no problem.

"On the wall behind the model," Jan had continued, "I'll hang van Baburen's *Procuress* and in contrast to the clear daylight flooding the first painting, I'll have subdued light and much shadow." On the surface it would be just another painting, wonderfully executed, of a lovely female at her music, but with a different tale to tell.

In the stage wagon Francesca looked out contentedly at the passing countryside with the neat farmhouses and the meadows where sheep and cows and horses kept one another company. No hedges were needed when narrow channels, gleaming with water, separated one field from another. Now and again the road passed close enough to a windmill to enable her to hear the unique "whomp" of the great sails as they turned majestically, grinding flour or keeping the land drained. She felt her heart expand with love for Holland, even as it did at the thought of Pieter when the tulip fields blazed gloriously into sight. There were many areas where the heads had already been snapped off their stalks and canal barges were constantly to be seen carrying away the multicoloured blooms, bright as jewels in the sun, for disposal. Yet another sight to see was the doorways and windows, wagons and carts and even the barges themselves adorned with garlands of tulip heads wherever children or patient adults had found time to string them together.

Francesca realized only too well that this was a frenziedly busy season of the year for Pieter and far from the best time for her to expect visits from him in Amsterdam. Then her heart leapt as a solution came to her. She would not let him know that she was home, but she would spend a day with him on her way back to Delft, having first ascertained from his housekeeper, Vrouw de Hout, that he was at Haarlem Huis. It would not matter how occupied with work he might happen to be, because she would be happy to be near him and even to help in any way possible. She had promised him once that she would visit Haarlem Huis at tulip time and here was a way of fulfilling the promise.

Since she was not expected at home there was nobody to meet her when she arrived in Dam Square. The noisy, seafaring atmosphere of Amsterdam was a blare of welcome in itself and made her realize how much she had missed the place of her birth. She had brought only one piece of hand baggage with her, for she knew she had all else she would need at home, and with it in one hand and her linen-wrapped painting under the other arm, she hurried homewards. Finally she ran the last yards and darted down the side passage to the courtyard. She sent the back door crashing open, skidded on the blue tiles of the corridor and burst into the kitchen. Only Griet was there and she almost dropped a copper pan in wide-eyed astonishment.

"Juffrouw Francesca!" she shrieked. "You've come home for my wedding!"

"I wouldn't have missed it for anything!"

Laughing, they embraced one another like sisters. Griet was overjoyed to be the first to give family news. Everyone was well in the house, Hendrick and Sybylla were dining that night with Adriaen and his parents and Maria was asleep in the family parlour. As for Griet herself, she would be going home in the morning to prepare for her marriage the following day. Then she would have three days on her own with her new husband before returning to her employment.

"Sijmon will be allowed to stay here with me until he sails again," she concluded. Then, in case Francesca might suppose it would mean yet another mouth to feed, she added, "He's a ship's carpenter and is going to repair a leak in the roof and make new furniture for eating outside in the courtyard and will complete many more tasks that I have lined up for him."

"I know you could never have chosen an idler for a husband! I'm sure

I speak for the whole family when I say that I hope he'll be here for a long time with you before he goes back to sea."

Griet was not optimistic about their having very long together, but stated cheerfully that they would make the most of whatever time they were granted. Then Francesca went to wake Maria, but at her footsteps the old woman opened her eyes and knew immediately who was there.

"You're home, child!" she cried out joyfully.

Griet set another place at the kitchen table, where she and Maria always had a simple supper when the two demanding members of the family were out.

Francesca did not mind having a few quiet hours on her first night at home. After supper Maria went early to bed and Griet's betrothed, a ruddy-faced, tow-haired young man with a ring in his ear, came to spend an hour with her in the kitchen. Francesca renewed her contact with her home and took note of any changes that had been made. There were new cream curtains in the dining hall and the Delft pot in which Pieter had brought the hyacinth had been added to a display of Delftware behind glass in the drawing room. In the reception hall she lifted the lid of the virginal, the inside of which was decorated with a Dutch scene of windmills and dancing children, which had so enchanted her as a small child when Anna had first shown them to her. It had always seemed to her that the little figures were dancing to the sound of the tinkling music. She closed the lid again after playing a few bars of a remembered piece.

In her bedchamber she found waiting for her the gold bracelet that Aunt Janetje had sent for the last feast of St. Nicholaes and she put it on, admiring the delicate Florentine craftsmanship and treasuring it equally for its donor's sake. Then she unpacked the two gowns she had brought with her, one for Griet's wedding and the other for Sybylla's betrothal party. When she had removed her painting from its wrappings she took it down to the studio, where she gazed once again on the portrait of Anna before going to look at Hendrick's latest work on the easel. It was covered with a cloth, which she flicked back to reveal a half-finished landscape with some magnificent trees. It was doubtful if he had found them growing together like that. He had probably sketched them individually at different places, a common practice

among landscape artists, who would leave out a wall if it blocked a view and cut out a building or anything else that did not enhance their composition. It was highly likely the sky would not be the one seen over the scenery chosen. Once when out walking with Hendrick, she had admired a particularly beautiful sky that was a clear blue with the right amount of cloud to capture an artist's eye. He had snapped his fingers contemptuously at it. "My skies are much better," he had said conceitedly. But it had always been his boast that on canvas he could improve on nature. What did surprise her was that the paint was hard and dry. Several days must have passed since he last put a brush to it.

Hendrick and Sybylla arrived home in a van Jansz coach, escorted by Adriaen, shortly before eleven o'clock. Francesca went into the reception hall to meet them and saw instantly that in looks and appearance Adriaen was everything her sister had ever wished for. Hendrick gave a shout of pleasure at the sight of her and Sybylla a delighted cry. Warm family greetings were exchanged and then her future brother-in-law was presented to her. He bowed in the flowery French way, watched by an entranced Sybylla.

"I'm honoured to meet you at last, Francesca," he said. "Sybylla is very proud of you as an artist and as her sister. Is Aletta here too?"

"No. That was not possible. I came home alone."

Sybylla pouted, but not enough to spoil the line of her mouth. "How disappointing. I so wanted her to be here for the party." She looked up sadly at Adriaen, who made suitable consoling remarks. Had they been alone she would have conjured up tears and he would have kissed them away. She knew how to choose her moments.

Francesca was well able to tell that Sybylla, in spite of the show she had made, had held little real hope that their sister would come. As for Hendrick, his clamped-up expression showed he was glad that Aletta had stayed away. It was time to pass on to Sybylla the message that had been given at the gates of the de Veere house. "Aletta sends you her love and best wishes."

Not long afterwards good nights were said and Adriaen left. No sooner had he gone than Sybylla, elated and radiant, flung out her hands to Francesca.

"Well? What do you think? Isn't he the handsomest man you've ever seen?"

Francesca smiled. "I believe he is."

"There! I knew you'd adore him! Every woman does, but he's mine! Mine! I'm so happy, aren't I, Father?" She darted to Hendrick and hugged his arm.

"Yes, and I'm happy for you, little one." He patted her head as if she were seven instead of seventeen. "Go to bed now. It's late and I want a few words with Francesca, although she must be tired too."

On their own in the family parlour, Francesca asked him first about his hands. He flexed his fingers to show her all was well. "They did trouble me again in the winter, but were not nearly as painful as before."

He was eager to know about her work and Vermeer's, questioning her keenly and forgetting the time. When she asked him about the landscape in the studio he explained that he had left it while working on a large commissioned painting of the Civil Guard, which had been set up in a corner of the Zuider Church. "It will not interfere much with my studio time, because I've taken on a young artist, Hans Roemer, to do almost everything except the faces and certain details. He's just out of his apprenticeship and is of the school of Haarlem, but he's come to Amsterdam to make his fortune!" He chuckled at such a wild dream for a painter.

"Did you decide on him because you are both of the same Guild?"

"I daresay that had something to do with it and I liked the samples of his work that he showed me."

"I'll take a look at the painting tomorrow."

Hendrick cleared his throat. "Pieter brought me that commission."

She could not keep back the rush of hope in her voice. "Have you and he mended your differences over what he did for Aletta?"

"We have."

"I'm so glad. Does this mean that you would welcome Aletta home again?"

"No! That's a separate matter."

She let the subject rest. At least one step forward had been made through his reconciliation with Pieter. She was sure that with time

4
0
9

Hendrick would soften towards her sister. "Pieter didn't mention to me in his last letter that he had met you again. To be blunt, Father, you are a man of such uncertain temper that I presume he didn't want me to be disappointed if trouble had flared up again before he could discuss it with me."

He was looking at her under his brows. "So you have been corresponding?"

"We've seen each other too."

"That was forbidden."

"Would anything have stopped you from seeing Mama when you first fell in love with her?"

"That was a different case altogether. Nobody stood between us."

"Vrouw Wolff did her best to carry out your extraordinary instructions. You mustn't blame her. I understand that you were melancholic when I left home and your concern for my well-being was out of all proportion, but those arrangements you made on my behalf were quite unnecessary. Pieter hasn't been a barrier to my painting." Her words throbbed. "He has inspired me. I can date the upturn in my work from the moment I began to fall in love with him. It was on the feast of St. Nicholaes. Surely you saw the improvement in my technique when I painted that hyacinth?"

He had been clenching and unclenching his hands on his knees and now he slammed his fists on the arms of his chair, making her jump. "Enough! No more talk of Pieter! At least not yet! Let's see Sybylla married first."

She smiled. "Don't get upset. There's no question of Pieter and me wishing to marry yet. I have to finish my apprenticeship first in any case. I've brought home one of my paintings and I'll show it to you tomorrow."

"Good. Now you must get some sleep after your long day."

"There's one more question I'd like to ask before I go to bed. How are you managing to give Sybylla a suitable dowry for this forthcoming marriage to a van Jansz?"

"Adriaen's father was most considerate and understanding. We had the usual meeting and I said straightforwardly that I could not offer anything but the smallest dowry, which would be, as you know, that

little sum of money that your mother left for each of you. He graciously accepted it as a token dowry and everything was settled."

"What a relief that Heer and Vrouw van Jansz were prepared to put their son's happiness before money."

Some distance away, in a great house on Heerengracht, that same couple were discussing their son's forthcoming betrothal. Heer van Jansz, tired and wanting to get to bed after entertaining his future daughter-in-law and her father to dinner, came close to exasperation that his wife should be in tears again.

"Why did he have to choose her?" she wailed, echoing a parental cry that had sounded down the centuries.

"Well, he has and that's that."

"But Adriaen could have had the choice of many fine young women within our own circle."

"Listen to me, my dear. We have gone over this again and again. Nobody hated the scandal over his long-standing affair more than you. Did you want him to stay a hamstrung lover to that married bitch forever?"

"No!" She was shocked at his blunt words. "But why a craftsman's daughter? Whatever can he see in her?"

Heer van Jansz knew exactly what his son could see in Sybylla, but it was not the kind of explanation he could give his wife. "There's no questioning a young man's fancy. Sybylla is the only one who has been able to entice him out of an unsavoury association we've both long condemned, which is why I waived a dowry. Be thankful that one day you'll be getting grandchildren, hopefully a grandson to carry on the van Jansz name and business, which you would never have done otherwise. Now I'm going to bed."

As he left his wife to go to his own bedchamber, he reflected that in all honesty Sybylla was not the wife he would have chosen for his son, but the old adage of any port in a storm held in this case. What was most important in his eyes was not the happiness of the young couple, but that the dreadful disgrace of Adriaen's blatant affair would be buried at last. At least Sybylla could be counted on to ensure that scandal

would never arise again about the esteemed name of van Jansz. To the father, if not to the son, she had all unwittingly revealed herself to be too shallow and greedy ever to allow anything that was rightfully hers to go to anyone else, whether it was Adriaen himself or the riches and luxuries that made her beautiful eyes glint like a cat sighting cream.

CHAPTER 18

When Griet left the Visser house in the morning to go home she had several wedding gifts from the family in her basket as well as from Maria and neighbours who knew her well. She also had a verbal message to deliver at the van Deventer house, which Hendrick had given her at the last minute. She was too excited to wonder anything about it and delivered it cheerfully to the manservant who opened the door to her.

"Please tell your master that Juffrouw Visser is at home."

Her duty done, she skipped back down the flight of steps and continued lightheartedly on her way.

In his studio Hendrick was nodding firm approval of Francesca's painting. It was small, less than a foot square, and was what was known as a "tronie," being a painting of a face executed as an exercise or for the artist's own whim, the identity of the sitter unimportant. In the case of Francesca's picture, it would be sold under the title *Head of a Girl in a Pearl Necklace*.

"It's quite good." Inwardly Hendrick was astounded by the immense quality of the painting, but although he was extravagant in all ways, including praise for his own work, he did not believe in turning any young artist's head with lavish phrases. Not that Francesca had ever been inclined to conceit, but that was beside the point. Although he had had to let Ludolf know she was at home, he was more at ease with her than he would have been if he had not had a rich son-in-law in the offing. The certainty had grown every day that his troubles would be over once the van Jansz wedding band was on Sybylla's finger. He would be able to snap his fingers at Ludolf and give his blessing to Pieter and Francesca. Luck had always rallied to him.

"The eldest Vermeer daughter posed for me," Francesca told him.

He had been leaning forward to study the precise brushwork and now he stepped back again to view the painting from a little distance. His daughter's work showed no trace of his bold technique with its echoes of Frans Hals's tutorship, but had evolved into an almost ethereal style as delicately as music from an Aeolian harp and yet with an underlying strength that compelled the eye. The sitter was looking over her left shoulder with light playing on the creamy skin of her face and neck, her dark eyes glowing as luminously as her pearls, embodying the power of life and beauty. All was held within a single second as if the whole painting had been begun and finished in that time, for in the next the eyelids would blink, a breath would be drawn and the moment lost forever.

"Your master has taught you well," he admitted, knowing that he could never have brought out her talent as Vermeer had done.

"I'll always be thankful for my apprenticeship with him," she said, unaware that she had touched a raw nerve in her father's conscience.

"Well, yes, it was all for the best. Weren't you going over to the Zuider Church this morning?"

"Yes, I'll be off now. I've asked Sybylla to come with me. She has told me that she was out both times that your assistant, Hans Roemer, was here and she hasn't seen your work there yet."

"She's had no time during weekdays and on Sunday she worships now with the van Jansz family at the Westerkerk."

"Has she ever said once to you that she is in love with Adriaen?"

"No, but that doesn't mean she's not." Then, seeing the questioning look on Francesca's face, he made a placating gesture with his hand. "All right. You and I know that she is dazzled by everything he represents, but she is fond of him too. I can tell. For mercy's sake, don't start casting doubts in her mind! The sooner she's married, the better. I've had no end of unsuitable suitors after her since you went away."

"In what way unsuitable? Do you mean they weren't rich enough to please her?"

"That was the main factor, but any bachelor or widower she smiled at seemed to think he had a chance with her. When they came calling to present themselves to me, interrupting my work, I soon gave them short shift."

Her eyes danced. "I'm sure you did."

He grinned at her, sharing her amusement. "It's good to have you home again, Francesca."

"It's good to be here. Now I'll leave you with your landscape. I like those trees."

"The tallest is growing here in Amsterdam and I took the other two from a sketch I made some years ago in Haarlem."

All the way to the Zuider Church, Sybylla talked about the gown she would wear for her betrothal party and of the silver brocade that was on its way from Florence for her wedding gown. "Aunt Janetje wrote that it has a design of Florentine lilies. Can you imagine anything lovelier?"

"Knowing her wonderful taste, I'm sure it will be a marvellous fabric. Do you think she'll come home for your marriage?"

"No. Her husband has been given some high civic appointment and for months ahead she will have to be at his side for great social functions and all the entertaining he will have to do."

They had reached the Zuider Church and they entered quietly. It was Basilican in design, lofty with pure clear windows. Together they made their way to a side aisle where Hendrick had told them Hans Roemer would be found at work.

The back of the massive easel holding the huge canvas in extended clamps was towards them as they approached. It stood on a large square of coarse linen spread over the flagstones to save blobs of paint staining them. There was no sign of the artist, although his discarded work smock, his palette and brushes with all the rest of his materials were on a table. The sisters went to the front of the canvas. The Civil Guard group was almost life-size, the men sitting at, or standing around, a table. As yet the painting was little more than the customary oil sketch such as an artist submitted on a much smaller scale for his client's approval before beginning commissioned work. Hendrick had completed three of the faces, including that of the standard-bearer, whose almost completed gilt-fringed cream silk garments and yellow-plumed

grey hat shone out from the dull ochre ground on which the paint was being built up.

"I wonder where the artist is," Sybylla queried.

A reply came from behind the railings of a side chapel. "I'm here."

A wall hid the speaker. Followed by Francesca, she went to investigate. She looked through the railings at a wild-haired, narrow-faced young man with reckless black eyes and a long humorous mouth that looked well used to laughter. He was seated on a praying stool, his back against the wall and his long legs stretched out in front of him as he tucked into a piece of bread and a hunk of cheese. The rest of the loaf lay on a spread-out paint rag. By it was a beaker of water. On his other side lay his hat like a tattered black saucer with a bright plume dyed to multicolours. He was plainly clad in clothes that had seen better days and wore a pair of wooden clogs.

"Don't make crumbs in there," Sybylla said automatically.

He made a comical play of looking around anxiously from where he sat and then giving her a bold grin. "I can't see any. Have you brought your broom to sweep up?"

"No, I haven't!" she retorted haughtily.

"That's as well, because there's a little mouse for whom I always leave a titbit. He comes out when I'm painting on my own and nobody else is about. I wouldn't want him to be disappointed. I've already promised him that he shall be in the painting."

"You can't do that!" Sybylla was outraged. "A mouse! In a serious militia group!"

"Oh, he won't be sitting at the table, leaning an arm on a piece of Gouda cheese. He'll be hard to find, but he'll be there."

Francesca was laughing. He was poking good-natured fun at the pompous poses many sitters adopted for such paintings. "Has this friend of yours a name?"

"I call him Rembrandt, after the great master, who once painted on this very spot."

Sybylla looked down her nose. "I don't think that's respectful."

Francesca disagreed with her smilingly. "My childhood memories of Rembrandt are of his being a very serious man, but I've always heard

that when Saskia was alive they led a merry life and none enjoyed a joke more than he."

The young man had risen to his feet, energetic in all his movements, and he came to the open gate in the railings. "I was certain he would have approved. I'm Hans Roemer, painting for Master Visser."

"We know," Francesca replied. "We're his daughters. This is my sister Sybylla and I'm Francesca."

"My compliments! Your father told me he had two daughters."

Francesca and Sybylla exchanged a glance. So Aletta was no longer thought of by Hendrick as a member of his family. "We are three," Francesca corrected, determined to set the record straight. "My other sister, Aletta, is living in Delft now. I'm home from there for a few days."

"So you're the one serving the apprenticeship and this sister is about to be betrothed. What is Vermeer's work like? I've never seen anything by him."

Sybylla became bored as they conversed. It never suited her not to be the centre of attention when a man was present. Admittedly this one was nothing to look at with his peasant garb and leonine mop of hair, but irritatingly there was something magnetic about him. But he was paying no attention to her, completely taken up with what her sister was saying and full of questions about Vermeer, whom nobody had heard of. She had felt quite shamed when she had had to admit to Adriaen's parents that her sister was training with an unknown artist.

"We should be going," she said imperiously. Yet she did not want to go. She wanted to go on standing there and to absorb the sight of this lithe young man, who probably hadn't a stuiver in his purse. He and Francesca were getting on remarkably well together. Then, as they laughed over something humorous about painting, excluding her, she felt an upsurge of savage jealousy. "Didn't you hear me, Francesca? With my betrothal only two days away I have no more time to waste here if you want me to go with you to the de Hartog house!"

They both looked at her then, Francesca with surprise at her acid tone and he with mirth still twinkling in his eyes. Sybylla was aware that her face was deeply flushed and knew she never looked her best when riled.

"Since when," he inquired impudently, "has anyone needed to rush about so busily before a betrothal that there is no time for a little leisurely talk? Perhaps you're having to exercise your finger to strengthen it for the weight of the van Jansz ring?"

She became like a spitting cat. "Such impertinence to your master's daughter!"

He was quite unperturbed. "Permit me to correct you. In this case your father is my employer and not my master."

"All the more reason why you should be working and not idling these minutes away!"

"True," he agreed amiably. "That was why I was here at first light and did not stop work for my breakfast until now. Perhaps tomorrow you would like me to save the one meal of my day until an hour when you could conveniently share it with me, humble fare though it is?"

"Stop making fun of me!" She did not know why she did not turn on her heel and stalk away.

Francesca stepped in, disturbed by Sybylla's tantrum. "I think we should go now." She looked back over her shoulder at Hans. "I'll call in to see if you have finished the standard-bearer before I go back to Delft."

"I look forward to seeing you, Juffrouw Visser. Good day to you both."

Outside again, Francesca looked curiously at Sybylla as they fell into step along the street. "Whyever did you become so aggressive towards that young man? There was no malice in him."

Sybylla tossed her head wilfully. "That's your opinion. I can say what I like and, as he certainly took no notice of what I said, don't you start telling me to go back and apologize as if I were five years old."

"I admit he spoke somewhat out of turn about the ring, but you must agree you did shout out rudely. It was quite unnecessary, because we had settled beforehand that we shouldn't stay long."

Sybylla gave a snort. "You appeared to be so lost in him that I thought you'd never be able to tear yourself away."

"Don't be childish. You should have learnt by now that you can't always be the centre of attention."

It was the last straw for Sybylla. She came to a standstill and blazed

at her sister. "I knew when you came home you would start ordering me and everybody else about! We've managed perfectly well without you. I'll soon be a married woman living in the finest house in all Amsterdam away from the moans of Maria and the moods of Father and—best of all—you can come home as often as you like and I'll be far out of your reach!"

Such blustering reminded Francesca of their father when he was unsure of himself and anxious to cover up something. "Indeed you will. So calm down and let's enjoy our walk to Willem's house. Remember, it's quite a while since I was here and I'll not be back again until your wedding, whenever that should be."

Sybylla bit her lip as they continued on their way. She wished she had not said what she had to Francesca, because she had not meant any of it. It was comforting to have her at home again. "I don't know what's the matter with me. I'm so on edge."

"Pre-betrothal nerves. It's not unusual."

Sybylla thought that was right. Even at this late hour she couldn't be sure of anything until Adriaen's ring was on her finger. She was always so afraid that Hendrick might make one of his noisy scenes and ruin everything. He did not like the van Jansz family's wholehearted support of the Grand Pensionary, Johan de Witt, who had governed the country since the death of Willem II over twenty years ago. She had had to beg Hendrick to swallow his tongue and not to voice his strong opinion that Louis XIV's demands, whenever they should come, should be opposed on all fronts. A recurring nightmare was of hearing her father, in spite of his promises to the contrary, letting his condemnation of conciliatory attitudes go bellowing forth after too much good wine and seeing those van Jansz faces freeze at his insistence on the military defence of Holland and the other Dutch states. On the evening three days after tomorrow when the betrothal had been safely announced, he could let forth as much as he liked, for Adriaen was too honourable a man to negate on such a solemn promise to her simply through some disgraceful uproar created by her father. Unlike Francesca and Aletta, she had never been interested in politics and was at loss to understand why men became so worked up about them. Her sister even thought women should have a hand in government, quoting the achievements

of Elizabeth of England in her time and those of Christina of Sweden and other strong royal women, the argument being that it was only an accident of birth that had given them the chance that many other women of ordinary status could have handled equally well.

On the way to Willem's house a short detour was made to Pieter's Amsterdam home so that Francesca could ask Vrouw de Hout if Pieter was expected to return within the next day or two.

Vrouw de Hout shook her head. "He's far too busy in his bulb fields at the moment to be anywhere else."

"Then there is no chance of missing him at Haarlem Huis if I should call as I have planned?"

"None at all."

As they left again Sybylla praised Francesca's resolve to see him.

At the de Hartog house Francesca received an enthusiastic reception from Willem. He asked her searching questions about her work while Sybylla chatted to his wife. When he heard Francesca had brought home one of her paintings he said he would accompany her and her sister back to their home to see it himself. When repassing the Zuider Church as the three of them walked along together, Sybylla glanced surreptitiously at the entrance in case Hans Roemer should emerge by chance. She had planned to regard him disdainfully, but he did not appear and this small score against him was denied her.

Francesca was glad that Willem was with them when she found Ludolf waiting at her home. She stiffened at his almost proprietorial greeting, having to avoid an embracing arm.

"I invite you all to dine at my house this evening," he said expansively to include Willem. "Please come with Vrouw de Hartog. We must celebrate Francesca's homecoming."

Sybylla responded enthusiastically, always welcoming an opportunity to dress up. "Oh yes! Will Adriaen be there?" She knew that he and his family were well acquainted with Ludolf.

"I invited his parents and the young man himself on my way here and they accepted."

As Ludolf accompanied Francesca and Willem into the studio where Hendrick was at work, he decided he had had enough of her dodging about as if he had no right to her. The time had come to speak. He

wanted a betrothed man's right to her kisses, which would be a poor recompense for what his whole body demanded whenever she was near. He must also make the situation clear to Geetruyd next time he was there. She was a sensible woman and an extra thousand or more guilders in her next payment should sweeten any disappointment she might feel. Perhaps the gift of a diamond brooch as a memento of what had previously been between them was also in order. Women always appreciated such niceties. He would make a point of implying that his marriage to Francesca need not put an end to what they had enjoyed together on his occasional visits to Delft. She need not know that once her usefulness to him was at an end he would never bother to see her again. By his reckoning Louis XIV would be ruler of Holland by the time Francesca's apprenticeship was completed a year from now in the spring of 1672. Even if a third year should be demanded of her it would make no difference, for by then he would have been given important duties at The Hague with enough authority to let his marriage to her go through. Since The Hague was only a short distance from Delft she could still attend Vermeer's studio two or three times a week. He had already looked at property in The Hague and had seen a splendid mansion that he intended to buy. He would have sold his Amsterdam house by now if he could have done so without arousing curiosity. These days he was having to exercise patience on all fronts and he found it wearying.

At first the evening went well. Francesca, in spite of being seated at Ludolf's right hand, had Heer van Jansz on her other side and he was an interesting conversationalist. Sybylla was elated and sparkling, thinking of when she would preside over far grander gatherings. She constantly exchanged deep glances across the table with Adriaen and little secret smiles. Once the unbidden thought came to her as to how Hans Roemer might have looked had he been dressed in clothes as fine as Adriaen's and seated opposite her, his hair brushed like silk and rings on his fingers. Then she dismissed the illusion quickly, answering some question that Willem, next to her at table, had put to her. If Vrouw van Jansz looked resignedly in her direction once or twice, she did not notice.

On the opposite side of the table Vrouw de Hartog, although seated

next to Adriaen, was entertained mostly by Hendrick, whom she knew well and who was in a jovial mood. It was proving to be the most pleasant occasion he had ever enjoyed under Ludolf's roof, a blight having been cast over all the others, but on this night he was on the brink of becoming free of his detestable patron and was full of mischievous satisfaction. Every time he noticed Adriaen smiling at Sybylla across the table he congratulated himself anew that she had landed such a wealthy fish out of the sea of her suitors. At the end of dinner he sat back in his chair to listen as Ludolf rose to his feet at the head of the table, a glass in hand.

"This could not be a better time for me to propose a special toast," Ludolf began, smiling at all seated in the sparkle of crystal and the glow of candlelight. "At my table this evening are two young people shortly to be betrothed. The name of van Jansz is to be joyously linked with that of Visser. Now, with my period of mourning at an end, I am able to announce my own betrothal. Please raise your glasses to my future wife, Francesca!"

Heer van Jansz and his wife, unaware of anything amiss, stood for the toast and the de Hartogs hid their astonishment as they followed suit a second or two later. Sybylla was openmouthed while Francesca sat deathly white and stunned by shock. Hendrick, forgetting that he was still far from being liberated by his future son-in-law, half rose from his chair with a congested face and slammed a heavy fist on the table, making the dessert dishes and the candelabra rattle, the candles casting wax.

"No!"

Vrouw van Jansz, who had never witnessed such a scene at a dinner table in her life, sank down weakly into her seat again and wielded her circular fan. "What is happening?" she appealed to her husband across the table. "I think we should go home at once!"

Francesca was on her feet. "There has been a misunderstanding. I feel no more should be said until I have discussed matters with Ludolf in the presence of my father."

Sybylla burst into tears. Regardless of what mistakes had been made, why had Hendrick made such a show about it? His roar had been enough to burst everyone's eardrums. The evening was ruined and

Adriaen's parents were already leaving, only his father saying good night to her. The de Hartogs were also departing, but both spoke to her and patted her shoulder. Adriaen had come over to her side of the table to stand by her chair. She thought for a panic-stricken moment that he was going too, but that was not his purpose.

"Let us go into the drawing room, Sybylla, and wait there. Heer van Deventer is seeing his departing guests out of the house and your father and sister are awaiting him in the library."

She saw then that they were alone in the banqueting hall, except for the servants, who had been waiting at table and now stood back against the walls, their faces expressionless. She did not think Adriaen's mother, or any of the van Jansz women, had ever wept in front of servants. She dried her eyes hastily and with as much dignity as she could muster went with him to the drawing room. There she deliberately fell into his arms and his kissing told her that his ardour had not waned. It was the first time he had ever been on his own with her and he intended to make the most of the opportunity.

In the library Hendrick stood pretending to look out the window, although there was nothing to see out there in the darkness. He could not bring himself to meet Francesca's eyes. She addressed his reflection in the panes.

"What do you know about Ludolf's extraordinary statement? Please tell me before he comes. I could see when you shouted that you were denying something you already knew."

He forced himself to answer her. "I hadn't wanted you to know yet. Nothing can take place before your apprenticeship ends, but a year ago I signed a marriage contract, promising you to him."

She could scarcely believe what she was hearing. All Pieter's warnings came back to her. She thought of the Dutch legend of a girl bargained for by a sinister suitor, who upon marriage revealed himself as a mass of putrefaction and was death himself. It was impossible for her to think of Ludolf as a husband in any other light. "Why did you do such a terrible thing?"

"I must have been drunk."

It was such a likely explanation that she did not question it. "Does Pieter know?"

"I told him when he called about the commission, but neither he nor I had expected it to be made public yet."

"I think he has always been afraid of this." She was filled with immense sadness that her only escape from Ludolf was in flight, which would mean leaving her family and her home for many years. A thought puzzled her. "You say you promised me to Ludolf twelve months ago, but that was when Amalia was still alive."

"No. He was so mad to have you that he gave me the contract to sign the day after she died."

She bowed her head and put a hand over her eyes, horrified by this disclosure. Amalia had been much in her thoughts on returning to the van Deventer house for the first time since that tragic evening. Now to hear of such callous indifference to her death was unsupportable.

Ludolf, entering the library, glimpsed her pose of distress before she whipped her hand away and stepped back, her face hostile. Matters had not gone exactly as he had expected. Not for one moment had he imagined that Hendrick, after his six weeks' experience of prison, would dare to make any objection, let alone indulge in such a furious outburst. As for Francesca, he had foreseen his announcement would cause her considerable shock, but relying on her proven self-control and good breeding, he had been certain she would not make any protest in front of his other guests.

He composed his expression to one of sympathetic understanding. "My dearest Francesca, don't be upset that this betrothal has been sprung on you. As I expect your father has explained, it is of long standing, but convention prevented me from speaking out before. Nothing shall interfere with your art. I want you to fulfil your ambitions. You shall have everything you've ever wanted. We'll not stay here when we're married. You shall have another house that you can furnish and decorate as you please. You shall visit Italy. I'll set Aletta up in a studio if that would please you. Your father and his household shall have all they need. Money problems will be behind him forever."

She spoke slowly and distinctly, her eyes hard and glittering. "Don't try to bribe me. I know there are parents who whip and starve their daughters into submitting to marriages with partners not of their choice, but never suppose that my father would deal thus with me! He

4
2
3

has never raised a hand to my sisters or to me and I know he won't begin now. I'll never marry you!"

"I can see you have no comprehension of the depth of my feelings for you. I've always wanted you to come to me willingly and I'll continue to hope for that. You have plenty of time before the end of your apprenticeship to make up your mind."

"I do?" She was wary, not trusting him. Hendrick had turned back to the room, equally suspicious. Ludolf was smiling at her.

"Indeed. You may decide as you please and I'll abide by your wishes."

"You'd tear up the contract?"

"Naturally. Unfortunately I'm sure that would cause your father lasting sorrow. Why not ask him to explain? It's time you knew all the facts."

Francesca looked questioningly at Hendrick, but his tormented gaze was on Ludolf, his face working. "Don't do this!" he pleaded hoarsely. Then he went charging from the room. Francesca would have followed him, but Ludolf caught her by the arm and restrained her.

"Let him go. He's too afraid to confess to what you have to know." She pulled free of him. "Then you tell me!"

"Very well. You had better sit down while I relate all that happened."

Hendrick had rushed back to the banqueting hall, thinking he might find Sybylla and Adriaen there, for he knew Sybylla would wait for him and Francesca. One of the servants clearing the table told him that the young couple had gone to the drawing room. He threw open the door and discovered them sprawled in an amorous embrace on the couch. Both of them leapt up, Sybylla, flushed and looking slightly dishevelled, hastily adjusting her low neckline.

"Get out, Sybylla!" Hendrick roared.

"But, Father, it was nothing! We were just—"

He lunged forward, took hold of her and almost threw her from the room. Then he locked the door to keep her out. Adriaen, not at all surprised by this display of parental wrath, hoped he was not going to have to grapple with the artist to save being cuffed. He had no intention of appearing at his own betrothal party with a black eye. An apology was in order.

"I'm afraid I let my love for Sybylla run away with me, Master Visser. I did kiss her several times—"

"Shut up! I haven't time to deal with that now! I'm in a desperate situation. Will you make me a substantial loan? I didn't intend to ask you until Sybylla was your wife, but events have precipitated matters."

Adriaen was relieved that his amorousness with Sybylla was to be overlooked so readily. "I don't carry money to social affairs such as this evening, but a loan can be arranged. How much do you require? A few hundreds?"

"That's not enough! I'm not talking in hundreds, but in thousands!"

The banker in Adriaen came to the fore. "In that case let us meet at my office tomorrow and we can go into the matter. I'll help you in any way I can."

"I need your promise now! For mercy's sake, I'm going to be your father-in-law. Surely you won't refuse me?"

"At least tell me the reason why you require the loan." Adriaen was more than prepared to step in for a critical emergency, but he wanted to know what it was all about.

"To settle gambling debts to van Deventer. If I can't return to the library free of all I owe him there will be dire consequences for Francesca."

Immediately Adriaen began to doubt the wisdom of becoming involved. Gamblers were a bad risk and he could foresee that if he made a loan to Hendrick now he could face a future of endlessly settling his father-in-law's debts. It must be every gambler's dream to have a banker in the family, but he must make no promises until he had discussed the matter with his father.

"I'm sorry, Master Visser," he said firmly, "but I see no cause for you to come to me. Van Deventer seemed pleased enough to be your daughter's betrothed at the table and I can't believe he'll negate on his wish to marry her just because you owe him money."

"You fool!" Hendrick was wild with fear and exasperation. "You haven't understood! She'll have to marry him against her will if I don't pay him. I want her released from that contract."

But it was too late. The handle of the locked door was tried and Francesca spoke. "Please let me in, Father."

4
2
5

Hendrick clapped his hands to his head with a groan and turned away, making no attempt to answer his daughter's request. Sybylla, having become hysterical when he had started shouting even louder, had rushed to fetch Francesca and met her, sombre-faced, coming from the library with Ludolf. Again Francesca rapped on the door, but it was Sybylla who shouted through it.

"Are you all right, Adriaen? Answer me!"

In the room Adriaen looked coldly at Hendrick. It rankled with him that he had been called a fool by a reckless gambler incapable of handling his own affairs. Deliberately he strode to the door and unlocked it. As it opened, Sybylla rushed to him and he began reassuring her that he was unharmed.

Francesca went towards her father, Ludolf remaining close to her. "Look at me, Father," she said quietly out of her own shocked state. She thought of Pieter's warning and how true it had proved to be.

Slowly Hendrick faced her. He spoke wearily. "Ludolf has told you?"

"He has. I only wish you had told me yourself long ago."

"I kept hoping to find a way out."

"I realize that. Let us go home now."

Hendrick and his daughters seated themselves in the van Jansz coach while Adriaen bade his host a courteous good night. As he came down the steps he could hear Sybylla shrieking at her father, but when he entered the equipage she stopped. No doubt she would prove difficult at times after they were married, but after glimpsing her beautiful breasts in those minutes when they were alone together, he felt he would be able to forgive her any amount of tantrums.

After Adriaen had seen the Vissers to their door and left again, Sybylla was still confused as to the cause of the uproar that Hendrick had created. She had believed he was about to use his fists on Adriaen and her relief that it had nothing to do with her or her betrothed's indiscretion made her overwhelmingly sympathetic towards Francesca when everything was explained to her. She uttered a long wail. Francesca put an arm about her shoulders and spoke to Hendrick again.

"Were all those restrictions placed on me in Delft at Ludolf's instigation?"

"They were," he admitted wearily, "and there's nothing I can do to lift them."

"Oh, my poor sister!" Sybylla cried out to her.

"Would you be very disappointed if I didn't stay for your betrothal party?" Francesca asked her. "I feel I have to see Pieter as soon as possible to talk everything over with him."

Sybylla was relieved. Her father would have to be present at the party, but he appeared too broken now ever to cause a scene again, whereas Francesca would be a reminder to Adriaen of the uproar in the van Deventer house and she wanted that forgotten as soon as possible. "No, I'll let you go if you promise to be at my wedding."

"I asked Master Vermeer if he could allow that before I came this time and he agreed."

"What will you do about Griet's wedding tomorrow?"

"I'll go with you and Father and Maria to the church and stay a while at the festivities afterwards to wish her well. Then I'll catch a stage wagon that should get me to Haarlem by early evening. There's one thing I wish you'd do for me."

"Anything!"

"Could you manage to keep a civil tongue in your head and convey my apologies to Hans Roemer for not returning to view the group painting again as I said I would, but I'll not have time to spare now."

Sybylla was not at all sure that she wanted to do what she had been asked. The prospect aroused disquiet in her while at the same time she felt a curious thrill at the idea of seeing the impudent rascal again. "Very well. I'll go one day."

"Don't forget."

Sybylla reflected that there was little chance of that. Then she kissed Hendrick good night, feeling a rush of love for him that brought tears to her eyes. He had been foolish, but then so had she on many occasions. The tears fell when she embraced Francesca, who had been landed in such awful straits by events in which she had had no part.

"Everything is not lost, Francesca." She wanted to offer the kind of comfort and the sense of hope that her sister had given her so often in the past. "Surely something will happen in the next few months to release you. Perhaps Pieter will think of a way."

"Maybe he will." Francesca smiled fondly at her sister attempting to cheer her. "Go to bed now. Father and I will be talking for a little while. Don't worry. I have no intention of upbraiding him."

As Sybylla went up to her bedchamber she marvelled that Francesca could talk rationally and without recrimination to their father. If he had put her in the same situation, preventing her from marrying Adriaen, she believed she would have gone on screaming until she drowned all the bells of Amsterdam, even the carillon of the Zuider Church.

Griet's marriage to Sijmon was a happy occasion. She had been true to him since they first met in spite of his two long absences at sea. Her gown was of blue velvet made up from a length saved from a time when Hendrick had tossed lengths of fabric to every female in the house after a win at cards. Its delicate lace trimming had been made by Maria and had a symbolic design of lovers' knots and roses. After the ceremony a merry time was had by family and friends, the food plentiful and barrels of beer set up to quench everybody's thirst. There was dancing to a flute, a lute and a drum, heavy feet making the floorboards shake at the home of Griet's brother and wife, where the festivities were held. Francesca had no difficulty in slipping away unnoticed after a word with the bridegroom and a kiss from the bride.

When she returned home to change for travelling and to collect her hand baggage and her painting, a neighbour, who had been watching out for her, came waving a sealed note in her hand.

"A woman named Vrouw de Hout was here looking for you. She said you mentioned going to Haarlem and asked if you would take this hand-delivered note with you whenever you leave."

Francesca saw it was addressed to Pieter and took it indoors with her to put it away in her purse, where she had already put Aunt Janetje's gift bracelet for Aletta. She gathered her baggage and made her way to Dan Square, where she boarded the stage wagon for Haarlem.

Throughout the two-hour journey she mulled over the events of the previous evening. What Ludolf had said to her drummed in her mind. All her and Pieter's hope to take flight to Italy as a last resort had been swept away.

"If the marriage contract is not upheld," Ludolf had said, "through any refusal by you to become my wife, or if you should hide away or run off somewhere, I'll take your father to court and do my utmost to see that he gets thirty years at least for his unpaid debt to me!"

She felt almost faint as she remembered his words. Shock still vibrated in her veins, but nothing should spoil her time with Pieter. The five days that were left to her before her return to Delft would now be his instead of the mere twenty-four hours she had thought originally were all she could take away from her family.

The stage wagon drew up near the Butchers' Hall in Haarlem and she set off at once to walk the two miles to Pieter's home. It was a clear evening, but dusk had already fallen and her baggage, into which she had packed additional belongings she needed in Delft, and the linen-wrapped painting were proving heavy and tiring. She went into the last tavern in the town to get a lantern, and this added to her burdens. By the time she reached the lane that led to his home it was dark, the stars were out and she was glad to reach her destination.

She passed the office, which was closed, and continued on past the cluster of trees to come in sight of Haarlem Huis for the first time. She could see that it was much larger than the average farmhouse with two floors and an attic, the thatch coming low over the upper windows, one of which shone with candlelight. Another window downstairs held an even brighter glow. She went up the path to the main door and banged on the knocker. Standing back, she saw the candlelight upstairs fade away as someone came with it to answer her knocking. When the door swung open Pieter stood there, a candlestick in his hand, his hair damp as if he were newly bathed after his day's work. The joyful surprise on his face at the sight of her was something she would always remember.

"Francesca, my love! Come in!"

"I'm here to stay for a while!"

She stepped inside, dropping her hand baggage, her painting and the lantern as he put down the candle on a cupboard. The next second they were in each other's arms, their mouths meeting in a kiss of passionate reunion. When they drew apart they began laughing and talking, asking and answering questions together. While he shut the door and rebolted it, she threw off her cloak and crossed the hall to pause on the thresh-

old of the lighted room. Her artist's eye took in its hues and proportions. There were cream-washed walls, a massive cupboard, an ancient chest thick with carving and a table covered by an Oriental rug in colours from her own palette of vermilion and indigo, lemon yellow, purple and Veronese green. A few old paintings on wood were comfortably at home in the general harmony.

"This is a lovely room!" she exclaimed, still looking about her.

"When my father built this house out of his tulipomania gains he concentrated on space. To please my mother, then a bride, he purchased stylish furniture, but he didn't want to part with what had been in the old farmhouse, and he stored it all in a barn. When the place became mine I decided to reinstate most of it. Over the years I've added a few extra things here and there."

She had gone to hold her hands to the fire, not because she was cold but simply to enjoy everything that was in the room. "How happy you must be here! The house has such a welcoming atmosphere."

"I think the house has been waiting for you."

"I'd like to think that is true."

He had come to take her by the waist and swivel her gently around to face him. "This is where you belong, my love. Here with me under this roof where I've long wanted you to be. There is a splendid room at the north end of this house that would make you a fine studio. It has three good windows, one with an east-facing view across the bulb fields." He saw a look he could not define flicker in her eyes. "What is it?"

She dipped her head, letting her brow come to rest against his shoulder. "I know that Father has signed a contract of marriage for me."

He held her close to him, stroking her hair. "How did you find out?"

She told him what had taken place. "Ludolf made it clear that any disappearance on my part would result in his taking Hendrick to court immediately. I could never, for the sake of my own freedom, let my father go mad chained up in a dungeon. Even flight is impossible."

He cupped her chin for her to look up at him again. "Not if he went to Florence too."

"Would that be possible?" She wanted to believe it, crushing down a wrenching feeling that it could never be. "He has always sworn he

would never live anywhere else except Amsterdam and he intends to die there, but in these desperate circumstances he would surely be willing to leave!" She seized on the idea. "Maria could have a home with Sybylla, and Griet could easily find a new place. Hendrick has always spoken of Florence as Michelangelo's city. He would be able to paint there!"

"I'd say there is no doubt about it."

She was already planning, clinging to hope. "He could bring what he treasures most in his home—the paintings of my mother, the Frans Hals and the one by Rembrandt of Titus. They could all be taken from their frames and easily packed. He would never leave his favourite palette and brushes behind, but those wouldn't take much space and so he could travel light."

"You can talk it over with him next time you're home."

"That will be for Sybylla's marriage, which is to be soon." She frowned slightly, pursing her lips. "Of course, I have to allow for his unpredictability."

"In what way?"

"It may take a long time to persuade him to tear up his roots." Nobody knew better than she how perverse her father could be. "He will procrastinate, always hoping that a more agreeable solution will present itself. It isn't as though I could take any extra tuition now. I have to gain Guild membership at the end of two years."

"Why is that?"

She looked amazed that he should ask. "Think of my father's debts. I couldn't inflict more on him!"

"That extra time has been already financed should it be needed."

Her expression was puzzled. "How do you mean?"

He grinned at her. "Can't you guess?"

"By you, Pieter?"

"I can tell you now how it all came about, which I couldn't do before."

When she had heard all the details she took his hand and pressed it to her lips. "So all I've achieved, and hope to achieve, is through you. I couldn't have wished for a better way, because it makes you an integral

part of my work and my life. Yet you scarcely knew me when you committed yourself to that bond."

"I already loved you."

She smiled and kissed his hand again before moving away from him to wander about the room looking at everything. Instinct told her not to waste a moment of these precious hours. It was why she had come. Ludolf was such a powerful and evil force in her life that a chance to be on her own with Pieter in this way might never come again, no matter what plans they made. "I'll be able to picture you here now when I get a letter from this house. That reminds me." She returned to where she had left her purse on one of the green upholstered chairs set back against the wall. "I have a letter for you that Vrouw de Hout asked me to bring here. Don't hesitate to read it."

He recognized Neeltje's handwriting and broke the seal. When he had scanned the contents he folded the note again and put it on a ledge. "Fortunately it's nothing urgent," he said.

"Where do you write to me?" she asked.

"At a desk in the next room."

"May I see it?"

"Come with me."

He took her by the hand. The rooms followed the usual pattern of opening one into another. In the dining hall adjacent to the kitchen a cold supper had been laid for him by a local woman who came in daily to cook, clean and prepare his meals when he was there. Francesca expressed a wish to freshen herself after her journey before eating and he showed her upstairs to a bedchamber where there was all she would need. It also had a fine old wall bed, enclosed on three sides, and he told her that all the upper rooms had a similar one. According to what she had been told, there had once been wall beds in her own home, but not long after her parents were married, Hendrick, enjoying one of his early gambling wins, had had them all removed and replaced by four-posters, including the one with extravagant giltwork that he had shared with her mother. She wondered if those original wall beds had had the same carved canopies as the one in this room.

Pieter had gone downstairs again, where he had set another place at the table for her and put a chair ready. When she reappeared in the

dining hall she had changed into the tawny velvet gown that she had worn earlier in the day to Griet's wedding, bunches of ribbons holding back the curls that danced over her ears. With ceremony he drew back the chair for her.

"If I had known you would be here this evening I'd have had a feast prepared," he said smilingly.

"This is feast enough," she declared. The crisp white napkins covering the dishes had been removed to reveal prepared lobsters, smoked meats, salads, fruit, bread and an almond tart with a jug of cream. Pieter poured the white wine that he had brought chilled from the cellar.

"Normally the good woman who prepared this supper for me cooks a stout repast, but these days when I'm working until dark I tell her to leave me something cold on the table or a hot dish by the kitchen firebox."

"I wouldn't have wanted anyone else to be here, Pieter." She met his eyes over the salad he was holding for her and then looked down as she took some onto her porcelain plate.

"Neither would I," he said softly, his eyes holding hers when she looked at him again. "We've never been alone before. There has always been someone else near at hand."

They talked while they ate, each wanting to know all that had happened to the other since the last letters they had exchanged. She related Aletta's difficult task in waiting on Constantijn, spoke about Griet's wedding and described Sybylla's excitement over the forthcoming betrothal, which she had chosen to miss in order to come straight to him. He told her of the books he had read, the plays he had seen and the games of golf and *kaatsen* he had played with friends in vigorous competition until the momentum of work had cut out those pastimes. He also informed her of his conversation with Neeltje, only withholding the woman's tale of murder and suspected murder, not wanting to cast a shadow over Francesca's first evening in his home.

"Incidentally, that note you brought was from her. She wrote that by chance she had found a contract of marriage between Ludolf and your father among his papers."

Francesca smiled wryly. "She's a little late with that information."

He turned their conversation to lighter matters again and she told

4
3
3

him about the Civil Guard painting she had seen, teasing him that she had viewed its progress before him, even though, as he was in the reserve, he would not be in the painting.

"It's coming on well, then?"

"Oh yes," she replied merrily, "and it's going to include a little mouse."

He chuckled with her over Hans Roemer's audacity and they tried to guess where it would appear. "Perhaps it will be under somebody's lace-edged collar!"

"Or peering through the captain's plume!"

All the while they had been talking and laughing each was aware of the enormous feeling of tenderness between them and that time was slipping swiftly towards the moment that had been inevitable since their first meeting.

As they rose from the table, he drawing back her chair, their eyes full of love for each other, she made a request.

"Show me the studio now. I want to set down roots here that nothing can ever wrench free." She needed to make some defiant gesture of her own against the great threat that loomed over her.

He took her face between his hands and kissed her tenderly. "I'll take you there. You'll be able to see something of the view too."

"Won't it be too dark?" she asked as he took up the candelabrum from the table to light the way.

He held out his free hand to her and she took it. "The shutters will be open and the moon should be up by now."

When they came to the room at the north end of the long house he went into it ahead of her and held the candelabrum high. It was completely bare of furnishings except for a large easel set up in the middle of the floor.

"Where did that come from?" she exclaimed.

"I picked it up for a couple of guilders in Haarlem market. Is it all right?"

"Why, yes," she replied, examining it. "It's a very old one, but that doesn't matter, because it's firm and sound. Not at all wobbly as some of them are after years of service. In the market, did you say?"

"About two months ago. It was with a lot of thrown-out furniture."

With a hand resting on the easel's middle bar, she looked through its structure at him, her face alight. "Suppose—oh, just suppose—that Frans Hals painted his canvases on it!"

He saw that she had spoken quite yearningly. "Maybe he did," he said, going along with her wish. "Are there any initials on it?"

"No. A master wouldn't do that, although an apprentice might if there were several pupils in the same studio and each wanted to make sure of his own."

"Are you disappointed there's no proof either way?"

She left the easel and went to the nearest window. "Nothing could disappoint me in this house. Extinguish the candles and let us look out together."

The room plunged into darkness as he pinched the wicks and left the candelabrum on the floor. Reaching her side, he heard her give a little sigh of delight at the view, which was long familiar to him. It was a sight of exquisite beauty. Beyond a canal at the end of the garden the tulips stood silver in the ethereal glow.

"Tomorrow in daylight you will see how vivid they are."

"Will they be gilded when the sun comes up as they are silvered now?" she breathed.

"Just for a few moments of the dawn before the petals come into their own."

"I'd like to capture that scene on canvas." She looked up into his face, illumined by the moon as was her own, their eyes dark, lustrous pools. Suddenly she was aware of making a vow. "One day I'll paint in this studio even if many troubled years lie between now and then and we are young no longer."

"May we have more time together than apart." He enfolded her in his arms.

"That's how I want it to be, but neither of us knows what lies in store." She raised a hand and touched his face lovingly. "That's why I came straight to you as soon as I could after hearing about the contract. No matter what the future may bring, let us make the most of the time we have now."

They kissed lingeringly. Then he swept her up in his arms and

carried her through the moon-washed house up the stairs to his bed-chamber.

He took the ribbons from her hair and unlaced her, her garments as silvered as the tulips had been, for there was no candlelight. She trembled, not from fear but from joy as he smoothed her cambric chemise from her shoulders and her breasts were revealed for his caresses and his kisses. At her waist he kissed her again. The chemise had lodged there on the loosened band of her last petticoat and he knelt to spread a hand over each of her hips and sent both garments cascading to her feet. Her spine arched as she threw back her head, her eyes closed, and plunged her fingers into his thick curls as his kisses burrowed into her with such sweet sensations that she could scarcely breathe.

"My love. My darling Francesca!" He lifted her effortlessly and laid her down in the great wall bed. A few moments later he came to her as pale and naked as a moon god, his muscled body rimed by the pure light. Yet it was a warm, vibrant and powerful man that she took into her arms, so full of love for her that his murmurs were almost as tangible as his caresses. She gasped deliciously again and again under his adoring exploration of her until at last passion overcame them both. There was a dagger thrust of pain as he pierced her, but it was immediately forgotten as suddenly there was nothing else for her in all the world except being one with him. They moved together in a rhythm of complete harmony, her heart beating wildly against his as she soared with him into an explosion of ecstasy from which she felt they would never emerge.

Slowly her surroundings returned to her. Once more the carved canopy of the wall bed loomed into place overhead, the dark furniture of the room took shape again against the light walls and outside the moon was still shining.

He lay across her, but he raised his head and shifted his weight onto his elbows to gaze down into her blissful face.

"I'll love you always," he declared quietly but with enormous feeling.

She smiled, closing her eyes and opening them again as if she had needed that second to absorb his tender words into her whole mind and body. "As I will love you," she whispered.

"Nobody can come between us now."

"Nobody," she agreed dreamily, blissfully oblivious to all else except his beloved presence.

Still balanced on his elbows, he slid his forearms under her back and held her. "You've come home to me, Francesca. Now your place will always be here."

It was what she wanted with her whole heart. Putting her hands behind his head, she raised herself slightly to meet his kiss. The passion of it bore them both deep into the soft goose-feather pillows.

CHAPTER I 9

It was just before dawn when Francesca felt Pieter kiss her and leave the bed to go into an adjacent side room to wash and dress for the day's work ahead.

She was just drifting off to sleep again when she remembered the tulips. By now the sky was lifting on first light. Throwing back the downy coverlet, she leapt out and ran through to the guest chamber, where the previous evening she had unpacked a lawn night shift. She pulled it over her head and thrust her arms into a robe as she flew from the room and down the stairs on her bare feet. The scent of coffee met her and a candle lamp glowed through the open kitchen door. Pieter, halfway through his breakfast at the kitchen table, saw her dart past, pale garments flowing and her hair full of red glints from the candlelight as it danced down her back.

"I hope I'm not too late," she called out.

He swallowed his mouthful of bread and cheese as he thrust back his chair to follow her. She had reached the studio and he went to join her at the east-facing window.

"You're in time," he said reassuringly. He put an arm about her waist and she leaned back against him as together they watched the dawn opening its fan across the sky. He knew the moment. "It will be now."

She caught her breath as the sunrays spread and suddenly the whole sea of tulips gleamed gold on their graceful stems. Her hand clasped his

tightly in her appreciation of what she was seeing. Then, as the strength of the sun increased, the gilding faded to let the blooms blaze into gloriously variegated hues of yellow, orange, crimson, scarlet, white and cream.

With a contented sigh she smiled at him. "What a shame it would have been if I'd missed seeing all that through being a lie-abed!"

"It's as well that you did," he agreed. "Later today all those cups, as they are called in the trade, will be taken from their stems. But there will be plenty left elsewhere kept for sale and you may pick armfuls if you wish."

"I may do that, but I also want to sketch every shape, feathered or plain, that you grow here."

When he had gone from the house, his workers having begun to arrive, she filled a copper carrying jug with hot water and took it upstairs to the guest bedchamber, where she had donned her night shift so hastily. There she bathed herself all over in a bowl that she placed on the floor, a sponge letting the rivulets run down her body.

She was dressed and had finished pinning up her hair when she heard the rattle of cart wheels. Going to the window, which she had already opened to the mild morning, she looked out. Through a gap in the trees some distance away she saw a cart and then another roll by on their way to market with a load of the newly picked tulips for sale. Her guess was that those destined for Amsterdam had been picked by lantern light and would have left some while ago.

When she went downstairs she found that the local woman, Vrouw Graff, had arrived and was clearing up. They greeted each other.

"I knew someone was staying," the woman said, a surprised look still on her face, "because of the breakfast crockery, but no ladies on their own have ever visited here before."

"I'll be staying for another five days."

"Then you may expect good weather. There is a full change from the cold spell we've been having and it smells like a summer morning outside." The woman glanced at the clock. "You're up very early for someone with leisure on her hands."

"I don't want to miss a minute of my time here. Now I'm going to explore until I know the whole layout of the van Doorne land."

"That will give you plenty of walking. You'd best make for the old farmhouse first and go from there."

Francesca followed the directions given and went along the lane down which the carts had passed until she came to the farmhouse and a cluster of old buildings, similarly thatched, that would have been byres, barns and storehouses in times past. Now they all played a new role in the bulb and flower business. She could see there was an additional orangery to the one from which Pieter had emerged on her first visit there. The windows had been opened inwards to let in the sun and avoid shadows, for the orange trees were still inside. She had heard it said that they should not be taken out until after the full moon of April and when May had come, which meant their winter hibernation would be over soon. She opened the door and went in.

There was a warm and fragrant atmosphere with an underlying waxy aroma from the warming lamps, now extinguished with the rise of temperature at the weather's change. The orange trees in their square oak boxes stood in orderly rows, their heights varying from two to almost five feet. Beautifying the lengthy orangery were pedestals on which stood pots of myrtle, laurel and jasmin. An old gardener was snipping unwanted slips from the orange trees in a time-consuming task and was glad of some conversation with her. He told her how Pieter had grown his first orange tree from the kernel of a well-ripened orange, such as was still done, for it was only in warmer climes that slips took root.

"He wasn't more than nine or ten at the time, getting the information he wanted from an old book. I knew then he wasn't meant for plain farming."

Outside again, she continued her tour of inspection and went into another building, attracted by the babble of women's voices. Here the tulips were being packed in layers, stem end to stem end, in shallow boxes lined with damp moss, no tulip head resting upon another. She had bade the women good morning, to which they replied, eyeing her with speculative curiosity. Then they resumed their own conversations while she watched, fascinated by the deftness of their hands. Now and again their stocks were replenished as other women brought in more tulips in long, shallow baskets. When a cart drew up outside the carter

came to carry out the boxes and load up. One woman was dealing with the last of the narcissi.

When Francesca left there she passed the stables, where the stalls were all empty now except for Pieter's saddle horses. Farther on she looked into a store stacked with boxes and the next one housed gardening implements of every kind. Then she began to wander the paths between the fields. Most of the picking was already over for the day, but weeding was in progress and the snipping off of the heads of the tulips she had seen at dawn was taking place. Many more fields had yet to have their blooms beheaded and at the far end of one of them Pieter sighted her and waved. As she went to meet him she knew that this was a scene she would paint one day.

They embraced happily. Taking her hand in his, he strolled along with her, talking enthusiastically about all that was around them from the quality of the soil to the importance of colour.

"Naturally no tulip grower strives these days to grow a black tulip, as was done during the three years of tulipomania."

"Nobody would want such a sinister colour, I'm sure."

"Agreed, and you also used the right adjective for it. Evil deeds were perpetrated to obtain such bulbs in those mad days. I'm aiming to grow a special colour that is the reverse of that ominous shade."

"May I ask what it is?"

"All I can say is that it will please you as an artist. You'll be the first to see it."

She fought back the unhappy thought that she might be married to a man she loathed when at last that tulip bloomed, keeping to her resolution that nothing should be allowed to spoil these few precious days.

The afternoon after the catastrophic dinner party Adriaen made a brief call on Ludolf. It was an amiable meeting, Ludolf dismissing good-humouredly Hendrick's outburst as a flurry of artistic temperament. He also made it clear that the promissory notes were not for sale. Adriaen did not pursue the subject and the conversation moved to other matters of mutual interest. They finished a second glass of claret and then Adriaen was shown around the garden before finally taking his leave.

He went straight to discuss the whole matter with his father now that he knew the whole situation. Heer van Jansz pointed out at once that van Deventer was a highly valued client who had banked a fortune with them, apart from considerable investments in several of their various enterprises, which would make it foolhardy to offend him in any way.

"You must realize, Adriaen," he said firmly, "that your forthcoming betrothal to Sybylla doesn't make you responsible in any way for her family. Van Deventer has told you himself that he is not interested in disposing of Visser's debts to him, and if we should loan the artist that large amount of money for him to settle them, it would only rebound on us. Not only would van Deventer be enraged, but he would let it be known among others of his wealthy ilk that the van Jansz bankers did not hesitate to undermine a client whenever it suited them."

Adriaen nodded. "The problem seems to be, according to a few words I had with Sybylla early this morning, that Francesca has her heart set on somebody else." He had not committed himself to any promise when Sybylla had appealed to him on her sister's behalf, simply saying he would look into the situation and see what he could do.

His father snapped his fingers to emphasize the unimportance of daughters setting their hearts in unguided directions. "Young women think themselves in love half a dozen times. Look at your sister, for example. If I had listened to her whims she would never have married her present husband, and then we should have lost an affiliation that has brought advancement to several of our ventures and ultimately great benefit to her. It is typical of an artist that he should not think logically and thus put his daughter's fancies before a most suitable marriage for her. Remember my good advice when you have grown daughters of your own."

"I will."

Heer van Jansz sat back comfortably in his chair. "Why shouldn't Francesca marry van Deventer? I suppose she thinks he is too old for her, but one can't expect a middle-aged widower to choose mutton when he can have lamb. So if he should exert a little pressure to ensure all goes according to his wishes, who could blame him? All Amsterdam knows that van Deventer was kind and considerate towards his first

wife, and Francesca should think herself fortunate to be gaining such a good and wealthy husband." He adopted a confidential man-to-man tone to his son. "It should be helpful to you to have a responsible sister-in-law in our social circle to keep an eye on Sybylla. Your betrothed is a delightful young woman, but she's still flighty. I've only met Francesca once at van Deventer's table, but she struck me as having her head screwed on the right way. None can deny the dignity and reserve with which she received the surprise announcement of van Deventer's claim on her. You'll find a staunch ally in her."

"I'm sure you're right, Father. I'll leave matters as they are."

"Well said." Heer van Jansz nodded approvingly. "Francesca will eventually come around to accepting the situation and then everything will be solved by its own accord."

Sybylla wished Francesca had not entrusted her with the verbal message for Hans Roemer. Yet although she could have passed it on for Hendrick to tell him she still retained the duty for herself. She had gone by the Zuider Church once or twice the day before and never failed to look towards it on each occasion. It was as if he knew she was in the vicinity and sent out rays of attraction to disquiet her mind and annoy her. She was already troubled enough about Francesca's future if nothing should be done. She could not exact any real pressure on Adriaen as yet, but after her betrothal tomorrow she would put her foot down firmly. According to her father, Adriaen had been very uncooperative, but then everything had happened so quickly. In the meantime she must wait and hope it would be different when there was time for sensible discussion. She had better see Hans at once and get it over with.

He was painting when she went into the church. It was almost as if he recognized her footsteps, because he spoke before she reached him. "I knew you'd come today, Juffrouw Sybylla."

She felt a shiver run down her spine. How could he have known? Then she told herself he was only bluffing. "Why should you have thought that?" she questioned derisively, moving past the easel to where she could see him.

He answered without looking at her. "Because it's the eve of your betrothal. Once that is official you'll have to think twice about coming to see me. Your betrothed might not like it."

"What are you talking about? I'll not be calling here after today. I only came to give you Francesca's apologies, because she's had to leave without a chance to view the painting again."

"That was courteous of her. I had promised to give her a clue as to where the mouse would be found."

"You can tell me instead."

He looked at her then, his eyes twinkling. "I think you should search for it."

"But why Francesca and not me?" She was aware of sounding petulant, but she felt slighted. He had shown himself to be much taken with her sister and so why not with her?

"Because you haven't had to go away." He resumed his painting.

She thought how she might get back at him. "Pieter de Hooch has been commissioned to paint the marriage portraits of Adriaen and myself."

He was not impressed. "That's a mistake. I would have done them much better. De Hooch should never have left Delft. That's where he reached his peak and then not in portraiture."

"I suppose you would like me to get the commission switched to you?" she taunted.

"No. I've never filched another man's work and I never will."

She was aware that once again he had deftly put her in her place. "Wouldn't you like to paint me?" she challenged.

He paused to reverse his brush and hold it vertically at arm's length towards her, closing one eye while he measured the contours of her face in midair, first one way and then the other. Then he nodded. "You may sit for me anytime you like."

Her eyes sparkled maliciously. "I could have my hand resting against my cheek to show off the van Jansz betrothal ring that is to be mine tomorrow."

"So you could," he agreed amiably, not rising to the bait.

She had had enough. "I'm going now. I'll not be coming back anymore."

When she had stalked away out of the church, Hans smiled as he continued to work on the hand of the standard-bearer. Sybylla would soon be back. In the meantime he had a purchase to make.

While getting ready for the betrothal party Sybylla found herself missing Francesca and Aletta as never before. They should have been with her and she wished that after all she had asked Francesca to stay, but it was too late now. Her gown was new in that Maria had turned out a roll of wide lace, made many years ago and hoarded for a special occasion. It had been used to cover the rose silk gown that was already more than a year old. The scalloped lace lay in filmy layers over the skirt as well as being stitched to the bodice, and a gathered frill of it fell from a neckline that had been more deeply scooped and also from the sleeves. With a hint of the pink silk beneath it was quite beautiful and none could have recognized the garment from its original appearance. Pink ribbons hung from the bunches of curls covering her ears and a tiny silver net, which had been Anna's, covered the twisted knot high at the back of her head.

She took up her hand glass to view herself from every angle in the wall mirror and preened happily, knowing she looked her best. It was not only Adriaen whom she would conquer with her beauty this evening, but every male in the room. She thought of Hans again and it grated on her anew that she had not yet summoned into his eyes the look of desire she was used to seeing in the eyes of other men. But why was she thinking "yet" when she wasn't going to see him again? She could not understand why it should be so galling that he had flirted with Francesca and not with her.

But this was no time to think about him. She was about to be betrothed to one of the richest and best-looking men in all Amsterdam. Already she had him at her feet. There was nothing he would deny her. Proudly she went from the room and down into the hall. Maria stood with Griet and Sijmon waiting to see her and they were full of praise and compliments.

Hendrick, waiting by the door and impatient that they should be on their way, nodded when she twirled for a general inspection. "Come,

Father," she said importantly, as if he had been the one keeping her waiting, and she sailed ahead of him out to the van Jansz coach.

She chatted happily to him on the way. He was also in the best of moods since hearing from her that, whatever Adriaen might have said yesterday, she was sure he would in time take note of her wish and those promissory notes would be handed over. Recently his hair had lost its last traces of ginger and had become completely snow white, which toned down his florid complexion and added to the distinguished air he had always had when conducting himself properly. Sybylla hoped that this evening he would be at his most charming and Adriaen's parents would forgive the scene he had made at Ludolf's table.

They had reached Heerengracht. A few bystanders had gathered by the van Jansz house to watch the well-dressed guests arrive. She alighted in the glow of candlelight from the open door. As she was about to mount the steps, Hans detached himself from the watching group and swept off his hat with its brilliant plume in a deep bow to her.

"I couldn't let this occasion pass without bringing you a gift," he said, handing her a tiny package.

Although taken aback, she was glad he should have seen her in her finery. "I thank you most sincerely."

She continued up into the house, her father exchanging a few jovial words with Hans before following after her. In the reception hall, even as her lace shawl was taken from her shoulders, she could not resist looking to discover what Hans had brought her. She unfolded the paper and there was a tiny pink sugar mouse. Unaccountably she was deeply moved by it, knowing it had been given out of goodwill and that it was all he could afford. She popped it quickly into the little silk pouch purse dangling on a cord from her wrist and went forward at her father's side to the chandelier-hung ballroom, where Heer and Vrouw van Jansz were receiving their guests. She could see Adriaen waiting for her.

It was an evening beyond her wildest dreams. She was feted and admired and—as she knew well enough—envied by all the younger women there. Adriaen in his coat and breeches of gold brocade, his fair hair gleaming to his shoulders, was her partner in the dancing more often than he should have been, but nobody could hold it against him on this special occasion that was their own.

The time came shortly before midnight when Sybylla and her father, together with Adriaen and his parents, went on their own into an adjacent drawing-room for the formal putting on of the betrothal ring. She held out her hand to Adriaen, her buffed nails shining like pearls, and he smiled fondly at her as he placed the fingers of his left hand under hers. Then with his right hand he took the ring from a little casket that his mother held for him and its ruby sparkled with a thousand lights as he slid the handsome jewel, set in gold and diamonds, onto her finger. It should have been the happiest moment in her life. But to her dismay she found herself remembering the pink sugar mouse which had been her first gift that evening and, thinking that excitement must be making her lose her reason, for a few crazy seconds she did not know which she valued most.

"My darling betrothed and my future wife." Adriaen was kissing her hand and dazedly she raised her lips for the kiss he placed on them.

"Dearest Adriaen!" She was herself again. What a glorious ring! She danced her fingers in the air and was dazzled by the ring's splendour. How fortunate she was! Even Vrouw van Jansz was being gracious to her, kissing her on the cheek and welcoming her into the family. Adriaen's father, who was not immune to her charms, which was almost like a secret shared between them, regarded her with the usual twinkle in his eyes and said how pleased he was that his son had chosen such a charming young woman. Hendrick, emotional as always, could hardly speak.

"I wish your mother could have been here," he said in a choked voice.

She nodded, but had the uncomfortable feeling that somehow Anna would not have approved. It was almost as if her mother were seeing through her again as in childhood when all her wiles had failed to deceive. Then she cast that thought from her, for the double doors were opening in readiness for the procession back into the ballroom. Heer van Jansz went first, clearing his throat for the formal announcement, and she and Adriaen followed, her hand on his raised wrist. Behind them came Hendrick escorting Vrouw van Jansz. The rest of the evening was a huge success.

When Sybylla came home, sated with triumph, she chatted inces-

santly to Griet, who had waited up to help her disrobe. But when she was in her night shift and on her own again she took the pink sugar mouse from the silk pouch purse and put it by her trinket box. There was something comical about it. She smiled and patted its head with a gentle fingertip before she remembered how it had ruined the actual moment of her betrothal. Angrily she snatched it up and went to the open window to hurl it as far as she could away from the house, but somehow she could not do it. She hesitated so long at the window that she began to shiver from the cool night air. Somewhat reluctantly she returned it to its place by the trinket box. Then, deliberately turning her back on it, she jumped into bed.

Francesca's stay at Haarlem Huis had reached its last evening. She had a stack of sketches that she had already packed and, dinner over, she and Pieter sat talking on a window seat. He had noticed that she had become increasingly thoughtful during the last few days and now she was almost pensive.

"What is it you have to say to me?" he prompted.

She raised eyes full of emotion. "We talked so glibly about living in Italy together, but there's one great obstacle that we haven't yet mentioned."

"What is that?"

"The fact that you belong here and nowhere else." She put her fingertips against his lips when he would have protested. "Hear me out. We've both known that for financial reasons alone you would have to keep on with this business, trusting in the honesty and capability of your manager. What's more, Dutch law couldn't touch you for breaking the marriage contract or my father fleeing his debts, which would leave you free to visit Holland sometimes, but that would never be enough for you."

"How can you be so sure?"

"Because now that I've seen all that you have here, your horticultural experiments, your orangeries, your bulb fields and all else that grips you to this land, I know you'd grow restless away from it."

"As you said, I can visit periodically," he reminded her.

"But travel is so difficult and hazardous with the complication of wars, the waylaying by thieves and murderers, privateers at sea and a host of other dangers, quite apart from the length of time that journeying takes. Circumstances might separate us for two or even three years. You need a wife and children here—a son to carry on after you."

"We'll have a son."

"One born on foreign soil, who would think of Florence as his home and Italian as his native tongue?"

"We could teach him to love all things Dutch and to know that Holland was his rightful place."

"But don't you realize what that would mean? There'd come a day when he'd insist on going back to Holland with you. Then neither you nor he would ever return!"

"Don't say that!" He caught her close to him. "I'd train him to take over here and then I'd return to you. We would never be parted again."

She thrust herself away from him. "But think of all those broken years before that happens. It would be no marriage between us. Only a series of interludes. Your suggestion that Father should leave with me for Florence has absolved you from making me your wife. Even if Ludolf should track me down the presence of Hendrick would be protection enough. Dutch law wouldn't stretch there to allow Ludolf to take him to court for debt and, free of that threat, Hendrick could dally over a marriage date indefinitely. In the meantime I'm sure that my Aunt Janetje's husband, who is a powerful man in Florence, would find a way to have Ludolf deported once and for all."

His face grew angry. "So you are reverting to your original decision never to marry!"

"It's not like that!" She sprang to her feet and moved to stand further away from him. "Yet I should never have let myself be swayed from it."

He had risen from the window seat and spoke with a wrathful and fiery bitterness. "So you would condemn me to an existence entirely without you! Has it not occurred to you that I would gladly take whatever time I can have with you, no matter how spasmodic, in preference to a lifetime of marriage with any other woman?"

"Do you suppose I don't feel the same with regard to any other man,

but I'm thinking of you! I can't in all fairness let you commit your life to me!"

He seized her by the arms and jerked her hard against him. "I made that commitment the first time we met. So it's too late to change now. We belong to each other, Francesca."

Her head fell back and there were tears glinting on her lashes. "Don't you care anything for your own good?" she asked helplessly.

"Naturally I do. That's why I don't intend to lose you. We shall love each other always."

Then he buried her mouth in his and she clung to him. Parting from him on the morrow would be the first of many such severances in the years ahead, but whenever they were together every moment would be as valued as it was now.

Later, in bed, drowsy after their lovemaking, she understood why her parents had found such sexual joy in making up their quarrels. Somehow everything was given a new dimension. Curled up in Pieter's sleeping embrace, she thought of the children she might bear in time to come when there was no longer any need to guard against conception. It must not count as any sacrifice on her part to let a son come to Holland. She would never deny her offspring his right to harvest on van Doorne land the most beauty-laden crops in the world.

In the morning, when Francesca was ready to leave, Pieter drove up in one of the market carts. Instead of just taking her to Haarlem to catch the stage wagon, as she had expected, he announced that he was going to drive her all the way to Delft.

They both appreciated the extra span of time together, she sitting beside him on the carter's seat. Towards noon rain began to fall and they took shelter in a derelict mill, where they ate the picnic that Vrouw Graff had prepared for them. Afterwards they climbed the wooden flights up to the top floor, where they looked out at the view. If Vermeer had been a painter of the open countryside the scene could have been his, for the rain had eased away and under a grey-blue sky there was a play of glorious light on wet grass and trees, hedgerows and canals, distant windmills and a single slow-moving barge garlanded with yellow and white tulips. She spoke of her notion to Pieter.

"So many of those cool colours are Master Vermeer's own and yet

they never chill on his canvas. Indeed in his paintings they warm the heart."

When she sensed that Pieter had begun to look at her more than at the view, she turned her head to meet his eyes, the pupils of her own softening and dilating with love. Gladly she lay down with him on the ancient, grain-strewn floorboards and he groaned aloud in an excess of passion for her.

When they left the mill, which had been their haven for a little while, they travelled on until, the hour becoming late, Pieter took a short detour to a village tavern, where they dined. Only the last lap of the journey remained. Delft came into sight when they reached the bridge where Constantijn had suffered his terrible injury and Francesca's thoughts went to him and Aletta. She believed that Aletta, although not yet realizing it, was in love with Constantijn. Perhaps their first meeting at the Exchange, brief and inconsequential though it had been, had instilled a sense of destiny in Aletta when she had seen him again in such tragically dramatic circumstances and she would never be free of it.

It was dark when Delft was reached. Pieter left the horse and cart at the end of Kromstraat and took advantage of the lack of any street lamps there to escort Francesca to her door.

"I don't want to leave you in this house," he said uneasily.

"You mean you don't want to leave me at all," she whispered teasingly.

"That's true, but you must take care."

"I will. You really must go now." She took her hand baggage from him. "We have had such a perfect time together."

"There will be other such times, my darling."

They exchanged a bittersweet kiss of parting. Then he stood back in the darkness while she opened the front door into the candlelit reception hall and went in. Nobody came to meet her. She took her hand baggage to her room but did not stop to unpack. In an upstairs parlour she found Clara with her foot on a stool, nursing a badly sprained ankle.

"It was such a foolish accident," Clara explained, wincing as she adjusted her foot slightly. "I tripped on a loose cobble in the street and went flying. See!" she added, pulling up her sleeve to reveal a badly

grazed and bruised arm. "I hurt myself everywhere. Geetruyd was cross with me for not looking where I was going."

"Where is she?"

"She's gone to a musical evening, which is why we dined early, but some dinner has been left for you."

"I'm not hungry, but I'd like some tea. Shall I bring you a cup?"

"That would be very pleasant. Bring yours too, and we'll drink it together."

"Are there any travellers staying at the moment?"

"One. I don't like it when they're here."

"Why not?" Francesca asked.

Clara had a ready answer, wagging a finger importantly to emphasize her words. "Geetruyd's never herself, always on edge, and then she snaps at me."

Downstairs again Francesca went along the corridor to the kitchen, where she found Weintje lolling against the courtyard door and giggling at something said by a young man making his departure. At her step the maidservant turned with a guilty start, not being allowed any dalliance during her hours of duty, but Francesca took no notice and ignored the evidence on the table of a meal for two having been eaten there. The young man went on his way and Weintje came at once to see what was wanted.

"Would you make a pot of tea for Juffrouw Clara and me?" Francesca requested. "I'll get the tray ready."

Weintje set about hurriedly as if expecting a reprimand at any moment, but when the tea was ready Francesca only thanked her and carried the tray away.

She had almost reached the stairs when the front door opened and the traveller entered the house. He was in his mid-thirties, thin and of average height. Francesca thought how easy it would be to sketch his features in a series of horizontal and vertical lines—straight mouth, brows and eyes, a nose sharp as an arrow and a square chin. He regarded her alertly, bowing slightly in greeting, but without a smile.

"Good evening," she said. "This tea is freshly made. Would you like a cup?"

"I thank you, *mejuffrouw*, but no." He unlocked the door of his room and went into it.

Francesca and Clara drank two cups each of the tea. As always when Geetruyd was not present Clara chatted almost without drawing breath. She fired questions at Francesca about her time in Amsterdam and asked about the betrothal party. Francesca, who had expected this problem, immediately launched into a detailed description of Sybylla's dress and style of hairdressing, by which time Clara's interest had waned and she began recounting all the mundane little things that had happened during the period of Francesca's absence. Her talk hopped from one subject to another and she returned again to Geetruyd's attitude towards her when anything went wrong.

"When the traveller who is staying here now arrived two days ago, Geetruyd became sharper than ever with me, because I can't do anything to help at the present time. I don't know why she bothers having any guests, except you, of course, Francesca, for it isn't as if she needed the money. She has an income from some other source, but what it is I don't know and wouldn't dare ask."

"She certainly likes the best of everything," Francesca said, thinking of the good wines, the food and the quality of Geetruyd's clothes and footwear.

Clara was enjoying herself. The opportunities for confidential chit-chat were normally denied her, as her benefactress's long-held threat of sending her to an almshouse if she gossiped had always had the double effect of keeping her silent and making her fearful of having friends in case she made a slip of the tongue. The fact that Francesca lived under a similar shadow of possible incarceration for any indiscretion made Clara feel there was a bond between them and because of that she could speak freely.

"I'm not stupid," she stated rebelliously, "even if Geetruyd should think so. When I first came to live here she was filling the house with anybody who could afford to pay for a good bed and wholesome food, but it was still a struggle for her to make ends meet. We had to observe countless small economies. She even sold kitchen scraps to a pig breeder and woe betide me if I threw away as much as an apple pip. We didn't live well in those days, but I made no complaint then and none now.

She did what she could for me." Clara lowered her voice conspiratorially, although there was nobody except Francesca to hear. "If Geetruyd only made a modest living with a house full of guests, how is she able to live well—even extravagantly—by letting a room occasionally?"

"I think it proves your point that she has another income."

Clara looked triumphant. "Right! I believe Heer van Deventer made an investment for her when they met again after some years and now it's paying off on a grand scale."

"Then why does she still have the inconvenience of lodgers in the house? Is it to maintain a front of genteel poverty?"

"I suppose so, but there's something else too. She likes to talk to them about their travels, however often they come. I think it's because she's never really been anywhere herself."

"How do you know this?"

"She has told me. I once dared to say to her that it was indiscreet to stay talking to men on their own when she took in their meals. She pointed out that she always left the door slightly ajar and anyone could hear it was only an interesting and respectable interlude."

Francesca, remembering how Geetruyd had raised her voice on that one occasion, thought how at that hour Clara and Weintje were both in their beds and out of earshot. "Have you ever met any of those travellers?"

"I've bidden them good day or good night, but nothing more." Clara wanted to finish with that line of conversation, because she had a question pent up in her that she had long wanted to ask Francesca. She had never had a romance herself, although she had come near it once with a quiet-natured carpenter who had been repairing windows and replacing rotten shutters on the house. They used to talk, she indoors and he on his ladder outside. Then he made the mistake of bringing her a posy of flowers from his garden one day and asking her out. Geetruyd had dismissed him, saying his work was not good enough, and another carpenter had finished the tasks. As if that were not enough, Geetruyd had poured scorn on Clara that she, at the age of forty, should have behaved like a lovesick girl. The flowers had been tossed away by Geetruyd, who had failed to notice that one pansy had fallen to the floor. Clara had retrieved it and pressed it in her Bible between two pieces of paper, where she had it still. The carpenter had died of lung trouble eighteen months later and it was her heartfelt regret that she had not been his wife to nurse him gently to the end. She felt that disappointment in love increased the bond between her and Francesca. "Were you very sad, Francesca, when you were banned from seeing Pieter van Doorne?"

Francesca looked down, smiling inwardly. "That's months ago now. So much has happened since." There was only one way to stem any more such questions from Clara. She looked up again. "Has Geetruyd not told you what she must surely have heard from Ludolf van Deventer? It is that my father has promised me in marriage to him."

"That can't be true!" Clara's face had become a mask of almost panic-stricken dismay.

"It is, and nobody wishes more than I that it was otherwise."

"But Geetruyd will go mad if she finds out! You must never let her know all the time you are staying here." Clara was highly agitated. "She's expecting to marry him herself!"

Francesca stared at her incredulously, not through any question of why Geetruyd should wish to marry again, but because it was a revelation that the relationship between Ludolf and Geetruyd was close enough for the woman to have considered the possibility. "She is far more suited to him than I am, but how do you know her feelings?"

"I know her so well that all the signs are clear. I remember her excitement when they met again after a number of years when he had been travelling abroad. After that it was never quite the same, maybe because he married someone else, but she loves money and he has plenty. It's very important to her and recently, since he became a widower, she has let slip a word or two without realizing it that shows she doesn't expect it to be long before she's living away from here and in luxury." All Clara's agitation returned in full force. "So don't, I beg you, tell of this marriage that has been arranged for you. She will make the rest of your time unbearable with every kind of pettiness. It is how she treats me whenever she is under strain or something has gone against her."

"What of you when I have left here?"

Clara let her hands rise and fall meekly. "She needs me in the house,

because she never likes to be wholly on her own." She winced as she lowered her foot from the stool to the floor. "Would you help me to bed now, Francesca? I'm in such pain that it wearies me."

Francesca helped her hobble into a smaller and less used parlour where a temporary bed had been made up on a day couch to save her the extra stairs. They bade each other good night and Francesca went to her own room. It saddened her anew that Clara should lead such a bleak life. How often gentle people fell under the control of bullies, either in marriage or in business as well as in other spheres. In return they gave loyalty and sacrificed themselves.

Before undressing, Francesca drew the face of the traveller, capturing his likeness in a minimum of lines before putting the drawing away with other work for the studio. She was in bed when she heard Weintje go up to her attic room. Not long after, Geetruyd came home. As Francesca had expected, she opened the door to look in on her and check that she had returned on the day arranged.

"So you're safely back from Amsterdam, Francesca. Did you bring me a letter from your father rescinding any of my rules of chaperonage?"

"No."

"There! What did I tell you? He has your well-being totally at heart and knows, as I do, that a strict hand is all-important until a daughter is wed, whether or not there is a young man on the horizon. Now good night to you."

In the morning Weintje escorted Francesca to Mechelin Huis. The maidservant was very amiable and seemed to think she should reciprocate the good turn Francesca had done her by ignoring her dalliance the previous evening.

"Now if there is any letter you want posted, or if there's anyone you want to meet on your way to or from the studio, you can trust me not to say anything."

"That's very obliging of you, Weintje, but—no."

"Well, remember what I've said. I'd have lost my free time indefinitely if you had told Vrouw Wolff about my beau."

"Are you going to marry him?"

"He hasn't asked me yet, but I'm hoping."

Jan and Catharina Vermeer welcomed Francesca back and the

younger children were as excited to see her again as if she had been away for months. Jan looked through all her sketches with her and together they decided which she should extend into a painting. She returned to him the portrait of the unnamed model, and he took the "tronie" away to his gallery. Before restarting her own work she studied his painting of the local woman by the virginals and saw that during her absence he had completed only one small section of the heavy lace on the woman's sleeve, but each precise stroke had been done meticulously to emphasize its silky texture. Then she cut a length from a roll of canvas for herself and began to thread it onto a wooden stretcher.

With Clara still unable to walk, Weintje accompanied Francesca when she took her first opportunity to see Aletta a few days after her return to Delft. At the gates her sister turned a key in the lock to let her in, but shook her head at the maidservant.

"I'm sorry, Weintje," Aletta said, "but I have only gained permission to admit my sister and nobody else."

"That's all right," Weintje replied cheerfully. "I've friends at a farm only a quarter of a mile away. I'll come back whenever Juffrouw Francesca wants me to be here."

It was agreed that she should return in three hours and she went off with an eager step. Francesca laced her arm in Aletta's as they crossed the forecourt of the house together.

"This is indeed a concession, Aletta. Is Constantijn being kinder towards you?"

"He's still extremely difficult," Aletta admitted, "but he took notice when I said I would go into Delft for a whole day once a week to be with you if he didn't permit me to offer you hospitality the next time you came. He can't bear the thought of my being away from the house, because he is afraid that I won't come back. He has also finally agreed to see his parents for the first time since he shut himself away here."

"I think you're making progress."

"In some ways, although not in others. He still gets drunk as much to challenge me as to relieve boredom. I've looked everywhere in his apartment for his secret store of drink several times over, but always without success."

"Perhaps it's in a neighbouring room."

4
5
6

Aletta shook her head. "Nothing would make him go outside that sanctuary he has created for himself. Some of his friends—those with whom he used to hunt and race and sail—come regularly in twos and threes, hoping to see him. They climb onto the gates, enraging Josephus and the dogs, while they cup their hands around their mouths and shout to Constantijn to stop being a hermit and so forth. He doesn't hear them, because his apartment is on the park side of the house, and it wouldn't make any difference if he did. He gets irrational fears. One is that the most staunch and determined of his friends will one day get together and make a concentrated sortie on the house to get through to him."

"Is this likely?"

"No. They would have done it already if that had been their motive. I think they come only to cheer him and to show that as far as they are concerned nothing has changed, hoping that eventually he will overcome his needless shame of his handicap."

"I like their attitude."

"So do I, although he is always ill at ease when he knows they've been at the gates. He sits with a spyglass to his eye like a seaman, scanning the park from the window. One night he roused the whole household with his shouting and ringing of his bell. When we arrived in his room he said his friends were coming with lanterns through the distant trees, but of course there was nothing to see. He's done that twice since. Now I've told Sara to stay in her bed and only Josephus and I go to him."

"Is it when he has been drinking?"

"It wasn't the first time, but probably on the second and third occasions."

They had reached the kitchen. Sara had gone shopping in Delft and they could talk on their own. Aletta poured milk into two glasses and they ate a slice each of a newly baked open tart of dried apricots, raisins and apples with a topping of caramelled almonds. Francesca handed over the gold bracelet from Aunt Janetje, and Aletta, delighted with it, tried it on at once.

"It's beautiful!" She held out her arm to admire it on her wrist. "Is yours the same?"

"No." Francesca displayed hers. "All three had different designs."

Aletta sighed with pleasure. "Aunt Janetje has always sent us lovely gifts." Carefully she removed the bracelet from her wrist and put it away in its little casket. "I can't wear it when I'm working."

"Is there ever a time in this house when you're not working?"

Aletta gave a little laugh. "Only when I'm sleeping. Now tell me all about home."

Francesca was uncertain whether or not to tell Aletta the whole wretched story when she had so many difficulties of her own to contend with, but her sister must know sooner or later and this was a time when they could be sure of being alone. She began with the good news that there was no deterioration in Hendrick's hands and a description of Griet's wedding, following with an account of the disastrous dinner party in Ludolf's house, the revelation of the hold that evil man held over their father, the marriage contract Hendrick had been forced to sign and finally her reasons for not attending the betrothal party.

Aletta's shock and distress were severe. She exclaimed over such misfortune happening to both her father and her sister. "But—Pieter," she said finally, "you—and—Pieter. Can't he do something?"

"I spent five wonderful days with him at Haarlem Huis," Francesca told her, "and he has plans as to how this terrible situation can be averted." She did not mention Italy. Aletta was so badly shaken it would have been cruel to add to her anxiety and grief by any suggestion they might be separated from each other for many years.

When Constantijn's bell rang, Aletta rose automatically from where she was sitting. "I'll be back in a second," she promised as she went from the kitchen.

On her way to Constantijn's room she could hear him playing the lute. Recently they had begun impromptu concerts together, she playing the clavichord in the anteroom and Constantijn the viol or the lute, both of which he played quite well. He also had a good singing voice, but so far he had only sung in her hearing when drunk.

"Sit down and listen," he said cheerfully as soon as she entered the room. "I've composed a new melody and I've jotted it down on paper. You can copy it out neatly later."

"My sister is here and I can't leave her, but if I left both doors of the apartment open she could listen from the stairs while I am here." She had said it all in one breath to stop any interruption.

He frowned, not pleased. "How long is she staying?"

"About another two hours."

There was a pause before he spoke again. "She must remain at the bottom of the flight."

"I'll tell her."

In the reception hall Francesca stood by the newel post, hoping the music was proving a distraction to her sister, as the notes of the melody floated pleasingly down to her. When the last note was played she heard Aletta pick up the melody again on the clavichord and then the lute struck up once more in accompaniment through to the end.

Upstairs Aletta rose from her seat at the clavichord and applauded Constantijn's composition with enthusiasm. "Why not write some lyrics too?" she suggested eagerly. "The melody is ideal for a love song."

"Is it?" he said bitterly. Before she could stop him he tore up the sheet of music he had written and crumpled the pieces into a ball, which he tossed fiercely out of the window.

"I'm going downstairs to my sister," she said quietly.

Francesca saw at once by her face that something had happened. "Was I the cause?" she asked anxiously.

Aletta shook her head. "No. There are a thousand ways to hurt him and I seem to blunder in on most of them. He threw his composition into the garden and I'm going outside to find it."

"I'll come with you."

"No, wait here. I can judge whereabouts to look."

She found the pieces scattered in a rose bed and knelt on the earth until she had retrieved every one. She returned to the kitchen and talked quietly with Francesca until Weintje returned. Later, in her own room before going to bed, she put the scraps together painstakingly and copied out the music onto a fresh sheet of paper. When the ink was dry she put it away in a drawer with the bracelet from Aunt Janetje and a few other things she treasured.

In spite of the shock and distress she had suffered so recently, sleep

came soon, her last conscious thoughts being that Pieter van Doorne with his love and determination would surely save her sister from the life of misery with which she was threatened.

CHAPTER 20

When the day of Heer and Vrouw de Veere's visit arrived, Constantijn insisted that Aletta stay in the room after admitting them. He had been morose ever since he had thrown his music out of the window, unpredictable in his whims and demands.

"But they will want to talk to you privately," she protested.

"I want you to be present. Is that understood?"

She had hoped to give his parents a little tactful advice when they arrived, but she had no chance. His mother rushed into the house and up to his apartment. There she promptly burst into tears at the sight of him, crying out that he was her poor helpless boy. As if that were not enough, her husband, obviously primed by her, tried to persuade him to come and live at their country house where he could receive the full care that he deserved.

"We've had a waist-high, pulpit-shaped screen made," his mother told him proudly, "and then you can be present at all social functions at our house without the least embarrassment about—anything."

"About the loss of my legs, Mother?" Constantijn said woodenly. "Is that what you mean?"

"Well, yes. Don't you think that's a splendid idea?"

Aletta despaired privately at such a demoralizing item being made and contrasted it in her own mind with the gift she had commissioned Josephus to make for him. She watched Constantijn becoming whiter and more wild-eyed as the visit dragged on. His face became desperate when his father said that two of the coach servants would be coming upstairs at any minute to carry him down to the waiting equipage.

"I've chosen where I want to live and there's an end to it!" Constantijn was afraid he was to be removed by well-intentioned force. Then he saw that Aletta had moved in front of the door as if to show she would never allow it and he became calmer. His parents left the apartment soon afterwards, disappointed and subdued. Aletta, following to show them out, was deeply saddened that the two people closest to Constantijn should have the least understanding of his mental torment. As they were about to go from the house she made a suggestion.

"There is something you can do for your son."

"What is that?" Vrouw de Veere implored, her eyes wet, for she had shed tears again when her son had kissed her farewell.

"We'll do anything," her husband endorsed.

"Last week I asked Josephus if he would make in his workshop two wooden stump legs with straps for your son and he was pleased to take on the task. He will attach two wooden feet and I have given him a pair of your son's shoes so that the feet can be of the right size and shape to be covered by his hose and footwear. I'm sewing the soft padding for the thigh cups, but perhaps you would like to provide a pair of crutches?"

Vrouw de Veere looked alarmed. "I've seen men manage with one stump leg but never with two." She pressed a hand against her chest in frantic anxiety, shaking her head. "Josephus must be stopped in that task at once! My son would fall! Perhaps kill himself if he fell against anything sharp! Oh no!"

But Heer de Veere was looking intently at Aletta. "He shall have those crutches. When will the stump legs be ready?"

"Quite soon." Aletta knew that Josephus also had the wood prepared for the crutches, but it was better for Constantijn, as well as his parents, if they contributed to the gift. "But I can't say the same for your son. He needs more time yet. I'll not give him the legs until I know the moment is right."

Even as she spoke she wondered how Heer de Veere would accept her taking charge, but he did not query her authoritative tones. "We'll leave the matter to your discretion and in the meantime I'll see that the best crutches I can have made are delivered here. What are the measurements?"

"I have them here." She took a piece of paper from her pocket and

handed it to him. He thanked her and then put a comforting arm about his wife's shoulders as he escorted her, still weeping, to their coach.

Constantijn drank himself into a stupor that night and was ill for two days afterwards. Irritable and gloomy, his parents' visit having set him back into a state of lethargy, he had no patience for either cards or backgammon. A half-finished game of chess on the table beside him was knocked to the floor when she suggested that they play it through. She could see he had withdrawn into himself again and was virtually back where he had started as far as taking an interest in anything was concerned. It would be doubly hard this time to draw him into life again, even to the point that he had reached before, but she was never going to give in.

As the balmy spring lengthened into summer her hopes of getting him to go out into the gardens came to nothing. He would sit on the balcony, but that was all, too sunk into shame over his helplessness to risk even a gardener seeing him from a distance. All that held his attention was the newspapers and Josephus had to buy a number of publications for him every week. Aletta, who read them when Constantijn had finished with them, discussed and argued political affairs with him.

It was a summer of unrest with many demonstrations throughout Holland in favour of the Prince of Orange being given leadership, a move that Constantijn supported. Being young himself, he wanted to see youth at the helm, and Aletta was in agreement. The fact that they were both Orangists created one bridge between them. But in the ancient Parliament buildings in The Hague, de Witt and the other politicians were resisting public pressure, more concerned with how to meet peaceably Louis XIV's exorbitant demands than listening to the voice of the people.

Since Aletta never went into town she had to get Josephus to make a purchase for her at an artist's supplier. Then she set to work to make a sketch pad as she had been taught long ago in her childhood days in her father's studio. When it was done she took it the next morning with a selection of reed pens and some coloured inks to Constantijn's apartment. He was always bathed and dressed before he breakfasted and he was still at the table when she entered after leaving what she had

brought with her in the anteroom. They talked as she cleared the table and he was in quite an amiable mood.

"I've made something that should interest you," she said, carrying the tray out to the anteroom. Then she returned to him with the sketching materials and set them down in front of him. "I know you appreciate art and have an eye for perspective and so I thought you might like to create a few sketches of your own."

He put his head on one side and regarded her with faint amusement. "That's most kind. You never tire in trying to chase my boredom away. I welcome your gift. You shall teach me to draw."

She was alarmed, for that had not been her intention at all. "You told me once that you used to sketch at school and so you've had some tuition. You don't need mine."

"But I do. You are the expert."

"What do you mean?" She was flustered.

"On your first day here you boasted to me that on one occasion in your father's studio you had been set to draw a beggar without legs. Am I to believe that wasn't in some routine of lessons in the technique of drawing and painting that you received? It certainly wasn't a subject plucked at random, was it?"

"Well, no," she admitted reluctantly. He had probed into her home background many times during their conversations, but she had never let him know of her once cherished aim to be an artist herself. Often when they had had these talks she had had a restless night afterwards, dreaming that she was painting again, only to awake to the plain walls of her room and her servant life with old wounds reopened. "But you forget I have no time for teaching. It cannot be hurried and I can't leave Sara to the heavier chores."

He saw she had seized on the only excuse available. "Will you at least give me advice and criticism?"

"I'll do that. Why not start with the view from the balcony?" She opened the glass doors wide.

"Yes, I will." His chair was already facing the view, as he liked to eat looking out across the park. He chose one of the pens, uncorked a bottle of ink and then gazed at the open sketchbook in front of him. "A blank space is daunting."

4
6
3

"That's why artists in their training like to get a ground onto their canvas as quickly as possible. Start with the horizon. Choose to make it high or low, but not straight across the middle."

She left him to his new pastime. By noon he had made a passable sketch that showed he was more able than he made out. From that time onwards, except when a bleak mood was on him and he would do nothing, he sketched quite regularly, she setting up still-life arrangements for him. When time permitted, Sara and Josephus took turns with her in sitting for him. At first it was emotionally painful for her to correct or demonstrate his mistakes, for it meant taking a pen into her own hand, but gradually that eased away and she managed to keep detached from his work since never once did he ask her to make a sketch of her own. It made her wonder if for all his quarrelling and taunting he was more sensitive to her feelings than he ever showed.

Francesca had not seen Pieter since they had parted at Geetruyd's door after her return from Haarlem with him. It was now late August and Ludolf was presently staying in Delft, his third visit since June, and she knew he would be waiting to escort her back to Kromstraat when she had finished her day's work. He would be taking Weintje's place as escort, for Clara's ankle had never come to rights again, showing that the original injury had been more than a sprain, and she walked with a limp, only able to go short distances without pain.

Jan had been painting beside Francesca that afternoon, and it was he who reminded her she had been working long past her time. "You started at seven-thirty this morning and ten hours is more than enough for one day."

"I stopped at noon to eat," she replied, "and a drink of tea twice."

"Anybody would think you didn't want to go back to Kromstraat," he joked, knowing how she disliked the company of the arrogant individual who had tried to buy off her apprenticeship.

She made an amused grimace. "Ludolf goes back to Amsterdam in the morning."

"So you'll be at our musical evening tomorrow?"

"I will! I shall be feeling free as a bird again!"

Outside she found Ludolf pacing up and down, for he would not step into premises where he considered he had been insulted by an ignorant artist. "You're late today, Francesca."

"I forget everything when I'm working."

"Naturally," he amended quickly. "That is to be commended. In any case it is a pleasure to wait for you."

She fumed inwardly. Why did he have to be so ingratiating? She found it unnatural and sickening. Crushing down her exasperation, she reminded him she still had much to learn during the next nine months. "I shall be submitting my work to the Guild at a sitting of the Committee, which will probably be held in April. I hope to receive my membership next May when I have completed my two-year apprenticeship with Jan Vermeer."

He began expressing his certainty that she would gain her membership easily, although he had seen nothing of her work since her portrait of him. On these walks it was impossible to have a reasonable conversation with him. He seemed to be intoxicated by being with her. She had never lied to him or made any false promises to ease her own escape from him, and neither would she do so now, but it was puzzling that he should be so infatuated that he seemed unaware of anything but his own desires when he was in her company. Once he had asked her why she had never told Geetruyd about the marriage contract.

"I can't speak easily about a matter that is abhorrent to my whole concept of freedom." Her truthful reply had not pleased him, but he appeared satisfied with her reticence.

She sighed inwardly as he began pressing her again for a marriage date. "No, Ludolf. I've told you several times that I won't discuss anything that lies beyond what I need to achieve from my time in Delft. Even after I've gained my Guild membership I shall need some time in Amsterdam with my father before I can arrange the changes that are to take place in the future."

"Very well. You're teaching me a lesson in patience that I've never had to learn before."

She looked at him out of the corner of her eye. Such a mild reply would never have come from him in the past, but he had become increasingly weak in his obsession for her, which would make him many

times more dangerous if he should realize that he was going to lose her. Sometimes he reminded her of a cowed dog grovelling for a titbit from the table when he looked at her, hungry for a love she could never give. Having secured her as his wife-to-be, as he believed, it was no longer enough for him and probably never had been, and throughout his summer visits she had seen this gradual change in him. Not that he did not show his displeasure when his temper flared. If it were possible to prefer him in any mood it was better when he was his normal, arrogant self.

As they came to Geetruyd's house she knew that once again he would be attentive to the woman just as he was to her. After what Clara had said about Geetruyd hoping to marry him, Francesca had been able to see that, for some obscure reason of his own, he was stringing the woman along with compliments and deep conversations as if she alone held his interest. Quite apart from Geetruyd's persistent chaperonage, Francesca felt she had a second shield against Ludolf through this front he was keeping up with the woman. She was certain that he intended Geetruyd should know nothing of the marriage contract until the wedding he was anticipating was about to take place.

That evening two regents and a regentess called unexpectedly to see Geetruyd on some urgent matter. Showing them into another parlour, she thought that Clara, who was limping along the corridor, was about to join Francesca and Ludolf in the room she had just left. Instead, Ludolf having swiftly closed the door, Clara limped past to the small parlour that was still her bedchamber, wanting to rest her ankle.

Francesca had risen quickly to her feet, for Ludolf was advancing on her. "I think Clara is supposed to be here. I'll call her."

"Let her be. I thought we were never going to have a minute to ourselves!" His expression alarmed her, for he looked almost ill with passion.

She moved swiftly, but he was quicker, reaching out an arm to hook her about the waist and hurl her into his embrace. Then his mouth was on hers, forcing open her lips, his tongue threatening to choke her. She felt as if she were being eaten alive, helpless as a doll in his grip, and her abhorrence of him soared as he thrust his hand into her bodice to squeeze her breast until she thought she would faint with the pain. He

seemed totally out of his mind, months of restraint released into this awful encounter. She flailed her arms wildly, hoping to seize something within reach with which to strike him. The back of her hand hit against a glazed surface. The next second there was a resounding crash as a Delft pot smashed into smithereens on the floor.

He let her go as if he had been shot. A few yards away a door opened at once and Geetruyd's footsteps came hurrying towards the parlour as he drew back from Francesca, an elated expression on his face. The obsessional look in his eyes terrified her. He did not seem sane.

"I can't wait for you any longer! Come back with me to Amsterdam!"

Geetruyd had reached the door and she flung it open. She had not heard what he had said, but she took in the situation at a glance. "What happened to one of my best pots?" she exclaimed almost hysterically.

Her voice had a sobering effect on him. "My fault entirely," he said carelessly. "I'll buy you another."

"But it was an antique and I was particularly fond of it." Geetruyd was determined to make the most of the situation. He should pay her far more than the measly pot was worth to get on the right side of her again. She looked calmly at Francesca's taut face as if she did not notice the crooked neckline and the crumbled collar. "Go and chat with my guests, would you? I must clear this mess up at once, because I had thought to serve tea for them and the three of us here quite shortly."

"Yes, of course." Francesca hurried thankfully from the room, closing the door after her.

Geetruyd turned to Ludolf with her hands on her hips. "Up to your tricks again, you lecher!"

He grinned, himself again, and pinched her chin playfully. "You should be glad to have such a virile lover. If ever I lost interest in flirting with a pretty girl it would be a bad sign."

She struck his hand away. "What you do in Amsterdam or elsewhere is not my concern, but, as I told you before, I will not have any girl molested by you all the time she is in my charge. And that pot was very expensive."

He was not deceived, knowing her mercenary nature only too well. "I've said I'd pay for it, but as you're upset about its loss I want to give

you a string of pearls or perhaps a diamond pendant to make up. Which would you like?"

She looked him straight in the eye. "I'll have both," she said bluntly.

He bought them from a jeweller before he left Delft. In her bed-chamber Geetruyd looked at the gifts with intense satisfaction. The pearls gleamed and the splendid diamond pendant sparkled handsomely, each gift in its own velvet-lined casket. If war should come—and the rising unrest of the populace against France suggested strongly that it might—jewellery would not lose its value as money might. It did not matter to her that she could not wear in public the jewels that Ludolf had given her from time to time, because each piece was a security better than any bond.

As she put them away in a safe place she considered the incident that had resulted in this gain. She had seen on Ludolf's first visit during Francesca's stay that he was greatly taken with the young woman. There was nothing unusual in that and it might have been a long-standing attraction, but on his subsequent visits he had gradually re-vealed himself to be totally besotted by her. This last time it was like a sickness on him. He watched hungrily for a door to open when Fran-cesca was expected in a room. He looked hangdog whenever she went to bed early, not having the wit to see she could barely tolerate his presence. Her cool politeness was in reality a scream of loathing at his lustful glances, his inability to refrain from touching her on the arm or hand or waist at every opportunity. Whereas one woman could always sense another woman's attitude, men in their puffed-up male conceit failed to pick up the signals. Ludolf was also one of those men to whom female hostility was an incitement to passion. Geetruyd knew from her own experience that in bed he was at his most savage and exultant whenever he met opposition to one of his unpleasant whims.

She regarded herself in a mirror and smoothed her fingertips over her temples, carefully checking that she did not have a hair out of place. It had never occurred to her until comparatively recently that Ludolf was behind the instructions she had been given for the protection of Fran-cesca. She could see now how Hendrick Visser, anxious to please his rich patron, would be totally influenced by Ludolf's suggestions as to how to keep Francesca from harm in a new town and surroundings

away from friends and family. Suppose—just suppose—Ludolf had long had it in his mind to marry Francesca after she had completed her apprenticeship. But the girl would never agree! Yet a daughter's disagreement with such a decision held no substance when parents had made up their minds. She herself knew that only too well from the fate of the girls who had been in her charge as well as from her own youthful experience. Then she straightened her shoulders. She was letting a foolish notion run away with her. Ludolf had not changed in the least towards her and when she had brought herself to speak out about their marrying as soon as Holland was subjugated to France he had not discouraged her. Quite the opposite. Once or twice it had been as if they were young again with all their hopes pinned on the demise of her husband as now they awaited the spoils of Louis XIV's victory.

Once again Francesca was able to settle to work without the shadow of Ludolf's presence in Delft looming over her. Pieter was coming to see her during Delft's annual kermis in September, a week of festivities when people from all walks of life rubbed shoulders in the general merriment. Last year she had been allowed a day off from the studio to enjoy the Delft kermis with the Vermeer children, but this year she would be with the man she loved. Jan was letting her borrow a mask and a red cloak from the atelier chest and with her hair covered by the hood she could be with Pieter without fear of recognition.

She counted the days as preparations for the kermis began to take place. Booths, tents and stalls were being set up in the market square and along the streets. There would be plays and concerts, archery contests and other sports, games of chance, processions, dances and fireworks as well as special entertainments for the children.

On the opening day people came early into town from miles around and a large crowd congregated for the procession of the local militia into the square. The Vermeers took up a position outside their own house where the children could stand at the front, Francesca helping to shepherd the youngest of them while Rina took her hand and remained at her side. Catharina had made them all little banners to wave, includ-

ing Francesca, and Beatrix jumped up and down with excitement as she waited for the procession to appear.

Fifes and drums, combined with the blare of long-stemmed trumpets, heralded the approach of the militia. Then came the standard-bearer in pumpkin-yellow brocade embroidered in gilt thread and sashed with orange silk, white plumes in his sweeping hat. He carried the standard in such a way that it whirled dramatically, although the air was mild and still with no breeze. Behind him marched the officers and men in all their finery. Cheers resounded around the square and Beatrix ran forward to join with the children running alongside them, Francesca and Rina rushing to keep abreast of her to make sure she did not get lost in a crush of people afterwards.

After returning the two girls back into their mother's care, Francesca and Jan went back indoors. He had stocked up his gallery with paintings and etchings over the past weeks and would have a busy time throughout the kermis, for people would be in a spending mood. She, as an apprentice, would have one day off on the morrow.

Next morning the highlight was to be a procession of the Guilds, in which Jan was taking part. He went off in his best coat and breeches of dark blue velvet to muster near the Old Church. Francesca in her mask watched from the studio window until she saw Pieter come to stand near Mechelin Huis at the end of the row of trees that divided off the square from the surrounds of the New Church. Then she hastened from the house by way of the gallery and ran joyously into Pieter's embrace. Nobody in the merry, milling throng paid them any attention. There was so much to see and to do. Vendors shouted out their wares or their entertainments in rhyme, which were often comic and brought forth roars of laughter. Pieter was not masked, but many were in carnival costumes and Francesca in her mask did not receive a second glance. They were able to join in the country dances together, watch a drama, eat and drink and try out their luck at various competitions. Once they saw Clara, a lonely little figure, who had limped painfully from Kromstraat to see the festivities in the square.

"I only wish we could let her join us for a little while," Francesca said after pointing her out to Pieter. "She has such a wretched time under Geetruyd's thumb, but I mustn't let her recognize me."

"She does look sad there on her own. Just wait here for me." He darted to a pedlar selling posies and bought one. Making his way through the crowd to where Clara stood, he swept off his hat, bowed and kissed her hand. Then as the little woman stared at him in blushing astonishment, he presented her with the posy, behaviour quite in order at a kermis, when it was acceptable to pay respectful tribute to any woman. As he left her Clara stared dazedly after him, a smile wreathing her face. He put his arm around Francesca, drawing her deeper into the crowd.

"I'm glad you did that," she said happily. "You've made Clara's day as wonderful as ours."

During the afternoon they left the festivities and walked out into the countryside, where for a little while she was able to remove her mask and let the hood fall back from her hair. They lay in the tall grass together and renewed their love for each other.

"When shall we meet again?" he asked as they wended their way back to the town.

"In Amsterdam when I go home for Christmas. Sybylla's marriage to Adriaen is to take place then."

"That's a long time to wait."

"The weeks will pass quickly. I have to be more careful than ever now that Geetruyd should not suspect we're seeing each other."

"Yes, it would be disastrous if incarceration stopped your gaining Guild membership at this late stage."

"It's not only that!" She halted and pressed herself close to him, throwing her arms about his neck. "Ludolf would hear of it and I'm terrified he might kill you!"

He put his hands on her waist, looking guardedly into her face. "Whatever makes you think he would go to such extreme measures?"

"He's so mad for me that I think jealousy might drive him to the most desperate deed. No normal man would have used such means as he did to snare me as a wife. I've given him nothing but rebuffs, made it plain that I'm not a willing participant in that contract and all I want is to be free of him, but still he will not let me go. It's a sickness. He's so obsessed that sometimes I wonder if he really sees me as an individual

anymore, but as some prize that he would maim or murder for if the need arose!"

Her head drooped forward against him and he stroked the nape of her neck with his fingertips, thinking how all unknowingly she had accurately summed up the character of the man who had already murdered once and most probably twice. "You mustn't ever be afraid for me. Remember, I'm a militiaman and trained to both attack and defend with my sword and pistol. Put all your fears at rest as far as I'm concerned."

She looked up anxiously at him again. "Nevertheless, we must take no more risks. I wouldn't have dared to meet you today if I hadn't been masked."

"Then it's farewell now until December," he said ruefully.

"It is, my dearest love."

When they reached the town they parted where they had met by the row of trees. She returned the mask and cloak to the atelier chest before she walked back to Kromstraat with Weintje through all the festive trappings of the kermis, where coloured lanterns and bright flares added to the general enchantment of the scene. Her thoughts followed Pieter riding back through the night, the bulb-selling season being in full swing and demanding his presence at Haarlem Huis just as his land would always draw him back.

Clara came with the posy to show her, full of it being a gift from a dashing stranger. "I wish you could have seen him, Francesca."

"I'm so pleased he singled you out."

Geetruyd, who was within hearing, sniffed contemptuously. "I expect the posy had been refused by every other woman at the kermis."

Clara's eyes filled with tears at the hurtful gibe. "That's not true! He was being courteous to me because I was on my own, not for any other reason. He could have given the posy to any one of the pretty girls there and not been spurned. As a matter of fact, he had his own sweetheart. I saw them together and the posy could have been hers if he had wished it, but he had bought her something else. I saw them earlier at one of the stalls."

"What made you notice them?" Francesca asked gently.

"The way they kissed as if they were alone on an island instead of

being in the midst of hundreds of people." There was a wistful note in Clara's voice.

Geetruyd had come up to her. "You should know better than to watch such abandoned behaviour in public!"

"There were plenty of other sweethearts kissing and cuddling," Clara retorted with unusual spirit. "It always happens at a kermis."

"That's why I disapprove of such roistering. The kermis is a tradition that should be abolished." Her glare silenced any further expression of personal opinion by Clara, who went meekly to her room to return her posy to a vase of water.

Francesca also went to her own room. There she gazed again at the ring Pieter had bought her at the stall. It was just a pretty bauble, but its significance went deep.

Constantijn looked at Aletta from under his brows as she dealt the cards for a game they were about to play. "Why haven't you been to the kermis?"

"I wouldn't go without you," she replied crisply.

He was taken aback. "What do you mean?"

"Only that I would have enjoyed it if you had had the courage to escort me." She was trying a tactic now of goading him in the hope of it having some good effect. The weeks since his parents' visit had been painful in the extreme.

"Huh!" he shouted derisively, sorting his cards. "What a spectacle that would have made! You could have put me in the tent for the freaks and gone off to enjoy yourself in the dances and games."

She lowered the fan of her cards to look at him angrily across the table. "Who would want to view you? You're only a man without legs. Why do you always imagine yourself to be so special?"

"You're damnably impertinent for a housekeeper!"

"And you are abominably rude for a master!"

He opened the play with a slapping down of a jack. It pleased him that she was never at a loss for words, even when he reduced her to this quarrelsome bickering. "How do you suggest I should have seen the entertainments of the kermis? By peeping through the drawn-down

blinds of a sedan chair?" He was remembering bitterly the many ker-
mises he had enjoyed with wild pranks and sports and the tumbling of
girls.

"You could have gone on wooden legs." She was scrutinizing the
hand she held. It was the first time she had even hinted at the stump
legs that had been ready for a long time, together with the crutches,
which had been delivered as promised.

"Why not on stilts?" he gibed. "That would be even better."

"I daresay you could manage that too if you had crutches that were
long enough."

He saw by her serious air that she had meant what she had said
about the wooden legs, but for the past two days the distant music and
noise of the kermis, which reached him through the open window, had
added to his despair, reminding him he could never compete dangerously again in any test of sporting skill.

"You mean well, Aletta," he said quietly, "but it's not just the walking. My previous life held so much that is lost to me forever."

"But—"

"The subject is closed. Let's get on with this game."

As they continued to play she knew he was as far away as ever from
what she wanted most for him. He had not yet forgotten the woman
he loved. Maybe Isabella, by breaking off the betrothal when he had
needed her most, had also broken him forever.

At Haarlem Huis, Pieter puzzled over the message from Gerard that he
had received that evening. It asked him to be in a certain place in
Haarlem's St. Bavo Church at an early-afternoon hour the next day and
no reason was given. For a wild moment he had hoped he might see
Francesca there, but he realized almost immediately that such a happening was highly unlikely.

He rode into Haarlem the following afternoon with ten minutes in
hand. He hitched his horse to a post by the Butchers' Hall and removed
his hat as he entered the huge church, its quietness falling over him like
a cloak. An old woman in black sat in meditation on a distant bench
and there was another in the little Dog Whippers' Chapel, so named for

those of that trade, who had made it their own in the past when employed by the church to keep out troublesome dogs. Neither the two women nor a stranger, who stood looking down at Frans Hals's stone, paid him any attention as he went by. He tried to be as quiet as possible, but inevitably the heels of his riding boots made some sound.

At the end of the church he came to the Bread Bench, by which he had been asked to wait. It was here in times gone by that Guild members had once sat and from which they had distributed bread among the poor after the services. He whiled away the time by studying the carving, which was a masterpiece of mediaeval craftsmanship. When footsteps approached leisurely he expected to see Gerard, but instead it was the stranger whom he had seen earlier, coming to view the historic bench. As good manners demanded, they bowed their heads to each other.

"What a treasure the church has here," the stranger said, placing a hand on the old wood. He was about Pieter's own height, similarly athletic in build, with sandy hair, a thin moustache and a small pointed beard. "Don't you agree, Heer van Doorne?"

Pieter raised an eyebrow in surprise. "You know me?"

"It was at my request that Gerard Meverden arranged for you to be here." The man indicated that they should keep their voices low, which they were doing to a degree in any case, being in a holy place. "Let us stroll together about this church as we talk and appear to be looking at everything of interest. My name is Paulus van Roos."

"What is your business with me?"

"It is not mine. I'm only the messenger. The duty with which I have been entrusted is to put two questions to you. The first is to ask if you would risk your life for our Prince and the freedom of our country."

"I have already dedicated myself to that purpose by my oath taken when I enlisted as a reservist in the militia. Before you ask me anything else I have a right to know who sent you and to what purpose."

Van Roos stopped as if to study a Spanish cannonball on display, a relic of the siege of Haarlem during the war with Spain. "Ah! May those days never come again."

"It's not Spain we have to fear but France!" Pieter commented strongly.

475

"Precisely!" Van Roos looked piercingly at him. "I have heard a clarion call to that effect in a voice that has been hushed far too long."

Pieter released a slow breath. So the twenty-two-year-old Prince Willem of Orange was about to assert himself at last against those who had long dominated Dutch political affairs. "Ask your other question."

"Can you be in Amsterdam tomorrow evening?"

"I can."

"Then go to the Margere bridge at nightfall. A boat will be waiting."

"How shall I know which is the one?"

"I'll be watching out for you. Now I bid you good day."

Van Roos strolled away and when Pieter judged him to be gone from the church he left too. He did not ride straight home, but went first to Gerard's house, only to learn that his friend had left that morning on a business trip and it was not known when he would return, as he travelled around so much.

Turning his horse for home, Pieter thought about the Prince, who had listened to the call of the people and had been waiting astutely until the time was right. Born a month after his father's death, reputed to be wise and intelligent beyond his years, he had been kept in the background while Johan de Witt, an admirable man in himself, straightforward and honest, had done much good for the country over a long period of time, but he no longer held the people's trust regarding his dealings with France. It would soon be the Prince's hour.

Pieter had a number of business matters to settle before he left for Amsterdam, having no idea how long he might have to stay there, and he worked late into the night and again in the morning before leaving his manager in charge. When he arrived at his city house Vrouw de Hout was surprised to see him, not having expected him for another two weeks. She fussed about, lighting the fire in the drawing room and apologizing for not having done so previously.

"I never come in here except to clean when you're away," she explained, "and there's not much in the house for dinner."

"Don't concern yourself," he said, sitting down with his long legs stretched out before him. It was good to relax and warm himself by the first flickering flames. "Anything will do, but I would like to eat as soon as possible. I have to go out again at nightfall."

That made her fuss more than ever. He heard the copper pans clattering in the kitchen. Before long she served him a perfectly adequate meal of leek soup followed by fish and rounded off with candied fruit and a selection of cheese. She would have served him coffee too, but he declined it.

"There's no time. It's getting dark already." He rose from the table. "I'm unsure of my plans. I may be back tonight and I may not."

It was a black night without a star. Pieter carried a lantern and the pale yellow rays caused the rain-wet cobbles to sparkle underfoot. He followed the streets that took him to the bridge. He was not going on this expedition unarmed, but had a pistol in his belt and a sword at his hip. It was a simple precaution against being set upon by robbers on the way and any unexpected danger that might arise through this curious meeting. The canals glinted gold in the reflected light of the windows and passing candle lamps. As he approached the bridge van Roos came from an archway.

"This way," he said without greeting, leading Pieter to some old stone steps not far from the bridge that led down to the canal. A boat was waiting, a man at the oars. Pieter took a seat, followed by van Roos. There was no conversation between them. The oars dipped in and out of the water until they came alongside one of the rear doorways common to houses backing onto canals, which gave access to either boat or sleigh according to the season.

It was opened to them. Van Roos motioned for Pieter to enter the house first and then went in after him. A manservant with a silver candlestick went ahead down a grey-and-white tiled corridor. Even without the light flickering on tapestries and gilt-framed paintings Pieter would have known himself to be in a house of some grandeur. Wealth had an aroma all its own.

When they reached a pair of double doors he and van Roos were shown through into a richly furnished room, which was illumined by scones shaped like hands, holding candles out from the panelled walls. Two men were talking together and they turned as Pieter and his companion entered. One was unknown to Pieter, but the other, young and tall with a brown-eyed, longish face, was instantly recognizable

from prints and coinage. Pieter, sweeping off his hat, made a low bow to the Prince of Orange.

"Your servant, always, Your Highness!"

"We bid you welcome, Heer van Doorne." The Prince moved to a carved chair and sat down. "This is an informal occasion and we appreciate your willingness to engage in a difficult and perilous task on our behalf. You are one of several loyal Dutchmen specially chosen to help smash the spy ring that the French King has established throughout the states of Holland. Our navy is strong but, as he knows, our army is in a shambles and our defences are weak and so he will attack by land. While there is still time left to amend whatever is possible and enlist foreign aid, we need to weed out his treacherous agents before word can get to Versailles as to what is afoot. It is essential to my plan that neither he nor anyone in de Witt's party has any inkling of the preparations I shall be making against him."

"How may I serve?"

"By concentrating on the district of Delft. It is believed the French agents have a headquarters there and that is what you are to uncover. We trust your caution and your judgment. You will be given a contact, a man already known to you, who has done some preliminary work. He will pass on to our intelligence section all you find out."

Pieter had no doubt it would be Gerard with whom he would be working and who must have recommended him. "I have a particular interest already in Delft."

The Prince smiled slightly. "We are well aware of that. The young lady is the daughter of the artist Hendrick Visser. You have been maintaining a degree of secrecy when you have been in the town previously, but that has to change. Now you will establish and man a stall in the market square and you will be seen selling your tulip bulbs as soon as it is seasonable. Meanwhile you can advertise yourself as a designer of fine parks and gardens. Let nobody doubt who you are. Frequent the hostelries and pothouses, gain an entrée into richer homes, always keeping an ear open for anything that might give you a lead. You must use your discretion as to how much Juffrouw Visser should know about your work. We were originally against her being informed of anything, but the same loyal patriot who spoke for you also recommended her as a

young woman of discretion, who comes from a family known as determined supporters of independence."

"I should be putting her in greatest danger," Pieter said, concerned. "She is under threat of incarceration already if she should ever be seen with me."

"It will be up to your initiative to see that what you fear does not come about. You have been successful to date. We feel sure you will do well in the duty we have assigned to you."

"I'm honoured to serve the House of Orange and my country."

"Well said." The Prince rose from his chair and stood for his equerry to take up his cloak and put it about his broad shoulders. "Heer van Roos will tell you everything else you wish to know. May God speed you on your mission."

Pieter bowed again. He turned to van Roos as soon as they were on their own. "Certainly there are a number of things I want to know."

"Yes, of course. Sit down." Van Roos went to a decanter of wine, beside which were four glasses, two already used by the Prince and his equerry. "This has been left for our refreshment and I'm sure you could do with it."

"Is this not your house, then?"

"No. Neither does it belong to the Prince. It is the city home of someone sympathetic to our cause." Van Roos handed Pieter a glass of wine and sat down with his own. "It should be a relief to you to be able to go openly to Delft."

"There are two ways of looking at that."

"Agreed."

"I realize it must have been Gerard Meverden who put in a report about me."

Van Roos appeared to study his wine. "Do you suppose you would have been brought into this intelligence organization on the strength of one man's recommendation? You were double-checked by someone else."

Pieter wondered who that person might be, but did not ask. In the game he was about to play names and identities would not be bandied about. "What is my first step to be?"

"Gerard Meverden will be waiting for you when you return to your

house after leaving here. Although he will not now be working in Delft he will return there at frequent intervals and will let you know how you can contact him. There is no time to be lost."

"Is invasion so imminent?"

"I fear so. We have winter as a breathing space, because no army moves when there is ice and snow, but by spring we can expect the worst. Our old success against the Spanish led us to believe we were invincible, but that is no longer the case. Inevitably our officers have thought more about their plumage and finery and their gourmet banquets than about keeping their soldiers primed for battle. Fortresses which withstood long sieges by the Spaniards without surrender have been allowed to fall into disrepair. Cannons drawn out of storage are collapsing on wooden carriages that have rotted from damp and neglect. Never has Holland been in greater danger."

"Tell me how I'm to play my part until the fighting starts. I have the Prince's instructions, but would be glad of further details."

"First of all, always go well armed."

Pieter indicated his sword and patted the side of his coat, which covered the pistol in his belt. "I came prepared this evening, not knowing what awaited me."

"Very wise." Van Roos then proceeded to list all that Pieter should look for in the task he had undertaken. "Stay at the Mechelin tavern. It's the largest in Delft and all kinds of travellers come and go, apart from it being popular with local people. Make a regular booking and then you'll never be without a room. Listen and observe and never draw unnecessary attention to yourself, particularly when people are in their cups and tongues are loosened. You've a hard task ahead of you, but you have been judged a man of courage and determination and the Prince has faith in you. With the fate of our country hanging in the balance even the smallest discovery might tip the scales in our favour, so never dismiss anything as being too insignificant to note."

Pieter asked several other questions, which van Roos answered to his satisfaction, and then they left by the same way they had come. By the steps near the Margere bridge Pieter alighted and the boat carried van Roos elsewhere. Gerard was waiting when Pieter reached his house again. They grinned as soon as they saw each other.

"So you have a new duty, my friend," Gerard said, clapping Pieter on the shoulder as soon as Vrouw de Hout was out of earshot.

"Yes, and I thank you for putting my name forward. I thought at first we should be working as a team, but now I find that is not entirely the case."

"No. I am concentrating on a section of the coast. We know weapons are being brought in by sea to arm those traitors prepared for their own gain to sell our country to Louis XIV. Nevertheless, we shall meet frequently in Delft."

They talked late into the night and met early at the breakfast table the next morning. They were able to ride in the same direction along the road for most of the way, autumn leaves flying up in rusty clouds from their horses' hooves. When they parted company Gerard made for the coast and Pieter covered the last miles to Delft. He left his horse in the Mechelin stables, secured a room at the tavern and then went into the Vermeer gallery. Jan was in the process of selling a painting, but when he saw Pieter he nodded a greeting and indicated the door that led to the living quarters of the house. There he met Jan's daughter Lysbeth, who took him to Catharina in the kitchen, where she was baking.

"Pieter! What a surprise! Have you come from Haarlem?"

"No, from Amsterdam."

"What a cold ride you must have had. Go and get warm by the fire in the studio, because I know whom you've come to see. Lysbeth will show you the way."

He found Francesca at work, and when she stood momentarily speechless at seeing him so unexpectedly, he embraced her, she with her brush and palette still in her hands. They sat down on painting stools by the fire, where they were completely alone. He began by telling her of the expansion of his business in Delft. "But," he said, "much as I want to be near you I would wish it to be in any other town rather than this one. My first thought when I was instructed to come here was that it counteracted our plans not to meet until Christmas for safety's sake."

"You say you were instructed?"

"What I am about to tell you is for you alone. You may well be able

4
8
1

to help me by being my eyes and ears, especially when I can't be in Delft."

When he had told her everything she spoke without hesitation. "What should I watch for?"

He listed what had been put to him and since he had decided to open a small office in Delft there would be no difficulty in her getting any useful information to him.

"There's one more matter to settle," he said. "I must let Vrouw Wolff know I'm going to be in town quite frequently and at the same time impress upon her that I'm here on business and not in pursuit of you."

"Yes, you'll have to do that. Talk spreads so fast in Delft that sooner or later your name would be spoken in her hearing." She raised her hands in a little gesture of uncertainty. "There was an incident in her house that struck me as strange at the time, but it happened months ago and couldn't have any connection with this new venture of yours."

"What was it?"

His eyes sharpened with interest as she told him how she had talked to the traveller from Utrecht on one of the rare occasions when she had seen those who stayed there, and how she had overheard Geetruyd's anger afterwards. "I don't hear anything from downstairs now," she concluded, "because after I located the loose brickwork I stuffed the space with old paint rags."

"Do you know which room the voices came from?"

"Yes. It can only be the bedchamber at the front of the house two floors below mine.

"If the paint rags were removed you might possibly hear something of interest again and in the meantime it would be helpful if you could keep a record of the travellers who come to the house, noting anything that seems unusual in the light of what I've confided to you. The incident you described may have been nothing more than a spurt of feminine jealousy on Vrouw Wolff's part, but it's odd that she should have said what she did about the possibility of you recognizing him again."

"I will remove the paint rags whenever I know somebody is staying. Normally it was only the bang of a door or very loud snoring that I heard and there must have been some trick in the acoustics that made

Geetruyd's voice so clear. If ever the chance presents itself I will inspect that room."

"Don't take any unnecessary risks."

"I'll be careful." Then she remembered the sketch of the traveller she had made and found it in a file. "I sketch faces that have character and I have a large collection now. The bone structure of this traveller's visage particularly interested me."

Pieter studied the sketch before putting it away in his pocket. "This likeness may prove useful."

Before leaving he was keen to see the painting on which she was presently engaged. It was of Catharina baking in the kitchen, exactly as he had seen her earlier, the flesh tone warm, the blue of her bodice and the red of her skirt clear and bright against the sombre tones of the kitchen. In the background Elizabeth was pouring milk into a bowl. A basket of newly baked bread was on the table. It was an ambitious subject, masterly executed.

"Your work is advancing to the top, exactly as I knew it would," he said.

They were standing hand in hand in front of the painting and she rested her head against his shoulder. His praise was always simply stated and deeply felt. There were many reasons why she loved him.

Geetruyd received Pieter frostily. "I remember your name very well. Francesca was forbidden to have anything to do with you and I thought the whole matter settled a long time ago."

"I've come here to your house specifically to see you, *mevrouw*, not Francesca."

"State your purpose."

He explained that he was extending his business to Delft and gave her some idea about his design work. She listened attentively, never taking her hard gaze from him. "So," he said in conclusion, "since I have no wish to cause Francesca any trouble, I ask you to accept my reason for being in this town."

Geetruyd eyed him suspiciously. Was this a ploy to put her off her guard or was it a genuine request to keep Francesca out of punishment

in case of a chance meeting? For the time being it seemed best to play along with him.

"How sensible of you to come to me first. I shall give Francesca permission to nod good day to you in passing, but I draw the line at any resumption of whatever was once between you."

He shrugged nonchalantly. "Francesca and I were only friends when she came here. A good many months have gone by since then. I have no wish to return to that earlier time."

She gave a nod. "I shall see to it that Francesca is left in no doubt as to why you are in this town. She is a proud young woman. You'll have no bother from her."

"That's all settled, then."

Geetruyd saw him to the door and was thoroughly amiable. "Unfortunately I have no garden for bulbs, but I may treat myself to a few tulips from your stall next year when they are in flower."

As soon as he had gone she dashed for her cloak and then followed him, determined to check that he did not make for Mechelin Huis. He did cross the square in that direction, but went straight into the tavern. She waited inconspicuously until Weintje passed by without noticing her on the way to fetch Francesca. When Geetruyd saw the two of them coming back across the square together with no sign of the young man darting after them, she hastened home ahead of them and was in a chair by the fire when they arrived.

Francesca was not in the least surprised when Geetruyd immediately demanded she turn out her pockets and her purse. In the early days these random checks had been made frequently to see if she had any secret love notes from Pieter or anyone else in her possession. It was one more indignity to be suffered under Geetruyd's regime.

At dinner Geetruyd informed her of Pieter's visit. "A fine-looking young man, altogether too worldly and mature for you. I can quite understand, now that I've seen him, why you were eager to keep contact with him during your first days here. You must have thought I was very hard on you at the time, but it was all for the best. He made it perfectly clear to me that he has no wish for you to go out of your way to talk to him while he is busy organizing his business."

Clara spoke up, hurt on Francesca's behalf that the young man

should have made such a point of rejecting her. "Francesca would never run after anyone who did not want her! She has no need in any case, being betrothed to Heer van Deventer."

Geetruyd dropped a fork onto her plate with a clatter. Only then did Clara realize what she had said. Geetruyd's face was venomous. "What was that statement you made, Clara?"

Clara could not answer. Her tongue seemed to have swollen in her mouth and her jaw had clenched. She had been terrified of Geetruyd many times, but never more than now. Without being aware of it she stared back at her with glazed eyes like a mesmerized rabbit. Francesca answered for her.

"It's true. I told Clara one day."

Geetruyd's glittering glare switched to her. "Why did you not tell me?"

"If you had asked I would have told you. My father and Ludolf signed a marriage contract without my knowledge. I knew nothing about it until I was home last spring. It's not my wish at all. If I could be free of him it would mean everything to me."

Geetruyd fought for control. "Ungrateful girl!" she shouted wildly. "He's destined for great heights one day! And it will all be wasted on you!" She threw her napkin on the table, thrust back her chair and swept tempestuously from the room. Her bedchamber door slammed upstairs.

Clara turned a frightened face towards Francesca. "I've done a dreadful thing."

"No, you haven't. Geetruyd would have had to know sooner or later."

It soon became apparent that Geetruyd was not going to emerge from her bedchamber again that evening. Clara and Weintje went to bed. Francesca, still in the parlour, decided to seize the chance that had come so unexpectedly. Taking a candle, she crept downstairs to the hall. No travellers were staying in the house and there was no danger of meeting anyone. Once in the hall, she crossed to the front bedchamber leading out of it and, finding the door was not locked, she entered swiftly, closing it behind her.

The wall bed was narrow, but had rich hangings and a brocade

coverlet. There was a table with writing materials and the usual furnishings. Crossing to the Delft-tiled fireplace, she stepped under the canopy to stand by the empty firebox as she searched for some cause for the curious transmitting of sound to her room. Then her candle showed her a cracked tile, half of which had long since gone and which appeared to have taken some crumbling brickwork with it. She judged that voices were magnified when people stood close to the canopy, which acted like a wide mouth to the funnel created by the cavity within the chimney breast leading up to her room. It explained why she had only caught a scrap of Geetruyd's conversation, as the woman had come near the fireplace and then moved away again.

Carefully Francesca removed the remaining piece of tile, which dislodged another that was loose. She took that for good measure, not wanting it to fall by its own accord and draw attention to the gap that was presently out of sight from anywhere except the unlikely place where she was standing. Weintje would wash the whole of the fireplace once a week, as she did others in the house, whether the room was occupied or not, but Francesca had seen she only stretched her arm inside the various canopies and never looked closely at the tiles themselves. Some brick dust had fallen to the hearth. Francesca wiped it up carefully with her handkerchief, into which she also concealed the tiling. It made a bulky little package, but she went back upstairs and reached her own bedchamber safely. There she removed the paint rags from the aperture in her fireplace and deposited the tiles within, where they would never be seen again unless the canopy and the chimney breast were ever demolished. After shaking the brick dust in her handkerchief out the window, she knew she had removed all evidence of what she had done.

CHAPTER 2 I

When Pieter left Delft after spending two weeks there, he felt he had laid good groundwork and also secured a small office in Kerkstraat where he could work on local projects while giving him a solid foothold in the town. As yet he had gleaned nothing of value to his assignment, but that would have been highly unlikely so early in his quest. During his stay he had spent every evening in the taproom of the Mechelin and had had no difficulty in getting himself known as a Haarlem man making ready to open up a new branch of his business locally. He had called on Vrouw Thin since she moved in wealthy circles and could establish him in another sphere of society. Unexpectedly, on her recommendation, he had gained two commissions for newly designed layouts of sizeable gardens. Both clients were wealthy men, but as yet he did not know where their political sympathies lay. All he could hope for was that sooner or later he would uncover something, however slight, that would set him on a trail.

He went back to Amsterdam, intent on speaking to Neeltje again. Previously she had concentrated on anything that might help him protect Francesca, but in the light of the strange little incident Francesca had reported to him, he felt anything Geetruyd Wolff had written to Ludolf might be of some interest. It was a long shot, but worth trying, because Ludolf was an unprincipled, self-made man with much to lose if war should come. One thing to be guarded against was too hasty a step in any direction that might lead to the capture of one man and the escape of many more, all equally dangerous to the freedom of Holland.

Disappointingly, he learned from his housekeeper that Neeltje had been given notice from the van Deventer house and was presently employed as companion to an old woman. Having acquired the address, he called on Neeltje, who was content to be looking after a kindly

person again, but she could think of nothing in the letters that would be of any help to him.

"It always seemed to me that Vrouw Wolff wrote of business matters and nothing else," Neeltje said, puzzled by this new line of questioning, for which he had given no reason. "Sometimes she actually referred to investments at the Exchange."

Although she promised to search her memory, Pieter was not optimistic that she would remember anything useful to him. He thanked her for all she had done and agreed to convey her good wishes to Francesca and her sisters.

When Pieter arrived at the Visser house, Griet showed him through to the studio, as Hendrick was working without a model that day. Hendrick proved to be in good spirits. There were days when his fingers still made it painful to hold a brush, but then he would take one of his breaks from work and enjoy the convivial company in the taverns with a game or two of cards with modest stakes. He had learnt a lesson and never forgot the outcome was still in the balance, even though it was weighed heavily in his favour with Sybylla's marriage to a wealthy bridegroom only a few weeks away.

"Is the Civil Guard painting finished?" Pieter asked him after giving him news of Francesca.

Hendrick frowned irritably. "No, it's not. I can't work only on that piece. I've been busy with other work. I hope you haven't come here to bring more complaints. Your fellow officers don't understand how difficult it is for me to remember appointments for sittings or, if I do remember, I may not feel like painting a face not of my choosing on that particular day."

Pieter had received reports that all was not going as well as had been expected. There was growing impatience for the painting to be ready. "When I leave here I'll take a look at it in the church. Is Sybylla home?"

"Yes, she is, and she'll go with you. I've never known her to take such an interest in a work of art before. Not only does she view it at least once a week, but she is nagging me constantly to get it done before her marriage."

"I hope you will." Pieter spoke firmly.

"All right!" Hendrick waved an impatient hand. "I'll do my best. I

488

expect you'll find Sybylla is still upstairs with the seamstress. Come and dine with me at a tavern this evening. I need some sensible conversation. There's no talk in this house that centres on anything other than the wedding."

They arranged to meet at a certain tavern. The seamstress was just leaving the house as Pieter went into the reception hall and Sybylla was delighted to see him, greeting him with a full kiss on the lips.

"How are Francesca and Aletta? Have you seen them? Say you have!" she exclaimed.

He suggested they talk on the way to the church and she rushed to get a cloak. Then she tucked her arm into his and set a swift pace as he told her all he could about her sisters. She also had something to tell him that linked indirectly to Francesca.

"Griet's husband, who is a seaman, as you know, told her something before he went to sea. She passed it on in confidence to me as a warning for Francesca, but since you are so close to her I want you to know too. Ludolf called at the house two or three times while Sijmon was here and that's how all this came to light. Sijmon recognized him as a privateer he had served under for a short while during his cabin-boy days, one voyage being enough under Ludolf's command, although van Deventer was not the surname he used then."

"Was Sijmon certain he had made no mistake?"

"He admitted he wasn't sure at first. The modulated voice, the curled periwig, the clean-shaven face and grand clothes, combined with the lapse of seventeen years, would have fooled him if it hadn't been for Ludolf's gait. I'm sure you've noticed how he throws himself into a certain swagger when he walks. It was that walk, which Sijmon had seen many times on the ship's deck, that convinced him as to Ludolf's identity."

"So now we know how Ludolf made his original fortune." Pieter was wondering if Geetruyd's friendship with the man went back to those days.

"I'd be frantic about Francesca having to marry him if I didn't know that Adriaen is prepared to pay Father's debts and set her free."

"Is that settled?"

"Not yet, but it will be. Adriaen has said over and over again that he

wants me to be happy in every way." Flirtatiously she snuggled up against him. "Oh, Pieter, you should see how generous he is to me. My betrothal gift was a glorious diamond necklace and eardrops. I have only to glance in a shop window at something and it is mine. Aunt Janetje sent me a Florentine silver brocade for my wedding gown, but Adriaen has allowed me to choose dozens of lovely fabrics for the many garments I'll need and his mother's seamstress and an army of assistants are making them up for me. Rich women don't go to shops to choose what they want, you know. Tradesmen will bring everything to the house."

"So you are happy, Sybylla?"

"Happier than I've ever been in my life!" she declared, her eyes challenging him to suppose otherwise. They had reached the church and she darted in ahead of him. Following her, he heard her disappointed exclamation and saw her expression droop. "Hans is not here!"

"Is he still coming to paint every day?"

"Just for a little while each morning. He has a room somewhere that is his home and his studio, and he does his own work there. Father's tardiness over painting the remaining sitters makes it impossible for him to finish this group painting as yet."

Her pace was slow as she led the way to the great canvas, her eagerness to get to it having evaporated completely. When Pieter viewed the painting he saw a vividly dramatic group, the sitters not just staring out of the canvas, but in animated discussion of how they would defend Amsterdam in an emergency, a map of the city spread out on the table around which they sat or stood. Five faces had still to be done, although collars and clothes and hair had all been completed. The hands of those men had also been left blank, for to an artist hands were as individual as faces. Pieter noticed that Sybylla was peering frowningly at a corner of the painting.

"Are you looking for the mouse?"

Her smile returned with dancing eyes. "You could only have heard about it from Francesca, because nobody else knows. You won't tell, will you?"

"You have my word on it."

"I don't think the mouse is in the painting yet, although I keep

looking. I believe Hans is waiting until Father finishes those faces before he adds it with the last strokes of his brush."

"It's a very fine painting, so any mouse should be proud to be in it."

She trilled merrily. "What fun you are, Pieter! Hans is like you in that respect, although he can make me very cross at times. He has promised to point the mouse out to me on my wedding eve if I haven't discovered it before."

"Why then?"

"Because once I'm Vrouw van Jansz I can't spend time here anymore. My social engagements will keep me busy from morning to night."

When Pieter left she stayed on, certain that Hans would come. Not once had he touched her or been in the least amorous towards her, but she was drawn to him by some magnetic quality that she could neither understand nor analyze. Whenever she saw him after an interim she felt suffused with joy. He would talk, rarely greeting her, conversing as if there had been no time between their being with each other and he was just carrying on with whatever they had been discussing previously. Her disappointment at not seeing him today was acute. How dare he not be there! Her temper began to mount as the minutes passed towards the hour of noon, when she would have to leave if she was to be ready in good time for a social outing with Adriaen's mother and sister that afternoon. Vrouw van Jansz was not a woman to be kept waiting and had a cutting edge to her tongue when displeased.

Sybylla's expression would have been a match for Hendrick's in a rage when finally she sprang up from the stool where she had been sitting, too angry to contain her temper any longer. She gathered up her skirts to rush out of the church and indulge her fury. Then she burst into tears and withdrew to a sheltered place by a tree so as not to be observed, although at the present time nobody was going past. Why didn't anything go exactly as she wanted? She had thought she would never have another care in the world when she was safely betrothed to Adriaen, but nothing was perfect. His mother was hateful and in her own mind she was having dreadful doubts about whether Adriaen would pay her father's debts, because he always changed the subject when she brought it up. Not that it mattered, because she was to have a large allowance and she could pay off Ludolf on a regular basis. She was

realistic enough to know she would begrudge paying out of her own purse, but she loved Francesca too much to let her become wife to that detestable man. Why was life so contrary? And where was Hans? How dare he not be at work in the church.

"Do you think, Sybylla," Hans said, breathing heavily as if he had run a long distance, and coming to a halt only a yard away from her, "that I could persuade Master Visser to let me complete the painting of the remaining sitters?"

She looked up quickly through a sparkle of tears. "I had something in my eye," she explained defiantly, wiping both eyes with a handkerchief.

"Shall I look?"

"It's gone now. You weren't painting this morning." Her quivering lower lip was accusing.

"I was kept waiting longer than expected when I went to see about a commission."

"Did you get it?"

"Yes. That's why I want to finish what has to be done on the group."

"Come home with me now and you can ask Father."

They walked together to her home and found Hendrick in his studio, where Hans posed the question to him. Hendrick made a great show of indecision, but inwardly he was thankful enough to relinquish the tedious chore. After all, Frans Hals had left half of such a group painting to another artist to finish, and what was good enough for such a master was all right for him too.

That afternoon Sybylla decided she loathed Adriaen's sister as much as she detested his mother. Both women walked past a most pitiable beggar without putting a coin in his cup as she did. One surprising fact she was discovering was that the rich could be horribly tightfisted when it suited them. Where was the pleasure in having money if one did not spend freely? She would show them how it should be done as soon as she was Adriaen's wife! Behind their backs she gave a little skip of anticipation. In the meantime Hans would be busy painting for longer hours again in the church, which would enable her to call in some time during each day to see how he was progressing. It was, she told herself, only to watch out for the mouse. For some reason everything seemed to stand or fall on her sighting it for herself without his having to tell her.

Pieter met Gerard at regular intervals, although so far each had little to report. A man had been watched on suspicion of spying in Gerard's area, but it proved a false trail. They sat in the parlour of Haarlem Huis.

"Have you seen this fellow anywhere?" Pieter asked, showing him the sketch of the traveller that Francesca had given him. Gerard shook his head, but he was keenly interested to know that Pieter was concentrating his attention on the Wolff house and those who came and went there. During the kermis, when every tavern and available room in the town had been full, many visitors even sleeping in stable lofts, Pieter had learned that the landlord of the Mechelin was under the impression that every room in the Wolff house had been taken, although Francesca had said nobody had been staying there. "Is Vrouw Wolff housing now only those engaged in undercover work and eliminating risk by confining the accommodation to them?" Pieter suggested.

"That seems a likely supposition," Gerard agreed. "It's fortunate we have Francesca under that roof. How often are you going to Delft now?"

"Once a week. Design orders that I never expected have given me a legitimate reason for being there so often at this time of year, and I'm now on conversational terms with a remarkable number of people in the town, and others living in fine country houses."

"When is your next visit?"

"Tomorrow."

The first snowflakes of winter were falling, only to disappear as soon as they touched the ground, when Pieter entered his Delft office. His clerk was an older man, not yet ready to retire, who had answered Pieter's advertisement for someone to do a few hours' office work on six mornings a week, this being sufficient at the present time. Pieter greeted him.

"Good day to you too, *mijnheer*," the clerk replied. "Have you just arrived?"

"No, I spent last night at the Mechelin. What is there for my attention today?"

Pieter sat down at his own desk while the clerk came from his to lay

letters and various papers in front of him. He had dealt with everything when the door from the street opened and Aletta came in with a laden basket on her arm, snowflakes melting into sequins on her cap and cloak.

"I hoped you'd be here," she said smilingly after Pieter had kissed her cheek and drawn her to the fireside. She looked around as she pulled off her gloves. "What a neat office! I've had no chance to come in before. I like those etchings of tulips and that painting of aquilegia on the wall. Most appropriate."

"You're not often in town, are you?"

"No, but I wanted to buy gifts for the Feast of St. Nicholaes. Constantijn still doesn't like me to be absent from the house for long, so I keep short my time away." They were able to converse without being overheard, for the clerk was partially deaf.

"How is de Veere? Has he received those wooden legs yet that Francesca told me about—such a good idea of yours."

"No, not yet, although he is well enough. You see, at first I had only thought of getting him into the right frame of mind to use them, but then I realized that was not enough. He needed physical strength too. He is strong in the arms and shoulders through hoisting himself about, but his thigh and pelvic muscles had to be strengthened again or else he would never manage those heavy legs. Josephus agreed with me and I left it to him to urge Constantijn into a routine of regular exercise. Now Josephus is in his element, seeing himself as a coach again, although he is training Constantijn for a different purpose than before."

"It's a sensible decision. Only good can come of it."

"I hope so."

"Have you seen Francesca this morning?"

"No, I don't call in during her working hours. Fortunately she can come quite often to see me at the de Veere house. I hear that the two of you are not meeting until Christmas."

"That's right. I only catch glimpses of her going in and out of the Vermeers' home, usually in the company of Weintje. Yet we keep in touch." It was easy enough with the Vermeer children or a tavern potboy as go-betweens. As yet Francesca had nothing to report. Two

4
9
4

travellers had stayed overnight, but not in the room with the funnel, and she had had no chance to catch sight of either.

Aletta glanced at the clock. "I must go. Josephus will be waiting for me by the Town Hall and I don't want him to catch a chill in the cold wind that is blowing today."

"I'll walk you there." Pieter took his greatcoat from a peg and thrust his arms into it. Then he put on his hat and carried the basket for her as they went out of the office together. It was a crowded market day with plenty of traffic. He raised his eyebrows when he saw the old-fashioned but well-polished coach waiting for Aletta with Josephus on the box.

"You didn't tell me you were riding in style today."

"It's the coach Constantijn's grandparents used to ride in. I could easily have walked in and out of town, but he always insists that Josephus take me these days."

Pieter put the basket on the seat for her and helped her into the coach. There was no glazing in the windows, but leather blinds helped keep out the draughts. He wished her happiness for the Feast of St. Nicholaes and the blessing of Christmas. She gave him her good wishes in return.

When they had exchanged a wave she let the leather blind fall back into place and the coach went bumping away over the cobbles. Pieter stopped to talk to someone he knew and was on his way back to the office when a sudden commotion occurred just ahead. He saw that a drunken wagoner, who had been leaving the market after delivering goods, had whipped up his horses carelessly, startling them both with an unexpected sting of the whip's end, and they had lunged forward to send the wagon into the side of a cart. No damage was done, but the wheels had locked.

Immediately Pieter ran with some other men to lend his strength in lifting the two vehicles apart. It was all over very quickly. The wheels were separated and the horses soothed. The wagoner, bawling his thanks to everybody, drove off down the lane leading into Volders-gracht while the two carters, sitting side by side in the cart, continued quietly on their way out of the square, disappearing from sight beyond the Old Church. Pieter sauntered thoughtfully towards his office, won-dering what it was about that commonplace incident that had left a question mark in his mind. Inside the office the clerk looked up and saw the distorted image of his employer through the small leaded panes of the upper half of the door. Then abruptly it vanished again.

Pieter was on his way at a run to the stables to fetch his horse. It had come to him what had been unusual about that incident. Carters and wagoners were notorious for their rough language if anything riled them, particularly if their horses or vehicles were harmed in any way, and frequently resorted to fisticuffs, always to the merriment of any crowd who immediately gathered. Such a fight could have been expected from the drunken wagoner, who had been brandishing his fists in readiness, as if he had been the innocent party. Yet the men on the cart had not uttered a word of rebuke, merely concerned that the load on their cart had not been jerked loose under its covers by the impact. Their horses had shown sweaty signs of having been driven hard, but they had come into the square at a slow pace and had left again in the same manner. There was nothing out of the ordinary in that, but combined with the uncharacteristic behaviour of the carters it demanded investigation.

As always on a market day, a good many farming carts and other vehicles were rolling in and out of town. Geese, newly purchased at the market, flapped their wings and squawked out of Pieter's path as he rode through and then a flock of sheep slowed him down. Two separate herds of cows further hindered him, one ambling along the road and the other crossing it from one field to another. The distance he had to ride before sighting the cart he was looking for showed that the man with the reins had resumed the former speed of his horses in spite of the hazards of livestock and the difficulty of passing other vehicles in places where the winding road narrowed.

He could see how swiftly the two men ahead were bowling along and he matched his speed to theirs at a distance. He no longer thought of them as being carters by trade, certain they were engaged in some special business of their own. They might be thieves having no connection at all with the mission to which he had been recruited. Twice the companion of the man who was driving looked back at him, although it was impossible to distinguish his features. Then Pieter realized they were testing him, driving still faster and then slowing again to see if he

altered his distance to any degree. He made his own speed irregular and when they settled to a steady pace again he was sure he had reassured them.

Suddenly the road formed an S bend through woodland and when he thought to come in sight of the cart again it had vanished. He spurred his horse into a gallop and discovered a crossroads. There was no way of telling which direction the men had taken. He studied the surface of the roads, but it was rock hard and there was nothing among the old tracks to give a clue. Undeterred, he searched diligently, taking one road until he could see the open countryside beyond the trees and then returning to search in another direction. Once he saw a cart in the far distance and galloped hard after it through a maze of farm lanes, only to find it was not his quarry. Finally he was forced to turn back to Delft.

That evening in the Mechelin he conversed with many local people, but he learnt nothing except that the cart did not come regularly to Delft, although one man was certain he had seen it twice before.

"When was that?" Pieter asked casually, buying his new acquaintance as well as himself another pint of beer.

"The first time must have been last spring," was the reply, followed by a slurp of beer.

"And since then?"

"About two months ago. Not long after the kermis."

"How can you remember that particular cart? It's no different from any other that is painted green with red wheels."

"I'm a whip and thong maker and I made and sold the whip that's on that cart. You know my place of work. Come and see me tomorrow and I'll show you how to spot my whips anywhere." The tankard was drained. "I thank you for the beer. You shall have a swig of my home-made brew in return. It's the best in all Holland." With a guffaw the whip maker left.

Pieter went to see the whip maker the next day, and found that the homemade beer proved to be extremely potent. He grinned appreciatively after the first swig as he stood in the man's workshop with windows that faced the road along which both he and the mysterious cart had passed the day before.

"How can you find a barrel strong enough to hold this brew?" he asked, wiping some foam away from his mouth.

The whip maker enjoyed the joke. "It's not easy. Now you take a look at the handles of those whips for sale in that rack over there and then you'll know why there's no mistaking a whip of mine."

The whips were standing upright with the thongs tied. After setting down his tankard, Pieter took one and examined the handle. It was bound in thin strips of soft leather in an intricate pattern that in no way detracted from the smoothness of the grip. One strip was stamped in gilt, enhancing the general effect, and others in the rack had variations of design.

"These are examples of splendid craftsmanship," Pieter commented. "They must be very expensive."

"They are. That's why it stuck in my memory when a carter bought one of them. Never before have I sold one of those whips to any but the well-to-do, who want their coachmen to be smart in every detail. I went outside to take a closer look at the cart itself, expecting it to be something special, but as you know, it was far from that. Why are you so interested anyway?"

"I once had a cart like it at my Haarlem bulb fields," Pieter answered truthfully. It had been an old one used on the farm before he had replaced it with another.

"So you think this might be yours? Stolen, was it?"

"Maybe. It was stored in one of the brick barns. All I can say is that I'll be glad if you'd let me know if you see it again."

"Indeed I will."

Pieter took Francesca's sketch from his pocket. "Was this the carter who bought the whip?"

The whip maker studied it and shook his head. "No."

"Could it have been his companion riding with him?"

"I can't say. I didn't pay him any attention."

Back in his own office Pieter studied a map of the area he had hanging on the wall. His gaze followed the lanes leading out from the crossroads, as he wondered where he had lost the cart. The most likely solution was that the two men had hidden themselves and their cart in one of the farm stables or behind a barn out of his sight. At least he

could be sure that if the same cart came this way again, the whip maker, who seemed to have eyes in the back of his head, would be on the watch and quick to inform him.

On the morning of the Feast of St. Nicholaes, Aletta exchanged small gifts with Sara and Josephus. Presents arrived in abundance for Constantijn from his parents and relatives, but several were more suitable for a bedridden invalid and defeated the purpose for which they had been sent. He would give his own gifts to the domestic staff in the hour before dinner, a tradition of the house from his grandparents' time. He had already handed over purses of money to Aletta for her to give to the gardeners. Sara was preparing a meal of his favourite dishes and Aletta had selected the best of the wines to serve with each course. She had already made up her mind to change that evening into one of her special gowns, unworn since she had attended events in the company of Francesca at the Vermeers. Normally in her role as housekeeper she dressed soberly with plain caps, although she wore dark silks in the evening and usually a more flattering cap of lace with a lining in a contrasting hue.

When the hour came she selected a lilac-blue velvet that was far from new, but which had always suited her. She brushed her hair well, pinned it up again and put on one of her party caps, which was covered in small glass beads. Lastly she took the Florentine bracelet and fastened it around her wrist. It was the first time she had worn it since trying it on after Francesca delivered it in the spring. She felt quite exhilarated to be dressed up again and her footsteps were light as she returned to the kitchen. Sara threw up her hands at such elegance and Josephus agreed she was a pretty sight to behold.

When everything was ready for the dinner, Aletta told Sara and Josephus to go to Constantijn for their gifts. As a housekeeper she would receive hers from him on her own. She knew what he had for them, because he had entrusted her to make the purchases and also those for his parents, which she had dispatched in good time. When Sara and Josephus returned to the kitchen they were well pleased with

his generosity. Then it was her turn. She had a present for him and took it with her.

Constantijn eyed her up and down with raised eyebrows of surprise. "You're looking very grand this evening."

"Only in keeping with this feast day."

He picked up a brocade-covered box from the table at which he was sitting and handed it to her. "Pray accept my St. Nicholaes gift."

"I thank you."

As she put out a hand to take it, while at the same time offering hers to him, he noticed the gold bracelet on her wrist. His brows clamped into a frown and he seized her fingers in a vicelike grip. "Where did you get this geegaw?"

"It came from Florence."

"I can see where it was made," he retorted, thin-lipped. "A lover's token! Name the man who gave it to you for this St. Nicholaes's Day!"

She sighed with exasperation. "Don't start imagining that marriage is going to take me away from here. My Aunt Janetje sent it to my home in Amsterdam and Francesca delivered it to me in the spring."

"Why haven't you worn it before?" He was still suspicious.

"It's not suitable for daily duties. Today is an exception."

He simmered down, releasing her hand, and let her take the brocaded box from him.

"I spoke hastily," he said, which was the nearest he had ever come to an apology.

"At my home we always opened gifts together. Please take the one I have here for you."

With a bow of his head he accepted the linen-wrapped gift tied with a ribbon, and thanked her courteously. While he unwrapped a book on great voyages she lifted the lid of the brocaded box to find a silver-topped crystal flask of the most costly perfume, which he could only have ordered through Josephus, and she appreciated the element of surprise he had planned for her. When they had both expressed their genuine pleasure in their respective gifts, she had dinner served to him.

Unexpectedly Constantijn did not appear to enjoy very much Sara's carefully prepared meal and he drank the wine as if he did not recognize the vintage in the glass, his mood singularly odd. Aletta was

relieved when he had finished eating and everything could be cleared away. All that remained was to fetch him a glass of brandy. Had he not been in such an unpredictable frame of mind she might have brought him the bottle on this special day, trusting in his restraint, but instinct warned her against it.

"Would you like a game of backgammon?" she asked him when she had put the brandy in front of him, it being the hour they usually settled to playing some game of chance.

"No. I want to be entertained in another way."

She thought he meant music. "What pieces would you like this evening on the clavichord?"

"Forget about music. Pray stand in front of me where I can see you well."

She obeyed uncertainly. "Do you wish to sketch me?"

"Not at the moment." He was looking at her under his brows. "I only wish to admire you. It's a long time since I've been in the presence of a well-dressed and comely young woman."

A faint blush ran along her cheekbones. After she'd been standing before him for a minute she became increasingly uneasy. "May I go now?"

He shook his head. "Not yet. Take your cap off."

If he had asked her to strip she could not have been more deeply shocked. "Indeed I will not!"

"Why? Caps are for wives and old women—not for a fine-looking girl. You should be wearing flowers or ribbons instead. I can't believe you sleep in that turban in which you appeared in the middle of the night after I'd seen those lights in the distance."

She regarded him suspiciously. She had wound up her tresses in a length of silk each time he had roused her and Sara and Josephus from their beds. "Did you play that trick just to make me come here with my hair down?"

"Not the first or second time." He grinned savagely. "And not that night two or three weeks ago, but maybe the rest of those summonses."

"So you ruined the night's rest of two old people and mine just for that? Your selfishness has no bounds!"

"I'll wake all three of you night after night from now on if you don't take off that cap."

She flushed. "You have no right to ask me. Please stop!"

"Isn't anyone ever going to see your locks?"

"My husband, in the unlikely event that I should marry."

"I'll marry you."

The colour faded from her face, which took on a paleness that was almost ashen, her eyes sparkling with fury. "How dare you!"

"Wait!" he thundered wrathfully as she stalked for the door. "Do you think I couldn't husband you just because I have no legs?"

She paused, shaking with anger from head to foot. "I haven't the least doubt about your manhood, but I will not be made the butt of your mockery anymore!"

"I've asked you to be my wife! What's wrong with that?"

"Everything! If you were now as you were before the accident you'd have the choice of any number of beautiful women and you'd never give a glance in my direction. I will not be asked because you think I'm the only woman available or ever likely to be! You can't even remember where we first met and it wasn't in this house!"

She rushed from the apartment and her heels went tapping away at speed down the stairs. He lay back helpless in his chair, raging at his fate that prevented him from going after her. What had she meant about a meeting prior to her coming here? He searched his memory, but all he recalled was the faint impression that he had seen her before when she had first come into his room.

She did not return to turn down his bed as she always did, Sara arriving instead. Suddenly he was scared that Aletta had packed and left. If she had he would send Josephus after her.

"Where's Aletta?" he demanded as Sara smoothed the sheet into place.

"Indisposed, master," Sara replied.

The relief that Aletta had not taken flight overwhelmed him. At present she was angry with him as she had been on many previous occasions when he had clashed with her, but she never sulked. She would come to wish him good night as usual. Not once had she missed doing that since her first night here. He waited optimistically, watching

the clock, but when the hour grew close on midnight, he knew she was not going to appear. Glumly he prepared for bed. He read for a while, but his thoughts kept drifting from the pages to Aletta until he realized he was taking nothing in from the book and closed it abruptly.

It was when he had snuffed the last candle that he saw the same sequins of light in the far trees that he had seen before. The old panic rose in him. His friends had decided that the Feast of St. Nicholaes was a suitable time to renew their efforts to see him! He reached for the bellpull hanging conveniently by his bed and jerked it hard while at the same time he shouted at the top of his voice. At night the bell rang in Josephus's accommodation over the stables as well as on the landing outside the bedchambers where Aletta and Sara slept. But nobody came. He snarled with rage. Aletta had played her old trick of disconnecting the bells, as she had done during the early days of her being in the house. Well, he had pistols handy, which he could fire over the heads of those oncoming friends of his. That should stop them in their tracks. But as he leaned over to pull out the drawer at the side of his bed he saw the lights had gone out again. He passed a hand across his eyes. Was it due to his imagination playing tricks with him after times of stress? There was a drive that passed through the woodland where the light appeared, but it was within the walls of his estate and none had access to the old gates there. Nevertheless, he would send Josephus to investigate in the morning. Anger against Aletta renewed itself. How dare she prevent those bells ringing! Now sleep was far from him. There was only one way of keeping at bay the melancholia that came in the small hours and that was to be found in a bottle of brandy.

At the other end of the house and one floor higher, Aletta lay awake on her pillows. She had heard the persistent clicking of the disconnected bell outside her door. She had also removed the kitchen connection with the stable to ensure that Josephus was not disturbed, for she had been sure that Constantijn would repeat his perverse prank that night when she had failed to see him again that evening.

Her fury with him had sprung from the hurt he had inflicted. That he should suggest marriage in that blunt, cool manner had been impossible to bear. She had put up with his tempers, his ugly moods, his melancholia and his apathy all because she knew she had patience with

him when anybody else would have walked out long ago. But recently
she had come to a new understanding of her motives. It was that she
loved him. The realization had not come overnight, as could happen
when someone fell in love, because there had been nothing romantic in
their association. Instead it had been a slow dawning and never once
had she looked for any reciprocation from him and never would she.
This evening his unwitting cruelty had nearly killed her with anguish
and it would be many days before she could face him again.

She tossed restlessly, unable to sleep. Suppose Constantijn hadn't
rung the bell as a prank? If he were lying there ill he would not be
attended to until Josephus made a first call in the morning. She turned
again in her bed. No, Constantijn would have gone on ringing if he was
ill. Unless he had fallen from the bed and was unable to move!

Deciding there would be no sleep for her until she had reassured
herself, she put on a robe and tied up her hair in the length of silk, even
at this hour tucking in any stray tendrils. A candle sconce was always
kept burning over the main staircase, being near the door of Constantijn's apartment, and she knew her way well enough from her room not
to need any light until she was there.

She had almost reached the landing that ran in a gallery to Constantijn's apartment when she heard a faint sound in the dark well of the
hall below. She listened intently, telling herself that all old houses were
full of strange noises at night. Then she heard the distinct tap of a heel
on the marble floor. It could not be Sara, because there had been
snoring from her room, and Josephus would never be roaming about the
house at this hour. Her heart began to pound. The tap came again.
Somebody was creeping slowly across the hall. There *was* an intruder!
Then she heard the bottom tread creak. He was coming upstairs!

There was nothing near at hand that she could seize as a weapon,
but Constantijn kept a pistol in a drawer by his bed. If she could slip
along there before the intruder saw her she could get the pistol. She
hoped desperately there was nothing seriously wrong with Constantijn,
or else the knowledge of an intruder in the house would distress him
even more.

She stepped out of her slippers and on bare feet began to creep along

by the wall. Then she came to a halt in complete astonishment at the sight of the man on the stairs, revealed to her by the sconce's glow.

It was Constantijn himself who was hauling himself up the flight, hand over hand along the handrail, the muscles rippling in his shoulders and back, for he was naked except for a belt around his waist into which he had tucked two bottles of brandy. Three keys dangled from a ring looped to the belt, one of which she thought might well be a duplicate of the key she had to the cellar door. It had been the tap of the keys against the glass bottles, and not a heel on marble, that she had heard.

As yet he had not seen her, being on the far side of the stairs. His speed and agility were those of an athlete. She knew now how he had been able to indulge in those drinking bouts and it was no wonder he had mocked her searching for a hidden store in his apartment. If he had worn a nightshirt or any other garment, dust from the cellar would have clung to the fabric and eventually given him away. Frowning, she advanced silently to the head of the stairs. He had almost reached the top when she spoke.

"I'll take charge of that brandy. You don't need it at this hour of the night."

He looked over his shoulder with a violent start. Then he let his head dip between his upstretched arms as he began to laugh, his whole body shaking with mirth. Letting go of the rail, he moved into a sitting position and rested an elbow on a higher stair as he flung back his head in a roar of uninhibited laughter. It was the first time she had ever heard him laugh without bitterness or cynicism and she began to smile. Tension between them melted away. She left him only to fetch his dressing robe and when she returned she saw he had set the two bottles on the top stair, but not the keys.

He grinned at her as he pulled on the robe and tied it. "As master of the house I have retained the keys to my own cellar."

She sat down beside the bottles. "If you had handed them over I would have given them back to you for the same reason."

"Yet you've always been strict over my consumption of grog."

"Only because I didn't want you to keep drinking until you couldn't stop. Now that danger has passed."

5
0
5

"Why are you so sure?"

"Because I realize now you could have helped yourself from the cellar every night if that had been your true inclination after I first stepped in to prevent Sara supplying you with whatever you wanted to drink."

"What made you suspect I've been helping myself from the cellar?"

"I didn't. I never noticed any bottles were missing."

"That's because one of those doors in the cellar leads to a smaller wine cellar and I took my supplies from there. So why were you on the gallery?"

"I started to worry you might be ill and that was why you had rung the bell. Why did you ring?"

"I thought for a few moments I'd seen lanterns again in the distance. So it was concern for me that brought you from your bed?" He levered himself up onto the top step beside her and moved away the bottles of brandy that stood between them. "I've remembered where I've seen you before. You used to look across at my window from Mechelin Huis every night when I was in Delft. You told me during your first day or two here that you had cared for the Vermeer children, but then afterwards I thought no more about it. But I'm right, am I not?"

"Yes, you are," she said, smiling. "Since you've remembered that much I'll tell you more. I was in the anteroom of the Amsterdam Exchange one day when you caught me looking through the window into the courtyard and you did the same before a crowd of your friends came to fetch you away."

He grinned. "I do remember now. How could I have not seen you then as I do now?"

She was not entirely sure what he meant by that. "There was a lovely girl among your friends. Was she Isabella?"

"Yes. But all that is finished."

"You won't be able to judge for sure until you're out into the world again."

"Maybe that's not such an impossibility as it once seemed to me. It's what you've wanted for me from the start, isn't it?"

She nodded, full of hope. The moment had come to tell him of the wooden legs that would enable him to stand again. But even as she

would have spoken, he seized her in his arms and was kissing her passionately. She was lost to all else until she felt him tugging the silk turban from her head. Total panic seized her. She began to fight like a tigress to free herself from his embrace.

He withdrew his mouth from hers, but did not release his hold as he stared at her. Her hair was the most beautiful he had ever seen, pale as moonlight, luxuriant and yet soft as spiders' webs. He said what he had long wanted to say. "I love you, Aletta."

She did not hear him, for she had begun to scream as if she were being raped. Abruptly he let her go, horrified by her reaction to his amorousness. She leapt to her feet and ran from him, her hair flying like a lovely cloud behind her.

In the morning when she entered his apartment it was in many ways as if what had happened in the night had never been. She was again soberly dressed, her hair out of sight under the plainest of her caps, her expression withdrawn. He reacted with cold hostility. They spoke with excruciating politeness to each other, their relationship having reached a curious impasse.

Josephus, as instructed, examined the old double gates to see if they had been tampered with, but they were securely padlocked as they had always been. He had some difficulty in getting through to them, for heavy snow had fallen just before dawn and once again the cloak of winter lay white and silver over the land.

Pieter had not been in Delft that day, but on his next visit the whip maker informed him that the green cart had been found empty and abandoned in a snowdrift. The carter and his companion, if there had been another man on this second occasion, had taken the horses from the shafts and made their departure.

"The whip went with them," the whip maker said. "So keep your eyes peeled for it."

Pieter went to the place where the cart had been snowbound. The hard snowbank still showed traces of the cart's removal in a need to clear the road when traffic had begun to flow again after the snowstorm. It was on the curve of a narrow lane just past the crossroads

where previously he had lost sight of it. He followed the lane and discovered it ran alongside the west wall of Constantijn de Veere's estate to peter out by a pair of wide padlocked gates. It seemed scarcely possible that the carter had driven through them, but if the man had had a key or an accomplice within the grounds, it would explain how quickly the cart had disappeared from view at the time when he had been following it. He recalled Francesca telling him of Constantijn's consternation at seeing distant lights in the park not long after Aletta went to work there.

A tree was growing conveniently near the wall. He climbed it high enough to be able to see what lay on the other side. Woodland hid the large formal garden that Francesca had said lay to the rear of the house, which was also out of sight. No snow had fallen since the night the cart had become stuck, but there were the softened indentations made by a man, probably a gardener checking the gates had not been damaged in the storm. By the way the snow lay it was possible to discern that he had followed a narrow drive that might well lead to the stables and outbuildings.

Pieter climbed down from the tree, remounted his horse and rode to the front gates of the house, where Josephus came with the guard dogs to ask his business. At Pieter's request Aletta soon appeared wrapped in a warm cloak and hurrying to speak to him. His first question surprised her.

"You told Francesca once that all were Orangists in this house. Does that still apply?"

"Yes, it does," she replied.

"You have no doubt about Josephus?"

"None whatever. He is a good man, loyal to the Prince. Why?"

He took her into his confidence to the point of telling her that it was highly likely that the lights Constantijn had seen could be linked to some nefarious business being carried out in these very grounds, a suspicion increased by Aletta's report that the most recent case of Constantijn seeing the lights had been on the night of the snowstorm. Sensibly she drew her own conclusions that something extremely important was at stake. There had been a query at the back of her mind ever since he had branched out in Delft, for it seemed foolhardy, in the

light of Francesca's vulnerability to punishment, that he should risk endangering her.

"You had better come into the house," she said, opening the gate for him. "This is something you should discuss with Constantijn. I take full responsibility for asking you in, although I warn you it's unlikely you'll be allowed into his apartment. I'll probably have to stand by the door and convey his remarks down to you."

When she explained the matter to Constantijn he regarded her from his chair with a steely gaze, no lifting of his expression whenever she entered his quarters now. "So it appears those lights might not have been a trick of my imagination after all. They could be consistent with a single candle lamp showing through the woodlands before being extinguished. You may send Pieter van Doorne up here since the safety of my house may be at stake."

For a second or two she stared at him in disbelief. Had she really heard aright? Then she almost scampered to the door. "I'll send him up at once!"

Pieter and Constantijn talked on their own for a considerable time while Aletta paced the hall, exulting in Constantijn having received his first visitor other than his parents, whom he had promised to see again on Christmas Day. Then Josephus was sent for and again she waited. When eventually Pieter and Josephus reappeared they both looked extremely serious. Josephus had one of Constantijn's pistols; Pieter had drawn his own pistol from his belt and in his other hand was Constantijn's ring of the three cellar keys.

"Where's Sara?" Josephus asked grimly.

"She's sorting linen on the top floor," Aletta replied.

"How long is she likely to be there?" Pieter wanted to know.

"Another three-quarters of an hour at least."

"That's as well. We want her out of the way, because we can't risk a careless word of gossip about an investigation we're about to make."

"Then I'll just check to make sure she wants nothing from down here." Aletta dashed up the flights to where she found Sara busily engaged, her task barely begun. Satisfied, Aletta went downstairs again and found the two men in the kitchen, where Josephus lit two lamps while Pieter explained the situation briefly to her.

"There's just a chance that the drive from the old gates beyond the woodland may have been used by intruders and there's only one place where they could have entered these premises unseen. Apparently there is a grating at the west end of the house, which, if removed, could give access to the locked cellars."

She remembered the grating, having passed it countless times, although she had never examined it closely. The thick bull's-eye glass behind the bars made it impossible to see within. "But nobody could get into the house that way, or any other, without the dogs barking. They are alert to any unusual sound."

Josephus interrupted, his voice thick with outrage at a possible intrusion under his very nose. "They're friendly enough and quiet when they know the person concerned."

Pieter nodded. "I showed Constantijn the sketch of a stranger that Francesca made and gave me. He identified the likeness immediately as that of one of the servants whom he dismissed the night he returned here. As you know, the dogs were kept originally to guard against poachers and I'm told they knew all the servants well."

Josephus opened the door to the cellar steps. When Aletta would have followed, Pieter stopped her. "There may be danger. Wait here, Aletta."

She did not obey. As soon as they were down in the cellar she moved onto the steps and watched from there as Pieter inserted the key in the lock of the long-closed door as silently as possible. Then he stood back, giving a prearranged nod to Josephus, who turned the key and flung the door wide to let Pieter dash through with his pistol cocked. Josephus rushed after him, but there was no sound of shots or voices. She almost leapt down the flight and rushed to the open door to see what was happening.

The lamps that Pieter and Josephus were holding showed the enormous length of the main cellar, which was divided into sections by walls and archways. They had opened another door into a far cellar where some daylight filtered through the bars of the grating and the bull's-eye glass. At first she could only see some old furniture wreathed in cobwebs, but when she drew level with the men she gasped at a huge cache of arms. Pikes and muskets were ranged against the walls, and a

large number of stacked kegs, which Pieter said contained gunpowder, stood to one side. He threw open the lids of some scores of boxes to reveal lead bullets that surely numbered thousands in all.

"How did all this get here?" she exclaimed in bewilderment. "Even if the dogs were silent I know I would have heard a cart on the gravel in the silence of the night! Can you explain, Pieter?"

"The cache must have been brought here in several loads and most painstakingly unloaded. The cart was driven through the old gates, to which the servant obviously had a duplicate key. Once in the woodland the cart lamps would have been extinguished and then everything you see here was carried from there. Between them, two men would have handed everything through that cellar window when the grating had been removed."

"But why should they do such a thing?"

"To be in readiness for traitors to give support to French forces when the time comes. No doubt there are many other such secret caches of arms not far from the gates of our cities. Now I'll report back to Constantijn."

"Shall you not bolt the window first?"

"No. Everything must be left exactly as it is. Our hope will be to catch the gunrunners next time they come, although it's unlikely to be until the snow goes again in the spring, because they'll not risk leaving tracks."

The doors were relocked and the lamps extinguished to be returned to a shelf. Pieter spent some more time with Constantijn and then left. When he had gone Aletta took the crutches and the wooden legs from the place where they had been kept until the time should be right. She had not the least doubt that it had come.

When Constantijn turned his head and saw what she had brought to him his eyes glittered with a kind of bitter mirth. "How is it that you so often read my thoughts?"

It was impossible to admit to him that being in love could give that extra empathy. "So you have made a decision to walk again?"

"From the moment I learned that an offence had been committed against my house. I intend to keep watch from now on and to defend it and my country by eliminating those traitors. Give those legs to me and

tell me how long you've had them in the house." While she explained everything he examined the straps and the legs. "Most ingenious. I can see that with the crutches my parents have donated I'll be able to develop a swinging movement, but at least I'll be able to stand upright when I'm stationary. You'd better send Josephus to me. There's no time like the present to make a start."

"He shall come immediately."

"Wait a moment!"

She had reached the door and paused to look over her shoulder at him. "Yes?"

"I thank you most sincerely." His voice was puzzled. "Why should you do so much for me?"

She met his gaze steadily. By his own will he had broken his bonds. He had renewed his contact with the outside world through Pieter and it was only a matter of time now before he left his apartment and afterwards this house and then moved back to Delft in his recovered self-respect. Soon he would no longer have any need of her.

"My motive has never been entirely unselfish," she admitted, coming back into the room. "I gave up being an artist when I left Amsterdam. In that accident by the bridge I was in the stage wagon with which your coach collided. I can't remember exactly how my resolve began, but after seeing you injured and out of your senses that day I became convinced that my own life would never come to rights again until you were restored to yours."

"So I have been holding you back?"

She smiled. "Not anymore. I believe we are both now on the mend."

"Sit down and tell me what happened in Amsterdam."

She obeyed and told him everything. When she had finished both were aware that the coldness between them had melted away again. "So now I may feel able to sketch a little sometimes."

"There's still something else I want to know. Since I love you with all my heart, surely you can tell me why you are dedicated to wearing a cap?"

Her breath caught in her throat at his statement. His eyes were full of love and she trembled, dipping her head to avoid his intense gaze.

Haltingly she explained the fear that had been on her for so long. "Now you know everything about me," she concluded in a whisper.

"So that night on the stairs you didn't scream in revulsion of me personally?"

"No!" Her head shot up in dismay that he should have supposed such a thing. "That could never be! I love you!"

Her confession was out before she could stop it and sent colour sweeping up into her cheeks. Such joy suffused his face that she was almost dazzled by it. He held out his arms to her.

"Then come here to me, darling Aletta, where you will always belong."

She remained sitting quite still for a few moments and then slowly she put up her violently trembling hands and removed her cap. Deliberately she shook the pins from her hair until it tumbled down around her face and down her back. He could see the enormous effort it had cost her and he loved her all the more for it. Now at last she came to him in a sudden little rush to fling herself across his chest and throw her arms about his neck. He crushed her to him and their kissing was long and passionate. She drew away from him only once and that was to take his hand and place it at the side of her face to guide his fingers into her hair.

"Marry me," he murmured urgently. "I have loved you for so long."

"I will," she answered lovingly, placing a finger against his lips to silence any protest, "when you can stand beside me in the church."

"What a little shrew you are, my sweeting."

She smiled, surrendering to his kisses again. The accusation of shrew had lost all its previous meaning, for he had turned it into an endearment.

From that day forward there began for Constantijn a time of trial and error in his attempts to walk, Aletta and Josephus constant in their encouragement. There was pain and stress, headlong falls and countless bruises. Once he cut his forehead open against a corner cupboard, blood dripping everywhere, and on another occasion he tipped backwards and knocked himself out, but at no time did he falter in his determination to master the cumbersome legs. In spite of the soft padding in the cups, agonizing blisters developed on his stumps until the flesh was raw, but

as soon as Josephus had changed the dressings on them he rebuckled on the legs and began again. He no longer stayed in his own apartment, but stumped and reeled and staggered and fell along the gallery and in and out of the other rooms on the same floor.

Although often exhausted by the exertions of the day, he took turns with Josephus in keeping watch in case the intruders should return, but the snow remained unmarked and it was gradually accepted that Pieter's opinion was correct that nothing more would happen until the thaw of spring.

It came as a shock to Sybylla to learn that she was expected to move into the van Jansz house to be under her future mother-in-law's supervision for the final two weeks before her marriage.

"But you won't be there!" she protested to Adriaen.

"No, of course I can't be. I'll be at my sister's house."

"But why can't I be married from home?" She had imagined Francesca helping her dress for her wedding just as Mama would have done if she had still been here. Griet, almost as excited as she would be herself, would be in attendance, picking up anything that was dropped. And what of dear old Maria, who had arranged with Hendrick that her chair should be placed in the reception hall where she could see the bride come down the stairs? Adriaen had already promised that one of the coaches should take Francesca and Maria to the church. He did not know that Griet would be included. In the van Jansz household there were many servants and it would have been unthinkable for any one of them to be allowed such a privilege.

"Dearest girl," Adriaen replied, "this is no ordinary wedding. You have proved already that you are able to win the hearts of all, even that of the Grand Pensionary when he dined at my father's table, but my mother wishes to show you exactly how to manage a fine house and a large domestic staff, such as we are to have, and where better than in my childhood home?"

"Very well," she agreed reluctantly. She was proud of the house on Heerengracht in which they were to live, even though she would have wished it to be more than five doors away from his parents' domicile.

Not that she had had much say in its furnishing and decoration, for Adriaen—on his mother's advice—had engaged an advisor to decide everything. "But I want Francesca to help me dress for our wedding. Nobody else!"

"Whatever you wish."

They were on their own in an anteroom, the door into the neighbouring drawing room left ajar for propriety's sake, his parents there with guests. Sybylla kept her voice low, as did Adriaen, which meant that Vrouw van Jansz would not be able to overhear their conversation, however much she strained her ears.

"There is something else," she said on an artfully wistful note.

"Tell me, my little love."

"What a sweet man you are!" She gazed at him beguilingly, thinking to herself that he was as handsome as her father's plaster cast of Apollo. "We need to talk very plainly."

He wondered what was coming. One never knew with Sybylla. She had already told him that she did not want to start a family until she had worn out fifty pairs of dancing shoes. But since he intended to have a son as soon as possible her dancing days were numbered until after that event. "What is it that you want to discuss?"

"When are you going to settle my father's debts and set my sister free?"

"I'm not," he replied with equal directness, able to see that the time of prevarication was over. "I had hoped that during these past months of our betrothal, and as the future wife of a banker, you would have come to realize that money can't be handed out on a whim."

"It's my sister's whole future that is at stake!"

"Don't dramatize. She has a wealthy man passionately in love with her. After the announcement van Deventer made to all of us at his dinner party, he let it be known to everyone of importance that Francesca is to be his bride. There is no way that the betrothal can be broken off now."

"It could be if only you would loan my father the necessary sum."

"That is out of the question. Van Deventer has the greater claim on the loyalty of the van Jansz bank."

"But Ludolf was a privateer and did dreadful things!"

A closed expression came over Adriaen's face. "It is not the bank's policy to question an investor's past or how he made his money. I shall forget what you said." He had his arm about her waist and now he cuddled her close to him, kissing her temples, her eyes, the corner of her mouth. His voice became soft and persuasive. "Think how you'll appreciate having your sister living nearby."

She moved her mouth to meet his in a more ardent kiss, for she enjoyed his kissing. One thing that particularly annoyed her about Hans was that he had never attempted to kiss her, although she had given him enough chances. Now Adriaen was murmuring all sorts of wonderful promises while in one part of her mind she was calculating how many months there were left before her sister went before the Guild. During that time she herself would be handing over the greater part of her allowance to Hendrick to enable him to pay off Ludolf month by month. Adriaen need never know.

When she confided her plan to Hendrick the next day, explaining that it was the only course left open, he exploded with wrath against the van Jansz family.

"That money-grabbing, miserly, France-loving bunch!" he roared, shaking his fists. "They've no right to call themselves Dutchmen! To think that they should make their wives sacrifice themselves to look after deserving relatives!"

"Calm down, Father," Sybylla said impatiently. "They don't. It's my choice and the only way we're going to get Francesca out of that awful marriage. You'd better not say anything to Ludolf about repayment until you have the first installment in your hand."

He calmed down. "I wish I could contribute financially to lessen your burden. I'd sell Rembrandt's painting of Titus if it would bring anything worthwhile, but Willem told me not long since that three or four hundred guilders would be as much as it could fetch."

"That's less than a week of my future allowance! I would never want you to sell it anyway. It's been in our home for as long as I can remember and Mama was always fond of it." She gave him a hug and a kiss. "Everything is going to be all right. Just leave it to me."

Hans finished the Civil Guard painting. Sybylla went to see it the day before it was due to be moved out of the church into its place at the militia's headquarters. She found Hans folding up the paint-blobbed linen cloth on which the easel had stood all the time.

"Is the mouse in the painting now?" she asked eagerly.

"It is."

She gazed low and high at the great painting, feeling she had come to know every bright eye and laughter wrinkle and fat jowl of the men depicted there, but still she could not locate the mouse.

"I can't see it!" She was desperate.

"Keep looking." He had put the folded cloth on the worktable and was packing up his belongings, which he had already sorted out from the pigments and oils and other materials that Hendrick had supplied.

"You should give me a clue!"

"No, you must use your eyes intelligently."

"That's not fair. Why can't you be agreeable? This is my last chance to find the mouse before I leave home for the van Jansz house."

"The painting will be on show to the public at the militia headquarters until the New Year."

"What good is that to me? I'll have no time to go there and anyway it wouldn't be the same as coming here." She tried wheedling. "Be good, Hans. You promised you'd tell me."

"On your wedding eve and not before."

"You're infuriating! You know I'll not be allowed to go anywhere that day now that I'll no longer be at home."

"Then maybe you'll never discover the mouse's whereabouts." He stood ready to leave.

Tears were spilling from her eyes. "You're cruel!"

He smiled wryly, remembering how she had tormented him with her flirtatiousness, her seductive wiles and her gibes about the wealthy life she was going to lead. "I haven't intended to be. I wish you well, Sybylla. May you have all the happiness your heart desires. Perhaps we'll meet again one day. I bid you farewell."

A sob clamped her throat. Her plea came brokenly, almost in a whisper, showing she knew how useless it was to utter it. "Don't go!"

He was already near the church door out of earshot and he left without looking back.

At the van Jansz house Sybylla's instructions from Adriaen's mother took up several hours a day. It was like being under Maria's rule again, except that now she did not dare answer back. She began to yearn even more for her wedding day, when, after the ceremony and the early part of the celebrations, Adriaen would whisk her away to their own home.

He called to see her once every day, but now his mother never left them alone. Sybylla was at a loss to understand why. Did the woman fear that at this late stage passion might sweep them away? Or was it that her maternal jealousy was reaching its peak? Unexpectedly one morning Adriaen's sister, who had arrived with him, mentioned they were on their way to view the splendid new group portrait at the militia headquarters, which everyone was talking about.

"You must be very proud of your father's achievement, Sybylla," she said with condescension.

"I should certainly like to see the painting in its final setting," Sybylla expressed hopefully.

"Then come with Adriaen and me."

Sybylla's faint hope that Hans might be there vanished when she saw that her father had added his signature to the painting, which was his right, and Hans would never receive any credit for his share of the labour. She overheard several remarks that endorsed her own opinion that the five guards Hans had painted in full were by far the most vibrant and alive in the painting. Not that she was paying any attention to the overall picture, for she was looking frantically, here, there and everywhere, for the elusive mouse. She bit her lip with frustration when she had to leave without success.

CHAPTER 2 2

Francesca left Delft for her Christmas trip home to Amsterdam the day before Sybylla's wedding eve. She carried with her Constantijn's formal request to Hendrick for Aletta's hand and messages from his parents expressing their goodwill. Uppermost in Aletta's mind was the dread that Hendrick would refuse to give his permission in order to punish her still more, but Francesca could not believe he would go to those lengths and had promised to speak to him on her behalf.

For herself Francesca was glad to get away from Delft for a little while. There had been a strange atmosphere in Geetruyd's house ever since Clara had disclosed her knowledge of the marriage contract. The following morning Geetruyd had been quite composed, nothing in her manner to hint at the emotional shock she had suffered, and to all appearances everything had carried on as before. Yet there was a subtle difference. Francesca felt she was being watched anew as closely and as strictly for some unknown purpose as in her first weeks at Kromstraat. It was a thoroughly uncomfortable sensation and yet there was nothing she could single out as direct evidence.

She had heard from Aletta that Pieter had said she was to be told everything about the discovery of firearms at the de Veere house, for that was something he dared not tell her in the brief notes they exchanged. In one of those he had asked her to redouble her efforts with regard to her sketching, which she knew to mean it was more important than ever that she should let him know if the man she had drawn should come to Geetruyd's house again.

The journey home was speedy on the hard-packed ice. Nevertheless, when she arrived there it was too late in the evening to call at the van Jansz house uninvited to see Sybylla and she had to wait until morning. Hendrick and Maria vied with each other in being the most pleased to see her, and to her enormous relief Constantijn's request was well received, even though it was for the wrong reason.

"Let them wed whenever they will," Hendrick said carelessly. "Draw up a letter of consent for me to sign before you leave again, Francesca. At last I'll be rid of all responsibility for a wayward daughter."

"But, Father!" Francesca exclaimed indignantly. "You shouldn't—"

Maria cut across her words. "Help me to bed, will you, my dear? You two can talk again afterwards." As soon as they were out of Hendrick's earshot the old woman confided her reason for interrupting. "You'll be wasting your breath trying to make him see sense about Aletta. I've tried so often, but he won't listen and is as stubborn as a mule."

"Aletta committed the unforgivable sin of hurting his pride at a time when he had other troubles. Does he never speak well of her even after all this time?"

"That's easy to answer. Her name never crosses his lips for good or ill. He's so proud of Sybylla and her forthcoming marriage to a van Jansz that he has no thought for anyone or anything else."

"What do you think of the match?"

"Sybylla has got what she wanted," Maria replied philosophically. "But it's well your dear mother is no longer here, because she would not have been happy about it."

In the morning Francesca went to the van Jansz house with a wedding gift of a Delft tulip bowl, to which both she and Aletta had contributed. Sybylla came flying to meet her as soon as she was announced, forgetting all Vrouw van Jansz's instructions on how to behave in front of servants.

"I'm so glad to see you, Francesca!"

"And I to see you," Francesca replied, made almost breathless by the tightness of her sister's embrace. She was startled to see how strained Sybylla looked, but she supposed it had not been easy spending two weeks with Vrouw van Jansz.

"I've so much to show you, Francesca." Sybylla's jubilation sounded slightly hysterical. "My wedding gown, my jewels, all my new clothes and the wonderful home that Adriaen and I are to live in!"

"I want to see everything, but are you well?" Francesca asked with concern, for Sybylla was clinging to her like a child.

"Yes, I'm just tired. Since I came to this house I've not been sleeping well. Adriaen's mother is a gorgon," she whispered, "and she criticizes my appearance and finds fault with everything I do until I could scream."

"You'll soon be free of her now. Only twenty-four hours left. Show me your wedding gown."

It was a shimmering cloud of silver and white, the deep neckline studded with pink pearls, as was the wide band that gave weight to the hemline. Francesca declared she had never seen a lovelier garment. At her request Sybylla put on the wedding headdress of silver and pink silk flowers, which suited her porcelain complexion, and, still wearing it, she began opening velvet-lined boxes and caskets to display a parure of sapphires and other jewels. Almost before Francesca had time to look properly at anything, Sybylla was throwing open the door of a great closet where gowns, looped on pegs or draped on wicker stands, vied with one another in elegance, the rainbow hues enhanced by delicate lace, rich braids, bunches of ribbons or embroidery so intricate that only hundreds of hours of eye-straining work could have produced it. Francesca saw that her sister had become more herself again as if reassured by these new possessions massed around her. It was the same when they went along to the house on Heerengracht where Sybylla and Adriaen were to live. It was ready for habitation and merely receiving the final touches. A thin man in an orange-coloured periwig was using a fashionably beribboned cane almost as tall as himself to point out things he wanted done to his assistants, who were hanging drapes and curtains, arranging furniture and rolling out rugs. Some chairs were being carried upstairs.

"Good day, *mejuffrouw,*" he greeted Sybylla, his deep bow a cover for his dislike of her. She had interfered all too much with the colours and furnishings he had wanted for her domain. To his relief she had not come to make any more of her maddening objections to this or that, but only to show her sister over the house.

"This shall be your room whenever you can come to stay with me, Francesca!" Sybylla swept ahead into a charmingly furnished bedchamber with walls panelled in azure Lyonese silk. She crossed to a window.

"You'll have a view of the garden. At my suggestion Adriaen asked Pieter to redesign it and he has submitted some splendid plans."

Francesca went to her sister's side and looked out with her at the snow-covered garden, wondering how many years would have to pass before she could enjoy that privilege and see it in bloom. She was tempted to confide in Sybylla about her proposed escape to Italy with their father, but she decided against it. The prospect of such a break in the family would cast a shadow over the wedding day for Sybylla and that must not happen. Time enough when she had the support of a loving husband, because even Maria had admitted Adriaen was clearly devoted to his future bride.

"I'm sure you'll find that Pieter includes flowers in every colour," Francesca said, "especially tulips, symbolizing faithful and passionate love, which will be most appropriate in the garden of a newly married couple."

"I suppose he will," Sybylla remarked vaguely. "Today I'm finding it difficult to concentrate on anything not linked to my marriage tomorrow." She turned to Francesca imploringly. "You will come early to the van Jansz house, won't you? I want you to be with me right up to the moment when it's time to leave for the church."

"I will," Francesca promised.

Again Sybylla clung to her. "I wish Aletta were here too."

"As I told you, she sends her love. I know that if it had been possible she would have been with you."

In the afternoon, after Francesca had left, Sybylla received more instruction from Vrouw van Jansz. It was how to deal with tradesmen impudent enough to present a bill too soon, how to conduct herself in shops, how to order goods to be brought to the house and other such matters.

"You will supervise the household accounts," the woman said, "but with any other bills to be settled Adriaen will deal with everything. By that I mean you may always have anything you wish to the figure of your personal allowance, but you will never handle money."

"But I like to pay for things myself," Sybylla protested, thinking of the cash she would want for Ludolf.

"What you like and what is decreed for your own good by your

husband can be poles apart. Adriaen knows you are too inexperienced in matters of wealth to be allowed to handle funds yourself. Don't look so bleak, Sybylla! His decision was made at the time of the betrothal on his father's advice. Adriaen would never go back on it." Vrouw van Jansz smoothed her hands together as if wiping them clean. "That concludes all the instruction I've felt bound to give you. There will be no guests coming here this evening. You will dine quietly with my husband and me."

Slowly Sybylla went with dragging feet up to her room. She felt weighed down by the disappointment she had received. To think of all the great wealth in the van Jansz family and yet she had been rendered powerless to release her sister as well as her father from their bonds. Again nothing was going right. Had anything really gone according to her wishes since Hans had come disturbingly into her life?

When Sybylla appeared at dinner Vrouw van Jansz saw how subdued and dejected she was and supposed she was suffering from eve-of-marriage nerves. Brides in their innocence were subject to last-minute fears of those yet unknown marital duties. Vrouw van Jansz remembered her own trepidation and showed more toleration than usual by pretending not to notice that Sybylla hardly ate anything.

When the night came Sybylla could not sleep. She left her bed to huddle with a shawl about her shoulders by the fire in her room. Her thoughts were no longer dwelling on anything except that it was fast approaching midnight and still she had not solved the puzzle of where the little mouse was in the great painting. She gazed into the flames as if she might find the solution there, despairing that all she truly wanted was slipping from her grasp.

A log crumbled in a shower of sparks, one of which landed on her bare foot, causing her to jerk away. Yet it was a moment of revelation. She threw up her head with a gasp. She knew where the mouse was! Not on a hat or peeping from a pocket or winking an eye under the arch of a shoe, but in a place so apparent to her now that she could not understand why she had not located it before.

Springing up, she threw off her shawl and ran to snatch garments from drawers and closet to dress with haste. Thrusting her feet into shoes and taking her darkest cloak, she opened the bedroom door and

listened. The house was still. Carefully she crept down to the basement hall of the servants' quarters, where lanterns were kept in a cupboard. She dared not be arrested by the Night Watch for failing to carry a light. Silently she drew back the bolt of the door that the domestic staff used and slipped out by the minor exit under the main steps of the entrance into the street.

With the beam of her lantern dancing ahead of her she ran swiftly over a bridge, having quite a way to cover before she reached the militia headquarters. By rights she should have been terrified of being on her own by night, the snowy streets menacing in the darkness, but she had only one fear and it sped her feet. She was desperately afraid that Hans would not be waiting any longer at the only place where she could hope to find him. He had given up his lodgings, because his new commission was taking him away from Amsterdam, and he had not told her his destination. It was now well into her wedding day and far past the time he had set for the solving of the puzzle.

At last the militia building came into sight. There were plenty of lights glowing in the windows, for the Night Watch would be on duty in the city and here the guards changed regularly. Breathless and tired from the pace she had set herself, she reached the steps and stumbled up them into the hallway, where a guard was on duty and another sat at a desk. Both were immediately on the alert, supposing she had come to report some outbreak of trouble, which was not unusual.

"Your business, *mejuffrouw?*" the sergeant at the desk demanded.

"I'm Sybylla, daughter of the artist Hendrick Visser, who painted the new group portrait. Is anybody with it now?"

"No. The banqueting hall is not in use tonight. Did you wish to see one of the officers?"

"No! A young man named Hans Roemer, my father's assistant on the work. Is he here in the building?"

The sergeant looked down at an entry of names. "He was here today, but visitors to the painting have to leave by six o'clock and nobody is allowed to view after that."

She swayed with disappointment. He had gone! She had missed him! For once in her life she was beyond tears, overwhelmed by the intensity of her despair at having come too late. The sergeant was saying some-

thing to her about sitting down and she supposed he thought she was about to faint, but in reality she was being crushed by heartbreak as she had never known it before.

Then the icy air of the snowy outdoors suddenly swept into the warm hall and Hans had seized her by the arms to turn her to him. His face was stark, whether from the cold or from some pitch of emotion she did not know, but the snow on his hat and shoulders showed how long he had been waiting somewhere in the street nearby. She gave a sob of thankfulness and grabbed at his collar to hold herself to him.

"I've solved the puzzle!" she cried out.

"Not here!" he said warningly, putting an arm around her to bundle her swiftly out of the headquarters and the hearing of the two guards. In the street he pulled her with him into a doorway. "Now tell me. Where is the mouse?"

"There and yet not there! What I thought originally to be a shadow where the standard-bearer's cloak touches the floor is, in reality, a mousehole. And one of those threadlike gleams of light is the mouse's tail as it escapes out of sight! Just as I have escaped!"

He gripped her by the arm. "Do you mean that?" he demanded.

"With all my heart! Don't make me go back to the van Jansz house! Let me come away with you!"

"Do you realize what you are saying?"

"I do!"

"You'd be leaving your family and everything you've ever wanted."

"Stop treating me as if I hadn't discovered that I love you above all else in the world!" she cried shamelessly.

His voice grew warm and tender. "That's what I've wanted to hear you say for so long. I love you so much."

They kissed, locked together, and snowflakes began drifting around them. After he had picked up her lantern, which she had dropped onto the snow for their embrace, he handed it back to her and collected a bundle of his belongings from where he had left it, slinging the strap that bound it over his shoulder. With his arm around her, he hurried her away with him through the falling snow as if pursuit were already on their trail.

5
2
5

Francesca, keeping her promise to go early to the van Jansz house, was waiting in the reception hall of her home for the sleigh, which Sybylla had said would come for her at nine o'clock. Francesca was in her finery for the day, her gown of tawny velvet and her hat dove grey with a golden plume. She was adjusting the brim in front of the Venetian mirror when she heard the sleigh draw up outside and a great hammering came on the door. She opened it and a wave of anxiety swept over her as she saw a stark-faced Adriaen, and not a van Jansz servant, at the stoop.

"What's happened?" she gasped, pressing a hand against her chest.

"I must see Sybylla!" he demanded, striding in. "I didn't realize how much it meant to her to be married from her childhood home!"

"Sybylla isn't here."

"She must be. Her bed in my parents' house has been slept in and so she could only have returned here at dawn."

"I'll go up to her room!" Francesca turned for the stairs, hoping that she would not find the bedchamber door locked and Sybylla too upset to open it. Yesterday her mood had been very strange, almost on the knife edge of hysteria, but she had become calmer by the time they had parted. Had something happened in the afternoon to cause her some unexpected distress?

To Francesca's relief the door gave at her touch, not even being closed. Then she stared in dismay at the state of the room. Clothes had been tumbled from drawers and chests. A stocking trailed across the floor and a glove dangled from a chair. Propped against the opened trinket box was a folded piece of paper. She saw it was addressed to herself. Full of dread, she read it.

I am running away with the man I really love. Break the news as gently as you can to Adriaen and say I regret hurting him. The same applies to Father. Tell him there was nothing I could do after all to save you from Ludolf. It will be up to Pieter now. Do not worry about me. I am happier than I have ever been in my life before. Your loving sister, Sybylla.

Francesca read it through a second time. At some hour in the night Sybylla, even if she had first slept for a while in her bed at the van Jansz

house, must have crept in here, knowing where a spare key was always hidden, collected a few belongings and left again as stealthily as she had come. Who had been waiting for her? With a heavy sigh, Francesca folded the note and concealed it in the palm of her hand. The reference to Pieter could not be disclosed to anyone other than Hendrick.

When she came downstairs again Hendrick was talking solemnly with Adriaen and they both looked at her anxiously, her serious expression telling them instantly that something was very wrong.

"There will be no marriage today, Adriaen," she said with compassion.

He stepped forward. "Why? Is she ill?"

"She's not here."

"But to whom else would she have gone?" He was bewildered, but irritated too.

Francesca moved to her father's side. Already his eyes showed fear, as if he knew that what she was about to say would strike him to the heart. "Sybylla left a note for me. She has gone away. I don't know with whom. You are both better able to answer that question than I, who have been away from Amsterdam since the spring." Her sympathetic gaze settled on the jilted young man. "Sybylla is deeply sorry to cause you unhappiness, Adriaen, but she wrote that she is with the man she really loves."

His lids narrowed in disbelief and he drew in a long breath. Then he reacted with thin-lipped, blazing-eyed fury. "The little whore!"

Hendrick gave a roar. "How dare you speak of my youngest daughter in such a manner!"

Adriaen regarded him with wrathful contempt. "You penniless oaf! You seem to have forgotten to whom you are speaking. I thought Sybylla had eyes for me only, but I was wrong. I don't know and neither do I care whom she has left me for. You may keep her whenever she should return. I want no more of her!"

He slammed his way out of the house. In the dreadful silence that followed Hendrick turned to Francesca and rested his hands on her shoulders. "It must be Hans Roemer whom she's gone away with. I can think of nobody else and he was leaving Amsterdam today. She was

always talking about him and going over to the church to keep track of the painting's progress."

"Oh, Father, you should have taken more care of her during the time of her betrothal!"

"I just presumed she was anxious that the painting should be finished as soon as possible, so I might receive payment for it before her wedding day. I never supposed for one moment there was anything serious in it."

Francesca sighed deeply. "Well, there was, but at least she hasn't gone thoughtlessly." She revealed the note and gave it to him to read. "I'd like you to explain what Sybylla meant about not being able to help me after all."

He told her. She almost shook her head at the foolishness of her father and her sister in supposing that Ludolf would agree to being paid in installments, but there was no point in bringing that up now.

"It was well meant," he concluded.

"I know it was and I appreciate her consideration. Have you any idea where Hans might be taking her?"

"No. All he said was that he had gained a commission that would mean leaving the city."

Francesca felt slightly relieved. "At least he has work, which means they won't starve. But we must try to find them!"

"How? They left here before dawn and could be anywhere by now. Do you think I wouldn't be out searching for them already if there was the slightest chance of discovering their whereabouts?"

"I shall let Pieter know. I'll ask him to watch out for them."

Hendrick shrugged as if he had no hope at all and he wandered over to the small portrait of Anna, which had hung there for as long as Francesca could remember. "What would your mama have said, Francesca," he said, weary with sadness, "if she had known I was to lose two of her daughters?"

"Neither of them is lost! Your estrangement with Aletta can be healed and Sybylla will return one day."

He deliberately ignored her mention of Aletta. "I'm afraid for Sybylla. She is such a child in so many ways."

Francesca spoke musingly. "I don't think she is any longer. I believe

that in going away with Hans she made the first adult decision of her life."

It was not more than an hour later when the van Jansz lawyer called. Hendrick summoned Francesca into the room to hear what was said, for they had already discussed the possibility of a demand for financial compensation by Adriaen's father for Sybylla's breaking of the betrothal contract. Whether it should be high or low it could only add to the morass of Hendrick's financial state.

"Now, Master Visser," the lawyer began, "whom have you told about this unfortunate affair?"

"Nobody outside the household," Hendrick replied sourly, resentful already of what he feared was to come.

"Good. It will be to your advantage if you agree to keep it that way. Heer van Jansz is most anxious that his son's name should not become subject to scandal and gossip through being jilted by your daughter. For that reason he is prepared to waive any claim to compensation if you will endorse his proposed announcement that the marriage previously arranged between the two young people has been dissolved by mutual consent."

Hendrick's expression had cleared. No compensation! "I'm in agreement with that. I wish to protect my daughter's good name as much as Heer van Jansz wishes to guard his son's."

Francesca spoke up. "There is one condition that must be included."

"What is that?" the lawyer questioned.

Hendrick also looked at her inquiringly. "Yes, what do you have in mind?"

"It is that no retribution will be made against the man, who is presently nameless, with whom my sister has made her departure."

The lawyer played the feather tip of his quill across his fingers. "I'm authorized by Heer van Jansz to agree to any reasonable request and I have no objection if it should be your wish, Master Visser."

"It is," Hendrick replied. He liked Hans and the lad could paint. It would be terrible to let those talented fingers be broken in torture screws, for there was no telling to what extremes Heer van Jansz and his son might go in a desire for vengeance should Hans be caught.

The lawyer added the amendment to the papers in front of him and when all were signed he departed.

It was a Christmas torn by personal distress in the Visser home. The faint hope cherished secretly and individually by those under its roof was that Sybylla would make a surprise return on Christmas Day, but that did not happen. There was no reason why it should have, for the runaway couple would not know they were not being hunted or that Hans had been spared any punishment for abducting her. Francesca's most desperate fear was that they would sail to one of the colonies and then there was little likelihood of ever seeing Sybylla again. Hendrick had gone to Hans's former lodgings but gained no clue, for nobody knew where he had gone.

She could see that deep melancholia was fast settling on her father again. At a carefully chosen moment she had put the suggestion to him that they should flee to Florence together.

"If war with France should come we would be going without Pieter, because I know that nothing could make him leave Holland until the invaders are driven out and neither would I expect it of him."

Momentarily Hendrick was speechless as he took in what had been said. Then he spoke slowly. "Leave Amsterdam? Is such a drastic move really necessary?" He moved to his chair and sat staring into the fire. "Yes, I see now it is inevitable. I can neither condemn you to life with that vile man nor face the horrors of prison myself. Leave me now while I consider all that must be done."

Knowing that Maria would neither wish nor be able to make the long journey to Italy, Francesca had assumed that their old nurse would live happily at Sybylla's new home, where she would have been well cared for. Since circumstances had changed and that could no longer happen, it was fortunate that Aletta could take Maria in, for all three sisters loved the old woman even if, in spite of those constant quarrels, Sybylla had always been her favourite. But when Francesca put the whole case to Maria an entirely different decision was reached by the old woman herself and she would not budge from it.

"I thank God you are to be free of Heer van Deventer," she said to Francesca. "It has caused me more worry than you could ever know. But I'll not go to Delft or anywhere else. There's a comfortable alms-

house for elderly women just along the street that will suit me well and I have three old friends there already. I want to be near at hand, because one day Sybylla will return and she'll want one of her own to welcome her."

"Oh, dearest Maria," Francesca exclaimed brokenly, kissing the wrinkled cheek, "don't you realize that she may never come back?"

"I know." Maria's voice quavered and she wiped an eye. "But I have to stay anyway."

Francesca's time at home was made even more harassing by Ludolf's constant visits. He treated the house as his own, sitting down at table without being invited, ordering Griet about and eventually swearing at Maria when she plodded into any room to act as chaperone every time he and Francesca were alone.

"Is this prearranged?" he snapped at Francesca, jerking a thumb in Maria's direction, where she sat solidly with her hands folded, watching them.

"It is. You have no right to expect me to be without chaperonage in my own home, or anywhere else."

Francesca noticed how his veneer was cracking. His impatience was raw. When he insisted it was time for her to wear his betrothal ring he held her hand and forced it on her finger, ignoring Maria's shriek of protest when the kiss he rammed down on Francesca's mouth went far beyond the approved limit. He no longer made any pretence of courtesy towards Hendrick and compelled him to agree to a marriage date for Francesca on the day after the appointment fixed for her appearance before the Guild.

"I'll not have time to get home from Delft!" she protested, alarmed at having no leeway of a week or two in which to leave for Italy.

Ludolf dismissed her protest with a snap of his fingers. "We'll marry there. I'll bring your father with me from Amsterdam."

Afterwards she asked Hendrick why he had not thought to postpone the marriage by a few days at least. "I didn't think," he admitted miserably. "I've too much on my mind."

Because of Ludolf's continual presence Francesca could not spend any daylight hours with Pieter, even though he had come specially to Amsterdam to see her. The only time that proved safe was at midnight

in her home, when they would be together by the fire in the parlour, content and loving, able to discuss many things, including a detailed plan to get her and Hendrick away from Delft immediately after her interview with the Guild. It had to be timed to the minute or else it would fail. Once the chance was gone there would be nothing to stop Ludolf summoning the law to his aid if he so wished, forcing Francesca into marriage. She shuddered with apprehension, but Pieter kissed her fears away.

"Trust me," he urged.

On their own they welcomed in the New Year of 1672 with a glass of wine and she wondered what it would hold for the two of them and for Holland in the months ahead.

Back in Delft, Francesca took the permit of marriage to Aletta and was prepared to tell of Sybylla's flight, but her sister already knew, having received a letter that day.

"They are married, but in terror of pursuit, and you and I are implored not to say from whence the letter was sent, although they will not be staying there."

"But how could they wed without Father's permission?"

Aletta's lips slipped in a sideways smile. "I expect Father will explode when he hears, but they found a foreign priest at the docks who was willing to marry them."

"Is the wedlock legal?"

"Father will only have to endorse the certificate one day. In the meantime they are man and wife in the eyes of God and the Church, which matters most, and any children they may have will be legitimate in that respect."

Francesca was given the letter to read for herself and saw that it had been sent from Rotterdam, but there was no address to which a reply could be sent. Since the runaway couple were at a port from which so many left for the colonies, Francesca's fears were reawakened that they might take ship from there.

"Father has to know where this letter was posted," she declared, "because they are running away from a threat that doesn't exist. What's more, he would never part them now that Hans has behaved responsibly in making Sybylla his wife."

Aletta agreed. She insisted that Francesca should write to their father and she herself would pay for a costly messenger to ride with the letter to Amsterdam. Her own marriage was to take place on the twenty-fourth day of February, by which time Constantijn should have completely mastered the use of his new legs.

Pieter happened to call at the de Veere house one evening when dinner was about to be served in the dining hall for the first time instead of upstairs. Aletta, delighted that he had come at such an important milestone in Constantijn's recovery, asked him to wait in the drawing room while she collected the crutches from Constantijn, who had reached the head of the stairs. He could not yet descend as he wished, but came hand over hand grasping the banister as he had done during his nocturnal visits to the cellar. His legs, rigged out fashionably, dragged with him, but as soon as he had levered himself upright again, wedging the crutches under his arms, he frowned, impatient with himself.

"This is the first and last time I'll come down for dinner, or any other meal, like this. I'd like some drugget fixed to the stairs. That will give me a grip on which to steady myself."

Aletta put aside visions of him tumbling headfirst. "It shall be done tomorrow. Pieter is here."

"Good. Let's invite him to dine."

"He says he has something important to discuss with both of us and so it must concern Francesca."

At table, after Sara had served the various courses and returned to the kitchen, Pieter asked Aletta if she had told Constantijn everything about the van Deventer marriage contract and how it had come about.

"Yes," she said, "as soon as we became betrothed we talked of family matters."

"Whatever it is you have to tell us, Pieter," Constantijn took over from her, "I want to inform you first that I have drawn up a banker's draft to cover the whole amount owed by Master Visser to van Deventer."

Aletta watched Constantijn as he spoke. Having no true knowledge of his financial affairs, merely aware from what Sara had said that his grandparents had left him an independent income, she had never sup-

posed that his funds could stretch to such munificence. When he had said, without her having the least expectation, that he would put forth the necessary monies, she had been rendered speechless.

"I should appreciate it, Pieter," Constantijn was saying, "if you would present it to him with my compliments, next time you are in Amsterdam."

Pieter raised his eyebrows appreciatively at such a generous offer. "There was a time when I would have had no hesitation in accepting on Hendrick's behalf, but circumstances are changing. It may be detrimental to our national security if van Deventer should be paid off now or if any other matter is allowed to arise that would bring forth a confrontation with him. I have long suspected that he is working for the French and I've just returned from Amsterdam, where certain incriminating evidence against him came into my hands through the courage of a servant woman, Neeltje, who is known to Aletta."

He described how Neeltje, to his great good fortune, had not forgotten the inquiries he had made to her about Ludolf's correspondence with Geetruyd. Although, as she had said, the contents of the letters had meant nothing to her, she had quietly decided to get hold of some of them. She was still on amiable terms with the housekeeper at the van Deventer house and so made a point of calling now and again to see her. Having learnt over Christmas that Ludolf was constantly at the Visser home, she had used one of his absences to get into his study with a key from the duplicate bunch she had kept. Her pretext for leaving the housekeeper's room had been to look for a silver thimble supposedly left behind in the sewing room. In the study she had taken a handful of letters at random, thrust them deep inside her bodice and locked up everything again. These letters had been duly delivered to Pieter's address and he had contacted Gerard immediately.

"In the light of these letters and other information that had been gained," Pieter reported, "it was obvious to the Prince's Secret Service that what Neeltje had taken to be people's initials also represented places where arms were unloaded or spies put ashore and embarked again, as well as identifying various individuals. Several caches of arms have already been discovered as well as the one in the cellars of this house, but the only positive identification of any person that could be

made was from the initials G.K., which are surely those of Gijsbert Kuiper, the servant you dismissed among others, Constantijn, on the night of your return here."

Constantijn's fists tightened angrily. "It must have been an unpleasant surprise for Gijsbert Kuiper when I moved back into this house, although I played into his hands by remaining helpless in my room."

Aletta put a hand over his. "That's all in the past. We must think only of the future now and what we can do to help Pieter."

"You're right, beloved." Constantijn studied the list of initials that Pieter gave him in the hope that a second servant, male or female, might be identified, but as he had not known the names of all the skeleton staff, none at all in the kitchen region, Aletta fetched the housekeeping records. Nothing helpful came to light.

"At least we have one name with Francesca's sketch to match it," she said, "and the confirmed knowledge as to why the guard dogs were silent and an entrance to the unused cellar was gained."

Pieter gestured agreement. "We also know that Geetruyd Wolff keeps a house where some spies come and go, even if other travellers who stay there are completely innocent. Although Neeltje did so well in getting me that batch of correspondence, she did grab at it in a natural haste and as a result the letters are not in consecutive order. Much vital information is missing and we know there are more caches of arms to be located. It has become apparent that an armed assault has been planned by the conspirators against The Hague, probably to coincide with some prearranged point of Louis XIV's anticipated advance into Holland when war comes. That's why the caches discovered have been deposited at a convenient range, ready to be snatched up and transported when the time comes for a force of traitors to capture the seat of government on the enemy's behalf."

"Would they have a Frenchman to lead them?" Constantijn questioned.

"Not if under the direction of a Dutchman already used to command in violent situations."

"Van Deventer?"

"He has the experience, having been a ruthless privateer. As you know, privateers don't always restrict their nefarious activities to the

sea, but frequently make raids on tropical islands where spoils are to be had, whether spices or slaves or some other valuable commodity."

Aletta spoke urgently. "Surely you'll arrest Ludolf at once, Pieter!"

"Not until we can be sure that enough caches have fallen into our hands to prevent the attack, or else his second-in-command will simply take over. For the same reason we must bide our time with Geetruyd too. None of those traitors must gain a whisper of what is rising against them."

"Does all this mean a flight to Italy for Francesca is no longer necessary?"

"I hope that will prove to be the case, but it's too early to say yet. Everything depends on what can be achieved in the three months that are left before her apprenticeship finishes towards the end of April. The time ahead is still full of danger for her. That's why, Aletta, I must ask you to be my messenger to her again and tell her all that I've told you and Constantijn. Nothing can be set down on paper. Too much is at risk."

Aletta felt a tremor of apprehension pass down her spine at his words. "I will see her tomorrow."

"I thank you. There's no time to lose."

When Francesca heard all her sister had to say it made her wonder again about Geetruyd's attitude towards her. That curious feeling still persisted that the woman was watching her as a venomous spider in a web watches its innocent prey.

On the same February day as that on which Aletta and Constantijn were to marry, the Prince of Orange, by popular demand, was finally made Captain General in charge of the defence of Holland and its states. Not all was going his way, for he was to be hampered by advisory councils formed to keep a hold over him, and the whole country was torn by conflicting loyalties. To the rest of Europe it had become apparent that the Dutch, having once proved themselves to be the bravest and the most staunch warriors in their defence against mighty Spain, had been undermined by peace and prosperity into a general reluctance to take up arms even to save their own freedom.

Yet this time the King of Spain, resentful over Louis XIV's earlier invasion of the Spanish Netherlands, had allied his country with Holland and it was largely due to the Prince of Orange's efforts that other allies were forthcoming. The Prince's treacherous uncle, Charles II of England, was giving his support to France, where it was known that two hundred thousand soldiers were preparing for the invasion of Holland and the strength of the French navy was being increased.

Yet the imminence of war seemed far away in the peaceful atmosphere of the Old Church, where Constantijn stood tall beside Aletta for their marriage, his crutches held for him temporarily by a friend in the role of the groom's right-hand man and guard. Francesca thought her sister had never looked more beautiful in a gown of blue-green silk with her lovely hair drawn smoothly into a topknot ringed with silk violets, gleaming drop pearls in the lobes of her pretty ears and more pearls about her neck, all wedding gifts from Constantijn. A natural wish for both sisters was that Sybylla could have been present, but in spite of every effort by Hendrick and Pieter, she and her husband had not been traced.

It was a quiet wedding. Jan Vermeer had escorted Aletta into the church and Catharina sat with Francesca. All the Vermeer children, except the eldest offspring still serving his apprenticeship, and Ignatius, who had a cold, were there too. On Constantijn's side only his parents and a few close friends were present, including one with whom he was in consultation about the breeding of Thoroughbred horses, an interest he had been planning to take up when the accident had occurred. When organ music filled the great church at the close of the ceremony, Constantijn received his crutches again. With the swinging walk he had developed he matched the moderate pace set by his graceful bride, both smiling happily at everyone. If Aletta glanced about a little more than was usual at such a time, few noticed and only her groom and her sister knew for whom she was looking in vain.

The whole wedding party had departed when Hendrick, who had been sitting out of sight in a side chapel, emerged and slowly left the church. Francesca had begged him during her Christmas visit to attend the ceremony, but his stubbornness and his pride prevented him from making the first move towards ending the estrangement with Aletta.

He told himself that he had come only for Anna's sake, refusing to accept that it sprang from the devastating blow of having lost contact with Sybylla as well.

Since nobody knew him in Delft and Francesca would be at the wedding feast, he went into the Vermeer gallery, hoping to see some of her work and that of her master. He was told by the girl in charge that Master Vermeer was away and she was Maria Vermeer, his eldest daughter.

"Is there something you wish to buy, *mijnheer?*" she inquired. When he replied that he was merely interested in seeing what was on display, she bade him take all the time he wished.

"Which are your father's works?" Hendrick asked her.

"There are none here."

He expressed his disappointment and wandered along until he stopped in front of a painting that he recognized instantly as being by Francesca. It was of a woman possessed of a sweet dignity in a rose-red gown, coming with a smile of welcome towards the man who stood with his back to the viewer, movement and repose faultlessly balanced. It was entitled *The Homecoming.* Hendrick could not take his eyes from the painting. He was aware of trembling at the beauty of the work, scarcely able to believe that out of his loins and Anna's womb had come such talent.

Maria, seeing how fixed his gaze was on the work, came to stand beside him. "My father travels as an art dealer and this shows my mother, Catharina, greeting him after an absence."

"It's very fine," he said huskily.

"It's not for sale," she said apologetically, thinking he had become tempted to buy.

"Why is that?"

"It's for Guild submission by an apprentice artist in the spring, but meantime my father has it here in the hope of future commissions for her. There are a few etchings on the table by the same hand, if you would like to see them."

He studied each one. All were scenes of Delft, with a single exception that was of his own studio with windows open to the street. Still he hesitated to leave. "I've heard so much of Master Vermeer's work. I

was told that after the death of Carel Fabritius in Delft it was declared here that your father had filled the gap, being as great an artist."

Maria gave a nod, intrigued that her father's name should be known by anyone outside Delft. "Locally he is held in very high regard. His advice is sought constantly by the Guild and other civil dignitaries in the valuing and purchasing of works of art. Recently he was asked by them to assess on their behalf a whole batch of so-called Italian masters that are to be auctioned and he will be exposing them as fakes, which will be much to the ire of the villains concerned!" She paused. "May I ask where you are from, *mijnheer?*"

"Amsterdam."

"So far away! In that case, since you are so interested in my father's work, I'm sure I'm permitted to show you just one of his."

"I'd be honoured."

She opened the door into the living quarters and took him into a rather grand anteroom where he supposed special customers were received. The painting was hung in solitary splendour. Hendrick knew it immediately from Francesca's description. Remembering what she had said of her master's looks, he noted the slightly frizzy hair of the man depicted in the work and took a guess at his identity. It was most surely Jan Vermeer himself and showed him in a studio seated with his back to the viewer, dressed in a costume fashionable a hundred years ago, undoubtedly from an atelier chest, with a flat velvet cap slightly at an angle. His brush was momentarily poised as he glanced towards his model while painting the wreath of laurel leaves, symbolically eternal, that adorned her lovely head. Illumined most marvellously by window light, she was robed in blue and ivory silk, posing as the Muse of history, Clio. She held a golden trumpet and a book in her arms. On the wall behind her was an ancient map of the Netherlands before the present boundaries existed. In all it was a totally allegorical tribute to the art of history painting, even the trumpet symbolizing paeans of praise to the painter's craft.

Hendrick beamed his approval. Master Vermeer was a man of his own heart. He was almost sure he recognized the model as being the woman in Francesca's painting when slightly younger. "Is that Vrouw Vermeer as the Muse?" he asked Maria Vermeer.

She gave a musical little laugh. "Father says that is his secret. How could the model be his wife when the painting is set back in time, any more than he could be the painter seated at the easel? But that is just his joke. He will never say yes or no to any questions put to him about this work. All I may say to you is that my mother cherishes it above all else that he has ever painted and therefore it must hold something special for them that is unknown to the rest of us."

Hendrick smiled to himself reminiscently. This girl was too young and virginal to understand those private moments that existed between a painter and his subject deeply in love with each other and which could lead to artistic creation. His own years with Anna had taught him that. A session of passionate lovemaking, the confirmation of the conception of a wanted child or the spiritual communication of tender feelings could well result in inspirational work. The atmosphere of this painting was full of it.

"This is surely called *An Allegory of Painting*," he remarked.

"Nothing is really settled on that point. Sometimes it is referred to by the title you've just given, but at others it is *The Art of Painting* or even *An Artist in His Studio*. Since it will never go out of our family's hands the title is of no particular importance in this house."

"I thank you most sincerely for allowing me to view it."

When Hendrick left the gallery he turned up his collar against the cold wind and pulled his hat well down. Yet he stopped to look through the small panes of a certain shop window. Anna was uppermost in his mind, memories strongly reawakened through the painting he had just viewed, and he was uncomfortably aware that she would have wanted him to send their daughter a marriage gift, whatever the circumstances. He knew in his heart what he should send even though his pride fought against it. The contents of the shop window might have been arranged by Anna specially for this moment, almost as if showing him the error of his ways. Well, he never had been able to hold out against her when she made a special appeal to him, even if his good resolutions seldom lasted. Doggedly, he opened the shop door. There he paid far more than he could spare for an order of goods to be sent anonymously to the bridal couple. Only in giving his name would he hold back.

Coming out again, he went to the stage wagon, which was almost

ready to leave. Soon afterwards he was borne out of Delft as unobtrusively as he had come. He had only two small coins left in his pocket. Not enough for food and beer at halts on the long journey. He sighed resignedly. At least he felt more at ease with himself, and Anna would have been pleased with what he had done.

At the marriage celebrations the feasting was over when Constantijn was told of a delivery that had come from the town. He escorted Aletta away from the company to see what had come and she asked Francesca to go with them. Set up in an anteroom was an easel and beside it several boxes of artist's supplies. At first Aletta drew back hesitantly.

"Who would think of sending all this?" she queried uneasily.

"I wish I had," Constantijn said, opening a box that held brushes and a pestle and mortar. "It's just what you should have, Aletta."

Francesca provided the explanation. "It can only have been ordered by Father from Amsterdam." She was thankful he had made such a conciliatory gesture. "You have already received gifts from anyone at home likely to think of it, even Pieter. Remember that it's only Constantijn and I in this whole area, Aletta, who know that you ever wanted to be an artist."

Aletta moved forward to the open box and her hands hovered over the brushes. "Such luxury! I've never used a brush I haven't made myself." Then she bit her lip. "It will mean starting all over again. I admit to having hoped one day to paint a little once more, but this has taken me so much by surprise."

Francesca picked up a brush and thrust it into her hand. "There! That doesn't feel strange, does it?"

Aletta's smile was tremulous. "No, I admit to that."

"I've a suggestion to make," Constantijn said to her. "How would you like me to ask Master Vermeer if he would be prepared to take on another pupil when Francesca leaves? By that time you would have done enough painting with all that is here for you to be ready for tuition again."

Aletta's love for him shone out of her eyes. "I'd like that more than I can say."

"That's settled then. Now we should return to our guests."

As they left the room together Aletta looked back over her shoulder

at Francesca, who was following. "I have accepted Father's olive branch, because that is what I've taken his gift to be, and when the time comes I'll present my own to him and then maybe he and I can be father and daughter again."

Maria Vermeer told Jan about showing his painting to an inquirer. He did not reprove her, but told her not to do it again. Nobody mentioned the matter to Francesca since the visiting stranger from Amsterdam had not given his name.

Gradually the snow and ice thawed as winter retreated again before the coming of spring. Although Constantijn and Josephus kept constant guard no further deliveries of arms were made to the cellar. Heer and Vrouw de Veere, who were at a loss to understand why no extra staff were being employed at their son's home, brought half a dozen of their own most trusted servants to relieve the burden of domestic chores from the shoulders of their daughter-in-law. Since Constantijn knew them all, he allowed them to stay, certain that he would have loyal support in any emergency.

"But don't usurp Aletta's authority in domestic matters, Mother, at least not again," he advised.

"I only did it out of love for you both," his mother replied, "and she was pleased and thanked me most sincerely. Your father and I owe her so much. If it hadn't been for Aletta you wouldn't be smiling at me from your good height just as you used to."

Aletta had entered the room in time to hear the last remark. "Oh, he would! He made his own decision to walk again before I suggested it."

Vrouw de Veere did not intend to discuss the matter anymore, having made up her own mind about it. "Constantijn tells me that Francesca is painting your marriage portraits."

"She is portraying us together in one painting," Aletta replied. As yet her own efforts were still tentative in the studio she had fixed up in one of the upper rooms and only Constantijn and Francesca were welcome there. Jan Vermeer was willing to consider her as a pupil providing her work reached a certain standing. As yet she had nothing worthy enough

to show him. "Francesca will submit her painting of us to the Guild on her special day and we shall have it afterwards."

Francesca had been delighted to receive the commission. The payment for it would go to Jan, but she would be able to add her own signature to it as soon as she had gained her mastership. She had never forgotten her mother standing in front of Rembrandt's marriage portrait of an acquaintance and his wife. Tears had trickled down Anna's cheeks, for she had been so moved by the tender embrace in which the groom held the bride as they stood side by side in specially chosen costumes of red and gold, adoring love in his face, sweet contentment in hers.

"Rembrandt said that a man and a woman in love should never be separated, not even by a picture frame," Anna had said gently. "How right he was."

Francesca had never forgotten those words or that moment. Her memory was standing her in good stead now as she captured the youth and happiness of her sister and brother-in-law on canvas in Jan's studio. Both had been for several sittings and she had done preliminary sketches before their marriage. Aletta was in peach silk with silver lace, Constantijn in grey-green velvet. Her fairness and his dark good looks made a splendid contrast.

When Truyd called her for the noon meal, Francesca paused by the studio window to look out at the square. Pieter had reopened his market stall there now and she could see him talking to a customer while two women assistants sold early-spring flowers, some arranged in posies with ribbons. The March wind was whipping his curly brown hair and flapping the flat brim of his hat. He had gained more business at his office than he would have wished, for that was far from the main purpose of his coming to Delft, but somehow he was managing to deal with everything. When the customer turned away without making a purchase she saw it was the local whip maker. Had he given some information to Pieter? She knew all about the special whip from Pieter's description and kept an eye open for it herself.

Ludolf paid spasmodic visits to Delft. Francesca never knew when he would appear. She had no idea what private conversation had passed

between Geetruyd and him when he made his first visit after the woman had learned of the betrothal, but there was no apparent animosity between them, she very gracious and he obviously relieved. It was Francesca herself who bore the brunt of his ill temper when he learned that she had left the betrothal ring at home in Amsterdam. He made a special trip to fetch it and came back again immediately. This time he put the hateful ruby on her finger in front of Geetruyd, whose smiling expression did not change even if her eyes were icy. Francesca wondered why Ludolf could not see that the woman's enmity was directed equally towards them both, but then nothing about him surprised her anymore.

France declared war on Holland and its states on the seventh day of April. Already Louis XIV's great army was on the march against its small, poorly armed adversary, which was still torn by political strife and dissent. The Dutch border towns and fortresses began to fall like ninepins before the French advance, some offering no resistance. Pieter and Gerard knew it was only a matter of time before the treacherous attack on The Hague took place, and as not all the arms caches had been located, a force of the Prince's men were wary as they waited for the first move to be made.

Not long after the outbreak of war, Weintje was agitated when she met Francesca at the studio in the late afternoon. "Would you mind hurrying as fast as you can with me to Kromstraat today," the maidservant requested, already striding out. "I've so much to do. Seven travellers are staying overnight."

Francesca was immediately alert. "Did they arrive together?"

"No. One came fairly early and then another. Two arrived later and I admitted the last three into the house just as I left to fetch you. Why do you ask?"

"What a rush it must have been for you to make up all those beds."

"Luckily for once, Vrouw Wolff knew ahead that they were coming and she has been helping me with the beds and other work since early this morning."

Francesca's blood tingled. Something was most surely in the air. Had

she needed confirmation it was awaiting her the moment she entered Geetruyd's house. Propped against the tall carved cupboard in the reception hall were three whips, one with ornamentation such as Pieter had described to her. The rumble of voices behind the door of the bedchamber that faced the street caused her to guess that, to her good fortune, all seven men had gathered there, which was not surprising, as it was the largest of the rooms that led off the reception hall.

She sped up to her own room, threw off her light cape and rushed to take the paint rags from the aperture in the fireplace. Disappointingly, she could not hear as well as she had hoped, but, as always when people talked together in a group, voices were slightly raised in volume. Since the company there would not expect to be overheard behind the security of a thick door, quite apart from Weintje being too busy, Clara too deaf and herself an unsuspecting innocent upstairs, they were talking freely.

She could hear from a feminine tone intermingling now and again that Geetruyd was with them. Her voice came through again.

"As I said at the time, there's nothing to worry about . . . Can't run fast on stumps . . . Five women servants, including old Sara, and two men, both over fifty and no threat . . . No, I wasn't including him . . . Leave the silencing of that fellow and the dogs to me. I've already made arrangements."

Francesca, her ear pressed to the aperture, was full of fear for the safety of those at the de Veere house. It must mean that there was to be a raid on the cellar this very night and that violence would be used to get the arms away. None of those conspirators, three in charge of vehicles, would be here to delay for a day or two. She had to let Pieter know! She must slip out of the house immediately before she was called for dinner. If luck was with her it would be served late this evening, with Weintje so overworked and Geetruyd finalizing plans with her fellow traitors.

Not risking being seen in any outdoor garment, she planned to slip out into the mild, light evening, see Pieter at either his office or the Mechelin tavern and then get back before her absence was noticed. But as she reached the hall and was on the point of turning for the main door, Geetruyd emerged from the conference.

"Ah, you're down in good time for dinner, Francesca. I was about to call you. We are dining slightly earlier this evening, for a little social gathering of my fellow regents and regentesses will take place here later upstairs in the east parlour. You shall join us as you have done on previous occasions."

Francesca could not help but be amazed by the woman's iron nerves. Geetruyd was carefully establishing her own respectable alibi while violence and most probably murder, planned under her own roof, would soon be taking place.

"Will the company stay late?" Francesca inquired conversationally.

"Until midnight at least. We are to have poetry reading, some singing and a little talk on a visit to Amsterdam from Heer van Golpen. Now come to the table. Clara is already there."

Francesca had never felt more trapped or frustrated. She dare not let Geetruyd suspect for one moment that she was desperate to get away, but somehow it had to be done. Never had a meal seemed longer. There was a hitch between courses when Clara, who was always excited when a social event was imminent, knocked over a glass of wine, which spread all over the fine lace-trimmed cloth. It had to be removed immediately and plunged into cold water to avoid staining, Geetruyd doing it herself while Weintje wiped the table, spread a fresh cloth and reset the dinner service. Francesca, looking at the clock, saw that the slim chance of carrying out her wish to slip out before the regents and regentesses arrived had gone.

When dinner ended she began clearing the table and Geetruyd did not object, well aware there was a lot for Weintje to do that evening, even though she herself had supervised the cooking. Francesca, putting down some dirty dishes to be washed, just had time to speak into the maidservant's ear.

"I must be out of the house for ten minutes this evening, Weintje. Would you help me?"

Weintje shot a wary look at the door, but Geetruyd was not to be seen. "I've long owed you a favour in return for a kindness you did me in not telling that my sweetheart had sat with me in the kitchen. What do you want me to do?"

"Cover for me. When it's time for coffee and cakes to be served to

Vrouw Wolff's company I'll come down as if to help you. That's when I'll go."

Geetruyd and Clara both came into the kitchen at that moment. Weintje gave Francesca a significant nod to show she would do as she had been asked.

By the time Francesca had finished clearing the table the regents and regentesses had arrived. As Geetruyd had not finished in the kitchen, Francesca was entrusted to show them upstairs, collect their cloaks and engage them in conversation. She was aware that none of them approved of her following the career of a painter and she found their disapproval irritating. Remembering her gentle Aunt Janetje, who had also been a regentess, she knew there must be many such kindly folk serving on the boards of institutions here in Delft, but unfortunately only the strictest and most narrow-minded ever came to spend time with Geetruyd.

The evening dragged. Then eventually Geetruyd jerked the bellpull for Weintje to bring the coffee and cakes. Francesca leapt to her feet. "I'll lend a hand!" she exclaimed, and was out of the room before Geetruyd could utter a word.

Francesca had been afraid the whips would be gone, but they were still there. She flew to the kitchen. "Are the travellers still at dinner in their rooms?"

"No, they've finished." Weintje gestured wildly. "Go if you're going! I've a lantern ready. Here! Take it."

Francesca ran out of the back door and into the street by way of the side passageway. Upstairs the conversation of the regentesses had turned to the weather and if there would be rain in the night. Clara obliged by drawing a curtain to inform them that the evening was still clear.

With fluttering petticoats, Francesca crossed the little bridge over the canal of Oude Langendijk and seconds later was in the market square. On she ran, her feet flying over the cobbles, until she reached the tavern. Before entering it she saw that a light was glowing in Pieter's office window and a man she recognized was standing outside. She rushed to him.

"Gerard! I have to see Pieter! It's vitally important."

He wasted no words and opened the office door for her. "Go in!"

She realized he must have been on guard, for inside the office Pieter was in discussion with several men, all of them armed. He forestalled any question in her mind about disclosing what she wanted to say.

"What is it, Francesca? You may speak freely."

"The de Veere house! The traitors are going there tonight! I can't stop."

Pieter turned to the men. "Get the horses!" Then he took Francesca by the hand. "I'll go back with you. Tell me everything on the way!"

They hurried along together, speaking quietly, for there were people about. "I knew as soon as I saw the whip in the hall," she explained, "that something was surely about to happen."

Near the corner of Kromstraat they halted, for by then she had told him all she had seen and overheard. He pulled her into his arms and kissed her hard.

"You've done so well, my love," he breathed.

"Take care!" she whispered after him. Already he had gone, running back and soon out of sight to where she guessed those who had been at the office with him would be already in the saddle, his horse brought forward in readiness.

She would have broken into a run again herself to cover the last short distance to the house, but as she turned she saw ranged ahead of her at the corner of Kromstraat the outraged faces of the regents and regentesses, Geetruyd standing with them, her expression showing grim satisfaction. Clara was there too, but looking worried. It was not Geetruyd who spoke first, but the fiercest of the regents, Heer van Golpen. He stepped forward and his voice thundered forth.

"You wicked young woman! How many times have you crept out of this good lady's house to keep immoral liaisons with the men of this town?"

Francesca tilted her chin and approached them. Her relief that she had given the warning and that the true cause of why she had been out had not been suspected was all that mattered. She wondered why they had come in search of her and supposed Weintje had been unable to keep them at bay. But as they all parted to let her through Clara gave her the explanation.

548

"I saw you from the window in the light from the opposite house. Are you angry with me?"

"No, Clara."

The little woman was suddenly conscious of the fury in the faces around her and in her nervousness blurted out, "I recognized the young man who just kissed you. It was he who gave me the posy at the kermis."

Geetruyd grabbed Francesca's arm and wrenched her around. "I saw him too! It was Pieter van Doorne! Were you at the kermis with him?"

"I was."

"But that was before he began coming to Delft on business. So it has been lies! All lies!"

Francesca regarded her calmly. "Neither of us has ever lied to you. You drew your own conclusions. Release my arm. I'll pack a few over-night necessities and go to the Vermeers', as I wanted to do the first night I was in your home."

She entered the house, the others following her and speaking in shocked tones among themselves. Her glance went immediately to the place where the whips had been propped. They were gone! As she reached the foot of the stairs Weintje appeared in the kitchen doorway, her face distressed.

"I couldn't stop them," she whispered.

"I know," Francesca whispered back with a smile.

In her bedchamber she put a few things together and then came down to the reception hall. Dread swept over her when she saw Heer van Golpen waiting for her with two burly-looking men in grey livery. Of Geetruyd and everyone else there was no sign.

"Francesca Visser," the regent said sternly, "you have flouted the kindly rules of this respectable home, abused its hospitality and by self-admission revealed your waywardness and defiance. I am chairman of the board of the House of Correction for young women and on Vrouw Wolff's behalf I have ordered these attendants to take you there for your own good until such time as you have learnt to mend your ways. I am accompanying you to register your name through my authority."

"No! I won't go! You have no right!"

He did not listen, signalling to the attendants, who took her by the

arms and hustled her out of the house in his wake. Twenty minutes later Francesca was alone in a sparsely furnished room on her own. There were bars on the window and the door was locked on the other side.

Geetruyd had a feeling that something was terribly wrong. It was early morning, neither Clara nor Weintje yet awake, but she was up in order to rumple the sheets of her fellow conspirators' beds to deceive the maidservant into thinking they had been slept in. One man should have returned. That had been essential to the whole operation, for she was to report to Ludolf as to how well matters had gone when he came later in the day.

She drank a cup of coffee to calm her nerves. By rights she should have been in high spirits, because at last she had put Francesca where she had long wanted her to be. It was a sweet revenge against Ludolf and would thwart his marriage plans for a long time to come. She had been watching and waiting for some small error on Francesca's part to justify an incarceration, never dreaming that it would happen with no fewer than three regents and five regentesses as witness. Most fortunate of all was the presence of Heer van Golpen, who had shouldered full responsibility and was a man of such integrity and standing that no appeal by the young woman's father for her release, or by Ludolf in whatever high position he obtained, could release her before her morals were considered secure by the governing board. It was not unknown for incarceration to be up to two or three years in extreme cases, which Geetruyd had decided would be her personal aim as far as Francesca was concerned. Ludolf could yelp all he liked, but it would make no difference.

Although buoyed up by this thought, Geetruyd could not dismiss her anxiety. She kept glancing at the clock. It was dawn and still Gijsbert Kuiper had not returned. Where was the man? Weintje would be up soon and he should be back in his room to save arousing the maidservant's curiosity.

Restless with apprehension, Geetruyd went to the hall window and looked out. There was a thick mist, but very early risers were about. A

carpenter driving a light cart drew up and began talking animatedly to an acquaintance on foot who beckoned another over to hear what was being said. Trying to reassure herself that the talk was of nothing more than the outcome of a cockfight or some such sport, she opened the main door into the street.

"Is anything amiss, gentlemen?" she asked.

They all three looked towards her. "Quite the reverse, Vrouw Wolff," said one, who knew her. The carpenter asserted himself as the bearer of the news.

"On my way into town I heard of an armed confrontation at young Constantijn de Veere's country house. I don't know yet what it was all about, but a farmer who helped catch one of the villains with a pitchfork said two others had been killed and four more arrested by the Prince's men. The sad news, which will grieve many in the town, is that old Josephus suffered a fatal wound and died in the arms of the new young mistress of the house."

"What had been going on?" Geetruyd asked stiffly. She was rigid with shock, but she had never panicked and she wouldn't do it now.

"Thieving of firearms from the de Veere cellars by traitors, ma'am, so the farmer gathered, but the matter isn't going to stop there. Others connected with the affair are to be rounded up, so he heard."

"Dear me! What times we live in!" Her mind was racing. "Are you busy today? I have need of a light cart such as yours."

The carpenter looked uncertain. The two men he had been talking to had moved off. "I've made a delivery already and I was thinking of getting back home to my workshop. What did you want transported, ma'am?"

"I would like to hire the cart itself for the day. I heard late last night that my sister is ill," she lied, "and I want to take her some things from my house that she needs, bedding and so forth. You could collect your cart here this evening. The matter is urgent and I will pay you well."

"Can you handle a horse, ma'am? This one can be speedy on a good road."

"I'm well used to horses. I had to drive my late husband on many occasions."

The carpenter thought to himself that she looked a capable woman.

Nothing frivolous about her and he could do with the extra money while he did other work. It would not be difficult to get a lift back home or another into town later. "Very well. Shall I help you load up?"

"That's most obliging of you."

Collecting what she wanted to take with her was not unrehearsed. She had long ago made preparations for flight in an emergency, although she had never expected it to come upon her as swiftly as this. There had been no liking between her and that Utrecht fellow and even Kuiper wouldn't be slow to give her away if put under pressure. The carpenter carried out a chest of her best linen, the table silverware, which she had always kept in a special box, two goose-feather pillows and a quilt and another chest containing her best garments into which she put an antique Chinese bowl and a valuable Delft vase to protect them from being broken. Silver pieces, such as a salver and some candlesticks, were wrapped into a velvet bag.

"You're taking a lot, Vrouw Wolff," the carpenter said without suspicion when she finally emerged from the house and shut the door quietly behind her. In one hand she carried a plain-looking casket that held gold pieces and another tucked under her arm was full of her jewels.

"My sister left some of her possessions behind when she stayed with me. This is an excellent chance to return them." She gave the carpenter his money. He thanked her and would have waited to see her drive off, but there came a clattering of hooves and a man came riding up to her. Geetruyd faltered when she saw it was Ludolf in the saddle.

"Where are you going?" he demanded.

She turned swiftly to wave to the carpenter. "How fortunate! I'm to have an escort. Good day." She shook the reins and as the cart moved forward Ludolf rode along beside her, asking her again what she was about. Succinctly she told him what she had heard. "I knew in my bones when Kuiper didn't return in the early hours that something had gone wrong."

He expelled a furious breath, his face flushed, hard and menacing, "What error did you make to bring all this about?"

"I?" It was because her nerves were so strained, fear of capture high

in her, that her answer burst shrilly from her. "I did everything right, as I always have done! Seek elsewhere to allot the blame!"

"Keep your voice down!" he ordered. He glanced about alertly, but the mist was like a protective veil and passersby were too busy about their own early-morning affairs to pay any attention to a rider and a woman driving a cart.

She struggled to subdue her high-pitched notes. "Somebody betrayed us."

"Yes, but who?" There was accusation in his stare.

"Would I be fleeing if I could seek protection from the militia?" she spat back.

He was forced to accept her defence. "The cache at the de Veere house was vital. Two others were uncovered yesterday and arrests made."

"Then look there for those who betrayed us."

He gave a nod. As yet he could not contemplate what this catastrophe might mean to his ministerial future. His immediate task was to try to salvage the situation for himself alone. If he used his influence to persuade some important Dutch cities to surrender to the French when the gates were reached it should surely compensate in Louis XIV's eyes for the failure of those plans to take The Hague.

"There's no more to be done here," he said sourly. "I'll delay no longer. I'll ride back to Kromstraat to fetch Francesca and take her with me to Utrecht, where I'll await the French."

"She's not at the house."

"Where is she, then?"

"In the House of Correction, incarcerated for an indefinite term, and you will never get her out of there, because there are bars and locks and armed guards. Lovers have tried before to get their young women out and failed!"

"Did you—?" he began savagely.

"No, it was a regent who took her into custody!" Then her feelings gave way. "Why should you care about Francesca any longer when we've been so much to each other and should be together now!"

He sneered at her in his anger. "I only sought you out again because I knew you'd be useful to me. Even that has come to an end."

She screeched, forgetting the need for caution, and lashed out at him with her whip. "Go to the devil!"

In her fury her aim was poor and the thong missed his face to catch him across the shoulder. Outraged, he swore at her, wheeled his horse about and rode away in the opposite direction. She turned the whip cruelly on the horse, weeping with temper, and it was as well the streets were all but deserted of traffic or else in the mist and half blinded with tears she would not have driven far without an accident.

She had reached a road leading out of town when Pieter began hammering on her door for admittance while another militiaman ran down the side passage to cut off any escape that way. In the country-side, as the laden cart jolted over the rough surface, the mist became thicker, rising from the river and the canals. Minuscule drops of moisture clung to Geetruyd's clothes and her hair, beaded her lashes and sheened her bitter face.

With a rattling of wheels she disappeared like a fading shadow into the dense white mist.

CHAPTER 23

Pieter, having learnt from Weintje where Francesca had been taken, went at once to see her, leaving the pursuit of Geetruyd to militiamen who had been called in for the task. He was told at the gate that the inmates of the House of Correction were allowed no visitors except by special permission, and he must apply to Heer van Golpen. At the regent's office he was coldly received. The fact that Geetruyd was being pursued as a spy met with disbelief and hostility. But it was more than that, because the regent made it plain he was not a supporter of the Prince.

"You have condemned Vrouw Wolff without giving her a hearing," the regent said, "In my opinion you have hounded a poor frightened and helpless woman out of her home, a woman whose only concern has

ever been the welfare of the people of Delft and of our country. I will not fail her wishes for the protection of Francesca Visser from wild desires and unsuitable company."

Pieter stood his ground. "Vrouw Wolff had fled from the house before I arrived to arrest her, and one of the men involved in the fighting at the de Veere property admitted she had organized the raid."

Van Golpen was puce with fury. "I have only your word for this, and in any circumstances a common thief would say anything to save his own skin. I have no doubt it is all a pack of lies. All the time I am chairman of the board Francesca Visser will not leave the care of this house without my permission. Depart from these premises and don't return."

Exasperated, Pieter left to shout at the barred windows from the street. "All's well, Francesca! I'll get you out of there somehow!"

She did not hear him, being engaged in scrubbing floors, clothed in a grey gown and plain white cap such as all the inmates had to wear. But one of the other young women had heard him and told her in a whisper as they stood at a long table with their heads bowed in readiness for grace. Francesca gave the girl a grateful glance and smiled. It cheered her to know that Pieter would be trying to get her released, although she had no illusions about how long it might take. She had discovered already that newcomers were treated with the greatest strictness and were given the worst of the menial tasks. None of that mattered to her. The enormous disappointment she had to bear was that she would not be able to submit her work to the Guild. When she would get another chance she did not know, for if the war encompassed Delft nothing would settle down again for a long time to come. To be so near to the long-awaited day and then to be denied the right to attend was a bitter pill to swallow.

Yet even that took second place beside the knowledge that Pieter, as an officer in the reserve, his duty done in Delft, which he had most surely meant by saying all was well, would be going to the fighting. His safekeeping came above all else. She wished with all her heart that she could have lain with him once more before war took him away.

Francesca and her fellow inmates, who numbered twenty-three, heard about the success of the armed confrontation at the de Veere

house, for local news and that of the war was given to them daily, all part of a scheme to awaken a sense of responsibility. For the same reason clothes were made for the poor and turns were taken in soup making for any who came hungry to the door. Francesca was saddened to know of the death of Josephus, who had been a friend to her sister and had done so much to help Constantijn.

She guessed that by now Aletta would have notified their father about this incarceration. Many times when a door opened she looked up from her work in the hope of seeing Hendrick with his broad red face and wide girth come striding in, full of indignation about what had happened, to snatch her away. But that did not occur. A fellow inmate explained why.

"When one of us is considered to be so wicked that even our parents can't be trusted to have charge of us, we are put under the authority of the city of Delft. That has probably happened in your case, even if it was no more than a romp in the hay. What did you do anyway?"

"It's too long and complicated a story to relate, but of one thing I'm certain. I wouldn't be here at all if I hadn't aroused needless jealousy in another woman."

The day Francesca should have submitted her paintings came and went. She heard nothing from Pieter or her family because those newly admitted were allowed no correspondence, except on compassionate grounds in the case of illness or bereavement in the family, until a period of six months had elapsed. The war news was not good. The French army, as if leaving nothing to chance, was taking every place whether important or not in their steady advance towards Amsterdam, which they intended to reach before sweeping south to The Hague and, if surrender had not been signed before then, Delft as well. Yet there was hope. The Prince had moved with his staunch little army into a strong position of defence, which it was hoped might soon change into one of attack. During a temporary absence of van Golpen from Delft, another regent, whose sympathies were with the Prince, supplied the information that apathy and disagreement were melting away among many who had been against the House of Orange, but there were still far too many pockets of nonresistance where the French were welcomed, either through fear or concern for personal wealth and position

or, in the case of Dutch soldiers, lack of adequate weaponry and good command.

Francesca came to know her fellow inmates well. There was much willfulness, tempers and screaming hysterics, especially among those parted from men they loved, whom their families had forbidden them to marry. She was full of compassion for them, not concerned with the rights or wrongs of any case, but understanding their heartache. Even more pathetic were girls, finally broken by incarceration, who were coming to terms with having to marry their parents' choice of a husband after long defiance had proved in vain. All those in her section were from what were known as good homes, most from well-to-do backgrounds. In another part of the building were young prostitutes, who were kept segregated until such time as they were considered reformed, and Francesca only saw them when they waved from barred windows whenever she and her fellow inmates strolled for exercise for one hour twice a day within a walled garden.

When she was given duties of digging and weeding she was at her happiest since coming into custody, even though she had been assigned to the vegetable patch and not to the flower beds. One glorious morning she paused in her work to turn her face to the sun. To be out of doors on such a day made her yearn to be sketching and painting again. She watched swallows swooping overhead, dark against a pure sky blue —azurite mixed with just the right amount of lead white paint. She smiled, certain that Hendrick would have added a wispy cloud or two.

"Francesca!" It was one of the women in charge striding towards her. Francesca sighed to herself. She had been caught loitering. That would mean a punishment of going without supper, or some such petty penalty.

"Yes, *mejuffrouw?*" she replied sharply, expecting a further reproof for her tone, but there were times when she did not know how much longer she could endure the injustice of her incarceration. There was no cruelty in this place—all in authority were quietly spoken and extraordinarily patient and kind in many ways—but the rules were as inflexible as the bars on the windows.

"You are wanted in the board room."

There were several doors to be unlocked by jangling keys before the

room was reached. Francesca was instructed to knock and go in. She had learnt through previous disappointments not to expect anything more than an interrogation as to her attitude and state of mind by the regentesses of the board, which took place at regular intervals. This time when she entered there were no white-capped, black-gowned ladies seated at the table. Instead Aletta and Jan Vermeer stood waiting to see her. She uttered a cry of joy and her sister rushed to embrace her.

"We've come to take you away!" Aletta exclaimed happily. "A letter ordering your release came from the Prince of Orange! Pieter put a request through to him!"

"How kind and generous of the Prince when he has so much to do and think about!"

"He knows how you served him and our country."

"It was so little." Francesca turned to Jan. "It's good of you to have come too! I've had no chance to draw or paint."

"I know. I tried to get materials in to you, but it was not allowed."

"I realized that." She was eager to collect her belongings and leave, but there was one question she had to ask her sister first. "How is Pieter? Do you know where he is?"

"Read for yourself." Aletta handed Francesca a letter. "It came with the Prince's order that your freedom be restored to you."

Francesca could not resist reading it through as soon as she returned to her quarters to pack. It was a love letter always to be treasured. All she would be able to tell the others was that he was with the Prince, but he had not stated his exact whereabouts. She feared he was in the thick of the fighting.

Her packing was soon done, because she had only those items she had brought with her on the night she had arrived. She changed quickly out of the institution's garments and into her own clothes. With a bundle looped over her arm she returned to her waiting sister and her master. The three of them rode to his house in the de Veere coach. Francesca was starved for family news. She learnt that all was well with Hendrick and Maria. What was more, Aletta had heard again from Sybylla.

"She wanted to let me know she was pregnant. I think she was longing to tell one of us her good news and this time she gave me her

address in Rotterdam. I was able to let her know that she and Hans have nothing to fear from the van Jansz family, which was a great relief to both of them. They have been living in fear of discovery."

"Will they be coming back to Amsterdam?"

"No. Sybylla has Father's touchy pride and she wants to wait until the whole affair has completely blown over and been forgotten." Aletta chatted on, filling gaps. Geetruyd had never been found. Ludolf was to have been arrested as a major spy, but no trace could be found of him and it was believed he was with the French forces. "So you are safe from that dreadful man at last, Francesca!"

Jan hoped in his own thoughts that Francesca had been spared the wretched marriage, but everything depended on whether France could be kept from overrunning Holland. Pieter had told him that Geetruyd had revealed once to Francesca that Ludolf believed himself to be destined for high places, which surely meant at least a ministerial position in a Dutch puppet government under Louis XIV. Then none would be able to withstand Ludolf, Francesca least of all.

Catharina and the Vermeer children were waiting at Mechelin Huis to welcome Francesca back again and a feast had been prepared, at which Constantijn was to join them. As yet Francesca had not mentioned her lost mastership and neither had Jan, but as so often in the case of children, Beatrix was unable to hold back a secret and she blurted it out, the shushing from her mother and her older sisters coming too late.

"The Guild liked your paintings, Francesca!"

Wide-eyed, Francesca looked to Jan for confirmation. "Did you submit my work on my behalf?"

"I did," he admitted smilingly. "We had planned a special surprise during which to tell you, because the children have written and prepared a song about it for you. It is to prelude our sitting down to table."

She turned to the younger children and to Beatrix, who had hung her head in shame at her own foolishness in speaking too soon. Francesca tilted the child's chin upwards with a fingertip. "Do you know, Beatrix, I'm glad to have been told first. It will make the song twice as enjoyable. May I hear it now?"

The young ones scampered to the virginal and were arranged in their

places by the older girls while Catharina seated herself at the keys. The song was simple and amusing and tuneful. Francesca clapped heartily. Then she spoke to Jan again. "Please tell me what happened on the day I should have been before the Guild Committee."

"I gave a full explanation as to why you had been shut away. Not all those on the Guild Committee are for the Prince, but art has no boundaries or politics, race or creed, and your work was judged on its own merits. As you know, no decision is ever made on the day itself, but I was hopeful. Then I had to approach them again when notification came for you to appear on the set day in May. Again they were considerate in view of the quality of your work and said they would see you as soon as you were released, whenever that might be."

"I can't thank you enough!"

"There's no need for thanks. You have worked hard and your painting more than deserves a mastership."

Constantijn had arrived by then and he came to greet her, managing his legs and his crutches even more deftly than he had done when she had last seen him, but she was dismayed to see that he had a bruise down the side of his face and a black eye. He grinned at her concern.

"I took a tumble down the stairs," he explained. "I smashed a crutch but I have a replacement. I'm touched by your sympathy, Francesca," he joked. "I get none from your sister. She simply brings me another crutch she has in reserve and tells me to get up again."

Francesca met Aletta's gaze and they exchanged a look of understanding. There were many ways of showing love.

Francesca stayed with Aletta and Constantijn while awaiting a call to the Guild after they had been informed of her release. She was shown how and where the armed conflict between the Prince's men and the traitors had taken place. Constantijn had been keeping watch and alerted all the servants, giving them firearms. One advance intruder was wounded and another roped up when the three who had come through the old gates were driven up the side gates with no attempt at cover, those with the whips believing they had nothing to fear. Then Constantijn opened fire and after that Aletta and the women kept firearms from

the cache primed with gunpowder, ramrod and ball. It was all over very quickly, for Pieter and his men approached from the old gate, and although one traitor made a dash for it he was caught eventually, two were killed and the rest surrendered. Tragically Josephus had already been fatally wounded.

Francesca went with Aletta to put flowers on his grave. She also visited Clara, with whom she had no quarrel. She found her quite content and busy baking pies.

"I didn't know what to do when I heard from Pieter van Doorne that Geetruyd was a traitor and had fled justice," Clara exclaimed. "I think I went around in circles, because I was so lost and frightened, but Weintje saved my senses. She said that if Geetruyd had gone and was never coming back, the house was mine. If I was agreeable she would continue to run the house as accommodation for travellers on condition her sweetheart could live here too as soon as they were married." The little woman beamed and clasped her floury hands together. "I'm so happy, Francesca. Weintje and I are partners and I'm allowed to help. We have only good travellers, respectable men and often married couples, who are sent to us by the landlord of the Mechelin tavern, and all is going well."

It was noticeable that Clara had lost her hunted look, for previously she had lived in constant dread of reprimands and slighting remarks from Geetruyd, who had always considered her incapable of doing anything properly. Now she had come into her own simply by being allowed to do whatever she could do well, including pie making, all with praise from Weintje where previously Geetruyd had poured scorn.

Francesca opened her purse and brought out Ludolf's betrothal ring. "My sister took this with my other trinkets and possessions when she collected them from here after I had been taken into the House of Correction. It should have been Geetruyd's and never mine. Since she has literally left you her house and everything in it I would like you to take this ring. Keep it for a rainy day. I should like to think it was capable of doing some good."

Clara was excited and Weintje was called. The maidservant added her thanks. "I will see that Juffrouw Clara keeps the ring secure. We are going to do well here, because neither I nor my husband-to-be is afraid

of hard work. I hope all will go well for you, *mejuffrouw*. You deserve it after all you had to put up with here."

Francesca was not allowed to leave before she had sampled one of Clara's cherry pies, which was delicious. Weintje's attitude towards Clara had become that of a niece protective towards an elderly aunt. Francesca could foresee only mutual benefit coming from the relationship.

Another source of pleasure for Francesca was that Aletta was painting regularly again. Although her work showed that she was badly in need of tuition, the same vital force was there waiting to be touched into an authoritative control of light and colour and movement. Francesca's eye was experienced enough now to see that her sister would never be a great artist, but she would be worthy of a mastership. Aletta was to begin her apprenticeship on the day after Francesca went before the Guild.

"Master Vermeer said he must see one apprentice safely launched into a mastership before he starts work with another," Aletta explained.

When the important day came, Francesca, through the generosity of Constantijn and her sister, had a new outfit to wear. The wide-brimmed straw hat, trimmed with white ribbons, turned upwards from her face at one side and her gown was of strawberry-coloured silk. Taking a deep breath, she straightened her shoulders and swept into the grand hall where the president and the dignitaries of the Guild awaited her. They sat at a long table facing her. A single chair, not as high-backed as theirs, had been placed ready for her in front of them. Her six paintings were on display easels and her drawings and etchings laid out on a side table.

The president, a grey-haired man in a velvet hat and crimson robes, greeted her. "Good day to you, Juffrouw Visser. Pray sit down." He indicated the chair facing him and when she had seated herself he continued. "Your work has aroused the interest of us all. There are a number of questions we wish to put to you."

It was not an ordeal. They talked to her of technique and subject matter and her answers appeared to satisfy them. Finally they all rose, she doing likewise, and the president took up a roll of parchment from which the seal of the Guild hung on a scarlet ribbon.

"Juffrouw Francesca Visser, I present you with documentation of

your mastership of the Guild of St. Luke. You have my most sincere congratulations. You may have been born in Amsterdam, but you will always be a daughter of Delft."

"I'm honoured, *mijnheer.*" She received the document from him and then curtseyed deeply. Dazed with happiness, she received the congratulations of the rest of the Committee and then walked with light steps from the room. In the anteroom there were more congratulations to come from Jan and Catharina, as well as from Aletta and Constantijn, who had been waiting there. Within an hour her work was back at Jan's studio and with joy she put her signature to each painting, incorporating a tiny tulip in a deep golden hue. It was almost too small to be seen, except by peering closely, but Aletta's sharp eyes noted the shaded colour she had chosen for the bloom.

"Why gold?" she asked. "It was cream when you signed Ludolf's portrait."

"This is a new beginning and a link with a certain time when as far as I could see the tulips were gilded by the sunrise."

Aletta asked no more questions. Whatever lay beyond that moment did not belong to anyone other than Francesca and the man she loved.

Francesca read Pieter's love letter many times over. He had advised her to go home to Amsterdam as soon as she had obtained her mastership and she was making ready for her departure from Delft. Aletta was against her going.

"Surely you would be safer from the warfare here in Delft? Every day we hear more of the French advance towards Amsterdam."

"Pieter would never have wanted me to go there if he hadn't thought it best. In any case, I want to be home with Father and Maria. They need me now with Sybylla away."

"I would come with you on a visit if I could. But I can't risk an upsurge in the war cutting me off from Constantijn."

"I agree. Your duty is to be with him and to make the most of the teaching you will receive from Master Vermeer."

Francesca found it hard to part from her sister and also from the Vermeers. Each of the children had drawn a picture or made a little gift

for her, an embroidered bookmark and a purse from the two older girls. In the studio she had a few minutes alone with Jan. He was about to start a new painting entitled *An Allegory of Faith*. She did not doubt it would be as beautiful as the rest of his work.

"It's a long time since my first day here," she said to him. "If the suggestion that I be your pupil had not been made I might never have become a master of painting in my own right."

"I think you would." His eyes were smiling. "Go to the heights, Francesca. You have it in you."

"I thank you for everything."

He and his family came to see her off, as did Aletta and Constantijn. "Come back soon!" they all called to her.

"I will!" She waved, but her gaze lingered last on Jan. She had a sudden sad foreboding that she would never see him again.

In Amsterdam it did not take Francesca long to settle down as if she had never been away, although that was only in the routine of the house. She realized that once a break had been made with one's childhood origins, for whatever reason, nothing can be the same again. She belonged, and yet her place was no longer here, for she had her own life to lead.

"If Pieter should ever get to Amsterdam, Father," she asked, "would you allow us to marry?"

Since the reports of the war were promising that day, Hendrick answered generously. "Indeed I would. You've been kept apart too long."

"Then give me that marriage contract to burn."

He found it and handed it over to her. She went into the kitchen and thrust it into the firebox to watch the flames curl the document to blackened ashes. Maria, who had come hobbling into the kitchen, tapped her cane approvingly on the tiled floor.

"Well done. That should have been burnt as soon as it was written."

It was not long before Hendrick began to regret his rash promise. The French army was advancing towards Amsterdam again, delayed only by the mopping up of quite ill-fortified places that could have done

little harm. It was as if Louis XIV's lust for conquest made it impossible for him not to place his seal on everything in his path for miles around. At Utrecht he had celebrated with ceremonial reviews of his troops and banquets while, according to rumours that sped around, quite ignoring the advice of his generals to take Holland swiftly and crush it instantly under his heel. Hendrick knew that if Amsterdam fell there could only be one outcome for Francesca and he himself dreaded coming face to face with Ludolf again.

He was seized with anxiety when he heard the sounds of a joyful reunion in the reception hall and came from his study to see that Pieter was there. The young man and Francesca were locked in a kiss, she being twirled around in his arms, her petticoats swirling.

She turned to Hendrick, her face radiant. "Remember your promise, Father! Pieter has something important to ask you."

Hendrick felt cornered and he played for time, holding up a hand. "First of all I have a question to put to Pieter." His gaze had taken in Pieter's travel-worn clothes, the dust on his boots and in his hair. "It looks to me as if you have come straight from the fighting."

"I have, *mijnheer.*"

"Then tell me this in an honest manner. Are we going to drive the French from Dutch soil?"

"We are indeed." Pieter spoke with total confidence. "It's not going to be easy and we may have many hard years ahead, but a tidal wave of loyalty and support for the Prince is rising on all sides. He is meeting it wherever he goes now. Things have changed a great deal since the city of Utrecht kept its gates closed against him because they were preparing to welcome the French. More and more volunteers are joining our forces every day. Our ultimate freedom is not in doubt."

"In that case," Hendrick stated, reluctant already to dash the look of joyous hope from Francesca's face, "you may marry my daughter."

"I'm honoured!" In high spirits Pieter bowed, but he had another request to make. "Would you let the marriage take place today? This afternoon?"

Hendrick blustered, caught off guard. "So soon! There's no need to rush matters."

565

"There is." Pieter was insistent. "Tomorrow at dawn I have to leave again."

There was something in the young man's eyes that conveyed a message of its own to Hendrick. It said that time and life itself might be running out. It was not hard to guess that when Pieter left Amsterdam in the morning some dangerous mission awaited him.

"Very well," Hendrick agreed. "You had better get the necessary papers from the Town Hall and present them to the minister at the Zuider Church. The ceremony should take place there."

For the ceremony Francesca wore the same silk gown in which she had received her mastership. She picked some roses from the courtyard flower beds and made them into a chaplet for her head. Pieter changed into clothes kept at his Amsterdam house. Hendrick escorted the bride to her groom and only Maria and Griet witnessed the ceremony. Summer sunshine filled the church, shining through the high clear windows, and the scent of the roses hung lightly in the still air.

The repast afterwards was the best Griet could produce at short notice and Hendrick provided the finest wine from his cellar. In the early evening Pieter and Francesca left her home to go to his house together. They had it to themselves, for he had given his housekeeper time off to stay with her daughter. Before leaving, the woman had placed flowers in their bedchamber.

When they reached the room Pieter took the chaplet of roses from Francesca's hair. She held him lightly by the wrists as he lowered the flowers. "Tell me where you are going tomorrow. I want to know."

He placed the chaplet down on a chest and put his arms lightly around her.

"Tomorrow I take command of troops who will be arriving in Amsterdam at dawn. Our task will be to defend the castle at Muiden from the French."

She knew the castle. It was only two hours from Amsterdam and occupied a strategic location on the Vecht River. All the ships that went to and from Amsterdam via the Zuider Zee had to pass under the guns of the castle. Equally important was the fact that the principal sluices by which the land around Amsterdam could be flooded were at Muiden. If the castle fell into French hands it would be a catastrophe.

"Let me come with you. The officers have their wives there, don't they?"

"Yes, but that's only because it's a peacetime token force that is still in charge. No more wives will be going there. In any case, be practical. You don't ride, do you?"

"No, but I could travel in an army wagon."

"That's forbidden. We have to be ready for action against the French at all times."

"But they are not so near yet."

"I fear they are. There could be advance parties anywhere now. My duty at the castle will be to await any order from the Prince to open the sluices and let in the sea to make an island of Amsterdam for its protection if the worst should come."

"Then we would be separated until the war ends! I'd be marooned here away from you!"

He reasoned with her. "Why do you think I wanted you out of Delft and here in Amsterdam? It was because I knew of the defences that had been planned for the city."

"But I'd be as safe in the castle with other wives once the land was flooded."

"In that event I would be relegating command of the garrison to someone else and returning to fight in the Prince's company. You'd still be marooned away from me."

"Yet we would have had a little more time together."

"No, my darling, no!" The set of his chin showed her that he would not alter his decision. She made one last effort. "If there should be any wives travelling with the troops tomorrow, then would you let me go too?"

Since he was full of mounting desire for her and knew he could agree to that request without any chance of it being fulfilled, he gave a nod. "On that condition only." His arms tightened about her and his mouth found hers, silencing all talk except that of love.

Their night together with the windows open to the soft air and a sky full of stars was all the more tender and passionate through the imminence of their parting on the morrow. He made love to her in a variety of ways, constantly aroused by her loving, often erotic response. They

exulted in each other's bodies, intoxicated by love, and no less pleasurable were the quiet, drowsy times when they lay entwined smiling and whispering until one slept and then the other, only to become simultaneously stirred by passion as each remembered again the swift passing of the minutes that would fade the stars and bring the dawn.

When the hour came they left the bed together, bathed together and dressed and ate some breakfast all without leaving each other. Then it was time for him to go from the house. He buckled on his sword, put on his orange-plumed hat and took up his riding gloves to tuck them into his orange sash. Then he held her to him and kissed her once more.

"I love you so much," he said softly. "Pray God this war will not keep us apart for too long."

They went out into the warm, clear morning, collected his horse and reached Dam Square shortly before a column of fifty men marched into view. He was concerned to see how tired they were and questioned the young officer in charge.

"Did you not camp outside the city as ordered?" he demanded.

"No, Captain. We were delayed and I had to march the men all night to get here."

"See that they're fed and let them rest for an hour. Then we must move, and quickly."

A coach, dusty from the summer roads, had drawn up in the wake of the soldiers, not far from where Francesca was standing. She could see a large, sensible-looking woman inside, wearing a white-collared dark gown and a white cap. Her gold eardrops and the rings on her fingers as she wielded a silver-handled fan suggested she was the wife of a well-to-do burgher. The coachman was already giving the horses water and the woman leaned out to address him.

"How long is it to be before we move on again?"

He stepped to one side where he could see her, still holding a leather bucket for the nearest horse. "About an hour and a half, I reckon, *mevrouw*, by which time the soldiers will have had a rest and their food."

"Is there a hostelry nearby?"

"Yes, I can see one on the corner." He left the horse to open the

coach door and lower the step for her. As she alighted, Francesca went forward.

"Your pardon, ma'am, but are you going to Muiden too?"

The woman looked surprised that Francesca should know her destination. "Yes, I am. I have special permission to visit my daughter at the castle. She is there with her husband and is shortly to give birth."

"I'm the wife of Captain van Doorne, who is taking command of the castle. Would you allow me to travel with you?"

"With pleasure. I'll be glad of your company. I'm Vrouw Vreeburg. Will you join me for breakfast at the hostelry?"

"I thank you, but now that I have the chance of transport I'll go home and fetch me some things to take with me."

Francesca ran to meet Pieter, who was coming back to her. He had been told about Vrouw Vreeburg and forestalled what she was about to say.

"The woman is not an army wife."

"No, but be fair, Pieter! She is the mother of one."

He sighed deeply. "Let's hire a porter for you at the hostelry and then you may bring a travelling chest from your home with all you'll need." One corner of his mouth lifted in a slight smile. "But don't bring an easel."

"I daresay the castle's carpenter will make me one."

When Francesca had finished packing she said farewell to Maria, who was still in bed, for the old woman rose later these days.

"God be with you, child," Maria said fondly.

Hendrick, well aware that Francesca might be travelling into danger, wanted to say something to cheer her on the way. "When all this is over I'll welcome Aletta back into the fold if she wants to come on a visit."

"She has been hoping for that."

"I never told you, but I was present when she was married."

Francesca held his hand in both of hers. "I know," she admitted. "One day when I was in that art supplier's shop I asked about the anonymous order that was sent to the de Veere house. The description of the customer could only have fitted you."

He grinned broadly at her. "You always were like your mother. I couldn't keep anything secret from her either."

When Francesca arrived back at Dam Square, Vrouw Vreeburg was looking out for her. Pieter, now in the saddle, seeing the porter trundling a sizeable box as well as the chest, guessed that the former contained a roll of canvas and painting materials. These were loaded onto the coach and Francesca stepped in to sit beside her fellow passenger. The soldiers, refreshed by food and drink, stood ready. Pieter at their head gave the signal and the column moved forward. The march out of the city and on to Muiden had begun.

Francesca and Vrouw Vreeburg found much of interest to talk about. It was not idle chatter but sensible discussion, and each had respect for the other's intelligence. They had both brought food, Vrouw Vreeburg having replenished a basket at the hostelry and Francesca had been well supplied by Griet. When the woman dozed Francesca looked out at the countryside, which was parched from the dry summer, the grass unnaturally brown at the wayside. It was the hard earth that had enabled the French to move their artillery at such speed and the low water levels had aided crossings.

They had completed half of the journey when Pieter came galloping up to the coach, his face very serious.

"We've sighted the French. They're advancing on us. I'm telling the coachman to detach this equipage from the column and drive on to the castle with all possible speed. Give warning there! There may be enemy troops advancing to attack it other than these! Good luck!"

Francesca heard him shouting to the coachman and then she and Vrouw Vreeburg were almost thrown from their seats as the coach took a leap forward. The horses set up a pace that would have rivalled that of any stage wagon. Her last glimpse of Pieter was as he gave orders to the soldiers, who were running to take up their firing positions.

"Well," Vrouw Vreeburg exclaimed, straightening her cap, "it's a good thing we came. If we should overtake more French troops on the road we can ride past, whereas an army messenger would have been stopped."

The remaining miles were covered without mishap. The round towers of the castle stood high against the sky as they entered the town of

Muiden. The way people were standing in groups talking solemnly together in the streets showed that something was wrong.

"I hope the castle hasn't been taken already!" Francesca exclaimed anxiously.

"Pray God that isn't so!" Vrouw Vreeburg cried.

At Francesca's instructions, the coachman, who had been keeping a moderate pace since they had come through the gates of the town, hailed three bystanders.

"Is anything amiss?"

One man exchanged a quick glance with the other two before answering. "That depends on your personal view, coachman. The fortress over at Naarden surrendered earlier to a troop of French cavalry and their commander has sent five of those marauding troopers here with a representative from Versailles to claim the castle of Muiden."

"I consider that to be bad news."

The man looked satisfied. "Then I'll tell you more. They have warned that resistance is pointless and all they wish to do is to save bloodshed. The magistrates are about to make their way to the castle now with the representative to authorize the handing over of the keys to him."

Francesca, who had heard everything, called quickly to the coachman. "Whip up!"

He obeyed with the same speed as he had done when they had first set out on their own, leaving the three bystanders gaping after him. Vrouw Vreeburg was full of outrage against the French.

"What villains! And what fools, those magistrates! Whatever can they have been promised in personal gain?"

"Maybe they are just frightened men who genuinely want to save the lives of the townsfolk," Francesca suggested.

"You're more charitable than I!" They had been rattling along the narrow streets when suddenly the coach began slowing down again. Vrouw Vreeburg fumed with impatience. "What has happened now?"

Francesca looked out once more and saw that the coachman had found his way blocked by a wider and larger coach gleaming with giltwork, a man mounted beside it in escort.

"It's the magisterial coach that is holding us up!" she explained

tensely. Then leaning out farther, she saw a group of the town dignitaries in their official robes come through the entrance door of a courthouse and begin to descend the flight of steps prior to entering the coach.

Urgently she instructed the coachman. "As soon as we come to a side street, turn down it! Somehow we must get to the castle first!"

"Very good, *mevrouw.*"

Francesca was about to draw her head back into the coach when she saw the horseman in escort to the gilded coach half turn in the saddle to speak to someone. A great wave of shock and fear swept over her as she recognized him. All colour drained from her face and she sank back onto the seat. Her companion peered at her in alarm.

"My dear young woman, don't pass out of your senses now!"

"That has never happened to me yet." Francesca sat bolt upright to dismiss the suggestion. "I was unprepared for recognizing the Versailles representative. He is a man called Ludolf van Deventer, a Dutch traitor whom I had hoped never to set eyes on again."

"What misfortune!"

The coachman was finding his way through the narrow streets. Then at last the castle of Muiden came into full view on the far side of the river. Reddish in colour, square in shape, it was surrounded by a wide moat with a drawbridge, which was down. Francesca called to the coachman that he should drive straight into the castle as soon as they reached it. Then she glanced back through the window and saw with alarm that the magisterial coach and its escort had already come into sight. Five French cavalrymen were riding in front of the gilded equipage with their officer at the head of the procession.

The Dutch sentries at the gatehouse to the single way across the river to the castle did not bother to examine Vrouw Vreeburg's paper of permission to visit, being used to the comings and goings of the wives and relatives of those in the garrison, and they merely waved the coach through. Their attention was fixed on the approaching procession and they were smartening themselves up for its arrival, a sure sign that they already knew that the castle was to be surrendered.

At Francesca's instruction the coachman whipped up the horses across the river and brought her and her companion into a wide court-

yard that lay in front of the moated castle. To her disappointment he was unable to drive straight into it as she had planned. A guard of honour was lined up in front of the drawbridge, barring the way and keeping it clear for the awaited dignitaries. Instead he was directed by a sergeant to drive on to a far corner of the courtyard, where he and his passengers would be out of the way. As he obeyed, Francesca and Vrouw Vreeburg had a passing glimpse of several wives, one highly pregnant, standing within the castle's entrance to watch the proceedings, some in tears at what was shortly to take place.

"I saw my daughter!" Vrouw Vreeburg exclaimed with relief. "But I wonder why my son-in-law was not with the guard of honour. After all, he is the commanding officer."

The coach had stopped. Francesca sprang out at once and threw herself into a run back across the courtyard, calling out to the soldiers as soon as she was within earshot.

"Don't surrender! If you do the French will have full control of the sluices. Amsterdam is already in danger from the enemy! We need the sea to help in its defence!"

The sergeant in charge, a large man with a protruding beer belly, was glaring. He had enjoyed his easy posting at the castle and intended to retain it under the French. His commanding officer was not of a like mind, but he was presently confined to his bed in the castle with a severe fever and was unable to receive the magisterial party and the Versailles representative. The surrender would be conducted without interference and the sergeant had no intention of letting a slip of a girl stir up trouble now.

"What's all this?" he boomed, setting himself solidly in her path.

"Defend the castle! Draw your men back into it while there is still time and hold it at all costs against the French! Those are the Prince's orders!"

The sergeant's reply was sharp and to the point. "Clear off! At once! Return to your coach and keep your mouth shut or leave! We have important duties here today."

"Listen to me," she implored desperately, clasping her hands in front of her in appeal. "I was travelling with a contingent of our soldiers coming under my husband's command to defend the castle, but they

were engaged by a French advance party. The castle of Muiden must not fall into enemy hands!"

The sergeant saw an older woman coming in haste from the coach. It was more than enough to have one female causing a furore, let alone two. A hasty glance over his shoulder showed him that the French troopers were emerging from the avenue, the magisterial coach coming behind them. He snapped an order to three of his guards. "Put this young woman and the other one back in the coach and keep them there! One of you make the coachman drive farther out of sight."

Francesca dodged, but two guards seized her. She kicked and struggled, calling again to the soldiers to make a stand against the French, but not one moved. Suddenly aware that she was in full view of the women gathered in the entrance, she screamed at them with all the force of her lungs as she was dragged away, the cords on her neck standing out.

"Pull up the drawbridge!"

She saw one woman spring into action immediately, but whether the others followed her example she did not know, for she was being taken swiftly away. In sickening realization she accepted that, however willing some of those women might have been, it would be beyond their physical strength to raise a heavy drawbridge. She saw that Vrouw Vreeburg was being hustled back by the third guard, who had gripped her by the arm, and her protests were fierce but in vain.

Francesca could hear the sergeant ordering his men to attention and there was a snap of heels and a clink of muskets. When she heard a single horse cantering forward from the approaching magisterial party, she closed her eyes briefly in despair, knowing whose voice she would hear.

"Release that young woman," Ludolf ordered. "I'll take charge of her."

The soldiers let her go and stepped away as Ludolf dismounted. She turned to him, her expression stony, her eyes blazing.

"You traitor!" she hissed.

He had believed her to be still locked away in Delft, confident that she would still be there when he was ready to collect her, and although his brows drew together in a frown at her fierceness, nothing could

dampen his pleasure at coming across her so unexpectedly. "Let's have no harsh words. Come into the castle with me, my dearest, and tell me how it is that you are here."

He reached for her, his intention plain enough that he would kiss her first, his lips parting and his expression elated. She raised both fists as if to hammer them against his chest and then spun about to run from him. One of the soldiers who had previously been holding her saw what was happening and gave her a thrust in the back as she passed him. She went crashing face downwards, the breath knocked out of her, her arms outflung. Gasping, she would have raised herself up, but Ludolf's booted foot slammed down onto the back of her wrist, crushing it on the cobbles.

"What is that?" he demanded wrathfully.

On her spread hand her gold wedding ring gleamed. She was ashen-faced with pain, fearing her wrist was broken, but she looked up over her shoulder at his brutal features with triumph.

"I'm Pieter van Doorne's wife! We were married yesterday!"

His reaction was to grind her wrist still harder into the cobbles, his face turning an ugly colour, distorted by jealousy. In the same instant there came a sudden uproar of shouts and a creaking and rattling. Automatically she switched her gaze, as he did, in that direction. The magisterial procession was in confusion. The cavalry officer at the head was trying to control his horse, which had taken fright when the drawbridge had suddenly begun to rise in front of it! Francesca let her cheek rest on the ground again with a sob of relief. The drawbridge was going up and there was nothing anyone this side of the moat could do to stop it!

"Halt that drawbridge!" Ludolf roared, leaping over her and running to where the magistrates, alarmed and disconcerted by this unexpected turn of events, were voicing their rage through the coach windows at those in the castle. In his inflamed mood Ludolf looked as if he would commit murder as soon as he came face to face with those responsible for the rebellious act and he let forth a torrent of abuse at the sergeant and the magistrates for allowing it to take place.

Francesca, nursing her wrist with no doubt now that it was badly broken and wincing at the excruciating pain, was thankful when one of

the guard of honour, all of whom were in disarray, came to assist her to her feet.

"My felicitations," he said with a confidential wink. "I can tell you now that as many men in the castle's small garrison were against surrender as there were those for it, but any who spoke up were clapped into chains."

"Do you think that some of your comrades in the castle helped the women to haul up the drawbridge?"

"You can be sure of that. How does it feel to have put a spark to tinder?"

"I'm glad of it!"

He was guiding her towards the coach, their steps slow, for every movement jarred her wrist. "That injury of yours needs a splint," he said. "As soon as you're seated I'll find a suitable piece of wood."

"You're most kind." She had to take a pause again, breathing deeply to fight the agony of her broken bones. As soon as she was ready to move on again there came a spatter of gunfire. She and the soldier looked back. All the military men had rushed for cover and the magistrates had crouched down in their coach while Ludolf had drawn his pistols and was shooting back at the castle's apertures. The dismounted French troopers had begun firing their long-barrelled matchlock rifles. The horses of the magisterial coach were frightened and restless, their reins held by their coachman, who had leapt down from his box to take shelter by a wheel. The sergeant had bawled an order to his men to fire, but it was noticeable that only about half obeyed him. A lull came, for there had been no return fire from the castle.

Ludolf shouted to those within. "Give up now! You haven't a chance of holding this fortress! It will fall to the French army, never doubt it! Muiden will be put to the flames! Blood will run in rivers through the streets and the moat here will turn red!"

At one of the castle's apertures, from which in centuries past arrows had been shot, a young military clerk looked down the barrel of his wheel-lock rifle and took the Dutch representative of Versailles into his sights. He had never aimed at a man before, and although his fellow countryman was a traitor of the worst kind, it was different from shooting game in the woodlands. His hand trembled as his finger tight-

ened on the trigger. The deafening report of the fired bullet and the acrid smell of the gunpowder were not the cause of his sudden turning aside to vomit. He had not realized a man could look surprised at the moment of death.

Ludolf had fallen, but he was not dead. Two of the guards pulled him out of range and the sergeant knelt to examine the wound. The bullet had torn into the upper left arm. Ludolf's own response to being shot was one of vengeance and frustration.

"The soldier who committed this misdeed must be executed! I'm here as the messenger of the King of France, not a militant." He ignored the fact that he had fired both pistols.

The sergeant was binding up the wound with Ludolf's own sash. "You must be taken to a doctor at once, *mijnheer*. The bullet appears to be lodged in a bone. Can you stand?"

"Yes, help me to my feet."

The sergeant hauled him upright and supported him. The magistrates were eager to get away, and they reached out their hands from the coach to assist the sergeant in getting Ludolf up the steps to them. Yet Ludolf resisted, staring towards Francesca.

"I want that woman to come with me. Bring her here!"

Francesca stood appalled, knowing she would faint from the waves of pain sweeping over her if she tried to run away.

"Leave me," she said to the soldier at her side. "This is something I must settle for myself." Then, as the soldier moved, she took one agonizing step forward, cradling her wrist against her chest, and called to Ludolf across the distance between them. "This is as far as I can go unaided. You must either come for me yourself or go out of my life forever!"

Ludolf jerked himself free from the support of the sergeant, who protested at his foolhardiness. "*Mijnheer!* Don't go! Get into the coach and I'll fetch her. You'll be within range of the castle's fire again!"

"They'll not dare shoot at me a second time," Ludolf growled. With his good arm he thrust himself away from the side of the coach, but there was no time for more. A shout had gone up from the avenue as one of the sentries had come running to yell jubilantly through cupped hands. "Our army is here!"

5
7
7

Ludolf grabbed the sergeant by the sleeve. "Get me on my horse!"

The sergeant ran to fetch it. Ludolf was barely in the saddle when Dutch officers at the head of their running troops came bursting out of the avenue. Swinging his horse around, Ludolf galloped in the opposite direction. As he passed Francesca he shouted to her:

"Nothing is ended yet! Never doubt but I'll deal with that so-called husband of yours!"

She watched him gallop on to disappear through the border of trees and plunge his horse down into the stretch of water beyond, making for the other shore.

Several hours later, weak from loss of blood, Ludolf lay at the edge of a cornfield. Some time ago he had fallen from his horse, which had galloped off on its own. He could see a farmhouse not far away, but he lacked the strength to crawl there. Yet sooner or later someone would come along and see him. His thirst was terrible, his parched throat making it impossible to shout. He drifted into blackness. When he opened his eyes again it was evening with the first early stars showing in the darkening sky, but he could see no lights at the farmhouse. There had been nobody about earlier, but he had thought the workers were all in the fields. Was the place deserted? It came to him in a few minutes of clarity that he had not heard a cow or the bleat of a sheep or the barking of a dog or any of the normal farmyard sounds. In fact, there had been a dearth of livestock for several miles before he had fallen at this spot, too dazed to consider the implication.

When he next emerged from the curious oblivion that kept sucking him down into its depths, the sun was up again and blazing down on him as it had done the day before. He was sweating with heat and fever. Somewhere in the distance was a curious roar and the ground on which he was lying appeared to be trembling. He seemed to see a sparkling in the sky above the corn. Then horrified realization dawned. It was spray from the sea. The sluices must have been opened at Muiden and the land was being flooded.

It was his last conscious thought before mercifully the moment of death came. He had no knowledge of being swept away by the thundering water like a piece of flotsam among fallen trees, broken buildings and pieces of thatch.

At Amsterdam, Francesca had not been to the walls to watch the sea approach as hundreds of citizens had done. She was posing in the studio for Hendrick, seated on a chair with a shawl hiding the binding of her wrist, which was in a sling. It was giving her plenty of time to mull over the events of the previous few days.

Pieter had not been with the first Dutch troops that had arrived at Muiden, but he and his surviving men had reached the castle in time to help ward off and defeat a French attack that had followed soon afterwards. The castle of Muiden had been left secure with a garrison of six hundred men when he had brought Francesca back to Amsterdam while there was still time to get through before the sluices took effect.

She had been exhausted by the speedy return journey, her wrist having been set by an army surgeon but still subject to severe pain. Despite her physical suffering, she knew intense relief when Pieter told her of the message he had received upon entering the city. They had hastened with the good news to Hendrick.

"Your troubles are at an end, Master Visser," Pieter had said. "Ludolf van Deventer is dead, presumably drowned. His body, washed up against a bank, was seen by passing boatmen, who brought it to the city. As a proven traitor he would have been executed had he been caught. Now, by custom, his assets will be confiscated by the state while any debts owing to him will be declared null and void."

"I can scarcely believe such news after all this time," Hendrick had answered, almost dazed by this unexpected release from the nightmare that had been hanging over him for so long.

Francesca recalled the brief farewell in the reception hall that she and Pieter had shared. They had faced each other, their eyes full of love.

"Come back safely to me," she had whispered passionately.

"One day there'll never be another parting," he had promised vehemently.

They had kissed, his arms wrapped around her. Then he had broken away and she had gone to the door to watch him mount his waiting horse and ride away. At the end of the street he had looked back and swept off his hat to wave it in farewell, the orange plume catching the

sunlight. Then he was gone from her sight, riding to rejoin the Prince's forces.

"You know, Father," she said from the rostrum, "I think it's time you gave me an interesting painting to look at on the wall whenever I pose for you."

"What do you want?"

"Rembrandt's portrait of Titus."

"We'll see," he replied, intent on his work.

His reply showed he had no intention of moving the painting from where it had hung for so many years. She decided to solve the matter for herself, knowing that he would expect her to sit for him many times yet before this war was over. Common sense told her that people in Amsterdam would have no money to spare for luxuries such as paintings until peace was restored. Hendrick would not be able to afford professional models.

"I'll paint my own picture to hang there as soon as my wrist is healed," she announced. "I'll paint Pieter, my tulip grower, on the morning when I saw him standing amid those acres of blooms. It's all in my mind's eye—the sunshine, the slight movement of the tulips in a gentle breeze, the workers bending as they collect the petalled cups into baskets, and then myself in the foreground."

The only sound in the studio was the quiet slap of Hendrick's brush against the canvas, a comfortable and familiar sound. Francesca forgot that the last time she had posed for him it had been for the painting of Flora, purchased calamitously by Ludolf. That was in the past. For Pieter's sake her thoughts dwelt on the future in the hope that the picture she was planning would one day become a reality. Then once more would he come to her through an ocean of tulips.

EPILOGUE

Francesca was painting in her studio at Haarlem Huis on the January day in 1689 when the Prince of Orange left Holland to become William III of England and reign jointly with his English wife, Mary. He was not leaving the rulership of his own country behind and Francesca was pleased that those ties would remain. He and his people had come through many trials and tribulations since that February day when he had taken command seventeen years before.

It had been a hard war for all, bringing starvation and tragedy and bankruptcy to many. She herself had known hunger and cold when Amsterdam was marooned by water. She had never forgotten what it was like and these days whoever came hungry to her door was given food and money. Amsterdam had been besieged for very nearly two years, but even then over three more terrible years of conflict passed before Louis XIV finally withdrew his armies with nothing gained, leaving Dutch freedom intact. Yet the prosperity of Holland and its states had been ruined, much of the land left unfit for agriculture from the flooding by the sea, and many bulb fields had been washed away. A great deal of overseas trade had been lost forever. Recovery had been slow and nothing would ever be the same again.

Francesca mixed yellow with lead white on her palette. Years ago, during the siege, she had painted *The Tulip Grower*. Now she was capturing a single tulip. Last summer, after years of hard work had been spent in restoring his soil, Pieter had finally achieved his aim to produce a new tulip. The petals rose creamy white from the calyx to shade through pale yellow to deepest gold, echoing the tulip she had long incorporated into her signature. She had made paint sketches at the time it was in bloom, unbeknown to Pieter, for there had been no chance at that busy time of year to settle to painting it as a surprise gift for him, but soon now it would be ready for his birthday. He supposed her to be working on a self-portrait she had begun before Christmas.

She was using more yellow on blue for the foliage than was usual for

her and she hoped the resulting greens would hold. Recently one of Jan Vermeer's paintings had been put up for auction in Haarlem. It was his *Little Street in Delft* and what had been green foliage had become decidedly blue in tint, although that in no way detracted from the unique beauty and tranquillity of the work. Pieter, knowing what it would mean to her to own it, had bid for it while she had sat beside him in the auction room, holding her breath in suspense. It had fetched very little. Nobody else had been interested, but she had been overjoyed when it became hers.

Pausing in her work, she looked at the Delft painting on her studio wall. Her foreboding that she would never see Jan again had proved right. His *Allegory of Faith* had been one of his last works. Not long after her departure he had caught a chill that had settled on his lungs. Three years later, when he had been made destitute by the lack of business owing to the war, he and his family had had to move into his mother-in-law's house and there he had died at the age of forty-three. Catharina had been left in dire straits. Although housed with her children by her mother, she had had to sell all she possessed to meet colossal debts. Two of Jan's paintings had gone to the master baker in lieu of payment for a single large bill. Most heartbreaking of all was that her most adored work by Jan, *An Artist in His Studio,* was taken from her by the law for her insolvency, even though she had done everything in her power to keep it.

Aletta had received part of her tuition from Jan until deterioration in his health had made it impossible for him to continue teaching, but he had transferred her apprenticeship to another Delft artist. She had gained her mastership, but an abundance of children, ten in all, had given her little time to paint. Her olive branch to Hendrick had been her first three children, one a babe in arms, whom she took to see him at the war's end. The breach had been healed between father and daughter as soon as they sighted each other.

Aletta never sold her paintings, working now and again for her own pleasure. Horses had become a favourite subject, which was to be expected with Constantijn's breeding of thoroughbreds. All their children had been taught to ride as soon as they were old enough and, almost from the start, Constantijn had begun riding again, in a specially de-

signed saddle, on horses he trained himself. He sold most of his fine animals to England, where there was always a demand, more than to his own countrymen, for even the richest, such as the van Jansz family, who had narrowly missed bankruptcy during the war, had never recovered their former great wealth in the hardships of the aftermath.

In Amsterdam, Hendrick still painted, although his hands were gnarled like the roots of a tree and it was excruciatingly painful for him to hold a brush. Strangely the influence of his old master had become more apparent than ever in these last works, and one of them was almost sold as a Frans Hals before the mistake was discovered in time. Although Hendrick scarcely ever found a buyer more than once or twice a year, he and his household lived in modest comfort on a stipend paid jointly by his two sons-in-law.

Maria had died, but not before seeing Sybylla again at the end of the war. Sadly, Sybylla had returned home a widow and her life was not easy, for Hendrick had grown still more cantankerous with the years. Sybylla never complained. Many times she could have married again, but her old flirtatious ways were quite gone and she would not consider it. Her loss of Hans, who had been killed during the defence of the town where they had lived after moving from Rotterdam, had changed her a great deal, for she had loved him with her whole heart, and since she could no longer have him she wanted no one else. Yet there was a widower of her own age whose companionship seemed to suit her well, and those who loved her hoped that with time they might find happiness together.

Her child, now sixteen and, for some reason known only to Sybylla, nicknamed Mouse since birth in spite of being christened Anna, was the apple of Hendrick's eye. He had taught her to paint, showing a patience he had never been able to maintain with his own daughters. Her cousins called her Anna-Mouse, which was a pleasant combination, but although she produced quite adequate still lifes, she would never reach Guild level and neither did she wish to, for she was already in love and had marriage on her mind.

Francesca considered her own output of work. The days when Jan Vermeer had been able to sell her apprentice paintings easily from his gallery for a moderately good price were long gone, for sales for artists

were few and far between these days. She did occasionally sell to art dealers and there was a collector of her work who came sometimes from Gouda, but she had become no richer through her work than any other artist she had ever known. Fortunately Pieter was a good provider for her and her sons. His investments made before the war in the colonies as well as in Holland had proved sound, not least in those three home commodities that would always be in demand by his fellow countrymen—beer, land and tulips.

As yet, circumstances had prevented Pieter from taking her on that long-promised visit to Italy, but before long the dream of her youth to see the Renaissance art of Florence, Venice and Rome was to come true. The youngest of their three sons, all of whom were born within eighteen months of each other, showed the true and unmistakable signs of becoming an artist, while the other two inclined to the land. Well named for a painter as Johannes, he was twelve years old and it had been arranged, to Francesca's mixed feelings of pride, pleasure and the pain of parting, that as soon as he was fourteen she and Pieter would take him to Florence and apprentice him to an Italian artist of high repute. The pinnacle of Dutch art had been reached in the golden span that had seen Rembrandt, Hals, de Hooch and Vermeer. Now it was in a decline with all else that had once made Holland great. But that was not to mean that such genius would never flower again. Francesca was sure, as were many others, that it would show its bright flame one day in the future. Perhaps even in her own child?

Aunt Janetje was too frail in health now to be given the responsibility of Johannes during his Italian apprenticeship, but her eldest son and his wife, who had visited Holland only a few months earlier, had expressed their willingness to act as guardians to the boy, having children of their own.

"Mother!"

Francesca looked up as the door of the studio was flung wide and Johannes came rushing in. He had discarded his outdoor clothes, but the cheeks of his lively face were still red and shiny as apples from skating outside.

"What is it?" she asked with an amused lift of her brows. He had a

boisterous personality and was only quiet when he was sleeping or painting.

"When are we going to Amsterdam again? I want Grandfather to see my new portrait of him."

"I think your father hopes to take you with him when next he goes to the Exchange."

"Shall you come with us?"

"Yes. I like to see your grandfather and Aunt Sybylla whenever I can."

"Good." He came to stand by her and tilted his head as he eyed her painting assessingly, he and his brothers sharing the secret of it being done for their father. "Do you think I'll ever learn to paint with light as you do, Mother?"

"I'm sure you will."

When he had gone from the room again, she thought to herself that the light in his work would not be of the crystal-clear quality that pervaded such works as Vermeer's and her own, coming as it did from the sparkle of the canals and the soft, sun-shot mists of the Dutch countryside. The light he would learn to master would have the warmth and richness of the Florentine sun reflected back from rust-red roofs, ancient time-weathered stone and the sapphire glimmer of the Arno. A whole new palette was for him.

Brush in hand, Francesca was facing her studio door when it opened again. This time it was Pieter who stood there. "Am I interrupting the painting of a masterpiece?" he inquired with a broad smile, leaning a shoulder against the jamb.

"No!" she laughed. "Not today."

"I came to see if you had time to go to the bulb shed with me. I'd like to show you the plans laid out there of the extension to be started in the spring."

She put down her palette and brush and rose from her stool at once. Separation from him throughout the difficult years of war had taught her the true values of life. She never took for granted a single moment that she spent with the man she loved.

ABOUT THE AUTHOR

Rosalind Laker's *previous novels include* Circle of Pearls, To Dance with Kings, *and* The Silver Touch. *She lives with her husband in Sussex, England.*